60

FARRAR
STRAUS
GIROUX

ALSO BY PETER HANDKE

Crossing the Sierra de Gredos

Crossing the Sierra de Gredos

PETER HANDKE

Translated from the German by Krishna Winston

FARRAR, STRAUS AND GIROUX   NEW YORK

Farrar, Straus and Giroux
19 Union Square West, New York 10003

Copyright © 2002 by Suhrkamp Verlag Frankfurt am Main
Translation copyright © 2007 by Farrar, Straus and Giroux, LLC
All rights reserved
Distributed in Canada by Douglas & McIntyre Ltd.
Printed in the United States of America
Originally published in 2002 by Suhrkamp Verlag, Germany,
as *Der Bildverlust oder Durch die Sierra de Gredos*
Published in the United States by Farrar, Straus and Giroux
First American edition, 2007

Library of Congress Cataloging-in-Publication Data
Handke, Peter.
    [Bildverlust, oder, Durch die Sierra de Gredos. English]
    Crossing the Sierra de Gredos / Peter Handke ; translated by Krishna Winston.
    — 1st American ed.
        p.   cm.
    ISBN-13: 978-0-374-28154-0 (hardcover : alk. paper)
    ISBN-10: 0-374-28154-8 (hardcover : alk. paper)
    I. Winston, Krishna.   II. Title

    PT2668.A5B5513 2007
    833'.914—dc22   2006031525

Designed by Jonathan D. Lippincott

www.fsgbooks.com

10 9 8 7 6 5 4 3 2 1

You will go
will return   *not*
die
in combat
    —Latin oracle

Have pity on her
who travels on such a day
    —Ibn 'Arabî

But perhaps knighthood
and enchantments nowadays must take paths
different from those of the ancients
    —Miguel de Cervantes, *El ingenioso hidalgo Don Quixote*
      de la Mancha

Crossing the Sierra de Gredos

1

She wished this were her last journey. The place where she had lived and worked for a long time now always offered more than enough new experiences and adventures. The country and the region were not the ones in which she had been born, and starting in childhood she had lived in several altogether different lands and landscapes.

Raised by grandparents who were avid travelers, or vagabonds, to be more precise, who seemed to change their nationality with every border they crossed, she had pined for a while in her youth for the long-lost land of her birth in eastern Germany, familiar to her not from her own memories but rather from stories, and later from dreams as well.

After several visits to that country, she then spent some years there as a student, in Dresden or Leipzig, let us say, a good hour by bicycle from the village of her birth, and eventually, several countries or two or three continents later, she even settled there, two hours by car from her alleged birth house, by now torn down and replaced by a new building. She lived there and worked, though not yet in banking.

Later still, again after several countries and continents, after alternating between work and the vagabond life, though not the same kind as her grandparents'—almost always alone—she gradually, imperceptibly, lost track of her birthplace, and one day the image of an expansionist, overweening Germany was gone from her consciousness, whereas for a while at least some traces of her own, small-caliber Germany lingered, a stream with the shadows of water-skaters on its pebbly bed, a harvested cornfield from whose furrows bits of chaff swirled into the air, a mulberry sapling that had wandered by mistake into that steppe-cold region.

And then these traces, too, faded away. The images no longer came of their own accord. She had to make an effort to summon them. And as a result they remained devoid of meaning. At most they turned up in an occasional dream. And eventually they, too, vanished from her dreams. That country no longer pursued her. She did not have a country of her own, or another country either, including this one here. And that was fine with her. Perfectly fine! The eternities spent in foreign parts seemed to have shaped her, enhancing her beauty, and not only the beauty of her face!

A clear, frost-cold night in early January on the outskirts of a northwestern riverport city. What was the name of the city? of the country? The author she had hired to write a book about her undertakings and her adventures had been forbidden from the very beginning to use names. In a pinch he could use place names, but it had to be made clear at once that they were usually false—altered or invented. Here and there the author, with whom she had negotiated a standard delivery contract, would also be free to toss in a real name; in any case, future readers were to confine themselves to following the larger story, and the story and the manner of its telling were calculated to make them free to forget, from the moment they turned the first page, any thoughts they might have had of hunting for clues or sniffing around. If possible, the first sentence of her book would banish any such overt or ulterior motives in favor of reading, pure and simple.

According to the contract, the same prohibition applied to names of persons and indications of time. Persons' names were admissible only when they were clearly products of the imagination. "What imagination?" (the author). — "The imagination appropriate to the specific adventure, and to love" (she). — "Whose love?" — "Mine. And indications of time only of this sort: One winter morning. On a summer night. The following fall. At Eastertime, in the middle of the war."

For a long while now she had had hardly any relatives left. And those who were still alive were out of sight and out of mind. Somewhere —"Where?" — "How should I know?"—she allegedly still had a half brother, who allegedly rented out recreational vehicles, or was a microchip technician? or both?

Yet for many years she had made her ancestors, starting with her parents, of whom she had no conscious memories, the objects of a quiet, private, and all the more fervent cult. These ancestors, with the possible exception of her grandparents, who for a long time were entirely too present, constituted—thanks to stories, no matter how fragmentary, indeed, precisely because they were fragmentary, and then also dreams—the love for which she wept anew, often daily, during a good "two dozen summers, and even more winters."

Did she long for her ancestors? Yes, yet not to be with them, but merely to be able to look in on them for a moment, to comfort them, to thank them, and to bow down before them, after taking the appropriate step backward.

And then these shadowy ancestors had lost all their hold over her. And that, too, had happened ever so gradually. Some summer or winter morning she had realized that her venerated dead belonged to the gazillions of those who were no longer present, having seeped into the ground since the dawn of time, crumbled, or blown away to the four corners of the earth, never to be recalled, never to be brought to life by any love whatsoever, irrecoverable for all eternity. They still turned up now and then in dreams, but only as part of a crowd, under the heading of "also present": this "now and then" no longer had the meaning it had once possessed of "at all sacred times."

And this second death of her ancestors was also fine with her, like the small and large birth country that had earlier slipped away from inside her. In the meantime she had come to see as delusory the type of strength she had long derived less from the entire country than from little pockets in that country, less from the wholly successful life of an ancestor (to be sure, there was not even one life that fit that description) than from misfortune and a lonely death (which was the lot of all her forebears). Such strength, she wondered: Did it not make one tyrannical and ruthless? Did it not add to the burdens of those with whom one now passed time, lived, worked, had dealings, in the present? Such strength was accompanied by a kind of arrogance, was it not, which could thwart, even harm, even destroy the days as well as the nights of one's contemporaries, those who somehow or other got close to one? Once free of her ancestor worship, did she become receptive to other kinds of strength? impulses? No, in spite of everything, it was not perfectly fine with her when the ancestors grew meaningless and dim. It was more a question of her letting it happen, with a bitter aftertaste, and not only on her tongue.

Week after week it had been bone-chillingly cold in this region where she had made her home for a long time now. At first she wanted to talk the author out of any reference to this detail, which hardly seemed to fit the "northwestern port city" they had settled on as her place of residence, a place where the Gulf Stream moderated the climate. But then she allowed herself to be persuaded that a "port" could also be a riverport, inland, far from the warming coast, on what was already a cold portion of the continent. Basel. Cologne. Rouen. Newcastle upon Tyne. Passau. What mattered: that her bank's headquarters were located in such a city. But the name of the bank was not to be mentioned in her story either.

On the morning of her departure she rose even earlier than usual. As before every journey, it had been a light, floating night, perhaps, too, because she had again slept in the bed belonging to her child, who had gone away. Her things were already packed—or rather, stashed in a bag purchased at the end of her girlhood and by now half as old as she was. It seemed immeasurably older, however: worn, torn, scuffed; like a relic from the Middle Ages, when travel had been very different from today; an ermine satchel? Time and again, before each of her solitary journeys, and not only into the Sierra, she had wanted to throw it away, or at least stow it in a corner. And every time it had been the one she decided to take with her—"just once more." As a child, her daughter, long since over the hills and far away, had begged her mother, whenever one of their games came to an end, for this kind of "just one more game," and after that "just one more": "Please, just one more, one more!" This was no longer asking; it was pleading. The author: Could he include that in her book? She: If not that, then what? All through the trip her bag remained half open. But nothing ever fell out. And her shoes? They were old and scuffed—good for rock climbing.

It was still completely dark, and outside the frost crackled on the windowpanes. She did not turn on the light; the moon, almost full, though waning, shone through the entire house with its many uncurtained windows. Here on its periphery, the riverport city extended to the foot of a ridge, partly wooded, partly bare cliffs. The hill, black with the moon behind it and very close by, appeared to form part of the spacious house, which at the moment looked empty. In each room—and there were quite a few rooms—the near emptiness projected a different image: here the resident had long since moved out for good; here the room had been cleared out except for two or three objects and pieces of equipment, ready for work to begin; now the deserted vestibule showed signs of a hasty departure; now the table in the parlor gleamed for a meeting about to take place; there, in the kitchen's one pot, the size of a cauldron, food had been prepared for a large gathering, or for a whole week.

A sort of fullness or, rather, stuffed quality, similar to that of her bag, manifested itself only in the first of the suite of rooms intended for a toddler, a schoolchild, and a student: even the corners were filled with games, action figures, toys, standing and lying next to and on top of each other. Except that in her bag each of the items had its place, its purpose, its plan; they all complemented and implied one another. But here in the playroom, the hundreds of toys were scattered every which way and did not reveal any recognizable game. Not even the rudiments of any familiar or reproducible game could be discerned, and not merely because of the moonlight. Yet games had been played in this room, with all the things lying about on the floor, and with all of them together, at the same time, and how! Full of enthusiasm, in the sweat of armpits and the brow, amid shouts of encouragement and the raucous singing of made-up songs, play, play, nothing but play. And the play seemed to have ended not all that long ago. Any minute now it would resume.

Before setting out, a cup of coffee (or tea) at one of the windows on the south side. That was the direction in which she was supposed to go. Yet it was a long time since a southern destination had meant anything to her, as was also true of the ocean and all the other points of the compass— and that was fine—including the Himalayas and a journey to the moon. The latter was suddenly reflected in her cup and promptly disappeared again. She tried to catch it. But it slipped away each time. She sat down on a folding chair, a so-called camp chair, and wished she could sit there forever.

Now a shock: someone was eyeing her, or her silhouette, from outside, from the dark: the author, the deliveryman. A first solitary peal of the bell in the church tower on the outskirts, and almost at the same moment the voice of the muezzin from the nearby minaret, answered by the repeated hooting of an owl in the wooded hills. The first early plane leaving a flashing trail among the sparkling fixed winter stars, and now, as a third element, a match struck across the entire sky and already extinguished: a January falling star.

No, no author. And yet he existed. He was even a reason for, and one of the destinations of, the trip she was about to undertake. And it was only tangentially or incidentally for the purpose of telling him her life story or whatever. The main purpose was money. He and she had first agreed on a contract for the delivery of her book, and now they were to sign a contract in which she and her bank—the bank and she, or at least her name, had long since become synonymous—were to have a free hand in managing and growing the author's fee.

Nowadays she did not normally concern herself with such matters. The bank had its own department for them, and by now she worked outside of and above the departments. But in this case she had to make an exception. She had got herself into this situation when she decided that she wanted a real book written about herself, instead of the endless newspaper articles and magazine features, a book about her bank, too, and its history. Of course the amount of money the author wanted to invest (or could invest) was a drop in the bucket, and not only compared to the sums her bank usually handled. And the author's personality, too, judging by the one meeting the two of them had had thus far, seemed like that of someone who would normally give her a wide berth.

How had she settled on him? Why had she not signed a contract with a journalist, or a historian, or, the most obvious choice, a journalist specializing in history? From the beginning she had insisted on a more or less serious writer, a teller of tales, or for that matter an inventor of tales, which did not have to imply that he bent or falsified the facts—just that he slipped in additional facts here and there, different, unsuspected facts, and, once in the swing of things, suppressed or, why not? simply forgot some that were obvious, not necessary to mention? "The Facts, Not the Myth"—that was what one of the historically oriented journalists had suggested as a subtitle when he offered his services for the book project. And among other mottoes, this one, this very one, had sent her off on the opposite track, or rather sidetrack, that of the author, although there came moments when she felt she had fallen into his trap.

Be that as it might, she was confident that he would smuggle all kinds of other things into the series of facts; and those things would be decisive for the story. Story? This was closer to the true state of affairs: as others might aspire to earn a place in history, she wanted to earn a place in the "story." And it should be a story that could not be filmed, or could be captured only in a film such as no one had ever made before.

At one time she had been a reader. (She still read now, but for her it was not real reading anymore. She did not read properly. Yet she felt orphaned without reading.) And in those days the author, that accursed author—and not only because of this trip he was forcing her to take—had served her less as a hero than as a pilot? No, she did not need a pilot;

served? Yes, served. And although his last few books had appeared quite a while ago, and she had not even got around to reading them, the idea had suddenly occurred to her of having him write her book. Him or no one. And he would get down to work for her right away. No one, not even he, could refuse her offer. Even that he might ask for time to think it over would be inconceivable to her. Once, when she had been in another part of the world, as the guest of a president, a man who placed great importance on his own dignity and whose cooperation was almost a matter of life and death to her bank—"let us say, the president of Singapore"—in the middle of the negotiations she had demanded that a certain document she had left in her hotel room be fetched, not by just anyone, but by the president himself. "And he promptly went to get it!"

The author, without a new book now in a decade, was, at the same time, almost to his own regret—"almost"—by no means forgotten. Without being anywhere near wealthy, he did not suffer from a lack of money. He knew nothing at all about her and her worldwide legendary reputation as a banker and financial expert until her proposal reached him, sped to his garden gate by an authorized courier, and his ignorance was not the result of his isolated life in a village in La Mancha (where did such a thing still exist, a voluntarily isolated life?).

And he, too, an explorer of forms and man of rhythms, and otherwise quite inept socially, or perhaps reluctant, and also growing old, complied with her summons at once. In the village's one *tienda* he purchased a telephone card, and from the village's only phone booth he announced his arrival for the next morning in the riverport city (even though he had half a day's journey to the nearest airport). And then the meeting in her penthouse office: "I will write your book. For as long as I can remember, money has been one of the great mysteries to me. And now I want to get to the bottom of that mystery. And besides, I have always hoped for a commission like this: not a work but a product to deliver. An order." A man of rhythms? What kind of rhythms? "Above all the rhythm of understanding, that most inclusive of feelings, hand in hand with the rhythm of remaining silent, and leaving things unspoken."

She had seen photographs of the author when he was much younger. But his face seemed hardly changed. Only his body was smaller than she had imagined, wizened, as if desiccated, prickly, like something blown in from the *meseta*. At the same time, he immediately looked familiar, as only one villager can to another; familiar as one villager could be to another especially in a different setting, whether in the nearest town, or, as happened more and more often, in a country where they were both strangers: for these days it seemed increasingly common for the inhabitants of villages and towns—these especially—to be scattered all over the world, less as tourists than as residents, working, married into the most faraway places, dragging the children they had had with Japanese natives or blacks down a side street in Osaka or Djibouti.

Yet the sense of familiarity did not persist. As the author stood there before her—he refused to have a seat—he soon became uncanny to her. Uncanny as only a person could be whom one had promptly wanted to take in one's arms, only to encounter an invisible wall of glass with the first step toward him.

There was nothing in her realm—and her realm was wherever she happened to be—to which she paid closer attention than proper distance. But the distance this man preserved toward her (and, as she later observed: not only toward her) was a kind of affront. There were people who positioned themselves practically in your face, no matter what the conversation was about, as if for a film close-up. He, on the other hand, for the duration of their discussion stayed at least one step farther back than was customary for people engaged in negotiations or conferring with each other; if she inadvertently stepped toward him in mid-sentence, he immediately backed away, acting all the while as if nothing had happened. People like this were boors, just as much as those who practically rubbed bellies with you. And at the same time: once he was standing there calmly, he seemed rooted in her office as if in his own soil (farmers had long since ceased to stand that way), legs spread, hands on hips—the picture would have been complete if he had gone into a straddle, the way some soldiers marked their terrain. And all the while he looked past her or gazed at the sky visible above her head through the skylight, or stared at her, or smiled suddenly, or once sighed deeply, or hummed a snatch of an unfamiliar song, or even remained so completely silent for a while that she, assuming that he was not understanding her language (yet didn't they speak the same language?) switched to English, French, Spanish, Russian, and only when he apparently could not understand at all—precisely then!—did he start to listen again or wake up, and the discussion of the contract could continue. He struck her as peaceable and at the same time irritable, or vice versa. Too peaceable? Too irritable?

Nonetheless she had eventually commissioned him to do the project. That same morning the delivery agreement was signed and in force; she had drafted it quickly, and when it came to the final version, he was firm and alert, paying meticulous attention, with something to say about every sentence. She regained a degree of confidence in the author, different from the confidence she had felt at first sight, once she realized that his insistence on constantly enlarging the space between them originated in a sense of guilt. It made sense to her as soon as her instinct saw or smelled it—all the articles claimed that she was "a creature of instinct"—and when she unexpectedly saw and smelled in the man her own guilt; a great guilt; but off-limits so long as one kept one's distance. And how was it with her? She protected herself in a different way. And as long as she was protected, there could be no mention of guilt; instead, she had a secret. And she was proud of her secret. She would defend that secret to the death.

The author probably was the right man for the job. In the meantime, however—now that she had ventured into the story—it seemed as if her book still called for someone else, not a reporter specializing in banking but a third type. What was that question the author had asked? Did she want the book to have a more spoken or literary style? For him the spoken aspect provided the foundation, or rather the subtext, and furthermore a counterexample. Literary style, on the other hand, was the essential additive to the story, its enrichment, *the* enrichment.

Her predawn walk around the house, through the grounds, in the lingering moonlight. One of the increasingly frequent airplanes passing in front of the moon, its moonlit shadow twinkling across the lawn, so different from the shadows of planes or birds in sunlight; owl-like. The countless tiny mounds thrown up by earthworms before the frost came, now frozen hard, an insult to her soles with every step. Newly arrived in Yucatán, she was mounting the steps of the Mayan temple before sunrise.

From the densely intertwined, frost-withered, and tangled ivy that covered the wall at the bottom of the garden, little brownish-blackish berries with a blue haze popped off and flew in an arc, having ripened only now, with the onset of winter; and from inside the hedge she heard a pecking, cracking, smacking. Downstream the Isonzo flowed, where it was not yet murky from the cement works, over white pebbles that also formed the banks—the million dead forgotten (no, not forgotten). The blackbird—the earliest daytime bird?—came shooting out of the bushes, as always almost grazing the ground, and as always taking the curve with its wings folded, and hurtling with a loud squawk into the open through the escape hatch it had long since had its eye on.

She paused. The coppersmiths' street in Cairo echoed with the sound of hammers on metal; smoke and clouds of metal filings eddied from the workshops, open to the street, and she saw and smelled the billows far more intensely and lastingly than on the day when she had passed through there, although at the time she had been all eyes and ears.

Such images came to her daily, especially in the morning hours. She lived off them, drawing from them her most powerful sense of being alive. They were not memories, either voluntary or involuntary; these images flashed before her too suddenly, like lightning or meteors, and refused to be slowed or brought to a halt, let alone captured. If you wanted to stop them and contemplate them at leisure, they had long since evaporated, and with such interference you would also destroy the lasting effect of the image, which had appeared for a fraction of a second, darted through you, and vanished just as abruptly.

What effect did the images have? They ennobled the day for her. They ratified the present for her. She lived off them, which also meant that she used them and made good use of them. She even employed them for her work; her ventures; her deals. If she had an almost magical ("legendary," as the articles put it) ability to focus on the matter at hand, to display "supernatural presence of mind at the decisive moment," not only having all the facts and figures in her head but also dazzling her partner or counterpart in negotiations by serving them up as "a numerical witches' brew," she owed this talent to something she had not yet revealed to any interviewer—and what words would she have chosen?—namely, to the intervention of these images of hers in her workday.

Does this mean that the images were subject to her will after all, there to be summoned at will or as needed? No. They remained unpredictable. But over time she had discovered various methods of activating her "reserves." It was not a question of specific techniques, certainly not of tricks, but rather of fundamental attitudes and a whole way of living.

Yes, she had aligned her whole life, not merely her profession and her existence as a "queen of finance," to accommodate these shooting images. What fundamental attitudes and behaviors were especially productive in this regard? She, who by nature (or by virtue of her profession?) was little given to shyness, proved shy when it came to speaking of such matters, but she could offer hints: a kind of mindfulness in everyday actions; a willingness to take detours; not avoiding moments of absentmindedness when in the presence of others, but rather letting herself succumb to them; physical effort—not athletic, preferably manual labor—for sustained periods and at a steady pace, to the brink of exhaustion, when the images might begin to glow . . . (instead of an exercise room in her house she had a workshop).

Just as she lived off the formation of images in every sense, she also lived for it. And she did not deploy her reserves—"Never use this word again!" she instructed the author—for any kind of war. A single image, mobilizing itself and her, was all she needed, and the day would acquire a peaceful aura. These images, although devoid of human beings and happenings, had to do with love, a love, a kind of love. And they had penetrated her since childhood, some days fewer of them, some days whole swarms of these shooting stars—always taking the form of something she had actually experienced in passing—sometimes completely absent, a nonday. And she was convinced that this happened to everyone, to a greater or lesser extent. No doubt the specific image always belonged to the individual's personal world. But the image itself, as an image, was universal. It transcended him, her, it. By virtue of the open and opening image, people belonged together. And the images did not impose anything, unlike every religion or doctrine of salvation. Except that as yet no one had managed to tell the story of these images properly? Had also not found this phenomenon as earthshaking as she had? Had also not found the courage? (She certainly had not?)

To tell the truth, she was not even all that shy or modest when it came to this topic so dear to her heart. Over the years she had often felt the urge to spread the word of her remarkable and memorable encounters with the shooting images, or image showers. Was it possible for a modern woman, not just a woman of the Middle Ages, to have a sense of calling? The idea became more and more compelling: she had to reveal what she knew. And finally the message had appeared in glowing letters before her eyes: Now or never. The moment had come to tell the world! And, strange to say—as if this were part of her calling—it would soon be too late, not only for her but for the world at large. Everywhere under the sun the images were dying out. She had to entrust herself to some author or other—not to lay out everything for him in minute detail, but to hint at this or that and let him describe the problem as he saw fit. For she was convinced it was a problem, one of epochal proportions, decisive for the future, one that should at last be made productive, but above all a lovely one. And wasn't a lovely problem the ideal basis for an expedition, including a narrative journey like this one?

This urgent sense of a calling was new to her. Some commentators saw it as an outgrowth of her success, which for quite some time had been consistent, unsurpassable, and above all invulnerable: missionary zeal as a result of unequaled success coupled with invulnerability. Others, on the contrary, saw her proud, self-chosen solitude as the cause. And there were still others, for instance the author she finally commissioned to write the story, who suspected, or "had the inspiration," that her "quest" expressed a "terrible guilt"—he unintentionally turned the tables on her this way during their first conversation. "And you expect to achieve some sort of expiation as a result of expressing these matters?" No reply.

In point of fact, even though this was not the source of her specific guilt, she had already fooled many people by letting images play a part in her everyday and professional dealings. It was hardly ever done on purpose. The images never came on demand; if they came at all, it was involuntary. But whenever one of her images shot through her, as long as it was with her, she emitted a special radiance that instantly filled the room. Those present when this happened could not help referring this radiance to themselves. In business situations they promptly felt as though she could see right through them, whereupon they surrendered all their ulterior motives and became putty in her hands; they followed wherever she led, essentially doing her bidding.

That almost never redounded to their disadvantage: usually both parties benefited. The effect of the images was no illusion! On those rare occasions when things went badly, again both parties suffered. Thinking himself betrayed, the other party might then try to attack her physically (in her business dealings she was never perceived as "a woman"); when this occurred, the images would intervene in perhaps the most remarkable way of all: in the face of a threat—and more than once when a weapon was involved—an image would turn up, as unexpectedly as consistently, and each time only one, which, however, was so powerful that it projected a radiant shield between her and the attacker. Poof! a deserted sandy playground by a canal in Ghent, and the enemy was an enemy no longer. Poof! the diminutive library along the city wall of Ávila, with a view from its windows of the foothills of the Sierra de Gredos, and the woman became untouchable to her attacker.

But in private life, according to the stories that made the rounds, the images inflicted quite a bit of harm, even destruction and devastation. In that realm the images could be mighty deceiving, so people said. The radiance or glow emanating from her, the woman, when they were in her, could be interpreted by the person who happened to be present only as benevolence—no, as commitment, compliance, surrender. Nothing brighter, more open, more naked than the face of this stranger, this woman who unexpectedly turned to me with this radiance brighter than any ordinary woman's smile. Desire, love, compassion: all wrapped up in one. And then the recoil. Yet the radiance persisted. And that was what turned us deluded lovers into madmen or wimps, or both. And since violence was out of the question with her, that woman! our only recourse was to curse and abuse her. "You did not keep your promise." — "You betrayed me." — "You lead everyone down the primrose path." — "She is the epitome of coldness and heartlessness." — "A sphinx who watches with eyes aglow as we tumble into the abyss."

But perhaps she really did love no one and no thing? Was in love with or passionate about only the mystery of that one image floating in from the void, each time filling her to the brim with presentness, crowning her once and for all—wasn't this what she wanted to be—the queen of the present moment? And could one blame those people, male or female, who, when at such moments she touched their hand, stroked their head, seized them by the forelock, nudged them with her hip, or even blew on them (not merely breathed on them), when she acted so loving toward them, embodying promise, and then an instant later turned away or pushed them away, charged her with unfaithfulness and even worse? Love: that was something she did not want to hear about. Likewise friendship. And that was how it had always been?

On the other hand she wished and wanted her story and ours to be set in a transitional period—a transitional period when there were still, and once again, surprises. "As you know, in the earthshaking periods, those in which this story is *not* to take place," she explained, "there are no more lovely surprises."

2

Now, as the book's time frame opened, a sound reverberated through the predawn garden in the wooded hills of the northwestern port city, at once moonlit and all the darker in some spots. (There were nights, especially in winter, that seemed endless; never again would day come on earth.) The sound had been that of a sigh, almost identical to the sigh that had escaped the aging author at the meeting in her office.

What, a sigh? reverberated? A sigh that reverberated? Yes. And it had come from her. And it had resembled a sound in Arabic, borne on the gusts of air, mimicking and amplifying them, consisting of nothing but *a*, *v*, *u*, *h*; and now it became clear to her why the sound brought such thoughts to the surface: in the Arabic text that her daughter had left behind when she disappeared, or fled the house, and which she was now studying every day, the introduction made particular mention of this sound as an example of how in Arabic often a simple aspiration, or a small exclamation, or a vibration of the larynx, or even the simple articulating of a word through transcription could become the basis or origin of a sound. And *avuh* was just such a self-descriptive word. According to the commentary, it was the most innate human sound.

Had the sound really come from her, this person here? Never had such a sigh been wrested from her. And now something like a response issued from the darkness. It came from one of the trees onto which the early ravens had already descended. Up to this moment, they had done nothing but caw and chatter. But now they fell silent for a while. And out of the silence one of them uttered a wondrous cry of yearning. Or was it all the ravens together? This yearning represented such a break with the ravens' usual shrieks that she almost laughed out loud. This yearning was so tender that she, who was never afraid of anything, almost took fright. And she called out a name. No, she almost shouted it. She did not even know whether such a name or such a word existed, and what or whom it described. But describe it did! From the hill came an echo, and in the house a shadow stirred. Another predawn bird, always quiet, became part of the pattern in the garden gate.

Today was not the first time she had noticed, but now, before her departure, it became strikingly clear how much the spacious, plantation-like grounds had changed during her time here. The ground especially, the form and consistency of the subsoil, had been greatly reshaped in these years, not so very many after all. (The trees, on the other hand, had remained largely the same.) The grounds had already had some slope to them. But when she moved in, they had still presented a level surface, intentionally leveled. Now, however, this plain appeared transformed into a veritable miniature landscape of mountains and valleys. The thick white coating of hoarfrost on the grass brought out with particular distinctness the rhythmic pattern of hillocks and hollows. A new, young earthscape, formed in only a few years, primarily by the rain and the winds from the west. On the crest of some of the hillocks there already stood, seeded by the wind and no taller than a thumb, a bristly little conifer. The hollows deepened "abruptly," and some of them had little swampy patches at their bottom, with the vegetation to match. There were even stretches of moor, also tiny natural ponds (with frogs and dragonflies in warm weather). The water in them could come up over one's ankles. Except that now it was frozen solid. No heel could break this ice. Not only on the ice but also on the leaves and needles of the trees the hoarfrost took the form of small, raised, prickly rings.

The only trees that had joined the others during her time there: a mulberry and a quince. The mulberry was grafted; a trunk without limbs—the dense branches grew straight out of the top of the trunk and curved uniformly downward and inward, layer upon layer, so that now, with the leaves gone, the tree looked something like an outsized beehive. At the same time, the trunk was pitted, with deep, branching cavities that served as a refuge for bats. At the moment they were hibernating there.

Now something darted out and fluttered on a zigzag course across the sky. So one of the creatures had slept its fill for the time being? Did that mean that the freeze was breaking? She, however, was wishing for more days of frost—the frost-clear air was one of the things that made her not want to leave. Or did this bat's flapping, closer and closer to her ear, mean: Run along, we'll keep an eye on things!?

Strange, the way she always picked up signs and portents before a departure. But she had never actually turned her head this way to follow the signs. Stepping a few paces to one side, she gained an overview of the bat's flight pattern, so confused and erratic from close up but consistent and marked by regular repetition as a whole. And then it became clear that one figure in this pattern pertained specifically to her. As the bat flew back and forth, up and down, it was tracing with great precision the silhouette of the mistress of this property, in the very spot where she had been standing a few minutes earlier.

All her life she had been surrounded by animals this way. Especially those generally considered timid came up to her; used her as a zone of refuge or repose. The story went that as a young girl she had traveled home from Africa with a snake under her shirt, crossing several borders and traveling on ships and buses. She herself preferred to tell anecdotes about less ticklish contacts and encounters—for instance about the muskrat that came so close in a large forest, advancing and retreating in a rapid rhythm, all the while snuffling, and staring at her out of little black eyes, eventually coming so close that its whiskers and pelt brushed her toes: at times she could still feel a bit of that sensation on her skin. Or the dragonfly above the miniature puddle here the previous summer: she, the large human being, stood there, had been standing there motionless for some time, and then the small flying creature, the dragonfly, was hovering there in the air, directly opposite her, quite high up for a dragonfly, an insect that usually stayed close to the water's surface, both pairs of wings whirring so rapidly that they remained invisible and it looked as though only the spindly body were floating there, with the oversized head in front, blue-black, a yellow circle in the middle, filling the dragonfly face, and eyeing her, the human being, even though this yellow did not actually mark its eyes: deep yellow, coming closer to her from minute to minute and ultimately drawing her into the dragonfly planet with this alien gaze. So was this something to fear? No.

She would suggest to the author in his village in La Mancha that the stories linking her with various animals also had something to do with receptivity to images. The most timid animals were precisely the ones that recognized (yes, "recognized") when someone was "in the picture," got the picture, registered the image. With such a person they forgot their timidity, and not only that. They pulled the person into their own existence, even if only for a moment, but what a moment! It was not only that they had no fear of the person; they all wished the person well, each in its own way.

Unlike the grafted mulberry, the quince tree in the former orchard on the outskirts of the riverport city was like all the quinces, or *kwite*, she remembered from her Sorbian village. Today as long ago, here as there, the trunk of the national tree in her former village grew slim and straight, branching at stepladder-height into a tangle of limbs, and in the crown, always low, the chaos of branches twisted without trunk or limbs, and here as there one could count on a few blackened fruit, from last year and previous years, to hang on through the winter. And the blackbird's profile had also formed part of the image forever and ever, as had the third traditional element, again in close proximity, the empty, ragged nest. Around the nest now, piercing laments from the father and mother bird, robbed of their young, while in the grass below the marauding cat trotted off, twitching feathers in his mouth. No, that had been the previous summer, or several summers ago. And it will happen again next summer.

And—what was this now?—the hedgehog running toward her from the underbrush (which surrounded her garden), *qunfuth!* as she involuntarily called to it, "hedgehog," in Arabic. Was this the baby born the previous fall? It was. And it had not only survived the intervening months, orphaned, all alone, but also, sleeping under the warm, fermenting leaf mold, had grown large, was almost a giant hedgehog. Upon being spoken to, it paused, then trotted toward her even faster, singlemindedly, poked her with its hard, rather cold, blackish rubbery nose, and said, "Don't go away. The grounds are so desolate without you. I like hearing your footsteps in my sleep." The hedgehog had roused itself just to give her that message, and now promptly burrowed into its leaf pile again.

The previous summer, during an entire week, its mother, or was it the father? had done something odd for a hedgehog: it had circled the entire property in broad daylight, without showing fear, at first merely squeaking softly but on the last day whistling more and more shrilly. In the end the hedgehog had halted its rounds at a flagstone path. The animal lay down on this spot, warmed by the July sun, but instead of falling silent whistled even more insistently, its head poking far out of its prickly armor. The whistling became trilling, more piercing than any alarm or police siren.

The trilling became blaring. The hedgehog's pointed mouth as wide open as it would go, and despite her, the woman's, hand on its face, no hint of a retreat. The blaring escalated to the wail of an air-raid siren—from such a small body, such a tiny face! Finally the screaming animal's leap into the air, with all four legs more than a hand's breadth above the ground, and now another leap, diagonally into the air, at least as high again. Then the hedgehog's stretching out on the sun-warmed flagstones as if to sleep. Its legs extended backward, its nose pointing forward on the stone. And hardly a moment later the prickly oval studded with iridescent blue flies, of which a few had been buzzing around the twitching nose earlier; in this sudden death the spines no longer in neat rows but pointing every which way, all in a jumble. And at almost the same instant the baby hedgehog groping its way out of the underbrush, hardly as big as an apple, briefly sniffing at its dead father or mother, and then already gone in the tall grass. And now that screaming of the father or mother also said to her, "Don't go away. Protect my young one."

During her travels in Asia, she had repeatedly come upon images of the death of the Buddha. Almost invariably he had been surrounded by animals. And in the images each of these animals represented a particular species; in the crowd around the corpse there was almost always only a single exemplar of a given kind: one horse, one cock, one water buffalo. Almost innumerable individual animals of this sort wept for the dead Buddha, who in each case was their own deceased, their relative, their dearest beloved. And they mourned him, as one could sense from the depiction, out loud, each with its mouth, its snout, its beak open, according to its kind. And all the animals there, the elephant, the tiger, the hyena, the goat, the ox, the crow, the wolf, wept real tears. Their lamentations could not merely be sensed; they also became audible, and not merely to the so-called inner ear. And those most audible were precisely the animals otherwise thought to be mute. The rain worm wailed its sorrow. The fish stuck its head out of the nearby Pacific and/or Indian Ocean and roared. A sobbing as if from a deep chasm issued from the wild pigeon, usually hardly capable of even a peep. And she, the observer, was in the picture. She was deciphering the images.

As for her neighbors, on the other hand, was there nothing to decipher? Did she even have neighbors? Yes, but their houses were so far from hers, originally a stagecoach relay station and inn, later surrounded by one of the large orchards once numerous on the slopes above the river, so that the inhabitants at most glimpsed its outlines through the trees now and then, on the far side of the road leading out of town. As time went by, she had worked at home more and more. Only now even fewer of her neighbors showed their faces than before.

And that was not her fault. She inhabited not only her own house and grounds, but also the immediate surrounding area. At night especially she roamed the densely settled outlying area, combed through the wooded hills. And increasingly she found herself drawn to places where people were. Yet she hardly ever caught sight of them, and not merely in the dark of night. Although she had the ability, without really disguising herself, to be disguised to the point of inconspicuousness or even invisibility, did her population avoid her? No, they closed themselves off from the outset, from one another as well. Every house formed a multiply gated and buffered precinct. Those who had recently moved there (of whom there were more and more), at first loud and uninhibited, with their windows open—having escaped at last from rented apartments, now living within their own four walls—soon hushed their voices and their noisy machines, until by now hardly anyone far and wide let out a peep. Only the idiot of the outskirts, differing from the traditional village idiot in that he was brash and tactless, shouted, sang, and whistled on the streets, which were almost deserted, and not only at night.

It was only in the past few years that it had become so quiet in these parts (except for one hour in the morning and one at the end of the day during the work week). Sometimes the silence resembled the calm just before or after a war. But usually the silent yet well-lit landscape of the outskirts radiated a breath of peace. Credit was due to various longtime inhabitants. Often they were tradesmen, and often they were still practicing their trades long past retirement age—a shoemaker of seventy, a mason of seventy-five, a gardener of eighty. Younger, more up-to-date practitioners of these trades advertised in all the papers. But because their companies were almost always located elsewhere, the old folks just kept on working here, especially on small jobs. They also did better work, and they were more reliable—not because they were older and more experienced but because they had their shops and houses here in the area, one street away or around the corner from the job or the client; they could not allow themselves to mess up or do shoddy work.

Whether tradesmen or others: these older residents, even when they did not open their mouths, were walking tales of adventure, or tales that had almost merged with the fruit trees' interlaced branches, the shoe leather, the shovels yellow with caked-on clay. Once they began to speak, the whole world became the topic. Nothing wrong with collecting the dream narratives and ghost stories of Tibet or the desert Tuaregs' nomadic songs: But why did no one pay any heed to the epics and chanted tales of these old-time residents of the outskirts, or those who had once migrated or fled here from other lands with their parents? Camera, film, video, microphones for them, too. For their numbers were visibly dwindling: the hand that closed the shutters there last week will have closed them for the last time; lost legend, lost lament, lost song of love; even the loss of a mere intimation—what a loss.

As time passed, she also picked up some information on the newer residents, no matter how they barricaded themselves in their houses. It always happened inadvertently, in passing. And it was precisely their shadowy outward existence that provided the background. These people were bound and determined not to betray themselves. There should be no hint of who they were, what they did, what their names were, where they came from. With them a new era began. If a piano could be heard once from behind closed windows, it always broke off immediately. No laundry was hung out to dry anywhere, or if it was, then only behind dense hedges, out of sight. Even the vehicles disappeared deep underground, into garages located beneath the basements.

And yet their stories did not remain entirely hidden. From time to time, and always without warning, fragments or particles of them would pierce the walls of silence. A single elementary particle, whizzing in from an often indefinable distance, was enough for a situation to leave a scorch mark. A situation? An entire story, more distinct and convincing than if it had been narrated from A to Z.

Such things occurred more at night and most often in the depths of the night, in the hours after midnight. One might be awakened by terrible wailing. Or what sounded at first like angry shouting, someone ranting and raving out on the street, turned to wailing. It was a woman's voice, with a brief response now and then from a man's voice, soothing or trying to be soothing. And something more serious than an ordinary quarrel was taking place. Something was drawing to an end; these were, or gradually became, sounds of dying. Eventually the wailing, impossible to resolve into individual words, became positively tender. Nowhere, not even in an opera, had she ever heard such an intense lament. The man's voice, still quiet and controlled, was no longer answering but providing a soft accompaniment to parts of the song; and finally it vanished altogether from the tonal image. A pause. A car door slamming. An engine starting up. Silence. And the lament resuming, at the same time fading away, as if coming from someone slowly walking backward. Then the force of the nocturnal stillness, equaling the force of the now silenced lament. And she was not the only person nearby who listened, and listened, and listened. But then no ambulance siren either. And the following morning no hearse; only a raw emptiness in the street, and in the house over there, or had it been the one behind it? And not one neighbor who said a word about it.

And lying awake again in the hours after midnight. Sometimes she liked staying awake when she had some problem connected with her work to resolve. And again a voice. But this time from very close by. And she recognized the voice, too, although it sounded so different from usual. And besides, she could make out every word of what was being said. The voice was that of an adolescent, the son of the people to whom she had rented the former gatekeeper's lodge, a remodeled carriage house at the entrance to her property. Although the contract called for the tenants to perform some gatekeeper's duties in their spare time, she had learned hardly anything about the little family. She knew nothing about the man's or the woman's job, or where the boy went to school, if in fact he did. He did not greet her; looked away when he saw her. Unlike his parents, he did not respect the property lines, either the visible or the invisible ones. The second gate, which marked the entry to her own private realm but which she left unlocked, he used without hesitation for his shortcuts, skirting her house on his way to a gap in the hedge that led to a side street that was apparently important to him. One time she had even found him in her kitchen (she usually left the house unlocked as well), where he was sitting at the table reading the paper; at the sight of her, his leisurely loping away through the former servants' entrance.

The gatekeeper's lodge was not near her house, not at all, and yet that night she had the son's voice in her ear as close as in a dream, and also just as clear. It was no dream, however. And the neighbor's son said the following: "The two of you want me dead. Thanks for the bones you tossed in my cage. You will not be seeing me again. My bed will stay empty. Thanks for the flowers on my grave. But at least let me play one more cassette. Why do you not want me? Why did you not abort me? Why did you not stick me in the oven? Or into the false-bottomed crate? Burning desert sands. Your loving . . ." And then silence, here, too. The next morning a void. And the morning after that the adolescent just as before, but now riding a scooter instead of a bicycle.

And another such night, this time not so late. Her return from the bank's headquarters down by the river, before midnight, in her Spanish Landrover, a sort of camouflaged vehicle (how fitting if she had been driving it in a veil). On the already deserted highway leading out of the city, by the turnoff close to her property, a lone figure flagging her down. She stopped. A very young woman, still a girl, really, about the same age as her daughter, with a face that seemed separate from her body, in the dim streetlights: "Don't you know a house abroad where I can go, preferably in North Africa? I have heard so much about the light there. I must get away. I am older than I look. I know you. You paint, don't you? How can one paint around here, in this country? A house where I can paint, in Tipasa or Casablanca, right now!" And without waiting for her reply, the girl disappeared into the darkness on the side of the road. And she, too, became visible again: sitting by a distant skylight, reading, as though nothing had happened.

Even the children of the newcomers arriving here in ever-increasing numbers during the last few years—on their front doors at most their initials, and then often of the sort that could belong to a Greek, Cyrillic, or even Arabic or Armenian alphabet—remained in the shadows. Bundled up and silent, they climbed with their bundled-up and silent parents or caretakers out of their outsize automobiles, and it was easy to mistake them for the supersize shopping bags being hauled into the houses from the supermarkets after work (the small shops, still numerous, and the local markets were patronized only by old people and longtime residents: hardly ever an unfamiliar face there, and certainly not that of a child).

Coming home from school almost every child walked alone, eyes on the ground, as if to remain unrecognizable. And in spite of that they made an impression on her, too, sooner or later, more vivid than that of the neighbor children in her village back home—had she also been a child keeping her eyes to the ground in those days? And this impression always formed when she heard crying. No matter how far away the crying was, every time it seemed to her to come from the immediate environs. And she heard it during the day just as clearly as in the silent depths of the night, even at times when the road leading out of town was at its noisiest.

Not all crying came this close, affected her this strongly: the crying of infants hardly, no matter how plaintive, also not the crying that followed a fall or some other physical mishap. It was the crying, usually without tears, brought on by a first major disappointment, already definitive: even sounds, not bursting spasmodically from the breast but closed up inside it, quiet sounds, actually, almost silent already, pitched somewhere halfway between sobbing, howling, wheezing, snuffling, with a deep, unidentifiable bass underneath, and all this continuing in an infinite loop, behind the closed shutters of a house, behind a tree in a garden, or somewhere on a street, in an alley, gradually receding, a one-person caravan.

She, the listener, remained glued to the spot and at the same time moved along with the caravan outside. What she heard from these neighborhood children was the sound of abandonment. This sound could be uttered at the same pitch by an adult—any adult? yes, any adult. (Except that in a grown-up it might be so piercing that the adult would be drawn and quartered by his own cry of woe?) In the past, long ago, one had gone around with just such a sound of abandonment inside one. And it stayed there for good. To be sure, it had receded into the remotest corner in the body's labyrinth. But sooner or later, from one moment to the next, it would resume its place in the midst of things, with the force of an explosion. She had seen a film one time at the end of which a woman did nothing but weep for a quarter of an hour. She was sitting in a deserted stadium or park or an unfinished building, and suddenly she was weeping, without tears, like the children here, and she wept and wept. From time to time she paused. Then she resumed her weeping, fell silent again, but the weeping would well up in her once more, and so it went, with the weeping eventually becoming like that of thousands, the mother of all weeping, till the end. (The author, to whom she mentioned this, told her that in his youth he had written a play that consisted of a single sentence or stage direction: "Someone sits on the bare stage and weeps, for an hour.") She herself had not wept in a long time. But occasionally she still heard her own weeping from ages ago.

Of late more and more such sounds of utter abandonment or rejection had reached her from the out-of-sight children of the neighborhood. And then she actually got to see one of these children at least. It was a spring evening, the starry sky already clear over the forest and outskirts. The child was passing the playing fields on its way home, alone. The lights around the field were just going out. Along the road a row of ornamental cherry trees. The child beneath them, seen from behind, almost big, long since of school age. As it walked along, again and again at regular intervals there was a shuddering of the shoulders under the flowering trees, their color particularly rich in the glow of the streetlights against the surrounding darkness. The constant shoulder-shuddering is weeping, the sound accompanying it hardly audible, despite the nocturnal stillness, yet, once one's hearing has adjusted to it, not to be drowned out by any airplane's droning or any railroad cars' clanking. And thus the rearview-image child trudged along with that shuddering of the shoulders until it had passed the row of trees and the athletic field. Who would tell of that sound of abandonment someday?

One had neighborly feelings precisely for these strangers, these barely visible people. From far away one could often not make out their profiles or silhouettes, only small white—no, pale—blotches amid the general gloom: their heads, their faces, their hands; their professions also formed pale gray blotches like this; where all the new residents worked remained a secret (concealed by them on purpose?); how a person earned a living no longer mattered; and their clothing revealed nothing: and all this simply reinforced the sense of neighborliness. What was clear was only that none of these people numbered among her clients. Or perhaps they did. Weren't they full of surprises?

On the other hand, the fact that they could not form a complete image of her brought the new residents even closer to her. True, her property, the former stagecoach station, occupied a significant location, at the point where the road leading out of the city began a steep climb (in earlier times, at least one team of horses had been added at this point). True, the house was striking simply by virtue of its age, its size, its construction, its form, its distance from the other houses. But no one, not even her tenants in the carriage house, knew any particulars about the occupant. And people did not want to know anything about her.

Once, however, at an Indian restaurant around the corner, she was asked by the proprietor whether she was a movie actress. And another time, in the nearby Chinese fruit and vegetable shop, the ancient greengrocer, who had just moved there and rented the place, asked, "Weren't you in Macao as a child?" — "When?" — "Fifty years ago." Fifty years ago! In Macao! It was as if the Chinese man were transferring some of his years to her and as a result instantly became younger. Or was this a manifestation of the famous Asian inquisitiveness? Which was usually more an act than genuine? At any rate, the others around here did not even pretend to be inquisitive. And that meant, to borrow a favorite expression of the stagecoach relay–owner and financial expert (instead of "I don't want to," or "You're not allowed to," she always said, "It is out of the question"): it was out of the question that anyone here should know any particulars or intimate details about anyone else.

Altogether, this area seemed to her to exemplify a new way of living. That people kept their distance from one another to such a degree (although it was by no means an upscale area) did not signify the end of neighborliness. Without showing off, people paid attention to one another, respected one another. When the moment came, and only then, they would be there to lend a hand; and then promptly keep their distance again, staying anonymous, and, after greeting each other for a little while, silent again.

In one respect she even seemed out of step with the times by comparison with the new neighbors (and it was out of the question, that she, the banker, should be out of step): the majority of the new people did not move into houses of their own but into housing acquired for people like this—who would be moving on in a couple of years; in the period covered by this story almost everyone was like this—by the companies, firms, corporations, research institutes, laboratories for which they worked (this housing could include old structures bought up by company headquarters). A growing number of her neighbors were not homeowners, in contrast to her. The cars, too, were company cars, or leased. The same held true for their household goods, including televisions and chain saws. Nothing, or certainly nothing large, heavy, or entailing responsibility, belonged to them.

And by now she almost envied them for this; or rather, she was jealous of them, just as it was not out of the question to be jealous, as an involved observer, of a game in which one would like to participate. For wasn't the pleasure she had so long taken in ownership pretty well exhausted? Above all, owning land had once given her a very special sense of space, a feeling of having broad shoulders. To buy a piece of land to add to her own, then another: pure joy. (She actually used the word "joy" in the author's presence.) To beat the bounds of one's property with head held high (not to say "ride the bounds"). But by now one tended to beat the bounds with lowered head or searching gaze: What needed to be done? What tasks were pressing? What had to be repaired? cleaned? replaced?

Free through property? In her case, at least, it was becoming a threat to her freedom. One's perceptions were no longer free. Only parts, and particles, nothing whole anymore. And oneself, as a property owner, no longer whole. Strangely enough, one way out, a form of liberation, was managing money, other people's money, but also her own—as if money, being a moveable asset, had nothing to do with "possessions" and provided an opportunity for free play, like that of the others in the neighborhood. Hadn't this free play turned into something particularly uncontrollable by now, hardly subject to rules anymore, dangerous, threatening, and not only to her?

Some of the new ways of living also had to do with the location of her city. After a period of decline for riverports, they were flourishing again. There had been a time without any shipping at all; the rivers on the entire continent deserted. But now the waterways were serving as the most modern traffic and transportation arteries, and the cities located on them were becoming hubs as never before in history, even during the Roman Empire. And her own city, at the confluence of two rivers, formed something like the hub of hubs. A financial center like Augsburg in the Fuggers' day, especially in the time of the family patriarch, Jakob—but less because of its wealth than because of the sheer volume of wheeling and dealing. A life like this, on and between two world-famous and commercially significant rivers, imbued the inhabitants, and the new arrivals more powerfully than the longtime residents, with a particular sense of place: stamped with self-confidence or even pride, quite different from that of the residents of New York or some other great metropolis by the sea, an inlander's pride, so to speak.

Part of it was that the rivers and their characteristic surroundings were increasingly shaping everyday life, were gradually permeating it almost to the exclusion of everything else. In the market stalls you could still see all the varieties of saltwater fish laid out. But the point was that these were "laid out," dead or half-dead, whereas the freshwater fish "cavorted" in glass tanks nearby; even if there were not quite so many varieties, each individual exemplar was almost a species unto itself, and not only because it was so palpably alive, leaping about amid the throng of other fishes. For many years out of style, they were now increasingly prized, purchased, and prepared according to the old recipes, and even more according to new ones, were a component of the daily regional cuisine ("regional" having become no less important than "national").

Similarly the old orchards and the vegetable gardens or fields or terraces along both rivers, which had long been left fallow, now, wherever they had not been turned into building lots, were experiencing a second spring—summer—fall. The varieties once planted there were being supplemented and enriched by imported varieties or varieties moving on their own into the area as a result of the abrupt warming of the climate all over the continent. Of course exotic fruits, as well as olives, wine grapes, pistachios, and such, continued to be imported into this northwestern region. But in the meantime it had become customary—this, too, part of the new way of living—that once the locally grown crops had been sold, used up, consumed, no substitutes were flown in from another hemisphere. No more fresh cherries or blueberries from Chile in the winter. No more early fall apples from New Zealand in the spring. No more cepes from South Africa with lamb at Eastertime. And in her two-river city, the ripening of the local fruits, rather than being accelerated, was actually held back.

And soon hardly anyone missed such luxuries. Now the very absence of a familiar vegetable, an accustomed fruit, imposed a rhythm on the year; this periodic absence could add a kind of zest. New ways of living? The return or recovery of the old ways? (Though without folk costumes, customs, songs and dances.) What a historian had characterized as the phenomenon of "cultural continuity," the most reliable rhythmic recurrence in history, indestructible (or was it really, over time)? Be that as it might: how the old varieties of apples, now brought back, stood out from the interlopers, on the trees, in the orchards, but also under the artificial lights of the huge warehouse-style supermarkets. How they gleamed, how fragrant they were, and this was no humbug. Or was she the only one who noticed, with her eyes and nose from childhood, from her Sorbian village?

On the other hand, it was not she who created the demand, and with it the return of the continuity phenomenon, but rather her odd, evasive neighborhood. And equally odd her sense of being at home there. She knew, after all (had experienced), that it took only a tiny jolt, a phrase picked up in passing, and one would tip from presumed continuity into an isolated moment, not historical in the slightest but torn out of any temporal sequence, into a unique instant of complete isolation.

3

She had many enemies. And she had made almost all her enemies through her work. And they were far away. But one enemy was stirring things up in her vicinity; nearby. It had begun as love. At least this was the word the man used, the moment they met, or the second moment. They ran into each other in a clearing deep in the woods. She entered the clearing on a corduroy road whose logs were already half-rotted. Without warning, the image of a deserted beer garden, shaded by chestnut trees, in the hills above Trieste on a midsummer morning came to her, and she spread her arms. Just then the man slipped out of the dense underbrush on the edge of the clearing and was right next to her. She did not start. Perhaps she would have jumped under any other circumstances, but with the image present nothing could harm her. It was out of the question that anything should affect her. So she stood there, arms still spread, and even smiled at the stranger. It was a spring evening, long before dark.

It was the man who uttered the word. Was he a foreigner? For he spoke the word with an accent. The majority of those living in the area were foreigners. Or did his excitement act as an accent-generator and tongue-twister? His outfit resembled that of an escaped prisoner, not because of the fabric or the cut, but because of all the rips (along with his disheveled hair), probably from his running through the woods. And he did not say, "I love you," and so on, but rather, "You must love me. You are going to love me." And continued at once, stammering, "You need me. You have been waiting a long time for me. Without me, you are done for. I will save you. You will not have loved me in vain."

She kept silent. Only her eyes gleamed, thanks to the persisting image, which it was up to her to intensify. In the center of the chestnut-shaded garden stood a limestone column, damp from the night's rain, a stalagmite. Water spewed from an iron pipe. An espresso machine hissed. And in the darkening clearing a gentle wind now sprang up. The man resumed: "Listen to me! Listen, I say. In the end, God, too, for whom the prophet Elijah, or which prophet was it? waited so long in the desert, did not come either in lightning or thunder or in the whirlwind, but in the softest, barely audible rustling." He advanced a step toward her, but then, on the recoil, dove back into the bushes. His nose had been bleeding, and the white handkerchief he had dropped in the grass of the clearing revealed a red, many-eyed, checkered pattern.

Next to that tavern in the hills—not a single guest—the Paris–Moscow express stood waiting; the place was a border-crossing point. The windows of the sleeping car were open; empty berths; through the windows on the other side the bare white limestone cliffs were visible. Didn't the stranger know that the god who had made himself heard in the rustling breeze was an Old Testament god? That his voice in that gentle whirring was not whispering about love but was filled with wrath? That that god wanted vengeance, vengeance, and more vengeance?

After such a beginning, it came as no surprise that the man soon found out where she lived; and that his voice was heard over the intercom around midnight: "In all these years here I never set foot in that clearing—and then to find you there. It was a sign: you love me. And although I had never met you in the flesh, I recognized you instantly. If that isn't a sign, what is? And the third sign: whenever I come to an unfamiliar place, I look straight ahead and pass through it without looking to right or left—but this time I looked to the side at once, to where you were standing, waiting for me. Unlock the door. You must let me in."

She did not unlock the door. For all the doors were already unlocked. But he did not press a single latch, did not turn a single knob; just rang and rang outside the garden gate, all night long. Eventually she turned off all the lights and lay down on a sofa in the dark parlor, her sword, a relic from one of her earlier lives, at her side. The ringing went on and on. But in time that was precisely what calmed her and finally caused her to doze off. And the next morning, after an almost restful sleep on the sofa, the bloody-nose handkerchief again, on the driveway, like a playing card.

Next a letter: "How easy it was to penetrate you. Your cunt was panting for me. Your sex instruments drummed on me, plucked me and rubbed me, danced around me. Your vaginal membranes rattled and fluttered, swelled and swirled, sailing from firm land over an ink-dark sea as a storm raged. No doubt about it, I was made for you. And I promise never to leave you!"

Now the time had come to sit down with the man, in broad daylight, for a sober hour in late morning. But where? Even the choice of a meeting place was critical. It was out of the question to meet in one of the many little eateries in her area: she had never been seen there with a man, and that was how it was to remain. The bars on the outskirts were also out of the question. The patrons there almost always stood or sat alone (she, too, was sometimes there among the guests, so briefly that she seemed like an apparition). And when people happened to come in as a twosome, it was to be assumed they belonged together, and in a slightly unsavory way; these couples usually spoke in lowered voices and huddled far from the others, in the darkest corner, behind a screen, if possible, where, one sensed, one of them would reach for the other's hand now and then. And she? She was clearly without a lover. And yet looked as though she were constantly and intensely loved, glowing from being loved, from having been loved, just moments earlier.

She chose a playground near the main rail line. In accordance with an odd principle, here, as throughout the river city, two benches stood facing each other, as if for two pairs of knees. An even crazier principle governed the chairs placed around the benches, each at a different angle, as if they had been shoved together or apart, like furniture in an outdoor display— yet when one wanted to straighten them: the chairs refused to budge, cemented in, bolted down, anchored.

So one day, before noon, they turned up, on two such chairs, almost close enough to touch each other, and yet, because the chairs' axes were askew, at an unbridgeable distance, while to the left and right of them the playground equipment creaked under the hordes of children, and the express trains roared by, with shreds of paper and white river gulls in their wake, their flight quite different from that behind the keels of ships.

She began, unconsciously imitating him, with "You listen to me!" and then said something like this: "It is not that I am against you. But for a long time I have had a sweetheart, a partner, someone who belongs to me. And the man I love is infinitely handsomer than you. You are nothing by comparison with my man. I will never abandon him. Only in his arms do I feel arms. His hips are the only ones for me. Only his arousal arouses me. His smell is the only one for me. And he is not merely my lover, but also my co-conspirator and squire. He is my up-hill and down-dale companion, my rope, steppe, and desert partner. He is my bodyguard, as I am his. He is my slave, as I am his. He is my judge—unfortunately not strict enough. He is my attorney, who wins all my cases. But above all this man is my chef. He is a chef such as you will find nowhere else on earth. Not a swindler like the others, not one of those phony magicians, conjuring up an illusion of ultramodernity with their overly clever dishes, a tart seemingly straight out of the oven, fish on the platter as if just reeled in, colors and forms as if shaken out of their sleeves just that minute—creating the illusion of a present that in reality almost always originated yesterday, the night before, or even the previous week, and thus tasting of anything possible, or rather of anything unreal, anything but the current moment, the present. My beloved, on the other hand, cooks mainly with left-overs. He neither throws leftovers away nor tries to disguise them in the dishes he serves me. He has a masterful way of combining leftovers with fresh ingredients, and the leftovers are the main part of what he prepares for us. On our plates it is the leftovers that create a full sense of the present. Combining what was there earlier with what we have now is his and our secret. You are the wrong man for me. And you are not the only wrong man."

"What was your man's name?" the unknown neighbor asked after a while. — "Labbayka," she responded after a while. "That is Arabic, and it means something like 'I am here for you.' But why do you say, 'What was his name?' instead of, 'What is his name?'?" — The unknown neighbor: "I ask, 'What was his name?' because I think your lover must have disappeared long ago, or is dead, or is imaginary. And if none of those, his name is something else entirely. And I think you, too, actually have a different name. You are living under an assumed name. You have changed your name several times in your life. I know all your fake names. I am on to you. I can smell your guilt. When that comes out, it will be the end of you. Look at the red dress of that girl on the swing!" — She: "The child in the red dress went home ages ago, and besides, her dress was not red." — The unknown neighbor: "Do you want to know my name?" — She, already getting up to leave: "No."

For a long time after that the suitor kept his distance. Nonetheless she constantly sensed his alien presence. She felt not only observed and spied-on but also recorded and registered. With her special perceptiveness, which in an instant could capture everything between the tips of her toes and the most distant horizon, she searched the surrounding area, without her stalker's ever showing up—or only as in a puzzle picture, where body parts belonging to the person you are supposed to find might be inscribed in the foliage of a tree, or in the pattern formed by cracked stucco on a house.

At the same time, it seemed as though she were holding him at bay with this capacity for perception. He apparently did not dare to venture closer, not yet. But then she began to catch sight of him with increasing frequency, always from behind: when she stopped at a traffic light, he would suddenly be there in one of the cars up ahead, or he would be on the overpass above the highway leading out of the city, visible from head to foot, but again only from the rear.

At last one morning, as she stepped out through the gate, there he stood in the flesh (she actually thought: "At last!") facing her, so close that he looked as if he were cut out of cardboard or plywood, a figure in a tunnel of horrors. What preoccupied her later was less the fact that he drew back to strike her than that he had both hands full of flowers that he had pulled up, roots and all, from the border along the drive, and that the unknown neighbor was dressed up, wearing a tuxedo that called to mind, as she later told the author, a dance on the upper deck of a luxury liner, complete with brass band and the Southern Cross. "Did he throw himself at you?" (the author). — "Do not ask! I cannot tell the story if I am asked questions" (she). Besides, the author should know by now that so long as she was under the protection of one of her images no one could harm her.

A path through the Montana Rockies wedged itself between her and the attacker, leaving the latter flailing his arms behind the spruces over yonder, scraping his knuckles raw on their Rocky bark. Unripe cranberries growing along the edge of the path formed little whitish ovals, with the occasional riper ones among them looking all the more red. Were those bear droppings beside them? Wasn't what she said next expressed in an Indian language, meaning in translation "Out of my way, stranger. This is my territory"? And in fact he did beat a retreat, backing away slowly, as she, too, slowly walked backward, he taking one step, then she taking one, until they were out of each other's sight. Never again would the nameless neighbor raise a hand against her. Finally, before their reciprocal disappearance, they even laughed. As she told it, she had also laughed earlier, from inside the image.

Instead he tried to get at her with words again, both spoken and written. And she let him try. And since the oral modality suited them both better, she also agreed to a meeting occasionally; by now it did not matter to her where—so long as it was not in her house—sometimes for dinner, and also at her office.

At such times she was the one who ordered food or picked up the tab (he accepted it as a matter of course). And that was not the only factor that would have led an observer to conclude that their relationship must be based on some collaborative project, with her making all the decisions and him merely taking orders from her. Some thought they were witnessing a medical consultation, or saw the man, sitting there with the woman, as her research subject. At such moments, the idiot of the outskirts—at the time of this story the idiots lived on the outskirts, where they belonged—would be crouching nearby, as her protector, and indeed everyone's, listening in silence, eyes wide open, and thus assisting her.

Only the suitor spoke. And onlookers would never have guessed that every time he spoke exclusively of her. Viewed from the street or from the kitchen pass-through, he sat there looking like someone who was revealing his innermost feelings to a chance acquaintance. And she seemed to be all ears, saying nothing, as could hardly be otherwise in such a case. His many gestures, flowing one into the other, seemed to refer only to him. They underlined what he was saying. Would the woman listening have followed them so attentively otherwise, even the smallest of them, her attentiveness concentrated in the corners of her eyes, as she read his words from his lips?

From the outside, a passerby one time could see him talking and talking at her, making an expansive gesture, pointing outward and upward to the outdoors. He swung his arm so vigorously that his sleeve slipped back. And she followed his index finger without specifically focusing on it, simply by widening her eyes and face somewhat. And in fact there was something to see in the direction in which he was pointing: it was summer, a thunderstorm broke out, from one minute to the next, and over there, on the far side of the plaza outside the restaurant, a mighty old cedar suddenly toppled over, coming to rest at an angle, then a jerk, and another; and then, as its roots were ripped from the ground, it came crashing down on the plaza, just missing a family running to take cover; the two children laughed out loud at the fallen tree, while the parents . . .

But the man talking and talking in the window had not noticed the tree coming down, and had gone on talking without a moment's pause, his apparent pointing giving way to a plucking and tearing at his own hair, while the woman took in the tree's fall but at the same time maintained her listener's pose—as if that were the way to bring the stranger to his senses? to placate him?

For his gesticulating directly contradicted what he was saying. Every time they met, she was his exclusive topic. Yet he never pointed at or indicated the woman he was wooing; he even avoided looking at her as his eloquence poured forth. He squeezed his own throat with both hands and said, "Everything about you is ugly. Your house is ugly. Your car is ugly. Your toes are ugly." He poked his fingers in his eyes and said, "The one who will be the loser is you. You have already lost. Just as your parents were losers and your daughter is a loser, you must become a loser, too."

Each of his meetings with her ended with his reviling her; predicting or asserting the worst possible outcomes for her. Sometimes he began with compliments or pleasantries: "This morning the wind carried your name to me . . ." — "Today I would like to intone a gentle psalm . . ." — "Only you know your secret, evasive companion . . ." — "It was on a morning in April, O woman with the warlike eyes . . ." But after a few such sentences he invariably began to scold her, which just as invariably gave way to swearing and cursing, during which he might box his own ears, strike his chest, or bite off his fingertips. Yet the scolding and cursing was never completely devoid of meaning. Among the empty phrases he stammered out, there was always one combination that hit home, revealing unsuspected acts and omissions, committed, she had thought until then, only in a dream. An act of cruelty, of forgetting, of malicious desertion—had actually occurred.

In the period just before her departure, the suitor/neighbor's vilification of her had applied exclusively to the future. Not that he threatened her—threats were out of the question with her—he spat out imprecations. What began like a poetic traveler's blessing ("Thou shalt find flower-strewn paths . . ."; "The dark and lowering sky will enrapture thee one night") unfailingly ended with an unvarnished curse. She would lose what was most precious to her. She would never return. She would be done in. Let mountain lions devour her, her still quaking flesh!—When the author asked why she wanted to have this tale of confusion included in her book, she said only, "The more confused the tale, the clearer the pain."

Where was her rejected suitor now, on the morning of her departure? Where was he standing, recording her final rounds? And what if this were indeed her last journey—something less to be wished for than to be feared? And at what moment had the owls stopped hooting amid the crescendo of morning sounds? And at what moment had the moon ceased to shine—casting light and shadow—as its disk sank silently into the sky, pale and without reflection? And at what moment did the last of the stars become invisible, leaving not the faintest flickering at the spot where it had just been shining on the horizon, already bright with day? And at what moment had the weather changed, the crisp, silent frost that had held the area in its grip for weeks now giving way, from one instant to the next, to a mild breeze?

How exciting to experience, with disarmed senses, without instruments and machines, all these transitions occurring in a speck of time, and yet, even if one seemingly succeeded in doing so—"Look! Venus is still there, no, now, no, now, now, yes! all gone!"—the awareness afterward of having missed the critical moment again, and that it had always been that way, and would be that way to the end? Having missed even that modest moment when, after stepping into a forest, one grew conscious of oneself as a complete being, surrounded by forest?

Unexpectedly, so the story goes, the "world champion of global finance" (as she had been dubbed in a magazine article) found herself whisked to the midst of the wooded slopes on the outskirts of the river-port city, borne through the morning air as if on the wings of the portion of the story that had already been told, and especially the portion that was yet to be told. And it was as if her journey had already begun; as if she were moving, as previously in the orchard on her property, in widening spirals, gathering impetus for setting out. No one but her in the forest that early, tremendously alone. And why was she alone? Where was her suitor? Was he asleep? He could not be sleeping through this, could he, missing her and this morning?

As she mounted the slope, she repeatedly wound up to throw one of the chestnuts she had gathered along the way and stuffed into her pockets. (Maroni! Wouldn't they give away her geographical location? No, by now these nuts grew almost everywhere, they were practically ubiquitous on the continent.) She wound up without throwing. "Just the act of winding up and setting one's sights on a target," she told the author, "brings this target into view—a hole in a tree, a crack in a cliff—as an image, together with its surroundings. Winding up without throwing: another way of generating images from one's own stock. But what is the point of such an image? With my target images I defend myself without defending myself—I attack without attacking—I wage war without having to wage war."

Marvelous walking: beneath her feet the hoarfrost, still sole-deep, crunching and crackling as no snow could ever crunch and crackle (not only much quieter but also much farther away, or more dreamlike)—and overhead in the crowns a new pliability and a transformation from hoarfrost-white to trickling-water-black in the gentle thawing breeze. And in the bare chestnut trees the spiky fruit husks, long since split open, but now and then releasing a chestnut that had been held there for months by the husk, a lighter brown than those strewn over the forest floor, and not soft or rotting like them but firm and healthy, with fresh, pale-yellow flesh. What, edible chestnuts in January? Yes. She to the author: "What is time? I am still as puzzled by it as long ago in the village." The magical emptiness of a Monday, the emptiness of the week's onset in the forest.

But remarkable walking, too, because the forest had been destroyed a few weeks earlier by a December hurricane such as even this northwestern region, accustomed to powerful storms, had never experienced. The hurricane came in the night, and although it raged for hours, she slept on, slept and slept, more soundly than ever. As had happened quite often in her life, she missed the event. After that, going into the forest was prohibited. "But of course I went in." The first time, the destruction looked to her far less extensive than what was shown in the newspapers and on television, and not only because around the small section depicted she could see the rest of the wooded area. But each time she returned, the destruction seemed more drastic. Did trees continue to hurtle to the ground after the storm was over? On the other hand, didn't the long period of frost that followed the hurricane anchor the loosened roots in the soil? And yet each time there were more trees, limbs, crowns that had apparently fallen overnight. Or had her eyes merely shied away from taking them in all at once?

Not a wood-road that was not blocked by trees or scattered debris. One had to scramble over, or slip under, or take a tedious detour—which brought one smack up against the next obstacle, and then another, with the result that one might inadvertently end up outside the forest. So she decided in favor of scrambling and crawling. Decided? No, it went without saying that she would court obstacles and danger, as she always had. Danger? Some of the trees she dove under were not yet resting completely on the ground, but were still hung up on splintered limbs sticking in the earth, often only one support, and not a sturdy one.

But what was there to look at amid this devastation? There is no secret to devastation, she thought on her first sortie into the forest after the millennial storm. Only with repetition were her eyes opened. Where the trees had been uprooted, huge masses of soil had been heaved up. These were almost perfect half-spheres or else pyramids of sand, clay, and scree, cross sections tipped up perpendicularly, from whose midsection the lateral roots stuck out like rays, their ends sheared off and shredded, while the middle consisted of a much thicker fragment of root that projected toward the viewer, the mother root, so to speak. The trees torn out of the ground by the hurricane had thrust thousands of such former root balls up into the air.

The cleanup had not yet begun; it would require a ten-year plan, an entire army: but even if all the tree corpses were to be sawn up over the course of ten or twenty years and turned into neatly stacked woodpiles, it would be out of the question to level the densely scattered halved balls, pyramids, and earth cones that now reared up before one throughout the forest, like primeval yurts; all the layers of subsoil dragged out of the depths into the light with the roots, from the horizontal to the vertical, would probably remain this way forever.

That would create a new landscape, an area such as had never been seen before, with new, crazy-quilt horizons here, there, and everywhere. And because the wood of the roots was particularly durable, it would continue to portray the spokes of a wheel, with the hub in the middle becoming even more unmistakable later on, when sculpted by wind and weather. She had little curiosity, a trait she shared with most of the inhabitants of her native region: but she was curious to see how the transformed landscape would look.

And then the craters in all the places where trees had stood before the hurricane, most of them massive old oaks: now one could see, layer upon layer, the material deposited by previous millennia. The snail shells at the bottom of the craters had not rolled into them recently, but seemed to have been there from time immemorial. And similarly the oyster shells were not left over from a picnic in the woods, were not trash tossed into the root cavities after a tour of the damage, but were stuck there, removable only with hammer and chisel, as if baked, a thousand years earlier, to their prehistoric oyster bed, lifted by the catastrophe from what had once been the sea. And the black basalt there in the next soil layer down came from a vulcanic vein. Where am I? When did that take place? And was that now? And when is "now"?

None of the other trees had such spreading crowns as the giant oaks, or oak giants. At the same time, the branches in the crowns were interwoven, forming a dense mass. And nothing made a more powerful impression of devastation than all the oak crowns lying smashed on the forest floor. Yet even these almost countless heaps of broken limbs offered something to observe. On its way down, one of these giant trees had fallen on its equally large, equally broad, giant neighbor, which in turn had fallen on the oak in front of it, and now they lay there as a single trunk, forming a sort of transcontinental line, all pointing toward a common vanishing point at the very end of the continent.

This line was rhythmically punctuated by the ruined crowns, or crown ruins, which had the appearance, lying on the ground, of enormous cages, cages intended for games, for they were wide open in all directions, with remains of tangled branches. And never, in fact, had so many birds cavorted way up in the crowns while the trees were alive as did now down there amid the deadwood. Behind and between the bars of the pseudo-cages, birds eyed each other and whirred about, especially the smallest birds, the titmice, the sparrows, the robins, eating their fill of food that was otherwise out of range of their usual low flight orbit. They pecked and swallowed, and to the outsider seemed to be playing jailbird.

Now and then there were also fallen trees in parallel lines, and inside the parallel zones almost inaccessible patches of forest had formed, which, in the meantime, had begun to serve as new habitats (and not merely refuges) for a number of species that in recent years had almost disappeared from the forests, driven away or seemingly extinct: although they did not show themselves this morning, foxes had obviously recently dug themselves new lairs in these enclaves, and all the uprooted moss, scattered around in clumps, was their doing; wild hares openly darted back and forth between their holes, without fear, now returned to daylight after a period of keeping hidden (where?), and merely hidden, so not killed off; and squirrels now zigzagged horizontally through the protected area, as before up and down the trunks, while among them peacocks stalked majestically in purple and blue.

Only the flocks of wild pigeons had become homeless as a result of the shattering of the forest, and even now, weeks after the night of the hurricane, they kept fluttering (a great rattling from hundreds of pairs of wings) away from one of the few treetops still standing and described their usual one-quarter or one-half loop to the next treetop—but it was no longer there, so they were left treading the empty air like figures in an animated cartoon, before they circled on to the next tree of refuge—but it, too, was missing, and so on and so on, day in, day out.

Here and there creatures new to the forest had moved into the small ponds formed by groundwater that had pooled in the many root craters: tiny fish and frogs now beginning to stir under the visibly melting ice— how ever had they got in there? For instance the osprey, missing the part of a wing that she saw lying next to one of the craters, it having fallen out of the bird's beak as the osprey was tossed by the hurricane into the wooded hills from the river valley and, less flying than flipping over and over, crashed into one of the trees? (She stuck the piece of wing into her belt.) Also strangers here were the moles, which had long since become a rarity in the gardens down below—but here in these in-between zones formed entire new peoples, having emigrated underground from all parts of the city upon hearing of the storm, finding the resulting spandrels of safety, and above all the loosened earth, easy to excavate for tunnels and more tunnels: note the mole hills, tent-city-like, between the downed trees, and one mole or another would burrow fearlessly, like the rabbits, right up to the surface. A damned shame that she had to leave just now!

Many trees, too, instead of knocking down the tree next to them, had been caught by the more robust younger tree. Often the uprooted giants hung with their crowns tangled in the branches of the still upright neighboring tree, usually actually two such upright trees, one on the right and one on the left, suggesting the inescapable image of a warrior fallen to his knees in a Homeric—or at least not present-day—battle.

Added to this the sounds, as a gentle wind sprang up, of the living and dead limbs scraping against each other overhead: a whispering and chirping. This sound, however, drowned out more and more by a splitting and crashing clear across the forest: as the subsoil thawed with lightning rapidity, many of the trees lost their last foothold, one after the other, trees that the hurricane had battered down to their very roots but which until now had been merely cracked. Although the wind now came only in mild gusts, there began, all around, out of the clear blue sky, a paroxysm of falling, sometimes gradual, sometimes sudden, but cumulatively massive. One giant began to tip, almost gently, a jerk at a time, until all that remained, without any sound of its hitting the ground, was the space where it had stood, with a shimmering phantom image of its branches; on another tree the heavy crown suddenly split off; a third had the ground pulled out from under it in an instant; and amid all the bursting and crashing sounds, seeming to answer each other from every corner of the forest, suddenly complete stillness would set in; not even a whisper from the wind. She did not stir from the spot. Was she so sure of being out of danger? Or might a single step of hers trigger a succession of falls around her?

Then, as the wind picked up, the falling suddenly ceased; not a single tree coming down. A glance at the sky: the majority of the trees that had not fallen were leaning steeply, and almost at an identical angle, which made it look as though those still more or less standing upright, clearly the minority, were leaning. Was one leaning oneself, about to tip out of the picture? And again: Was this now? And wasn't it something other than, and more than, today's date?

A glance at the ground: in the thawing mud, and all the more distinct, the marks of paws, hooves, bird feet, shoe treads, crowded together, as if on a path, imprinted there as if from long ago; and someone with bare feet had also joined this procession; is joining it; will have joined it. And now, at forehead level in the more than merely thinned-out forest, at sunrise, the glow of the luxuriant wild rhododendrons typical of the northwest, hardly any solitary bushes, but dense colonies girdling the hill, as tall as a full-grown man, picked out of the gloom and barrenness, at the moment of the wind's breaking through and of the first rays of sun, as the only bright spot in the battered forest, a swaying radiance emanating from these earth-hugging creatures; from head to foot and, from the vanguard to the rear guard, a violent yet also even, small-caliber blinking, gleaming, flashing from the rhododendrons' evergreen foliage, in the same sunlit moment representing a sort of procession, caravan, or, most persistently, work detail or squad, marching in place and at the same time advancing and passing by, lingering while also constantly setting out, and the glinting comes from belt buckles, from headbands, from the braid on sleeves, but above all from the tools they are carrying, pocket calculators as well as sonar devices, hand telephones with a screen as well as the apparently long since obsolete handsaws, masons' spatulas (in a strange, streamlined form), kerosene lanterns. Involuntarily she broke into a run, unaccustomed though she was from her native village and in general to running: an obstacle course, which seemed most appropriate for her.

No, it was now after all; with the wind in the branches, it was the present, though with an admixture of other time periods; the present as it had always been. In the thumping of trains over the railroad ties could also be heard the booming of cannon firing a hundred years earlier and the creaking and screeching of wheels as horse-drawn conveyances mounted the steepest stretch of road through the forest, where they always slid back a bit, a backsliding that occurred despite the extra team hitched on at the relay station at the base of the hill. And the root craters from the hurricane would soon merge with the nearby bomb craters from the previous century, in this very forest.

This grander present, this grander time: "Behind the hubbub of the storm, behind the trunks and limbs fallen helter-skelter and lying on top of one another," she told the author, "one glimpsed the present, the unadulterated present, as a park? as a garden?—as a clearing—as an enclosure. What just a moment ago had been a hurricane-blasted forest now revealed itself as an enclosure, and so these words came to mind: The enclosure of the grander time, and one thought: When will this kind of time finally prevail? When will it finally determine everything else?"

The author's response: Was this thought part of her mission, like her belief in images? Her only reply: "No questions!" and she went on speaking as though she had not heard him. "What a delight time can be. No, what a delicacy it is. One would like to bite into it and eat it, nourish oneself with it. And it is nourishing in a way. When my daughter was a child, she would express her sense of time like this: 'It has been a long time since I have eaten an apple!' And now, when I came out of the forest, it occurred to me that I, who am famous for having time—'She has so much time, and in a position like hers!'—had to set out at once."

To stay here. To stay here? Now she clearly heard a cuckoo calling, in the middle of January, an echo from a dream. Did she jingle the change in her pocket? She hardly ever carried cash, and certainly not coins. Yet shortly before her departure she gave herself permission to be superstitious. Clinging to her hiking shoes was a mountain thistle, a kind that did not grow anywhere in the woods here. She ran into a neighbor whose obituary had been posted for days in all the local shops. So he was alive? And who had died in his stead? Long ago, in the Sorbian village, more than one person had greeted her grandfather, when he came into town after a longish absence, with the question, "What, you're not dead? Everyone was saying you died the day before yesterday!"

The enclosure of the grander time: what powerful gusts! And what phantom gusts now. At last she was sure about her journey. One way or the other she would learn something from it. And she would find a treasure, though not the kind one could seize possession of. Yes, was she a treasure-seeker, then? She had always been seeking a treasure, and always for others.

4

In that hour of departure, her rejected suitor had also crossed her path. In spite of the early hour, he was sitting on a bench by the railroad tracks, and she changed course to meet him, as if even from him she expected to receive a portent, as earlier from a flight of birds high in the sky. He gazed right past her, however, and not intentionally: he had simply failed to recognize her. Had the two of them ever really exchanged a word? And besides, he was not alone: at second glance he could be seen to have a small child on his lap, the child and he forming a pair—the pair on the bench, above a long, swooping curve in the rails, following, with simultaneous and perfectly coordinated head movements, the trains, of which one came into view every few minutes, gathering speed as it reached the city limits or already at full throttle.

And that morning she had also wanted to find an omen in the idiot of the outskirts, who had been circling, as usual, starting early in the day, with his long stride, back and forth and going nowhere in particular, and this all day long and all days long. She plucked at his jacket sleeve as she passed, thinking that she would give him a coat if she ever returned to her region (an odd thought, since the journey was planned for hardly more than a few days, and besides there would be no ocean to cross).

As always, the idiot had been marching down the middle of the street, in goose step and swinging his arms, playing the part of a local dignitary, walking and walking, and he had continued on his rounds with sovereign indifference to her plucking, showing the world his Caesarian profile, like that on a coin. He merely turned his bald, spherical head toward her as he sped past (his round face looking back between his shoulders) and burst out with one of his oracular utterances, to which others, and she as well, usually paid no attention. He bawled it out with all his lung power, his lips smeared with black as if with coal: "Ablaha! That means: idiot woman! For other women the sex foam, for you the octopus cloud! Octopus in the mountains! Madness is my currency. And what is yours?" (The author's comment: "Ablaha—a good name for you. That's what I'll call you from time to time in your, in my, story.") And then the idiot suddenly stopped dead, drawing in air with his throat and head, and saying: "I have a long story to tell about you, too. Woman, a tale told by an idiot, full of sound and without fury!"

Time and again, thresholds of departure before she finally set out. Much time has elapsed since that morning, but at least two of these thresholds still exist, in memory and physically, in that location, and someone familiar with the place will gladly guide one reader or another to them. One of the thresholds consists of the rows of stalagmite bumps on the bottom landing of the staircase that leads up to the small suburban railroad station; for as long as anyone can remember, there has been dripping from the rails above down through the leaky ceiling, and the dripping will continue: up above it takes the form of whitish, nail-shaped stalactites, dozens of them, crowded together, while on the ground below it forms round humps or bumps, which, when one makes a point of walking on them, fit into the tread of one's shoes and give one's steps a sort of bounce—the steps of those departing as well as of those arriving: in short, a threshold.

And the second threshold: in the most densely built-up area, a patch of unpaved road, impossible to pave, for the roots of two enormous chestnut trees protrude mightily from the ground, grown into and crossing each other, forming a root skein wider than a brook, diagonally across the road, poking up majestically like mountain ranges, and the hollows between them gorges, and one of the roots, all knobby, surmounting the others, skyward, forming what geologists call the *Gipfelflur*, the summit plain: as if prefiguring the mountain range she planned to cross in a three-day hike on her way to the author in La Mancha—the Sierra de Gredos: the pointed knob here representing the highest peak there, the Pico de Almanzor.

Now and back then, balancing from root to root, from ridge to ridge, committing to memory distances and footholds. Fortunately the hurricane had left both chestnut trees standing, and since that time no storm remotely as violent has swept through the area around the riverport city.

Other departure thresholds that had no external form and no visible existence, that exist only in the telling?: a glimpse into a garden familiar and beloved from before the storm because of the cedar there: no more cedar, which meant that the house had become a different house. And, on the other hand, houses that had always looked completely abandoned—and now after the storm it became apparent that they had been secretly inhabited, and would remain inhabited, and obviously so in the future. And the layers of the past revealed around the houses by the storm: in a garden, as if behind a curtain suddenly ripped away, the spoked wooden wheel of an antediluvian farm wagon; in the next one the outdoor pump that had been heaved out of the ground; and on one of the houses here on the outskirts the porch roof, supported by round granite columns that had remained hidden all these years, their capitals carved before most of the city's monuments: an eagle with eyes wide open and wings also spread wide—whose dance she imitated without anyone's being able to tell that she was dancing.

The smallest pretext used for delay. Was there such a thing: energetic delaying? Gathering energy from delaying? Narrative delaying?

Back on her property, turning off the switches (even the light switches, in the latest style, actually turned again), and turning on one of the lights again—let that lamp stay on for her not-distant return. Stopping at the door and going back to shake out her bedding, all the bedding, as if for the evening of that same day. Likewise half-opening the closed shutters. Taking some leftover food out of the freezer again. Amid the meticulous order left behind by the janitorial crew—she used the same one as her high-rise bank down by the confluence of the two rivers, the entire crew for just one hour each month—messing things up in one or two places (it looked almost like an escape route). Slicing an apple (the cut surface would turn brown even before nightfall). Turning off the alarm. Putting logs in all the fireplaces, ready to be lit. Switching on the radio on the kitchen table (at the lowest volume). Putting milk out by the bush for the hedgehog (several bowls at once). Retrieving some of the balls hidden everywhere in the bushes and rolling them back and forth between the fruit trees. Sniffing the withered quince. Unlocking one of the garden's side gates (after a period of electronically operated locks, keys had come back into their own; everyone in the riverport city carried a bunch on his belt, or somewhere else—the idiot of the outskirts had the largest bunch). Pausing in front of the boy from the gatekeeper's lodge, who was standing just then by the main gate, had the hiccups, and held out his two fists to her: Left or right? Picking one fist (one hand seemed as left as the other): Is this crumpled-up drawing supposed to be her? As a girl? Pocketing the drawing and placing her key in his open hand, the one and only key to open almost all the doors on the property.

On the side streets—with the exception of the road leading out of the city, which becomes a gleaming highway at its vanishing point, just past the city limits, there were only side streets "in my town"—moving vans could be seen in several places that morning; unusual for people to move away from here, and evidently to somewhere entirely different. What has got into them that they are leaving "my area"? No, they are not doing this of their own free will; they must go, driven from their homes, poor things, especially the children! The piano hoisted out the window, the four-wheeler next to the tricycle, next to the bicycle: What good will they be far from "my land"? And that clan setting out with the heaviest luggage imaginable—even the wheels make it no lighter—for the railway stations: Why must you leave this place, you pathetic figures, and why for so long? why going so far? But isn't she also one of these figures, dragging themselves with stooped backs out beyond the city limits? "No, I am traveling light, with my hands free. The one you see over there is only my double."

The winter/January traveler was last seen turning and walking backward until she disappeared from view: a considerable stretch on the straight, steeply rising main road out of town. From the two rivers down below the crackling of the thawing ice floes as they gallop toward the sea, one piggybacking on the other. Up there the crest of the throughway, with the glint of a pass.

It is still early in the day. Plenty of time! (The greeting customary in these parts.) Before night's end, which had been just a short while ago, almost her only companions being objects and their outlines, trees, houses, empty streets, the only sound the hooting of owls, taking on the contours of an endlessly repeated Arabic letter; and just after that the great majority of the animals, morning birds, ravens, blackbirds, falcons; and just after that the suddenly swelling swarm of pedestrians, among them not a few schoolchildren, all still in the darkness; and after that an hour in which machines dominated the scene, cars, planes, tractor-trailers, helicopters, with the passersby reduced to background figures, the animals (especially the birds) to sporadic undertones; and now, with the woman's,

"Ablaha's," vanishing up on the pass, that interval, still half-morning, half-midday, when with or without sunshine the whole region is going full blast, and yet stillness returns, a sort of second stillness, in which the machines, too, including the noisiest ones, have subsided into a kind of backdrop of activity, the occasional clatter of a helicopter, the drone of a motorcycle now almost reduced to memories, like the TV antennas, whether arrow-shaped or parabolic, and only the smoke rising straight up from the chimneys represents the present and creates a foreground reaching to the horizon on all sides ("hearth": Wasn't that once another word for "home"?), one step at a time the area around the rivercity was re-created in its morning guise, this time as well, today once again, or it re-constituted itself, embodied a being of flesh and blood, earth and fire, din and silence, a mighty being, a planet that in spite of everything still rose from the dead each day, stretching to its outer limits, not so much burst-ing with life as infinitely elastic.

Yes, a special planet had forced, pushed, fought, elbowed its way into the light of the world (so yesterday morning had not been the last time af-ter all). And what reinforced this impression was precisely the fact that the area served as a transit point or passageway and as an intersection or junction and place of exchange—witness the bank building at the conflu-ence of the rivers—for all continental and transcontinental movements. How would her area manage without her? How would her planet survive without her?

Perhaps she continued to walk backward for a while longer. But by the time she reached the top of the pass she had been striding full speed ahead for a good while. She did not even look back; presumably the so-called lady banker did not look back even once at her so-called riverport city down below, at her so-called planet! Not one thought for us here, no image of me in my narrow galley of a room, no good wishes sent from up there to us down here, the hiccups of the boy in front of the gatekeeper's lodge long since switched off, the drawing tossed in the trash, the draw-ing with her face most likely twisted into the grimace on a clumsily forged banknote!

Yet as she crossed the first lane of the highway she had almost been run over by a truck. And even before that, the garden gate, snapping shut, had almost jammed her fingers. And while still in the house, luggage in hand, she had missed one of the several stair steps and for a scary mo-ment had teetered on the verge of a major fall (a young woman in the neighborhood, whom she of course did not know—only I know of this accident, and hardly anyone shares my dismay—recently fell to her death this way).

And far from being relieved at having been spared, she had actually been indignant. Indignant? Yes, indignant at the thought that her trip might have come to naught; she would have missed the Sierra de Gredos; she would not have seen the village in La Mancha where her so-called author lived; she would not have been able to recount her other life, unofficial, but for her all the more characteristic, to this self-appointed, so-called author! In reality, this disloyal woman was even glad to get away for a while from her "leeched-out" country, from "this suburban life, beset by tedium—suburbaniting being the equivalent of rusticating," "the life there, often measurable only in numbers and in countdowns, only in seconds, minutes, hours, instead of in moments, daydreams, surges, inhaling and exhaling. Desiring, letting go, desiring all the more." What kind of desiring? What kind of desiring? Already she is too far away; she cannot hear me anymore. Did she ever hear me? Will she ever hear me? (The narrator here, dear reader, will not chime in again for quite a while.)

While crossing the top of the low pass, up there on the highest crest of the straight-as-a-die highway, she sang. Exotic singing, even for this day and age when the most unfamiliar tones, those of pygmies or other aboriginal peoples, can apparently belong to everyone. Singing without words; or rather with words, but in an idiom that no one understood, not even the singer herself—but what was there to understand? A singing analogous to riding; high in the saddle? but without a horse.

She had become once more the adventurer she had always been. And she had already survived the first adventure of this sortie, if only a minor one, right after she crossed the city limits: a man in a car had recognized her despite her disguise, which excited him all the more (a celebrity defenseless in the wild), and pulled up next to her, not only pointing to the backseat with his thumb but at the same time grabbing for her with his other hand. Through his open window she had struck him in the face with her bag, which she was still carrying over her arm, so hard that he tipped forward, his foot slipping off the brake, and involuntarily stepped on the accelerator—the car lurched forward and was already shooting past; what else could the driver do now but get out of there—but from the look in his eyes it was clear that she had made another enemy, an irreconcilable one, and he would take revenge, not immediately, for this was not the moment, but the moment would come. And once again that was fine with her: beyond the borders of her area she knew she was in enemy territory.

A strange state of affairs: back home hardly anyone knew who she was, and that helped her feel at home there, but elsewhere many people recognized her, and this recognition was usually accompanied by hostility. Threats, danger, exposure: so there were times when one experienced oneself out there in the real world only this way, as an adventurer more or less against one's will? And now she suddenly found herself back—at last—in just such a period (which in the meantime had faded from memory, relegated to the realm of legend). Heroic life? From now on, nothing but the heroic life! (We shall see.) She swung her bag onto her back and now had both hands free. And she stuck one of the feathers from her belt into her hatband.

It was a man's hat. Except that in the period when she undertook her legendary journey there was hardly anything for men that could not also be for women (the reverse, however, was hardly the case). From the top of her head to the tips of her boots she had on nothing that a man could not have worn just as well. Yet the way she wore it, and the way she strode along: there, under the open sky, on the shoulder of the highway, this was a woman if ever there was one, and not a woman disguised as a man, but a woman with rather broad shoulders, unusually large hands, and also rather large feet, recognizable from a distance, at first glance, as a woman to the core, as never before: Good God, what should one look at if not at her? And will she favor me now with so much as a glance?

Yes, she did look at me as she passed, in fact straight at me, and so sweetly, it seems to me, with a positively kind smile, or was she just making fun of me? Or did she not even register my presence, and her miraculous smile was inspired by her mental images—remembered or anticipated? As I turned to look after her, expecting her to do the same, all I can see is her rolling shoulders, already at a distance, and I see her pull a handkerchief out of her deep pocket and ceremoniously unfold it to the rhythm of her stride and blow her nose in the same fashion (and yet heartily), a handkerchief, or snot rag, as if from olden times, with blue and red checks, an embroidered monogram, not hers but that of her village grandfather, from whom her tight-fitting, seemingly bulletproof vest may have come as well, with braid woven of fine bronze wire, broken in many places and sticking out like jewelry, her only jewelry? No, she was also wearing earrings, a necklace, and bangles, which had jingled as she passed, and she looked made up, without any added color, even painted, her features seeming traced, her eyes in particular outlined to emphasize their shining. To whom was she on her way? To what party? And why was she walking alone, did not invite me to walk with her?

And what did she have back there in her apparently weightless bag, that of a parachute jumper? A parachute? Whose cord she would pull when she needed it? Certainly none of the following were in it: a hairdryer; flares; a framed photograph; a gold-plated ballpoint pen that could double as a flashlight; a bathing suit; a sleeping bag; a compass; suntan oil; today's newspaper; a nightgown; binoculars; a magnifying glass; a microscope; a lighter; a razor blade; a novel, a volume of poetry, a travel guide (at least not an ordinary one); small gifts; slippers; a survival kit; a spare hat, a spare vest, a spare pair of pants, spare boots, a spare vial of perfume.

So she was wearing perfume? No. But as she passed me that time on the highway, she seemed to be surrounded by an invisible nimbus, a nimbus made up of the breeze caused by her motion and coldness, a perfume of unparalleled freshness, and she positively exuded this breath of coldness, her lips most of all. I wanted to turn back at once and follow it, follow her; catch up with her. But she moved too fast for me, and not only for me. (This kind of narrative, too, dear reader, this bowing and scraping, is supposed to remain a rarity as events unfold, if it in fact intrudes at all.)

5

The day of her departure fell in the middle of the week. At any rate, Sunday was still far off; she already knew where she wanted to be by then, and was looking forward to it. The sudden change in the weather, the break in the cold, also swept away the last obstacle to her wanderlust: perhaps in compensation she would experience the frost, the continuation of pure winter weather that she had wanted to last as long as possible, as all the more persistent on her expedition, even if this expedition would be taking place far down in the south, which, with a view from the Pico de Almanzor, was almost all the way to Africa (didn't *al-manzar* mean "the view" in Arabic? or did the name come from *al-mansûr*, "the victor"?, hadn't a victorious Arab general and king during the Middle Ages borne that name?).

In the Sierra de Gredos, the summit plain, extending from the eastern massif across the particularly high central massif and all the way to the western massif, a distance of almost two hundred kilometers along the ridge, would certainly (or "without a doubt," one of the phrases in common use at the time of our story) be snow-covered, with the snow extending down into the highland valleys, and would no doubt remain so well into springtime. And when the January sun, so consistent during all the weeks leading up to her setting-out, veiled itself and then disappeared behind cloud banks moving in quickly from the west, that only contributed to her old, new, returning high spirits. The inky gleam of the asphalt, the clear, dark horizons, so far, far off, and the blue of the olives, covering the ground in a circle under the trees on the Sierra's southern slopes, where the time for shaking them to the ground and harvesting them would just have arrived! Even now, a thousand miles from there, up here in the northwest, she jogged a few steps toward that blue-shrouded world.

From the beginning she had been one of the pioneers of new ways of life (which in turn might represent the return of ways of life that had been forgotten or seemingly rejected for good). But ways of life did not mean sensational carryings-on, a whole new terminology, ear-shattering parties, dreamlike couplings, futuristic organizations; did not mean anything generally considered future-oriented, but rather present-oriented or present-enhancing practices; did not mean anything public or officially sponsored, either, but arose only from her and for her, without any reference to society or even to a community, and it became a way of life only through example and suggestion, and because it was perhaps already in the air; nor did it lead to anything more than having something in common with this person or that, without any sense of belonging to a clique, an avant-garde, an elite; such nonconspiratorial and sporadic sharing with people who were otherwise strangers, who could go back to being strangers after an amused or timidly deferential meeting of the eyes, such sharing represented to her during that period not exactly the most lofty but just about the most truthful feelings; at any rate, people like her, she thought, did not need—at least for a transitional period—a sense of community, let alone a sense of society; what she was aiming for was a sense of life independent of society and all systems (except, of course, in her profession, but for now that was to appear in her story only as a blank, unwritten, white space, making the adjacent passages—everything was adjacent to it, after all!—appear all the more vivid and colorful). And from such a sense of life the new or revived old ways of life usually took shape on their own, and in turn preserved the sense of life and kept it vibrant.

What ways of life? Neither climbing trees nor plunging into holes chopped in the ice. Neither running marathons nor retracing old pilgrimage routes. Neither mushroom hunting nor sleeping in caves. Neither spiritual exercises on Mount Athos nor journeys on the Trans-Siberian Railroad. Neither love-ins nor joining the Peace Corps. One example (which, truth be told, is no example at all): as a child in the Sorbian village, when it was raining, she had often dashed from her grandparents' house across the courtyard to the woodshed, because there, behind the slats that let in every wind gust, with her head almost bumping against the thin tin roof, she was so much closer to the action, the experience of "rain," and it surprised her that she was always alone there, standing among the stacks of firewood, within earshot of and facing the rain: a way of life!—but no one followed her and shared it with her. No, it did not merely surprise her but after a while actually infuriated her that she did not get anyone to share the experience with her: so even as a child she had the sense of mission that later appreciated in value with each article written about her.

A further example (which again is not an example): as a schoolgirl, and then as a university student, too, on all official occasions and at all public or political speeches, she made herself scarce as soon as possible, yet without leaving the hall: she would stay there, but would render herself invisible by going to sit or stand behind a curtain. And at such times there was always a curtain suitable for hiding behind—she would spot it immediately, and if it was not a curtain, then a blackboard, a screen, a map rack, or a wardrobe would serve the purpose. But it worked best, was most full of life, behind a real curtain, if possible a stage curtain, in front of which, at a lectern or such, the solemnities or whatever were taking place. Through the years, the schoolchild and later student of economics crouched in the dim light behind just such a stage curtain at every "event" (though in those days they did not yet use the English term), and felt surrounded by a space entirely different from the one out there in the social realm, felt that an entirely different time was in effect—but why did no one ever join her here, either? for wouldn't even her enemies—from childhood on she already had a large flock of enemies—if they had only stepped behind the curtain where she was hiding, have promptly if not forgotten their enmity, at least put it aside for a few moments—decisive moments?! Where are you, you fellows? Why do you not come out and admit it: This is the right way!? What do you expect to accomplish out there in that phony light; have you forgotten the rest of the world? Was she a Cassandra? No, to people like that she would not have pointed out impending disaster. No catastrophe-early-warning mission. No treason. No messing with destruction. But all the same, a child, a girl, a woman with a mission?

Not until much later did she find here and there some who shared her little idiosyncrasies when it came to ways of life. But that was in a period when she had long since ceased to be surprised and annoyed that no one cared to imitate her. That, for example, she kept the identity of her child's father a secret: in those days quite a few women did the same; and, like her, these women managed to live without a man. Another, rather small, example, more a feature of everyday life than of the larger arc of life: among a minority (though not a statistically relevant one, and not merely in her region but throughout the world), it had become the custom not to listen to music anymore, either at home or at concerts; merely the custom or a deliberately chosen way of life? A way of life. And a further, even more insignificant, example: another tiny minority had taken to turning off the lights in their houses and simply sitting quietly in the dark, at a window or in front of a screen: a mere habit or a way of life? A way of life.

Another such new or old way of life could be seen in the way she set out for the airport now. She walked to the airport, which lay almost half a day's journey on foot from her city in the northwest; she hiked to her plane. She had started undertaking such hikes long before this, whenever she had time, and as we know, she always had plenty of time.

She had undertaken the first such hike in Berlin, when she walked from a street off the Kurfürstendamm all the way to the entrance to Tegel Airport. Although it was a weekday, in her memory it became a Sunday. She followed Schloss-Strasse, looped around Charlottenburg Palace, first taking a slight detour into the Egyptian Museum, followed Tegeler Weg along the perimeter of the palace grounds, unexpectedly found herself walking along the Spree—which she remembered from her childhood in the Sorbian village as a rivulet, unprepossessing yet deep—almost close enough for dipping one's hand into and at the same time fast-moving, winding, meandering, alternating between river-breadth and brook-narrowness, then, before the branching-off of the West Harbor Canal, even coming up with a real island, the water pulsing westward in wide, rhythmic curves, following the drainage bed of the ancient river valley, with a hint of long ago in the wind currents and the shimmering at the bends, which detracted not at all from its presentness. And onward, then as now, turning north, away from the Spree, on the shoulder of the city autobahn, with the Jungfernheide on the left and Plötzensee on the right—was she still in Berlin?—scrambling half-illegally through allotment gardens and over fences, pinching fruit from the trees, slipping under barbed wire, dodging ferocious dogs (although after their first, feigned lunging they backed off even faster, into the farthest corner), shouting at fleeing rabbits, whereupon these halted just before their bramble bush and pricked up their ears, and a few moments later came the automatic doors of the terminal, with its monitors and loudspeaker announcements like "Moscow," "Tener- iffe," "Faro," "Antalya," "Baghdad" (as she was still crawling through the brambles onto the tarmac, the destinations were being called out, sound- ing as though they were coming from the airplane engines just being started above her head).

Later she almost preferred walking home after a landing in her area, often hiking from the runway over hill and dale straight to her house. And in this practice, too, she was not alone. By now quite a few people made their way home in this fashion, especially after long trips; hiked the last stretch, which could sometimes take longer than the whole flight. Be- sides, when going in this direction one had no need to fear arriving in a crowd, as could happen at the airport: initially one might be more or less accompanied by others, in a fairly large (though usually rather small) group, but then one person after another would peel off, and one would reach one's destination alone.

Now homecomers of this sort could also be recognized even at a dis- tance by their (deceptively) light luggage, which nonetheless was clearly luggage, well traveled (without stickers), and by a certain self-assurance, almost arrogance, in their gait that allowed them to walk along the shoul- der without wasting so much as a sideways glance at the vehicles rushing by them, often passing perilously close on purpose and honking sense- lessly. Among themselves, too, they acknowledged each other at most with a once-over out of the corner of the eye: such an acknowledgment providing a sort of sustenance to keep them going.

Nevertheless she then wanted to persuade the author of her story to come up with a different beginning for her journey: hadn't too much been revealed already, less about her—she perhaps had something en- tirely different to reveal—than about the circumstances prevailing at the time, which, as previously mentioned, were supposed to be portrayed more "ex negativo," through things that did not make up the foreground? The author: "But isn't that what has just been described?" — She: "Why not let me take a boat down the river? or: 'She walked to the large new bus station on the very edge of the city, where buses depart several times a week for all the other riverport cities on the continent: for Belgrade, for Vienna, for Düsseldorf, for Budapest, for Saragossa, for Seville, and across to Tangiers by ferry, each of these modern buses more fantastical or dreamlike than the one before, hardly recognizable as buses anymore, interplanetary transport modules—only the clock in the bus station still the same as when I moved here a decade and a half ago, still showing the wrong time, five hours fast, or seven hours slow.'"

The author: "But what will happen to the message of your book?" — She: "What message?" — The author: "For instance the one about the new or recaptured ways of life." — She: "Well, have you ever had a message?" — The author: "Yes, messages and more messages. But only the kind my book unexpectedly presented to me." — She: "Happy messages?" — The author: "Up to now, almost exclusively happy ones."

With scratched forehead and muddy boots, her, and our, arrival at the terminal. So much fresh air earlier, and now, from one step to the next, in a different element. Element? Almost exclusively revolving doors now, holding back the world outside. But even where an old-style door stood open for a bit, no breath of air made its way into the hall. On the gleaming floor no footprints but hers. Nothing but scrape marks from suitcase wheels and luggage carts. Not a speck of free space; every inch of the airport floor occupied by people walking, standing, queueing up, running— each sticking to the beeline to which he or she had laid claim. Many talking loudly to themselves—no, they were shouting at people who were not there. But not every one with a hand to one ear was holding a so-called mobile telephone: here and there amid the racket a person simply cupped his hand over his ear and kept silent.

In one place there were drops of what looked like a nosebleed, in a dice pattern: one of the passengers, of whom there were not a few, had walked into an interior glass wall, perhaps seeing a reflection of the outside and thinking he was outdoors? On all sides, illuminated maps of the world and globes rotating as if four-dimensionally—was this the atlas of distant places from her childhood? Or is the atlas of distant places instead the view from my window here? Where are you all trying to get to, with destinations you have been talked into or forced to choose, at times, on days, and for a length of time over which you also have no control, that you must allow others to determine, and all of which—destination, departure and arrival time, duration—have nothing to do with your former and perhaps persisting love of travel, as well as your still possible spontaneous longing to set out, rendered impossible, however, by this dictatorship of money and the computer? Didn't the current restrictions on travel conflict with the right to freedom of choice, one of the fundamental rights enumerated in democratic constitutions, and the need for spontaneity—the pleasure of surprising oneself and others? ("End of message")

Wild dove feathers on a conveyor belt, and one person or another also picked them up and pocketed them. Some people dressed in black, about to take off to attend a village funeral. A family sleeping on a bench off to one side, even the parents barefoot. An army of deep, gleaming reflections that catch our eye and make us turn our heads, but nowhere an image, a live one? A child, staring straight ahead, ignoring the motley scene, and thus also ignoring it for me.

Single raindrops on the dusty road. Walking up a creosoted plank, as wide and thick as a door, from the wharf to the ship. Where had she seen this plank before? In the maritime museum in Madrid, in a display of the equipment with which the sailors of the Spanish-Austrian empire had sailed across the seas, especially the western ones, to "West India," Venezuela, Mexico. The board was so thick, and it was seated so firmly on both ends, that it did not sway or bounce once under her feet, all the way to the railing. So when was that? In the sixteenth century, around 1556, to be precise, shortly after the abdication of the *emperador*, the emperor Charles the Fifth, and at the time of his crossing, in a litter because of his gout, of the Sierra de Gredos, on the way to his retirement in the cloister of (San) Yuste, in the southern foothills. And where was that? In the largest Spanish international port of the time, Sanlúcar de Barrameda, also a kind of riverport, on the río Guadalquivir, below Seville, where they hauled in the Indian gold from afar. The gangplank was not yet positioned vertically, fastened to a wall with ropes, as later in the museum, and it was also not creosoted, but scoured white by salt (from the famous salt mines of Sanlúcar, with their "salt unequaled for drying cod"), and she had walked up it barefoot, like the sleeping family from overseas today, or whenever, on another morning of departure here, or wherever, in the airport terminal.

She was famous in a way that allowed her pretty much to decide for herself whether people would recognize her or not. And thus she usually went unrecognized, even though someone always stopped short in front of her and involuntarily traced her face and her outlines in the air—and was then at a loss as to what to do with her: the drawing erased.

Becoming blurry and interchangeable in this way was difficult to sustain in airports, however. That was where she was always most likely to be recognized, for better or worse. Usually for worse. It never happened immediately upon her being recognized that people wished her ill. At the first sight of her, many eyes even expressed surprise and pleasure. Someone or other seemed almost happy to run into her. Even those who had some prejudice against her were at first taken aback and barely refrained from greeting the woman warmly. She looked completely different from the impression people would have formed from yet another report, article, photograph, news item, portraying this devious string-puller and puppeteer.

First of all, in real life she was infinitely more beautiful. And then, in contrast to her occasional staged appearances on television, where she displayed a grimly noncommittal expression, she was open and accessible. The very way she moved revealed that from everything and everyone she passed she absorbed some feature and took it with her, in her swinging shoulders, at her temples, behind her ears, in the curve of her hips, in her wide knees, and it was precisely that feature that stood for one as an entire person—the feature discovered by her in a flashing glance and scanned into memory, that reminded one of oneself as a figure that bore no resemblance to a type or to one's role in the current situation.

A jolt, and just as quickly it was over. The attentiveness and empathy shown by that person were all an act. Didn't everyone know that in her youth, before she took up her few previous professions—before her present one—she had starred in a film (a film, by the way, that was still shown, not only in certain movie theaters in Europe but also in clips during her television appearances: a tale from the Middle Ages in which she, one lay performer among others, had played Guinevere, the wife of King Arthur and at the same time the mysterious beloved—was she or wasn't she?—of the knight Lancelot).

This era, the time in which her present story was taking place, was one of distrust, by now unprecedented. No one believed anyone anymore. Or at least people did not believe others' displays of affection or friendliness, compassion or desire, let alone love, of no matter what kind. If a person beamed and expressed joy, others did not accept his assertion of happiness—even when the person in question was a child. A person might scream in pain—but after a moment of hesitation and concern, all too brief, the person he was with would look at him askance: not just with distrust but also with disdain.

None of the true or perhaps primal emotions were taken at face value for long, with the exception of hate, disgust, contempt. Were those primal emotions? The primal emotions from the dawn of time? At any rate, this was an era of spectators who were not simply malicious but actually evil-minded. Perhaps not at first or second sight, but later, and then relentlessly, they wished those who crossed their paths ill. This woman's beauty now: ah, yes! But as they turned away, the spark of pleasure and reflectiveness changed abruptly to thoughts of violence: of hurting her for her beauty; humiliating her for it; punishing her for it. Was there such a thing as primal hate, primal rage, primal disgust, initially undirected, then seeming to find redemption in taking aim at beauty, this most rare phenomenon? I, the spectator, as judge and hangman? Redeemed in this manner from the hate inside me?

Airports seemed in those/nowadays to have become the breeding grounds for the spoilsport activities of the millions of malevolent spectators. At least in these surroundings their hostility was not subject to any soothing influences (which, on the other hand, were hoped for? after all, didn't I myself suffer from this blind rage?). Was it the stale air and the ubiquitous artificial lighting—even in places where the natural light, coming in from outside, would have been adequate—that made us all the more irritable? Or the impatience, unavoidable in such a place, that also provoked ill will? Airports, especially the large ones—and there were almost nothing but large ones, or enormous ones, now—irritated people into hostility. And a person who had already been a sort of enemy was almost always transformed, when we bumped into each other there, into a definite, definitive enemy (without words—precisely because we did not exchange a word).

Thus she now ran into one of her enemies from work, who was clearly on his way to some other place entirely, but crossed her path again and again in the labyrinthine complex, or was walking in front of, behind, or even next to her. Finally he turned white as a sheet, and she heard him grind his teeth with hate as he lit a cigarette, clicking his lighter fiercely and making it flare up as if he were about to burn someone at the stake, while at the same time he punched the airless air with his metal attaché case. And countless strangers, at the sight of her well-known face, were ready to hurl insults at her. The insults could come unexpectedly, from a side corridor, or when someone passed her on the moving walkway, or from behind her, hissed by someone she could not see—who remained out of sight, either because after launching the sneak attack he promptly disappeared or because as a matter of principle she never turned to look at such people.

Now, in the hour before her flight, a voice became audible, close to her ear, the voice of a woman, not soft, just shaking, with rage? with age?: "You should be ashamed of yourself. You have brought shame on your father and your mother and your country. Shame on you!" Beauty as provocation? It seemed that in this transitional era it had become a wicked provocation—her kind of beauty made people turn wicked? And how did the woman react to this contempt? On the one hand, it left her unscathed, this woman who was happy to have no parents and no home. But on the other hand, as a mere rebuke, it awakened and deepened her awareness of guilt—no hour passed when that did not suddenly intervene in her life, between one step and the next. And yet on the other hand: an ants' trail there beside the moving walkway! The dead pigeon, skeletal, way up on top of the glass dome, where it had lain for years. The rustling of the palms of Jericho. Or are, and were, those the equally towering palms of Nablus? She had sat, was sitting, is sitting, will have sat, all alone in the sun on a deserted terrace with a view of the desert. The dog half rolled in the sand; next to his stomach, the much smaller cat, likewise.

With these images she did more than keep her attackers at bay. She struck back at them. The image of the moment served not only as armor but also, whenever more was called for than peaceable disarming, as a weapon. With the images she had the power literally to do the other person in and "eliminate" him. Without his knowing what had hit him, and without his registering the image, it struck him, launched from her eyebrows or shoulder blades, catching him with the force of an electric shock that darted through him from the soles of his feet to the top of his head.

So now the metal attaché case belonging to her enemy from work was knocked out of his hand and went flying across the terminal, and he staggered after it. Now the old woman's voice that kept hissing at her from behind became a choking sound, and a moment later the ghostly figure was swept from the scene by one of the needle-sharp palm fronds from Nablus or Jericho. At any rate she wanted the author to slip these incidents into her story. The author: "So they are invented?" —She: "No. Actually happened, for the retelling."

During takeoff, it seemed as if it were no longer early January, as it had been just that morning; as if the onset of winter were long since behind one, and as if, with dark clouds overhead threatening rain, one were somewhere in the middle of the year, or the action were being resumed at least a month later. A thistle poked out of the concrete runway. Then the bunches of fox grapes down below along the edge of the runway had faded; no more silvery sheen in the gray; and their wintry garlands hanging there limp. And as the plane gathered speed, one of these withered garlands swirling up toward her window, beating against the glass with an otherworldly sound, as on the door of a stagecoach. And moments before, the rumbling of the landing gear like the rumbling of a bus on a potholed road through the Pyrenees. And outside on the tarmac, bouncing and tumbling along, the burrs ripped from the prairie thornbushes, in clouds of desert dust, the image precisely prefiguring a sequence, an hour later, or how much later? in the film playing above the passengers' heads, obviously shot against the bare brown of the Iberian plateau, seemingly final and unchanging, to which the green of the northwest will long since have given way.

"Love quest!" she had thought, with one eye on the film above her head, the other on the landscape far below, feeling simultaneously stared at from the air, from the film, quietly, fixedly, from a distance, unapproachably, from as close as anyone or anything could possibly be. Desire set in, or intensified, took center stage. For her desire was always present, was constant. "Not a moment in which I do not feel desire," she told the author, and she said it matter-of-factly, as if it were something to take for granted. "Desire or longing?" (the author). — "Desire and longing."

Except that her desire was such that hardly any person in her presence could recognize it (and presumably it was not directed at him in any case?). Anyone who did perceive it was more likely to be filled with alarm. Never mind whether I am the object or not: Get me out of here! She has gone mad. What a rough voice she has. What faces she makes. She will tear my head off. She will plunge her sword into my heart. Or she will simply spit on me and show me her nine tongues. Or she will wring the neck of the child in the seat next to her. Or she will hurl the child and herself out the emergency exit, above the río Ebro now, over the río Duero now, onto the cathedral coming into sight down below, no bigger than a child's block, dedicated to "Our Lady of the Pillar," of Saragossa, not the northwestern but the southwestern riverport city already: without exception, men as well as women, even children, even animals, we promptly turn tail and flee from this wild woman's longing, desire, fulfillment, helplessness—all in one. On the kitchen table in her deserted house the passion fruit, or pomegranate? or lemon? and laid out next to it the knife, clouded by the exhalations of fruit flesh forcing their way through the peel.

A love quest? Love? At the time the word "love" was all the rage. (She had urged the author to use tasteless or clichéd expressions like "all the rage" now and then in her story so as to "muddy" and wrinkle it a bit.) Not only was there no longer any hesitation to utter the word "love," and then why not several times a day. It also blared constantly from microphones and loudspeakers, in churches as well as in railroad stations, in concert halls, stadiums, courtrooms, even at press conferences; you could see it, red on white, and not in fine print, either, on every other election and advertising poster, see it flashing in every third neon sign.

"Loving punctuality" was a slogan for the railways: which meant that instead of departing late, the trains departed early, so that one was always missing them. At the executions now being carried out daily, in Texas or elsewhere, as the convict lay there with the lethal injection already dripping into his vein, there was routinely a reading from the Epistle to the Corinthians, ". . . but the greatest of these is love." Nothing but love songs, broadcast by Radio "Longing" or "Seventh Heaven" Channel, echoed through the subway and suburban railroad stations, where, likewise day and night, heavily armed soldiers patrolled, and the towering metal barriers, long since far too high to be jumped, and not only for children and old people (who in any case were banned from the premises), clanged shut on the heels of the lucky holders of luckily valid tickets who had slipped through in the nick of time, shut behind the "beloved passengers" with a thunderous crash that echoed through all the subway and suburban tunnels, repeated and amplified a thousandfold, to the accompaniment of Elvis singing "Love Me Tender" and Connie Francis singing in German "Die Liebe ist ein seltsames Spiel," on Radio Paradiso or Radio Nostalgia.

After an era of peace, not phony but healthy, robust, confident peace, when many of us felt happy about their era, "our era," the present, the darkness of a prewar period had closed in again. But this was a prewar era such as had perhaps never been experienced before. Peace continued to dominate the picture, the word "peace" written everywhere in the sky by planes, traced in the night by torchbearers, just like "love."

And at the same time war had already started, the old kind that pitted peoples against one another, as well as a new kind, pitting every individual against every other, the second kind more ruthlessly bent on annihilation than the first. Not only did she, as a lady banker, or whatever, have many enemies: by now anyone could be surrounded by enemies, and was their archenemy in turn, their enemy to the death, and that included the participant in a friendship banquet or lovefest just as much as Delegate No. 248 to the International Peace Conference, No. 2 in the Council of the Twelve Wise Men of the World, as well as Dying Man No. 3 in the ward of the House of Death, and us idiots, hiking through the woods with our fellow idiots (who said this, who was narrating this story?—the Council of Idiots).

This war of each against each—often most cruel against those most like me, against those closest to me—was never formally declared. In the past, if someone said, "From today on, we are at war!" or "I will destroy you!" or "Your hearse has been ordered!" or merely "Die!" that was more like a joke; at least one could ignore it. The current war was waged without a formal declaration. It took place wordlessly, behind the façade of the streaming images, sounds, and pictographs of "peace," not limited to a dove with an olive branch in its beak. Instead of "War!" as a threat, one was now more likely to hear "I love you, and I will always love you!"; instead of "From today on, I am your enemy, and you will find out soon enough what I can do to you!" it was "As your friend, I . . ."; and a threat that meant almost certain death was "We will never ever abandon you folks!"

Do the minutes of the meeting of the Council of Idiots end here? No, they continue a bit, something along these lines: in the current era, ancient enmities between peoples, usually going back hundreds, if not thousands, of years, had flared up again. After a period in which we thought we had finally and definitively been saved from them, at least on our continent (what deserved the name of salvation here, if not that?), all the hereditary enmities had bubbled to the surface in Europe, in their most naked form. Long ago, very long ago, even among the prejudices peoples had against one another, there had been a few affectionate ones and many that were at least ambivalent: if the X were lazy, at least they were jolly; if brutal, at least reliable; if bad cooks, at least good musicians; if bandits, at least not sociopaths; if reeking of garlic, at least the best beekeepers. But now all that mattered between peoples were the terrible memories, the most terrible ones, which completely dominated the present. Where did people today get these memories, when they had grown up with history books from which any trace of antagonistic allusions to other countries had been expunged?

Grotesque memories in our part of the world, meanwhile unified as a legal and economic entity and thus almost a single state, as once before in time immemorial; all intracontinental borders eliminated meanwhile, so that one could travel by reindeer sled from Lapland to Thessaloniki, on water skis from the Wörthersee to St. Petersburg: "You Spaniards stabbed my brother with a spear in Cambrai in July 1532"; "The Liechtensteiners betrayed us to the Turks back in the Middle Ages"; "The British are mining the English Channel as they did under Henry VIII"; "The Swiss are swearing fealty just as they did long ago to a land where the sun never rises"; "There's not a single Frenchman who does not bear collective guilt and will not have to make amends for the beheading of Marie Antoinette . . ."; "Your goalkeeper killed our defender." End of the Council of Idiots executive summary?

By now every people detested every other—and detested completely—detested each other as never before in human history. Declarations of friendship between peoples and celebrations of eternal reconciliation held official significance only, and were merely temporary, not for the long haul: soon evil thoughts emerged among the official representatives, too, among them especially (what the population as a whole thought was not expressed openly, as had always been the case?, and only a god could have articulated it?).

The "people's representatives" on the one hand and the "political educators" on the other were the first to drop all restraint toward the opposing country and appoint themselves leaders in the war of words. This phenomenon, too, was no novelty in history. What was new and unheard-of in this transitional period—or will it turn out to have been the end of time?—is that the "leading statesmen" and the "opinion-molders" were saying precisely those things, which they then put into action, for which in previous historical eras the mob had been known, or which had at any rate been ascribed to it.

There were no longer any borders? Yet restrictions and prohibitions as perhaps never before. When a current leader of one sort or another found his prohibitions colliding with the many recent restrictions, something coalesced in his person that we had thought consigned to the distant past, long buried in the obscurity of legend: in him, things that played a role only in historical-recreation films, and were increasingly fading from human memory, all the malice, murderous impulses, lynching fantasies, and bestialities buried in the ancient rubbish heap of his country's mob, found their new mouthpiece and third rail. Everywhere the perhaps over-rated mob of formerly existing countries, reduced long since to dust and bone fragments, was reembodied in the current leaders; and each of these revenants rivaled his predecessors in defiance of the law, blind rage, and homicidal hatred.

But strangely enough: the old mob now became visible to us only and exclusively in the person of the revenant—no mass of people presented itself as the new mob, only those who in each other's company styled themselves the "leaders." Our memory preserves from earlier times a specific image of the traditional mob: how after a speech in a hall or a stadium by the leader of the day, in the surrounding streets and squares, up to then deserted or peaceful, the manhole covers begin to pop up, and his followers, who have been lurking underground, are catapulted into the light, an instant majority, for the moment just grinning palely like ghosts and shoving a bit, not yet pouncing and crushing—but wait, just you wait.

And almost the same image fits the modern mob: it, too, in the guise of the so-called leaders, suddenly hoists itself out of a sewer opening, one over here, another over there, ready to pounce and strike—except that they remain isolated, without a trace of a following or a people behind them—and why do they not wage their wars in single combat, as used to happen in the Middle Ages or in legend, man-to-man, woman-to-woman, etc., stabbing, shooting, bombing each other out of existence—instead of their respective peoples—after posing for a photo opportunity for posterity, for all I care?

The prewar gloom: the wars between the countries of the continent, outwardly united and border-free, had not yet broken out; would perhaps not even break out in the true sense; would not be declared and would also no longer be called "war" but, for instance, "peace operation" or "love action" (see above). Yet one of the new leaders, from the former cornflowers-in-the-gun-barrel movement, made a revealing slip of the tongue when his favorite slogan—"Not war—love!"—reversed itself in his mouth into "War *and* love!"; and in fact, during his last "Operation Out-stretched Hand" (against another country), his wife, barren for many years, finally got pregnant (his caressing of her belly in public).

And at any rate, the incidents preliminary to war were piling up, and again it was indicative that they were always mob actions committed by the leading personages, and that these mob actions were directed against what was probably one of the first basic laws of primitive, still stateless, societies—that more and more leaders, invited to visit another country, trampled the ancient law of hospitality underfoot, worse than any old-time mob.

One of these characters took his morning jog, dressed accordingly, by zigzagging through the valley where the host country's kings were buried (a photo that later appeared on the dust jacket of his how-to book for jog-gers). A picture of another leader made the rounds showing him in a bomber flying over a country that had been almost completely wiped out in the last world war by his forefathers. He was laughing uproariously, his feet in tennis shoes propped on the improvised map table at 5,000 me-ters. A third leader (wasn't it always the same one) could be seen at a compulsory peace conference jabbing the host in the chest with both hands, one finger on each hand extended like a dagger. And a fourth, while touring a foreign city destroyed in civil unrest, did not go on foot or by car but had himself pulled in a small cart by a couple of natives, so that he towered above the crowd, with an expression on his face as if he were also the camera by which he was having himself filmed for television, along with the city and the victims.

And the fighter-bombers now far below the passenger plane, menac-ingly close to the plateau: Wasn't this the long-awaited open war against the legendary people—these days a mere tribe, a mere sect—that had al-legedly retreated into the most remote reaches of the Sierra de Gredos?

6

She had never spoken of the fact that she had another brother. In all the articles and brochures featuring her, the only brothers mentioned were the alleged microchip–half brother and the one who had died as a small child in an automobile accident, along with her parents. She was the eldest of the three siblings; the unmentioned brother was the youngest, born just before the parents' death, and plucked unscathed from the wreck.

On the very day in January on which she set out on her portentous journey, her brother was released from the prison, or "detention center." For several years he had been locked up there as a "terrorist," not merely over the hills and far away but in another country. She to the author: in the accounts of herself and her business prowess her brother had obviously had no place. But now he was to appear in her book. She had not withheld information about him because she was ashamed of him. (On the contrary? Also not on the contrary.) And she wished, she wanted her brother not to be merely mentioned in the current book, "my definitive book," but rather to figure as one of the main characters, "of course along with me and also various others."

What should be told about him? The events leading from his childhood up to his crime, from the trial to the completion of his sentence? Primarily his story from the current morning on, when he steps through the narrow discharge gate of the "Institution for Implementation of Justice" a free man, his hands now free like hers, over the hills and far away and even beyond the dunes. Unlike the visitors' gate, which is as wide as a barn door and opens onto the beltway, this gate lets out into a cemetery, the size of about ten stadiums, with light-colored smoke eddying at that moment from the crematorium there, in which flakes of rust mingle with snowflakes, the smoke now intersected abruptly by a flight of wild doves, shimmering in exactly the same color, as if the birds had just been given birth to by the smoke or had slipped out of their shells there.

"Along with my adventurous journey I want you to tell my brother's as well," she directed the author, "describing how he will have made his way from the prison gate across very different lands, during the prewar period and later in the middle of war, to the country he had chosen in his youth as his future home—but he is still young, of course!" — The author: "But how? Should I invent a story?" — She: "Don't pretend to be dense! And stop making yourself out again to be more insignificant than you are! If I picked you to be the author, you may be sure I had my reasons." — "And what were they?" — "Although you may have invented a detail or two in your books from time to time, and perhaps even everything (I have not the slightest interest in knowing that): all in all, your long tales have always been accurate, and in particular will remain accurate for the foreseeable future, infinitely more accurate or real than any conceivable factual accounts, and they were, and are, also infinitely more real than the alleged reality that people boast one can touch and smell."

The author: "But I do want to capture something you can touch and smell." — She: "You're splitting hairs again. Fortunately you do this only in conversation, not in your writing! Enough! There is a kind of touching and smelling that is different from grabbing and sniffing out. And besides, you are famous for being able to take a gesture, a hint of movement, a voice—that has come to you from afar, for only an instant, often only from hearsay—especially the gesture, movement, or voice of a stranger, and transform yourself completely into the other person. Someone down at the other end of the street limps ever so slightly, and you embody him here until he has disappeared around the corner, and long after he is gone. That is how my brother, just released from prison, stepped out of the cemetery that morning—" — The author: "—which lay beyond the Baltic dunes, and in heavy snow pressed the access code on the hand telephone given him as a going-away present by one of the guards." — She: "You fool!" — The author: "But that is what happened, is it not?" — She: "Yes, that is what happened."

She had visited her brother often during his years of incarceration. Each time it had been a long and momentous journey; and she wanted from now on to undertake only this kind of journey, if any at all, not necessarily to some legendary foreign prison or other, but certainly journeys with an undercurrent of uncertainty, fear, sorrow, pain, and the threat of no return.

She had stolen time for these visits to her brother from her busy schedule at the big bank. Flying in the morning into the city where the prison was located and returning, at the latest, on the evening flight. One time she arrived at the visitors' gate after two hours on the plane and a two-hour taxi ride and did not see the usual long line. She was the first one there that day, and felt exultant. It turned out to be the only day of the week without visiting hours. And she had to go back that same evening. No admittance, no exception, even for her. She walked around the entire facility, the size of a small town and heavily guarded, sat on a bench in the cemetery, where she ate an apple and dozed off briefly; not a sound from behind the walls, and yet the sense of being close to her imprisoned brother as hardly ever before; in her one-minute dream on the cemetery bench he was bending over her and breathing on her.

Another time, as a participant in the annual conference of the World or Universal Bank, being held in the prison city, she was able to stay overnight, and took a penthouse suite in a hotel in the dunes offering a view of both the sea and the compound, with its electrified fence, search-lights, and watchtowers. At sunrise the rolling North and Baltic seas in the distance, and the momentary reflection of the prisoners taking their morn-ing exercise—they themselves not visible—in the tilted sight-blocking screens mounted atop the far side of the wall over there, where for short stretches they consisted not of concrete but of smoked glass. Allowed in then, after hours taken up with the usual security checks and backups—one stalled line after the other, in the course of which the visitors at a standstill there eventually developed a kind of tribal solidarity, not only with the prisoners they were waiting to visit but also among themselves—allowed in and escorted to the so-called visitation room in groups of five or six at a time; in actuality it is a windowless shed, divided by a row of tables and chairs, and down the middle of the tables a glass panel, without an opening for speaking through; in the case of short prisoners or visitors, the top above the level of their heads; and this shed suddenly full to bursting with the five or six visitors on one side and the five or six prisoners on the other side of the panel (to which had to be added two guards on the right and left flanks); these dozen people all talking at once, in pairs, with a hug hardly possible because of the high panel separating them, at most a quick brushing over the hair or a stroking of the forehead with outstretched fingertips; no talking, just a din, increasing steadily during the brief visiting period, almost always cut short because of the noise; each visitor had to drown out the others to be heard at least somewhat by his imprisoned family member, or vice versa; but given the general necessity for shouting and yelling, with more and more words becoming incomprehensible, and even lip movements impossible to decipher after a while, because the mouths were opened so wide; at the same time the entire clan pretending to understand and make sense of what was being said amid the racket in the shed; and yet at the same time, even though they were now standing and speaking over the glass panel, on tiptoe, with one ear long since within spitting distance of the speaker-shouter, not making out a single word; and not even hearing their own words as they uttered a response at random, not a single word—and then "Time's up!" and the next instant the prisoners, without being able to exchange even a last glance, already out of the room and on their way back to their cells; now deafening silence, in which each visitor separately, no longer part of a family or a clan, will have departed in a daze, making for the outside, for freedom.

Even discounting the pandemonium, she could follow little of what her brother said, and less with each visit. For one thing, he expressed himself more and more in the language of his chosen country (just as in the letters he wrote her, which she had to have translated—a problem: because outside that country hardly anyone knew the language, and anyone who did kept the knowledge to himself like a guilty or shameful secret). And then, with the passing years in the distant penitentiary, her brother expressed himself more and more exclusively in riddles and incomprehensible images—yet spoke and wrote in the same quiet rhythm as before (not falling silent or becoming frenetic).

Just moments ago his glowing eyes and his almost elegant, collarless white shirt, not at all prison-like, in the shed steaming with sweat and spittle, and a few heartbeats later she was in the parking lot outside the visitors' entrance, facing the flags of all nations displayed outside the luxury hotel diagonally across the way (from the outside, the prison, built far below street level, was unobtrusive and easily overlooked); the chauffeur of a hired limousine waiting for her, and a few breaths later opening the door for her by the seaside conference center, where she would deliver her keynote address on riddles so unlike her brother's: "The Riddle of Money"; the hands of brother and sister clutching each other above the dividing panel, the leathery softness of the limousine, with classical music (immediately turned off on her command), the flashbulbs going off around her, the star of the conference, and all as if in the same moment.

In the meantime, however, the chauffeur had unexpectedly revealed that he was intimately acquainted with the penitentiary, as a former guard, also with the visitors' shed, known to all as the "port of good fortune."

On the morning of his release, her brother probably did step through the special discharge gate into the cemetery by the sea. But he was not alone. Two plainclothes policemen and a staffer from the attorney general's office of the country that had incarcerated him escorted him. He did not walk through the cemetery to the highway, but was led straight from the gate to a car just then parking along the first row of graves. The car was not a hearse, and he was driven by the shortest route to the main airport. (The bird that had come flying out of the smoke from the crematorium, as if having just slipped out of its shell there, had not been a dove.)

At the airport ticket counter her brother was handed a passport from the country he had chosen as his home. That country no longer existed as an independent entity. During his imprisonment it had been annexed to another, newly created, country. His passport was no longer valid. The country to which he was to be deported now, bordering his homeland, was the only one on the continent where his passport would still be accepted temporarily as identification (though it was still valid in an island republic near the South Pole and in two dwarf states, one in the Himalayas and one that had been an Indian reservation and had declared its independence from the United States).

The official from the attorney general's office read her brother the deportation order. Henceforth he was forbidden to set foot on the soil of this country. If he ever again created the situation that had led to the years of incarceration, it was not merely not out of the question but a likelihood bordering on certainty that he would forthwith be convicted of a criminal offense, just as before. Away to his homeland with him— wherever that might be; to his family, wherever some of them might still be found: after landing he would make his way to them, somehow or other. And thus her brother was deported that morning by air, in downright princely fashion, with a free ticket, and, also in princely fashion, alone, without any possibility of return? without any necessity to return; free, freer than he had ever been.

And no one had given him a hand telephone as a going-away present, certainly no cell-unlocker. He could have used the phone to call his girl-friend of many years, down below in the prison city on the northeastern sea, whose houses now, from the plane, which had immediately climbed very high into the clear sky (no, it was not snowing that day), had blurred with the ocean foam.

But telephoning was forbidden on board, and a hand telephone like that would have been no good for a call from the other country, either. His sister did not know who his girlfriend was, or whether she even existed. As she flew high over the Iberian plateau—with the tracery of its arid valleys so clear from certain angles, as were their likewise arid, lichen-white side branches, that one could have the impression of being very close to the ground, with these patterns almost near enough to touch, in the form of what had been a primeval forest, never cut but long since turned skeletal, from which clouds of wood dust swirled, stirred up by the airstream—, her brother was sitting, like her, at a porthole, perhaps above a similar, and why not the same? barren residual landscape. His skin was slightly tanned as always, despite the winter and his life in confinement, not merely from the outdoor work of the last few weeks, and he was wear-ing his eternal white collarless shirt of heavy fustian, which was never even slightly dirty, at most a bit frayed (and therefore all the more ele-gant), and today, in celebration of his journey into the unknown, he had on over it a claret jacket and a long, black, fur-trimmed coat, the person-ification of elegance, not only compared to her, who today as always, and at least in this respect similar to him, has some unusual feature, more no-ticeable than their grandfather's checkered handkerchief, a seemingly conscious and intentional clownlike touch or even something comical, in the present case, for instance, the partial wing of a bird of prey that she stuck into her belt that morning in the hurricane forest and later into her bosom.

"Write that I, she, this woman, suddenly felt a hand touching the feathers and my breast, and then actually saw it, too," she told the author. It was a child's hand. The child was sitting next to her. This hand, small though it was, was unusually warm. "And I noticed that my own hands, whose warmth others immediately remark upon, were unusually cold. They had become so cold during the flight that they ached down to the bones. And the unknown child now took my fingers without more ado and warmed them between his own."

Yet she felt almost as though nothing had touched her, and indeed the touching of her breast had been gentler than the brush of a veil. She closed her eyes and opened them almost at once, wide, to look at the child in the seat next to hers. He was evidently traveling alone, without the usual unaccompanied-minor card around his neck (but hadn't these been abolished long ago?). What he had instead was something like a purse, which looked unusually heavy around his frail neck.

Suddenly she felt as though she and the boy were about to be filmed; as though the camera were diagonally above them, quite close, and the command "Action!" or "Movement!" or merely an almost inaudible "Please!" that could be read from unidentified lips had already been given. Ever since she had acted in that film set in the Middle Ages, such notions had repeatedly inserted themselves into her days and her everyday life (although in her case, one could hardly speak of "everyday life," whether from an internal or an external perspective). True, that had been her only role, albeit a major one. Yet even now, almost twenty years later, in certain situations, always different, she still felt the camera focused on her, one far, far larger than the actual one. There was no pattern to the situations, and generally there were one or two other people present (it never happened when they were more than three—perhaps a pattern after all?).

For the most part, however, she was performing in this film alone. And for the most part it was not daytime. She was sitting one evening in an easy chair by the window, holding a book, and once she reached a particular line she felt the camera at her back. She herself a blurry profile in the image; only the print in the book in sharp focus, and her finger following the sentences; the turning of the page almost a ceremony, before which she paused for an appropriate interval and then finally, if possible without the slightest sound, turned the page (if there was rustling, the scene was repeated, and if the paper crackled, like a newspaper page being turned, the shooting would be called off for the evening—an end to the reading).

Or she was lying in bed at night, half- or already sound asleep, and suddenly she became aware of the camera above her on the ceiling. All she had to do now was go on sleeping—not pretending to sleep, as in other films, but rather sleeping soundly and peacefully while also portraying sound, peaceful sleeping, for the benefit of the whole world; for the "public at large." And having the camera running even helped her: in portraying someone sleeping, she "really and truly" slept (the expression used by children in her Sorbian village), and more soundly and peacefully than at any other time.

But she had never had to do a take with a child this way. She looked up at the invisible camera to see whether there might be lines for her to read: nothing but the blank sky, almost blackish-blue (it was the period when airplanes, like buses and high-speed ferries, as well as the coaches that had come back into circulation here and there, were more and more equipped with glass roofs). Instead she heard the boy next to her. Speaking softly, yet as clearly and audibly as the first birdcalls before dawn— despite the almost deafening roar of the engines—, he said, "I must see what you have in your backpack." She said nothing. She had no need to say anything. She had no script—"fortunately," she thought.

The child was already busy loosening the pack, the many knots posing no difficulty: a few tweaks, and he had one after the other undone. "What a smell!" he said, delving into her personal effects not only with his fingers but also headfirst, and it remained unclear whether he meant a stench, a lovely fragrance, or simply a smell. And already some of her possessions were laid out on the tray table in front of him. "Chestnuts, freshly peeled!" he said, letting them roll out of both hands again and again. "The size of blackbirds' eggs. The color and form of a plucked and scalded chicken's hindquarters. In other words: cream-colored. A smell like new potatoes, dug only yesterday, the first of the year, the best, the famous ones from the island in the Atlantic. Taste [already he was taking a bite out of one] of nuts? of almonds? of peach pits? No, unlike anything else: of pure, raw chestnuts. Number [he counted them all at a single glance]: forty-eight!"

And on to the next thing, but without haste, carefully, as if it were something precious: a travel guide, an unusual one, in fact with the title "Guide to the Dangers of the Sierra de Gredos." The child leafing through it, cautiously, section by section, reading out some of the titles: Mountain Brooks and Floods; Thunderstorms; Free-Range Mountain Cattle; Snakes; Wildlife; Dangerous Plants; Forest Fires; Getting Lost (the longest chapter); Snow- and Icestorms; Avalanches; Razor Cliffs; Poisonous Waterfalls. — Author: Aruba del Río — "That's you, isn't it, under a pseudonym, you've taken along your own book as a guide for the trip!"

Now a third object picked up with both hands by the child: another book, the Arabic reader belonging to her vanished daughter. The boy was small but must have been of school age already, for he read, and fluently, too: "*Bab*, gate. *Djabal*, mountain range. *Sahra*, desert. *Firaula*, straw-berry. *Tariq hamm*, highway. *Bank*, bank. *Harb*, war. *Maut*, death. *Bint*, daughter." He hesitated over one word: "*Huduh*, silence. Silence, that's a word I do not know. I do not know what it means. I do not need to know that, either. I do not want to know, either. *Huduh*, silence." And he read on: "*Haduv*, enemy. *Chatar*, danger. *Djikra*, memory. *Zeit*, oil. *Hubb*, love. (I do not know that word, either.) *Batata*, potato. *Nuqud*, money. *Asad*, lion. *Fassulja*, bean. *Hassan*, the handsome and good. *Thaltz*, snow. *Bir*, well. *Chajat*, tailor. *Banna*, stonemason. *Ja*, oh dear, and oh."

He stowed the book carefully in the knapsack and suddenly struck her on the thorax, with a tiny fist, a single blow, but one that really hurt. She felt not only struck but also injured—wounded. She would die of the wound, now, during the flight, during the journey. Meanwhile the child continued rummaging through her things. "A snake skin. A mountain thistle. A fan. A veil—how strange that it is wet, as if it had just been pulled out of the water—strange, something wet among the dry things. A chef's tocque. A chef's neckerchief. A chef's tunic. Cooking mitts. A chef's belt. A chef's apron. A chef's knee pads. Chef's clogs made of linden wood. Everything but the clogs linen-white."

Finally the boy's hand dug carefully to the very bottom of the bag and emerged at last holding a bookmark: a present from her daughter, made during her first year in school, a photographic self-portrait, glued onto a strip of cardboard, with a colorful design painted around it: she thought she had lost it years before, during a walk with a book through the woods of the riverport city: she had missed it for a long time, had hunted for it in vain, on wood-roads, under the deepest layers of fallen leaves, also the following year, and even the one after that: and now here it was, as in-tensely as anything can be. She closed her eyes; opened her eyes.

The child in the seat next to her unbuttoned his shirt. Curled up on his naked chest was a dormouse, squirrel-like but smaller, its tail shorter but all the bushier. The animal was breathing; it was alive; it was sleep-ing; its sharp claws partially extended, harmlessly touching the child's skin; its soft fur ruffled by the air from the vent above them.

The child gazed unblinking at the woman next to him and said, "You will never go home. You are lost. But perhaps you are not yet lost, not completely. Why are you so alone? Not even in a dream have I met any-one so alone. And perhaps you will die and be even more alone in dying. Without anyone. La-Ahad. Ahada, another of your assumed names. And what beautiful and tender hands you have. And what gentle eyes—like those of people who doubt they will return home."

And while the unknown child continued to speak, softly yet distinctly, she noticed that for the first time, since when? yes, since when?, she was close to tears. And she was utterly amazed; and just this once she wanted to be seen this way on film, in a full-screen close-up. The author: "Should this go in the book? May it?" — She: "Yes."

While the child was speaking, sentence after sentence, a strip of light traveled beneath the plane, which was flying at a perceptibly lower altitude now, moved across the plateau, and caused a band of asphalt to shimmer, a reservoir to glitter, an irrigation canal to flash. A topsy-turvy new world on the first day of the journey (but hadn't several days passed already?): the sky above the glass roof almost black as night, with a hint of the first stars, and down below the sunlit earth. In similar fashion, on the way to the airport, an ancient crone, without her dentures, had come toward her, driving a factory-new race car, as if trying to set a new record, the car's number emblazoned from stem to stern. And similarly, that morning the outskirts' troop of drunks had been hauling cases of beverages from the supermarket to their lairs in the woods—without exception bottles of mineral water. And was it possible?: a flock of wild geese, flying past the plane window in a long, jagged V, from right to left: "Arabic writing," the boy commented. And could there be such a thing?: in the same fashion a swarm of leaves swept by the window, holm oak leaves typical of the plateau? And where and since when did this exist?: and next, a pale-pink drift of snowflake-like blossoms, as if the almonds were in bloom and almost finished blooming, now in late February, early March.

The child had moved on to another subject some time ago. He was talking about money. — The author: "Didn't you stipulate that this topic should be kept out of your book, at most implied, through not being mentioned?" — She: "At a few points it belongs in the story. And this was just such an exception." The monologue of the child in the seat next to her began with his taking a packet of banknotes from the purse hanging around his neck. Leafing through them, he exclaimed, "Oh, money of mine!" The author, interrupting, to her: "And what would be your equivalent exclamation?" — She: "Oh, dear, money. Ja, an-nuqud. And yours?" — The author: "Ah, money!"

The child said more or less the following: "My money is nice to look at. And it has such a friendly feel to it, my money does. And it does me so much good, my money, my cash money. It is my first money. And it is money I earned myself. I did not find my money. I did not steal my money. And my money was not given to me, either. For my first money they wanted to open an account for me and deposit my money in it. If my money had been a gift, I would have said yes at once. But because I worked for my money, giving lessons in math, Russian, and Spanish, shoveling snow, helping with the potato harvest, herding cows in the pasture, mucking out the barn, I wanted to see my money, each bill and even the smallest coin. And I insisted that my cash be given to me in person each time, on the spot, right after the completion of every job, without involving anyone else. When I saw other people going up to the counter in the bank with their money in bundles and briefcases, to get rid of their banknotes in exchange for a teller's receipt, in my eyes that meant it was not money they had earned themselves but dirty money. Every one of them, I thought, was bringing to the bank money that had been either found or stolen or extorted—at any rate it was not theirs, and they converted it into mere numbers, to launder it, by the numbers. But my money, even if it looked a bit soiled on the surface, was clean money. And even if a bill had really and truly been dirty in the hands of a previous owner, as my banknote it was washed clean in the twinkling of an eye, and, unlike at the bank, the whole thing was on the up and up. When I exchange my money, it is only from coins to bills. I know that you are one of the few people who no longer touch money, in the form of either coins or banknotes; who no longer even carry credit cards; and whose fingerprints are accepted all over the world as a form of payment. But how beautiful my money is. And you do me so much good, money of mine, my cash money."

She closed her eyes and promptly opened them again. A gull, white as ocean spray, flew past her porthole, and this in the middle of the plateau, far inland. But of course there were reservoirs even here, and not all the rivers had dried up. If they had ever been aloft, now the passengers were no longer flying. Without having noticeably touched down, the aircraft was taxiing along a rather narrow landing strip far from the city, at first speeding like a race car, then, on rather bumpy ground, bouncing along evenly as it slowed and circled the terminal, as if they were on an old bus with ruined springs or in a carriage, an impression that was reinforced when, as the propeller vanes became visible—prop planes were in style again—they appeared to be turning backward, like wagon wheels in

Westerns. It was a small airport by today's standards, when even midsize cities had runways stretching from one horizon to the other, unusually small, surrounded on all sides by empty steppe, with at most a couple of rusty tin shacks and automobile carcasses, a few stalks of steppe grass so high they almost grazed the window. And this prop plane was that low to the ground, although it was the largest thing on the broad field, with nothing else around but a few one- or two-seaters.

And yet this was the airport of Valladolid, formerly the capital of the plateau region, the city of princes and kings, and today a city of half a million?! For almost every crossing of the Sierra de Gredos she had landed here rather than in Madrid. But the last time was now several years in the past. And as if in keeping with the topsy-turvy new world: the Valladolid airport had not been expanded but instead been reduced considerably in size—just as the local soccer team (of which she was fond, for no particular reason, and whose fortunes she followed on the Internet) had meanwhile slipped from the top league to the third, and any local princes and kings one approached would have been transformed instantly into frogs if one had kissed them.

Ceremonial taxiing around the steppe airport, as if to salute every side. Meanwhile the child next to her was reading a comic book. He had already read these pictorial stories at the beginning of the trip, and now he was rereading them. He flipped the pages rapidly, yet it was clear that he was absorbing each frame completely. He swallowed image after image with his eyes, blinking after each narrated event. Only toward the end of each story did he slow down. And once the story was finished, the child did not go right on to the next, as one might have expected, but paused for a while, motionless, his eyeballs protruding as if made of glass, even holding his breath, which he released late, audibly even, amid the plane's taxiing roar, a prolonged sigh. (And she noticed that she involuntarily sighed with him, almost silently.) Before the child reader finished the last story, the aircraft came to a stop and the signal for deplaning sounded. Out on the airfield, there were hares and foxes in the high grass, a sight that had vanished from airfields everywhere else.

Along with the few other passengers, the child stood up, having promptly closed the comic book. But in the moment immediately before that, he had glanced from the page he had just read to the next and read it, skimmed it, as if he wanted to soak it up like a map showing the direction in which he was to strike out.

"Vladimir!" she said, and that indeed turned out to be one of his several names, as Ablaha, Aruba, and Ahada were hers. And suddenly a dream from the previous night came to her, in which she had set fire to a child, first hesitantly, then mechanically, carrying out an order—"It is the law"—until the child and its little animal were in flames. How violent her dreams had become of late, and not only hers? With other people, was it not merely their dreams? And now at least this child here was as unharmed and healthy as a child can be, and as only a child can look. And they were seeing each other at this moment for the last time. I, on the other hand, have seen them forever.

7

It was almost night on the great plain of Valladolid. In the airport, the conveyor belt had clattered like a mill wheel. Next to the airfield a bonfire was burning. Tree roots from the steppe were being burned. The flames were small, whitish blue, and very hot. This fire had been going for several days. Soldiers were standing nearby, warming themselves. It was winter on the plateau, too. Valladolid: seven hundred meters above sea level. Other soldiers were standing in the small arrival lounge, which was also the departure lounge, keeping in the background, half in the shadows, and unarmed. She was the first to set foot outside the terminal; all the other passengers were still waiting for their luggage. There was no wind. A single bush, *shudjaira* in Arabic, was swaying violently next to several other bushes that were not moving at all. A very large, heavy bird had flown out of it just moments before. And the bush is still shaking and quaking.

And the stranger did not strike out in the direction of Valladolid. She is walking along the highway, *tariq hamm*, which branches off just past the airport into the desert, *sahra*, no, the steppe, into the grassland. And then someone ran after her, a man with a suitcase, one of the people from the plane. And she turned and smiled, but the smile was not meant for him. And she unlocked a vehicle parked, or standing, in the tall grass among a hundred and twelve wrecks, apparently ready to drive, a Landrover built in the year such-and-such, from the Santana Works in Linares, mud-colored like a military vehicle, but without any lettering.

And she had the man climb in next to her with his suitcase and drove off, heading almost due southwest, in the direction of Salamanca, Piedrahita, Milesevo, Sopochana, Nuevo Bazar, Sierra de Gredos. Above her the first stars were out. And next to her flowed the río Pisuerga, which soon merged with the great río Duero. And the road was increasingly free of traffic, because of a war? *harb* in Arabic, don't know, don't know what that is, either, a "war." And the Arabic book in her knapsack did not smell of her, the stranger, not in the slightest.

All during the flight the heroine had expected that when she left the plane she would suddenly see her brother behind her. In her mind's eye she pictured him initially striking out in the same direction as she had taken and sitting in the same aircraft, after changing planes. This image was so powerful that she assumed the shouting behind her was part of it, and only much later, when the shout was repeated over and over, did she turn to look. No, it did not come from her brother.

But the man who was calling to her was also no stranger. It was one of her former clients, once a major entrepreneur who had then gone bankrupt. (In the meantime there were hardly any entrepreneurs left, at most manufacturers and vendors of toys of all kinds—with almost every item, every product, the main selling point was no longer its usefulness or nutritional or some other value, but its value as a plaything, or as a brand, or as a pastime—and swarming around the leaders in the toy business were the hordes of game players and speculators.)

From a certain moment on, she had refused to extend him credit. And besides, he was already so deeply in debt to her bank that the bank seized all his company's assets and then almost all his personal property. He viewed her, the head of the bank, as responsible for his failure. Against the background of all his faceless competitors, who had in fact collapsed even before he did, and more wretchedly, the victims of impersonal market forces, of an economic situation to which one could not attribute blame or malice, this woman was the only person, the only individual who now, embodying these incomprehensible forces, but also as a particular being, or beast, of flesh and blood, represented something he could identify as his adversary, his destroyer, his executioner. He hounded her for years, and not only with letters. He had to get revenge, but did not know exactly how. Revenge, that was almost his only thought during that entire time.

But no action to match the thought occurred to him. With this woman, there could be no question of killing or beating or rape, of setting her house on fire or—the only thing he had briefly considered—kidnapping her child. All that remained was to wait for her punishment to be carried out by someone else, someone who had also been plunged into misery, or perhaps by the gods, or, best of all, by her herself, for with the passage of time her guilt vis-à-vis him had to become unbearable; at the thought of the injustice she had done him, one day, and he hoped it would be soon, she would throw herself off the roof of her office building into the confluence of the two rivers or, an even more delicious prospect, go stark, raving mad.

For the time being he took satisfaction in seeing her—this woman who could sometimes be remarkably clumsy—stumble, lose a shoe, bump into a door frame, try to open a door by pulling it instead of pushing, or, conversely, pushing instead of pulling; he witnessed such incidents from time to time, if only from a distance, or even only on television. Village bumpkin! A village bumpkin has me on her conscience! And upon hearing the news of her (almost grown-up) daughter's going missing and then disappearing altogether, he had had no thought at all, or at least none that he put in words. Everything had gone very still inside him, and from that moment on had remained so, as far as that "evil woman" was concerned. No more letters. Once, in the company of a former competitor, who had also been dropped by her and then began to spew hate and threats, the silence in which he listened to the other man was such that the latter felt compelled to interrupt his tirade and say, "But let us speak of something more pleasant!" In the meantime, however, he had finally launched a new company, producing toys for all ages, from the youngest to the most doddering.

Outside the Valladolid airport, the once and future business leader called after her, not because he was sure of having recognized her but because he was not sure it was she. Just as she was probably preoccupied at the moment with her recently released brother, he was preoccupied with her, and not only at that moment, but so much so that if she were to be suddenly standing before him, he would most likely assume she was a look-alike or a mere apparition. And indeed, each time one saw her, she looked so different that at first one took her for someone else altogether, someone completely unfamiliar; and each time, her appearance of the moment made such a deep impression that the next time, one again could not (and did not) associate her appearance with the earlier one.

She, however, had recognized him at once. And he identified her from the uncomplicated way she behaved toward him after that glance of recognition: as if he were still her client, and a good one, an important one actually. The friendly manner in which she invited him into the Land-rover was not that of a powerful person or one of higher station but of one who was at his service; as if she still cared about managing his money, and, as his money manager, famous banker or not, were of course at his service as no one else was; as if this service were second nature to her by now, or had always been.

And of course she then proved to be fully informed about him and his business; she knew that he had a meeting the next day in Tordesillas, which was more or less on her route. If they had met anywhere else, at home in the riverport city, in an international airport, or in one of the well-known metropolises, he would have avoided her, even hidden from her, and, if forced to be in her presence, would have preserved an obstinate silence. But in this environment, far from the beaten path, it seemed curiously easy for them to deal with each other. And his speaking seemed to come of its own accord. It may be that the war impending not far from here did its part. (Except that by this time there were so many reports and such contradictory ones every day, and from all over the world, that we could hardly lend credence to yet another.)

He talked and talked, and almost all the while she listened in silence, as she chauffeured her once and perhaps future client across the plateau, deserted now that it was evening. Especially at this hour it became obvious, as at hardly any other, how ancient this region was; one could see it in the residual mountains, silhouetted against the very distant horizon and without exception bare of trees, in the residual hills, in the remnants of cliffs poking up from the earth, worn down and eroded over millions of years. And yet precisely this ancient land here seemed to have the strength to rejuvenate one. At least it rejuvenated them, the two new arrivals. At least it rejuvenated him.

His speaking was lighthearted, and in the course of the drive, over which night soon fell, it grew more lighthearted still. This was a period in which the atmosphere, the "ether," was buzzing, humming, reverberating with dialogues. The word "dialogue" itself constantly crackled from all channels. According to the most cutting-edge dialogue research, a newly established scholarly discipline that promptly boasted of attracting a huge groundswell of interest, the term "dialogue" by now occurred more frequently—and not merely in the media, the interfaith synods, and philosophical treatises—than "I am," "today," "life" (or, alternately, "death"), "eye" (or "ear"), "mountain" (or "valley"), "bread" (or "wine"). Even among prisoners in the exercise yard, "dialogue" was registered with greater frequency than, for instance, "motherfucker," "scumbag," or "bitch"; and likewise "dialogue" was recorded ten times more often among the insane and the mentally retarded taking supervised walks in town or in the woods than expressions like "the man in the moon," "apple" (or "pear"), "God" (or "Satan"), "fear" (or "meds"). Even the few remaining farmers, located at least a day's journey from each other, were understood to be involved in ongoing dialogue, or at least they were shown again and again engaged in dialogue, and children were also shown dialoguing, even in the last picture in the children's books approved for adoption as school texts.

But here and there a voice made itself heard, without being raised or seeking a public forum, asserting that in the meantime the truly authentic conversations were taking quite a different form, for instance that of the monologue—while the partner, who could also be many in number, an actual audience, was all eyes and ears—the form of telling a story and listening, listening and passing the story on, listening some more, and passing the story on and on. And the most intense conversation (which, to be sure, was not suitable, not suitable at all, for just any old audience) occurred nowadays, especially nowadays! without words, not in the silent exchange of glances but in the interplay of your sex and mine, not merely without words but if possible also almost without sound, but all the more eloquent and emphatic, in the course of which I transmit to you each of my conversational fragments with even more than all my senses, and in turn absorb each of your conversational fragments with more than all my senses? yes, absorb, and inscribe them on myself from A to Z: a conversation, or dialogue, if you will, more enduring than almost any other nowadays, or at the time when this adventure took place; a dialogue-narrative of which not one of the exchanges, however minute—toward the end of the telling, more and more intense in the pattern of question-response-response-question-response-response—will ever be forgotten; the most unforgettable of all the conversations in our lives; ineradicable from your and my memory; even if later we will become strangers to one another, or even enemies.

"When I was young, I was full of enthusiasm," the entrepreneur told her during that drive, on which after a while they were the only ones on the road. In the fallow fields, nocturnal bonfires were burning here and there, with the silhouettes of feral dogs flitting by, no humans in sight. She drove very fast, as if through enemy territory (but she always drove that way).

"In all the pictures of me as a boy I have glowing eyes. My enthusiasm mystified children of my own age. It even put them off and made me an outsider, also a figure of fun. But older children appreciated me all the more, and adults still more—some of them, not all. Even as a very small child I was always bouncing with enthusiasm; in my baby pictures I already had that glowing look, always turned toward a sun and not blinded by it. My original enthusiasm was completely unfocused, it seems to me. And at the same time I—or how should I refer to that earlier being—was completely caught up in my enthusiasm; possessed by it as by a demon, though a thoroughly benevolent and lovable one; that entire newborn body a bundle of unfocused enthusiasm.

"As I got older, it remained unfocused for a long time. Except that after a while it no longer emanated from the center of my body, radiating from there to all my limbs—making it seem as if I had nine times nine arms—but became concentrated in my head: my eyes, my ears, and especially my tongue. I would talk a blue streak, until there was a rushing in my ears, my eyes bugged out, and my skull felt as if it were about to burst (as is happening again now, by the way).

"On other occasions, when my enthusiasm did have a focal point for a change, it was always a human being, always an adult, to be specific. I felt enthusiasm for some adult or other. How I could venerate him then, send my thoughts in his direction, summon him in a dream, believe in this person, yes, believe in him! An adult who could elicit my enthusiasm in this fashion was never my father or my mother—or was it? search your heart—but rather, for instance, a distant relative or a teacher (usually in a so-called minor subject, who perhaps came to our classroom only once a week), but it could also be a businessman, a soccer player (perhaps merely a local celebrity, or precisely such a person), and, strange to say, especially a person who, according to hearsay, for instance my parents' stories, had been stricken with misfortune. Ah, once you were filled with enthusiasm for the unfortunate—not the unfortunate of your own age, but the unfortunate adults! And then you yourself became an adult, neither unfortunate nor fortunate, but bent on success, and very soon successful, and how.

"If only I could recall when I lost my enthusiasm, and why. The energy remained, or a sort of thrust, always stirring, or ready to leap into action. Yet you no longer radiated light. Instead of your head's glowing and your tongue's shooting sparks, after a while all your doings, your entire existence, came more and more only from the back of your head, and finally withered into mere calculation. Instead of enthusiasm, nothing but alertness, and alertness was eventually crowded out by hypervigilance. Instead of your childlike enthusiasm, drives and a sense of being driven.

"And with your business failure, signed and sealed by the beautiful lady banker, came hate, your period of enthusiastic hate. Does such a thing exist, my friend, enthusiastic hate? No, it does not exist. Hate is no form of enthusiasm. This hate, in any case, insinuated itself into my days even before my collapse. Time and again, even in the period of hypervigilance, you would wake up in the morning under a vast, clear sky feeling inspired, inspired?, yes, inspired with your indeterminate enthusiasm. Only it usually became twisted, with the first wave of thought, into a quiver of at least a dozen arrows of hate, ready to be shot at this man or that, at this woman or that. You wanted to kill? Perhaps even worse: see someone dead. You wanted to destroy? See someone destroyed. Force someone to the ground? See him on the ground.

"And suddenly you yourself were on the ground, primarily thanks to her. Thanks? Yes. For after the period of sheer hate came my period of gratitude; and with it my enthusiasm returned, now no longer childlike but mature, and this period continues to this day and will not end until my life does. Gratitude and ideas: only ideas of this sort deserve the name. She who caused your ruin reminded you. Reminded you of what? Just reminded, without a whom or a what. Reminded you unspecifically and all the more tellingly. And thus, thanks to her, you also discovered for the first time, after an interlude of impotent and inactive hate (more and more directed against yourself), what it means to work.

"Yes, I realized that up to my fall I had never worked, had merely made money. Thanks to her, I learned to work, first under duress, later voluntarily. And eventually you worked enthusiastically, as a baker, a stonemason, a truck driver on the narrowest and most winding dirt roads through the mountains. And not once were you out for profit, old boy. Yes, I wanted nothing but to do my work, slowly and methodically, as well as possible, and that now became my kind of success.

"So you've become an entrepreneur again? Yes, but without intending to and without ulterior motives. As an entrepreneur, now, I have come to see myself not as a moneymaker but as someone who works, slowly and methodically, one step at a time, one word at a time, as carefully as possible. And thus I live as if my losses were profits, and am certain of this much: when I lose, I win; when I am enthusiastic or happy, I am enriched and loved. Just as one of the ancient cities here on the plateau has the motto *Sueño y trabajo*, dream and work, the logo of my new enterprise bears the motto: 'Enthusiasm and Work.'

"But then, too—oh, dear, we enthusiasts of today! In contrast to the enthusiasts of earlier times, each enthusiast today remains solitary, no longer joins forces with the others.—Yet, for the time being, for this transitional period, isn't that the way it ought to be?"

At this point in his speech he is supposed to have suddenly bent over his chauffeuse's hand on the wheel, which she held like reins, and brushed it with his lips, or even touched it? if so, even more softly than with a veil, and he allegedly added, "Your child will turn out not to have vanished for good; your sweetheart will not be absent for many more years; your brother will not have been detained long at the border."

During this drive she toyed with an inexplicable notion, and not for the first time, a notion somewhat reminiscent of her sensation in the airplane of being filmed: what was taking place just then in the present, as the present moment, was being narrated at the same time as something long since past, or perhaps not long since past but certainly not of the present moment. And besides, it was not she who toyed with the notion that the two of them were traveling—no, not simultaneously, but rather exclusively, in a narrative: the notion acted itself out for her, without any involvement on her part. And since she had been on the lookout for signs from the time she set out, she took this, too, as a sign. And to see and feel herself being narrated was something she considered a good sign. It gave her a sense of security. In the notion of being narrated she felt protected, along with her passenger.

A sort of shelteredness had already made itself felt simply in the act of listening. The man had conducted his monologue in the form of a conversation with himself, instead of directing it at her. And pricking up her ears for such conversations turned out to be much easier than having to play the role of the person being addressed. Long ago, in the village schoolhouse, she had absorbed her teacher's lessons most effortlessly when he stood by the window, for instance, and murmured into space, or seemed to confide the material casually to a treetop. Being addressed head-on, however, often rendered her deaf, even when she was an anonymous member of a large audience, and thus shielded from the speaker's direct gaze.

The road shrouded in darkness. By now she must have long since passed the village of Simancas, located on a river, where the archives of the old kingdom and sometime empire were housed; archives with holdings richer than those of Naples or Palermo, archives that even held the records of the 1532 grain harvest in her Sorbian village and the rate of infant mortality between 1550 and 1570. All that had been visible of Simancas as they drove by was a tent city near the mouth of the río Pisuerga, where it flowed into the río Duero, domed tents, all the same size, reddish in the light of the rising moon above this residual territory, in her daughter's Arabic book a fragment of text pertaining to this phenomenon, "red tents, love tents." The one hitchhiker on the *carretera* had not been her brother.

And shortly before Tordesillas, with mad Queen Juana de Castilla in her tower, a dialogue had sprung up between the two travelers after all. The passenger pointed to a medallion attached to the windshield and asked, "Who is the white figure in that image?" — She: "The white angel." — The passenger: "Which white angel?" — She: "The white angel of Milesevo." — The passenger: "Where is Milesevo?" — She: "Milesevo is a village in the Sierra de Gredos. And the white angel is all that is left of a medieval fresco there." — He: "What is the angel pointing to?" — She: "The angel is pointing to an empty grave." — He: "What confident pointing. Never have I seen a finger extended so energetically."

They were not expecting him in Tordesillas on this particular evening. He had not reserved a hotel room. Since his first business failure he had given up making special preparations for the future. For his trips, including business trips, he planned only what was absolutely necessary. More than one appointment was out of the question. And this appointment he did not allow others to schedule. He was the one who decided on the time; and it was never to last more than an hour. For the time beforehand and afterward he remained in charge.

If he planned anything else for his travels, it was the uncertainties, and any number of them: missing this connection or that, failing to meet a possible business partner, or perhaps not recognizing him, or better still: not revealing himself to him, remaining unseen as he watched the other person scan the restaurant, the hotel lobby, the railroad platform, for the important stranger; and more than once he had let the person he was supposed to meet simply depart again, and not out of dislike or distaste but for some reason he could not explain to himself—held spellbound in his hiding place by a sort of magnetic effect, yet all the while filled with pleasure and a sense of adventure—and afterward he would spend an enjoyable day or evening alone.

And now the time had come to look for a place for the night. And besides, he was hungry. She, too? Yes. She knew the area and turned off the dark highway onto an even darker side road. Branches scraped the car windows. They had not seen the large city of Valladolid; almost nothing of little Simancas; and now there was nothing to see of medium-size or small Tordesillas but a glow on the underside of a single low-hanging cloud, or was that already another town, farther to the west, Toro or Zamora, or did it come from a wildfire?

But suddenly they had halted in the middle of the barren plateau in front of a castle-like structure, no, really and truly a castle; for wasn't that the escutcheon of the former dynasty above the entrance portal? And the building and grounds were so vast that it could only be a royal castle, not merely an imitation or a dream of one.

No indication of a "hotel": neither neon lights nor a sign; also no cars in the courtyard, not even one or two modest ones with local license plates that would show that although there were no guests, at least a few employees were there waiting for them. To be sure, although all the windows were dark, at the main gate a light was shining, in fact a pair of torches, one on either side, and as if they had been there a long time.

They got out of the car. A night breeze was blowing; "from the southeast, from the Sierra," she said. A buzzing and rattling from the acacias that formed an avenue leading up to the entrance: the sound of the black, sickle-shaped seedpods, with which the bare trees were bursting (the rattling came from the dry seeds in the pods). On the ground of the avenue each of their footsteps caused a crackling in the fallen sickles. The chauffeuse stuck her index and middle finger in her mouth and blew; her whistle circled the entire castle. (In her Sorbian village such a whistle had been called for in the middle of the gentlest village song.) All the acacia branches, from the fork to the tip, had dagger-like, razor-sharp thorns, each thorn outlined against the star-bright Iberian winter sky, once the car's headlights were turned off. Did that mighty rushing come from below, from the río Duero, here not so far from where it flowed into the Atlantic, and was the castle located on a bluff high above a broad valley? "No," she said, as if he had asked: "No river, just a little brook down in a ravine."

An answer like this was consistent with her viewing the imposing structure as a roadside hostel placed there to accommodate them. When her whistle drew no response, she clapped her hands as she stood there on the graveled circular drive, bordered by box shrubs, in front of the entrance. And to do so, she put down the suitcase. Which suitcase? Which would it be but the one belonging to her passenger, which she had lifted out of the car herself and carried this far.

Still no answer, so she bent down to pick up a pebble, just one, and aimed it at a certain window among the twenty-four on the second floor, dark like all the others. She hit it squarely in the middle: a sound not of glass, or at least not of modern glass, but of very old glass; less of glass than of soft stone or very hard wood.

As our newly minted enthusiast told it, the lord of the manor now opened the window. Lord of the manor? The epitome of one. And he was alone, as a lord of the manor must be nowadays. But she is said to have shouted up to him as if he were the bellhop and supposed to hop to it: "Two rooms!" And in no time: the lord of the manor was coming downstairs from his second floor to meet them, who by now were standing in the flickering light of the hall, having scrambled over the threshold, almost knee high. Before he was even close to them, he held out two keys, keys with bows as shiny as if they were made of crystal. And he smiled briefly, as if in greeting, as if he had been expecting the two, or at least her, the woman; but he spoke not a word, either then or in the hours that followed, as the traveling entrepreneur likewise kept silent from this moment on, as if he had nothing more to add to the long speech he had made during the nocturnal drive.

The lord wore a black suit, a white shirt, and a black tie, as if he were simultaneously the hotel manager and the maître d'hôtel, in charge of the restaurant. The curved staircase looked as if it were of marble, and had steps so shallow and broad that one floated up it as if being carried. Their rooms, located in opposite directions, were as spacious as ballrooms, the bed in each case tucked into a corner, and they had floors of something like red brick, with uneven spots, dips and miniature valleys and chains of hills, which made her feel, as she told the author, as if she were walking back home in her garden; "the only thing missing was the swampy patches."

And when she opened the casement windows and leaned out, gazing toward the south and the Sierra, it looked as if down below in the manor grounds, now brightly lit by the moon, "in my eyes a farmer's pasture," a hedgehog hobbled by, the same one as at home; with teeny glittering eyes, as if to say, "I am here already." And in the castle pond, "in the village puddle," the glaring reflection of the moon, now transected by the reflection of the familiar matitudinal bat. When, not until their last morning? And the bat mirrored in the still water with a clarity of contour never seen in reality.

8

The two travelers supping on the ground floor, not in one of the reception rooms but in one of the corner rooms, to be reached by way of a labyrinth of corridors, some of which ended at blank walls or trompe l'oeil doors. The corner room no larger than a niche, yet with a domed ceiling set with thousands of tiny enameled tiles whose colors and shapes formed a repeating pattern, so that at first it looked as though the dome were growing larger and larger, and then as though there were no dome at all but a low, flat ceiling, almost low enough to touch with one's fingertips from a seated position.

The small chamber was reminiscent of certain almost inaccessible places into which people used to withdraw in earlier times, not for any clandestine activities but because they wanted to be alone with their own kind—close friends, members of their own social class or sex. And in fact this had once been a smoking room, a place reserved for men. Only now it was the woman who led the man there, unhesitatingly taking this turn and that, and, playing hostess, pointing out his place at the table, barely large enough for two, making as if to run her finger over the likewise enamel-tiled wall, to wipe away centuries-old soot. And in fact her hands were now sooty, from the fire in the fireplace, whose dimensions matched those of the niche, the opening no bigger than the stovepipe aperture low in the enameled wall. A mere hand's breadth from the "firehole" (her term for "fireplace"), the enamel was already cold.

A cold winter night, cold as only winter nights on the plateau can be. Distant thunder. Explosions. In the still damp piles of firewood? The once and perhaps future client had changed for supper; was dressed like the lord of the manor or whomever (who in the meantime was standing in the invisible, inaudible, unsmellable kitchen or wherever). The lady banker or whoever was still in the outfit she had been wearing earlier. At most she picked up from time to time, as if playfully, one of the fans lying next to her plate and ran her finger over one of its five, or six? classic segments, always the same one, painted with landscape images, in this case depicting the Sierra, the Sierra de Gredos?—in this country everything was a "sierra," from the Bay of Biscay to the Straits of Gibraltar, and this sierra or whatever on the fan could just as easily be the Sierra Cantabria, or the Sierra Guadarrama, the Sierra de Copaonica, the Sierra Morena, or the Sierra Nevada. And appropriately, the traditional term for the obligatory landscape images on all fans: simply *país*, countryside.

And as if the entrepreneur had tacitly asked the lady banker what she was doing in the Sierra de Gredos, of all places, and in winter, of all times, and with the current world situation, of all things, she then, speaking on her feet (or sitting), delivered one of those pronouncements for which she was famous all over the continent and beyond. (The designations "lady banker" and "entrepreneur" no longer fit the two of them, and not only since their arrival at the castle or hostel; from the moment of their landing at the remote little airport of Valladolid, they had become something else besides; and then, during the evening drive along the road, almost exclusively that something else; a different reality; the second wind of being no one in particular.)

During that meal, eaten in the orbit of the queen who had gone mad, she had a deep voice, hardly recognizable as a woman's voice, and she said more or less the following: "To me the Sierra de Gredos is the mountain range that epitomizes danger—not just physical danger, but danger per se. I have known this Sierra for almost two decades now. The first time I came, I was pregnant with my daughter Lubna, in my next-to-last month. The child's father was also there. It was summertime, and we were driving along the southern flank of the mountains, coming from the west, from Portugal, from the Atlantic, where we had landed, and heading east, toward Madrid. The plain, or rather lowlands, across which we were traveling, between the Gredos massif and the Montes de Toledo, was and is in the grip of blistering heat. It seems to me we were not making any headway there in the valley of the río Tajo; hardly stirred from the spot, although at the same time we were traveling along at a good clip. That had to do with the Sierra in the distance: a single naked mass of rock stretching to infinity, always at the same distance and unchanged every time we looked, although in the meantime we had covered perhaps ten kilometers and some twenty miles.

"Finally it became clear that we would turn in that direction. That occurred on the heights of Talavera de la Reina. And the route led north toward the foot of the Sierra. And as we approached, the Sierra remained the same pale blue, almost white (yet even on the sharp Almanzor peak there was no snow left), at any rate paler than the sky. And the night was spent in the *konak*, the guest house (still in existence at that time) belonging to the cloister of San Pedro de Alcántara, near the only town for miles around, little Arenas de San Pedro.

"The following day we began to climb, on fairly overgrown paths through the wilderness. The child in my belly was quiet as a mouse, much quieter than usual. I could not walk fast, and soon we separated. The plan was to rendezvous in El Arenal, or Mahabba, its earlier name in Arabic, the highest mountain village on the southern slope.

"Along the way I rested one time in the shade of an overhanging cliff, and fell asleep, perhaps for a short while, perhaps a long while. Perhaps I did not sleep at all, just closed my eyes. When I opened them again, I found myself in an image from an alien world. Everything that had just now been familiar had been jettisoned, and me along with it. Nothing about the vegetation, the granite boulders, the path, was familiar, nor was this hand, this belly, this navel, this big toe. The whole world, and I along with it, stood there twisted and displaced, completely awry, without one's brain being able to straighten it out one way or the other, everything either crooked or upside down, and the sky, too, upside down.

"Despite my round belly I broke into a run, up the mountainside, which in reality meant down the mountain, and promptly fell flat on my face, luckily into one of the many natural water basins on the south side of the Sierra, troughlike hollows in the otherwise slippery-smooth granite beds of the innumerable mountain brooks. Glorious swimming then, and for years and years after that, soon with the child by my side.

"And curses on the Sierra de Gredos, and not only on the almost insurmountable southern flank, and not only because of the fiendish flies, which you are not spared even in winter, which surround you in swarms that grow larger with every step, which although they do not sting, fly into your eyes and ears, into your nostrils, and, since you cannot keep your mouth shut tight while climbing, eventually get into your throat, into your airway and gullet, which corroborates the story told about King Charles V, the later and only Emperor Charles (the first and last): since childhood he had stood around with his mouth open so wide that even when abroad, in Flanders or elsewhere, he was tracked down and besieged by those famous flies of the Sierra de Gredos, on whose southern slope he then in fact died, though by then almost an old man. Curses on the Sierra de Gredos!"

Suddenly she broke off her scarcely begun narrative: that was another habit for which she was known. She went to the kitchen, which was far away, not merely around several corners but also up and down several staircases, and brought back food. And with every dish it was plain that she was the one who had put the finishing touches on it.

They shoved the little table over to the one window, "the flue" (her expression) for the former smoking room, so as to have a view during the meal, if only of the blackness of the night. Later the chef and lord of the manor came and ate with them; and as a threesome they then had even more room than as a twosome earlier.

She named each of the dishes in turn: "smoked bacon"—actually slices of the superb ham from the "boar of the black claw"; "cellar salad"—actually the cress that grows in star-shaped clusters even in wintertime on the steppe, above subterranean veins of water, with an especially delicate sourness at that time of year; "ragout of pickled herring, salt cod, and chicken drumstick"—actually she brought in a brass bowl in which strands or strips of freshly steamed brook or river crayfish, trout, and equally light-colored little cubes of lamb were meticulously arranged in meanders that nestled against each other, reproducing the courses of the brooks or rivers of the plateau; "prunes and dried apples"—actually oranges, oranges, and more oranges, which had just ripened, in wintertime, their freshness and juiciness unequaled by any other fruit; "with the last bits of dry cheese rind"—actually dry and actually hardly more than bits of rind, but how pungent; "the last smidgen of cider, from the year before last, the last drops from the last cask"—actually a last smidgen, though of wine, and what a last smidgen.

In between she appeared with a portrait, framed in rock crystal, of Juana, the allegedly or supposedly mad queen, a work painted by Zurbarán, painter of saints, almost a century after the death of the allegedly or supposedly mad woman; she placed it on the windowsill—the painting's height exceeded that of the window, for it was not only Zurbarán's saints that demanded height—and offered the following description: "a charcoal drawing by the local village idiot, a portrait of a stable maid here, who is also the village idiot's mother, father unknown."

In the oil painting, mad Juana, painted very dark, was gazing out the window of her tower in Tordesillas; far below and at a considerable distance lay the río Duero in the last or first light of day, with glittering banks of granite, still there today in almost the same locations. And this queen showed no signs of insanity whatsoever; at most perhaps in the brightness of her long garment, with no source of light visible in her chamber; bright, positively glowing against the dark masonry, also her hand, with which she was pointing not outside but rather to some interior space, perhaps the room next to hers?: she had just risen from her chair—but there was no chair in her chamber, the chamber was empty—no, jumped up, no, she had dashed there from somewhere else, had run there, and now was pointing, with eyes wide and gazing upward and her mouth open, into impenetrable darkness, while holding in her other hand an open book, a single page of which was standing straight up in the air from her running. How the palm of her pointing hand glowed, as did her abnormally long index finger, which against the dark background resembled a flashlight.

"How differently this supposedly insane woman points out of the picture than the white angel toward the empty grave. She seems to be pointing out something to herself alone, and not in a regal or commanding fashion at all, but in inexpressible astonishment, terminally astonished. Never again will she emerge from this moment of staring in wonder and amazement. At one time, when children became distracted in the middle of a game or some other rhythmic activity and just stared into space, people might say, 'Hey there, stop staring into the idiot box!' But this supposedly insane woman is certainly not staring into any idiot box." Who said that? None of the three at the table could have answered the question. Perhaps no one had really spoken at all.

If they had been somewhat on edge earlier, the evening meal had calmed them. And if they had been calm earlier, it had calmed them still more. And if they had been fighting fatigue before, now they let it have its way with them, and at the same time part of them became wide awake. And at the same time they were porous, unusual nowadays during a meal?, porous in the direction of both day and night, as porous as sometimes on the borderline between the clarity of being awake and the very different clarity of a dream.

She looked through the key bow at the lord of the manor / chef. The wrought-iron bow was so wide that it could accommodate both of her eyes. Behind the interwoven Oriental motifs they appeared as if behind a grating. And she said he had not yet learned to stand at the stove as a whole person. The way he cooked left part of his body disengaged. The idea that one should be completely involved in any process and any activity—"The whole person must take part"—applied especially to food preparation. One's toes, knees, thighs, hips, shoulders, all had to pitch in. In his case, only the hands and eyes were active. And the result?: despite all the seasonings he had obviously tracked down for his kitchen, didn't one seasoning seem to be missing, or rather a rhythm, from the individual dishes as well as from the sequence of dishes?; didn't rhythm have to be the main seasoning for a chef?

The chef replied, which means that he did open his mouth after all in the course of this night, with this story ("Do not be afraid to let something contradictory appear now and then in these pages!"), and commented that "The whole person must take part" probably applied as much to a baker or a hermit or a lover as to a chef. And, he said, he had just cooked for them as a "whole person," and then he had tasted the difference himself. Except that occasional breaks in his rhythm had been caused by this dear visitor's presence. He did not mean her in particular, he added, but the presence of a stranger in general, no, not a stranger—but anyone. The minute someone watched him cooking, he lost his rhythm, even when the observer was kindly disposed toward him or truly enthusiastic about what he was doing—especially then. In his profession he could not stand observers of any kind.

And that was also true of actions that had nothing whatever to do with food preparation. If someone stood beside him while he was hammering in a nail, he was "guaranteed" to bend it. Even if someone watched him simply tying his shoelaces—and the person in question did not have to be looking straight at him; the mere presence was enough—: the laces were bound to end up all knotted.

As a child he had already feared any kind of observer, he continued. He had learned early to ride a horse, in secret. But the first time someone watched him ride, he had promptly fallen off. When he and others had shown off how well they could shinny up an oak tree, he had been the only one to get stuck halfway up the thick trunk (he could still see himself hanging there, on the lone tree in the middle of the cow pasture, and slowly sliding back down the trunk)—and when he had tried it again alone, he had reached the top faster than the fastest one in the group. And his fear of observers had then become a sort of hatred of them. Yes, he hated observers—of whatever sort. Even love was in danger of turning to hate, or to irritation, which was just as bad, when the loved one stood watching him do something he could do only when he was alone. And (here he laughed once) almost everything that mattered to him, and particularly his cooking, was something he could do only completely alone and unobserved.

Here his second guest chimed in briefly. The entrepreneur—or whatever he was on this evening—said that precisely a rhythm that was broken here and there, the interruption at some stages, the loss of all rhythm at certain moments while the food was cooking, the cook's palpable state of intimidation and his hesitation during individual transitions in the complicated preparation process, made the phases that came before and after—when he was working alone in the kitchen, undisturbed by her, the other person—all the more significant, accounting ultimately for the lasting impression, the "fabulous" aftertaste, which was no less "real" than the first direct impression this evening meal made on the palate, "which I—and this is no mere turn of phrase—will never forget. O infinite alphabet of taste." Hadn't the tasting they had all done been a form of spelling-out and also memorizing or recollecting?

The last word in their dinner-table conversation belonged to the banker (or whatever she was, and not only on this night). She remarked that it had not been her intention at all to call the meal into question. On the subject of "my lord chef" as a person, she had also meant something else entirely. In contrasting his way of doing things with the notion of "the whole person must take part," she had been intent on working through a problem, "which in turn is part of my profession." And now as a threesome they had just worked through this problem.

As far as she herself was concerned, she had recognized during the working-through that she was exactly the opposite. She could undertake a task as a "whole person" only in the presence of someone else, a "third party," even if the third party existed only in her imagination. So as "to walk," or "merely to take one step," "to calculate," or "merely to type up numbers," "to draft a plan," or "merely to fiddle with possible combinations" as a whole person, she had to be able to picture observers, and beyond that inspectors, "judges," so to speak, as if she were "in a contest, no, a competition!" "onstage, no, in an arena!" Even when looking at something as simple as a spoon or a piece of string, for instance, she felt a sort of obligation to view the string "as a whole person," "or vice versa, when being looked at, to allow myself to be looked at by the other person, or animal, as a whole person!"

Yet as she sat there now: no one else's gaze could get to her, and not only because of her eyes behind the giant key. There nothing was looking at me, let alone a whole person. And above all nothing allowed itself to be looked at by us, let alone . . . "In her way of not letting herself be looked at from time to time she resembled less an actress on the screen and definitely more a policeman on the street. He may look at me—if by no means as a whole person—, but does not allow himself to be looked at, not in the slightest, even when he is standing a hand's breadth from me." So that night she did not have the last word after all?

Who said that?—The author in La Mancha, in his village, much later. And he will have added, "The whole person must tell the story!" And she will have replied, beaten and battered as she will be by then, and still shaky from her time in the Sierra de Gredos: "What you call the policeman's gaze has in reality been my defense and my armor. And if I positioned myself time and again this close to another person, it was to leave that person no room for killing, and likewise no room for any kind of embrace. I moved in so close simply in order to become unapproachable. During a long period in my life I crowded in close, body to body, so that my enemies or adversaries could not lift their little finger against me. It has finally become clear to me: I acted this way—it was a constant, uninterrupted acting, and woe to me if I ever shrank back—because I feared death." — The author: "And feared love?" — She: "For a long time that, too, was a kind of fear of death, a particularly bad, acute form."

There are insinuations that my heroine spent that night near Tordesillas with a lover. In one version it was the chef and lord of the manor, in another the failed entrepreneur, in yet another an unnamed third person. But whatever the source: he is the false narrator. And the fellow is a false narrator not only because he offers false information, because he lies— and he is lying, in fact; he lies the gray slime out of the cracks in the ground—but the apocryphal swindler and slippery speculator is a false narrator furthermore because he is telling something that in my view ought not to be told—that in my view does not belong in a story, certainly not in this one here.

Our story here, even on the darkest night, and, I would hope, at some point also the hottest night, must take place beneath the sky, the most spacious of skies. The aforementioned insinuations, however, do not take place under any sky. And besides, they do not take place; they are merely insinuated. And insinuations and ulterior motives are the very opposite of the sky, the one that arches above our heads, as well as that of storytelling—the antithesis of anything remotely connected with the heavens, including your heavenly body. The scoundrels who want to sneak into my book are merely pretending to tell a story. They are feinting, as in fencing. The minute they open their mouths, or rather their traps, they lie—and at the same time they lie like a book, and that is what is special about these literary liars, and what makes this old expression so appropriate again nowadays. But the problem is not that these no-goods and would-be competitors lie. If only it really were a problem; problems, as we know, are productive.

I, too, lie, when the moment is ripe; I can lie the blue out of the sky and even more out of the darkest cracks in the ground. Yet the lies you false storytellers dish up—just to finish with this topic—are not exactly fiendish (you're all too dodgy and at the same time too stodgy, abandoned one and all by any kind of spirit, including the evil ones), but exactly the opposite. How, for instance, can my heroine spend a night with a toy merchant? And what serious reader would not shake his head at the suggestion that she lay that night in the arms of a chef (even if, on the evening in question, he may have had a golden touch in the kitchen for a change and is perhaps in fact a master of his métier—a métier grievously overvalued these days, in my humble opinion, by the way)?

The most likely scenario I could imagine for our woman would be a night of lovemaking with an unknown and invisible third person. Not a night of love but a night of struggle. A life-and-death struggle. In which she remained victorious in the end. Will have remained. Luckily for me. This way our story can continue.

But such a third person would also be counterfeit. He must not exist. He does not belong here. He does not come to my mind. He does not enter my mind. First of all, this story of ours takes place in a time when for not a few people physical union had come to represent something wonderful again, and accordingly something rare. And then, too, the moment for that, and especially the place for that, had not yet come in the story. A night of love in a castle was out of the question, even in the vicinity of the Sierra de Gredos.

The only touching that took place: she placed her hand on someone's shoulder before going to bed. She did not say whose. And when it came to the next touch she was already alone: having stepped into her room and closed the door behind her, she leaned against the door frame. As for the chef, he had already almost fallen asleep at the table; all his strength and sense of urgency had gone into the preparation of the meal. And as for the traveling entrepreneur, as he himself reported, he had been positively relieved to trot off to his solitary bed: ever since his collision with the lady banker, but not only because of that, he saw only danger in any encounter with a woman, and left the scene afterward with the thought: Scraped by again! Got out alive again!

Her brother traveled only by night, and that had always been the case, not merely since he had become a fugitive, or, as now, a deportee. They said it was because the accident involving his parents and the other brother had occurred in broad daylight. But what didn't "they" say. After a few weeks, he had run away from the boarding school (in those days they still kept the pupils locked in) to which his grandparents had taken him, hardly more than a child—at his own request, for he wanted to become a priest—after nightfall, and had set out, only ten years old, on the nocturnal pilgrimage, yes, pilgrimage, along country roads and across fields, back to the Sorbian village, more than thirty miles away; before sunrise he was suddenly standing beside his sister, who had been awakened by an unusual weight on her bed: an armful of early apples that her brother had picked in the orchard behind the house (it was the end of September). And this child who had returned home promptly named the different varieties: "Shepherd's Apples, found in the woods by a French shepherd.—Alexander Lukas, found in the woods around the year 1870 by a certain Alexander Lukas.—Princess of Angoulême, an old French variety, named after the daughter of Louis the Sixteenth, the king who was guillotined.—Dear Louise of Avranches.—Cox Orange: bred in 1830 by an Englishman named Cox.—Ontario: bred in 1887 on Lake Ontario in Canada."

This time, too, her brother was traveling by night, through the long winter night, almost without stopping. Even his intermittent pauses were part of his traveling: waiting for a train connection; waiting for a car that finally stopped; waiting in a hiding place for guards and patrols to pass.

Cold, and hardly anything to eat: and yet he did not mind in the slightest traveling by night. So long as it was night: he did not need much more. Unlike her, he was in his element moving around at night. If she was not already asleep, she had to be at her destination by midnight at the latest, in a house, close to a bed. He, on the other hand, even when he was not traveling, made his rounds in the dark, between dusk and dawn. During his years in prison, when he was not pacing or dancing around his cell at night, he lay on his cot, drawing spirals in the air, and if he happened to fall asleep for a bit, he felt even more imprisoned during such nocturnal sleep than he already was. The nights for him were made for sniffing out, tracking down, rummaging around. As a fifteen-year-old he had written poems, all of which had night as their subject. She still knew two lines from one of his night poems by heart: "Snakes on the prowl rummage through the stillness, / Night—and only the will lives!" Since that time she referred to her brother as "the night-rummager." And now for all these years he had not been able to rummage through a single night. And waiting to be set free had had nothing in common with the waiting during his nocturnal journeys.

Sometimes her brother struck her as uncanny. At such moments she was afraid for him. And this fear was usually connected with fear for others, not merely for this person or that but several, many, a great many. True, he had not killed anyone yet; he had been sent to jail only for "violence against objects"—though destructive and repeated violence. Yet it was her fear, gaining strength with the years of his incarceration, that in the meantime he had set his heart on killing, or at least striking, massively.

Yet as a child, and also for a long time afterward, he had been completely incapable of hurting anyone; he simply could not defend himself or hit back; and even in the penitentiary, where he was stronger than most, on several occasions when he got into a scuffle, he let himself be beaten up without resisting—at most he cried out, in helplessness and rage, rage directed more at himself for having no talent for violence against people, against his own kind, for being absolutely incapable of violating the taboo zone—the other's stomach, chest, face; for not even being able to bring himself to trip the other man up or grab him by the nose or ear or put him in a headlock.

Fear for her brother: for in the end he had taken to signing his letters to her with an expression that had been popular long ago, used to brand history's notorious evildoers: "an enemy of mankind." And since the contents of these letters seemed to fit this expression more and more—though in a sort of code; the two of them had had a secret language since childhood—his sister finally could not help believing it, not completely, but almost: yes, her brother, the one with the litany of apple varieties, the one who had sat next to her for years in the dark of night, had really and truly become an enemy of mankind. And he would not be satisfied to leave it at that colorful epithet. Yes, wasn't her brother aware that, at the time of this book, fighting against anything or for anything was no longer possible? And that if he died in such a fight, his death would move no one—except her: as a man without parents, he was no victim, was a desperado from the outset; the death of a man without parents held no significance and did not count.

But for now he was traveling through the night with the impertinence of a newly released prisoner. It was as if there were no differences or transitions between the airplane ride at the beginning, then the trip in a car with a chauffeur, then walking, then riding again. He seemed to be swept along in a single, expansive, gravity-free movement. As he rode, sitting by the window on the night bus, for instance, where the passengers all became people like him, whatever they might be otherwise, he was also striding along with airborne hundred-yard steps, which ran through his head like a sort of counting song, from one into the thousands. And in walking down the dark roads he was constantly rolling on the balls of his feet. And it could also happen that, as he continued along the shoulder of a nocturnal highway, he might suddenly hop on one leg, as if a game of hopscotch were marked out in chalk on the asphalt.

Even when he walked backward for a stretch—a habit he shared with his sister—it was less for the purpose of flagging down a car than out of high spirits. During his repeated sprints he would also run backward, often for an entire nocturnal mile, with his back to the next border he would have to cross. Borders were his element, just as the night was. The more notorious a border, the more it attracted him. Where most others disguised themselves before reaching the border, cloaked themselves or hid (for example, under a tarpaulin on a truck, as the author had done as a child, or in some other way), he presented himself if possible even more elegantly than usual, and moved with the openness of one who feels at home at borders, and during this first night's journey also with challenging bravado: "Nothing can happen to me. No one will stop me. I have nothing to lose."

While it was one of the aging author's nightmares to be forced to cross that forbidden and dangerous border of his childhood again, and this time in the middle of the night, on foot and alone, in a suit, shirt, and tie (but where, for God's sake, are his shoes and socks?—doubly nightmarish!), the newly released prisoner approached such a border like the fulfillment of a wish-dream, and in this dream he then crossed the bridge over the border-marking river like a man without a care in the world, barefoot, his shoes in his hand, and no one stopped him—it was night, after all, and nocturnal borders could only be his accomplices; and besides, he had a passport that was still valid, if just barely, and besides, he had served his time, and besides, he had been convicted in a different country altogether.

Not a soul, also no vehicle, during the first seven nocturnal miles after the border crossing. Moonset. Deepest, most silent night. Sporadic glitter of mica in the tar for a short distance around, accompanying the pedestrian. No sound but that of his still-bare feet; not even that of a night plane high in the sky—no airplane flew over this country, had not for a long time now, not even by day.

Then a cry, of alarm? of joy?: someone was walking along the nocturnal road, ten paces ahead of him, and as he caught up with the figure in a single stride, she turned toward him, her face glowing in the pitch darkness, and he recognized, no, it struck him: a girl, no longer a child, but as young as a person can possibly be, a human being—his sister's child. The cry—if it was a cry at all—had come neither from her nor from him.

"The history of the world is a mess," he had written to his sister from prison one time, using no code for a change. "The race of man is an evil apparition and deserves to be wiped out." In this nocturnal moment, however, he saw his own dictum as inoperative, and how. The face before him signified: he would not kill, not yet. A major act of violence was not for him, not yet. First he would sit down with his sister's child, at the "Night-Travelers' Lodge" up ahead.

9

As she did almost every night, she awoke after a couple of hours of deep sleep. She groped for the light switch, noticing only then that she was not sleeping in her own bed; that she was not at home. The initial discomfiture gave way to astonishment, and the astonishment energized her.

She sat up and fished the Arabic book from the citadel room's uneven floor—fished: that was how high the bed was, and how far below the book. The child on the plane to Valladolid had spoken the truth: the book did not smell of her. It smelled of her vanished daughter. The girl had been reading it, lesson after lesson, example after example, quotation after quotation (the fragments of classical Arabic poetry with which every lesson ended). The book had been systematically studied and mined by her, word for word; traced; copied; glossed; threaded with marginal notes that eventually came to mean as much as, and then clearly more than, the print on the page, and referred only vaguely or not at all, or not obviously, to the text. The book—a mere brochure, actually—looked even from the outside as if it had been carded, kneaded, pulled lengthwise and widthwise and licked, as it were; rained on and snowed on.

And inside the covers things were even more exciting: the impression of an athletic contest continuing page after page, a wrestling match to the bitter end, which also had something joyful about it, not only because of the constantly changing pencil colors and the changing script, from Roman to Arabic, from Greek to shorthand.

And again from the outside, from the side, one could see where the reading had stopped, even before the book's midpoint: the part that had been read or explored was gray—no, not "dirty gray"—, the pages curved, bent, thickened, crisscrossed, and sprinkled with little strokes or dots—traces of the marginal glosses inside, which often wanted to spill over the edges; then a white borderline, and after that nothing but the unread white layers; the gray next to this white like a different rock stratum; a different one? no, the same material in both layers of the brochure, with one layer simply transformed and corrugated by chemistry and warmth, the chemistry of sweat from the reading finger lingering for hours on a single pair of pages, the warmth of the writing hand.

And the mother took up the reading where her child had left off. She, however, never added anything to what she read. No underlining. She even opened the book carefully, her fingers moving as if she were wearing gloves. Reading the book from a distance, looking into it as into a remote niche. Anything not to leave traces. Nonetheless, a reading second to none: spelling out, with lips moving silently, bursting out with a word-sound here and there, and then again, and again, pausing, her eyes raised from the book as she mulled over the section she had just read, in its context, the more immediate and the wider one.

And this hour in the depths of the night seemed particularly favorable to her reading. These days one read to get away from the world even less than was perhaps usual; indeed, exactly the opposite was the case. Here stood the chair, with its woodworm holes. Over there the door latch curved downward. Over there was a ladder, leaning as only a ladder can—what an invention, the ladder! On the highway the milk truck loaded with filled milk cans, stacked one on top of the other, clicking as they jostled each other, and among the cans a refugee family, including the author as a child (here sneaking into her book and her story again—but for the last time, please!). Way off, on the farthest horizon, the train rattling by—already in motion for a long, long time, but audible only now as a result of her reading; in one compartment her lover, her missing life companion, without a ticket, without identification, suffering from a high fever, heading in a direction in which he did not want to go, the direction opposite from hers—but at least he was not dead, he was alive, he existed. And impaled on one thick thorn in the acacia avenue outside the window, a very small bird? a cicada? a dragonfly?—The door to the chamber where she lay reading was pushed open, and in streamed human body warmth.

No comfort in her reading-herself-out-into-the-world? Fortunately? Reading to find comfort was not real reading? Another pause at an Arabic word and then the word-sound bursting out: as if precisely these words demanded to be heard. And this explosive voicing of the sound provided additional illumination to the field of vision: each foreign word a sort of flashbulb that gave whatever was in the field of vision (and beyond it) contours, surging with life; as if with the ex-pression, the chair, the ladder, the latch, the thorn, were instantly created anew.

And the nocturnal reader soon fell asleep again, as if after a great expenditure of energy, and slept deeply, deeply. And after her reading she had an image of the bed on which she was lying as a map of the world. But the thorns now, longer and fatter than swords? They belong to an old wooden statue in the church of the Sorbian village, where they pierce, at all different angles, the bodies of martyrs—in the thigh, belly, thorax, neck. Perhaps her reading of Arabic was a mere backdrop. But sometimes this backdrop meant everything.

While she took a shower the next morning (a long, long one), got dressed (slowly, one article at a time), gazed out the open window on the south side (her eyes moving from her fingertips out over the entire plateau, which grew hilly again as it disappeared in the distance), more and more additional images zoomed into her, or merely brushed past her; no more images of martyrdom and menace. These new images were the kind of which she was convinced that one was sufficient to arm her—and not only her, but everyone (see her sense of mission)—for getting through even the most oppressive day.

And again she contemplated the conditions or laws that allowed such an image to seek a person out. The genesis, the origin, the source of these images must be explored at last; a necessity that made one all the freer; as, indeed, every time she said, "I must," "one must," a little smile seemed to float around her. At any rate, to be receptive to images one had to remain focused on the matter at hand, whatever it was (see showering, see gazing out the window). And no special slowing-down or even acceleration of the current activity was needed: whether one moved deliberately or rapidly—the decisive factor was to be fully engaged.

Likewise irrelevant were distance and proximity; only the proper interval yielded, or oscillated, the image, and a proper interval could be that of the thread to the needle, hardly a hand's breadth from the eye: for instance, a bend in the Bidassoa, the river marking the border to the Basque country, appeared—image, a jolt into the world, a jolt, all the more necessary for everyone, into reality.

Another law of sorts that determined the generation of images: they arrived—and again she was sure this was true for everyone—primarily in the morning, in the hour after waking. Though for her, something about the images had changed of late, in the last few years. The images still came as if without reason, unbidden; primarily at the beginning of the day; and so forth. Yet more and more the images originated in one particular part of the world, and those that flashed in from all over the earth—now a tree root in northern Japan, now a rain puddle from a Spanish enclave in North Africa, now a hole in a frozen Finnish lake—were becoming increasingly rare.

She regretted that. It made her uneasy. For the images she had previously received from the world were all linked, as if obedient to a law, with places where, when she had actually been there, she had experienced unity or harmony—of which she had not been aware at the moment—that, too, such a law? Even if these areas were "beautiful," "lovely," or even "picturesque" (that in itself already constituting a sort of image of an area), that did not contribute to their subsequent image-worthiness; rather, they had to have left an imprint on you, without your knowledge, from which later a world at peace, an entire world in a still possible peace, or perhaps precisely that "enclosure of the grander time," will have taken shape, unexpected and unhoped for.

In the meantime now, the images, specifically those morning-fresh ones, were increasingly limited to an area, which, every time she was there, had shown her a peaceful face for only brief moments, but more usually a hostile, menacing one, yes, more than once a cannibalistic face, the face of death.

And this region was the Sierra de Gredos. On some days she reminded herself that she was a survivor; that if she belonged to any people or tribe, it was the tribe of survivors; and that the awareness of having survived, and of surviving along with one unknown survivor or another, far off or nearby, had to be the thought that forged the strongest bonds. And she had become this kind of survivor through her crossings of the Sierra de Gredos.

When she made a point of calling the Sierra to mind, the massif presented primarily memories of adversities, major ones or merely small ones, such as the absence of air in the dense, light-blocking conifer forests, and the wood-roads, where one had felt cheerful only moments earlier, narrowing over the course of a few steps into impassable mud slides. In the images, in the unsummoned image, however: the Sierra de Gredos and peace, or peaceableness, were one and the same; and it could be no other way with these images, this kind of image—a fundamental law of the image: make peace, and hop to it! Take action. Become active. But how? As the image dictates!

"Doesn't that deserve a serious research project?" she challenged the author. "To find out why, in recent times, most of the images, and not only mine but also everyone else's, originate in regions where in reality one has experienced hardly anything good but rather the very worst; and, with me as the experimental subject, to study as well why the images from the Sierra de Gredos keep nudging one almost constantly, as insistently and as gently as the wooly heads of a thousand times a thousand sheep, ever since it has been rumored that war is about to break out there?"

The shadows of water-skaters on a riverbed: Where was that?—By a stone bridge, known as the "Roman" bridge, over the río Tormes, which rises in the Sierra and, although in some stretches as wide as a river, remains a rushing brook all the way to the end of the central massif in Barco de Ávila, overflowing into innumerable still pools.—A fawn, separated from its mother, its coat soaked in a downpour, standing a hand's breadth from her, likewise drenched, the animal too weak to flee, or merely curious: Where was that?—On a stone-paved road. A stone-paved road; in the mountains? yes, right below Puerto del Pico, the main pass through the Sierra de Gredos; the flagstones cracked in many places, some missing, truly the only remnant in the Sierra of the Roman colonial era, a Roman road winding down the southern flank in lasso-like S-curves, the "calzada romana," and, unlike the modern road over the pass, clearly part of the mountain range even two thousand years ago, less built there than simply laid along the slopes, following what was already present, sketched out beforehand by nature.—On a wall above an outdoor sink, a broken mirror, reflecting the crowns of the fir trees in the sun, and behind them, multiplied by the cracks, the pyramid-shaped summit of Pico de Almanzor: Where was that?—Back by the main river of the Sierra de Gredos, the río Tormes, at a children's summer camp, deserted long since when she hiked past it, or closed down, and not only because it is autumn (no, it is not "autumn"; no specific season ever appears in the images), the faucets either unscrewed or without water, the mirror shards opposite her at hip level, so that she must bend over ("I must"—she smiles), to look at herself; above her head the Almanzor forming a tricorn hat.

Hop to it! Do something. Help. Reach out. Serve. Serve? Yes, serve. Do good? No, be good. Lend a hand. Mediate? No, we know about you mediators and intermediaries rushing blindly to serve as go-betweens and thereby merely hastening a truly disastrous disaster. For heaven's sake, do not mediate! Participate and be there—and in this way mediate after all, or rather facilitate something, even if only with your eyes, what? The image? No, that is not possible: not the image but an intuition of it; that is sufficient.

And thus, for instance, the financial powerhouse, the adventurer, the former film actress, or whatever she is, sews on a button early that morning near Tordesillas, or wherever, for the toy manufacturer, or whatever he is, in the citadel, or dive. And the man takes it for granted and does not even object, sitting next to her again at the same small table by the window hardly the size of a loophole. And she also darns a glove for him: for it is bitter cold on the southern plateau, colder than in the northwestern riverport city, according to the radio. And for their departure she then fetches his suitcase from his room. And the suitcase weighs her down, even her, this inconspicuously strong woman with the large hands; that is how heavy toys are these days. A toy market in the vicinity of an impending war?

With that the woman has finished serving him. From now on he must make his way alone, and if perhaps not alone, then at least without her. With the help of her images she has given him a push, and that must be sufficient. But why does he look at her in the hostel courtyard as if he still lacked something?

And so the two of them fall into another dialogue like the one they conducted the previous night in the car. She: "Did you find the light switch in your room?" — He: "Yes." — She: "Was the bed wide enough?" — He: "Yes." — She: "Did you see the lightning after midnight?" — He: "Yes." — She: "Will you stay in Tordesillas?" — He: "No. Today I am heading west already, along the río Duero. And without the suitcase." — She: "On the old pilgrims' route, to Santiago de Compostela?" — He: "Heaven forbid. Not on any pilgrims' route, and certainly not an old one."

And if the man still lacks something, now he is resigned to lacking it; even strengthened by it? Their voices seem to be amplified by the walls of the various little sheds built in a circle around the main structure. And just as she placed her hand on his shoulder in parting the night before, now, for this morning's parting, she strikes him in the throat, making him stagger backward. And so he goes, looking over his shoulder at her, as if a third parting were still in the offing, not right away—the culmination of their partings. And then, already on the *carretera*, the highway, the *cesta*, the *tariq hamm*, he pauses briefly, sets down the suitcase, and tosses a handful of pebbles in her direction, so violently that several skitter all the way to her feet. She has retained the almost unblinking gaze of her childhood. Except that it has nothing childlike about it. Perhaps it did not have that even long ago.

The man heading toward the Atlantic. And the woman toward the Mediterranean? On this morning the sky above the *meseta* was blue. The highland plain of grass, stone, and sand extending in all directions from the hostel was green, brown, red, and silvery gray (the silvery color from the flecks of argentine mica in the weathered granite sand). By daylight, the hostel, with its gaping chimney, its roof sprouting thistles, its crumbling stucco, and its empty window frames, where black jackdaws with yellow beaks constantly flew in and out, uttering their hoarse cries, now had only the silhouette of a *castillo*, or castle, and was almost as black as the jackdaws, black without the sheen of their feathers. Then the jet contrails—it was an era of black jet contrails—even a shade blacker than a black background as they passed in front of the sun, at which moments it became palpably colder, as during a total eclipse.

All colors seemed to be gathered here, and the objects also revealed a new color—which had existed nowhere in the world until this morning—which had never before been seen by a human eye—and for which there was also no name and never would be—and rightly so. Was the unknown new color purely a wish? A wish awakened at the sight of the slowly wandering line separating sun and shadow, between the area of rigid white hoarfrost and the glistening, seemingly windblown thawing area in the steppe-grass-filled courtyard of the hostel? At the sight of the thawing grass, whose tips stirred not from the wind but rather from the steady melting of the layers of hoarfrost, which accumulated in droplets, causing one stalk after another to sway?

Yes, a wish—a wish that sprang up at the sight of that one dewdrop in the sun which, in contrast to the myriad glass-clear, transparent, white-flashing droplets, stood out from the dewdrop field as a bronze sphere, not glistening and flashing but glowing, shimmering, shining; no mere glittering dot but a sphere, a dome, challenging one to discover—not some unknown planet but the old familiar one, the earth here, challenging one to engage in unceasing daily discovery that led to no specific outcome, nothing that could be exploited, unless perhaps for keeping possibilities open—discovery as a way of keeping possibilities open?

A wish for a new color on, in, with the earth, a wish that became even more intense with the discovery that simply by looking, and without stirring from the spot, without stretching out one's hand, one could generate and also multiply this one bronze-colored—no, nameless-colored dew-globe—how monumental it appeared among all the other merely glittering droplets: with nothing but a slight movement of one's head, back and forth, up and down, with one's eyes as wide open as possible: suddenly in the thawing field an entire aisle or loop of new shades scintillating between bronze, ruby, crystal, turquoise, amber, siena, lapis lazuli, and especially the unnamed color.

Why was there no legend, like the legend of the ancient giant whose strength drained away as soon as he lost contact with the earth and returned the moment he touched the earth again, of someone who found his strength, an entirely different kind of gigantic strength, to be sure, by simply looking down at the ground? Wish-color, wish-strength. But didn't a letter from her brother, the enemy of mankind, contain the diametrically opposite wish?: "Were it not for the children, I would wish that the final world war might break out and that those of us here now would be wiped out, one and all."

No one must know that she wanted to make her way through the Sierra de Gredos. Neither the people at her bank, her banks, nor the author, nor anyone else, not even her old acquaintance here, the hostel-owner and chef. (Only with her daughter would she of course have shared her intention at once—) Were anyone to learn of her plan, it would be—so she thought—"as if my secret came to light, and that would mean humiliation, whereas unrevealed it remains a source of riches."

Where was he, the chef? The chef was out in a corner of the courtyard, busy with his morning preparations for the day's cooking. And without a word she deposited the whole bunch of shelled chestnuts from the forests outside the riverport city among the other ingredients on his work counter. On this morning-between-frost-and-thaw, the chestnuts, too, appeared not merely "light or quince yellow," but gave hints of that new color.

For that afternoon a wedding party was expected. By then she would be far away, and at the same time she would be present. If the previous evening the hostel had seemed about to close its doors forever, today it was filled with activity, as if this were its usual state and yesterday's deserted atmosphere an illusion. One delivery man after another appeared, and not only from the nearby yet invisible Tordesillas, but also from Madrid, and from the Galician fishing ports. In between even a refrigerated truck from a distant foreign country, with river crayfish, perch, and pike; where could they possibly come from? and then a little hand-drawn cart with rather wizened mountain apples and potatoes, which had come a long way, from the Sierra de Gredos. At the same time, arriving from all points of the compass, crews of masons, carpenters, and roofers, who promptly went to work.

She would not be there to see the outcome, and yet she would be: by the time the wedding party arrived, the dive would look more or less like a castle again. In the midst of all this a postman appeared with a stack of mail, for the innkeeper, for the guests, but also for her, a letter from her brother, written while he was still in prison. Almost at the same moment an itinerant knife sharpener turned up and sharpened the innkeeper's knives on his grindstone, driven by a foot pedal, and her scissors, at no charge. And then at one point a soldier came by, in uniform and armed, but without a cap—hair flying and face flushed—, bummed a cigarette and rushed on, searching for his lost unit?

With the change in circumstances on his property, the innkeeper had also become a different person. He had risen at the crack of dawn, while the others were still sleeping, to get to work on his cooking. He felt as if he were doing these things for his many children. Standing on one leg, shifting, while cooking, from one leg to the other. Chefs, the race of one-leg-standers. Even throwing his whole body into it when washing up. His pleasure at the heat rising from the stove. Applying final touches, to the nonedibles as well. Letting the seasonings fly to him—his elegance an additional seasoning. The chef, a different kind of embodiment. His cooking performance as a performance of the world.

Now it stimulated him to have someone watching. While peeling, grating, slicing, dicing, and turning, he repeatedly stood up and strode back and forth in his courtyard work corner, constantly busy, less a chef than an athlete, gathering strength for the competition. She assisted him, or rather: she was allowed to assist him, if only peripherally, by bringing a bucket of water, for instance, and collecting the trash. In between, the moment arrived when she was finally allowed to hand him her present; he took it matter-of-factly and ran one hand over it, while with the other, his left hand—a left-handed chef—he continued with the preparations for the wedding feast. This was a period in which women were more likely to give men presents, and what presents, too, and—at least where this woman was concerned—without ulterior motives. And meanwhile he was also cooking up a stew, on the side, for a mortally ill neighbor on the *meseta*. The man's child then carried the heavy ceramic pot home to his father.

And worthy of describing was also the particular corner of the court-yard where the *ventero* (= innkeeper) was working that morning. There were remnants of the former park surrounding the castle, such as a box hedge and a small almond tree. But the ground already showed less of the gravel spread there long ago than of the reappearing sandy-stony-grassy subsoil of the steppe, yes, desert, along with the polygonal pattern of cracks caused by the dryness. It was indeed *"bel et bien,"* a corner or nook formed not by the *castillo* but by two sheds standing at an angle to one another, nowhere near a right angle, one shed half-finished, evidently left that way for centuries, the other half in ruins.

Next to the chef's work counter in this corner, not hidden but clearly visible from the drive, the following items lay about: an old window frame, leaning against a door jamb; a pile of half-broken roof tiles; a rusty wheelbarrow; several large and small balls that had long since deflated; a rabbit coop without rabbits (only tufts of fur caught in the wire); a cement mixer, missing its cord, its drum full of hardened concrete; a stone-lined well with a pulley but no rope; an empty refrigerator missing its door; a child's swing attached to a broken beam, with the seat's single slat sticking up at an angle; a bathtub (the only object that was partly hidden, in the box hedge); a pyramid of animal bones—seemingly washed clean. A small open fire of knobby broom roots was burning in a pit, and roasting on a spit above it was a lamb, and she was allowed to turn the spit from time to time.

As was usual on the southern plateau, away from the mountains, the biting winter morning air yielded from one moment to the next—a leap that could be felt in body and soul—to a nonseasonal mild warmth. The chef on his work stool gazed at the woman through an opening in a knife handle, as she had gazed yesterday through the key bow, and said, "I have left the corner like this on purpose, and even arranged it this way. My nickname for it is 'the Balkan courtyard,' and if it were not so bad for business, I would also use that name publicly for the entire complex, with a neon sign up on the roof ridge: *El corte balcánico.* If the name scares off my guests, that's not true of the thing itself, this place, this spot. On the contrary: you will see—even if you are not around to see it—that along with my cuisine and the name of my *venta*, *El merendero en el desierto*, The Snack Shack in the Desert, it is above all this courtyard that accounts for my popularity. Thanks to it, I was able to pay off the loan you gave me, ahead of schedule. All the tables in the three dining rooms have a view of my Balkan or Lithuanian or Lapp courtyard with its broken ladders, empty cable spools, and sideless baby carriages. Unlike the usual views of a park or the ocean, the nook offers a sense of reality, if perhaps a mournful or painful one, and helps the guests focus, while eating, on the thing at hand, on the important things, and thus makes them value eating here as something out of the ordinary and at the same time enjoy the food both heartily and lightheartedly. The people who seek me out need the view of this courtyard, even if they are not aware of that.

"And—" (a transition that was a specialty of the innkeeper's?) "—you have, so I hear, commissioned someone to write the book about you. You did not want to write it yourself, and not only to avoid the first person. And the author was not to be a woman but a man, absolutely had to be a man, but why this one in particular? And now you want to, no, you must, head farther south, and, worse still, to the almost treeless Mancha, and are counting every hour, even this one here, until you are back home again, or at least over the roof-tile border, away from the curved southern tiles and back with your flat northern tiles! And at the expression 'you must,' you still have that smile.

"Yes, you must continue heading south, for the sake of your book and for something else. And you have never turned back in the face of anything. Ah, and you do not allow anyone to touch you. For you have a plan. And you have almost always had a plan. And at times you have the eyes of a madwoman. Nowadays it is almost only in women that one sees these crazy eyes.

"Why don't you let me write a chapter for your book, too. Or at least a paragraph? *Albanil*, meaning mason, is a word from the time of the Arabs here. Look at the *albaniles*' cigarette butts here in the Balkan courtyard: only masons smoke this way, down to the butt of the butt! And listen to the loud voices of the roofers; they constantly have to shout, from the roof to the ground, and vice versa. And listen to the carpenters: so quiet, almost silent. And when they do speak now and then, while fitting beams and hammering laths in place, it is of something entirely different— whatever comes to mind, more like talking to themselves. And are there really any *carpinteros* left? These here, at least, come from abroad, as do the masons, as do the roofers, all from different countries, and no work crew understands the other. During the last war here, the well shaft was used by the resistance for a radio transmitter. Today the radio operators would be tracked down immediately."

On the little almond tree a few blossoms were already opening: from the closed bud a single feathery petal stuck out. She involuntarily began to count: three, four, five . . . She closed her eyes. She opened her eyes. In the air in front of her floated the afterimage of the trees at home near the northwestern riverport city that had been felled by the storm, along with their upended root masses, the image of a vast shipwreck from olden times, an entire Viking fleet. Was that possible, an afterimage with one's eyes open, and a day and a night later? She closed her eyes, opened them. And above the flat Iberian high plateau floated the jagged peaks and pinnacles, the knife-sharp points and wind gaps of the Sierra de Gredos, along with the sun-bathed fields along the ridges and the pools of shadow in the hundred and twelve gorges. Was that possible, an anticipatory image of something that still lay beyond seven horizons?

Her principle, her ideal, her project: having time. Yes, as almost always in her life up to now, she had time. She had time and stood up to take her leave. It was up to her now to go forth into the land, the embodiment of that old German expression, now fallen into disuse, according to which the days went forth into the land; she would go forth into the land, just as, in another age, one that had never been graspable and countable or counting and valid, the days went forth into the land; had gone; will have gone.

Yet now a sort of dialogue sprang up between the innkeeper and the adventurer, as they stood facing one another in the Balkan courtyard in the middle of the *meseta*, and this, too, running counter to what was called dialogue in the era that is to be bypassed by her story, yet owing the energy for that bypassing to the era and, in the process of bypassing it, circumscribing the era all the more powerfully and making it recognizable, leaving it as a gray zone, untouched (similar to our heroine's arcane banking knowledge): the gray zone of a present day—"which does not deserve this name!" (so who was it who said that?)—left gray; hence nothing of the gray current era in my, your, our story, unless as a negative image, in which the gray may grow lighter or for moments begin to flicker and vibrate. And the scraps and fragments of many languages in the speech of the masons, roofers, and carpenters, Slavic, Berber, but also some native, as it were, Castilian, a suitable accompaniment to the conversation between the two of them, which was not at all contemporary.

It was she who began, with a question: "What is your guilt?" (It remained unclear: emphasis on "your"? Emphasis on "guilt"?) — He, after a pause: laughs. — She: laughs, too. — He: "Explain high finance to me." — She: "I find it uncanny, too, and increasingly so. — Will there be war?" — He: "I do not believe in war. A war is an impossibility in our story. — When will we taste the morning again together this way?" — She: "When the dog rose forms an arch at sunrise." — He: "Look in a different direction with your crazy eyes; I do not want to cut off another fingertip." — She: "Perhaps I will encounter my greatest male enemy today, and my greatest female enemy. That would be nice." — He: "On the border between La Mancha and Andalusia they're still mining mercury, to separate gold and silver for coins from the lifeless rock." — She: "That was once upon a time. And besides, there are no coins any longer. Look, a bird's nest in the drum of the cement mixer." — He: "And do you remember what causes the sound down there in the gorge?" — She: "The pounding? It sounds like a giant hammer beating on a hard pad, but with something soft inserted between the hammer and the pad? The blows landing at regular intervals, four or five times a minute, and all night long, and all day long?" — He: "The drumming, the thumping, the stamping, the giant water-driven wooden hammer on a flywheel, the as-yet-undestroyed remnants of the long-gone tannery that used to exist at the bottom of the gorge, abandoned hundreds of years ago and hammering in the void when your predecessors, traveling on money business, passed through here on their way to the kings and the one and only emperor, whose realms without your loans would have fallen apart like grown-ups' playthings, which is what they really were behind the shield of gold and money, and correspondingly childish and deadly, and for you, their successor in the world of finance, equally or differently powerful, the tanning hammers, drive wheels, and fulling pads have continued working, without raw materials and without any product—except that in the meantime the pads sound as if they were the hides themselves—and as long as this rhythmic knocking and banging continues, I, too, would like to continue with my dicing, slicing, turning, shaking, and sprinkling from morn till night."

And then, already on the way to the car, she looked back along the line formed by her shoulder (no one could sight along the shoulder as she could, into the near and far distance at once), and said: "Listen, the foot-steps in the gravel of the plateau. How the ground of every landscape one walks through produces its own unique sound—as here, in this old, drowsy, silently weathering residual area, the ever-thickening layers of soft, coarse-grained sand consisting of granite and mica, mixed with bits of rotted wood and plant stalks: a crunching so different from the gravel in any garden or cemetery you might think of; crunching? a sound with-out a name, new, like a new color." — And here one of the roofers chimed in loudly from the almost completely repaired roof, understandable de-spite his foreign tongue: "Yes! Walking in the Berbers' sand makes a dif-ferent sound. Absolutely not to be compared with the sound here. Not a sound—a tone!" — A mason spoke up, already dismantling the scaffold: "Yes, and walking through the mountain pastures below the Gran Sasso d'Italia: every blade of grass a taut guitar string, and every step—ah!"

And finally the carpenters, usually so silent, spoke up. Since their profession was seldom called upon, in this period they had become spe-cialists in all sorts of auxiliary trades, and here at the hostel, after quickly accomplishing their main business, had also pruned the acacias for the innkeeper, repaired the rickshaw-like shopping tricycle, had ironed the tablecloths and napkins, and installed a satellite dish, with which their employer could bring in all the local stations from Alaska, the land of his persistent longing. And at the moment they were sitting in the back of their pickup truck, ready to depart, their legs dangling over the tailgate, and they said, "Back in the Balkans we walked only on limestone. And the limestone was porous and hardly made a sound. And certainly no tone. We hardly heard ourselves walking on the limestone there. Our steps were swallowed up by the lime subsoil. But our walking did become audible in the mud of the lowlands, from Voyvodina to the plain of Thes-saloniki. One half of our Balkan lands consisted of this mud, the other of limestone. And back in the days when there was still work in the Balkans, we went from the limestone to the mud, and vice versa, and vice versa again."

Finally—all the workmen were gone, but a brigade of sous-chefs and waiters was arriving, and the woman had just turned the key of the rough-terrain vehicle—the chef came running toward her, knife in hand, the point aimed at the ground, handed her a bundle of provisions, wrapped in white linen, through the window, and said (this, too, belonged to the dia-logue): "Do not start eating this too soon. One's first hunger is not real hunger.—In the books it used to say that one could not set out on an adventure without clean shirts and money and, in case of need, salves for the healing of wounds. And a long time ago you said you wished you could walk somewhere with me, out there—not for a hike, simply walking. And then you walked so fast that soon I could not keep up." — And she: "Look—" What was it she said: "a wood pigeon"? "a flash of lightning"? "a polecat"? it was no longer audible; she was already driving away.

1 0

There was another recurring passage in the old books: "He" (the hero—why were they almost exclusively men, with a woman rating at most an intermezzo? why, for example, was there no detailed story of a woman to be read, from the sixteenth or seventeenth century?) "traveled on the road for many a mile without encountering anything worthy of telling." And now, during the drive south toward the Sierra de Gredos, she encountered hardly anything that, according to the more or less established conventions or rules, would have been suitable for her story, which she did want to be thoroughly adventurous.

The sun shone. A still haze hovered over the unvaryingly bare and crumbly tableland. The poplars in the few riverside meadows, or *vegas*, or *lukas*, stood ramrod straight and leafless. The olive zone, where a harvest would have been under way, did not begin until the southern foothills of the Sierra. She rolled along, hers almost the only vehicle in her lane. Coming in the opposite direction, at close intervals, however, were mostly trucks, and each time the same model and the same color, bearing the name of one and the same firm, which apparently owned a huge fleet, all with seemingly identical mustachioed men sitting high behind the wheel, all without passengers; yet each accompanied by a dangling, rocking rosary, complete with dagger-shaped cross, in the front windshield, identical to that of the driver in front of him; one after another of these drivers in his cab raised his hand to greet her with the same gesture, each smiling at her with his eyes as a sign of comradeship but also friendly concern, wishing her all the best as he passed: as if she needed that.

And dangling in her windshield was always that same medallion with the white angel pointing rigidly out of the image toward the empty tomb of the resurrected Christ. And no one was walking along the side of the road. And in the sky floated a single cloud that did not change during the entire trip. And no city came into view. And no fire burned in the thousand fields of the *meseta*, which with time came to represent a single field. And although during those hours nothing worthy of telling occurred, it seemed to my heroine as if one event were following the other, as if the happenings were coming hot on each other's heels and overlapping harmoniously with one another, as in a traditional story, yet also in a completely different way; as if the narration of her book were moving along all the more emphatically during this interim.

"I experienced spells of faintheartedness, something previously unknown to me," she told the author later. "This faintheartedness—what a word—urged me to turn around and go home. One time I stopped the car and made a half-turn. And at that very moment I felt: my story was breaking off. And you know how it is with me: feeling myself being narrated— my be-all and end-all, my one and only standard. And I must endure that, I must. Not that I am addicted to danger: but danger is part of it, without danger, no story; without my story: I have not lived, I will not have lived. And so there was only one thing to do: press on. And then came the moment when I accepted the idea of never returning home. It was even all right with me. Inwardly I crossed a line and was ready." — The author: "Ready for what?" — She: "Ready." And for the time being she wanted to be alone as she continued her journey.

The only thing that occurred on this stretch: she filled her tank. Where a male hero seeking adventure would perhaps have grown grouchy and impatient, under the same circumstances she drew patience and lightheartedness from the absence of particular happenings; patience she would need for what lay ahead, of that she was certain.

Usually practically a race-car driver, she drove in a leisurely and steady fashion, and at the filling station—this, too, far from any city, along the deserted highway—she inserted a pause after each self-service operation. It suited her fine that the station owner, actually just a shopkeeper, came from his field behind the building, where he was plowing under the previous year's cornstalks with his tractor, and engaged her in a lengthy exchange about nothing of significance. She even dragged out the conversation, with if possible even more meaningless comments, such as, "Yes, and almost three months till Easter," or: "Right: the cans of motor oil are heavy," or: "Yes, soon summer will be here."

And the conversation ended more or less this way: — The station owner: "Your husband back safe and sound from Africa?" — She: "Without a scratch on him." — The station owner: "Your mother released from the hospital?" — She: "A week ago, still looking very pale." — The station owner: "Your children still doing well in school?" — She: "The boy's been slacking off a bit lately." — The station owner: "I remember how much I enjoyed watching you dance, Mahabba. And then your voice. No one in the whole area sang like you. You should not have given up your singing. Why did you give all that up after your wedding? stop dancing? stop singing? The softer the song, the more your voice went through and through me." — She: "I will take it up again, perhaps not the dancing but the singing. What I need is a new song. I can feel it coming on. All that's there now are a few notes, a few words. What's missing is something to pull it together. Perhaps on the other side of the Sierra?"

She wished the station owner would go on speaking to her as this woman for whom he obviously mistook her. Or was he merely pretending to be confused?—All the better: she would drive off feeling easier in her mind. To let him go on and on about her in the role of that stranger; and if adding anything, doing so without asking questions of her own, or asking why, with no intention other than to get him to digress, again and again, every digression having as its focus the unknown woman, who in the meantime could equally well be her. As she left the filling station, the owner or farmer suddenly took her hand and kissed it. The benefit of an interlude, in which one allegedly wasted only one's own time, and time in general, and gained so much time. A rich interval. Bright trumpet blasts across the entire barren *meseta*.

Then nothing at all happened, and for a considerable length of time, once she was alone again with the road and the tableland. That for a while nothing at all happened: what an event these days—what a special circumstance. Nothing but repeated flashing of lightning. The flashes did not come out of the consistently clear blue sky; they came out of or lit up inside her. A flashing of images began inside her such as had never before erupted in such variety and such quick succession; like meteor showers, coming so thick and fast, yet often at distant points in a firmament which for that very reason seems impossible to encompass; the eye cannot keep up, yet does not want to let a single falling star go unnoticed. And again a curious phenomenon: that these image flashes were generated by patience, and almost happiness—yet always pointed instead to something disheartening or even grievously sad.

In front of the car a whirl of chopped cornstalks, long since withered, blew along the *carretera*, whipped together by a wind spout into a sort of leafy column that spun past a few feet above the asphalt; and at the same time she, the driver, felt the brook flash through her, the brook called Satkula that circled the Sorbian village, more than a thousand miles away, in a great arc.

She put her finger to her forehead, which meant: be mindful. The image of the brook, the glittering of the water oppressive? First of all because she viewed any recollection of her childhood and its setting as over and done with. And then, that village signified to her falling prey to death. In her memory, the villagers there had been obsessed with death, day in, day out, including the children, or perhaps them above all, the children? Yes, the children's awareness, above all, at least there and at that time, had been riddled with village tales of people's dying, almost always gruesome, never peaceful, never? no, never. A neighbor had been tied up and his head stuck in an anthill, where the ants had eaten him alive (although it happened during the war, before her time, she had experienced it, as a child, as happening in the present). Another man broke his neck simply by falling to the ground while picking apples, and not even from high up on a ladder but simply from a chair (that could happen to them, the children, just as well). A neighbor woman choked to death simply because a horse whose smell she could not stand passed by. Another woman, so one heard, young and healthy, simply did not wake up one morning, and died, according to the priest at her open grave, in a state of sin, unmarried, with an unborn child in her womb. The miller—for a couple of years there was such a person there—lost the third and last of his children when the little one drowned in the brook, which was especially rapid below the dam, where the millrace joined it.

Perhaps it was less these accumulated deaths themselves than the tales of them circulating from dawn till dusk that populated the entire village for her, even in broad daylight, with terrifying ghosts; for all that was left of her own parents, of whose accidental death the villagers did not speak, at least not to her, the child, was trails of light, primarily due, no doubt, to her grandparents, who dwelt exclusively and insistently on stages of the parents' lives—and wasn't that characteristic of old folks? And any death in the village that she witnessed with her own eyes affected her very differently from one described by a third party or, worse still, overheard in passing: the person, the neighbor, whose death, even the most wretched one, she experienced with her own eyes, present until the final breath, would never crouch on her chest at night or pluck out her heart and then jump out at her the next morning as she was on her way to school or in the afternoon as she drove the cows to pasture—for a while this was still done in the village, by some little girl or other, outfitted with a whip and rubber boots—from behind a barn, from the slippery rocks where one forded the brook, from an empty root cellar stinking of rotting turnips.

Yes, the innumerable tales of death and dying, or, more precisely, anecdotes, at times made her village seem toxic. Never again a village, or at least not that one. And in retrospect it seemed to her as if it had been chiefly that sense of being pursued by the villagers' obsession with corpses that had awakened her interest in money, when she was still a child. In money, simply the concept of it, she saw something that suggested an escape from the grim cycle of cadaver-worship, the hereafter, and apparitions. Money circulated toward life, embodied the living world, and meant *now!* (and now, and now . . .). And in the beginning it was just a healthy distraction. The thought of money gradually banished all the ghoulish stories.

And even then her urge to deal with money, to handle it on behalf of others, was far more powerful than the urge to have it for herself, to possess it; even then she had the idea (yes) not so much to multiply money as to let it be fruitful; to manage it—which then became the focus of her university studies—to use money to open new avenues, and still more new avenues, consistent with one of her later guiding principles: "He who steps into the same river has ever different waters flowing past him." Setting things in motion with money: thus she became the first person from her death-obsessed village to go into the money business. (That she was a woman doing this was no longer particularly remarkable even then.)

And now she said, talking to herself sotto voce, as usual: "'Thou shalt manage money!' is a commandment like 'Thou shalt not steal!'; its positive counterpart, like 'Thou shalt make it be fruitful and multiply!' And who knows, perhaps I accomplished as much as I did in this business because the thought of money enabled me to shake off those village death-and-doom stories? That thought gave me the energy to immerse myself completely, to my own and everyone's benefit, in the world of the here-and-now, of life? But why are the village images coming to me now? Flow on without me, village brook!"

Another image flash: it pertained to the adolescent in the gate-keeper's lodge at the entrance to her estate. Like all the images that flew to her so unexpectedly, this, too, was thoroughly peaceful; was set in peacetime; generated peace—the image was peace itself. And at the same time the image-spark that lit up the boy, Vladimir, for her appeared, like that of the village brook, accompanied by, or primed or shot through with, a lack—something was missing, if not from the image itself, then all the more tangibly from the subject of the image, the person in the image, and dreadfully missing!

The boy was sitting, just as he had one time in reality, at the kitchen table in her house, not as an intruder but instead very matter-of-factly, as someone who belonged there. He was reading. The kitchen was clean, sunlit, and warm. The large wooden table was bare except for a bowl of quinces, yellow as only quinces can be. Peace? Silent contentment. And nevertheless she sensed, at the very moment the image passed through her, empathy, no, pity, for the actual distant figure there in the, in his and her, in their northwestern riverport city. It—it? a surge—drove her to him; or he was supposed to be here with her in this instant. That he was so distant—from her? from what might it be?—simply far away, separated, isolated—was her responsibility, struck her as her own omission, her (un-specified) guilt.

The image, along with its powerful calm, meant: she should be close to the boy, this other person. Contrary to appearances, this burly Vladimir, who passed her in her own space as if she were not there, was as much at risk of going under as any human being could be; the very personification of a need for attention. He was in danger of falling out of the picture, and she had to rush to his aid. ("I must," and that smile of hers.) His parents alone would never be equal to the task, ever, and for anyone. (Her "sense of mission.")

And this lightning image, too, was also followed after a few moments' hesitation by an audible conversation with herself: "If I ever return from this journey, I shall open an account for you at my bank, Vladimir. For a boy, that kind of thing can be as important as his first bicycle or motor-bike. And for you it will be something else besides. And for your sake I re-gret that I cannot turn back: if this is not my last journey, at least it is the decisive one. And I would like to bring something back for you. What that will be, I do not know yet. But it will be right for you. And you will continue to look right through me, though perhaps in a different way." As she said this, she turned her head, still driving in a southerly direction, and, accelerating now, she glanced as usual along the axis formed by her shoulder, and blew into the air with a breath that would have extinguished a candle from a great distance or would have made a small branch sway.

A different image—an interpolated image, intersecting the others—lit up her vanished daughter like a flash of lightning. It, too, told of peace. It, too, and that was the unusual thing about this wild succession of images, seemed weighed down by dark embellishments. She saw the girl, grown up by now, as a child. (What she saw in this fashion was always something she had also experienced; usually long ago; the images represented a kind of unexpected and astonishing recurrence, an addition to the usual memories.) The child was sitting on a sofa in a corner of the room, playing the guitar. The music was inaudible; the image was silent, like all the others; but in that fraction of a second she saw that her daughter was not playing a proper tune but rather isolated chords: this was evident from the child's eyes, focused more sideways on the hand holding down the strings on the instrument's neck than on the fingers plucking the strings farther down. She was just learning to play. And nonetheless that simple sequence of sounds made the impression of accomplished playing. That had to do with the girl's gaze, now, in the moment between the last chord, its reverberation, and silence: still completely engrossed in playing and already full of enthusiasm for what had just been played, and full of joy at the anticipated praise, and full of eagerness to continue playing—if not the guitar, then another instrument—eagerness to play, play, play, on and on forever. (It was in fact not a guitar but an *oud*, an Arabian lute.)

And again an awareness of guilt came over her, though this time a less unspecific one. For she saw and simultaneously reflected (images of this sort could be counted on to bring about insight) that, when it came to her child's infinite passion for play, she, the mother, had if not betrayed her daughter at least not taken her seriously enough. She had shown no interest in her games, or merely a fleeting one. Even on the occasions when she had played with her, she had rarely given the game her full attention. In contrast to her daughter, who had paid constant and rapt attention to the ball or dice, and likewise to her, her grown-up partner—as witness the little-girl eyes gazing straight at her, with a presence of mind found only in children at play—most of the time she had merely pretended to be playing. She had hardly ever succeeded, even with the best will in the world, in becoming truly involved in the game.

She felt it would be imperative to tell all this to the author when she reached La Mancha, and she actually began now, during her solitary drive; launched her words with great intensity into the air, into thin air, consistent with the way she wanted her whole book to be, setting the air currents in motion: "Just as one speaks of playing at being serious, people could speak of me as playing at playing with my child. And in doing so, I was not doing her any good. I took care of her. I protected her. I caressed her, yes, caressed her. I hugged her. I loved her. I adored her, yes, adored her. But when she played, I was criminally negligent of my child, in my capacity as spectator and playmate. If you ask me whether that is my secret guilt, I will say no. But there is something to it. Perhaps.

"Listen: my child was the personification of play. Whether she was speaking, studying, eating, or walking, whatever her activities, she could not help playing. For her, as well as for anyone who became her audience and/or playmate, that was a joy and a source—yes, a source—of exhilaration. This ability to play meant, and this I came to recognize too late, a magical gift. To be able to transform anything in life into a game, even simple breathing, or turning one's face into the wind, or blinking, or shivering in the cold: that strengthened the existence and the presence of the player and at the same time that of her playmates and/or observers. It was my child's playing and my being-in-the-game that made us a family in the first place; would have made us a family. How the house, with all its rooms, was aired out by my child's playing—there was no need to throw open the windows. How our property became enlivened. What singing had been to my grandfather, playing was to my child. Even when she talked about something that hurt, she talked excitedly, as if it were a game.

"And thus my daughter's wanting to leave me was also part of her game, part of her inability not to play, as I also recognized too late. Just as she played at shaking her head as a child, as an adolescent she played at being sad, being bored, despising money (and hence my profession), and then wanting to leave. While as a child she was fully aware of my inadequate involvement in her play, yet graciously ignored it—that was how self-sufficient and total her play was at the time—as an adolescent she increasingly needed me not merely to play at joining in, needed me to participate fully as the number-one playmate and/or observer! If that person had laughed heartily at her wanting-to-leave game, she would have moved on to the next game, and so on, as before. As it was, as a solitary player, she became the prisoner of this one game, increasingly dangerous, and then one day had to play it out—"

As she often did, she broke off the story in the middle and said, now talking to herself again, "If I gave up my child, my vanished daughter, I would also give up the world.—When did I forget how to play? Or was I never able to play? Does that have something to do with one's having been a villager?"(She in particular missed few opportunities to speak of herself in the "one" form. In her story, the moment would not come until later, much later, when it was "she," the woman, and then what a woman that would be, what a "she.") "Or one's being the eldest sibling? And yet precisely as a person in banking one really should be a player? No, no. And yet more and more people in banking are players? In a more and more dangerous game?"

And turning anew to the air, to the engine hood, facing in the direction she was driving, heading south, toward the Sierra and La Mancha: "What a mess. And no coherence. No continuity, no continuity. And yet: life. Glorious life. How grand life is. Let's have that book. You must record my story, our story. How lost one is otherwise. Getting to the top, victories, and triumphs: the worst form of lostness! One must make sure something continues." And again, in the end, nothing but an exclamation, a single word, one that did not exist yet in any language, like a distorted word, or the sound made by an idiot.

She was still far from coming up with the song. Perhaps she would never be able to sing it, she who fell silent after a few notes of any song, whether sung with others or solo. But the song, just one, was hiding, or waiting, inside one, had always been there, always wanting to burst out into the open, and for almost an entire lifetime already. And of course it was a love song, a nonspecific one that included one specific person or other, or rather merely grazed the person. Merely?

"Our book," she said to the author (she unconsciously used "our" instead of "my"), "should omit my early history if at all possible, including the village, my ancestors, also my work in banking—which I prefer to assign to my early history—except for just a few details. And one such detail is the fact that my grandfather was a singer of songs, known far beyond the immediate region, still giving concerts in half of Europe as an old man. A classic singer of the German *Lied*, who at the same time maintained his residence in his native village all his life: here the house of the smith and wheelwright, there the sawmill, here the farm, there the schoolteacher's house, here the constable's house, there the tailor's house, here the singer's house, a house of wood, set in an orchard, actually even smaller than the others' houses (only the constable's was equally small). Let that flow into our book, casually, in passing."

Then the series of flashing images of her brother, who in the meantime was where on his journey, parallel to hers or perhaps not, to his chosen people? Traveling only at night, he was sleeping now during the day, but not in the hay in a barn or a stable, but warm and well cared for in a bed. The correspondences he had conducted daily in prison had resulted in a long list of addresses, all of which represented possible places to spend the night. Not only in the country toward which he was heading but also throughout the world, the released prisoner would have been taken in immediately, here as well as there, with hardly a day's journey between one place and the next. In every town, even small ones, at least one house stood ready to receive him, a sort of network almost like that of a certain sect or a people scattered all over the earth. And should he happen to find one door barred, his sister was certain that one right next to it would immediately be opened to him. Her brother, the enemy of mankind, was at the same time the quintessential social animal. He was aware of thresholds, true, but instead of impeding him, they gave him momentum; he drew the strength from them to open himself up, and others.

Precisely when encountering strangers he was immediately all there, as a matter of course, yet made no assumptions, with the result that he infected every new acquaintance with his attitude, always liberating or refreshing. Women in particular tended to respond to him, and after exchanging two sentences with him began to use the intimate form of address. Accordingly, her brother was at this very moment sleeping, if not at one of his thousands of correspondents' addresses, then under the coverlet of a young or older "motherly" woman he had met only an hour ago at the bus station (or in the next room), who meanwhile was at work somewhere, having pressed the key to her apartment into his hand after the third sentence they exchanged.

But the present image had nothing to do with her sleeping brother. It, too, obedient to the rule or law governing such images, came flying or flashing out of the depths of time, and this one even from a long-ago past: in it her brother appeared to her as a very small child, almost a nursling still (but nursing from whom? his mother had died in an accident the day before). And this child—like the adult in the present—was sleeping, though not in a bed in a closed room somewhere but rather on a wool blanket outdoors, under an apple tree, back home in their village orchard. Yes, she had seen him this way once, and she had squatted next to him, in the role of the one who was supposed to take care of him, the guardian of his sleep. Her tiny brother lay there on his back, in the light summer shade of the tree, and slept deeply and peacefully, the sleep of the righteous, almost the self-righteous, as only a nursling can sleep, with cheeks puffed out and lips protruding.

This image, like all the rest in the image shower, told of (dealt with) a kind of peace. And this fragment from a very different era likewise contained an element of melancholy, or, worse still, a danger, a threat. And with unabated amazement she recalled that at that moment it had been crucial that her brother not wake up. He was very ill, and this was supposed to be his healing sleep. He had to sleep for a long, long time. If he woke up too soon, or suddenly, it would kill him. And soon the blazing sun would reach his face. Should she pick him up and move his bed? Sit down and shield him? And the tractor sounds growing louder. And the saw blades howling as they sliced into the tree trunk. And now, as she drives steadily southward over the mesa, along the almost always deserted *carretera*, with the image of her endangered brother before her, a small branch hits her windshield with a pop (in reality more a cracking sound), making her jump. Unlike with the previous images, she remains silent; avoids any sudden noise in the car. Not squirming in her seat, which could set a defective spring to humming. Not turning on the windshield wipers (to remove the sight-blocking branch)—risk of squealing. Maintaining a steady speed so as not to shift. Having to brake suddenly now would be the end, once and for all!

Then, even when opening her brother's letter with one hand: no ripping, as little noise as possible. Reading, silently, the single sentence: "That the world is still there—wonderful!" (Not to be taken literally, see "secret code"!) The branch blown onto the windshield: from an acacia, leafless, arrow-shaped; studded with sharp, pointy thorns; arranged in pairs, in the form of bulls' horns.

Then all the image meteors—didn't "meteor" mean "between heaven and earth"?—outdone in brilliance and duration by one whose content she did not want to reveal to the author. The only thing she told him: "It was just a word." And then she explained to him: "Even single words can arrive from a distant place and time as images. And perhaps there is no image more penetrating and intense than a pure word image like this."

Even now, long after the fact, when she spoke of it, the word was present for her as hardly any present could be. Although she kept the word secret, she revealed herself terrifyingly to the author. If he was terrified, it was in this sense: suddenly he viewed her with different eyes; he no longer recognized in her what he thought he knew; he saw before him a total stranger, and at the same time someone familiar; he wanted both to back away and move closer; his terror: not so far from what was at one time called "holy," at least with a hint of it. And yet she remained unapproachable? Or on the contrary? And he, or one, or whoever, simply did not find the right way to approach her?

After the arrival of that word image—"It flew to me, came sailing to me"—she had driven on at her steady speed. She drove on. She is driving. The highway over the upland plateau is bumpy, and the car bounces and sways like a carriage. While driving she pushes back the Santana's canvas top. She sticks something between her lips, something that suits her even less than a cigarette: a toothpick, and not even one made of ivory, let's say, but a wooden one. She takes off her hat and lets down her hair—which does not suit her either, or does it now?

Empty blue sky, devoid of airplanes, devoid of the kites and buzzards so common on the mesa, with that motionless dark cloud still hanging there, though by now low on the horizon, sinking out of sight, like a mountain. In her open rough-terrain vehicle the heroine shows herself to the author for a moment from high above (although he has never written a film script). Then she moves in close again, in a veritable close-up, or a torso shot. And for the first time now he sees her eyes, as if they had always been veiled to him previously, even though he has been preoccupied with her story for so long, including their color, which again does not seem to suit her at all; or perhaps it does, and how! though not her origin and her country, but then what did that have to do with her story?: an indescribable black.

"Indescribable"? How could he, such an experienced writer, let a word like that slip out? And now he tried at least to describe that black, at first mainly for himself, as usual: it was a black that could resist any light, even the most glaring, even the winter sun hanging low over the fallow disk of the earth. The adventurer's eyes did not merely face down the sun; they literally absorbed it—perhaps, too, because although they were open wide, they did not dry out, at all, at all—and sent the rays back, transformed, and how! A black like the black of the eyes of the white-robed angel on the medallion, whose one finger pointed sideways toward the empty tomb? No! How extinguished those eyes appeared now, almost wondrously extinguished; for how they would flare up again when—. In ancient books, the word for the black of her eyes was *gagat* or *azabache*, meaning something like pitch black. But not that either: this was no film. After all, hadn't the movies made it impossible to find a color and a face? These were supplied ready-made, in close-up? Besides, our heroine bore no resemblance to any angel, including the fallen ones, and least of all at such moments! This black sucked in the light, absorbed it; tasted it; savored the aftertaste. Her entire face, then her neck and shoulders as well, were engaged in silent tasting, motionless, without biting, chewing, or swallowing. Along with the light of day, the air was tasted, the air-stream, the hues of sky and earth. And also striking to the author—which subsequently struck him again and again, if anything at all—was how, in addition to her eyes, all the parts of the woman's body, even the smallest ones, unveiled and unclothed, revealed themselves in the light surround-ing her; as aspects of the light, stretching, billowing, arching, even when the woman did not raise her face as she drove along, but rather kept it lowered. Visible even now the seemingly eternal abrasion on her brow, al-ways in the same place. Visible, too, her hardworking villager's hands: she was strong. But the physical strength was not her own. And nonetheless the many scars on her body.

And how the author will stare when these patches of light he is contemplating on the woman's body are suddenly joined by one that is considerably more extensive—that is, when a few milestones after the arrival of the aforementioned word image, one of her shoulders, again seen from above, is suddenly bared, her shirt having seemingly slipped down to her elbow of its own accord? And although the bunched material perhaps interfered with her steering, she did not pull the shirt back up. She drove on quite some distance with one shoulder bare. Her skin re-flected the light. The lashes above her black eyes stuck out distinctly, without mascara, ever more distinctly, like the acacia thorns from the windshield. And finally she bit the toothpick in two.

"But even this image or word," she indicated to the author later on, "had a black mourning border. It arrived as pure energy and was accompanied by impossibility. The more insistently it called for unity, the stronger was the echo, and that proclaimed: separation, once and for all! Not mere mourning: pain, almost screaming; pain at the impossibility of staying together forever. So then I tossed the falcon's wing, picked up in the devastated forest after the hurricane, out the roof of the car."

And here the moment has come in her story to indicate that, according to tradition, her clan does not belong only to the Sorbian, i.e., Slavic, minority in the easternmost reaches of Germany. More notably it descends from a minority within this minority: from an Arab trader who came to the region even before the turn of the first millennium and conducted his business there. Hence her vanished daughter's Arabic book? Hence the blackness of her eyes?

Myriads of images, constantly brushing past her, plummeting down on her, shooting up inside her, shining through her, tickling her awake during that solitary drive. As much internal as external, high above as down low, horizontal as vertical. And each of the images, even if it was switched off after a microsecond and at most had a bit of an afterglow, was tangible, and accessible to both the senses and the mind, both leaving an aftertaste and clarifying one's thought processes; was each image, albeit surrounded, as now, and undergirded by the glow of missed continuity, a treasure that would never be lost, even if one allowed a particular image to disappear again without making a point of tasting and contemplating it, and a treasure whose value—she of course knew all about "value"—exceeded anything one could ever "have" in life or call "one's own"; the fundamentals underlying any "goods"?: "love" (was love a good?), "loyalty," including to oneself (was loyalty a good?), "beauty," and "goodness" (was goodness a good?), "renunciation" (was renunciation a good?), and of course "peace"?

At any rate, each image among the thousands was under the control of its receiver, even if it had flashed by in the twinkling of an eye, as if the receiver were also the transmitter. What remained of the image was the imprint, which, before it faded, sooner or later, and in some cases not at all (in this respect comparable to an unusual dream), could "bear fruit," and this without exception (whereas with dreams this was the exception). And one could decide which of these images would bear fruit—as the selection and utilization of those just described rested on the intensely personal choice made by the one "image person" in question.

"Those images," she dictated, for the moment more a *"banquière"* than an *"aventurière,"* to the author, "are a form of capital. Capital without any exchange value, but with all the more use value. Capital whose owner one remains only if one chooses to use it to the utmost. If one allows this capital to sit unused, it collapses, and—this is the unique feature of these moveable and/or immoveable image assets, my most liquid holdings and at the same time my soundest real estate—one collapses with it, even if the opposite appears to be true. Having and owning as a process of constant trading, yet not speculating and lining one's pockets but rather pure usufruct, as much to one's own benefit as to others'. By putting the image-capital to work, and why shouldn't one?, for profit and enrichment, shared profit and joint enrichment, without claiming to be an owner, without the title of ownership: a way of handling property that has hitherto gone unrealized in any economic and banking system—" She broke off; end of dictation. But had the author taken it all down? His scribbles indecipherable; his private shorthand.

Over time the lightning flashes of images had become sparser. In this barren countryside all one saw, as far as the horizon, was this barren countryside. The cloud behind her had dissipated, as clouds sometimes do over the ocean. Oh (in Arabic, *ja*), how fruitful this interlude had been: it was right that now the images dwindled and finally disappeared altogether. Although outwardly nothing was happening—which, given the rocky baldness of the mesa, perhaps contributed to the hail of images?—, the lone driver felt like someone who had just crossed a newly discovered and at the same time tranquil, strangely familiar continent. This had been the time for images, and now there would come a time without. Yet she could have spent an entire day, even an entire month, alone in their company. And hadn't she just experienced an entire month, an entire year?

But at the end she pursued a final image, one that had filled her with particular astonishment. With it came the idiot from the riverport city at home, the "idiot of the outskirts." He was perched on the site of the weekly fish market. As befitted such an image, she had actually once seen him sitting there in just this way. She walked past him, and he looked at her. He was bald and barefoot. The day was windy and cold—even if in the image now neither wind nor cold played a role. Or, rather, yes, at least the wind did. For between the woman walking past and the idiot, papers and plastic bags are swirling around, intermingled with the gleaming of fish scales. The market is closed. The stands are dismantled; the square is empty, although not yet cleaned up. Fish heads and lemon slices in wooden crates, or littering the ground. The idiot not perched as usual by the side of the road or on the curb, but on one of the hydrants that will be used to wash the trash out of the marketplace. He sits there as on a throne, at eye level with her, the passerby, who has known him, as he knows her, for a long time.

And one day the idiot had been standing beside her in the narrow little Armenian church on the outskirts, both of them equally strangers there, or perhaps not? the others at the mass not any less strangers, only less noticeably so? More than once they had crossed each other's paths on the way to the forest, he meanwhile riding a motor scooter without a muffler, and now and then with a woman, a different one each time, all of them appearing normal, so to speak, at least in comparison to him, who was constantly throwing his arms in the air and babbling in fits and starts, either in a deep guttural voice or a falsetto—normal, and, in the idiot's company, in such high spirits that one would not have recognized them if earlier one had happened to run into these particular women or girls alone. And one time he had shouted enthusiastically into her car, from one of his favorite spots, a coach's brake-chock inscribed with a king's crown, left centuries earlier along the road leading out of the city: "I know everything about you. I've read all about you, everything!"

Now there/here on the market hydrant the idiot is trembling. He is freezing. His teeth are chattering. In a moment he will be shooed from his perch and soaked through, which will make him freeze even more. Far and wide no female companion in sight. And his elderly parents, who have taken care of him for decades, have both died, she the day before yesterday, he yesterday, or at least, mortally ill, were taken away, and now the idiot is living in the house all by himself, an excessively spacious old building with espaliered fruit trees out in front, and many paths through the rear garden, where one sometimes saw him strolling with a small book in hand, like a priest praying from a breviary in earlier times—though merely pretending to read, or perhaps not?

The square smells of fish, the often rather oily kinds from the rivers. The sky northwest-gray. The idiot hungry. And without any money either, except for the two coins he has always jingled in his pocket; which he lays on the counter in the suburban bars; and which would not pay even for the sugar in the coffee to which they always treat him, which he sweetens with so many cubes that the cup almost overflows. And how strange that outside of the office she almost always ran into people who had no money and, stranger still, had no interest in money, and that this suited her, strange or not?

In contrast to the others, that shower of images with the idiot as its central figure was not set in peacetime. The figure on the hydrant there was suffering. Not merely that he was cold, and so on; there was also a terminal hopelessness; the imminent prospect of being dragged away from his house and from the region where he had spent his entire life; of being removed, perhaps in an hour, from the only sphere of existence halfway possible for the idiot.

And yet, also in contrast to the rest of the current image series, not a trace of grief in his face; no sorrow at parting; no hint of fear of dying or perishing. In the midst of the swirling market debris, and his dire straits, the idiot remains untouched, and untouchable. On his temporary perch there, he is the essence of untouchability, beyond peace and war, heaven and hell. He crouches—no, sits "enthroned"—there, defying death—and life as well? no, transcending all our stupid thoughts of imperfect continuity, transitoriness, and irrevocability; the epitome of presentness, beyond my sorrows and joys; the embodiment of the current moment; simply there, and above all, as only an idiot can be, there and then.

And thus one sees oneself perceived by that figure on the cistern in a manner unlike any other; a form of perception that accompanies one, step for step, and meanwhile registers one, word for word, or sentence for sentence—note the movements of the idiot's lips; if not narrating one, then enumerating one, in an impartial, merciless, seemingly inhuman manner; precisely the kind of enumeration specific to an idiot, which, however, can occasionally validate and acknowledge one like a particular kind of narration; a registering that does not categorize—a blessing. How affirming such enumeration by the idiot is, in that it challenges one to do a better job at anything one does in his field of vision, or at least to do it more clearly, which means more rhythmically! And so, as she passed him back then, she set her feet down more firmly and let her shoulders roll back a bit more. And now on the highway she does nothing for the time being but drive.

She drives on. Dust flies up. The sun shines in her face. She does not squint. It is possible she will be dead soon. She is wearing a ring. Her belt is broader. Her mouth is the broadest. I caress her. She does not notice. Maybe she is a man? In her heart a white lily blooms. Her ribs are sharp as a knife. You stink. She turns the wheel. The road is straight. By the side of the road lies a skull. Another over there. The fields are gray and yellow. There stands a tree, full of dried-up leaves. The leaves tinkle. From that tree hung a black boar. It was slit open. The intestines were spilling out. Who will wash them? On a pole sits an owl in the bright sun. My girlfriend has a small mole in the hollow above her collarbone. Now she drives faster. My mother smoked, one cigarette after the other. One time I beat her because of that, in a dream. Another time she had an operation, but thirteen nurses blocked my way to her. Where will she turn in to spend the night? An empty bed is already waiting for her somewhere, or perhaps not. She is hungry. There is a line of dust around her nostrils. She is alone. I have never seen her not alone, except in photos. In the company of others she is unrecognizable. She plays at being sociable. And she does not play very well. She would play better with me. And in the pictures she plays particularly badly when she is in the company of a woman. She looks disfigured to me then, and ugly. Or no, not ugly, worse than that, a beautiful caricature. And her gestures and body language toward the other woman. She seems to be waving five hands in the air, jerking two heads, shifting from one foot to the other, jiggling like a millipede, her hips constantly bent like a tailor's dummy. My father was a tailor, down in New Orleans, and in his deserted shop still hang a couple of suits and garments dropped off for alterations. And nevertheless, nonetheless, despite everything, and even so, I would like to see her in her story with someone else, at long last. Perhaps she just cannot stand being photographed? Even though she was a film star in her youth? Although or precisely for that reason? (This expression I picked up during the time when my parents listened to "Radio New Europe.") To see her with someone, where she would be more, by a factor of one, by a factor of one hundred, than she is by herself.

She drives on. The dust flies up more and more. The sun shines on the nape of her neck. She pins up her hair. She pulls her shirt up over her shoulder. Her knees are sharp as daggers. She clamps her legs around me and draws me home into herself. There I curl up blissfully. There is a fragrance of lilies. And perhaps she will die this very night.

11

Toward evening, traffic on the *carretera* swelled. It was not only from both directions that the number of cars increased. Vehicles also came lumbering onto the road from the previously empty fields, steppes, and semideserts, fewer tractors than trucks, many of them with flapping tarpaulins, all grayish yellow like the earth, a sort of camouflage, and now and then convoys of tanks and armored personnel carriers, as if returning from maneuvers, and likewise ordinary automobiles, not only those made for rocky slopes but also many sporty little cars more suited to city traffic, hobbling along oddly from the trackless savannahs.

And all these vehicles, most of them, like her Santana, heading south, merged onto the highway, which continued almost straight as an arrow. And still no village in sight, let alone a city. Beautiful old Segovia at most a felt presence, as a strip of haze above the seemingly infinite mesa, to the east, at the foot of the Sierra de Guadarrama (not her destination), which was white down to a fairly low altitude—suggesting that the considerably higher Sierra de Gredos was even whiter? Or was this whiteness the result in part of the craggy massifs in the distance, lit up by the rays of the sun?

And then, just as abruptly, planes in the sky, flying quite low, not sport or private planes but dark, quite massive wide-bodied four-propeller bombers, zooming in from the south, seemingly springing up out of the ground, flying even lower as they approached and slowing to a speed that almost matched that of the stream of vehicles directly below them, and with their flaps set almost perpendicularly, describing a sort of landing curve, a broad ellipse, heading for which airport? the one at "Nuova Segóvia," nearby according to the highway sign, yet out of sight, despite the roar of planes landing in quick succession, on the otherwise still apparently uninhabited mesa; and bombers like these returning to their base, each with its nose almost touching the tail of the one in front of it, each with the same sound, something between droning, rumbling, growling, and clattering, maneuvers inextricable from war, unlike those of tanks.

And now the shattering of her windshield, as if simply from the sound waves; glass shards in the car, also on her; not a single remnant of glass left in the frame there in front of her. And then the sign "Deviación," detour. And was this possible: In the middle of the seemingly endless high plateau, almost unvarying except for the occasional rock outcropping, suddenly a "straits"? The road a cut through an outcropping, from a distance hardly distinguishable, yet from close up clearly higher than all the other outcroppings and also infinitely longer, crossing the entire countryside, forming a natural barrier, traversable only at this one notch, which had been carved out deeper for the *carretera*, forming a "straits," or an *estrecho*, like the straits or *estrecho* of Gibraltar between the Mediterranean and the Atlantic.

And there, with walls of rock on both sides, the road did in fact narrow. Two vehicles could barely pass one another. For a truck, the vehicle approaching from the opposite direction had to stop to let it go by. A pedestrian would have had to flatten himself against the cliff (if that was even possible), and not only during the evening rush hour, as now. "Estrecho del Nuevo Bazar"—that, according to the sign, was the name of this pass. And, again according to a sign, it was more than a thousand meters above sea level. That meant that the *meseta*, to all appearances completely flat since the beginning of her drive, had imperceptibly gained about four hundred meters in altitude.

Immediately after the straits, after the *cordillere*, came the detour; the *carretera* blocked with steel chevaux-de-frise, a type of barricade now known almost exclusively from early war films and old newsreels, spirals of barbed wire wound through metal spikes. The highway sign, with "Ávila—Sierra de Gredos" crossed out with a thick line, barely legible, and further obscured by splashes of tar and bullet holes. The names of these places no longer occurring after the detour arrow, except for "Nuevo Bazar," phosphorescent, and not only from the deep-yellow evening sun.

The straits was familiar to her from many previous trips. The settlement known as "El Nuevo Bazar" had also existed for years. She had spent the night there, in one of the many new hotels. And yet she no longer knew where she was, sitting in the line of vehicles, now moving at a snail's pace, on the turnoff with which she was supposedly familiar. After the straits, had this huge hollow or basin in the landscape been there the last time? Was she on the right road? Was this even a road? With all the cars, bumper-to-bumper and rearview-mirror-in-rearview-mirror, and with the constant rumbling and pounding from the stones underneath, with dust flying at her, as well as thistles, steppe grasses, wild bees, and the occasional hornet—what, in the middle of winter?—even that was soon no longer a certainty.

Then the moment when she did not merely wonder, "Where am I?" but also, "Where is this place?" An area such as she had never encountered before. As if, with the passage of time, this familiar countryside had been transformed into something entirely different. As if it had been stood on its head; tipped over; turned upside down. As if this place, including the blueing sky and the greening patches (fields of winter rye dotting the fallow land), were ultimately not "here" anymore, but where? at the antipodes? on a distant star? As if this region, despite the bronze-glittering patches of water and the swaying dog rose bushes here and there—the little fruit capsules glowing reddish purple on the canes, arching against the evening sky—could not even be called "a country"; "a province"? (misleading); "a region"? (even more misleading); "a stretch"? (too innocuous); "an evil star"? (too pretentious).

And yet: as if one were nevertheless being ineluctably drawn in, breathing freely despite the dust, drawn into an atmosphere inimical to life, one that pulled the ground out from under one's feet, now, now; that tipped one over or swallowed one up and let one tumble into a pit called "nowhereland," into its non-name.

Time and again, often merely as a result of deviating from the beaten path a bit, she had landed in a sort of white hole. And after the initial blow to the head (literally), it had done her good, and now? "Don't know," she said to herself. "Who knows." And still no sign of the "Nuevo Bazar," announced, with each rotation of the wheels, along and above the road, also up in the sky, with banner in tow: no plantation or lone farm, not even a shed out in the fields. Instead billboards, one crowding and blocking the next, and then, out of nowhere, broad, smoothly paved sidewalks, with no one walking on them, accompanying the road, which meanwhile had become a distinctly good one, with electronic temperature displays on every light pole, the degrees differing markedly, not only because of sun and shade, as did the times flashing on the screens. Then floodlights, from a stadium? Suns infinitely more glaring than our familiar sun; the latter setting.

Finally, among the billboards—on which one often saw not merely a picture of the item offered for sale but the actual object, a house, a yacht, a car, an entire garden, a castle gate, in the original, on poles, suspended, on wheels for taking with one immediately (including the gate and even the garden)—a small, seemingly forgotten sign: a turnoff after all for "Ávila—Sierra de Gredos," probably the last one. And this little sign was not crossed out, not blackened, was unharmed; and the road, albeit narrow, led in a curve, shimmering with emptiness, in the direction she wanted. The peak of one of the foothills of the Sierra already visible beyond the curve of the horizon. Yet she stayed in the pack with the others, on the road into Nuevo Bazar.

She shook off the shards of glass. Was that a bullet hole? She closed the roof of the car; when the sun went down, it got cold in this highland hollow. She put on makeup; she could do this while driving—still at a snail's pace and hindered further by the traffic lights, increasingly frequent, yet without intersections, without any other sign of a settlement, the land to either side still lying fallow. She piled her hair on her head and wound it into a knot. She took the acacia branch, which had fallen into the Santana when the glass shattered, broke off the thorns one at a time, and stuck it diagonally through the knot of hair. She tied on a gauzy white cloth whose hem partially concealed her eyes. She turned on the car radio and set the dial to the station indicated on other roadside columns, now illuminated for the night, these columns, too, coming up at every rotation of the wheels, and, unlike the temperature and time indicators, always giving the same call numbers for the station.

She had been warned about Nuevo Bazar. From several quarters word had reached her that the place had changed recently (and the warnings had nothing to do with the current rumors of war); it was no longer a good place. The author of the most recent travel guide—whom, to be sure, one could not trust any more than most of the proliferating advice- and hot-tip-dispensers, assigners of plus or minus points, for all sorts of regions, no matter how out of the way—wrote: "Nuevo Bazar, a mixture of Andorra, Palermo, and Tirana. Every morning ten truckloads of blood-soaked sawdust to be disposed of. Mounds sprinkled with lime, growing daily, outside the city, which does not deserve the name of 'ciudad' but has become a death zone, popularly known now simply as 'La Zona,' and no longer Nuevo Bazar."

But not a word about this on the radio. For a long time, local news briefs, and these dealing only with the weather, the water level, prices at the indoor market, the times of movie showings and church services. Not until almost the end did the word "war" occur, or rather a denial: "no war"; allegedly only scattered skirmishes were taking place, far off in the mountains to the south. And only at the very end, but then for a while, and repeated every few car lengths: "War!"—but somewhere else entirely, not merely in another country—in Africa; no rumors of sporadic slaughters of the mountain tribe in the Sierra, or of tribal members among themselves?, no, "the" war was world news: and yet how involved the two announcers on Radio Nuevo Bazar, a man and a woman, both with unmistakably very young voices, seemed to be in this real, universally acknowledged war, as one could hear from their rapid-fire question-and-answer, and also reporting, game. The war over there in Africa—actually not that much farther than the Sierra—: that was the thing; that was it; that was where things were happening; and what are you people doing here, what are we young folks doing here, in this backwater?

Yet the two announcers were for the most part reporting only what was being reported over there in the African war-torn area. "Reported," that was a word that occurred in every sentence in their accounts, and when an incident, always having to do with mass death and destruction, was introduced with that word, the incident was considered proven; "reported" meant, as far as the war was concerned: this way and no other way; uncertainty impossible; "confirmed"—the usual conclusion of the report; "allegedly" or "probably," as in the case of the "vague rumors" from the Sierra: out of the question.

And the height of unimpeachability was achieved when one also gave the person doing the "reporting" the status of eyewitness ("one"? the reporter? the war itself?): "According to eyewitness reports . . ."—no greater truth was knowable. And such reporting, the definitive evidence, could only go hand in hand with the horrific?; reporting and horror were inseparable, and not solely on the news? also in books? or had this always been the case? reporting without horror was not really reporting? commanded no attention? was not heard? no longer heard? was not taken seriously? reporting-and-war-and-atrocities: only that was taken seriously?

Without turning off the radio, leafing at random through her vanished daughter's Arabic booklet, then even reading bits here and there (that was possible during the stop-and-go drive into Nuevo Bazar): "Al-Halba was a place in Baghdad . . ." "in the presence of this sheik one felt as if one were in a garden . . ." No matter how this New Bazaar might have changed since her last trip, from one moment to the next she suddenly had time for the place, at least for this night—time? yes, and not only for the place.

And so what if Nuevo Bazar represented a threat or an obstacle, according to the guidebook? That was all right: after all, danger—not to be confused with "war"—was her element. And the infamous masses of people in the "Zone"? Even there she caught a whiff of value, and certainly not out of nobility on her part (the very notion of catching a whiff contradicted that), but out of animal instinct: an instinct that did not derive from her profession, her managerial activities, but rather had brought her to them in the first place? Without a whiff of value, no adventures that extended beyond conventional banking and benefited business undertakings, and not only these? One of the few sentences the author underlined in the hundreds of articles he was reading in preparation for his book on her: "The secret of this businesswoman: in almost everything, even unfavorable circumstances, she catches a whiff of value. Not a gambler but an adventurer."

The story, and she as well, wanted my adventurer to remain unseen on the evening of that drive into Nuevo Bazar. Despite the shattered windshield, not one gaze from all the thousands she encountered came to rest on her. And that had to do not only with her partial disguise and the cloth over her eyes. She simply willed people not to register her presence, and so it was.

The author of one of the earlier articles, who had been allowed to shadow her during a workday at the bank and then also accompany her through her riverport city in the evening, had noticed this ability she had, and had ascribed it to a special feature of her office: she sat there alone, inaccessible, closed off, visible to no one, behind a door that could be opened only by a button on her desk; and at the same time she had before her, in the same wall as the door, a pane as large as a shop window that provided a view, not of the outdoors but of the office space, with the cubicles where the bank officers sat and received their clients or whomever; through this pane she could keep her eye on everything happening out there, while those on the other side saw only their own reflections in the matte, silvery, foil-like surface.

The author of another feature on her, who had also written a soccer novel, explained the phenomenon of her not being seen (or the non-phenomenon) by saying that her way of looking past others toward something in the distance, a vanishing point or goal, and of tracing with her eyes a possible passage between the people around her, was reminiscent of the "divinely talented Libero," who, with the ball on his foot, having glimpsed an opening among the opposing players, would distract and mesmerize them into position, thereby preserving the gaps his eyes had detected, after which he, Libero, now invisible to those who had been thus magnetized and blinded, would kick the ball as he wished, past the other team's players, or over them, and usually score.

Whatever the case: that evening she did not want to be seen, and no one saw her. Everybody looked away from her; at most someone might follow her gaze: for the way she focused on the horizon suggested that something remarkable must be going on there. But there was nothing to see, not even a horizon.

Suddenly, after stopping, starting, then stopping again, one was in Nuevo Bazar and surrounded by buildings, tall ones, as if already in the center of town. No actual center: every street corner could be central, also a side street, a passageway, a stone staircase with four or five steps. Because the town was located in a hollow, which unexpectedly dropped off even more and at the same time formed a curve, perhaps following the meanders of one of the rivers that had at one time been numerous on the mesa, it remained hidden up to the last moment, until one turned onto the steeply descending curve, where, instead of the barren, wide steppe, one was instantly surrounded by façades close enough to touch, and instead of the uninterrupted highland sky saw narrow ribbons of sky following the configuration of the streets below.

And after a long day on the road, often fraught with uncertainty, that could be a blessing. It could be pleasantly stimulating; stimulating and calming at the same time; welcoming without a welcome sign. And like an evening *corso* in a southern city, the sidewalks, earlier completely unpopulated, once one reached the first cornerstone of a building, were black, white, colorful with pushing, crowding, or merely standing and leaning pedestrians (as in a *corso*), the unwritten law being that they could not venture one step beyond the boundary of the prescribed evening promenade, in this case the edge of the settlement, and if an individual by mistake violated this law, he had to turn around immediately.

As a result of this welcome, a surge of appetite: a desire to taste this town for an evening. And what had the author of that travel guide meant by that reference to daily tons of blood-soaked sawdust in Nuevo Bazar? Certainly it was not to be taken literally, but there was also not the slightest indication that the image was supposed to be interpreted metaphorically. The pedestrians, and likewise the people in cars, driving by very slowly, had nothing evil in mind and simply wanted to enjoy the moment. As a group, they even made an unusually carefree impression; and that had to do with the convertible tops, open in spite of the January evening at this altitude, the rolled-up sleeves and sleeveless blouses: an innovative feature was the streetlamps, which not only produced light but also heated the air. The streets, including the side streets, were as bright as day, and that, too, in marked contrast to the area before the entrance to the town, already shrouded in night: light coming from the many floodlights on poles towering above the town, whose gleam, even when one looked straight up, remained mild instead of blinding; reminiscent of a veiled sun on a morning just before the onset of spring.

And listen: even a few cicadas could be heard, as loud as in summertime, a grating and warbling, though not from actual live insects but rather from deceptively good imitations of them, dear little machines in the shape of cicadas, attached way up on the streetlamps here and there, even programmed to make artful pauses, so that no chorus of shrill sounds resulted; just sporadic bursts of sound, which then continued in a casual, even rhythm. And look: olive trees in cask-sized pots, and feel: genuine, proper, olive-green fans of leaves that one could break off, and even ripe, genuinely bitter fruit.

Should she make her way to her bank's branch in Nuevo Bazar, where, as at each of the branches throughout the world, above the lobby a visitor's apartment was maintained for her use, to be accessed by means of a series of codes, stored in her hand telephone, for the four or five doors? This time that was out of the question. After all, this journey had to do with something other than an article or a feature: with a, the, her, our, book. Spending the night in such a comfortable, and, what is more, familiar apartment did not belong in the book; and besides, she was not traveling on business. The story forbade that, and consequently she forbade it to herself.

She did not even have to make a point of forbidding herself. It went without saying that she must hunt down a place for the night. (Smile.) The bank apartment "did not count." And besides, for a while, "or for good?" she thought, she was more than merely "not in service"; for the book she had to be someone other than her everyday role—not necessarily someone different: someone in addition, who could, to be sure, provide service if necessary. The book, the adventure, required that she be a stranger here, a nobody. And at this thought a hand was placed on her shoulder. *Katib* was Arabic for shoulder, and *kitab* was the book.

Searching for a bed for the night provided a foretaste of the pending adventure. The many hotels, at least three times as many as the last time she had been here, were all full, or, conversely, were empty: "Waiting for the Refugees," as the vacancy sign outside announced. But at first she did not even inquire about a room. That was as it should be. Parking the car on what was apparently the only lot in the entire settlement not yet built up, and setting out on foot. A sort of happy anticipation of a night without a bed, among the glass shards in the car, or elsewhere. Easy does it: in the course of events that will not fail to come about.

Eventually she found a room in a place that was neither a pension nor a private home, and, in spite of the first impression, also not a shelter for the homeless. Crammed in among dozens of identical buildings, it called itself a *venta*, even though it was in the middle of the town (as everything in Nuevo Bazar suggested the middle), *venta* like a hostel out along the highway, standing alone, the only building far and wide, at a crossroads that had been important centuries ago, but in the meantime was no longer important, and perhaps not even a crossroads anymore.

A *venta* without rooms: the floors above the ground level, where the taproom and dining room were located, consisting simply of four corridors that met at right angles, opening onto an inner courtyard, actually more like a shaft, at the bottom of which was an empty square of concrete, hardly as big as a Ping-Pong table, called the "patio." Nothing but corridors, without doors to any rooms—so where to sleep? In the sleeping compartments along all the walls of the corridors or galleries: an unbroken succession of wooden sleeping cupboards or boxes or cabinets (the ceiling so low); looking very narrow from the outside, but inside halfway roomy, even if one's head or feet bumped against the adjacent bedcupboard; a heavy, dark curtain to close off the compartment; and these berths, suitable only for sleeping alone, like litters, stacked as in a litter storage shed, lined up around the four corridors, and almost all of them already booked for the night.

She (does the *ventero* even notice that she is a woman?) is given one of the last berths, one with a wall lamp, so that with the curtain closed she can do her usual after-midnight reading. And also, as usual for travelers, a key, in spite of the unlockable litter, in case she comes in late. And how small this key is in comparison to the one she had the other night, how light and inconspicuous, like the key to a mailbox or a bicycle.

After the evening meal in the *venta* I saw her outside, mingling with the passersby, whose numbers had at least doubled in the meantime. The drivers from earlier are among them; hardly anyone is driving now. And no one notices her; as if she were still invisible, or—this, too, a trait she displays occasionally—utterly nondescript.

As part of such casual strolling in a crowd, there is a common phenomenon, or natural occurrence: time and again, a face, a voice, even a mere gesture, reminds one of an acquaintance; usually someone from earlier in one's life, a person one lost sight of long ago, often someone already dead. But here not one such an encounter. Instead the pedestrians all resemble each other, probably as a result of the artificial lighting from high above, like people hurrying, some in one direction, to a stadium for a game, and others in the opposite direction, toward a bullfighting arena or an open-air concert.

Many children in the crowd, as usual, and they, too, resemble one another, and not only one child resembling the other, but the children resembling the adults, and not as children resemble their parents, but rather as adults resemble adults; children with grown-up faces. No excessively loud voices; any talking is steady, subdued, as on the way to, or on the way back from, a so-called communal experience.

Gradually one was able to see that these masses, instead of forming a uniform procession, were moving back and forth in innumerable little groups, troops, clusters, and units, with gaps between one team (even as few as two could form a "team") and the next, at first almost imperceptible, but after a while distinct. At the same time, from one group to the next, a great variety of languages, all spoken in the same subdued tones; not entirely different languages, as becomes clear when one listens carefully, in fact almost always from the same source, from the same language family, but pronounced, accented, aspirated, in entirely different ways, apparently intentionally, by the squads strolling by; and this most noticeably and emphatically in the case of mere dialects and patois, where each of the hundreds of little troops is showing off its own particular variant (of the written language shared by all of them) with the most extensive possible display of unique features; distinguishing itself in this manner from the next little unit, as if that group's members spoke an incomprehensible Chinese or Siberian mumbo-jumbo, and only here, among us, could pure Castilian or Bazaranian be heard; and thus planting each entity like a standard, announcing, as it marches past, a newly declared language, as a challenge; which matches that image from earlier, during the evening drive, of the line of cars into Nuevo Bazar: the banners, flags, and pennants being frenetically waved from every car, with the windows and tops open, and each cloth bearing different colors and coats of arms.

And among these individual squads—hardly any impression of a *corso* and evening stroll anymore—none who have eyes for another person, behind them, in front of them, coming toward them, or indeed for any individual. People intentionally look away from one another; not out of scorn or hatred, but rather out of a new kind of reticence (in this respect, too, Nuevo Bazar has changed since the last time); these people have become timid toward and foreign to each other, and above all toward themselves. All of them have become afraid of strangers, even in their own country (perhaps it would be different in another country?). And tomorrow they will also turn their head away with a jerk when they are alone and encounter someone from the smaller or larger clan in whose company they are today.

And it is not only the nine thousand nine hundred and ninety-nine faces that resemble each other—almost all of them wear their hair the same way, for instance the old and young men, who have one long, bleached strand of hair tucked into their belt in the back. And all these mortally shy, orphaned, abandoned, and/or widowed men are dressed in the same style, and their shoes or high heels have the same little metal plates tapping a chorus into the night. Night? And many push and bump into each other, unintentionally, in this crowd, so uniform and apparently timid, where no one any longer knows the fine art of stepping aside; and the response to the bumping is an expletive or a hastily drawn weapon here and there; the words and gesture initially not a hostile act but rather an expression of the irritability common to all in Nuevo Bazar, or even more of nervousness—as indeed one peal of a church or temple bell, actually melodious, now leaps out at one as a cold, dry clang, something between a threat and a warning tone, a sort of dog substitute, and makes one—one? many—recoil in alarm.

1 2

At some temporal distance from the events outlined here, a historian later provided an exhaustive account of the Nuevo Bazar of that period. Let his ramblings—for that is what they are—be introduced here by a few excerpts, on the suggestion of our protagonist, who sees it as an essential feature of the book devoted to her, first of all, that she disappear occasionally from its pages (though with her presence still felt, for instance as its reader) and, second, that in this book, albeit not too often, a problem of rhythm!, some passages occur that are not exactly filthy, but certainly grubby, bordering on the tasteless and abstruse, to be sure only bordering, and playing fast and loose with reality—instead of, as is otherwise a basic principle of her story, seeking and exploring reality in a sort of quest.

Let this point also be made to preface the historian's passages: he appointed himself the representative of the profession and furthermore a "specialist, respected throughout Europe, on the Nuevo Bazar Zone"; his statements, despite their carefully cultivated tone of historical objectivity, are dictated by overzealousness and ill will (the author of that tendentious travel guide could have been one of his predecessors); and finally, it would be plain to a blind man that he had spent his entire life or half-life as a private historian in a zone very similar to Nuevo Bazar, perhaps even identical with it.

It begins with the historian's wanting to see each of the many peoples in the Zone as manifesting only the worst, most evil, or ugly of its "historically conditioned peculiarities and characteristics." The good, better, attractive, likable traits of any people in the Zone were long ago eradicated, precisely by the elimination of borders and barriers between the individual peoples: the elimination of historical ones "rightfully and indubitably" to be viewed as progress and liberation, but with them went the "natural" ones as well, which, along with threshold anxiety, also drove out of the people on either side any of the "threshold awareness" that had functioned as a "basis for national education," as an "instrument of national refinement": leaving no ability to distinguish between here and there.

"One people, in the territory of any other people, behaved more and more as though it were in its own territory, in the sense of behaving all the more badly—uniquely and exclusively badly—for over there, beyond the former borders, it is of course not our people, but since the elimination of the borders it is our territory. Our territory? our free range, our space for wallowing and mucking around, our surrogate battleground. If the individual peoples in the Zone would simply regard the entire area as their own, at least now and then one of their good qualities would manifest itself.

"Thus as far as the Zone is concerned, the comforting concept formulated by one of my historiographical predecessors, that of *cultural continuity*, meaning the indestructible qualities of the peoples, which includes those legendary ties to a place and to a historical mission that persist even in the face of near extinction, exile, destruction of traditions, of economic systems, of compilations of legal precedents—this comforting concept, when applied to the Zone [one of those typical private-historian utterances, so complicated that the beginning has to be reiterated at the end!] is actually tinged with mockery.

"The only cultural continuity maintained among one of the peoples there is the coarseness and obscenity for which it has been known since the Thirty Years' War (not a trace left of its love of celebrations or its hospitality); among another people nothing remains but the habit, for which it has been known since the early Middle Ages, of yelling and elbowing others out of the way—its newspapers are even so large that when they flip them open anyone sitting nearby has to move—and at the same time a penchant for pussyfooting around (without their once famous ability to turn inward and suddenly step elegantly out of the way); and the cultural continuity of the third or other Zone people, praised in antiquity and earlier still, even by foreign chroniclers, for their love of children, knowledge of the stars, expertise in fruit growing, and skill as mariners, now expresses itself exclusively in two characteristics mentioned previously only in passing by hostile historians: gluttony and a passion for foul language and negative attitudes (not a single statement without a tacked-on opinion, always a bad one, or a profanity, never intended humorously—an honest-to-goodness curse). Thus only negative characteristics as cultural continuity among the peoples of the Zone? Only those characteristics that lash out."

And that is by no means all. This would-be historian has even worse things to say. He works himself up to describing the people of Nuevo Bazar in terms that bear not the slightest relation to any visible reality, less descriptions than figments of his imagination.

Thus he mentions, as a custom shared by all the different ethnic groups in his day, that they do not clip their mobile phones onto their belts or elsewhere but drag them along, in the settled areas, on a line or a leash, almost as long as for a dog, "on a rail specially installed for this purpose by the Zone administration." Furthermore, according to him, all the inhabitants, without exception, including any children who know how to count, are required to have such a device with them at all times, and to keep it switched on.

"On the other hand there was a regulation stipulating that if one received a call one had to put on a special helmet, which concealed the speaker's or listener's face, along with its expressions, from the eyes of others on the street, and muffled his voice, at the same time distorting it to the point of incomprehensibility. Time and again it happened in the Zone in those days that a person telecommunicating out on the street without the prescribed facial shield would have his hand knocked from his ear by one of the specially appointed enforcers, with a stick designed just for that purpose (and not a few civilians played policeman, using their bare fists), and time and again mistakes were made, when a presumed violator was merely holding his hand to his ear as he walked—mistakes that did not always simply end with an apology and the apology's being accepted.

"Altogether, the entire Zone was notable for being a source of mistakes and mix-ups. The residents of the Zone did not even become aware of most of them, or if they did, fortunately there were no serious consequences. To mention (for the last time!) those long-distance-calling minis that everyone had to carry: especially in the spring, which still occurred in the Zone, though very inconspicuously, quite often one of those out on the street would mistake the sudden squawking of birds, whether close by or high up in the air, for his telephone's ringing, and would promptly press the little button, after obediently popping on the helmet. And one never saw anyone in Nuevo Bazar doing actual work; certainly there were people slaving away, but they were kept out of sight or were so far off that they no longer had any significance. And all the wares from the wide world seemed to be available, but when one really needed something, it was nowhere, but nowhere, to be found. And while all the alleged monuments glowed and glittered, the hordes of pedestrians below waited in vain for the simple headlights of buses and other means of transportation.

"And since each of the approximately nine hundred ninety-nine ethnic groups in the Zone had its own ring tone, when a titmouse squeaked, only the Galicians would answer; when a blackbird chirped, the Valencians; when a falcon screeched, the Andalusians; when a lark trilled, the Carinthians; when a woodpecker rapped, the New Spartans; when a jackdaw squawked, the Chumadians. But no one in the throng would react to the clattering, or rather rattling, of the storks, which periodically drowned out all the other sounds or noises. Here, as everywhere on the mesa—in spite of everything, the Zone continued to be a part of it—the storks built their basket-like nests atop the church towers, but their sound not only did not match any of the different rings; it was not even heard by the people of the Zone, or if it was heard, it was mistaken for a stick caught in a vehicle's wheel. No one knew that there was life up there among the presumably dried-out twigs atop the tower; not even the children looked up to see the dagger-like beaks poking out of the nests, or the fighter planes overhead.

"Among the innumerable mix-ups occurring daily in the Zone at that time, others were less innocuous: the mere sound of the wind had become so unfamiliar that a person hearing a rushing behind him would take it for a truck bearing down on him, and would involuntarily jump out of the way, and precisely thereby . . . Another person might hear the crunching of footsteps growing louder and louder on all sides, and, assuming that he was surrounded by enemies, would fire blindly in all directions—many adults in the Zone were armed, and not only adults—yet the crunching was actually the croaking of frogs, which continued to have their moist places, though hidden from view."

And the height of the Zone's self-appointed historian's ridiculous imaginings, an example of his utter disregard for the principle articulated long before him by a narrator of an entirely different sort—"to present this and that to the reader without drawing any conclusions!"—could be found in his conclusions, which he prefaced with a few final aspersions, cast not only on the people of the Zone but also on the animals, plants, and objects there.

"To be sure, there were still a few original inhabitants in the Zone who referred to themselves as being 'of the old school.' But they were dying out. All the others had moved there from elsewhere, most of them already two or three generations back, without displaying any trace of the regions and countries from which their ancestors came, indeed without any knowledge of those ancestors. Each person stalked around as his own hero; there was bragging even in the eyes of the infants: 'Whatever you people are, I've been for a long time already. In a pinch, I'd be a better singer than Orpheus or Bob Dylan. If I wrote a book, Cervantes and Tolstoy would be rank amateurs by comparison. If I had to direct movies, they would make *Birth of a Nation* and *Viridiana* look like home videos. If I were asked to paint a picture . . . ,' and so on. Admiration and enthusiasm for the actions and accomplishments of anyone else was considered old-fashioned and embarrassing, or was merely feigned, and in such a way as to be intentionally transparent. Yet in the Zone and on the street, as well as on the Zone TV and the Zone Internet (which was limited to the Zone!), one of the most frequently used words was 'love.' 'I love this salt shaker, I love this purple, we (couples always spoke in the first person plural) love New Zealand wines, we loved the latest work by . . .' (even the booksellers used nothing but the first person plural, whether they were several or only one) . . .

"In truth, what had once been love had long since disappeared from the Zone. And that revealed itself above all in the fact that each person had his own way of measuring time; in fact, all the digital watches beeped to mark the hours at completely different intervals. And each person followed his own clock, lording it over everyone else with his personal time. Not only the credit cards but also the paper currency displayed their owner's picture almost immediately after coming into his possession. While on one street veritable hordes of judges paraded in full regalia, on a nearby parallel street the daily procession of felons took place. Even the worst criminals (often former statesmen and their ilk) moved about freely in the Zone, openly and as a matter of course, aware that they would never ever be punished.

"As far as I am concerned, perhaps here and there a hint of that extinct love may have revived. But the person in whom it revived remained hopelessly alone with it. Only the haters still formed a community. Even the children in the Zone were handicapped by bad qualities, at first imposed on and instilled in them, soon innate. If one of the last two or three original inhabitants happened to speak to such a child from the heart, saying, 'Be yourself!' (this might be an old photographer, setting up a school photo), the child would promptly, at a complete loss, make a whole succession of faces, not one of which was anywhere near 'the right one.'

"Another thing was that any child in the Zone, if asked about the points of the compass, would be incapable of pointing out south, north, west, and east (and most of the adults could not do so either). Bees were called wasps, or vice versa. Chestnuts, although people enjoyed eating them roasted, on a plate, were not recognized when they were lying under their tree (in spite of everything, there was still the occasional chestnut tree on the edge of the Zone). An apple, if it was not arranged in a basket in front of a store, but was hanging from a tree, among the leaves (in spite of everything, there were still . . .), was not recognized as a fruit, and was left there to rot.

"Of course one also from time to time saw the Zone, which, by the way, was not in a world of its own, dotted with the colorful neckerchiefs of all sorts of scout troops. But instead of exploring nature, these troops behaved more like militias, with casually worn daggers (whose forms could be ascribed to the many ethnic groups that had moved into the area), under the motto 'Do one bad deed every day,' even if that consisted merely of pushing someone from another ethnic group off the sidewalk. In the Zone, even gardeners, who are favorably looked upon everywhere else, were likewise no longer considered 'good folk': even they, the good gardeners of yore, went all out to make life miserable for their neighbors, perhaps by deploying all their equipment, enough for ten fire departments, against every individual blade of grass, and with blaring sirens to match, and preferably on Sundays; or else these battalions of gardeners, the most avid patrons of taverns after work, would move in like an eviction squad and beat up a person standing alone at the bar, preferably a former hunter from the steppes, a remnant of the original population, quietly sipping his drink by himself.

"It is uncertain whether the many mutations among the plants in the Zone can be traced back to the gardeners' constant spraying with toxic chemicals, etc.: what was clear, at any rate, was that the stinging nettles that still sprang up vigorously here and there, in spite of everything, no longer stung—yet some of them stung all the more savagely: one of the increasingly cruel perfidiousnesses of the Zone's gardeners, who had mutated along with the plants—just as during that period the Zone's sparrows more and more mutated into vultures, and the small black ants into termites (overnight all that was left of the Zone's parliament was its façade. But even before the building was gobbled up it had become a mere stage set)."

The conclusion drawn by our would-be archivist followed: "In light of all this, one could ask oneself whether these very conditions in the Zone might not give rise to a longing for another world, for entirely different possibilities, or any possibility at all. Except that there was no other world or possibility anywhere." (So the person drawing this conclusion did not consider such a longing worthy of even a question mark?) "On the contrary, one of the influential books of the time, entitled *The New Candide*, argued that the conditions prevailing in the Zone were the best of all possible worlds!" Yet didn't precisely the crowding, the large number of inhabitants of Nuevo Bazar, argue for the opposite? How can one imagine forming such a large number? Imagine? Image? For shame!

1 3

Back to my woman from the northwestern riverport city. In contrast to her hired author in his village in La Mancha, she had no objection to the tendencies manifested by that would-be historian from whom we have heard in the interim. For during that night in Nuevo Bazar, a night as bright as day, she found his seemingly groundless assertions confirmed in some fundamental respects.

It was true that almost everyone on the streets strode along as his own king, and also expected anyone he encountered to make the appropriate obeisance. And because each individual used his personal sense of time to tyrannize over the person in whose company he happened to be, repeatedly the apparently peaceful bustle would experience from one moment to the next an audible and visible jolt: shouting, screaming, hitting, violence (which would then subside just as suddenly); among the faces that looked so similar, and so balanced, wherever one went there would be one, two, or several that in the twinkling of an eye could turn into grotesque masks, with teeth bared, tongues lolling or stuck out, and the well-tempered, almost overly civilized voices—which everywhere, even among the older children, could easily be mistaken in intonation and pacing for the sonorous tones of radio and television announcers—after an abrupt catching of the breath were transformed into the screeching, growling, and hissing of apes? hyenas? beasts of prey?, no, of human beings turning savage, with a savagery utterly different from the putative primeval variety.

And immediately afterward—the grimaces and howling suppressed and silenced with such uncanny rapidity that the bared teeth and screeching seemed to have been a chimera—the earlier monolithic equanimity and radio-announcer sonorousness restored; except that now one increasingly suspected general pretense, masquerade, and playacting; as if it were already Carnival time here in Nuevo Bazar; except that each person, following his self-declared time-reckoning, was making his way to his very own celebration; intent upon appearing as the particular historical figure and assuming the particular role that had been reserved for him since birth.

Then she, too, felt almost infected by the constant oscillation between sonorous magic, shrill unmasking, remasking, and growing suspicion. She also noticed that the longer she stayed in Nuevo Bazar, the more she herself regarded people, and hence also the smallest phenomena, with suspicion, even at a distance and with gun cocked, as it were, no, not merely as it were. And she realized that suspicion and the proliferating mix-ups in the Zone went hand in hand—although in her case without the terrible consequences so common there.

"Mix-ups?" — "Yes, at first I mistook the heartbeat in my ear," she told the author later, "—not surprisingly, after a long day of driving alone—for someone pounding on a steel door or the rumbling of a wrecking ball. But that was all. Or I more and more often mistook the books that quite a few people had in their hands for dog leashes. Or when someone raised his cane, I saw it as a gun pointed at me—except that I did not immediately pull my own trigger, as is said to have happened more than once in Nuevo Bazar.

"What continued to haunt me: the suspicion that every phenomenon in that place had been tampered with—and the sense of irreality. That became most clear to me at the time, at the time? when I, who usually derive my perceptions of real shapes and colors from a kind of tasting, tried to recall the evening meal I had eaten at the hostel: I simply could not remember what I had eaten there barely an hour or two earlier, and in particular I had not the slightest aftertaste.

"But," she continued, "unlike the Zone historian's, my gaze did not remain fixated. Or I used whatever I was fixated on as a point of departure. I willed it that way, for my story." — The author: "Is that something a person can will?" — She: "Yes, it can be willed and resolved. I willed and resolved to push off from my fixations, and by means of them, and that came to pass. And thus it was that there, in the so-called Zone, I found my way back into my story and our book.

"That *historiador* and those who consider themselves his successors or disciples, the whole tribe of 'friends of history,' with their cultural continuity: all well and good. Yet our book has an even greater continuity as its subject, which should not preclude—on the contrary—the narration of equally brief, even the very briefest, moments, and the inclusion of various things that verge on dreams—though only verge—, in which time leaps, or is suspended, or piles up, becoming concentrated and even dense enough to touch, as occasionally happens in a Western; remember *The Searchers*, when the family waits in silence, alone on the prairie, for the Indians' attack and for death; and the compressed time in *Rio Bravo*, where all night long the trumpet of death is played for the group under siege in the jail, and in the end it feels as though not just one night has passed but an epic year, an epically compressed eternity.

"Your task is to describe not cultural continuity but the grander time, and it cannot happen, it is simply not permissible, for the future to appear as an impossibility, as is the case with the Zone archivist." — The author: "Please accept my thanks for this lecture. But in my previous life as a writer have I not done quite a bit, or tried to, to develop a sense of this grander, or also merely different, time, and to make it strong enough to bear the weight of this long story and that, and this and this, and another and yet another?" — The woman from the riverport city: "What do you think induced me to select you, of all people, to write this particular book? Idiot." — The author: "But why a man for this assignment? Wouldn't a woman be more suitable, and also more appropriate to the spirit of the times, as the teller of your adventures?" — She: "Storytelling is storytelling is storytelling, whether a man or a woman tells the story. The minute you begin to tell a story, you are neither a man nor a woman anymore, but simply the storyteller, or, better still, you are the pure embodiment of storytelling. And by the way: be more sparing in your use of 'so to speak' and 'as it were.'" — The author: "And should I assume that when someone's story is told it does not matter whether the subject is a man or a woman?"

The riverport woman: "No, no, no. Our book must be about my story, a woman's story if ever there was one." — The author: "In what respect, for instance?" — She, gazing along the line of her shoulder to the distant horizon on that side: "To begin with, simply by virtue of telling a long story, a very long story, perhaps longer than all your previous ones. If a story is to be told about me, and in general, about a woman, it must be a long, long, long story—and something other than a woman's novel or a chronicle of life at court. If suited to our times, then something of this sort. And simultaneously, my, and our, story should run counter to our age, as is appropriate for a book, or is it not?, should circumvent it, transcend it, subvert it, no? And by the way, be more sparing in your use of 'for instance': it is obvious that every detail in our book suggests an example, no?" — The author: "A story as long as *Gone with the Wind*? And about a woman in finance, whose image as a woman is distorted or even destroyed by the image of money?" — The woman from the riverport city: "For all I care, equally long, or almost as long, or half as long—even that would be something—as *Gone with the Wind*, but in other respects with no resemblance to it. Or perhaps not, after all?"

And she continued to gaze along her shoulder, and said, after a long pause, "And besides, I have nothing to do with financial matters anymore. I am, so to speak, no longer a banking princess, as it were. I have changed professions." — The author: "Since when?" — She: "Since last night. An eternity ago. Since my crossing of the Sierra de Gredos. Since the evening, night, and morning in the Zone of Nuevo Bazar." And she gazed along the line of her shoulder, which swiveled gently as she did so, toward the far-off horizon, now at her back, and fell into a silence that lasted for some time and became more profound with every breath, eventually giving way to something like a pulsing, and gradually drawing in the author.

She had moved through Nuevo Bazar as if along a diagonal or the line formed by a cross section. The images she encountered, also in her pushing-off from the established "track" (the word supplied by the Zone archivist), with the omnipresent images of shopping, organized events, happenings, and other stimuli in the foreground (and in N.B. these foregrounds predominated), prevented even one of those images from poking her, images that, according to her conviction, represented and refreshed the world for her and for everyone, and were the main point of her book.

But that did not matter now. First of all, it had been her experience that in any case those world-conjuring images, whether here in Nuevo Bazar or at home in the riverport city, did not show up in the evening. They belonged to the morning; were part of the morning; brought with them and brought about what made the morning the real morning.

And besides, she had always trusted sleep and the revitalization it could be expected to bring. Nor did it disturb her that the glimpses through the few gaps, actually mere cracks, into the background of the settlement revealed images of desolation, of despair, or of sheer nonsense; that just kept her more awake. From the beginning to the end of the diagonal line, there was no building on the right or the left whose ground floor did not have a shop window. These shop windows usually took up the width of the entire ground floor, and often the entire façade as well, from the street level up to the top floor, the fifth, sixth, seventh. Quite a few of the façades had no front doors, suggesting that the rooms behind them, from bottom to top, were merely display spaces? Next to them almost identical shops, all just as brightly illuminated, the wares laid out in exactly the same way, except that automatic doors let one enter and buy, the stores still open at this late hour, the clerks lit up like statues and as motionless as the solitary mannequins in the neighboring buildings. Each showcase façade showing only one type of item, from bottom to top, but in multiples, masses of them, so that next to one display with thousands of fur coats came another with equally many suitcases, and next to that, one with ten thousand wall clocks, and so forth.

The sensation of moving between two stationary railroad trains, with multiple decks entirely of glass, or are the trains gradually beginning to move after all?; the sensation further reinforced by the music, which remains the same from car to car, from the six hundred thirteen garden chairs stacked up in one, to the three thousand four hundred bicycles symmetrically arranged on stands up to the roof in the next, and the thirty thousand wine bottles in yet another.

And the gaps and backgrounds in this cross section: What is going on with them? They exist, though perhaps not every time in the literal sense. One of the stores, depots, showcase buildings, annexes, although as glaringly lit as all the others, is empty, white walls without shelves; not a clothes hanger nor carton nor even thumbtack to be seen, not merely cleared out and awaiting a new shipment, also not newly erected and therefore standing empty until the following day or the following week, but empty this way for a long time already, and for the duration, yet in its emptiness, even without a sign, or the name of a company, or a street number, in business, like the other stores along the diagonal, or at least ready to go into business.

For first of all there is the usual automatic glass door, opening and inviting even someone passing at a distance to enter; and then in the background (yes, background) of this store that has always been empty, one person, obviously the manager, in a three-piece suit and tie, on a chair, low and extremely narrow, at a very small but immaculately polished table, on which he has placed both hands, his fingers extended, spread wide, his nails rounded and manicured as only a salesman's or businessman's would be, while he sits there very erect, keeping his eye on the door—in contrast to the clerks in the neighboring compartments (most of them constantly talking to each other, some of them apparently distracted)—the epitome of presence of mind, without a trace of an item for sale, without a catalogue, without a computer, without a telephone, without paper and pencil, without toothpicks, without a Jew's harp, without an ammunition belt.

Another such gap and background is formed when, for a change, the stores along the diagonal of Nuevo Bazar are not constructed in an unbroken line but leave between them a crack to slip into, not large enough to slip through—for that there is not enough room. In one of these very rare niches one's eye then encounters, as elsewhere the metal shopping carts that have been left standing, pushed away, allowed to crash into each other, similarly overturned baby carriages, which seem to have careened off course, a pile of similarly rusted lower and upper frames, the fabric long since gone, the wheels sticking up, as if these conveyances, like the pushcarts, had been merely borrowed (and simply left standing after use, or shoved out of the way).

And yet another background image of this sort came from the duplicate posters pasted on every display window, photos or artists' renderings of children and adolescents who had gone missing here in the Zone—there were dozens of these posters—and dozens upon dozens of the equally many wanted terrorists: and since the children had often been missing for so long that their photos had been altered to make them recognizable at an older age, and, conversely, because often the only available portraits of the long-sought perpetrators of violence were from their youth, the posters, which all had the same size and the same format, resembled each other to the point of being indistinguishable.

And another such background forms precisely in conjunction with these other images, the prevailing, conspicuous ones—from which one pushes off or allows one's gaze to be propelled like an arrow from a special bow: for instance (there it is again, "for instance"), up high, on the seventh and top floor, the attic of a bookstore, all of whose floors up to that one are chock-full of piles, in the form of temples, pyramids, pile dwellings, from level two to level seven the same title, all the millions of copies equally thick, with the same colors on the dust jackets, with identical spines; but under the roof one book that apparently slipped through the cracks and was hung, facedown, its pages open, on some rope or in a fishnet used as decoration, of a thickness different from the others', without its dust jacket, obviously already partially read, so that, if one had a good telescope handy—which one does—in whose sight the book and its individual lines could be brought as close as certain figures on the cornice of a medieval tower could be brought to an observer on the ground, from whose naked eye they were far, far away, they would allow themselves to be deciphered thus: "In a village in La Mancha, whose name I do not wish to recall, there lived not long ago . . ."

Despite the winter night and the icy cold, which blew in all the more piercingly because the settlement itself was heated by the banks of electrical coils, for a long time you could not see anyone's breath in the crowd; but suddenly there was one breath cloud here, and then another there, literal billows of fog in front of their faces; and finally one of the nocturnal passersby completely shrouded in a ball of white vapor, having just stepped out of a walk-in refrigerator? or from out there on the crackling-cold dark steppe on the mesa?

And now the lone farmer's vehicle on the diagonal street, a small delivery van, the back filled with sacks of potatoes and fruit, the vehicle and its load evenly covered with a thin layer of snow, which, regardless of the heaters, remains frozen solid, the snow reproducing the wind out on the savannah, in ridges, ripples, small mounds like dunes.

And the lone pedestrian now, who surprisingly looks unlike the others, otherwise so similar to one another, and in general stands out, more staggering than walking, not because he is drunk, but rather out of seemingly terminal despair, his eyes crisscrossed by it as if by ceaselessly scratching and scraping razor blades, in his hands on either side two knives at the ready, no, not yet at the ready, not yet snapped open, and why not? why not yet? when will he brandish them? what is holding him back?, and how does he even manage to place one foot in front of the other, to hold himself halfway upright, to avoid collisions?; extraordinary that he can make his way alive from one curb to the other without being torn apart halfway across by wretchedness and howling misery, which dribbles from his lips in the form of thick spittle and from his nose as snot, and bursts from his thorax as a howl (mistaken by the passersby for the roar of a distant Formula One engine as it accelerates on the final lap). Yes, when and where will this kind of despair finally tear this citizen of Nuevo Bazar to pieces? with a violence so terrible that it will have to tear each and every one of his fellow citizens and neighbors to pieces as well?

And if the crowd of people along the diagonal, gradually thinning out and becoming sparse and no longer constituting a *corso* for quite a while now, moves along in procession as if on an invisible line, this happens out of uncertainty and fear: stay out of the wind and in the shadow of the person ahead of you at all costs! shielded by him as much as possible, as by the person behind you; eyes on the ground, so that you will be able to say with a clear conscience that you saw nothing of the explosions, the flames, the bloody tangles; and likewise blocking out the sound of the bombers droning high above this dome of artificial and warming daylight at midnight; talking at the very top of your voice, to yourself? on a satellite phone?; each person in the single-file procession uttering sounds with wide-open mouth that are neither Catalan nor Asturian nor Navarrian: a new language that has no adjectives, and especially no verbs, but only nouns; and these exclusively in abbreviations, such as MZ for *manzana*, apple; SDD for *soledad*, solitude; DS for *dolores*, pain; MC for *merced*, mercy; GRR for *guerra*, war; CBL for *caballo*, horse; SRR for *sierra*; CHN for *chesnia*, longing; and so forth; almost exclusively consonants; a vowel a rarity, a chance to take a breath; and all of these abbreviations or chopped-off words following each other in crazily quick succession, at the same time issuing from the throats as drawlingly, sloppily, and indistinctly as if this language were not being spoken by local residents, Spaniards or speakers of Romance languages; as if it were not a language at all but a mere intonation; and that of a very different language, borrowed from another language family entirely; outdoing even that people's exaggerations and puffed-up, self-assured way of speaking, including the use of abbreviations and consonants, as if this ostentatious style helped them, in their solitary rushing along behind one another, banish their nocturnal fears by stalking along boastfully and giving them additional cover and protection.

And not every building on the diagonal artery is exclusively a store or a warehouse; at least here and there some floors are occupied, especially basements, with awning windows high up on the walls, at street level; and every two dozen or so paces one hears a kind of music issuing from these semicellars into the loop being constantly repeated along the entire diagonal, always solitary drumming; but this, too, always the same from basement to basement, the same rhythm, the same volume; the drum always tuned to the same note, struck as if by the same youngster home alone— his parents gone, on vacation, or vanished, never to be seen again; all the boys, and not a few girls among them, pounding on their instruments in the same monotone, whether with their fists or drumsticks, in a devil-, or whoever-, may-care fashion.

And once, for a moment, for hardly as much as a measure, a third kind of music: suddenly chiming in and then immediately inaudible again; darting in from an unidentifiable direction, the instrument also hard to identify, a guitar? perhaps a lute? a gusla? a Jew's harp? or maybe just a voice, after all? or, yes! a voice and an instrument, hovering in the air for a measure before falling silent, coming together, merging, melding; a single moment during the night along the diagonal line, when, out of the very meager backgrounds, instead of hopelessness and blind indignation, that sheltered preserve of the grander time came into focus, if only to the ear? precisely to the ear! insistently audible; two or three notes from afar and at the same time from just around the corner and heart-piercing, like a stiletto or a scalpel; stabbing as deep as possible, but not lethally.

At last she turned off, to the side, to the outside. What? in Nuevo Bazar, where any and every spot represented the center, there was an outside? Yes, in the sense that all her life, whenever she had been in a place where she could not find her way out of the center, but was trapped there, encircled by foregrounds, superficial images, and other such provocations, she had made a point of hurling herself at the center; instead of darting to the side to escape, she had headed straight for the middle of the center; just as in a bazaar (and not only an Oriental one), assailed on all sides (and not merely by hissing Oriental voices), one could find peace and a space of one's own by resolutely heading in the direction of the (not only Oriental) disturbers of the peace and taking a seat in their midst, as if one were one of them—which one was, after all, wasn't one?

And in this spirit, my, our, adventurer suddenly turned aside, that is to say strode straight toward a tent-shaped structure, the same height as the others, which, according to its neon sign, was apparently called LSC, or "Lone Star Café," and took a seat at a small round table that seemed to be waiting for her in the middle of the tent. But why did she not go home to her *venta*, where the bunk was waiting for her in the same way, yet entirely differently?—First of all, she had forgotten how to get to the hostel, and in particular it was out of the question for her to capitulate in the face of such centrality, all-encompassing and devastating to any alternative sense of place and time. There was an adventure to undergo here. Even here, in this off-putting realm, there had to be something worth telling.

But do the things that happened subsequently in the Lone Star Café fit the spirit of our book? "They do." (She to the author.)

In the middle of the night, on the tent site at the heart of the center of Nuevo Bazar, a familiar face finally crossed her path (though hadn't it been the morning of that same day that she had been in the company of the businessman she had ruined and the cook?).

It was as if all those who had not yet found their way home, local residents and new arrivals, had gathered in the Lone Star Café. Much jostling at the hundreds of glass-topped tables, even among those who were already seated. If one was not at home—wherever that might be—at least here in the tent, which, like the tables, chairs, and counters, was of glass, one had to stake a claim to one's place and one's seat.

And amid the pushing and shoving (especially when a seat became free, as in the subway during rush hour), suddenly at a distant table she saw the face of a woman with whom she was almost friends—"almost"; for she did not have any women friends; and the situation with her vanished daughter entailed something altogether different.

The other woman was in the same profession as hers, in a similar key position, but less visible. At the global "monetary experts' conferences," at that time not yet and no longer held under police protection, the two of them had repeatedly interacted and had grown closer. Why? Because they had both studied economics (to the extent this subject could be taught and learned)? — No. There was no more bitter rivalry, despite their putting a good face on a bad situation, than between businessmen, and especially businesswomen. Each expected to be stabbed in the back by the other man, and especially the other woman. Why, then? Because both of them had found their way into banking and finance more or less by accident, because it had just "turned out" that way, and both of them, the minute they left their workplaces and business hours, at the drop of a hat, in the twinkling of an eye, when the lock snapped shut behind them, forgot their jobs: not merely refraining for the time being from mentioning the money markets and the power of money, but also not giving the matter a second thought, and each time setting out for a completely different life?

Almost all our tycoons—and this has been confirmed by more or less thorough surveys conducted by the author—landed in their profession without plan or purpose; when they were students, if they had any goal in mind, it was certainly not "that kind of thing." And once in the profession,

they had no sooner stepped out of their temples than they metamorphosed in a fraction of a second into carefree mountain climbers, kayak-
ers, gardeners, lovers (source: the author).

Because both women's ancestors had had nothing to do with the
business in which their descendants were now involved, because they
were both descended from villagers, though from different countries, and
both had been born and had grown up in a transitional period, when, at
least in a village, goods and barter played a greater role than money, and
in the villages "money" was not yet automatically associated with "bank"?
Because both of them had lost their parents early? Because both of them,
without otherwise resembling each other in figure or facial features, radiated a similar beauty, when the moment was right?: a twinlike beauty, that
of a very rare type of twins, able to be mistaken for each other only at
certain moments, but then what a beauty! a rustic beauty, which was certainly quietly aware of itself yet did not thrust itself into the foreground or
make much of itself, and could, in the next moment, turn into homeliness
or even repulsiveness, or simpleminded, idiotic, no, moronic, ugliness—
because both of them were in every sense noncompetitively beautiful,
also of an "old-fashioned," no, "timeless," beauty, no, of a beauty belonging to a different time—which did not mean, did it, that the two women
stood outside of current reality; did not help shape this reality; had no
power?

Because that other woman, before she landed by accident in her current field, had, in her youth, just like the woman here, been a star for a
year or so, the woman here by playing the lead in a film, her only one, the
woman there on the strength of a song, a soft ballad, which in the middle
suddenly erupted in cries for help and cries of rage and then returned to
its starting point: a song still often broadcast today, at least in her country
(portions of it also used in tourism promotions), which had been imitated,
in contrast to the film role of her current "colleague," by several other
songs, performed in a provocatively similar style, in the same rhythm, and
with a melodic line that hardly differed from hers?

Or, on the contrary, had it not contributed to the vague attraction between the two of them that our heroine, often without identifiable reasons,
found herself suddenly confronted by people with hostile intentions toward
her: acquaintances, who up to then had been the soul of considerateness,
or at least had displayed unfeigned respect, and now suddenly bared their
teeth, and likewise strangers, men as well as women, repeatedly smearing

her out of the blue, as the one person responsible for all misfortune, including their own—while the other woman, her occasional twin, had the reputation of having never had an enemy; of being incapable of speaking a single unkind word or making a face; of being unable to raise her voice, let alone utter a scream as in her hit song long ago (indeed, so her almost-friend told the author later, "I never heard anyone with a gentler voice, a voice that came more from the heart, and consistently so, without fluctuation, in the work setting as well as outside, and no contradiction between her business dealings and her voice")?

And now, in the depths of that night, in the Lone Star Café, she saw her almost-friend make a face, and then another. The other woman, the former singer, was not alone at her table. Across from her sat the man who, it was said, had been the love of her youth, and had then become her husband, and at the same time, at least up to now, had remained all the more the love of her youth. If the woman witnessing the scene had been asked to name one couple among her contemporaries one could have faith in, only these two would have come to mind. To put it more emphatically: to the extent that one could have faith in this couple, no, had to, one could have faith in something else, something that transcended these particular two people and their particular case.

Until that nocturnal hour in Nuevo Bazar, she had thought that their love story had been pretold by the author for her book, if only in passing and as a prelude, and above all as a contrast to her own "harebrained and hair-raising" story (her words): how, even when separated, each of them remained so present to the other that when they came together again in person, after no matter how long a time, even after a month, a year, they without ado resumed a conversation from time out of mind, in the same tone, the most amiable tone imaginable, usually beginning with "And . . ." (". . . and how the ravens cawed . . . ," ". . . and the plate is still warm . . . ," ". . . and then you clean my glasses for me . . . ," ". . . and at Whitsuntide you eat the first strawberries from my palm . . ."; how, sitting across from one another, after a long silence they began without transition to speak again, and again in the most amiable of tones, and were promptly in the middle of the dialogue they had already been conducting in silence ("just as you say . . . ," "I see it the same way . . . ," "and where were you after that?" "and I you, too!" "and I you, since that day when you are sitting in the bus and are about to leave for boarding school, while I remain behind at the bus stop!").

Altogether, up to then their entire life had been an unbroken conversation, continued during the intervals, often lasting for days, when they did not open their mouths, as well as during the even longer separations occasioned by their work; continued in their sleep, whether with dreams or without, and, so to speak—no, not "so to speak"—confirmed each time in the sexual union of their bodies, the eternal conversation, as it were— no, not "as it were"—raised in complete silence to the acme of physical and mental awareness, impressing itself on the memory with primeval force, so to speak—no, without "so to speak" and yes, "primeval force"— and utterly independent of time. (How does the witness know this? Or isn't this a case of an author's letting himself go—not the certified, authentic, legitimate author but rather one of those would-be authors, who hardly miss an opportunity to elbow their way into our joint story?)

It is true: the couple's conversation took place outside of any time and remained unaffected by any ordinary sequence of time involving past, future, present; with their dialogue, the two of them had each other constantly present, in the past as well as in the future, from alpha to omega; for them there was no passage of time, and thus neither a beginning nor an end, no "Once upon a time" and no "It will come to pass," only "You are," "I have," or vice versa; like children, perhaps, who, when one tells them that in the summer they will go swimming in the ocean, point out the window and reply, "But it's snowing!" or, when an adult tells them that he was a child once, can laugh out loud at such an obviously nonsensical notion.

And now, in that midnight hour, the witness saw her almost-friend, after making a face at her husband, open her mouth and say—she read the words from her lips at a distance: "And I hate you. And I have always hated you. And I will hate you until after you are dead." And having said that, she turned her head away from the man sitting across from her and looked up at one of the televisions playing everywhere in the place, each tuned to a different program. On the screen she looked up at, a squad of soldiers was just storming an enemy position, shooting everything in sight, including dogs, hens, and, with particular gusto, pigs. And then the former ballad-singer stood up, pulled out a knife, not a very long one, and plunged it straight into the heart of her husband and lover of many years. He did not even have a chance to close his eyes, and did not slump to one side, but remained seated right where he was, at first with wide-open, then with still half-open, eyes.

Why this murder? For in a contemporary book reasons must be given? there must be no unexplained elements? — One possible explanation can be found in the descriptions offered by the historian of the Zone. He expresses the opinion that the Zone creates states of mind, and compels them to manifest themselves in deeds, that never existed before, not even in secret, and not even unconsciously. According to him, the new arrivals in particular suffer from this phenomenon and make others suffer terribly in turn; and precisely those among the new people who are the soul of gentleness and never raised a finger to hurt anyone before.

He thought he could provide a graphic image of this mechanism with the example of the oxen—as if the word "gentle" were appropriate to them—who, no sooner than they had been driven from the open steppe of the mesa into the Zone, rushed at everything that moved, like fighting bulls. In the Zone, the sheep—who actually were more or less "gentle"— also knocked down children and even adults, and the sparrows dive-bombed passersby, bloodying their foreheads. In Nuevo Bazar, a sort of arch-enmity, arch-disgust, arch-rage, flared up out of the clear blue sky, directed at everything and everybody, more virulently at the familiar than the unfamiliar, without any particular cause, insisting on expression through violence; and directed primarily at the people closest to one, and most nakedly and fiercely at the person one loved most intimately: the Zone, at least in this initial and transitional period, could be fatal to love and conjugal life. In Nuevo Bazar, he said, one was two thousand light-years away from home and from love.

And since here, too, the historian had merely made assertions rather than providing explanations, at the end of his insinuations he threw in just one explanation, a single one, and one that seemed deliberately shoddy: a reason for the sudden switch from nonviolence to often lethal violence was the artificial daylight in the Zone. "Murder and manslaughter can be attributed to the light." Yet he said not a word about the properties of this light or what there was about it that produced such effects. Only this: "Toward midnight the light suddenly begins to be too much, especially for those who are not accustomed to it."

There was some truth to this, according to my heroine: the artificial light around the glass tent of the Lone Star Café seemed even a few degrees harsher, also more palpable, than the light elsewhere in Nuevo Bazar. Besides, it had a different coloration from the rest of the light, which was a hazy yellowish gray; it was pale violet, similar to the light after sunset over an ice-smooth glacier, and in this light, the bodies of objects, of the cars parking outside (apart from which there were no other objects there), and of people (only those sitting inside, no more pedestrians) acquired even sharper contours, yes, sharp edges, like sliced laboratory sections.

Midnight around the bar lit up by an ambulance and a police car? Perhaps: if the lights have stopped flashing and merely illuminate the space. But that, too, was not accurate, for the impression was deceptively like that of "day," of a day that should long since have turned to night, and which simply refused to become night, "come hell or high water."

And in this light the witness saw her almost-friend continue plunging in the knife, no longer into her husband and best beloved, who was long since dead, but indiscriminately into those seated at the next tables, with screams like those that had occurred in the middle of her successful ballad (or was I merely imagining this? Wasn't she silent as she wielded the knife?): a woman's attempt at running amok; as if she had jumped in to take the place of the person staggering along the diagonal street earlier—and now she was promptly stopped by a couple of policemen, or members of a military patrol?, in plainclothes, with whom, as it now turned out, the glass tent was packed.

The moment in which the woman stood there handcuffed, waiting to be taken away (the image instantly appearing live on all the television screens): the essence of gentle beauty, as if transfigured. Next to her, in place of her husband, who had been taken away even faster, in a different way, sawdust strewn on the ground. And only now can one see: she is dressed like a woman wayfarer from a much earlier century, riding in a coach to one of the kings of the time, Charles the Fifth, Philip the Second, with a shipment of money to deliver, and she, the donor of the money, is equal in station to the queen. And aren't the other guests also in costume? A midnight costume ball at the Lone Star Café in the center of Nuevo Bazar on the mesa? An incident or scenario that was actually a sort of placeholder for a prologue, such as she had in mind for her book?

Television off. Music off. Lights out, not only in the bar but also in the entire settlement. No more artificial day: a pitch-dark postmidnight hour; then the night light gradually creeping in, the night sky arching overhead. Everyone leaving, including her. And, now, in the night, no problem finding her way home to the hostel. With the flood heaters in the air over Nuevo Bazar turned off, the cold of the wintry steppe streaming in from all directions. A rushing in one's ears, as if in the barrenness high overhead, in the pitch darkness, the crowns of trees were stirring. A return of the sense of taste, tasting of the air and the icy wind.

Not another person out and about, from one minute to the next, as was almost the rule in this southern part of Europe (although the region had nothing southerly about it). Only an idiot, astonishingly old, by the way, almost a graybeard, with a harelip, making his nocturnal rounds, seemingly as always, with a flashlight, shining it first on her, then on himself, and doffing his knitted cap as he passed: "Buenas noches, señora andante!; Buenas noches, señora de mi alma!" (Good night, lady out walking . . . lady of my soul!).

14

Back at the hostel, with the help of a tiny light attached to the front-door key, she lit her way up to her compartment in the gallery off the interior courtyard. The curtains to all the sleeping compartments were drawn and hooked from the inside. If there was a light on in any compartment, it did not show.

On the other hand, at considerable intervals, and each time from far-apart sections of the patio, came a variety of noises and sounds; yet hardly the usual, more-or-less regular sounds made by sleepers; rather almost inaudible ones here, more distinct ones there, and in particular sudden sounds that ceased abruptly, like voices responding to each other, or like certain voices involuntarily led by others, amid the all-the-more-powerful silence that enveloped the hostel from top to bottom; a silence as physical as only the deep sleep of a very disparate crowd can generate; a crowd in which each person is not at home in this place, having found his way there from quite distant parts, by difficult, if not life-threatening, paths, and, in his sleeping compartment at last, and safe for this night at least, has tossed and turned for hours before finally falling asleep; but then from sleeping berth to sleeping berth; and one person right after the other, the first as a sort of sleep-leader among maybe a hundred, drawing the rest along into the now general deep sleep; and as if this sleep had come only with the arrival of the woman, the last guest to turn in.

Yes, not until their numbers were complete was it permissible for this little band of lost, dispersed, and asylum-seeking folks, united by nothing but their restlessness, to give themselves up to rest (a palpably only temporary rest). A great breath of relief sweeping through the *venta*, now in the form of a soft whimpering, now in the form of a sighing that expressed itself only in the moment of falling asleep; here as a giggling, a release from the earlier daylong stress, even a burst of laughter, such as the man or woman in question could never have uttered while awake; then over there as a cry, so brief that one cannot believe one's ears and thinks one must have been mistaken, but on the other hand so piercing that one still recalls it decades later and wonders whether it was not a death cry—so shrill and at the same time broken off in the middle: that could not have been a cry of sexual pleasure, or at least not only that? Or: a cry of pleasure, long held back, welling up, and at the same time a death cry? And thus she made her way to her own sleeping berth—now and then jingling her key on the stairs and in the gallery, as if to provide additional reassurance to those who had had such a hard time finding rest.

The curtain to the compartment drawn back. But the space was not unoccupied. In the glow of the lamp affixed to the wall sat a lovely young girl with an overly serious mien, playing chess with herself in her nightgown. Glancing up, she said only, "Too early—," and pulled the curtain to. The chess pieces had been of transparent rock crystal, powerful, almost lumpy shapes, such as once upon a time the caliphs, and in particular King Almanzor in Andalusia, had taken along to pass the time during their campaigns against the Christendoms.

The next compartment over was the right one (her mistake). Here she now sat, like the girl next door, with her back to the walnut partition, as thin as it was solid. "For those of our tribe, it is more fitting to keep watch than to sleep." Calling to mind the few people who were the point of her story. But for that she had to read first. Immerse herself in the Arabic booklet belonging to her faraway daughter. "Time to read!" Upon her opening the book, a sound as if of lips parting, very soft and gentle.

She pronounced the individual words and phrases over and over under her breath. The Arabic script looked to her like the tracks of wild animals running through a field of grain: loops, leaps, circles, and, at the end, in the middle of the wheat field, a large rest-circle. Intermittently she switched on her hand telephone and spoke to the answering machine in the office of her temporary replacement, back home in the banking citadel in the riverport city; made suggestions, gave instructions; analyzed and predicted. In one breath she recited an ancient Arabic sentence from the fifth or the sixth, the Christian eleventh or twelfth, century, in the translation written in the margin by her daughter. "I departed from the paved ground, away from the teeming throng, and strolled in the sand." And in the next breath she murmured into the speaking device that fit into the palm of her hand phrases like "clear strategy," "aggressively implement the new technologies," "warning on profits," "additional earnings impetus," "stagnant employment picture," "remain on the road to growth," "bull market." And turning in the twinkling of an eye back to the book, she deciphered and spelled out, "I turned my cheek to the dust and felt nothing more than affection." And then, again switching on the telephone nestled in her fist: "The inflation horizon will certainly brighten soon," "gratifying market trends," "a very attractive investment—shows imagination!" "In the coming months the growth rate could explode in a war of 'fundamentals versus growth,' and certain fundamentals will have to be given a timely burial." And continuing in the other text: "Love possessed me in such a fashion that I neglected myself as well as my beloved . . . my innermost heart was burning to know what path he took through the mountains . . . when in the year 532 I stood on the inland dune outside Fez . . . said the bird on the edge of the desert, the lovers spoke a language used otherwise only by madmen . . . the word for 'tears' had the same root as the word for 'to cross' . . . and the breath of mercy came from Yemen (or from 'the right'—'Yemen' was the word for 'right') . . ."

And so on, turning from one of these locutions to the others and back again, back and forth, back and forth. Was this really possible? Could it be done? Yes, it could be done. And as time passed, the dictating came to resemble the murmured reading, as if all the banking formulas and stock-market clichés were part of the desert tales from bygone times. "The earnings potential of the traditional blue-chip stocks when I disappeared amid the stirring tamarisk branches close by the main tent before the ascent into the mountains, where we tugged at the camels' nose rings in the shadow of the world financial markets and trade deficits." Her professional language eventually interwoven with the other language and recited by her in the same soft incantatory tone, yet also with a peculiar urgency, as if she were using it here and in the present hour for the last time, for now or for good.

And then in the booklet a word in Arabic script, which, without any effort on her part, spelled itself out, deciphered itself, illuminated itself—read itself, lent itself to reading; the first word she recognized without needing to focus on it or follow it with her eyes from right to left. It was no longer "she" reading the foreign script; "it" read, and this "it read" surpassed for that one word-moment all the previous instances of "she (or I) read." Such reading-recognition was accompanied by something different from the writing on the wall by an invisible hand that prophesied my, the despot's, demise, the handwriting that could not be deciphered by me and would be interpreted only by one versed in such things, a third party.

And although the unexpectedly legible word—and then another, and then a few more—might simply mean "wood," *chasch(a)b*, or "hornet," *zunbur*, "mustard," *chardal*, a window now opened up, or a prospect. To the reader, curled up in her narrow sleeping berth with the book resting on her raised knees, the characters began to resemble monumental writing outdoors in a landscape, painted on a mountainside or formed of stones. Except that they did not express anything monumental, anything resembling propaganda or advertising. Rather the signs inched along like a small, exceptionally delicate caravan on the most distant horizon, beneath a sky that they rendered material and tangible; to the sound of an inaudible music, snatches of which she sang along with, with the recurring word she knew by heart, *murranim*, singer.

And she drew back the compartment's fleece-thick curtain, just a crack; but that was enough to allow the postmidnight air to waft in, and with it a cry issuing from one of the dozens of other sleeping berths in this hostel of the dispersed, a hollow gurgling from the bottom of a well shaft going way down into the bowels of the earth. From the neighboring berth the clicking of chess pieces battling each other.

It had not been the first time that her daughter, her child, vanished. As an adolescent she had already left the house several years earlier; also the riverport city; also the country. And even then she had gone without news of her child. Now, with the book meanwhile laid aside, she began to talk to herself. (Author's observation: that at the time of this story, more and more people, especially the most beautiful women, carried on conversations with themselves.) A person standing outside would not have believed that the speaker was alone: she must be sitting or lying there with someone else; a man or a woman who kept as still as a mouse, all ears, as the woman's soft yet clearly audible voice addressed itself to him or her, calmly, quietly, with many a pause, borne on the nocturnal stillness.

She spoke of herself there and then in the third person; almost in the tone of a chronicle. At intervals she addressed a "you"; and that, too, gave the impression that she had company. And the adventurer could be heard saying the following: "You know, her love for her child expressed itself from the beginning in her always wanting to rescue her. Merely to be there and to protect her was not enough. The mother had to be prepared at any moment to provide first aid and rescue. And thus the lives of the two women, with the father absent, teetered constantly on the edge of drama. And listen, she often rescued her child when there was hardly a need for rescue. She jumped forward and snatched her out of the path of a car that had long since turned off in another direction. She pulled her back from an abyss that was either miles away or only two feet deep." If this were a film, her daughter would have got hooked on drugs, and she, the mother, would have been jealous of her youth. But this was no film plot.

"And let me tell you: at the school gate, this mother knocked a man to the ground who was actually another girl's father, not a kidnapper. And time and again she rescued her child from bad company, male and female. And one day she pried her out of the embrace of a boy she had never seen before. And then one day the adolescent girl disappeared without a trace.

"And the mother promptly set out to find her child and rescue her, to fetch her home from hell, or from the land behind the looking glass, or from the bottom of an enchanted lake. For months and months she searched, from country to country, continent to continent, from new moon to full moon to new moon. And when she found her child at last, it was indeed not in a hellhole, but behind an invisible looking glass or in a second reality at the bottom of a lake. I tell you: after four or five months she came upon her vanished daughter on an island in the southern Atlantic— you need not know its name, let's say beyond Lanzarote. The girl was living on the western coast in a shepherd's hut—with nothing but ocean between there and Brazil—several miles from a town whose name I do want to mention to you, Los Llanos de Aridane (not Ariadne).

"This time the mother undertook the rescue operation differently from the previous times. She did not rush to the spot and come storming into the situation, but sneaked up on the rescuee, crept on all fours across rocky pastureland toward the cliff with the hut, crawling from bush to bush. From afar she then saw the girl with her back turned toward her, standing tall—she was no longer half-grown—in the flower border she had planted herself. The woman sneaked around her child in an arc; she did not want to call out to her, not from behind. Having reached the bluff, she had to scramble down the cliff a bit and work her way back up in a zigzag. And look: when she was only a few steps away from her lost daughter, she stood up straight behind the last shrubbery before the Atlantic

Ocean, one of those briar bushes that send clouds of loose seedpods rolling in balls across the high plateaus.

"Can you explain to me why I seem to recall that all this happened at Eastertime? Because of the white cloths hung up to dry in the sun in front of the stone hut? Because of the little garden so glowingly, so intensely green in the rolling landscape? Because of the barefootedness, those very white feet of hers (they, too, seemed to have grown in the meantime)? And would you believe it: even though her daughter again had no need of being rescued—mother and child were both overjoyed to see each other; and this one time, an exception in their relationship, they were happy in each other's presence at the same moment. And as they then celebrated this moment, without any special extras, you can really speak of a festive occasion. And the woman subsequently stayed on the island for a while, in the hut, close to the town. (During the first night the daughter put her mother to bed, in her own bed, and exhausted though the woman was from the search, when she awoke, she had recovered completely.) And in the end mother and daughter did not leave the island together; the girl did not rejoin the mother in the northwestern riverport city until a month later.

"In the years that followed, together again in the house, they found their relationship reversed, just imagine! Now it was the child, long since grown up, who wanted to be rescued by her mother, only by her. And if perhaps not rescued, at least constantly cared for, hovered over, spoken to, interrogated, advised by her; not simply mothered but rather challenged, and indeed as sternly as possible; evaluated, judged, and without maternal indulgence, please.

"The mother, on the other hand, now no longer saw the grown woman as a child or even as her own daughter, her flesh and blood, but only as a family member, and that even in her dreams; as one who, despite their life together, was increasingly pulling away. That fundamental lack of synchrony, which, except for that moment of reunion on the Atlantic island, had always existed between mother and child, persisted between the woman and her grown daughter, but now with the signs reversed.

"Imagine, the woman would never have guessed that her big, beautiful, strong, self-reliant housemate would seriously have expected; needed; wanted anything of her. And imagine: whatever the daughter undertook or chose not to undertake during those last years was done with complete seriousness in reference to her mother: What will my mother say to that?

What will she think? And whatever is wrong with her? Why is she not there for me anymore? Why does she not help me? Why does she not rescue me? Why does my mother not love me anymore? Why is suggesting games the only thing that ever occurs to her to do with me (although she still does not know how to play)?

"And you should know that one day the daughter, the child, the woman, let out a whimper in the middle of a conversation between the two adults; a whimper as if coming from all the lost children in the universe at once; the leap between the down-to-earth discussion and the misery that suddenly broke through was again a reversal of the earlier state of affairs, when the little child, if she had a bad fall or was hit by another child, would sob so hard that she could not say a word, even to her own mother—and then suddenly, after drawing a deep breath, would begin to speak in a perfectly calm voice, picking up where she had left off. And do you believe me when I say that on one of the following days this child again disappeared from her mother's house, and has remained gone to this very night?"

Finally pain; pain: finally! And while she cowered in the berth, her shoulders slightly hunched beneath the low ceiling, she was swept out into the open by it, this final and seemingly infinite pain. And at last she could fall silent, stop talking to herself; no longer had to open her mouth to tell her story: the story continued on without her; with the help of pain, her story moved forward, beneath a not only open but also vast sky. Before that only one last little question: "What happened between her and her child: Was it connected somehow with her 'secret guilt,' or what she herself referred to as her 'delicious secret, guilt only if it came to light'?" And the answer was?: "No."

And now, as if a weight were being lifted from all those sleeping and more or less suffering nightmares in those berths extending to the edges of the hostel's roof, there and there, and down there and up there, the oppressed sighs and near-death cries gradually fell silent, also the simple coughing and sneezing, until suddenly complete silence descended, not only over the *venta* but far beyond it as well, disembodied, overflowing, rushing in through every opening and pore—transforming the bodies themselves into openings and pores—pushing into the distant refuges of the nocturnal animals and the woodworms' last holes, and filling these, too, with silence; that entire part of the world a bowl filled with silence, followed, accompanied, and undercoated by expectation. Preceding this, two or three final sounds: in her berth the switching-off of the wall light; in the neighboring berth the falling-down or rather laying-down of a fairly heavy chess piece, the king: checkmate; and finally, from outside, a single owl's hoot, unexpectedly not repeated—how so? in the middle of the settlement of Nuevo Bazar? yes—, and precisely the same blowing into cupped hands as—when had that been?—back home in the riverport city.

She threw off the blanket. Despite the curtain's being open a crack to the winter sky, it had become almost hot in her niche. The wood panels, surrounding her on all sides in the short, narrow bed, felt sun-warm. And her skin adapted to this solar collector and expanded. In contrast to the Spartan decor of the hostel, the bedclothes were of a luxurious splendor. The linens were not merely old but from a rich and glorious time, and had acquired their splendid sheen only as they aged. "Luxurious" referred not to the number of pieces, colors, or layers, but to their weight. The two top sheets, pure white like the bottom sheet, lay heavily upon her, more heavily than the rather ordinary cotton blanket earlier, and yet, unlike the latter, did not weigh her down in the slightest. And although they were tucked in up to her neck and hardly left a hand's breadth of space between themselves and her body anywhere, as she lay there the woman did not feel at all confined by the sheets. She would sleep lightly under them as seldom before.

And at the same time she, or a part of her, no, something that went beyond the usual, everyday, mundane "she," remained awake. Under these bedclothes there was a sense that weight and floating, warmth and cooling, were in equilibrium; and she felt as though she could taste that. Hadn't she once reached out her hand to someone under just such sheets? Or, on the contrary, hadn't someone reached out to her? Pain and desire? Desire and pain?

And had that actually been her? Or hadn't it rather been the young woman from the Middle Ages whom she had portrayed long ago in her first and only film? The story goes that in that scene in the film, which has been lost in the meantime (not a single copy to be found?), she was covered with the same white linen up to her shoulders, first seen from the front in a full shot, the camera high above the bed; then a torso shot, again from the front, with the camera closer; and then finally a long shot, but this time with her profile in sharp focus, her facial expression unchanged, with an additional turning-away at the end to what is allegedly known in technical terms (author's research) as a "lost profile" shot.

And the story goes that in that final long shot, her face, which in any case was already very white, along with her shoulders, which were also already very white, became whiter and whiter, and imperceptibly dissolved into the white of the bed linens. And the story goes furthermore that during this night in the hostel berth, without a camera present, without opening of the shutter or any other cinematographic tricks, this blending into the white of the bedding was repeated, for heaven's—or hell's—sake. In the Australian desert the hot wind swept from one solitary bush to the next, a few dunes away. On the planet Mars an avalanche of ice came cascading down the sky-high mountain there, the Olympus Rex? In Nuevo Bazar, in the middle of the smoothly paved diagonal artery, a rock ledge broke through. Hazelnuts and chestnuts bounced off the belly of a woman, a different one? (Which suitor said that? Or wanted that? Or wanted to imagine that?)

That same night her brother, released from prison, crossed the last of several borders since his departure from the country of his imprisonment and arrived in the country he had chosen as his new home. It was snowing there, as almost always in wintertime. By now he was driving a car, lent to him by the woman with whom he had stayed all day until an hour after the early nightfall. At a signal from him, she would follow him to a place yet to be determined. There was no woman who would not have done everything for her brother, after spending at most an hour with this almost silent man, who alternated constantly between monumental weariness and flashes of alertness.

It is said that even to her, his sister or somewhat older sibling, the brother meant more than any man, suitor, wooer, especially in their early youth. Yet that supposedly had nothing to do with their personal relationship, also not with the fact that they were orphaned early, but was a tradition with this Slavic Sorbian or half-Arab population, small and becoming smaller with each day that passed—the last villages almost completely absorbed into the German ones around them, and these long since incorporated into cities—: the love between brother and sister, as the author's research discovered, had remained a prime characteristic of this people (see also cultural continuity); "the attitude peculiarly characteristic of all the women there consists in the exceptionally lively friendship they bring to their brothers; the latter sometimes seem to have greater worth in their eyes than their husbands. Their most sacred oath invokes the name of their brothers. And one of the most common formulas goes thus: 'By the life of my brother!'" (historian from a previous century). And on each of the rare occasions when she, the sister, had seen her brother again, the terrorist and enemy of mankind, after she had kissed him on both cheeks she had also kissed him on his brow and shoulder, that, too, part of this tradition—or did she merely think she had done so, in retrospect?

Yet her brother despised his Slavic people. (He refused to believe in any Arab ancestors.) He despised them because they had not merely affiliated themselves with the infinitely larger, all-powerful state majority, for the sake of money, positions, the right to participate in decisions and live under the flag of a world power, but had also sold out to this people, body and soul, heart and mind, language and "customs" (?, yes!). Her brother hated his people because they had given up their identity as a people, without war, without mounting even the slightest resistance.

And he hated them even more because they nonetheless continued to call themselves a "people," or rather allowed themselves to be characterized as a "minority"; while in reality they had long since been reduced to appearing as a merely tolerated folkloric ensemble, one of twenty or thirty song-and-dance numbers trotted out for a festival produced by the national tourism office or in a promotional video, and beyond that?—nothing, nothing at all. Did this imply that her brother, in contrast to her, the sister, still believed in something like a people? Yes. And such a thing was even a necessity to him.

"I am lost without a people," he had told her once, close to tears (and at the same time had jabbed a knife into the table). And since he was convinced that his maternal and paternal people was now no more than a "national propaganda lie," and was "worth nothing and good for nothing" as a people, a minority, a population, or whatever, he had chosen another people for himself, "the only one far and wide," as he was also convinced, "that still deserves the name"; whereas his sister was careful, and not only lately, not to take sides for or against anything, or even to get worked up over a sports team, for or against it—if for no other reason than that the few times when she had committed herself to a cause, a movement, or a group, after a very short while that same cause, movement, or group had dissolved, fallen apart, with such regularity that she had come to believe that this had occurred precisely because of her advocacy and support, as that soccer team she had rooted for as a girl whenever it played, merely on account of a certain player or even just the appealing sound of its name, had promptly begun to slide farther and farther down in the standings.

And now her brother was driving on this snowy night through his chosen country, with the window open, heading for his chosen people, which was at war with almost all the neighboring states, out-and-out war (not merely an undeclared or rumored one like the war in the nearby Sierra). And among other things, his chosen country and his chosen people would be saved, thanks to him; would emerge victorious; and would show the world. Thanks to knights errant such as him, a new era would dawn, or an old one, the forgotten one, the legendary one that still existed only as an object of ridicule, would be reinstated as never before. But wasn't the country of his choice hopelessly lost? A defeated people, defeated once and for all, which had long since given up on itself and yet behaved as though life went on—precisely the sign of being defeated? And wouldn't heroes like him actually help administer the coup de grâce?

And now, in the depths of night, in a heavy snowfall, he took the secret route through the mountains with which he had long been familiar. All the roads across the valley were blocked off. The country was blacked out. He drove without headlights, no faster than a walk, except when he accelerated as the road climbed. A woman was sitting next to him; not the one from earlier in the day. A little light came from the trees laden with snow, enough to make the shadows, or rather shapeless specters, of the snowflakes outside dart across the faces of the two people in the car. The knight Feirefiz, Parsifal's half brother, had had just such a body with dark and light speckles. "Feirefiz"—that would have been a good name for her brother.

Somewhere halfway into the mountains he had come upon the young woman standing by the road, with a basket on her arm. Her brother had started: a seemingly congenital jumpiness, which had nothing to do with fear—constituted, as he had always appeared to be, of fearlessness, sheer courage, and excessive, ridiculous jumpiness; sensitivity to anything abrupt, whether a sound or something visual—and yet he himself was an abrupt person, given to sudden anger, sudden friendliness, sudden displays of goodness, sudden violent impulses (although directed only toward things, for the time being).

Driving at the speed of a walk up the mountainside, the new pair will now consume their middle-of-the-night meal. Until now they have not exchanged a single word, and from one rotation of the wheels to the next, they are more and more in agreement that until they touch each other for the first time, and altogether until the end, they will remain wordless like this; leaving it to their bodies to act, stretching toward, tensing against, arching over each other; or merely leaving it to the snow, sporadically blowing into the car, or to the spruce branches, likewise sporadically brushing against the sides of the car.

They will have helped themselves from the basket between them to slices of cold leg of lamb and corn bread. But while the young woman drinks wine diluted with water, the brother will drink milk—not that he always has, but as he has done since the time when he came to believe that he could rinse away all the darkness, blackness, blind rage inside him by drinking that white liquid. And again there were not a few people who, seeing him constantly drinking milk, sniffed his glass for disguised whiskey or vodka.

And in the most silent hour of the night, the one before the predawn graying of the sky, still at the speed of a walk, the two of them will have neared, by way of the secret route, the crossing point, recognizable only to her brother, devoted to even the smallest feature in his elective country, and thus to the alpine-hut-like shelter of his new lover. In the meantime, that moment when the brother will have become aware that he has just shaken off the last breath or scent of the years in prison, the mustiness swept away and out of the world by a clump of stones under a snow tire: a powerful push from deep, deep inside, which is followed as a matter of course by his free hand's groping for the hip of the strange woman.

15

The principal traveler awakened as if someone had been moving through her all night, crawling through her armpits, stepping on her ribs, balancing above her legs. She opened her eyes: in spite of the heavy curtain, the red light of dawn filtering into the berth. A body next to her; or no, her own body, her chest and stomach and knees, nestled against the back, buttocks, and knee hollows of someone else, almost as if her body and the stranger's were one.

She found herself waking up in the company of the young girl from the next compartment. Had the girl crept in with her during the night? No, again the opposite: in her sleep she had sought out her neighbor. So she was sleepwalking again, as she had done long ago in the village, as a child, but never since then. And how she had nestled against the other person's back! This person, the girl, lay there sound asleep, with sleep-puffy lips; the rock-crystal chess pieces set up in orderly ranks for a new game, within easy reach.

Moving, as if weightless, from the stranger's berth back to her own. Everywhere else, blessed stillness, not only in the *venta*. "Saved!" Falling asleep again in her own bed, this time without any dreams. Awakening refreshed, after a couple of deep breaths. Pulling open the sleeping compartment's curtain, carefully, so as not to wake anyone.

She wanted to be the first one up, and to remain alone like this for as long as possible, surrounded by the thousands who were sleeping peacefully at last, if only for the time being. In the morning chill of the mesa, gusting from above into the open inner courtyard, a larger, intensely frosty, almost breathtaking cold: a breath of the air from the peaks of the Sierra de Gredos, invisible from the new settlement down in the hollow.

She made the hostel bed, shaking the bedclothes out over the patio, smoothing and stretching the linens, as if the bed were located on her own estate and she were beginning the day there with simple household chores. Yet she carried them out several degrees more meticulously than back home in the riverport city; she could not leave a single wrinkle or lump in the bed—from which the hostel maid would later promptly strip the bedding. In the same way, after her solitary, ceremonial morning ablutions in the still empty common bathroom, as big as a hall, she applied shoe cream and polished her laced boots with more obvious care than ever at home; combed her hair longer than before going to a party there (not to mention before going to the office).

She did notice that, unlike on the other mornings, not one image from other places where she had once been flashed before her or came dancing along, although she performed these everyday actions so much more carefully and calmly, but this fact did not trouble her: she ascribed it to the peculiarity of the "Zone" of Nuevo Bazar, including its location in the hollow.

It gave her pause that one of her bootlaces broke and that her brush split in half while she was brushing her hair. She had always experienced such misfortunes, often precisely after a confident awakening, and from one time to the next, the more trivial they were, the more menacingly they restricted if not the day then at least its first hour, which had seemed so open to possibilities. No matter that the author indicated to her that according to his research "all truly beautiful women" ("truly beautiful" in the sense that they goaded everyone who saw them to go forth and seek his own lost beauty) were clumsy, and that precisely this trait animated their beauty and produced a soothing effect: she herself remained cross at her clumsiness, did not consider it harmless, but rather an expression of the guilt she was keeping to herself—whereupon the author, as was actually to be expected, retorted that "all truly beautiful women" were afflicted with a more or less vague sense of guilt, and precisely that . . . and so on.

After breakfast from her bag, which resembled something not just from the Middle Ages but from an even more bygone time—leftovers, but what leftovers! packed up for her by her friend the chef—in the gallery, at the one small table there (making constant noises, but the softest possible, so as to allow the others to continue sleeping, better and more gently than complete absence of sound), she went down to the ground floor. There, surprisingly, the entire hostel staff, which was numerous, already up and preparing for the day: filling out orders, writing up menus, carrying cases of wine down to the cellar. And from them, too, came no loud sounds. Voices uniformly quiet, yet without whispering, and thus also no hissing.

And overnight various *venta* people seemed to have switched roles in some way. One who the previous evening had stood way in the back of the kitchen as a dishwasher was now sitting in the booth at the entryway, obviously the boss. The girl in the taproom the day before, hardly out of school, was now his wife, her hair drawn back tightly, wearing a gray suit and holding a child in her arms. The only other guest, at one of the neighboring tables, was busy today in the boiler room, serving as the house electrician and plumber. The chamber- or compartment maid from before, who had shyly backed away from every stranger, was the boss's sister, now a teacher by profession, sitting this morning in a corner and, with a stern face and expansive gestures, correcting the last of her pupils' notebooks.

And similarly, out on the otherwise empty street, one of the falling-down drunks from the previous evening's crowd had become a traffic policeman, on duty but with nothing to do, standing all the straighter out there with no one around. And in the next figure, the only one far and wide, she recognized the person who, the night before, had been filled with wild despair and looking daggers, but in the light of the new day had been transformed into a brisk jogger and, dressed accordingly, was bounding lightfootedly over all possible obstacles, even seeking out wheelbarrows, traffic barriers, and garbage cans as he circled the Zone for the sixteenth or twenty-fourth time.

To the vacant lot, the only one remaining, where she had left her car the previous day: the site built up overnight, the exterior walls already erected, only the roof still missing. Had that really been the place? Yes; the splintered medallion with the white angel still lay in the construction debris, among other tiny fragments. On a side street her Santana Landrover: smashed and burned out. No surprise: she had already dreamed this. And no thought of reporting it to the police, but on the contrary: "All right. Time to go. Now everything can get under way." (Here the author characteristically deleted the exclamation point—merely hinted at in any case—in contrast to his positively elaborate question marks.)

So off to the bus station, to which no sign had pointed for a long time already, but which was familiar to her from earlier, together with the *venta* the only somewhat older structure in Nuevo Bazar, with a round inner courtyard in place of the hostel's rectangular one. In this circle now dozens of buses, their engines running, roaring with readiness to hit the road, the rotunda mottled with blue clouds of exhaust. Boarding one particular bus without hesitation, taking the last free seat—how many people had suddenly turned up in the bus, after the hour of emptiness that morning—, the door closing, and off they go. In the mirror above the driver, her face, one among many: she almost does not find it, almost does not recognize herself in the violently vibrating bus-mirror image. But the turnoff from the previous evening is the same—except that the sign seems to have become even smaller and more out of date, as if no longer valid, scrapped: "Ávila—Sierra de Gredos."

The faces of quite a few of the passengers looked familiar. While boarding the bus, she had involuntarily nodded to them, and her greeting had been returned promptly and as a matter of course. And the driver seemed familiar as well. And she knew where she had seen him before, unlike the others. He was the one she had taken the previous night for the new settlement's idiot, the one who had looked almost like an old man, with the harelip, shining his flashlight into her face. By daylight, in the rearview mirror, the same harelip, only less noticeable, under a broad pug nose. Yet no more resemblance to an idiot or an old man.

As usual the driver was engaged in conversation with someone on the seat diagonally behind him, without ever turning to look at this passenger. But the person he was talking to was not the young girl who would usually stand next to the driver, displaying herself to the other riders and thus making herself the star of the bus trip, but a child, the driver's young son, still far from adolescence. And several more children on the bus, all crowded together in the back; the vehicle also serving as a school bus. And the windows in the midsection blocked all the way to the roof by bookshelves, every inch of space filled with books, a sort of darkened corridor; the bus also serving as a traveling lending library.

From where did she recognize one fellow passenger or another? These were no cases of mistaken identity. They had met before, and not merely once, though not in this particular way and constellation, which was as new to her as to the others, but rather in their everyday settings, where she, the adventurer, and the familiar faces likewise, in contrast to here, were all at home. They had had a relationship—but where? in the riverport city? or earlier in the Sorbian village? or at some other way station in her life and his and theirs?—if perhaps not a daily relationship, nonetheless a fairly constant, regular one; and even if such a relationship far away in their shared setting had no doubt been a rather impersonal and fleeting/momentary one, for instance that of seller and buyer, of mail carrier and mail recipient, of cemetery superintendent and visitor, or simply of passersby on the, her, their, particular street, on opposite sidewalks each time, here and now in this unfamiliar and remote region, very early in the morning, unexpectedly together in this somewhat unusual vehicle, heading for a not exactly frequented region, they appeared close and familiar as never before, familiar half an eternity already, familiar almost like accomplices or even desperados who had already been involved in some pretty unsavory schemes together and were now setting out on a particularly shady adventure.

And each of them brooded, for at least part of the way, over where he or she had had something to do with her, under what murky circumstances? And what guilt they had incurred toward one another back at home? Or she toward him? Or him toward her there? Or had it been only in their thoughts? And now deeds would follow here. But if the few of them in the bus really (really?) did know each other from earlier: no one remembered from where or how. And the brooding soon ceased. They were all simply riding along; letting themselves be driven.

They were heading south, with numerous roads turning off to the left and right toward villages far from the main road and invisible from it— often merely appearing to be villages, for once the bus passed the first houses, they often turned out to be towns, with a network of narrow, twisting streets and in the center a large, if unpaved, sandy square.

The terrain rose, fell, and rose in long waves, dips, and elevations, almost imperceptibly, as was usual on the mesa. But after a while the land climbed noticeably for quite a long stretch. Ice flowers formed around the rims of the bus windows and then melted away in the hour after sunrise. Despite the climb, hardly any curves. Instead, where previously there had been turnoffs, there were now repeated detours, taking them away from the *carretera* in great arcs and then back to it, traversing the bleak, barren landscape, an utterly uninhabited in-between region, on gravel tracks. No one had got on or off the bus.

The only inhabited place visible from the road, at a distance, was the city of Ávila, on its hill, far to the east; the houses of the old town almost hidden behind the encircling wall, bumped out in hundreds of places;

round about it on the high plain, New Ávila, La Nueva Ávila, the larger of the settlements, half cordoning off the hill with buildings, forming a second, very different perimeter. The black clouds above the cathedral tower were flocks of jackdaws, as always.

The bus had bypassed this old and new Ávila, maintaining always the same distance. The detours in the uninhabited area now occurred in the same rhythm as previously the turnoffs to the villages or towns. Later, when she described the bus trip to the author, she kept falling into the first person plural. "We had long since taken off our earphones." (Yet at most one or two girls were listening to their music this way in the beginning.) "Instead of watching the film on the monitor above the front windshield, we looked out the windows, and despite the low angle of the sun had drawn back all the curtains." (Yet only she and the children in the back, whose view of the screen was blocked by the library shelves in the midsection of the bus, were not following the film. "We sat ramrod straight, our hands on the backrests in front of us. Although we were familiar with the route from long ago, at every turnoff and detour we wondered where we were now; was this really the route to the Sierra? was it possible that this familiar village had changed so much since the last time we passed through? only the name still the same? and over there, was that still the cliff from all the previous years, in the form of a rabbit stretched out on the ground? and is it only because of the detour that today we see in its place a kneeling camel?

"And on the one hand, as unfamiliar as the foreland of our Sierra de Gredos appeared to us in almost every detail, on the other hand it seemed tremendously homelike to us; the more novel, the more homelike. The more unknown the fountain in the marketplace there—iced over, by the way—the clearer; we had had it before our eyes all along, and had merely overlooked it. The more surprisingly the medieval stone bridge arched away from the concrete bridge over which our bus drove straight ahead, the clearer: from the very beginning we had been crossing this section of bridge, we knew every stone, we could balance in our sleep on the remains of the parapet high above the rushing brook. The foreland was strange to us during that morning bus ride in a way that an area could appear strange only when we had not only traveled through it many times but had once actually resided and lived there, if very long ago. Resided long ago? Perhaps the entire time."

And she continued her story: "Perhaps it was not so much in this landscape that we had always lived but more or less together on this special bus. When I recall our trip into the foothills of the Sierra—you should remember, we should remember, one should remember—, from a certain moment during our travels together I can no longer say which of us passengers, or, more accurately, travelers, was who, which of us did what, or to which of us what was done. The one who bit into an apple was the old man there wearing the mountaineer's hat, and at the same time the driver, bent over the wheel, as well as the young city girl next to me with a student's briefcase, and me myself. The person with one arm in a sling was, among others, also me.

"Several people in the bus, including me, had taken off their shoes or boots. One time this person or that, no, all of us, heaved a sigh, in the same moment, a deep sigh, a brief accompaniment to the hardly changing sound of the engine. You and I, and likewise he and she, turned a page. One woman was in the late stages of pregnancy, and I with her. For a while our ears were blocked from the change in altitude, and we could no longer follow the conversation between our driver and his son, which continued uninterrupted during almost the entire journey. One time I vomited, no, that was one of the children in the very bumpy back, or wasn't it me after all, in addition to this person and that?

"We cried from toothache, held our heads to counteract sinus pressure, expelled clouds of breath when we got off at the first rest stop. In between we laughed in unison during one-minute naps. We jumped when a heavy blackbird crashed into a window. One woman had a nosebleed, as did the man over there, and I over here was also bleeding from the nose, even though only one nose was bleeding, drops so hot that they almost burned a hole in my clothes when they fell. From a certain threshold on, *chataba* in Arabic, in the area or merely on the bus trip, we had become communicating tubes, and what happened to one of us flowed at the same time into the other travelers and equalized its level.

"And the most obvious thing we shared was the sensory impressions. Blinded by the first sunlit patch of snow, all of us shut our eyes at the same moment. Together we tasted, yes, tasted the steady morning wind during that first rest stop in the foothills. And what united us the most during that entire time, for better and for worse, in patience or in tranquillity, in fear or in worry, was our shared hearing or listening: to the way the engine kept running; to when a plane would break the sound barrier again; to the way the children in the back, and thus the rest of us with them, played their games, calmly and thereby generating patience, as uninhibitedly and loudly as if nothing were wrong; to the way the library books in the flexible bumped-out midsection of the bus constantly rubbed against each other, pounded against each other, or, when it was a question of movie cassettes, clicked and clacked against each other, they, too, as if nothing were wrong."

"It sounds as though the bus provided a kind of shelter or refuge for all of you," the author remarked. She continued: "If we were all of one mind during the journey into the Sierra, it was against the backdrop of a constant threat and a heightened vulnerability, exacerbated by our sitting still so long in that large, overly long bus, whereas, on the other hand, riding along, precisely in that immensely long vehicle, created the feeling, or the illusion—but: the main thing was the feeling and illusion! *¡sentimiento y ilusión!*—of safety.

"In becoming open and receptive to one another this way, between anxiousness and gentleness, we formed, for the duration of the travel interlude, a society, a lovely one, full of life. It's up to you, writer, to transform it into a lasting one." — The author: "Please go on." — The client: "We drove, whether uphill or occasionally downhill again, at an even, slow pace, as if that, too, provided a kind of security. Although for quite some time now no more detours had been marked, the driver sometimes turned off onto side roads, parts of the old road, narrow, curving, along rushing brooks, between towering cliffs.

"This old road had been out of use for so many years that what remained of the paving was overgrown with ground-blackberry runners. Here and there bushes were also growing in the middle of the road, and our bus snaked between them and drove over them, hardly slowing down, and since not only the roof but also porthole-like portions of the floor were glazed, as is the case with quite a few of the most advanced vehicles nowadays, with shatterproof glass, we could see, time after time, all around us, overhead, to left and right, but also underneath, the branches whipping together and bouncing apart.

"It was almost an eternity since another vehicle had traversed these byways, at least any motorized one, and certainly not a bus—this was probably the first time a bus had passed this way—and in two or three places a tree had grown up in the middle of the road, if only a spindly one, a birch, a pine, an ash; whereupon the driver, who among other tools also had a saw with him, got out with his son and cut down the obstacle without more ado. After one such stop, as we drove on, a bunch of winter grapes bobbed above the front windshield, silvery balls with black pistils in the center.

"In contrast to the new road through the mountains, the stretches of the old one onto which we turned off did not run through a completely unpopulated area. At least some stretches of it seemed inhabited—though the houses, all of which were separate structures, with nothing else far and wide, revealed themselves on our approach to be in ruins, and not only since yesterday, apparently, but rather at least since several decades earlier, even centuries. For the most part they were remnants of mills and animal sheds; but also in one place of a school (so, beyond one granite hillock or another there must have once been farmsteads with many children), and in another place of an inn, located where six or eight mountain paths, long since abandoned and half-buried, more likely old cattle trails, crossed each other, forming a star, an inn for which the name *venta* must have been literally appropriate years ago.

"Our old road was one of these roads crossing the others, the only one that was still passable, if barely, and there it reached its first pass summit, a dip in the peaks of the Sierra de Paramera, the range in front of our Sierra de Gredos and not nearly as high. And there, where a bit farther on, already visible from below, the new road branched off from the main pass, the Puerto de Menga, open on all sides, and rejoined our *carretera antigua*, reassuringly, yet not so reassuringly after all, we stopped for the first time for a brief rest.

"Even the couple of trees around the tumbledown inn looked rather like ruins, were split, partially stripped of their bark, and seared with burn marks from lightning strikes. The one healthy tree amid the rubble, which elsewhere in the south and up into the lower reaches of the mountains would be a fig, its roots further splitting the walls, was an oak here, a sturdy tree, yet almost like one growing high in the mountains, whose ball-like burls, looking like sharp elbows, seemed to be jabbing at the remains of the building around it and taking them into a headlock; the inn's roof had in any case long since been sent flying by the tree's hard-as-a-rock crown. We sat and stood during our rest period between what remained of the walls, under the tree, which still had all its leaves, though they were dead, rattling in the mountain wind.

"No one spoke except the driver and his young son, who carried on their conversation as they had since the beginning of the journey, without interruption, in dreamy voices, sounding more and more alike, the little boy's at the same pitch as the father's. The group of children also listened in silence, one of them turning out to be an adult once out in the open, yet his face still indistinguishable from the others'. The driver and his son had hauled a crate with refreshments—more than just apples and nuts—from the bus to the ruins of the inn; each traveler could help himself, and did just that.

"Only once were we startled: when the driver and his son, breaking off their dialogue, shouted in unison to a child who had wandered just a step away from the vicinity of the ruins/bus. Mines? A precipice? Overgrown cellar holes? Or did that simply mean: Everyone stay together!!"?

She went on telling her story, in a voice that was increasingly less that of a woman than that of a woman, man, child, and old person, young and old in one, yet with a frequency coming through from time to time, as a tonic or dominant, that could only be that of a woman: "For a long, long while we remained in the roofless and windowless tumbledown inn at the top of that old pass into the Sierra that had outlived its usefulness decades or centuries earlier. The noticeable feature of the few crossings into the mountains is that the weather changes constantly in those hollows, because of the warmer upwind from the much steeper southern flanks. Even in the case of that pass through the foothills, the wind kept colliding with the cold northern air and promptly produced a rain cloud, followed by a snow cloud, then a fog belt snaking along the gentler northern slopes. All around, the sky maintained an unchanging blue, while only at very brief intervals did this blue aloft reach us in the hollow with the ruins.

"And even during the brief stretches of blue sky and sunshine, without a cloud or wisp of fog, now and then heavy, dense drops of rather mild rain would plunk down on us, out of the clear blue sky, as if coming from a sky somewhere behind the other one—just as, when a few moments later the appropriate cloud came over, despite the dampness and near darkness, only single drops would fall—or out of this blue would also flash single yet steady snowflakes, as if coming from outer space, which, when they hit the current of southerly air, were blown back up into the blue of the atmosphere.

"Those of us who, unlike the children—who stayed together in pairs or groups—did not perch in the almost entirely empty window openings, squatted for the most part on our heels in a circle around the driver, his son, and the crate of provisions; and a few stretched out in the corners, on the ground, on paper, the adults as if taking cover, while the children everywhere in the ruins' window openings constituted a sort of peace-keeping force. In one corner of the former *venta* still stood a cast-iron stove, not all that rusted, but minus its pipe, and next to it, and looking even older than the stove, a heap of firewood, as if stacked there in ancient times, whose bottom logs, however, neither rotted nor mildewed like the others, produced a remarkably fresh, almost smokeless fire in the open stove—which, however, gave off hardly any heat—and it is true that none of us wanted to warm ourselves, whether we needed to or not.

"Even in its better days the inn's floor had consisted not of wooden planks but, in all of its three or four rooms—in the meantime merged into one—of packed clay, and in one corner was a stone-lined tub, full of water: rainwater channeled in from the outside by a gutter? no, an actual spring there, inside the building a barely visible pulsing and swirling from way down below, and one of us who stuck his hand in exclaimed in surprise, made a face, and we all followed suit: the springwater in the niche, or, to use a current expression, in the 'wet room,' of the medieval *venta* was warm—unexpectedly so for us, coming from the wintry air, even hot to the touch, and it emitted or rather exuded that smell 'of rotten eggs' that indicates sulphur, as I hope you, an author who should know his science, will realize, the stench now growing stronger, invading the nostrils of even those most impervious to smells: the stench was so powerful for a few moments, the sulphurous wave so overwhelming, that we, with the exception of the children, who merely laughed, as at everything unexpected, at first reacted with an almost imperceptible impulse to flee, which expressed itself in our holding our breath or failing to blink: gas attack? ptomaine? But then: the driver and his son stretching out on the clay floor by the sulphur spring, and, on their stomachs, their faces half in the water, drinking from it, 'good for sore throat, stomach problems, panic attacks,' while they continued to converse, calmly, as they had done all the while, their speech intermittently reduced to a gurgling, but nonetheless still comprehensible.

"And we followed the lead of those two, whether it was really and truly a healing spring, and whether that had been the case since Roman times, indeed since the original inhabitants, the so-called Numantians, or not; even the children gulped the water, lying on their stomachs, and how. And at the same time an airplane, very low over the old pass, flying excessively slowly, to the eye hardly faster than the falcons overhead; with a heavy belly, its dark-green paint like camouflage (which, on the other hand, clashed with all the natural colors in the area, whether in the air or on the ground), its fuselage as broad as it was short, and its roar menacing. As the children had previously waved to everything along the way that showed a sign of life, they now did the same, gesturing from their windows in the ruins, arms flailing, voices yelling. And a hand up in the cockpit waved back, as if it could not help it, just as on the previous stretch of road the children's impetuous and enthusiastic greetings had been answered from the trucks, from the horse-drawn carts—there were more and more of them—and also from the cars of the police patrols. We adults presumably remained invisible to the pilot under the crown of oak leaves, and likewise our bus, or was it taken for a wreck or a greenhouse?

"Where the old road, beyond the *puerto*—which means, as you will know, if, as I hope and trust, you are familiar with foreign languages, both 'pass' and 'harbor'—joined the new one down below, a hiker was walking along the shoulder, heading south and toward the Sierra, with a knapsack over his shoulder, and although the airplane's shadow swallowed him up for a few moments, the man continued on his way, calmly, or at least without missing a beat; without glancing up or to the side; his gaze fixed on the granite gravel, as if he were walking in someone's footsteps.

"Before the bomber appeared, when only its roar was to be heard, whatever was in motion in the sky or on the ground had fled. Everything scattered; or seemed to scatter. A hare dashed off in a zigzag, followed in a straight line by a herd of wild boar. The falcons scattered, or rather swooped off in all directions—a provision for actual fleeing clearly not part of their natural endowment? Even the clouds and billows of fog taking flight."

She continued her narrative: "Yet that was only an isolated incident, a colorless one, seemingly bleached-out, among thousands of colorful ones during our bus trip. That we were constantly biting our lips during the meal was actually caused by the cold. As far back as childhood, on particularly cold days, time and again we had unintentionally and painfully sunk our teeth into our frost-swollen lower lips, even drawing blood. In the ruins of the inn up there at the top of the long since abandoned pass, everything tasted delicious. Even if that same morning we had eaten an apple or a chunk of the very kind of juniper-cured ham that was in the crate of provisions, we thought: How long it's been since we ate an apple. We've never tasted the difference between mountain and lowland nuts so distinctly.

"And it is not only the person who first came up with the wheel but also the person who first combined ham and juniper berries who deserves to be called an inventor. We consumed with gusto even foods we had hated up to then, as I had hated pickled mushrooms." — "Perhaps also because you were all entertaining the thought that this might be your last meal?" (The author.) — She: "No. If we felt in danger, it was the same as every day, there for a moment and then gone again; and sometimes for another moment, and so on." — The author: "Why do you constantly use the first person plural in your narrative? 'We, we, and we'? Even when it's only 'I'?" — His client: "To keep us together. To keep us us! To keep me only me is not right, at least not for this book of ours!"

And then she fell silent. She closed her eyes. Her eyes remained closed for a while. She said nothing, just breathed, deeply. When she finally opened her eyes: a blacker black than usual, unblinking, the pupils pulsing evenly. Then she said: "In earlier times quite a few people had the ability to summon to the inside of their eyelids the residual image of a place, weeks or months later. But what I was seeing just now was not an image of us bus passengers during our rest stop by the ruins, but rather writing, lines that ran both from left to right and from right to left." And turning her head away and gazing to one side along the line of her shoulder, she ordered her hired writer: "I want you to take this over! Take it over from me, author, more freely. Let it emerge. Let it acquire its own shape."

16

Then to the north a group of people on foot came into view, and among them the litter with the gout-plagued abdicated emperor was carried past the *venta* and over the pass. The annual reenactment of the final journey of Charles V, which had taken place almost half a millennium earlier, over the Sierra de Gredos and down to its southern slopes, to Jarandilla de la Vera and to the final stage of his life in the Yuste monastery? Four young fellows, familiar with the area, in summery clothes, some of them barefoot, carried the old man on poles over their shoulders. Yet Emperador Carlos was not really that old—"about my age when I was hired by the banking queen to write the book" (the author)—, and was actually peering like a child from his litter, or perhaps like someone about to die, on the way to his place of burial.

As during all the years when the woman and the emperor had held meetings, she was bringing him a chest full of money, transported on a horse-drawn cart and now hauled up by her entourage (far more numerous than that of her business partner), but this time it was simply meant as a gift, no longer for financing one of his dozen or two wars and for paying his army of mercenaries scattered throughout war-torn Europe, and farther afield in North Africa, in South America. But the abdicated emperor, the dying man, merely waved it away; did not want the money; did not even wish to see it.

All he wanted or wished for was that she might let herself be carried in his litter, by his side, for a few paces, until just over the top of the pass; which was then done. There was ample room for both of them, and the bearers actually seemed to find the double load, that of the winter emperor and the winter queen, lighter, far, far lighter, and not only because after the long climb the road finally leveled out and then headed downhill. They almost ran, dancing and skipping, and the man marked for death, face-to-face with his unfamiliar-familiar friend-foe, bit his lip; but unlike the bus passengers in the previous episode, did so voluntarily.

A trained falcon perched on the emperor's forearm, on the ermine sleeve of his robe; so much smaller than its mountain relatives wheeling in the air above, and looking not at all bird-of-prey-like or avid of the chase, but just as greatly in need of help and childlike in its beseeching manner as its litter-borne master. A flock of ravens, black as only ravens can be, caught up with the group, not cawing or screeching, but bawling, as if from one throat and one body, in bloodthirsty rage and murderous lust; and again the pinkish-white almond blossoms wafted past the solid raven-feather cloud now dispersed in all directions: against the sky-darkening raven blackness, spots of brightness never before seen in this way.

And among the innumerable colorless water droplets on the blades of grass, where was that one bronze-colored one from yesterday, or when-ever, near Tordesillas, or wherever? There it was, at the feet of my adven-turer, as she squatted in the circle of her traveling companions in the ruined inn, even if it was not melted hoarfrost as before, but a drop of melting snow, and instead of on a blade of grass on a folio volume poking out of the debris on the ground: a tiny but glowing bronze lamp just a bit above the earth, no larger than the head of a pin and all the more blind-ing, at least for a moment, just as, at night, also for moments, a single glow-worm can be.

In a corner of the wall, overlooked until then, the wheel of a barouche, it, too, having followed her here from elsewhere, along with its tried-and-true twelve spokes, counted at one glance—but from where? from the hurricane-lashed garden behind her house in the riverport city, or from elsewhere. And on the interior walls of the ruin, inscriptions, familiar from long ago, even those in Hebrew, Cyrillic, Arabic, one or another of which she had already deciphered, again effortlessly and without any spe-cific intention of reading them: "Here begins the land of the swine—death to the swine-eaters" (*al chinzir*, "the swine"), and: "Here ends the elephant kingdom and begins the donkey kingdom."

One of the travelers found in the rubble an old, or perhaps not so old, wanted poster, as large as a movie advertisement: a search had been un-der way, or was still under way, for a band of bank and armored-car rob-bers; and the likeness of the only woman on the poster resembled her so much that for a while some of the travelers kept glancing back and forth between the photo and her; the children even pointed at her, and, as they did whenever they thought something was afoot, whatever it might be, waved and clapped.

For a while the entire group held their breath, then breathed all the more deeply; an audible puffing and expelling of air, pushing air out of the deepest recesses of the lungs, as if in a game; the clouds of breath thicker and whiter than ever before, eddying from the throats and floating away from each traveler's mouth into the surrounding area and, entirely unlike the fire-spewing of dragons, marking the contours of all objects in their path, the rounded notches in the oak leaves, the half-buried folio pages, the snowflakes floating past the faces—how sharp their crystalline forms became in the expelled breath—the intermittent rays of the sun, the bundles of rays distinct enough to touch, like writing emerging from a plain background. And in the mountain air, the features of this person or that in the group took on sharp outlines from this playful blowing at one another from filled lungs, outlines at once alien and familiar: no mistake, no confusion of identity—I know you. The hissing and crackling of the fire in the open-air stove matched the general puffing and rattling expulsion of breath. Now someone or other was already opening his mouth to speak to someone else; then hesitated after all.

After a while the driver will have given the signal to resume the journey, swinging a hand bell, a rusty one that still clanged, also found in the rubble, from the inventory of the inn that had once stood there. The travelers will have risen from their squatting position. The children are promptly seated in the back of the bus. The driver's son, whose head comes up only to the hips of the adults, has punched them in the stomach, an additional signal for departure. With some he also had to take a running leap to get at them; and that included the women as well as the men. Finally, for her, a particularly energetic, remarkably powerful blow, below the belt, for which he hurled himself at her.

She acted as if nothing were amiss; as if she did not even notice. As was so often the case, she continued eating, whereas all the others had long since finished their meal; she had postponed starting, as usual; had first sampled with her eyes and then eaten with provocative slowness; left not a shred, not a crumb; savored every morsel, as she now did the flakes, the kernels, even the bits of membrane in the cracked nut, until there was nothing left; let the aftertaste of every molecule linger on her tongue, not allowing herself to be disturbed or hurried.

The others had all been sitting in the Sierra bus for more than a while, some of them already asleep, others with their eyes closed, when she finally joined them. She simply had her own sense of time, and, when circumstances warranted, this sense also had to prevail over the people around her, who had always tacitly accepted being ruled by her casual attitude toward time; even bowed to it willingly and often full of curiosity and anticipation. Thus the passengers now sat there in the bus as if something were about to be offered to them; as if they were about to witness a special performance. Even the driver and his son waited in patient suspense, their dialogue interrupted.

Upon her joining them, the engine of the completely silent vehicle started up; and for the moment it sounded as if there were several engines. A blast on the horn rather like the steam whistle of an old paddleboat, halfway into the mountains, and now they were rolling along the old pass, on a road out of use since peace had come to the region, since the civil war, that is, heading down to where this road merged into the so-called new road, no longer all that new; enveloped all the way to the merge in a cloud of dust that matched the name of this intermediate stage of the bus trip, "Polvereda."

They drove along for a while without any noteworthy events. If there was a village somewhere in the Polvereda region, hidden behind the lower ridges that accompanied the *carretera* and gradually closed in on it, no road sign pointed to one. The stretch of road they were traveling had no side roads branching off, and if there happened to be any, they soon ended at a mountain pasture, where, however, no cows or sheep or any other animals were standing, only here and there a solitary raven, no longer molting. The name "Polvereda" was still appropriate once they left the hard asphalt road; for, at even the slightest breath of wind, plumes of dust rose here and there and formed narrow funnels, swirling into the air.

They rode for a while beneath a sky where, whatever looks might suggest, no airplane had ever appeared, or Leonardo da Vinci's flying man either. No jet contrails way up high; and if a cloud occasionally could be mistaken for one, none of the passengers made the association; not one of them saw anything other than a cloud. And no trucks came toward them. No electric poles. No pasture surrounded by wire fences; instead interlaced fieldstones, branches, and broom twigs. The colorful scraps in the bushes were not paper or plastic but cloth, fleeces, also skins.

The only vehicle approaching from the other direction: a bus in which not a soul was sitting but the driver, who, contrary to custom, did not wave to his colleague; also no engine sound, as if this other bus were rolling down this steep stretch of road with the engine off, coasting. And not a soul outside, except the hiker, the one from earlier, from some past era, still walking along the shoulder, with his knapsack, his pack, from which dangled, no, not a camera and binoculars but a mason's hammer, chisel, square, and compasses, the latter two made of wood, monumental in size: the stopping of the bus, on her, the adventurer's, command. The itinerant mason had then not climbed aboard the bus—had peremptorily waved the travelers on, without stopping or even raising his head. His gait, with long strides and arms swinging rhythmically, his hair fluttering behind, his sleeves and trousers flapping and whipping like sails, his tools—or *hadatt*, as she thought, not "tools"—bouncing around him, circling and swinging like the gondolas on a carousel: and all this happening for just the second—again she did not think "second" but *thania*—of the bus's stopping and opening its door. And the hiker in close-up, chewing, as he walked, on a raisin, *zabiba* in Arabic.

Ah, to get off the bus and go on foot, too; to walk like this stonemason, or whatever he was; to place one's feet like him in the footsteps, deeply imprinted in the natural gravel along the roadside, of one who had passed that way before, which—and these, too, as also became clear in that one moment of the bus's stopping—not those of a human being but rather of an animal, a hoofed animal, not a horse but an animal with smaller, more delicate hooves, evidently a long-legged one; ah, to stride through these seemingly oceanic spaces between mountain ranges with as much verve as that figure already disappearing in the distance; with ever new horizons or frames of vision; horizons entirely different from those visible from the vehicle, even if they were the same ones, stimulating appetite, creating desire, touching one's lips, breast, and belly, even when, and precisely when, they were still a day's journey away; even if the horizons were an illusion.

The bus drove for a long time through the Polvereda, from time immemorial a far-flung region of sand and dust clouds at the foot of the Sierra. Now and then little clouds and wisps of wood dust even came puffing out of the bark of the ancient trees, more and more isolated from one another. Almost all of these trees had broken crowns. Was it possible that the hurricane that had struck the riverport city, back home in the northwest, had also swept through these southern mountains? No, this destruction had occurred long ago. Furthermore, these beheaded trees displayed streaks of soot, although not all the way up the trunks (which would have indicated a forest fire), but only at the points of breakage or beheading; and unlike that of a lightning strike, the damage had come not from the top but from the side, had swept through horizontally, had split the trees' necks without leaving traces of fire, the soot mark looking like a black ruff placed around the headless neck as it stuck up into midair.

It had been neither lightning nor storms nor forest fires. No, these trees, so crippled that they were no longer recognizable as oaks, birches, or mountain acacias, often not even as living things (they might just as well have been the ruins of pile dwellings or telephone poles), had been shot in two, and if not with full-sized rockets, then certainly not with mere pistol and rifle bullets either (these had turned every single road and advertising sign into a sieve, such that the holes, if one took the time to look at them, formed their own unique symbols, words, and outlines of images).

Here in the Polvereda region a battle had taken place; even, over the centuries, several battles; and the most recent one could have been fought a week ago or a dozen years ago already—the destruction seemed at first sight a thing of the distant past, but at second sight as if it had just now swept across the landscape with a single massive karate chop—the splintered wood so white, the fibers so fresh and marrow-moist.

And in old tales and books, this Polvereda here, this dust-cloud region, had already been mentioned as a perpetual theater of war. One of those old stories, however, suggested that this region, the *comarca*, the marches, merely presented travelers with phantom images of war and battles (see "dust clouds"). In that book, the Polvereda figures as a generator of hallucinations for any stranger; and since the region has always been largely uninhabited, it is almost only strangers who find their way there. The Polvereda as the "enchantress turned to dust," "the deceiver": and it deceives people also with respect to time: the stranger who goes astray and sees those mysterious dust clouds, now here, now there, experiences even things from the distant past, things that have become the stuff of legend, as very much of the present, all the more terrifying and unexpected.

And, inversely, the stranger is incapable, according to this book, of recognizing all the incidental occurrences, both large and small, of the current moment, of the day and hour in which he is crossing the region, as the actual, harmless, peaceful, vital present and letting them govern him: all the tiny birds whirring by—in the Polvereda, too, there are titmice, sparrows, and robins, for example—the rust-yellow lichens on the largely flat ledges that protrude everywhere from the upland savannah, the brooks that cross the road in various places, actually mere rivulets: all these the newcomer to the region sees and hears only in connection with the mirages of battles appearing to him momentarily from the depths of the decades and centuries, the armies clashing or the campaigns about to be waged. The sparrows are the harbingers of the cannonballs. The yellow lichens are artificial, camouflage for the tanks concealed under tarpaulins, not ledges. No matter how reassuring their gurgling sounds, the mountain brooks cascading so rapidly have a reddish cast that by no means comes only from the iron contained in the granite and quartz sand, which also hovers constantly over the brooks in a haze of weathered particles.

From their seats high up in the bus, now, in this hour, the passengers' gaze as if sharpened by the slightly curved glass all around: clear across the Polvereda more and more wild dogs' cadavers on the road; a bull's head impaled on a thornbush, the eyes seeming to open and shut in the dusty wind; in a freshly dug ditch all along the road, the skull of a ram, not slaughtered, not separated from the—missing—rump with a knife, but as if torn from it with great muscular force, likewise the hooves and legs lying nearby, a single last puff of breath bursting from the encrusted nostrils after a blast of sand.

And the falcon, pursued through the air for ages by the army of ravens, has meanwhile landed in one of the shrapneled trees, on the stump of the sole remaining lower limb, and in the next moment all the ravens have fallen upon the sick or old, or perhaps in fact young, animal—here no enchantment by a whirl of dust was necessary; for a change, this was completely clear and up to the minute—a gigantic, dense black murder machine, with a sound exceeding that of any chorus of raving ravens, absorbing all possible sounds made by even the most powerfully destructive beings and, like a machine, leaving behind a rumbling, bashing, ramming, banging, stamping, and, finally, pounding.

And while this pitch-black execution machine's pistons moved up and down, more and more regularly as time passed, its steel joints bending and extending, and its wheels sliding powerfully back and forth, there appeared once more, caught in its mechanism, the seemingly quiet gray of the falcon feathers, the yellow of an eye or talon, bit after bit, and then not the slightest bit anymore.

And in the bus, the driver and his little boy were still carrying on their conversation, if now no longer in such soft, dreamy voices. The child was even quaking from head to toe, to borrow a comparison in the tale from the Polvereda that had survived the centuries, "like quicksilver" (when this was still an important metal, used to extract gold and silver from less valuable substances), and this quaking also imparted itself to his speech.

And it thus became apparent that their earlier conversation had its roots in fear and terror. When the father and son talked to each other so unusually quietly and evenly, almost in a singsong, and uninterruptedly —anything to avoid a pause—it had been in order to keep the monster from awakening. — . . . The father: "Do you remember the time we saw the snake exhibit?" — The son: "Yes, that was before we went to the movies. And then I sat in the front seat next to you in the car for the first time." — The father: "You never wanted to wear short pants." — The son: "One time Mother left me alone all day in a clearing in the woods." — The father: "When she came for you, it was already getting dark." — The son: "But I was not scared even for a moment, or if so, only for her." — The father: "You went on picking berries, even after the two buckets were full." — The son: "One with blackberries, the other with *firaulas*, with strawberries. And Mother cried, but not because something bad had happened but from joy and amazement that I was still there." — The father: "And at the very spot where she had left you that morning."

Son: "And one time you were nowhere to be found, supposedly over in America." — The father: "That was someone else, a brother of my grandfather's, and besides, that was sometime in the last century." — The son: "Yes, he emigrated, and we never heard from him again." — The father: "Perhaps he became rich, and someday you will be the owner of a brewery in Milwaukee or Cincinnati." — The son: "But poling through the reeds in a boat that time, that was you and me, wasn't it?" — The father: "Yes, in the summer, long before sunrise, and one plank was leaky." — The son: "And black water seeped through, or was that black stuff leeches, and click! they bit?" — "Our ancestors used to earn extra money with leeches. Those insects were exported to the northern countries, where they were coveted for medicinal purposes." — "And even more coveted were our swine here; remember how your grandfather's grandfather herded a hundred of them in night marches over hill and dale, crossing the border, sleeping by day with them in the oak underbrush, and sold the *chinzires* at the famous livestock markets of Toloso, Hajat, and San Antonio.

"How long we have been living in the Sierra de Gredos now!" — "Were you present when I was born?" — "Yes." — "Did I laugh?" — "Yes." — "Were you happy to have me?" — "Yes." — "Did it snow that day?" — "Yes." — "And do you remember that time when we were walking on the road through the fields when the first drops fell?" — "We sat down side by side on a milestone into which a king's crest was incised." — "Was there enough room?" — "Oh, yes." — "And when the first drops carved deep craters in the thick dust, they were so heavy?" — "Yes, Son." — "And how I did not need glasses anymore from that day on?" — "Yes, my son."

"Where are we now, Father?" — "Still in the Polvereda, and we will turn off soon to the village of the same name there." — "Will we stay in the Sierra all our lives, Father?" — "I probably will, you certainly not, Child." — "Will I learn to ride soon?" — "Tomorrow, or next week." — "What day is today?" — "Friday. *Viernes. Jaum-al-dzumha.*" — "Friday already! Will you let me drive again?" — "After the next stop, Child." — "After Polvereda, Father?" — "After Polvereda, Child." — "Have the ravens just done something to the falcon?" — "Which ravens? Which falcon? There have been no ravens here for centuries, dear child! . . ."

17

To the accompaniment of these and similar exchanges between the bus driver and his son, the travelers reached the village, which, like most of the small settlements in the Sierra—not one city, not even a very small one, in that whole large area—lay hidden in a basin between high cliffs.

From the main road, which, as usual, passed the village at some distance, there was hardly a tumbledown stone barn to be seen; but then—this, too, no particular surprise by now—as they made their way past the first houses, a succession of several distinct districts, and each time they rounded a building, a section of the village that was clearly larger, covering more space than the charming one they had just passed, would lie there spread out before the windshield, until finally the bus rolled into a central square that in no way resembled that of a village, but not that of a town either, and indeed defied all comparisons: with colonnades, a well (half fountain, half drinking trough), and a covered market, unpaved, sandy, intended to serve also as a bullfighting arena; here, too, eddies of dust, though unlike those out on the vast, empty high plateau, *en miniature*.

And like most of the *pueblos* situated north of the crest of the Sierra, alias *sela*, also known as *qurjas*, Polvereda—the village—lay just below the tree line. The Plaza Mayor or *arena*—didn't *arena* mean "sand"?—was deserted, although at this late-afternoon hour one would have expected strollers, even in the villages, even up in the mountains, albeit exclusively elderly ones here. Only behind the windows of the Plaza Bar, far into the otherwise seemingly empty interior, could one see, picked out in the dusk by the slanting rays of the winter sun, at one of the occupied tables, the hands (rather old) of card players, and at the other table the hands of dice players.

The bus stopped by the livestock trough, which had ice around the edges, also a beard of icicles hanging from its wooden spout; in the middle of the square, which was surrounded by buildings, constructed of massive blocks of worked stone, that nonetheless left the sky visible (one of them the rectory, the other the town hall, the third a stable, another a ruin), the square that formed the village within the village in the village of Polvereda.

All the passengers got off except the children way back in the rear, who at first did stand up like the rest but then sat down shoulder-to-shoulder on a barrier now lowered in front of the library in the bus's midsection. As they stood up, it became apparent that some of these children were already adolescents. Today was their library day; their school had sent them out to become acquainted with the northern foreland of the Sierra, and particularly, in that connection, to familiarize themselves with borrowing books, with the people lending them, and likewise with the books themselves, with locating titles and authors, with books as artifacts and articles of value.

At almost the same time as the bus, a tractor-trailer had pulled into the square, announcing itself at a distance, from the houses on the outskirts of the village, which suddenly seemed quite far away, by a rhythmic honking that continued here on the square, like that of a car carrying newlyweds. In contrast to the entirely transparent bus, the truck consisted of a white metal box, completely sealed except for slits in the front for seeing through, until the moment when the driver opened the back of the container and transformed his vehicle into a market booth, slightly raised above the square, its shelves and crates stocked with products that were to be found nowhere else in the mountain village, which, like most of the others, had not had a general store for a long time; in addition to bananas, oranges, and cleaning agents, also bread, ham, and cheese (despite the fact that close to the village, in the hollow, stretched fields with wheat stubble, and before that, after the great expanse of wasteland, goats and also cattle and black-hoofed swine had been nibbling at the sparse grass).

In response to the honking, people flocked to the square; less the rural housewives one would have expected, "aprons and black kerchiefs," than more urban figures, such as one would find in the capital; the older ones among them were also bareheaded, often in long coats and shawls, with freshly polished street shoes; the female contingent, at first in the majority, seemed to have come directly from the beauty parlor and swayed their hips, even those who were not so young; shoes with extremely high heels no rarity.

The truck driver, metamorphosed into a vendor in the vehicle metamorphosed into a shop, had lowered a running board for these customers, with steps leading up to it. But not everyone came to buy, at least not at first. At the library bus's open door, one of the children or adolescents had sounded the aforementioned hand bell simultaneously with the honking of the cross-country supermarket, as a sort of reply, but in a different rhythm. A few of the Polvereda folk, and not only women, made a beeline for the bookshelves. More of them, however, hesitated, first doing their shopping and approaching the lending library only afterward, if at all.

But since the book borrowers over here needed considerably more time than the shoppers over there, they were soon lined up in the aisle; and the line in the meantime stretched partway into the arena, whereas to the shop on wheels—which, in a curious optical illusion, had attracted a much larger crowd than the bookmobile—only an occasional latecomer hurried; and in the end the traveling shopkeeper closed up his store and, before he headed for a quick stop at the bar, took up a position in the line of borrowers, by now quite short again.

The lending itself went quickly: the child librarians did the finding, stamping, recording in a jiffy, and the borrowers, some of them the same age but others much older and elderly, almost always knew what they wanted. They were slow only to turn away and leave; skimmed their books while standing next to someone still waiting in line—but avoided showing what they had picked out, covering the titles with their hands or with a videocassette they had also borrowed, seemingly ashamed of what they had borrowed as they trotted back to the square in the reverse line, which moved almost as deliberately as the parallel line of waiting borrowers—or was it shyness rather than shame?—and then one or the other disappeared among the houses with an embarrassed grin and downcast eyes, as if he had just made a fool of himself before the assembled community; "at the same time," she continued, "you could hear some people's mouths watering, and not just the young people's, as they went on their way! A couple of them tossed their books to each other at some distance from the bus, back and forth, like handball players in training, or jugglers.

"I was squatting on my heels again, like my fellow travelers, by the frozen-over drinking trough, or fountain, and then looked up from below, past the glass-sided bus, with the silhouettes of the librarians, the books, and the borrowers, and saw for the first time above the one-story roofs of Polvereda—no curved roof tiles as in the south, indeed, nothing characteristic of the south here—the entire central array of peaks belonging to the Sierra de Gredos in miniature and all the clearer, as if viewed through a reversed telescope, the peak of the Mira, of the Galana, of the pointed Three Little Brothers, and, approximately in the middle, a peak so jagged that, at least to all appearances, it alone, of all the peaks, did not lie under the otherwise unbroken blanket of shimmering snow: Almanzor, 'The Outlook.'"

The author: "Is it correct if I add to the description of the book borrowers that they also hid the books among their purchases, their heads of lettuce, their rolls and detergent?" — She: "Yes, if you mention that at the same time they did not remove their hands, or their one free hand, from the books hidden there and constantly bent over them as they were leaving and stuck their heads way down into their plastic bags and emerged with their noses looking dusty."

The author: "During one period in my life, I, too, did not want to be seen with a book anymore, and if I were, I wanted no one to be able to read the book's title. In the meantime, of late, I make a point of leaving my house, or my residence, my *almacén*, with a book, and have it with me and visible everywhere, and if someone tries to peek at it, I promptly move it into the light—in case the light is not already shining on it!—so that anyone who has eyes to see it can do so. Another aspect of this is that in the meantime—unless there is real urgency, as with you and your heart's desire, your story—after a period of using the most speedy means of communication, if I cannot talk directly face-to-face with a person, I send a letter, and by the classic form of mail, too, perhaps destined to disappear soon, and by the least rapid delivery. An airmail letter, even if it is in transit for two or three days, reaches the recipient too fast for my taste, and I choose regular delivery" — "*Barran*" (she, inadvertently) — "and not, as my mailwoman in La Mancha thinks, because that is 'cheaper' — or, in the case of letters going overseas, surface mail.

"This is not intended to be praise of slowness or anything of the sort. No: for me it is appropriate for the lines I have addressed to various people—of whom there are only a few left, and only a few letters, and a few lines—that they have time to wend their way to the recipients. In my imagination—" — "So we are back to the imagination again—" (she, interrupting him inadvertently) — "—not to say anything against imagination, if it broadens instead of narrowing—well, in my imagination, precisely this kind of long or 'leisurely' traveling on the part of a letter adds to the words I have written something they would have lacked if they had been hustled along electronically or whatever. Of course my letter must also be conceived and executed for this manner of transportation, almost quaint nowadays. An angry letter, for instance, is out of the question. So is, obviously, a business letter—" — "Obviously?" (she, inadvertently) — "or, on the contrary, yes, perhaps precisely certain business letters.

"Most suitable, it is true, for this kind of slow and steady progress, keeping close to the ground or the earth's surface and wending its way to the addressee, are letters of friendship and love—" — "Friendship? love? you?" (she, inadvertently) — "—for whatever resonates in them in the way of friendship or love (which need not be explicitly mentioned) is enhanced, as I imagine it, by their particular journey over land or sea; and not merely enhanced, but furthermore validated, given validity in a way different from a photogram—" — "Fax" (she, or a third person?) — "—or a u-mail—" — "e-" (she, or who?).

The author: "Simply the thought that my envelope will sit in the village mailbox for a while, even overnight or over the weekend, with all its little words. The mailbox rumbled when I tossed in the letter, that's how empty it was! And then the letter being driven to the railroad station beyond the seven plains of La Mancha. Resting in the mailbag during the train's umpteen stops, day and night, at stations or along open stretches in the various countries it traversed. Being sorted at the junction. Being transferred to a postal bus, and so on.

"And with every additional leg of the journey, I imagine, my letter becomes more believable, and each of its sentences gains effectiveness and truthfulness, or validity, becomes valid in a way it would not have if I had conveyed its contents over the telephone or even here, face-to-face. Only in this fashion can my few words, launched into the distance, become credible to you, clearly coming from my heart, or at least that general vicinity.

"Which brings us back—(some) letters are like (some) books—to books. You and I have in common a village childhood, if in very different villages—or so I picture it. And thus I take the liberty of speaking in passing of my native village's lending library, long since dissolved into dust. It is evening now, and as happens from time to time on the evenings when I am not alone, my tongue is finally loosened, and I feel an urge to tell stories, and more and more they are stories from long, long ago that are, so to speak—yes, so to speak—of no import.

"That library was located in the schoolhouse and did not have its own room; it was simply a glass-fronted cabinet against a wall in the one room that housed all the grades. At the time I had a sort of terror of cabinets in the village's houses; also of those in my own home. They were all armoires, crammed full of clothing, most of it old, often worn out and moth-eaten, some of it going back to our forebears and the forebears of our forebears, or the Sunday best of a son who did not return from some war or other; just about every house had one or two such keepsakes.

"And my terror became acute whenever such a cabinet was not locked, as repeatedly happened, but was left half-open, probably to air out the contents, and I was alone in the house and in the room where it stood. The doors would open gradually, one jerk at a time, often without a sound, and behind the rows of clothing hanging in the back of the cabinet—I still cannot get used to using the proper word, 'armoire'—there would be a concentration of energy, something poised to pounce, soon scraps would be flying, and not only scraps of cloth. On the other hand, whenever the lending-library cabinet was opened, once a week, before my eyes in the classroom—"

Like his heroine or business partner, the author frequently interrupted his narrative in mid-sentence and began to pose questions as usual: "And your image of libraries? Your images? Surely no books ever turn up in these images, as you understand them and want to see them conveyed in our book? Usually nothing but places, landscapes, and if sheets of paper, then without writing, no? Surely you do not want to tell me that you were ever tapped on the shoulder by an image in which something like a library flashed?" And again, as he not infrequently did, the author tried to provoke the woman into talking, which he did not by saying, "Tell me a story!" but rather by coming out with "Do not tell me anything!"

His guest, the client, gazed awhile along the line of her shoulder, focusing on some distant vanishing point, and then raised? or rather lowered, her voice: "Yes, no image, no images of various national libraries where we spent a short or a long time, and if the image of one that burned, then not the library in Alexandria but one from a house fire long ago in the village, the remains of books all mixed up with shattered windowpanes, and apples roasted by the heat lying in the grass under a tree, far from the actual site of the fire.

"And another image: that of a lending library on the outskirts of a metropolis situated by the ocean, installed in a former customs agent's hut, between the path once used by the customs officials and the steep cliff nearby, the path widened into a promenade, and the hut a single room, rendered much brighter by the windows, which had been enlarged on all sides, and a view, past the people strolling along the customs path, far, far out over the surface of the water, and not a single reader in the image, nothing but the silhouettes of the books between the ocean in the background and the pedestrians, bicyclists, and roller skaters in the foreground, and that, day in, day out, year in, year out, always the same image before my eyes, or perhaps sometimes also an image of this library late at night; the silhouettes of the books and the salty deep way out there viewed together through the display-window-size panes in the near darkness, with not a soul in sight." — "And in the reality-outside-this-image, this branch library has certainly long since been turned into a branch bank?" (the author) — She: "More likely converted into a customs-path museum." — Both at the same time, inadvertently: "As it should be." — The woman, the guest: "Which puts us back in the bus traveling into the Sierra de Gredos."

Almost as often as she had crossed the Sierra she had also passed through the Polvereda, the dust-cloud region, and the village of the same name. And each time she had encountered almost the same people, evidently mountain-dwellers from way back, similarly dressed, all with a similar accent, similar mannerisms, and especially a similar skin tone.

But on the day described here, much appeared entirely different to her. True, the natives were walking and especially sitting—the older card and dice players indoors in the one bar, those who were too old to play outside in the sun, low in the sky—as if they had always been there. Except that now they no longer dominated the scene. They shopped and borrowed books from the bus in about the same proportion as those wearing big-city clothes, who likewise came from Polvereda, or at least were not strangers here. Yet between these two groups, involved in the same activities, was a third group, apparently a distinct minority, and this one constituted the new and noticeable element in the mountain village. Groups? No, none of the three different sets of people formed anything like a group, not the returnees or vacationers from the capital, not even the natives, and certainly not the last category; they all came and went independently of each other.

The third or last type seemed particularly separate from one another. Was that because each of them had a different skin color, if only in small but obvious variations, from deep black to bronze to reddish brown, from olive to peach to lemony to rich yellow, from quince yellow to yellowish gray to blue-green to snow-white, this last unusual precisely in this mountainous region? Earlier it would have been said that these individuals, one after the other, exemplified a "race" or its "variants" and "subvariants." And now? At the time of this story the word "race" had long since disappeared, and was used, if at all, merely to designate external, superficial traits, such as skin tone, but preferably it was avoided altogether.

Or did these people with differently pigmented or overly white skin stand out so markedly because some of them turned up in garments and with headgear entirely unknown in the Sierra, and furthermore known nowadays only from archival pictures: so to speak, in tribal or native costumes (words like "tribe" or "native" also long since out of use, if not suspect and frowned upon), in "caftans" (?), "saris" (?), "burnooses" (?), with a "fez" (?), a "turban" (?), a "kaffiya," or God only knows what they were all called?

Yet individuals of the third type were apparently not so unknown in the village after all; or no longer, and for a considerable time already. They moved across the Plaza Mayor as matter-of-factly as the others; spoke the language of the country halfway fluently, although each with an immediately recognizable, not seldom transnational, accent; except for that one ancient Chinese (the term "ancient" otherwise to be strictly avoided), wearing a visored cap and an all-blue tunic buttoned up to the neck, padding in silent cloth shoes with a sort of delicate shyness, such as had not been observed anywhere else in the country and thus striking to the eye—the eye was what mattered—and describing a monumental arc of courtesy, of "deference," around everyone, even the dogs, and then, in the bus, pointing mutely but firmly to the one book for whose sake he had made his way to the library. It was the book in his language, with Chinese characters, stepladder-like.

And like the ancient Chinaman, others from the races, peoples, and tribes foreign to this region would borrow, along with a, let us say, domestic Spanish, Romance, Latin, or European book, one from their land of origin: obviously the one they asked for, whether requested ahead of time or not, was available in the traveling library. Initially amazed at this scene, she soon experienced no further amazement as she perched on the drinking trough and watched; or her amazement became so powerful and exclusive that it was no longer recognizable as such?

1 8

And again the signal for driving on. Departure from Polvereda, away from the dust clouds. But this time no ringing of a hand bell: ordinary honking, though considerably more insistent, more shrill to the ears. Nor did it come from the glass and library bus, but from another vehicle, which at that moment came backing out of a shed previously assumed to be an abandoned storage building.

The second bus was an ordinary one, not exactly new, but more suitable than the first for the mountain switchbacks. The travelers changed buses, except for the children, who will ride back with their library, driven by the bus driver, who in the meantime has fallen silent, next to him his silent son—their dialogue having in the meantime become unnecessary? Already they have driven off. But the new driver likewise has a companion sitting next to him, an enormous, very quiet sheepdog, his face, in profile, pointed constantly toward his master.

In this connecting bus it had been cold, not only as they set out but also long after that, and it had reeked of cigarette smoke and various other things. And trepidation had crept through the thinned ranks of the passengers; as if, with the children gone, they no longer saw themselves protected.

No one said a word. No one turned his head, not to any other passenger and certainly not to the mountain landscape, now growing increasingly precipitous, where, after the first switchback—part of a system of serpentine curves laid out evenly over the entire width of the last rise and barrier before the Sierra—the summit plain, visible just a little while earlier from the village square, was now blocked out again.

No one responded, not even the new driver, when a farmhand waved from a wheat field no larger than a garden, located just over the tree line and separated from its rocky surroundings by a stone wall of granite, the wheat shocks scattered among the stubble; no one took the time to interpret the old man's gesture as a wish for good luck or even a blessing for the journey; nor did anyone take the time to be surprised at seeing wheat fields at such an altitude, almost two thousand meters above sea level, if only one such field.

She alone, the adventurer, seated directly behind the driver and the dog, seemed to have time again, as since the beginning of this journey,— "her last, it was to be hoped"—time and more time. "And having time," she indicated to the author, "meant to me: being free of anxiety, of worry, of constraint; no fear of winter, of slippery roads, of getting stuck on this otherwise long impassable stretch of road, of a below-freezing night in the mountains, of pitch-darkness, of anything of any sort.

"Nonetheless I naturally—naturally?—had an awareness of the dangers, perhaps more acutely than my fellow passengers; and of one danger in particular, the great danger. But on that stretch of road my feeling of having time was more powerful than my awareness of danger. It was like that game where the paper covers the stone and therefore the 'paper' player beats the 'stone' player: in this instance, feeling trumped awareness, while in a different situation, at a different time, awareness could certainly have been the scissors to my feeling of having time—my feeling would have been cut to shreds by my awareness . . ."

Awareness of being in danger and the feeling of having time: if this was in fact a game, it was one without a winner and a loser. Instead one complemented the other, and, furthermore, both together gave birth to a third factor. In this confined, tinny, drafty vehicle she felt the kind of jolt go through the story for whose sake she had set out on this journey; a tightening, a powerful tugging and pulling, a pull. She sensed, no, she saw and felt, that her book, after all the intervening explications and descriptions, which of course were just as much part of it (a little like the lasso-like, looping serpentines along which the bus was rolling uphill), was now back to simply being told, or, even better and lovelier, was telling itself; was approaching that most sublime of narrative sensations, when "it narrates itself," "I, you, it, all of you, she, we, we are freely narrated, out of one country into another, at least for a while, and again and again in this fashion, and now and then, as the entirely appropriate rarity and precious thing in the book of our life."

She was the one passenger in the bus who looked out the window; who waved back at the farmhand in the enclosure, with a mere shimmer in the corners of her eyes; who turned around to the others, all of whom gradually got up from their scattered seats and moved toward the front, huddling together, more around her than around the driver, forming a cluster in the front of the bus similar to that of the children in the back of the bus on the earlier stage of the trip.

Only a few passengers were left, and as she gazed at them one at a time, it seemed to her that not only the bus had been changed in Polvereda but also, except for her, all the passengers, and at the same time that each of those few faces was familiar. They had already had something to do with each other, and in a life-altering way at that; their life lines had crossed at some point, but in what manner? under what circumstances?

And again the bus was approaching a pass, in the first twilight, which could just as well be the first light of dawn. After that the Gredos massif would finally stand there without any foothills, with the upland valley to the north carved by the río Tormes, whose headwaters lay in the Sierra. And again this crossing point was marked by clouds welling up thickly against the deep blue, almost black, air over the notch in the rocky ridge, and alternating with swaths of mist and light snow and moments of clear weather.

From this weather-basin haze emerged now and then the silhouette of one of the flying men letting the rising air currents carry them aloft on their artificial, brilliantly colored wings. Initially some of the flyers were swept so high that they were bathed in the last sunlight, while for the earth below, including the crests of the foothills, the sun had already set. And in very slow, snaking curves, almost as gradual as the winged creatures tracing their spirals in the air, the bus drew closer to, then farther away from, then closer to the pass and the kite-flyers, or whatever they claimed to be. Alongside stretched a short, naturally formed plateau, used by the sportsmen for their running starts and takeoffs. It was swept by uninterrupted courses of clouds rushing by, and lay there in a haze.

And when the bus had almost reached the pass—the sign reading "Puerto de Peña Negra [= Black Rock Pass], 1900m" all the more legible for moments at the threshold to the cloud kitchen—one of the birdmen landed, instead of taking off like his companions, there on the flat spot, and having hardly touched—almost crashed—down, ran, no, dashed out of the picture, as if sucked into and dissolved by the mist, including his wings, crossed or tangled on his back.

Wherever was the place, necessarily much higher up, from which he had pushed off earlier? And hadn't his flying apparatus actually been a parachute, which had briefly billowed behind and above him again as he ran? And no brightly colored sports parachute, either, but rather one in rock gray or Swiss-pine brown, in camouflage colors, so to speak, and not only so to speak? A military parachute?

Or had all the peculiar cloud formations in all the Sierra passes, or could it have been something else? cast such an evil spell on the passengers in the bus that they saw war in peacetime? saw instead of a boulder one made of papier-mâché and painted stone-color, "in reality" a covering for a tank concealed underneath? saw behind the façade of an apparent woodpile the storage place for a stack of machine guns? just as the hero of the book set in that region had once seen a marauding knight in every shepherd?

Or was this in the meantime a period unlike that one long ago, and did the vanes of the windmills sawing the air now in fact represent something other than mere "windmill vanes," not exactly "evil giants," but certainly something else? and the same was true of the ball-like object that came rolling unexpectedly around the foot of a cliff? of these scarecrows mounted clear across the valley? of these naked mannequins stacked in the back of a passing truck?

And who could know whether "in reality" the ugly-as-sin or perhaps imaginary chosen lady of the hero in that immortal book may have been, and perhaps is, just as beautiful and noble, yes, infinitely more noble and beautiful and especially more real than her suitor portrayed, and portrays, her? and that she was waiting, and is waiting, for him in precisely that village in La Mancha where he imagined her, and, the epitome of beauty and youth and reality, will continue to wait for him?

Be that as it might: what was certain was that these travelers here had not set out in the spirit of adventure, in contrast to that literary hero. They even visibly feared adventure. If it had been up to them, they would perhaps not have set out in the first place. Even when they were children, tunnels of horrors had held little attraction for them. It was not only the old folks whose heads bobbed back and forth like those of helpless infants as they were driven along. The only adventurer among them was the woman sitting up front in the bus, at once a total stranger and familiar.

She looked as if she were lying in wait or poised to throw: to throw herself into an adventure, to hurl herself completely off balance—wasn't the word "lance" part of that concept? What a glow in her eyes as she had turned to watch the paratrooper, or whoever he was, dart among the sport-flyers. And when the bus had driven through the Puerto de Peña Negra, or whatever the pass was called, and scraped against the side of a cliff, and, after veering this way and that, seemingly no longer under the driver's control, come to a halt diagonally across the road, with its engine stalled, she was instantly up front at the wheel, where she grasped the driver, who had slumped over it, under the armpits and carefully bedded him down at the feet of his enormous dog, who was whimpering almost like a small child.

"Not something like a stray bullet?" the author asked: "The very expression 'stray bullet' is something I could never bring myself to write, at least not in your, and our, book!" — "You could have been one of the passengers in the bus with me," she replied. "But not to worry: if there is to be any adventure, it will have the most limited or strictly abbreviated episodes of overt violence or fighting possible. How else would you have been the one I went out of my way to hire to write the story? If there is to be action, there will generally be less emphasis on purely external action than on the kind that from time to time erupts from the inside to the outside in the rhythm of a long, long story.

"Accordingly, you may go ahead and write that at the last summit of the last pass before the Sierra the driver was not struck by a bullet, either a stray one or any other kind. He just felt sick all of a sudden. He had probably had a heart attack, or it was an asthma attack that ripped the steering wheel from his hands. Another woman in the bus helped me drag him outside, where he promptly regained consciousness." And she helped him up. He did not want to sit; stood leaning against the cliff by the road. The color drained from his rooster- or birthmark-red face. She scooped up icy water gushing from the cliff and sprinkled it on his wrists. The dog trotted back and forth in front of its master in a figure eight, whimpering, and then lay down quietly on its belly beside him, its head raised.

After that, no one will have moved. The two women also motionless, one of them right beside the driver, her hand on his shoulder. Not one word was spoken, either, the other woman having turned off the bus radio the minute she came forward to help. Nothing but the rattling of tall thistles in the wind from the Sierra. The tableau held. The sick man repeatedly tried to straighten up and get back on the bus, and again and again his knees buckled. The two women—it was clear that no one else was allowed to help them—picked him up by his arms and legs and carried him inside, bedding him down on one of the unoccupied rows of seats toward the back. The dog followed and lay down parallel to him, its back so high that it would keep him from rolling off.

By now the adventurer had taken her place in the driver's seat and turned the key; the bus drove on, heading downhill, just as steadily as before. Although for some time now she had hardly been playing her professional role as the lady banker, the skills peculiar to this profession continued to manifest themselves in the situations typical of this altered world, allowing her to take charge, make decisions, and determine the sequence of events: the combination of service and authority so characteristic of her work; patient, almost somnambulistic waiting for results and seizing the one favorable moment in a seemingly brutal yet at the same time gingerly fashion; forestalling, saving the day, promoting one's own interests.

But there was one adventure-averse passenger or another who saw in her intervention a missionary zeal at work: a zeal that was "characteristic" in a different sense, stemming from guilt and intended to cover up a specific guilt. Were there not numerous examples of this sort of thing in history? The kind of person who gravitates toward being a helper, and at the same time a trendsetter or even leader, out of a guilt impossible to assuage in any other way? And then a third party chiming in, our author, let us say, with his daily view of the stony steppe of La Mancha, who wanted no truck with such opinions and explanations, and explained and opined that his protagonist simply was the way she was, and whatever she did or declined to do was simply what she did or declined to do.

And he asked—a rhetorical question that already implied its own answer—whether she, the woman there, had not, on the contrary, become a queen of banking precisely as a result of her innate capacity for service and for leaping into the breach, or because of the fundamental presence of mind that made these capacities possible and, in the case of the person in question, also worked hand in hand with the gift of foresight—the ability to foresee developments, structural shifts, overt and covert warfare, or a false peace born of inertia and an active, energetic peace, opening paths into uncharted territory: in the same sense as one of her historical predecessors, the banker and trader Jakob Fugger in sixteenth-century Augsburg, who was said to have displayed the powerful gift of foresight as "a form of perfect hearing" (here, too, he, the author, said he had done his research, actually more in contrast to his usual practice)?

It went along with this, and with foresight and presence of mind, he said, that she, like Jakob F., the greatest man in history when it came to "fructifying money," had her roots, or whatever one called them, in a village. Early life in a village, opined and explained the researcher-author, himself a longtime refugee from the city, reinforced the aforementioned gifts, giving them a foundation and at the same time illuminating them, in the sense of "making them shine forth."

And in the end he further explained these gifts of his heroine's as resulting from her having spent her village childhood without parents—which meant that she, as the older child, always had to be responsible for her "little brother," that—but fortunately for her and for the book, he interrupted himself here with a laugh, as if this explaining had been nothing but a game. She had been about to point out to him that he was creating the impression he had to defend her tooth and nail against someone, "almost like an admirer"; and he should refrain from this, in the interest of the story, up to the very last paragraph!

19

Remarkable how, with the adventurer at the wheel now, the passengers relaxed; likewise the sick driver, lying next to the enormous dog and only a short while ago still fighting for breath. After surviving these moments of mortal dread and loud, premature lamenting, the two of them were enjoying a sleep as sound as it was deep; snoring and wheezing. Yet she was driving considerably more briskly than her predecessor, and not merely because they were heading down the mountain (the serpentines on the southern side of these last foothills had even more extended loops, as if that were possible, and in the Sierra, going downhill usually meant: slow down).

Along the entire stretch, zigzagging across mountain meadows sparsely punctuated with dwarf firs, the arrayed peaks of the Gredos remained clearly in view, as if all at the same distance, on the upper periphery of one's field of vision, no longer hidden by any range in between.

Also not another trace, except behind them, up on the Black Rock Pass, of a puff of mist or cloud. A clear winter-evening sky, although it remains uncertain whether the darkness forming the basis of the blue—no longer the "blueing" of that morning or afternoon—stems from the blackness of outer space, already perceptible in the high mountains, or from the impending night. No more smell of smoke, it having been drawn out of the bus up in the thinner, or finer, atmosphere; but also no more freezing and shivering.

On the sloping meadows, in contrast to the grazing places somewhat farther down, which tended to be deserted, there are herds of cattle almost everywhere, as well as scattered families of horses, the horses, like the cattle (many bulls), with coats so short that they look like a skin stretched taut over their bodies, for the most part as dark as coal: so a portion of the livestock from the mountains are not driven over the Sierra to spend the winter months in the much warmer and always snowless southern region, the valleys of the río Tiétar and the río Tajo beyond?

"Was it always like this up here?" wondered the driver, she who knew the Sierra inside out. "Yes, every time I came through here in wintertime, there were animals grazing, and only in the pastures here in the central region—but in no other year as many as are here now, and also—this, too, is new—as carefully and strictly guarded: around every herd and tribe a small team of herders with walkie-talkies—, as if in case of an accident."

From the pass up above, she had still seen some of the mountain pastures on the southern flank below bathed in sunlight, a field of rays that visibly gave way to pitch-darkness—with an afterglow lasting but the twinkling of an eye—until only a single cow, separated from the rest of the herd in a dip below a ridge, had a yellow gleam on its flank, or was that part of its coat?

After sunset, a similar yellow, then reddish, then yellow-red-blue gleam on the clustered peaks of the Sierra de Gredos, far off against the sky. These might have been the central European Alps now, with the all too famous alpenglow on the snowy expanses in the background; and, to complete the picture, the clanging of the bells belonging to the cows and the bellwethers in the foreground and the veil of frost over the high valley carved out below, already shrouded in darkness, from which the thinly scattered lights of houses stood out, clearly nowhere dense enough to signal the presence of a larger village or town.

What was it that brought her back, time after time, as on the current evening, to this Sierra de Gredos, hardly distinguishable, especially now in wintertime, from the Swiss mountain ranges along the Italian and French borders, and whose highest peak, even the Almanzor, was hardly more than half as high as Mont Blanc, the Jungfrau, or the Matterhorn?

What in the world was she seeking or expecting in this mountain range without ski slopes or ski lifts, a range completely unknown outside the tableland area, known even in its own country only from hearsay as one got farther away from it, a destination at most for the inhabitants of the region, and perhaps also for those from Madrid? Weren't even its principal types of rock, the granites, gneisses, and mica schists, the same as in the far more rugged Alps, which seemed to beckon with very different sorts of thrilling adventures, the only variation being that the Sierra ridges were older by so and so many millions of years, though not old in the sense of "phenomenal," "rare," "record-breaking," or even "venerable," but rather in the sense of "worn down," "crumbling," "cast off," "written off," in short, "aged," in contrast to the still youthful Alps, in whose substrate something continued to stir, mountains that rose up year after year, pushed higher and expanded, while the Sierra de Gredos was steadily diminishing, eroding, shrinking, not quite perceptibly, but measurably, and someday, millions of days from now, would be hardly more than a somewhat elevated table in the tableland?

Why, if she was already taking a detour to seek out the author, did she not choose a more exciting one, especially one that would lead through sites of general interest or places where an audience was concentrated—whether the reading public or not—also a more contemporary area, that is to say, a more relevant, and, well, what the heck, a much, much longer detour than this one through the Sierra, which, properly speaking, was no detour at all—for instance, a detour in a great arc by way of North Africa to the author's hole-in-the-wall in La Mancha, through the Mauritanian deserts, across the High Atlas in Morocco, through the Straits of Gibraltar, and heading inland across the Sierra Nevada, then the Sierra Morena, and finally the Sierra de Calatrava, the "Death's Head Sierra"—all landscapes she had traveled and hiked at least two or three times, and where she had had almost exclusively good, heartening, happy, and life-enhancing experiences, unlike here in the Gredos massif?

"It is true," she said, continuing to talk softly to herself at the wheel and turning in her thoughts to her so faraway author: "Whenever I think of my previous hikes through the Sierra de Gredos, unless the familiar images come to me unbidden, I usually find myself recalling a borderline situation, not seldom one between life and death, or at least something simply unpleasant and bad. And yet, since that first time, when I was pregnant with my daughter, I have set out to cross these mountains almost every year and sometimes twice in one year, far, far more often than I have made my way through all these parts of the world where I was consistently filled with ecstatic feelings—no, not with illusory ecstasy but rather with a state of love, yes, of love, and of which I have only fond memories afterward. Whereas one time when I was on my way through here I found myself in the middle of a driving snowstorm, with flakes so wet and heavy that I could hardly breathe and was afraid of suffocating. I almost died of exhaustion. That was in January, like now—"

She corrected herself again: "No, that January it was the torrential downpour. Or was it a different January? No, the lost shoes. The snowstorm was in May—in the Sierra I always get all mixed up about time, and that is partly the fault of the Sierra de Gredos itself.—I had just been walking in the mountains in the May sunlight. I was walking as light-footedly, even with my knapsack, *mochila* in Spanish, *mihlatuz zahr* in Arabic, as a person can walk. As always when I am going somewhere on foot, I assessed my condition, the moment and hour, and my relationship to the world or to life, by whether I involuntarily spun around myself at least once as I went along.

"And the spinning occurred there again and again, as if at regular, predetermined intervals. Likewise I encountered from time to time, amid the short grass, some of which was still a wintry gray, sorrel, always growing in clusters, all fresh and green, and I repeatedly plucked a leaf and munched on it, and soon it was not merely against thirst but just because, out of contentment, and as if to savor and enhance the contentment with the sourness.

"I was already so high up in the Sierra that there were no longer any ravines to get around. Up to a certain altitude, just below the tree line, let us say, the Sierra is transsected by deep, narrow ravines, yet from a distance it looks so smooth and accessible, at least on the northern side. Yet instead of climbing straight to the ridge—calling it mountain climbing in the technical sense would be something of an exaggeration, since on the northern slopes, unlike the southern slopes, it is seldom necessary—I dawdled across the mountain pastures, devoid of ditches and almost entirely without trees, and also no longer fenced in every few feet, going gradually uphill for a while, then downhill again when I felt like it, and instead of having to wear myself out scrambling over barbed wire every few steps, now, imagine, I had to wade through or simply jump across a little brook that had just welled up and ran almost level with the rocks and the grass, and would not dig itself in until farther down, and on this meandering route toward the Puerto del Pico, the crossing to the south I had chosen for that day, you know, one of these bubbling-up brooks after another, also the rushing of these brooks along the ground, similar to my periodic turning-in-circles yet continuing without pause, in a seemingly preestablished and -determined order.

"I need not tell you what's up with the passes and crossings in the Sierra de Gredos. And the Puerto del Pico, the north–south crossing, approximately in the middle, between the eastern and central massifs, is carved infinitely deeper and especially more steeply out of the ancient rock than most of the other notches, and can be seen from far away as a deep trough in the mountain range, which is oriented along an east-west axis and falls off sharply from the Puerto on both sides. And if there is a clear and classic border between north and south anywhere, it is there on the crest of the Puerto del Pico, the classic kind of north and south you read about.

"The southern air here, you should know, where it wafts in freely from the lowland, unhindered by any foothills, blows considerably warmer than in the other Puertos, and also with far more force and energy between the steep walls of the trough; it moves—not constantly, but on certain, not infrequent, days, at a specific time, usually at noon—right along the line of the northerly air, which up to this point has tended to hover there and remain cold, or even turn colder and colder in the innermost reaches of the mountains, and slips under it, while the northern air by contrast falls upon the southern air, and the result, as you can see back there to the left at the Puerto del Pico, is no longer mere huffs and puffs of fog and clouds with scattered snowflakes, but thunder and lightning, along with cloudbursts that unceasingly and mercilessly dump cold water over the landscape, refusing to let up before nightfall, and, somewhat higher, around the steep escarpments, snowstorms and blizzards, a sudden hurricane of flakes like the one in which I reached the pass that time in May when I was on my hundred-brook and thousand-sorrel-leaf trek.

"One step and I was out of the May sunlight, with a vista eastward across the open and obvious void to the Escorial and likewise westward all the way to the Plaza Mayor in Salamanca, if not straight into polar darkness, then into the prepolar contourless fading of the light on the wintry Bering Sea; no driving snow, but a kind of spewing, and soon no longer individual flakes but an almost solid, suffocating, spongy mass, being hurled at me again and again, soon not snowy white, but deepening the darkness, except when sporadic, almost welcome, flashes of lightning lit up the air for a moment.

"And strange, and stranger still, that this becomes clear to me only now as I am telling you this story: how quickly I, who had been so filled with joy in life, my own, and in all existence, imagining that there in the treeless waste I could smell the June linden blossoms, from one bend of the knee to the next, was on the verge of giving up and being dead. Soon it will be all over with me, I thought. Just a few more steps, and I will not be able to do anything but let myself fall. And once I have fallen, I will remain lying at that spot and will not get up.

"The clumps of wet snow plunked onto the ground. The ground was vernally warm and along the foot of the cliffs already summery warm. But soon the snow stopped melting. It accumulated. It grew deeper and deeper, as rapidly as a brook flooding in a storm. Soon it rose above my knees. Then it was above my belly. I stumbled. Then I fell, or almost. I scrabbled along. You can still see me creeping along for a stretch, on all fours, half blinded, panting, whimpering, dribbling spit—and then no more spit."

She interrupted herself. "I see you are hardly listening to me anymore. Your mind is wandering. I know you, my listener, my author, I mean: that is because I am telling the story in short, dramatic sentences. A narrative style like that can drive you away. And the kind of adventure that goes hand in hand with such narration—no, not hand in hand at all—has no validity in your eyes. According to you, any external adventure counts, and can be narrated, and is worthy of being narrated, only if it also elicits an internal adventure: when thanks to what befalls you, you are surprised at yourself, startled at yourself, or puzzled by yourself, or simply find some aspect of yourself strange, and thus discover a problem and ponder this problem, and describe it as your problem, or, no, an existential problem, in connection, of course, with the external adventure, so that now the external and the internal actually do go hand in hand, literally and in reality.

"In the course of that snowstorm at the Puerto del Pico, I once again found myself in the realm of the pasture fences, of which only the top strands of wire and the tips of the fence posts were visible. To get over them seemed to drain my last strength, but these obstacles also served as my reference points and provided a rhythm that each time yielded a bit more strength.

"The moment of 'It's all over!' did not hit me until I was standing in the noontime darkness in front of a seemingly insurmountable chainlink fence, as high as a house, that appeared to stretch forever in both directions, and when I then found the gate, it was secured with chains. Had I wandered through an invisible breach into the territory of an abandoned but otherwise intact mountain barracks that blocked any escape route, or a long since deserted Sierra prison (which in my case was again serving its original purpose)? Couldn't I have turned around and crawled and crept back into the May sunlight?

"Yet stranger still, any turning back was out of the question, just as during the previous times in the Sierra when I had fought for my life there—and not just for an hour in a blizzard but one time for almost a whole day, and once for a whole lovelong, yes, lovelong, night—I could still have turned back at a certain spot, before the snake clearing, before the burned forest, but it was simply impossible that I, that anyone, that we, should have turned back, strange, so strange. When I came upon that chainlink fence, at any rate, I knew this was my point of no return. But that was when the transformation occurred, strange, so strange, of me into my brother, far off behind the walls of the penitentiary in the dunes—"

In her usual way she broke off her tale here before reaching the end and turned to her invisible listener: "Ah, you were about to drift away from me again into your absentmindedness. And not until that little word 'we,' and with it my brother, came into play did you prick up your ears again, and did your eyes, which had gone dull, light up. And I also know why my snowstorm story has so little meaning for you, aside from the fact that it seems to you too mired in external adventure: you, my listener and my author, dislike stories that deal constantly with one person, and in which only one person, alone and unaccompanied, does things, experiences things, moves about, even when this solitary person is me, the woman—which really should appeal to you, in that it first presents a surprise—a heroine familiar from entirely different images, all by herself and prostrate in the deep snow—and then a problem worth telling about. No, in my, and our, book you want to see me experiencing things in some sort of company—rather than alone this way—and described accordingly.

"Yet except for my first trip through the Sierra de Gredos, every other time I was alone here. And even on that first trip I soon struck out on my own, accompanied only by the child in my belly, without her father. It is only since the current day and evening that I have not been journeying through the Sierra alone! So the story can move along the way you like it!"

And again she interrupted herself: "And it seems to me now, my listener and author, that the one commissioned to write the book is not you. It was not so much I who gave you the commission as you who gave it to me. I am the one you commissioned—at your service!" And as she momentarily took her hands off the wheel of the bus, she laughed; laughed out loud into the dark, silent bus. "How may I help you?"

What was the seemingly familiar stranger laughing about up front at the wheel, in the pitch-darkness, which was even more intense outside than inside; which made one think from time to time that one was no longer being driven on a road but over bumps and humps, where outside and inside, except for the sound of the bus's engine (more a grinding than the calming hum of the sparkling glass bus earlier) and the screeching, groaning, and rattling of the whole, whole? bus, everything had become as silent as the grave?

The idiot at the wheel laughed, and did not stop laughing, and if she paused now and then, it was clear that she would immediately burst out laughing again, in the same hearty, childlike way, which after a while infected even the last and most resistant of the few remaining passengers and likewise the regular driver, apparently risen from the dead, if not entirely recovered and still lying there in back on his reclined seat, and made them laugh, too. The story goes that all the people in that night bus laughed out loud, at the same pitch as the woman at the wheel, although the bus then actually did make a detour over bumps and humps—when the road was partially buried by a rock slide—across a pasture, where cattle, looking in the dark like buffalo, scattered at a gallop; even the driver's enormous dog showed his white teeth and seemed to laugh along, silently.

In a film, the vehicle now meandering over this hummocky grazing area would have been visible first from the side, apparition-like, with the equally apparition-like silhouettes of its occupants, and in the next shot would have been seen from above, with the camera moving higher and higher, until the bus could no longer be identified as such, a small object crawling over the earth's curved surface, and the occupants' laughter would have filled the theater as the only sound accompanying the image. "With the laughing idiot as our driver, we felt idiotically safe," even when she fell silent, and even when the coach rumbled through a mountain torrent that cascaded for a moment over the coach's roof: the bridge there smashed, and, as later became apparent, not only this one, as if dynamited.

Silently she resumed her conversation with herself, intended for the distant author: "Listen, just like my other landscapes scattered throughout the world, the Sierra de Gredos has come to represent for me, every time I am here, an example of something indestructible, in defiance of history and the present era, promising a life on earth that if not lasting an eternity will at least last half an eternity. Hear this, my listener and witness to my view of things: at some moments when I was on my way through the Sierra de Gredos—" (here she paused in her monologue) "—I have experienced this region as blessed, like many other parts of this planet, including cities, of course. But every single time, this Sierra de Gredos, offering a possible place where not only I but also we and those like us might live, has abruptly become a hostile, even deadly sphere, and each time I have counted myself incredibly lucky to have escaped with my life. Accursed Sierra!

"So now you know the two reasons that spur me to set out whenever I can for this blessed/accursed Sierra de Gredos: on the one hand the world up here, which changes so abruptly, more powerfully and predictably than I have experienced in any other part of the world; and on the other hand, each time when I have escaped and am safe and sound again at home, the rendezvous every morning with images from here in the Sierra—peaceful ones, you understand—image and peace are ultimately one and the same—: images such as did not appear nearly so often and especially so comprehensively—the part for the whole—from those other regions where simply being there immediately filled one with hope.

"And listen as I tell you and repeat what 'image-forming' means and signifies: the world is still standing. It has not perished, contrary to my brother's belief. And listen as I tell you also that earlier on, before my crossings of the Sierra, I liked to travel with others, and often did so, and that soon I will be traveling with others again, here in the Sierra de Gredos and elsewhere."

Before the bus reached its destination, the route passed through several more watercourses. The bridges over them, too, destroyed. But the road swerved aside from the bridge and in the water became a ford, as it had probably been before any bridges were built, returning to asphalt on the other side. And during the traversing of these very shallow fords, in contrast to earlier in the mountain torrent, the water hardly rose and also did not wash over the sides of the bus; nothing but a splintering of ice floes along the banks.

It also happened that the elderly vehicle, which creaked at the slightest unevenness, rammed into a block of granite in one of the fords. But that did not make any of the travelers uneasy. With her as the driver, nothing troubled them anymore. The very fact that a woman was driving cradled them in a sense of security, and the repeated traversing of the fords added to the temporary state of dreamlike carefreeness. None of them even looked up when the alder branches hanging far into the water whipped against the windows, sweeping from left to right; and even if a falling boulder had hit the roof or a grenade had exploded in front of the bus, they would not have been startled out of their peaceful reveries.

The woman holding the reins up front on the coachman's box also fell into a reflective daze, while remaining completely alert. Fording the brooks reminded her of the film in which she had played the youthful heroine. In that saga, set in the Middle Ages, she had also been constantly fording bodies of water, less brooks like these than rivers, often broad ones with deep spots, where the story required her, dressed in a kind of chain mail, to sink, fight for her life, and so on. Also a proper single combat, the final and decisive one—which, to be sure, was then broken off in the middle—between her and a, the, man, took place in just such a ford, complete with clashing swords, snorting steeds, and so on, the only variant being that, instead of slashing away silently at each other, they had to alternate shouting at one another, uttering tirades of insults that were by no means purely medieval and, in the course of the scene, gave way to an entirely different kind of speaking, and so on: cut, end of the film, man and woman up to their hips in the water of the ford, motionless, facing one another.

And driving along cautiously and briskly, at the same time deep in reflection, she then brought to a close on this final stretch her silent monologue addressed to the absent author: "Whenever I cast my mind back to myself in all my misadventures and not seldom life-threatening solitary passages through the Sierra, I experience it not as something from the past but as the most intense present, assailing me and piercing me infinitely more keenly than during the moments, hours, or entire days and nights when I hovered between life and death. If in that blizzard I just missed letting myself fall down in the snow for good, the moment I revisit the situation I am threatened even more by that ultimate surrender: with the snow already up to my chest, I take one last step and after that will let myself tumble into the depths, never to return. And from an even earlier point in time, yes, point, from that first time in the Sierra, with the child in my womb, when I unexpectedly found myself completely disoriented, found? I am still there in the blazing sun on the southern flank, and the next time I recall that hour I will die, along with my unborn child, of heat stroke and abandonment.

"But the images that come flying or flashing to me from the Sierra after the fact are also very much of the present. All such images—the only kind that matter to me for my, and our, story—not only those from the Sierra de Gredos, take place in the present. Yes, in contrast to my terrors and bad situations, the images become present to me playfully; the image itself as a game in which an entirely different present is in effect than my personal one. The images play out in an impersonal present, which is more, far more, than mine and yours; they take place in the grander time, and in a single tense, for which, when I consider them, the images, the term 'present' is not really appropriate—no, the images do not take place either in a grander or grand time, but in a time and in a tense for which no adjective, let alone a name, exists.

"And listen, look: are not the images therefore, is not 'the image' a thoroughly epic problem, material for Homeric tales by the dozen? Material for a different odyssey, whose action takes place both externally and internally?"

2 0

To the accompaniment of these and other conversations with herself, she drove her fellow passengers, including the incapacitated driver and his dog, toward the late-evening bus's destination, the village of Pedrada.

Pedrada, which can be translated as "stone toss," or "rain of stones," or "hail of stones"—"siege of stones" would also be possible—is located in the innermost reaches of the Sierra region, or, as it says in that book set there many centuries ago, "in the bowels of the Sierra de Gredos." And this Pedrada is one of the few villages at the headwaters of the río Tormes that lie right on the banks of the river and not, like Navarredonda ("Round Hollow"), Hoyos del Espino ("Thorn Hole"), Hoyos del Collado ("Hill Hole"), Navacepeda ("Vine Hollow"), and Navalperal ("Pear Hollow"), at a safe distance from the floodplain of the river, which here near its beginnings is not regulated anywhere. The houses of Pedrada are scattered through the river's far-flung source area, slotted in between several streams and also mere rivulets, which singly and collectively, as they snake along from various sides, from the gentle slopes, flanks, and mostly treeless high plateaus, are referred to as the río Tormes.

The sparse settlement lies among these almost innumerable, still narrow watercourses, which often meander through mountain-grass meadows, and it becomes a bit more prepossessing only at one spot, where the thousands of tributaries have gradually converged to form one river that quickly and unimpededly shoots over rapids and cascades, finally deserving of the name.

The road that branches off toward Pedrada in Navarredonda de Gredos was a dead-end spur terminating in the village. From there no passable route continued; there were only livestock trails, and for a long time now there had been no paths for crossing the mountain chain to the south; those that had once existed were overgrown with broom, which by now had spread everywhere, forming a thicket as dense as a jungle, or, closer to the ridge, the path had been blocked by scree and boulders; the only exception the partially preserved path, or *cordel,* still used for driving the cattle caravans down to the flatlands in late fall or back into the mountains in spring.

The author, not given to enthusiasm for such things, or simply lazy, had commissioned someone else to do research on that *cordel,* and on the *transhumancia* (= cattle-driving), "just as"—thus his excuse—"Flaubert did not snoop around himself at agricultural fairs or whatever for his Madame B. or whomever, but had an acquaintance describe such things for him in letters": that trail, that *cordel,* or whatever, ran on the other side of Pedrada more or less from west to east, from El Barco de Ávila toward the deep trough of the Puerto del Pico, to spare the animals' hooves the mountains with their razor-sharp wind gaps, and this route, with its bomb-crater-deep gullies and washouts, coming one after the other and taking up the entire stretch, had been impassable for decades to even the most heavy-duty vehicle or conveyance, whether with four-wheel or all-wheel drive. Even a hundred-wheel tank would have tipped over there sooner or later; not to mention a bus, and especially this one, driving through the night, even when driven by this stranger, this woman to whom the region around my Pedrada seems to be more familiar than to me, almost a native of the area, and under whose care—how nice and straight she sits at the wheel, her arms extended like oars, hardly moving the wheel—so does it turn itself on the curves?—I would like to stay on the road as far as the last stable of Pedrada and even up to the ridge of the Sierra, and then on and on forever.

Almost all the passengers then got off the bus before its final destination. Each time they made their way to the front, stood beside the driver, and placed their hand on her shoulder shortly before the desired stop. Each was loaded down, as if returning from a long journey. Each turned in the open door once more to say thank you and goodbye to her, each using the same words but in an entirely different accent; and each, before he or she opened his or her mouth, cleared his or her throat and then said, "Thank you, good night, see you next time," in the same raspy voice, as if he or she had not spoken for at least the entire day.

All those who got off went on their way alone, immediately heading downhill from the dead-end road, never toward a house, at least not one that was visible, lit up; were promptly swallowed up by the darkness, in which at most an open fire burned, isolated and a long way off, from which now and then pitch-laden smoke wafted through the bus.

When the bus reached the sign saying "Pedrada," the only people left besides her were the driver, his dog, and the other woman who had helped her with the two of them. She noticed a new sign that announced PEDRADA in several other languages and scripts. And where was the familiar old hotel at the entrance to the village, at the spot where all the tributaries came together to form the río Tormes? What, the inn El Milano Real, "The Red Kite" (named after the bird of prey most common in the Sierra), no longer existed?

In its place, between the streams, at the wellspring of the river, a tent, no, more like a colony of tents, a sort of tent village. And there were no streetlights any longer. Or had there ever been any? Yet in spite of the moonless night—hadn't it been a full moon here not long ago? or was it too early for the moon to have risen?—all of Pedrada, or what was left of it, could be made out clearly.

The light came from the sky above the source area, which was a sprawling, slightly concave, high plain, hollow and highland at the same time, the highest inhabited one in the Sierra? This sky seemed even bigger by night than by day, and twinkled or flashed with stars, in different colors, yellowish, bluish, red, white, green, and the light was collected on the ground and thrown back by the shiny deposits of quartz and mica, which seemed to be everywhere in this headwaters region, more so than anywhere else in the mountain range, reflecting the light of the firmament even from the clear bottom of the brooks and rivulets, though no higher than, let us say, the waistlines of the villagers, who were bustling about outside in astonishingly large numbers—their faces, and even more the space above the crowns of their heads, remaining in darkness.

So many more and unfamiliar stars were visible that instead of the usual constellations one saw entirely unfamiliar ones and wanted to give them new, entirely unheard-of names. And although the snow-covered expanses on the summit plain that seemed hardly a stone's or a boulder's throw away contributed to making the night brighter, these stars hardly suggested wintry images. Did that perhaps have to do with the fact that Pedrada, like a few other places in the northern Sierra, had a sort of microclimate, lying beneath a dome of relatively and only intermittently warm air?

Upon leaving the bus, one involuntarily splayed one's fingers—that was how surprisingly mild the air was as it brushed one's skin. Or did the warmth come from the open fires, even more numerous around the tents here in the heart of the village, especially the large fire, the size of several bonfires, glowing red-hot by the main tent, which looked taller than the vanished Milano Real? In Pedrada one could at first make sense of nothing. And one accepted that.

There was also artificial light in the village, of course, but only inside the tents, and hardly any of it penetrated to the outside. This light, produced by generators—every brook dotted with them—rendered the tents phosphorescent, as it were, or not only as it were, lent them a dimly glowing shape from within. Did that result from the hairline fissures and holes, invisible to the naked eye, in the tent walls? And likewise from the material of which the tents were made?

For the tents did not consist of the material commonly used today, either canvas or some other fabric or plastic. Each of the tents, including the central one, was a cone constructed of wooden poles, lashed together with branches and vines, and layered from bottom to top, or was one mistaken? with leaves, grass, and broom twigs, held together with clay—didn't "Gredos" mean "clay"?—in which the myriad fragments of mica contributed to the phosphorescent effect?

So these were not light, easily transported tents but more like yurts, or what people imagine yurts to be? Earth-brown, clay-yellow hummocks, sprung up cheek by jowl from the earth like termite mounds (or what we imagine termite mounds to look like), into which the people here had needed only to hack a sort of narrow opening for a door, over which they then hung a pelt?

As far as she was concerned, this former lady banker and sometime coach-box lady: Hadn't she, in that moment of getting off the bus in Pedrada, "my driving duties fulfilled," seen the tents or yurts as those tree roots, ripped from the ground and tipped over to lie horizontally, in the hurricane-ravaged forests back home near the northwestern riverport city that she had visited the morning she set out? And hadn't various things from home also followed her during the entire time of her journey? or traveled with her? or seemed to have got there ahead of her whenever she arrived?

Not one ordinary house still inhabited in Pedrada. Or did it merely look that way when one arrived by night? And all the houses, including the barns and stables, in ruins: another nocturnal-arrival apparition? And if ruins: Hadn't those already been here the very first time she came?

What was certain at least was that except inside the tents no light was burning in a building. Across the entire high plateau the rattling of generators, but as if one of these sounds muffled the other, almost swallowing it up. And was that music in the tents? Were people singing? Or did the hubbub of voices outside, merging with the roaring and rumbling of the various watercourses, create the impression of voices and instruments sounding in unison?

In quick succession some surprising and unexpected aspects of Pedrada, seemingly so remote. Satellite dishes mounted on the tents? A paperboy making his way from tent to tent, with the next morning's papers? An Asian, or also non-Asian, deliveryman heading at full speed with bouquets of roses toward the main tent, the converted inn called At the Sign of the Red Kite II? —Listen, let me tell you: no, no paperboy, but perhaps, yes, definitely, a pizza-delivery boy, younger than young, swerving out of the darkness on his motor scooter, zooming back and forth, still unsure of the address for his delivery, finally, in his confusion, asking for directions, and whom did he ask? whom else but her, just arrived in the village—every time she is the one, she of all people, whom local folk approach for information when she is in a strange place—and promptly sent on by her, buzzing off, only to come to a halt around the next nocturnal corner, utterly at a loss, with his pizza box strapped to the rack on the back of his scooter.

And right after that, on his way to the main tent, the daytime roamer, the stonemason, with his tools dangling from his belt, who back on the *carretera* did not board the bus but wanted to continue on and on, on foot: so he, the pedestrian, reached Pedrada before her with the bus, and slips into the tent ahead of her.

And already as they were pulling into the village, the regular driver, having regained his strength and, sitting upright in front next to her in a long, lightweight fur coat, seemingly whisked there by magic, holding his Labrador by the collar, inseparable from him, pointing out the parking lot to her, an orchard—so in the meantime such a thing existed even up here in the mountains—and later clearing a path to the inn-tent for her and the other woman through the nocturnal throng of pedestrians in the semidarkness, and once inside leading the two of them straight to the quarters assigned to them for the night, transformed from a bus driver, a role he was playing perhaps only for the day, into the administrator of the yurt village and the district.

And on the way from the bus, now parked in the orchard next to another that resembled it like a twin, the other woman traveler identified herself as someone who had accompanied her once before, and actually for a not inconsiderable length of time, for days, indeed—memory now chimed in—for weeks, not on a journey, but rather from workplace to workplace, from appointment to appointment, from outskirts to downtown and back again, to write the cover story on her for an Italian? Brazilian? magazine—the heroine of the feature no longer remembered which—but now, walking somewhat behind her and addressing her back, explained: she was traveling the Sierra on her own this time, not as an author, let alone as a journalist, which she had been, by the way, only for a while and for the purpose of earning a living, and she had intentionally not brought any of her professional tools with her on this journey, neither her computer (she said *ordenador*) nor her hand telephone (*portable*)—besides, there was "no service" for the Pedrada region, at least at the moment—not even a notepad and pencil; in fact, she had set out for the Sierra without any luggage, any encumbrance, so as to forget how to speak and in fact forget all her languages; whereupon a memory image of this former author finally came to the woman to whom she was speaking: the image of a terribly young woman always tottering along on high heels, constantly blushing, with tears forever welling up in the corners of her eyes for no apparent reason, the image most sharply focused on the wheel-less suitcases, weighing a ton, and the equally heavy gear bags dragging down both her shoulders, all of which she had hauled from a great distance, if not from far-off countries, to their fleeting rendezvous, and always without help, always "alone" (in the sense in which a woman in her land of origin, when company arrived unexpectedly or a telephone call came and she had a man with her, would say defensively, "I'm not alone just now").

And on the basis of the image she turned to face the other woman, now following in her footsteps with hands completely free: how "terribly young" and "alone" the woman, the girl, still was, and yet how small, how tiny she appeared in the current surroundings, out in the orchard as well as inside the hotel tent, although today, too, she was wearing high-heeled shoes, but this time more sturdy ones: "My God, you're so little!" said her former feature-article heroine, in a hoarse voice and clearing her throat, as if for her, too, this were the first time she had spoken out loud this day; and this exclamation, furthermore using the intimate form of "you," uttered by her, who in the past had never exchanged a personal word with this writer, expressed a friendliness surprising even to the speaker herself—sounding entirely different from the way "My God, she's so big!" would have sounded—conveying immediate affection, after which she grabbed her fellow traveler under the arms, as if to confirm that she was really walking along without luggage, with hands and arms free, this woman to whom she had extended only the tips of her fingers back in the days when they met in major cities.

Ultimately one was most surprised there in Pedrada, in the innermost reaches of the Sierra de Gredos, by oneself, above all by the way one interacted with others, for instance with this woman whom one knew more or less, or hardly at all, from the world outside: by the words and gestures that became possible when one met, words and gestures unthinkable "out there in the world," and by how matter-of-factly they came out of one. Did these expressions, of which one would previously have considered oneself incapable, perhaps have to do with the so-called remoteness of this place? And also with a shared sense, perhaps imagined, of vulnerability? And what did "remote from the world" mean?

The individual sleeping quarters in the Milano Real II consisted of tents inside the tent, arranged more or less in a semicircle at the back, along the walls of the mother tent; not made of wood and clay like the big tent, but of classic tent material, though not of one in common use; each one—there were only a dozen such "tent rooms"—in another color of the spectrum, from which the little tent also got its name; and instead of being conical or pyramidal in form, cube-shaped, except for the concave back wall, which at the same time was part of the wall of the main structure.

She had never seen and touched a material like that of her tent chamber, dubbed "Orange," or *Burtuqal*. Completely opaque from the outside, although a bedside lamp was lit, from the inside the material allowed one in some places to see the neighboring tents and especially the front part of the tent inn, which was left free of smaller tents and was several times larger than the sleeping area in the back.

For a moment she thought she was at home in the riverport city, in her office, likewise located way at the back of the floor for top management, where, without having been visible herself, she had been able to follow the goings-on in the open-plan office outside through a wall of one-way plate glass instead of a cloth wall. ("Had been able to"? "having been visible"?: Did this mean that all that was a thing of the past? over and done with forever?)

The tent material somewhat resembled a patchwork, though without detectable seams; in one place it felt like brocade, in the next like jute, in the third like silk, and in another more like a man-made fiber, with what seemed like temporary patches here and there of plastic or even waxed paper. Although it would have been possible for her to look outside through the holes, tears, and slits that seemed to have been made intentionally in the rear wall of her night-tent, forming a sort of aperture and at the same time delicately chiseled ornamentation, she decided instead to survey the neighboring sleeping tents and the wide interior space under the dome of the main tent. After this day of being in constant motion, almost always with very distant horizons up ahead, she did not want to see any more of the world outside; did not want to have to see anything outside the walls of the inn; also did not want to set foot that night outside the curtain at the entrance to the tent.

But certainly to look through the cloth walls: at the likewise opaque tent walls to her right and left, which allow one to sense a forehead leaning against the material or a fist being clenched—this one called "Violet," or *Banafsadzi*, the sleeping place of the former magazine writer, still blushing blood red; the other one, "Gray," or *Aswad*, where the hiker or stonemason who refused a ride is sleeping; and looking straight out at the great hall, as big as a barn, or the barn as big as a hall—the area in front of the semicircle of rooms is in fact something between the great room of an inn and a threshing floor—empty except for a long supper table, extending from one mud-and-wood wall to the other, set with dishes in some places, cleared in others, and in places crowded with useless stuff.

Nothing else but these many tables, pushed together along a ragged diagonal in the front portion of the lodging tent. And this area without any partitions: a single high, broad expanse, illuminated by lightbulbs dangling from the dome, which in the uneven flow of current from the generators sometimes glow, sometimes flicker, sometimes just splutter and intermittently go completely dark for a fraction of a second, and in this fashion give the impression of being constantly rocked back and forth by a draft (but aren't the light fixtures actually rocking?).

No kitchen in the place; no sideboard; no heater; no reception desk (if El Milano Real Roman Numeral Two is even supposed to be a proper hotel); no credit-card stickers at the entrance or exit, or were there? that one, lone little sign there, a logo completely unfamiliar to her—and that was something—also faded and seemingly long since invalid, that particular card out of circulation, from a prehistoric credit-card era, so to speak, the emblem unrecognizable from a distance, even if she had eyes as sharp as the red kite.

The only place where the dining hall has other decoration is on the walls, at the same time forming the exterior walls of the structure. Hanging cheek by jowl on nails of all sizes, driven at random into the clay stucco and wooden ribs, on hooks, some of them bent downward, and on loops, are—not pots and pans but fire extinguishers (loose, not screwed to the wall), strikingly many of them; also guns (they, too, like the credit-card plaque, seemingly no longer current, but on the other hand no mere souvenirs, not decor, but ready for firing); first-aid kits and pouches (at least as numerous as the extinguishers); gas masks (these being the most numerous wall objects, from infant- to hydrocephalic-sized, a whole slew of them—was that expression still used?—a question thrown in by the Mancha-author, who had been away from the land of his mother tongue for a long time); and in between, there, and there! a stringed musical instrument, one unfamiliar to her, hanging by its strap, but for the most part wind instruments, trumpets and clarinets, and also an accordion.

And the floor of the inn-tent—only now does she take this in—is covered with carpets, some fairly shabby, partially covering a wild-strawberry-red kilim or a peacock-blue Isfahan. And the man sitting motionless in one of the particularly dusky corners of the hall or barn or tent, seemingly waiting for the supper guests, in a collarless white shirt, ripped in places, and an all the more flawless waistcoat trimmed with silver braid under his ermine, is the same older man who was being carried in a litter over the old Puerto de Menga during the day, who reminded her of the *emperador* who centuries earlier was carried the same way to his place of retirement in the southern spurs of the Sierra de Gredos.

And the stocky dog lying at the threshold to the tent, on a particularly thick carpet, still belongs to its owner, the previous bus driver who is just now entering, but it is not stocky, but—only now will she have noticed this, through the wall of her chamber—pregnant ("One does not say 'pregnant,'" she corrected her author, "one says 'with young'").

21

The bus driver or hotelier drummed the guests together for the mountain supper. In point of fact, he did not actually bang on a drum, nor did he blow one of the trumpets; he merely ran a bow over that one stringed instrument, over its single string, thickly plaited out of horsehair or whatever, moving the bow back and forth, forth and back, without stopping: a bellowing sound, in which the woman who alternately blushed and went pale heard a "sobbing," while the other woman heard "an animal in heat," a third person heard "the opening measures of a long ballad, which will accompany us through the meal and after that into sleep"—a narrative song that then did not materialize after all.

It was not only the three of them but almost a dozen who came, a few at a time, to the table under the dome of that high tent or barn, most of them from the cloth chambers, but also some from the outside.

It was also from the outside that the innkeeper brought in the food. There were several courses. What they consisted of in particular—as she indicated later to the author—was of no relevance to the story. "I contributed only a couple handfuls of the chestnuts I had brought along from the riverport city, a rare delicacy in the northern Sierra—strangely enough, some of them were already starting to sprout."

But what did matter: that the dishes were brought in each time from the outside. One sensed, smelled, and tasted that they had been cooked in the open air, on outdoor fires; that local water had been used, from all those tributary brooks, one of them right behind The Red Kite, and the river they converged to form; and that the dishes were served almost the instant they were ready. Did not one row of tents in the village, the one directly on the Tormes, consist of fishermen's tents, open on the side facing the water?

"Served"? No, they were wheeled in—by the chauffeur, aka innkeeper, who moved with the light-footedness found perhaps only in someone who but a short while ago had been lying there as if weighed down with stones—wheeled in on a four-wheeled serving cart similar to those that at one time—this story was taking place in an entirely different time—had been standard equipment in the state-operated hotels and restaurants of the communist states or countries of various stripes: the familiar squealing of the wheels, seemingly a thing of the past, even more piercing indoors on the carpets, on which the vehicle repeatedly got hung up, than outside in the alleys between the tents, but always audible there from almost infinitely far off as it approached the diners, creaking around innumerable corners, in that respect, too, a throwback to the achievements of the Eastern bloc or some other bloc that had hurtled into the pit of time.

Unlike the usual waitstaff in those days, the man steering the cart today hopped from one foot to the other as if in a surfeit of high spirits, dancing from guest to guest and serving each one with heartwarming delight.

And one's heart needed warming. As in the glass bus during the day, throughout Pedrada, despite the tents, a persistent menace, growing from one second to the next, could be detected.

The fact that it was night, that no more low-flying planes and big-bellied helicopters were to be heard, nothing but a sporadic, almost outer-space-like, quasi-peaceful hum (could one still use the term "quasi"?), surely from an intercontinental aircraft, did nothing to assuage the almost universal feeling of defenselessness, of vulnerability, of teetering on the edge.

With the faltering of the generators, the lightbulbs kept going out and then coming on again with apparent difficulty (causing those dining beneath them to alternate between opening their eyes wide and squinting), which made for great uncertainty; the filaments in the bulbs, which they instinctively turned their heads to look at while engaged in the most enjoyable eating and most animated conversation (in spite of everything), appeared each time they met the eye as the fine, superfine, spiderweb-fine threads that they indeed were; which also suggests, however, that this sensation of being in danger was not the prevailing one and could be felt only on the edges of the group of diners.

From the very beginning, even before everyone had taken a seat at the table, a general exchange and mutual sharing sprang up in the center of the group, independent of the external uncertainty.

The *emperador*, or the actor playing the emperor in a historical film being shot just then in the Sierra, or whatever he was, had taken his place at the head of the table as one of the dinner guests. In spite of his ermine cloak, he was visibly shivering as he sat there surrounded by his bearers or fellow actors. His seat was an upside-down fruit crate, padded with an old automobile tire. His plate was of an alabaster- or quince-blossom-white porcelain, his cutlery, however, of plastic.

At the foot of the table, or the other head, the actual one, sat a small family, a very young father and even younger mother, barely even a teen-ager, and an infant with enormous blue eyes: their spoons, forks, and knives were of heavy silver, as if just fetched out of an old chest, while their plates consisted of fragments of earthenware held together with wire, and for drinking—the beverages also came from outside—the boy and girl, that is to say, the parents, had a single paper cup, with which they toasted the others, who raised their various coffee cups (with something other than coffee in them), crystal goblets, tin cups (like the drinking vessels in Westerns), athletic trophies, or entire bottles and the like to the youthful parents, he perching on a bus seat, still attached to its frame, while she lounged in a sort of choir stall, as if in a wing chair.

In similar fashion, the table, which took up the entire length of the hall, was not all of a piece. On closer inspection, one saw that it consisted of several tables, of varying heights and widths; here and there a door removed from its hinges, a plain board, even the roof of a car, all resting on sawhorses; a barrel, a chest-high library stepladder, a piece of a raft. This entire table was covered with empty fruit and potato sacks of a coarse material, true to a Pedrada tradition: as the innkeeper explained, this was supposed to assure good harvests in the coming year.

What, harvests at such an altitude? Yes, hadn't they seen the apple orchards? And the fields of stubble near the Peña Negra Pass? And Navalperal de Tormes, the pear-growing village? And up here, where oats, rye, wheat, and even peaches grew (the latter in sheltered spots) amid the cliffs and boulders, didn't other crops flourish even more reliably—the *patatas*, potatoes, also known as *krompire*, or, in the Arabic still alive in many expressions, *batatas*?

The story goes that during that evening meal no one spoke while others were speaking, or interrupted anyone else. Only one person spoke at a time, and all the rest, even those way down at the other end of the table, listened; apparently no one had to raise his voice, and the rattling of the generators outside actually served as a kind of sound carrier.

As the story tells us, the first to begin to speak was the former Friulian or Argentinian magazine writer. And at the same time it was clear that everyone would have a turn to address the others during the time they spent together. Without blushing, the young woman, instead of looking around while speaking, gazed directly at the person who had been the subject of her magazine piece years earlier.

What she said, however, was not meant only for the ears of the powerful banker, or whatever she was, or had been. We are told that she probably fixed her eyes on this person because her face was the only one she recognized in the gathering, and even more because she believed, no, was convinced, that she would come to know this person, encountered unexpectedly and, what is more, in a decisive, yes, decisive location, set apart and remote from the places familiar to the two of them, in a decisively different way, yes, decisive from this day on, just as she, speaking here in a foreign setting and teetering on the edge, would show herself in an entirely different light to her former interviewee, as well as to the others and to herself.

As she spoke, she occasionally twisted a rusty tin can that stood in front of her, filled with a bouquet of dog-rose canes covered with fruit, red as only rose hips can be; while the speakers coming after her twirled in the same fashion rock crystal vases, jade goblets, old beakers missing their caps and handles, discarded baby bottles, ink wells, tin tea caddies, bronze mortars, and so on, while in each of these "vases" were the same bright rose-hip-red rose-hip bunches, which, according to the bus-driving tent-innkeeper, had been used for centuries in the Sierra de Gredos to ward off melancholy or to protect one against snow-blindness, a life-threatening danger especially for those crossing the mountains now in the winter months, and emphasized in the guide to local dangers. Like the rest of the company, the pale young woman had not changed for dinner. And likewise everyone's hairdo had remained the same.

And nonetheless she looked, as did those next to her, as if she had not come there from the present, or rather, only from the present. Without being in costume or dressed up, with the possible exception of the "emperor" or "king" or whatever he was—but was that really a costume?—they sat there as if at a time boundary, on the one hand clearly in the current era, and on the other hand, in the next moment and breath, perhaps even more clearly and distinctly in a second era, from which a curtain had been suddenly raised behind one, not a bygone period, not a historical one, also not one at odds with the present or a merely imaginary one: no, a period as undefined as undefinable, one that existed in addition to the current one, a present offering expanding possibilities and all the more real or tangible.

This new era found its clearest image in the persons of the adolescent couple and their small child. They sat there, as one can sit there only now, in the moment, on a winter evening, quite high in the mountains, with flushed cheeks, tired yet intermittently wide awake (the woman who had commissioned the book rejected the expression "full of beans" proposed by the author): also very contemporary, she with yellow and green streaks in her hair, he with blue and silver streaks in his, both of them wearing their hair cropped short, both of them wearing an identical single tiny earring, of aluminum or some such—and the next moment this very up-to-date couple, moved as it were ("Strike 'as it were'!") into a new dimension, distant and deep, out of sight and at the same moment unexpectedly close—"something artificial and virtual images can simulate only feebly and deceivingly"—were vouchsafed an additional present, incomparably stronger and above all more durable than the previously mentioned presents, which nonetheless also remained in view, "and the durability of this image in comparison to a virtual one is like that of infinity to zero!"

She then tried to explain to the author that a splendid present like this, "beyond any doubt the most splendid possible," in the image of the youthful couple, had its origins, among other things, in the distance between them as they sat there, a distance not entirely usual "nowadays": "This distance between her and him was now, and more than simply now."

And, as she explained, part of it was that both the boy and the girl held themselves remarkably erect, their torsos, necks, and heads, one the spitting image of the other, and likewise hardly turning toward each other, each of them constantly looking straight ahead, their eyes focused on the rearmost horizon of the tent hall, yet "not at all" fixedly, and their upright, erect sitting beside each other was remarkable not in the sense of "strange" or "weird," but rather in the sense of "noteworthy" or "wondrous" or, yes, "moving": "first re-presenting" that which was present.

Accordingly, she said, the young couple, together with the infant, who chewed alternately on his mother's and his father's finger with his first teeth—they allowed it without wincing—seemed to be inside yet another tent, an invisible one, not measurable but just as, yes, just as substantial as the one of mud and wood, as the ones of tent material or whatever.

She went on to mention that this scene suddenly brought to mind the only remaining photo of her parents, killed in an accident: the two of them likewise almost still children, long, long before her birth, during or shortly after the end of the war, side by side, ramrod straight, sitting on a felled tree trunk at the edge of a clearing near the village, and, in addition to their similar way of gazing into the distance, dressed almost exactly the same, as far as fabric, pattern, and cut went, as the couple here with their very trendy hairstyle and -color—"timeless"—neither urban nor rustic, and certainly not in folk costume (Sorbian or any other)—simply white and black—which had nothing to do with the fact that the photo was in black-and-white. And just as every time she envisioned her (future) parents as perching there together in a prewar period, contrary to the facts, now in the present she saw their two revenants ("not at all returned from any kingdom of the dead") the same way.

And drawn into this present, perhaps preceding a war but on this night even more tangibly peaceful, was the "itinerant stonemason," having seemingly drifted there like a ghost, previously on the *carretera* and then, upon entering the tent-inn, from some medieval period, and likewise the "first and last local and pan-European emperor," as if on the way to a *son-et-lumière* spectacle, in the park at Aranjuez, let us say, conceived as the crowning event in the annual historical reenactment there, carried over the Sierra in his legendary litter to his final resting place, together with his entourage: all of them, though seemingly disguised and their bodies transported by their disguises to a distant, dusty, dilapidated past, which no living images could revive (they least of all), protruded from their earlier time—if they indeed came from some such—with their shoulders, necks, and heads, into a present as vivid as any, and next to this one the current present seemed dimmer than any allegedly dark past.

"Sometimes I have the same sensation," the author is said to have replied, "when I see portraits of people from earlier centuries, paintings, copper engravings, woodcuts: initially the faces usually look not only remote in time, but also entirely foreign, alien, incomprehensible, belonging to a human type diametrically opposite to me, as a man of today, but as I gaze at them, they often come alive for me as wonderfully approachable, colorful, lively beings, such as are now revealed to me in my daily surroundings only at sacred, or rather blessed, times. Goodness gracious!" — Her reply: "That evening only one person was entirely rooted in the present, in nothing but today. But I do not want you to have him appear in our story until later." — The author: "A photographer?" — She: "Yes, a photographer, among other things. But how do you know?"

The earlier writer of the magazine story, constantly turning toward her earlier heroine, began to speak and revealed herself as follows: "Once I was a friend of other people's stories. *Fui una vez amiga de historias ajenas.* At least I played that role, or wanted to play it, or had to play it. Now I know nothing of others anymore, and have no desire to know anything, and above all do not pretend to know anything about this person or that or about you. *No sé nada.* I know nothing.

"And I am no longer a friend of knowing about others' lives. *No soy amiga de saber vidas ajenas.* How alien, cold and abruptly alien, clearly alien for all time, every person, in truth, appeared to me from the outset, men as well as women, also children, closer relatives as well as much more distant ones, aunts and uncles, nephews and nieces, once to three times removed. Especially the aunts and uncles, the nephews and nieces. How incomprehensible people appeared to me, and how little I understood how anyone could describe another person, tease out traits, characteristics, and idiosyncrasies, and knit them into an ostensibly recognizable figure. What I perceived instead was a cloth doll. Even when someone did this only in the presence of one other person, even when I recognized the person being described, or thought I recognized him, it seemed to me that the whole thing was a swindle, and that even a—what is the term?—lifelike description of a person was simply not right, was indecent, presumptuous.

"Just as there is a prohibition on images that is rooted in our consciousness, or in instinct, above all in respect to the human face, it seemed to me that there was also a sort of prohibition on description, again where the human face was concerned.

"And all the more so when the describing no longer occurred only in the presence of one other person but in society! And all the more so when it became public! And all the more so when it was done in writing, in an article or even a book! And why did it have to be me to whom all the individual strangers became even more alien, if possible, in descriptions, or ceased to exist altogether!—the pseudo-descriptions and imitations, especially those considered most successful, had the most devastating effect—why did it have to be me who came upon or stumbled into a profession or business whose stock in trade was public description, captured in black-and-white, of individuals, of 'people'!

"If it had at least been a question of capturing a nation, or of people in the aggregate. Human masses and crowds were alien to me, too, but alien in a different way, at least sometimes, not as indescribably foreign as all the nine hundred ninety-nine individuals whom I pried loose and nailed to the page, from the color of their eyes, to their gums, to their shoe size, to their way of walking, shaking hands, brushing the hair back from their forehead, their voices, the shape of their ears, the shape of their chins, their shoulders, their furniture, their pets, their gardens, their vehicles, their preferences, their recurring dreams, their perfume, their failed suicide attempts, their hidden guilt, their forbidden love, their secret ambition in life.

"And even when all the details were correct, and as a rule they were, I knew that my descriptions, my descriptions of people and persons, were nothing but a deception and a distortion. How did I know that? I just knew it. I knew it if for no other reason than that every detail had to be striking. There was no demand for a detail that was not striking. I knew it? My disgust knew it, my disgust at describing your lips, your skin, your nostrils, your way of driving a car, your way of crossing your legs, or not, as the case might be, of opening the door for others, of keeping your eyes closed for a long time, of remaining constantly attentive, of reading people's lips and eyes, of suddenly clenching your fists, of striking your head with your fist. My disgust at describing, and then at you and at me.

"But now that I no longer need to find anything striking about my subjects, now that I do not need to publish such things, these people have become a tad less alien to me, and above all alien in a different way. Now that I no longer pretend to be a friend of others' lives, to understand them, to write and put in circulation true stories about them, I have begun to discover a new world. Now that I do not need to know anything about you—now that I no longer have to focus on someone as the subject or object of a story that must be written, I know that I can be more open with you, with him—" (turning toward the stonemason) "before him—" (turning toward Carlos Primero, alias Charles V) "before all of you—" (opening her eyes and taking in all the others at the table at a glance) "more open in general." (With each gaze now, and now, and now, a blushing deeper than ever before, as if on the verge of a great anger or some other powerful emotion.)

"Only now, with my fundamental ignorance, my ignorance as my foundation—heaven knows, facile paradoxes and plays on words still crop up from my story period!—instead of writing *about* you, I could write you *up*, write you *off*, write *around* you.

"And I was never as frank as tonight in Pedrada, here in the innermost Sierra. I sense, I know, that today I could discover you, you and you, and all of you, instead of revealing this or that about you, guessing, and putting it into a false context. During the bus ride, with the first rotation of the wheels, everything I had known about you earlier was already canceled—no previous life, no roles, no position, and in its place the desire to discover you, to tell your story again in discovery mode, the very opposite of the scoop that was once my first commandment.

"Except that now I no longer write, not out of disgust at writing, at writing implements, at paper, at the computer. My not-writing-anymore comes from a sort of lightheartedness; giving up writing has left me more light of heart and friendly. And now that I keep my hands off anything remotely connected with script and texts, I see that I am, in fact, yes, fact! a friend of others' lives. The more alien your life, your lives, the more open I am to them.

"And how strange our story seems to me, precisely here; ¡Soy amiga de vidas ajenas! ¡Soy amiga de historias ajenísimas! Mi emperador, let us see a few moments of your unknown story. And you, you are not really the banking empress I once had to interview across three continents, are you? Or you are no longer that? Ah, goodness gracious, I still have all these questions. But at least they are only spoken and are not intended for publication."

Now the response of the woman to whom these remarks were primarily directed: "And you ask different questions now. For I recall how in the old days you talked almost constantly, always in the same soft, childlike voice. But simultaneously, gazing into my eyes with your own large eyes, you were ready to pounce. You were intent on trapping, catching, pinning down—not necessarily me as a person but a predetermined, predictable, printable—what was the word I used at the time?—scenario, extending beyond me to a situation, a state of affairs, a current issue. You also talked constantly about your own stories, worries, dreams, adventures, including your adventures in love, perhaps not entirely made up on the spur of the moment—for the purpose of worming corresponding confessions out of strangers.

"Not even for a brief second were you free of suspicion. The suspicion implicit in your questions was the very foundation, the basis of your profession, and once your suspicions were confirmed in one way or another, you stripped me, and all the others, of my, and their, little and not-so-little secrets and then left us there, the way a pickpocket, or rather a nest-robber, leaves his victims, even if the word 'victim' is not entirely appropriate? No, it is. And what are you living on these days? How are you earning your living now that you have given up describing people?"

The fellow passenger: "For a while it was an important piece of information in a story whether a person had money, and where it came from, and so on. But for this story of ours, this evening's story, that has become irrelevant." Did that mean that she was in on the undertaking?

And the lady banker, replying only now to the question posed at the beginning and showing her hand: "It is true. Or at least it is likely that my banking days are over, and not only since this evening. It seems to me that all of banking is in a bad way, and not only since today. Yet I know that the core of my profession remains sound. It embodies, and continues to be, an idea that is not merely useful but essential. And this idea is almost unique, in that it pertains entirely to others, my contemporaries, and it can be summed up thus: being a big wheel. Wheeling and dealing. The banker as a trustworthy driver, with both hands on the wheel, moving other people's money. Showing forethought, foreseeing, forecasting, forestalling. Launching initiatives. Managing. And primarily seeing to it that you, my contemporaries, have time; that you do not waste your time worrying about money, hoping for profits and dreading losses.

"At present, however, a person in my profession manages less than he gambles. We gamble, and we gamble whether we want to or not. We are forced to gamble with money, with numbers, with products, with the markets. If our activity previously may have included an enjoyable element of play, in the form of an element of adventure—no, not of adventure, simply of entertainment—our work now consists of an excess of gaming; of gambling for profits, a compulsion to gamble for profits.

"And I reject this game. It is a misuse of the hands on the wheel, of the trusty driver's role. It should be prohibited. But who would prohibit it—when it is entire countries and the powerful who are most deeply involved? It has become a game that not only does not get things moving or move things in the right direction, but actually destroys them. I myself do not enjoy playing games, have never really learned to play. Yet the form of play that has been required of me recently is even more evil, cold, and lethal than chess: it is true that its main moves continue to consist of exercising forethought, foreseeing, forecasting, and forestalling, but all this has acquired a profoundly different significance. Banking and the stock exchange have come to consist almost exclusively of a cold, ruthless gambling for profit that has nothing to do with my idea of how I should be working.

"Being forced to play the game leaves me hardly any room for free play. And those who have recently entered our profession, because, as natural gamblers, or whatever they are, they have come to expect of it, and rightly so, a life like a game, now live in constant fear, even when they assert the opposite to their paying public. For this game cannot be mastered by even the most skillful players. In their dreams, and perhaps all too soon in reality, they are devoured by it from head to toe. They do not want to play anymore. But once started . . .

"Anyone who starts this game has to play it through to the end, and that is its most damaging feature. Luckily for me, in this case at least, I do not know how to play, and thus never began . . ."

The former magazine writer: "In our interview you did not so much as hint at any of this. Nor did you want to answer any questions about your brother in prison, your vanished child, the child's unknown father, and/or your lover at the time / at present. The only things you agreed to discuss were sturdy shoes, fruit trees—you favored me with a complete lecture on the particular white of quince blossoms—, chefs, seasonings (O saffron, O coriander), mountain-climbing techniques, the most remote island in the Atlantic, children's toys in the Middle Ages, weight distribution while one is ascending and descending mountains, the fragrance of linden blossoms in June—'the fragrance that seems to come from farthest away'—*My Darling Clementine*, and Westerns in general, hedgehogs, the beauties of night hiking, the best pencils, and so on, for days and nights on end.

"And now this brutal frankness—which would not have been suitable for the magazine anyway, or would it? And what will you do without your profession, without your wheeling and dealing? Establish a different kind of bank? An anti-gambling bank? Make a second film? Write a story about different types of pencils?"

She: "What I plan to do? Practice even more forethought. Do even more foreseeing and forecasting. Forestall even more usefully and necessarily. Make even more sure that along with me, now that I myself have time, plenty of time, this person or that also has time, plenty of time, time and more time. And perhaps learn to play at last. Not the profit game but a finder's game. Or simply become playful. And find my daughter again, here in the Sierra de Gredos. And find, here or elsewhere, my unknown lover. For he is alive, and he exists, just so you know, just so all of you know. And speak with my brother, not as I did during the last few years from the visitors' perch in the prison behind the dunes, where a dozen of us had to shout, and could not hear our own voices, let alone those of the people we were visiting. And perhaps also find the various small items I have lost here in the Sierra over the years, a scarf one time, a hair comb another time, a cap, a shawl—especially the shawl. Each time I was sure when I set out that along the road one of the objects from the previous year or the year before would gleam up at me, unharmed, in spite of storms, rain, and snow, and each time I ended up losing something else. But this time, just wait!

"And how in each of you here I see one of my near and dear. In you, dear interviewer, I see my daughter, whom I actually so often failed to recognize as my own child, even when she came through the door and stood before me. Ah, even on the day she was born, when she was brought to my room, I said to myself in that first moment: So who is this splendid newborn with this self-confident, seemingly cocky face, at the same time so vulnerable, looking ready to play? And later, when I was visiting a strange house with her, an unknown child unexpectedly came in the door from the garden or somewhere else, making not a sound, very pale—the pallor that you now display as well—and I thought to myself: Who in the world is this solemn, quiet child; never have I seen anyone so solemn, pale, and quiet in all my life—until it struck me that this was my own child, from whom I had been separated for less than a day. And even later, after her first disappearance—now that you are not interrogating me, I can reveal this to you—when I had hunted all summer, fall, and winter, always with her image in my head, and finally found her on the last island in the Atlantic, near the village of Los Llanos de Aridane, I want you all to know, and we were celebrating that evening, the two of us in the San Petronio restaurant—if you need these details—where I told her for the first time who her father was and that her father was alive: toward midnight, then, as today in the Milano Real Dos of Pedrada, when she had gone off for a little while, perhaps out to the street, to a boyfriend or someone, suddenly there was a young woman next to me, just as you are now, in profile, and I wondered, and not just for a moment, what this beautiful stranger was doing at my table; from what country she had washed up on this remote island; and how it happened that the stranger seemed so motherless and fatherless, or without any need of parents? And why, although it was not cold in the restaurant, a shiver kept running over her forearms, making the little hairs there stand on end?

"And turn your face to me now: Yes, she is the one. Yes, you are the one. And that man there in the ermine cloak, representing the abdicated king and emperor on the way to his final resting place on the southern flank of the Gredos, I greet as my grandfather from the village back home. He was a singer, but—if you want to know—not a singer of folk songs. Just like that old singer, you hold your head very high and will sing us something in a few minutes, with your high-pitched voice, as effortlessly and uninsistently as only an old singer can, nothing but pure voice, with at most a quarter of an eye on us. And just as with that singer in the last days of his life, together with your ermine and your gold-braided waist-coat, a strong odor emanates from you, almost a stench."

"Do you walk in your sleep?" (Here a question interjected by the former feature-article author.) — She: "I always have. And I see the itinerant stonemason there, or whatever he represents, as my brother, on the verge of killing a person for the first time. At the moment it is still just a ghost of a notion in him. But as soon as he speaks it out loud, he will, willy-nilly, be held to it and veritably obliged to do the deed. It was already the same with your violence toward objects, which landed you in the penitentiary: for a long time destruction was only one of your thoughts among many— but as soon as you had put it in words to one person, then another, then everyone you knew, it had to happen someday; you had no choice; no sooner said than done; having said it meant having to do it."

The stonemason, now revealing his feelings: "Never fear, sister. I will not say it, not tonight. But it is true: time and again I have been close to speaking the words, especially lately. Just a slip of the tongue, and the word would have been out there, with all the guards listening. And you, sister, made no small contribution to my destructive rage. Of course it is also true that in our village days you exercised forethought for me, foresaw for me, kindly forestalled things for me, forecast the coming day and the coming year, with my interests at heart.

"And it is also true that you never wanted anything for yourself, or at least not for yourself only. Everything you undertook was undertaken for the sake of someone else, also several someone elses, but primarily for the sake of me, the parentless child, the orphan. And although you were also an orphan, you did not see yourself as one, not once; as a child you were already self-sufficient, independent, the child of no one, the descendant of no ancestors, from the outset a person without any frame of reference: as little a villager as a person defined by the Slavic minority or the German nation, and then not someone from the economics department, either, or a person whose manner gave the slightest hint that she was a tycoon, just as you never behaved in a sisterly fashion, or as a lover—but that is something of which neither I nor anyone else has any knowledge, perhaps least of all your lover himself, if he in fact exists. You defied definition; you stood, moved, and acted solely and exclusively somewhere outside/on the periphery.

"Everything you did, as you conceived it, had to be done for someone else's sake, and at the time this someone was above all me, the orphan. It was impossible for you simply to do, look for, collect something without the thought that it was for me. But that did not stem from goodness, or from any intention to be helpful and useful—you just were, and are, that way; that is your nature, and perhaps, I often thought, your need to do things for others, and the way you become incapable of lifting a finger when you lose the image of a person, or persons, is even a sort of defect—your own personal sickness. Even in the old days, whenever you had to buy something, it could not be for you, even if you needed the item; and not until the idea of buying something or other came to you in connection with me could you set out to make the purchase.

"To pick an apple hanging just outside your window and eat it was out of the question, out of the realm of possibility: but to scramble up to the most precarious treetop for some fruit or other, so long as it was for me—no hesitation! And out in the woods you never popped the wild strawberries, or whatever you were picking there, straight into your mouth, not a single one: no matter how luscious you found all the little fruits of the field, no matter how avid you always were for the fruit and berries—you were capable of picking, hunting, and gathering only when thinking of someone other than yourself. And how dispirited and unmotivated you became when it was a question of harvesting only for yourself! That is sick, sister.

"And just as it is said of some people that they 'do not know how to share,' you, with this sickness of yours, sister, had the opposite compulsion—to share all the time. You no sooner got something in your hand, somehow or other, than you were already offering it to me or someone else—everyone in your vicinity—so as to share it. This gesture was completely involuntary; you could not help yourself—you had to share. Sometimes I experienced your gesture of sharing as aggression—you pushed the thing to be shared in my face, thrusting your arm at me violently. It was as if you had to crush me, and, later, various other people, against your ribs—

"One time you told me how you pictured yourself dying: while saving someone else's life. Ah, my poor sick sister. And you crushed me against your ribs in an entirely different way, too: by standing in for the father, not ours but one from the Old Testament. Just as the Old Testament fathers were ordered to beat their sons preemptively, again and again, so that evil would have no chance to take root in them, or would be nipped in the bud, you beat me in those days even before I did anything wrong, prophylactically.

"And I, and I, and I? How little I can say about myself, and then almost only what I am not. I am not like you—if for no other reason than that from the beginning I saw myself in relation to others, measured myself against others, compared myself with others, defined myself with reference to others. I was a villager if ever there was one. I was a Slav, or simply what was considered Slavic. I became a servant of God if ever an orphaned Slavic villager became one. And then, always a child of my time, or not of my time, and continuing to understand myself almost exclusively in relation to my contemporaries and in reaction to the spirit of the times, I became a destroyer."

The stonemason or wanderer fell silent for a while, took a deep breath, and then resumed speaking: "For a very long time in my life I hardly lived from within myself. Whatever I did or failed to do, wherever I was: I was dependent on someone or something else. A few dependencies actually helped me stand on my own two feet and enriched me. These were more like safety nets, signposts, lifelines, reference points. But the majority of my dependencies did not strengthen me but diminished me. That was especially true of my dependency on people.

"I do not know why, when I found myself in the company of others, and perhaps not even reluctantly, I would instantly feel like their slave, or at least like a subordinate. In the twinkling of an eye I would be transformed into an appendage or accessory; did not exist on my own; just flailed at the end of the more or less imaginary leash that tied me to the other person, or was transfixed, in a bad sense, under the person's spell, paralyzed.

"And each time this flailing or paralysis also made itself evident, too. Even when I was with strangers, on streets, in subways, in stadiums, I no longer acted but only reacted, magnetically attracted to the others, slavish, unfree. Even my way of walking, looking, standing, sitting, was determined entirely by my reaction to the walking, looking, standing, and so on of my fellow pedestrians, fellow onlookers, fellow travelers. Either I imitated them slavishly or I did the exact opposite, another form of slavish behavior: when they ran, I walked with exaggerated slowness; when they all looked into the arena, I pointedly looked away, at the sky or their faces, and so forth.

"Even in the presence of animals, especially that of pets, cats, dogs, cows, hens, rabbits, I fell into this kind of dependency and lost my freedom, fell under the spell of animal eyes, under the spell of animal movements. It was almost only in dealings with inanimate objects that I escaped from this flailing and paralysis under the yoke of others. Lacking any connection to others came to be the freedom that could replenish me. To create a frieze, consisting of the gazes of contemporaries! To be splendidly relieved of relationships, I thought, would mean to be ripe for what is real.

"As a stonemason I knew I was free of the community tether at least for the duration of my workday, yet not entirely alone. But soon even at work I fell into a kind of dependency, though one that for a while propped me up instead of crushing me: constantly stumbling in the others' present, and in the present altogether, I decided, as a stonemason, and this time not slavishly but full of determination, of my own free will, to forge a relationship with the historical period that I saw as most suited to me, the Middle Ages."

The mason paused. He took another deep breath. Not a soul interrupted him. He resumed his narrative, in a voice seemingly not emanating from him, with no visible movement of his lips, although in no way with the ghostly quality of a ventriloquist.

"I made up my mind not to be a person of the present day, to be someone not of today. I wanted to be, and then actually was, associated with the stone structures, and even more with the stone sculptures, from the eleventh, twelfth, and thirteenth European centuries. These faces, whose ears often stuck out, whose noses looked squashed, whose lips were thick, whose eyes protruded from their sockets, these were my people. They absolved me, and I, crisscrossing Europe for years, on one pilgrimage after another, from one extended family carved in stone to the other, absolved myself in their company, face-to-face, listened to them, let them infect me with that thick-lipped grinning, that way of listening while attending to what was going on inside one, with that imperturbable yet quietly empathetic gaze, which registered me and my background at once playfully and kindly.

"For whole days and years my sole contact, my exclusive communication, was with those stone dream-dancers, fortunately seldom hewn out of marble, mostly out of granite or a more friable stone. And, listen, all of you, I did not become eccentric as a result, but rather, through my daily involvement with them, I shook off any kind of eccentricity from earlier. And in silent conversation, face-to-face—yes, in their presence I felt my own blurry, slack face broaden, tighten, organize itself—I aired out my skull, into the farthest recesses of my brain, and then set out on my path with a clarity and energy such as I had rarely experienced, no, never experienced, in conversations with flesh-and-blood human beings.

"In the company of people from the Middle Ages, my chosen era, engaged day in, day out in dialogue, which was accompanied by tapping, sniffing, tracing their outlines, mimicking, in dialogue with my chosen people, which had long since ceased to be limited to those figures and works in stone, having expanded to include the heroic epics from that era, their plots continuing in me, as well as the illuminated initials in the old manuscripts and such, I envisioned spending the rest of my life in this period and passing my days on earth both peacefully and fruitfully, without ever again coming into contact, let alone collision, with present-day contemporaries, not a single one."

And this was the moment when, out of the clear blue sky, the stonemason and wanderer spread his arms before the Argentinian or Sardinian woman sitting next to him, or whatever she was, and the pale young woman, with a blush engulfing her entire face, let herself fall against him.

He hugged her. She threw her arms around him. The story tells us she embraced him. And he, as the story tells us further, locked his arms around her so tightly that she uttered a noise that sounded, though only in the first moment, like a wail. They held each other.

Or did the apparent wail actually come from him, or did it come from both of them? Or did it come from the male storyteller, or the female storyteller? And the story goes that the two of them remained in that position, eye to eye, as the wanderer and/or stonemason resumed his tale.

"But now it is all over with me and the Middle Ages. And the story of my involvement with the stone faces did not end only today—although perhaps it is not being fully recounted until today. The end of my relationship with them, and along with it that particular relationship to the world altogether, did not occur unexpectedly. These stone and painted and written models of composure, of fervent acceptance, of surrender, and of confident and sun-bright reason, which I saw as quintessentially medieval, inseparable from their hip angulation, faded only gradually, almost imperceptibly, did not leave me all at once, did not cease communication with me from one day to the next.

"Yet the way in which I found myself increasingly alone, almost imperceptibly yet steadily, struck me as all the more threatening. And finally I was left without them. They no longer said anything to me. I no longer said anything to them. I now had nothing to say or to give to anyone, to take from anyone, and likewise there was no longer anyone to say or give anything to me, to take anything from me. I no longer reacted to anything, either for good or for ill. I was alone. I was without a reference point. I am alone. I am lost."

The woman at his side said, more affirming than interrupting: "I, too, am lost."

The stonemason is said to have continued speaking, in an even deeper, more resonant voice: "But I am not giving up. My chosen era, the Middle Ages, is gone, once and for all. And so I must move to another period. I must find my way to others, against whom I can measure myself without shriveling up in their presence or letting myself be hemmed in and limited by them, or letting them clip all my antennae. I shall set out to find other people, people of now and today, in whose presence I can breathe a sigh of relief when I measure myself against them: people, living people, whose presence strengthens mine, as I do theirs. Such people must exist, even in the present. They do exist. It cannot be that I am lost and done for in the present. It cannot be that nowadays people like us have no choice but to perish."

The woman at his side: "No, we are not lost and done for."

They say the itinerant stonemason drew a deep breath, hit the table with one of his hammers, and picked up the thread again, addressing himself particularly to the woman who had commissioned the story: "In a transitional phase I was focused exclusively on destruction, just like your brother. I used these tools here no longer for constructing, shaping, laying stone upon stone, repairing, but for smashing, tipping, toppling, ruining. With my chisel I no longer struck shapes out of stone. I struck again and again, but not forms, and it was no longer only blocks of stone before me as earlier. With the mallet I split and smashed whatever lay in my path, anything that might have been used as a building block, let alone a cornerstone or a foundation. With my masonry saw I no longer sliced roofing slates and thresholds. With my masonry bit I drilled everything but friezes and ornaments, vents or drainage holes. With my level I measured everything but level surfaces. With my acetylene torch I cut everything but steel girders. Quite a few of the piles of rubble you encountered on your way through the Sierra were my doing."

As he spoke, the mason, so the story goes, fell to gesticulating, more and more wildly and less and less in control of his movements, and in the end he was so tangled up in his fingers, arms, and legs—the fingers of one hand jammed between his knees, one leg wrapped around the other and as if bolted to it, his second hand caught in an armpit, incapable of moving backward or forward—that he crouched there completely immobilized, tied in his own straitjacket, violently scrunched up, and with every attempt to free himself from this position merely squeezing himself more hopelessly and painfully into his self-induced jam.

And subsequently, so the story goes, the other one, the pale young woman at his side, the former magazine-story girl, took charge of this almost grotesque figure, entangled in itself like a medieval gargoyle, as follows: one after the other, she unraveled, separated, loosened, freed the various limbs of the man beside her, with astonishing effortlessness in fact, just plucking at one hand, tapping the other, patting a knee, rubbing an ankle.

And then the woman did the final untangling by blowing on him from a slight distance, that, too, without straining, very delicately, a mere puff, which reached, however, not only his face, but the entire body of the stonemason and solitary wanderer, widened his eyes and nostrils, expanded his shoulders, arched his thorax, bumped out his hips, curved his buttocks, tightened his thighs.

And then, according to the story, a first kiss was exchanged between the woman and the man, before the eyes of all the others in the midnight clay-wood inn-tent of Pedrada, in the innermost reaches of the Sierra de Gredos, a kiss from mouth to mouth, again something that had become the rarest of the rare in the particular period in which this story takes place, especially with others looking on, and, as in this case, downright festive. At this time one had to earn something like this! And the two had earned it.

And furthermore: the two kissed each other without touching in any other way. They remained seated with a space between them. And their hands were completely uninvolved. They both kept their hands motionless, wherever they happened to be. Before this the woman had taken a swallow from her paper cup. And even this drinking had been done without the assistance of her hands, merely with her lips, which she allegedly dipped into the drink, with her head bent. And the two are said not to have closed their eyes. On the contrary, as the story goes, they kept their eyes fixed on each other, without blinking.

And subsequently, in the background of the barn or hall of the Milano Real, for a moment a long-legged animal flitted past the sleeping tents, a deer? a gazelle? an ostrich (in the meantime they were being raised even up there in the mountains)? a Great Dane? And after the long kiss, *qubla* in Arabic, which lasted past the stroke of midnight—impossible to tell whether their tongues were involved; that was apparently superfluous— the new couple leaned back with a laugh, a soundless one, supposed to have lasted almost as long as the main thing just now. It was chiefly the stonemason, or whatever he was, who laughed, and, according to the story, it was the longest laugh of his life up to then, also one unlike any he had laughed before. ("'Laugh,' *djahika* in Arabic," the woman who had commissioned the story dictated to the author.)

That night he, like the woman, did not speak another word. But if he had said something, it might have been this, for example: "I once spoke twenty-four languages, and now I do not speak a single one. There: the spot of sunlight deep in the underbrush, by the ruins of the wall I knocked down: my departed mother!" Or he might perhaps have said:

"From now on I shall give the widest possible berth to all the people of to-day who are not my type, and not our type, and no good for you and me—I know that immediately, do I know it?—give the widest berth to the overwhelming majority, I know that—how do I know that?—and shall pass outside the range of their seeing and hearing and reality, but no longer slavishly and constrained by them, but rather of my own free will and with verve, strengthened by their kind of being or reality, pushing my-self off from that type, moving, with the help of their tyrannical omnipres-ence, away into a different, at least equally promising realm of reality, into a no less real reality, and thus, full of joy and in good spirits, staying as far as possible from those others, and at the same time, thanks to them, trac-ing or plotting the world around its edges, arc by arc, and this will be the world, this will yield a world; and those who are not my type, not our type, and not good for you and for me, and who fill me with the most profound disgust, will thus at least have been something for us; beyond the bound-aries of their world, the world of my world will begin, the genesis of the world will come into view, the worlding of our world—but what does 'my,' what does 'our' mean?"

And the woman would have said, "You wonder whether I am all dressed up this way for a man? For whom else? To be nothing more than a body, entirely body, all body, a single body. To matter. And for whom else but a man?"

And then, so the story goes, sometime after midnight, the king, em-peror, the one in costume, the actor or amateur player, or whatever he was, got up from his metal drum, or whatever it was, at the end of the table, or, more precisely, was heaved to his feet by his bearers or assis-tants, with considerable effort, and now began to sing, no longer sup-ported by anyone, in an ageless voice, clear and almost too high: "No more journeys! And no more flies flying into my mouth. And no more bat-tles, either in Tunis or in Mühldorf or in Pavia, either on water or on land. And no business transactions, no money chests, no more gold and silver routes. And no more popes, and no more of that alleged community of faith, which has long since become the greatest and most brutal of all sects. And no painter, and no paintings, and no more picture galleries.

"And no more summer residences. And no rivers, no río Guadalquivir in Seville, no río Guadiana in the Sierra Morena, no more río Tormes in the Sierra de Gredos. And no more love affairs, either in Regensburg or in Lodi or in Pedrada. And no more king and no more emperor. And no more music and no more fading of music into silence. And no more olive trees with roots like rocks. And no more reek of cadavers.

"And no more Flanders and no more Brabant. And no more godforsaken, seemingly insane mother. And no more sour milk. And no more woman and no more tears. And neither Turks nor French, neither Augsburgers nor Würzburgers nor Innsbruckers, and neither marks nor talers, neither dollars nor escudos, neither maravedi nor gulden for my songs anymore. And no more ibexes. And no more Sierra, Almanzor, Mira, or Galana. And no more apple trees. And no more wooden ladders propped against the apple trees. And no more blue pickers' tunics on the rungs of the ladders propped against the apple trees. And no patches on the blue tunics of the pickers on the rungs of the ladders propped against the apple trees.

"And no Lord have mercy, and no lift up your hearts, and no transubstantiation, and no more go in peace. And no more children's voices. And no more fountainheads and deltas. And no more Incas, Aztecs, Mayas, Cheyenne, Sorbs, Wends, Sufis, and Athabasques. And no more salt mines. And my lonely-hunter heart no more. And no more white angel. And no more moons in my fingernails, and no more nails on my fingers, and no more fingers on my hands. And no more sun never setting over my empire. And no more empire. And no more feral dogs. And no more dirt on my comb. And no more mountain passes and mountain taverns. And no more wild strawberries."

The singer, so the story goes, was carried back to his tent as soon as his song ended, as if to die. And in that night the last word belonged to that guest at the table who had barely been mentioned up to then (except that he seemed to be the only one "entirely of the present," "unmistakably of today"). He set down his cutlery—he had been the first to start eating and now was the last to finish—and said, in a voice that sounded as if it had been trained for years in front of microphones, in radio studios, or elsewhere: "To an outsider such as myself, it immediately becomes apparent that your most frequently used expressions are 'not,' 'no,' 'neither this nor that,' 'not he, not she, not that, but.' You express yourselves chiefly in negations, evoke and define yourselves and your concerns almost exclusively *ex negativo*, by reference to something that you and your concerns are not, or are no longer, or are on the contrary or in contrast to. To judge by the words you use, your experiences in particular consist almost entirely of things you have not experienced, or at least not in the way that would be considered experiences elsewhere. To all of you, experience often means something diametrically opposite to what is commonly called 'experience' elsewhere. As a result, almost all of your so-called stories consist chiefly of negations. They are the stories of things that did not happen. You did not go to war. You did not cross the tracks. No one has read today's paper. No one fired at you. You did not see anyone throwing stones. No black smoke billowed out of any window. No one placed the noose around someone's neck.

"What kind of happenings do you have? What kind of stories are these, without observations and without images—at least without planned, balanced, and well-observed images; without recourse to anything a contemporary audience would consider eventful; without reference to the realities, either individual or even societal—which you people either proudly avoid or about which you sanguinely keep silent—as if the rest of us, *nosotros*, could guess them by ourselves or could figure them out.

"Stories like yours, which primarily tell about things someone does not do, and furthermore without any illustrations, without close-ups, without the camera's viewfinder: to the rest of us, these without a doubt simply do not count as stories. They are actually a kind of stinginess. You stint with yourselves and your experiences. Instead of plunging into life in front of the rest of us, you hurl yourselves into thin air.

"Your way of eating and drinking conforms to that. I have been observing you all evening; I am here for purposeful observation, you know, not for pointless fantasizing: you leave not a single crumb, not a scrap, and not only on your plates. You pick up the tiniest morsel that has fallen to the ground and shove it into your mouths. Not a speck on the table or on your clothes that is not scraped off by you people and licked up. You people, *vosotros*, lick every bowl and suck every glass to the last blob and the last drop. That is what I have observed.

"No doubt about it: you all live in a state of inexpressible deprivation. You doubtless lack most of the basic things that create social bonds between people of today and make them contemporaries of the rest of us. You convey to us the image not merely of cardsharps but of possible criminals, capable of an appalling act of violence, which you perhaps committed long ago and keep secret here: which is no doubt also the reason for your non-stories, consisting primarily of evasions, distractions, avoidances, and deflections."

The postmidnight speaker had delivered these remarks with that un-wavering, pasted-on smile for which he was known throughout the civilized world at the time of this story, known from newspapers and even more from television, the smile that viewers of the day found "simpatico," to use one of the terms fashionable at the time: according to contemporary viewers, his lips were always drawn back in a friendly expression, which created "dimples" in his cheeks and a steady "warm glow" in his "fawn-colored" eyes, or, as others would have it, "tawny eyes."

And while speaking he had propped his legs on the table, "not as a provocation, but to show that in spite of everything he felt at home even here among them, even in the notorious region of Petrada, and to make the others less shy." For the same reason he had slipped in the two little words in their native language mentioned above, even though *nosotros* and *vosotros* were all the Spanish, or Iberian, or whatever, that he knew.

Now he stood up and prepared to leave, still with his tried-and-true smile. Of course he did not pay: that would presumably be taken care of by the organization by which he had allowed himself to be sent out, since early in life, as an observer and reporter, and, after missions here and there, now into the Sierra? Unlike the other supper guests, he would not be spending the night in The Red Kite but "in modest private lodgings," in one of the infinitely smaller and less comfortably appointed tent huts with a local family, as he always did, "to be as up-close and personal as possible to the pulse of the local happenings." And according to his fellow observers, as he made his way out of the hall, in the flickering of the light-bulbs, his "boyish freckles and chubby cheeks" and his "eternally rebellious Irish-red hair" showed all the more distinctly.

Other eyewitnesses, however, did not see him leave on foot but rather on a low-slung wheeled chassis, as if drawn by invisible spirits, while he looked straight into a camera being pulled a slight distance ahead of him, whereupon his presence in the half-barbarian mountain hamlet was beamed simultaneously to all the civilized channels. The way in which he moved along just above the ground: was that not in fact a form of being driven, pushed, and pulled, in which he bestirred neither knees nor arms nor shoulders, unlike a person walking?

And now, when he had already reached the door, and stood there for a few seconds, as if expecting the door to the clay tent structure to open automatically, a woman got up from among the crowd of those other eyewitnesses, approached him with giant steps, and, forgetting her image, her office, and her feminine dignity, gave him a kick, only one, but a powerful one, sufficient to propel the reporter through the door, which, before it closed, briefly swung out again, like the door to a saloon.

The report on his stay among the people of Pedrada that he later published all over the world claimed not to be influenced in any way by this incident. Some of the observations captured in the report are supposed to be incorporated later by the book's heroine into the book on the loss of images and on crossing the Sierra de Gredos; but this is not yet the place for that.

2 2

She stayed up all night.

The others were sleeping in their tent compartments at the back of the big tent, or at least were lying there in their beds. She cleared the table as usual, washed up, put things in order, stacked the dishes. Then she sat alone for a while at the bare table—the lightbulbs out at last; no more roaring of the generators—in a shimmer of light that came from the mica cliffs outside.

Later she sat in her tent, almost without light, and later still she made the rounds of the other tents, going from one to the other. She kept watch. But it is also possible that as she sat there, her eyes open, she occasionally dozed off.

And all night long, whether she was awake or dozing for a moment, a pain was gnawing inside her ("an ache," she told the author), which, if it were to continue, would break her heart. Not only her more or less random entourage, but all of Pedrada, the entire population of the innermost Sierra, was asleep or lying in bed.

At one point she felt cold, in a way that otherwise only a person abandoned by God and the world can feel cold. She was freezing, wretchedly, from inside out. Had she been abandoned by God and the world? "No." Little by little, the inhabitants of the village came to mind. Although she had seen them for only a few seconds, upon the bus's nighttime arrival, on the way to the parking lot in the orchard and to the Milano Real, an image had remained with her. And as she thought of the images, she felt warm again.

She had been in Pedrada several times before. Each time there had been some small change or other. But this time almost everything seemed new, and not merely the tent colony at the confluence of the various tributaries of the Tormes. In the crowd of nocturnal roamers outdoors, the natives were clearly in the minority. For one thing, most of them, as quasi-mountain-dwellers, were unaccustomed to a *corso* and had long since withdrawn into the few ancestral stone houses. And then, since her last sojourn here, the last stop before any crossing of the Sierra, the population had evidently increased considerably. A mighty influx had occurred.

And the new residents were apparently all still up and about, despite the lateness of the hour, outside the tents, which in general had long since ceased to be provisional housing. And what was special about all this bustle: though elbow to elbow, cheek by jowl with the others, each person seemed entirely alone. This movement also no longer had anything in common with a *corso*. Not that those walking side by side and those coming toward them paid each other no mind: it was a given that for all the individuals, there were no others, or, rather, he or she, that particular man or this particular woman, existed for and mattered to no one but him- or herself (and even that was questionable).

Each person in the crowd was making his own circuit?—and at the same time followed attentively in the tracks of the person just ahead of him; paid attention to the space between those next to him and behind him. Every one of them must have moved to Pedrada from a different place, an entirely different place. And every one of them was afraid of all the others who had moved there from entirely different places. Here he was far more foreign to them than they to him. He could not allow himself, or could not allow himself yet, to be intimate with any of them, no matter whom.

And so each person, when it happened, as it repeatedly did, that someone made eye contact, would instantly look away from the other, as if he had just done something improper, something that he, of all people, had no right to do. So when one person bumped into another, as was inevitable with all the shuffling and shoving, each jerked back as if a crime had been committed, by him, one of the untouchables. Yet no one in the hordes of people who had moved to Pedrada since her last time here resembled in the slightest a pariah, or a refugee, or an expellee. Each had come voluntarily to this area, and also to the new groups of people here, and more than merely voluntarily: of his own free will; had made the decision almost confidently or proudly.

The tents were no refugee tents. (So what was the source of the mutual timidity?) The garment of each of the new arrivals was not merely appropriate, without defects, neither too new nor threadbare, but also seemingly made to measure, his alone, so that it was less his suit that seemed elegant than the person. And they were all dressed very differently, by no means in the latest styles, their clothes suggesting ever so subtly, almost imperceptibly, all the parts of the world from which they might have set out for this region: America, Africa, Arabia, Israel, China, India, Russia, but neither were they wearing the traditional dress or costumes of those places.

And although each of them moved through the mountain village completely alone, by himself, stumbling, shyly brushing past the others, and although each of them looked so unique, in his clothing as well as his hair color, the form of his eyes and skull, and although each of them obviously also thought of himself as infinitely alone and unbridgeably different from all the others, nonetheless in that crowd they all expressed the same thing, both in the gestures and grimaces with which one and all talked to themselves or to some invisible, absent third person, and in their actual subdued, constant conversations with themselves, which often coincided word for word—for by now they all spoke the Sierra vernacular—with the murmuring of those in front of and behind them: "Never to be alone again, never to lock a door behind oneself," and so on. So in the image these newcomers generated they belonged together as much as any of the established residents. (But how did they get themselves into the image?)

Yet they also came together now and then outside of the image: it happened whenever something like a transaction, an offer, an inquiry, an exchange, a purchase developed between two of them, serendipitously, as they were pushing past each other: they would then stand still for a moment, and although they hardly opened their mouths to negotiate, for that moment things were pretty lively between the seller and the buyer. And only then the actual exchanging, step by step, of wares and money (for anything but cash was out of the question here): a relieved smile on both sides, without reservations and suspicion, openhearted and at the same time with a reserved ceremoniousness, with almost more pleasure at handing over the money than at receiving it, mutual agreement and affection brought about by the money, the bills and coins, which made her recall why she, of all people, with her village childhood, had once wanted to study the manifestations—rather than the so-called laws—of commerce and economic activity.

And she, too, wanted to lay in cash for the following day and the rest of the journey. Was the way in which the new people of Pedrada had revealed themselves to her that night in the Sierra a fact, or was it only her gaze that made them appear so? Only? Only her gaze? A gaze could create (and destroy, and declare null and void). The gaze, hers—that was how she wanted it to be for the book—created something.

She kept watch until daybreak. Or did she merely stay awake? No, she kept watch. She kept watch over the whole area, over those who were sleeping there. Although she remained alone, she felt as though someone were watching with her and keeping her company, invisible but no less palpable, all night long.

For a while she also read again, in the glow of her flashlight, in her vanished daughter's Arabic book. "It is all right to read," she told herself, "all right to read on." And then, in the middle of reading: "She is alive. My child is alive! And tomorrow I will inquire about her here. And I will receive information."

She also watched over herself. If she were to lie down—this was her thought—she would die then and there.

Not until she made her rounds through the hostel did she enter the sleeping tent of the youthful parents. The infant was sleeping quietly between the two of them. They were turned toward him, and each had placed a hand on him, one on top of the other. At the same time they were talking to the sleeping baby, their eyes closed, an almost incomprehensible murmuring and muttering that merged into a stammered duet, without a single distinct word, and finally into a twofold whimpering, as when in a dream one is supposed to speak a magic word and cannot get it out, no matter how one tries.

The one who was sleeping deeply and peacefully was the infant. His sleeping penetrated the dream lamentations of his adolescent parents and finally silenced them. The entire tent filled with the breathing of the three sleepers, peaceful at last, and a scent wafted forth, only from the tiny child, the *niño*, the *tifl* (without any effort on her part the Arabic word came to her): the child's unique, intensified sleep scent. A perfume unlike any that had been produced and marketed anywhere. What a coup that would be. How such a perfume would stimulate the senses—she told herself—sharpening all the senses into one; into the most sensual of the sensual.

She kept watch out of love, or the urge or thirst for love, and that was why, if she lay down now, she would not be able to avoid expiring at that very moment? How great, how enormous was her longing, almost always—no, not that "almost" again. "Is my longing too great for my time? Is my longing too great for all time?" — Where was the one she loved? Why did that wretch not realize of his own accord where she was, and come looking for her? Why was that no-good wandering far away along the main road, his trousers eternally flapping in the breeze, not away from her, but also not "back this way"? "Clueless idiot! Phony adventurer? Lazybones!" And the sounds of the tributaries of the río Tormes rushed into the sleeping tent, each of them audible discretely, as an undertone, overtone, background tone, with only the dominant missing; or was it missing?

In the next tent-room—"Guess its color!" she said at the end of the journey to the author—lay her brother, lay the stonemason or building-smasher, or whatever he was, and the Mexican or Armenian woman, or whatever she was, the one who did not want to collect any more strangers' stories. They lay in each other's arms, utterly motionless, even their half-open eyes motionless. No sound either, not a peep from these two, holding their breath and completely united, motionlessly united, and that for a long, long time.

Instead, sounds from outside, most noticeable again those of the mountain torrents, which here in the love tent sounded as though they were coming from above; as if they were all cascading with a pounding noise right over the tent peak, rushing down the sides in all directions, streaming around the tent with a crackling sound, and sounds from much farther off entered as well, from the mountains, from the summit plain, the peak "cirque"—the local expression—way up in the Sierra, of the Mira, of the Galana, of the Galayos, of the Almanzor: a rockslide there; the crossing of a ridge by a heavy-bodied ibex, the fabled animal of the Sierra de Gredos, actually not extinct, not even rare, bursting with life for the moment—in the villages there statues of the ibex instead of famous human historical figures—a dull sound that carried far; the crash of stags' antlers colliding, as if in a dream; a sound now like a whip, then like pizzicato on a gigantic bass string, caused by the expanding and contracting of the ice layer on the lake up there, on the arena floor, so to speak, of the cirque at the peak, called La Laguna Grande de Gredos—each sound of this sort, also those from the most distant background, drawn into the play or the sleep of the couple here in the tent, its walls serving to amplify and deepen each of the far-off spatial sounds, a membrane being made to resonate and vibrate—here, where the two bodies lie interlocked even more soundlessly, as if listening; and with each sound, no matter how reedy, penetrating and resonating from the nocturnal Sierra like a gong, a shared ("Is the word 'conjoint' still in use?"), an increasing shuddering, "or, more precisely, shudder going through them," a boundless one, in the last analysis (was that expression still in use?). And will these two who once went astray have wept as a twosome then, silently?

Next she looked in on the litter-bearers, or whatever they were just then, of the abdicated emperor, or whatever he was just then, the four of them sleeping in the same tent-room, one in a child's bed, one on the floor. They were all lying on their backs, probably because they were so exhausted from hauling their burden for days. And they were all sleeping in their clothes. Although they seemed to be wearing costumes from a by-gone century, their faces, all pointing toward the roof, were thoroughly of the present time, part of this night; as only human faces, and particularly faces plunged so deeply and soundly into sleep, could be of the current time, the present, the embodied, tangible present.

Laila, night; *bil-lail*, at night; tonight, *hadjihil-laila*; present, *hadjir*; now, *al-aana*; face, *wadj*. Each of these words, spoken out loud, was a breath that brought the four sleepers closer to her and confirmed their presence. Now!—and she leaned over each one in turn and stroked their faces, swollen from exhaustion—not merely the lips, nose, and eyes beneath the visibly heavy lids swollen, but also their temples and their ears, even the earlobes. She kneaded the swellings without waking even one of the four. One bearer had a checkered skin, almost a chessboard pattern. A second had had a nosebleed before falling asleep—his nostrils darkly encrusted—and a handkerchief lay next to him, white, with the blood spots inscribed on it, little blackish-red, slightly indented circles evenly distributed over the cloth (where he had stuck one corner after the other into his bleeding nostril), the circles forming a pattern on the white surface like those on a die.

She stood then, and stood and stood, lost in contemplation of the die pattern. It reminded her of nothing and of everything. At this sight she felt her guilt, now free, however, of a guilty conscience, not as a burden, weighing on her, but rather as something unavoidable, and at the same time the state of being guilty as justified. There must be guilt! "Must"— and she laughed, or so it seemed to her. And it also seemed to her as if the nosebleed pattern were her own. And she considered stealing that handkerchief from the sleeper.

As a child, even as an adolescent in her Sorbian or Oriental village, she had been a chronic thief, though only of fruit—other thefts repelled her—and only of apples and pears. She had raided all her neighbors' land, from the first moment of ripening. And even later, wherever she happened to be in the world, she could never pass a tree without stealing at least one piece of fruit. That would remain the case all her life! and she then in all seriousness suggested to the author that a possible title for their book might be *The Fruit Thief.*

Handkerchief theft: it did not go beyond the thought. Her hand, already reaching for the item, stopped a span before it ("span": hadn't that word gone out of use long ago?). She stared and stared at the reddish-black dots, more than just six, more than twice as many. Instead, as the story goes, another hand now approached her hesitating one, that of the sleeper, who was perhaps only feigning sleep?

Yet this stranger's hand likewise stopped halfway: two hands, motionless in the air, without the hint of a tremor, in the glow of a flashlight. She, the fruit thief, was untouchable. She, too, an untouchable? Yes. Except that it was she who projected the sense that no one could touch her, no one anymore, no one yet. Her untouchableness was active. She made herself this way. It was like the film in which she had played the heroine: she herself did not fight, but whenever someone came storming at her, she held out a lance, a sword, or a stick in front of her, and that alone stopped or felled the other person, kept anyone who was not the right person at bay.

And if the right one happened to come along (that was how it should be in a film), the long-lost man? Obviously. But his appearing, his merely showing himself, and their standing opposite one another, face-to-face, that had already been the final scene in the film: "All my longing"— that was the final sentence she had to speak in her role—"had only one object: to have you there in front of me again and to see you again at long last."

The story goes that during that night in Pedrada the last tent she entered was that of the abdicated world ruler, "over whose empire (thanks to the addition of the empires of the exterminated American Indians) the sun never set," and so on. The emperor or king, or her business partner or accomplice, or the one on the prowl for what had once been history, was lying in his ermine, stretched out on a bed as if on a bier, and seemed to be dead, more dead than any living being can appear, dead as only a dead person can seem.

The tent bed was the broadest imaginable, and she lay down beside him; stretched out like him. Except that although she lay there as still as he did, completely still, she did not seem dead at all. No greater contrast than between these two bodies, stretched out side by side, a hairsbreadth apart, yet not touching anywhere.

To the degree that the man had become emaciated, presenting an image of progressive wasting, the woman at his side now blossomed. As his cheeks shrank to the last shreds of skin still attached to his facial bones, sunken like those of a mummy, the woman's cheeks swelled and took on the sheen of a freshly plucked apple, polished with a cloth. All of her forms expanded, grew taut, stretched. Altogether she acquired volume, grew larger and firmer, and at the same time became heavy and heavier— warmly heavy, beautifully heavy. While his forehead shriveled, acquiring creases and cracks "like the varnish on an old painting," his eyes sucked in by their sockets, his lips drawn back over his teeth (which would never bite again), his legs transformed into cold sticks, she experienced, right there beside him, a generalized swelling, one which "in contrast to the four sleeping vassals had nothing at all to do with any kind of exhaustion."

Her thighs, next to the wretched male quasi-skeleton, rose, curved, and filled out, as did her breasts; her mouth, the reverse of the man's cadaver-like one, stood slightly open, showing the tip of her tongue, "the smile of the flesh and the woman victorious"; and above them the woman's eyes now opened as wide as possible, with a gleam despite their blackness "that represented the triumph of life and survival, the triumph heightened by the man lying there next to her on the tent bed, so waxy and wan, from head to toe, body and soul, in his ermine. And how in that moment, during the night, this night, her hair gleamed, came loose, fell over the head of the bed, spread over the pillow and the bolsters, snaking toward the bald, deader-than-dead skull of her neighbor, of that witness to her aliveness, all the sweeter now, in this night!" In a film one would have seen the two of them from above, from the dome of the tent chamber, first in a long shot, then in a close-up.

In the course of her life she had become a ruler, for better or worse. "And this sort of ruler," she then told the author, "is something I do not want to be anymore." But the realm in which she had always been eager to reign was that of the sleepers, with her as the only one still awake, as during that night in Pedrada. From early childhood on, she had had the notion that sleepers were not bad people. Even evildoers and unkind people, she had thought as a child, and still thought, were harmless and peaceable when they slept, and not only for the moment, but for the entire period of sleep; by making use of their sleep, and in consideration of their sleep, one could certainly discover them as peace-loving, well-intentioned, indeed childlike folk.

Sleepers, she imagined, embodied their true being. And the true being of every individual, she had always thought, and still thought to-day, was good! This goodness came to light in a sleeper and could be studied. That was an area of study that had not yet been "exploited," something like "dormant capital." This notion, that all people, yes, all, when asleep became childlike and were good, and in the process embod-ied and even prefigured the best of all possible worlds, had perhaps been, she thought, one of the keys to her power over others: in the con-frontations, indeed struggles, with even her presumably most ferocious adversaries, she had pictured them as sleepers, and that had at least contributed to turning one opponent or another into a partner and accomplice.

The author countered by asking how it happened, then, that she had incurred so much hostility, and he added that in his eyes, becoming "childlike" in sleep, and in general, did not at all mean being a good per-son, or an unsuspecting person, or a pure person, at least not in his expe-rience of "contemporary children"; and then he told her that at one time he had had an opinion of sleepers not so different from her own. But over the years he had noticed, and specifically in himself, that in sleep the mo-mentary surges of hate he experienced while awake, likewise the out-bursts of anger and hostility, had not fallen silent as in his earlier years but had erupted even more forcefully.

And by now, he said, evil raged in him even more furiously at night, while he was sleeping, than during the day, when he had tried-and-true techniques for shooing it away whenever it showed its face: lacking any such technique as a sleeper—no matter how much he practiced before closing his eyes—he sometimes roared and bared his teeth, or did so at least in his dreams, all night long at someone he did not know, or darted into a crowd of strangers brandishing a knife, thus embodying only the worst of all possible worlds and in the end feeling nothing but relief at waking up. "It seems to me that today we sleepers are to be feared. Steer clear of sleepers, even those who seem peaceful and quiet! You no sooner bend over them than they will jump up and stab you."

She was keeping watch. Was she keeping watch? She sat up. She stood up. She walked up and down inside the main tent. Not a sound from the Sierra. Even the tributaries of the río Tormes had fallen silent, as if switched off, or as if they no longer reached her ears.

In her early days back there in the riverport city, at night she had heard every train, no matter how distant, and every steamer's whistle blowing at night—and after a few months, after a few years, nothing.

So she had been in the innermost reaches of the Sierra that long already? Eyes wide open, for true dreaming! ("Avoid the word 'true,'" she dictated to the author, "instead use 'comprehensive.'") So eyes wide open for comprehensive dreaming. It was the last hour of the night, and as so often she had the notion that a final decision was about to be made, something good or something terrible, a decision affecting not her alone but indeed the entire planet. It was also the hour when the earth always became most perceptible to her as a planet, a newborn one— dependent on its solar system and yet alone in the universe, as alone as anything can be, vulnerable, perilously vulnerable: precisely in this hour it would tip, not, as usual, toward day but into so-called eternal night. Decision? Turning point? Eyes open. Among the constellations of the northern hemisphere—Orion, the Pleiades, the Great Bear—the South- ern Cross, actually not visible in these parts, inserted itself, as if gently slipped in.

That snake, no longer than her forearm, as narrow as her little finger, patterned in yellow and black like a salamander, which she had encoun- tered during one of her previous crossings of the Sierra de Gredos, when she stumbled yet again in the trackless wilderness without being able to brake herself, at this moment slithered away in a leisurely fashion—no raising of its head or darting of its tongue at her—and, as she tumbled downhill, let her slide by in the scree, stepped aside ("Can one say of a snake that it stepped?") ahead of her, leisurely and gracefully.

Poisonous though it was, the snake had not frightened her when she fell toward it: that moment with the viper had even been a helpful one during that crazy hike through the Sierra: with the help of the snake she had achieved equanimity where previously she had been almost too cocksure, also hasty and not always mindful while walking or beating her way forward, and from the viper moment on, she maintained her composure, step after step, even if later she briefly lost her footing time and again. She had borrowed from her snake the rhythm she needed to wend her way out of the rocky maze, which, when one found oneself in it, sometimes seemed to offer no escape. And long after the crossing she drew on or called up the image of the snake to stay on top of certain situations, or simply to remain focused and to follow through on something, intensely and calmly, not allowing herself to be deflected from her course, yet concentrating entirely on the moment, on the now, now, now . . .

And once again from far, far away in the eastern village the image came to her of herself, the older sister, pushing the baby carriage with her summer-naked brother in it, still a nursling (nursing at whose breasts now, after the accidental death of their mother?), and losing her grip on the carriage, which plunged off the path and tipped over the bank, into the jungle-like thicket of tall stinging nettles there, and again she plunged after the vanished brother-bundle into the dark-green, hairy nettle flames.

And once more she plucked at the unknown love of her life, lying facedown in the damp steppe grass, then stepped over his body, again and again, back and forth, back and forth, and asked him why he was so afraid that she would suck out his blood.

And on her estate, the former stagecoach relay station, on the edge of the riverport city, long since left behind by her, sparks from horseshoes pierced the darkness, the piles of pots in the kitchen shifted, the quinces, the *kwite*, the *dunje*, the *safardzali*, rolled among the piles of laundry, no letter lay on the bare table, no one played with the toys set up in her vanished child's nursery.

And out here, among the dozens of brooks, rose thousands of mossy mounds, apparent islands, the *turbari*, softer than soft, which, when someone stepped on them, slowly twisted and sank, now, now, into the depths, into the bogginess, into the bog.

And the author in his village in La Mancha, in the chamber with the narrow cot, against the windowless wall, he, too, on his stomach, his hand over his eyes in his sleep, as if the night were not yet dark enough for him, him of all people.

"I have nothing to do with banking anymore, at least not as it is today," she told him later. "And yet I am preoccupied with the idea of founding a new kind of bank—an image bank, a worldwide one, for the exchange, use, and investment of all my, your, and our images—" But when the author urged her to expand upon her project a little, as so often, she broke off her flight of fancy when it had hardly got off the ground.

2 3

But then the new day after all. The feeder brooks once more audible. The tent crowd holding a brief farewell meeting, out of doors in the morning mountain air in front of the Milano Real of Pedrada.

Each person also drank his coffee or whatever outdoors, from porcelain cups, yogurt containers, toothbrush glasses. She, the heroine, adventurer, or vagabond, had her Blue Mountain Coffee from Jamaica with her as always, which she shared with one person or another: a rich black oily gleam, that mirrored the summit plain of the Sierra. It was wrong to be stingy with these most precious of beans: if you used too few of them, the coffee would turn out more bitter and weak than any other coffee.

No one ate. Although it was allegedly winter and, according to the thermometer, a chilly morning, no clouds of breath showed in front of people's mouths, just as in certain films where snow and a wintry landscape are a mere backdrop; only the beverages were steaming.

Now everyone here would set out by himself, or remain on the spot, or take the early bus, already waiting in the orchard, back to the plains and the cities.

Despite the bright daylight, not a single inhabitant of Pedrada was to be seen; the tents closed up tightly, as were the gray wooden shutters on the ancient granite-block houses: yet a living, breathing stillness (in his report, the observer, sent by the World Council, or whomever, who now burst out of his observer's tent for his morning run, five to ten times around the colony, would characterize it as "hopeless," "unmotivated," "apathetic," "eccentric").

No one spoke at first. That night of dying and being dead had apparently had a good effect on the *emperador*, emperor, king, or the historical reenactor playing that role—perhaps a local historian from the provinces here, in his civilian profession a savings-bank employee who thought he would gain insight into the past through this role-playing: he decided not to continue the journey in the litter; would cover on foot the rest of the way to the retreat of Charles V and I, without the real or artificial ermine cloak, together with his four colleagues from the Caja de Ahorros (= savings bank) in Piedrahita or elsewhere, who would no longer have to carry him.

The medieval stonemason and the young woman no longer on the lookout for anyone's story but her own—never again would she blush—stood with their arms around each other, as if since they first touched one another that night they had not been a finger's breadth or a hairsbreadth apart, when sitting, then falling down, then lying, later getting up, and now stepping outside: not a chink between these two Siamese bodies. How would it end? Well, there was enough for the stone man to do here in Pedrada (= place of stones), and her simultaneous and parallel activity could at least cause no harm.

And the terribly young couple? Overnight they had become adults, he broad-shouldered, with a suitable hat, she visibly also larger, with a proud womanly face and wider pelvis, from which her stomach already protruded a little with their second child, while in the morning light the first-born now appeared to have grown out of his diapers, having become a year or more older during the night, now able to stand on both legs, walk, hop over one of the feeder brooks of the río Tormes; and if his mouth did not yet produce any recognizable words, his eyes were already speaking, taking in everything that happened, could have said things about the others that they themselves did not even guess or know. Soon he would board the bus with his parents and sit between them during the entire trip and remain to the end, come what might, surrounded by these parents of his.

In the moment of parting they finally spoke. A strangely animated farewell for a group that had come together by chance, and so fleetingly. How full of enthusiasm each person there seemed, for himself, for the path ahead, as well as for the others and their very different paths. And hadn't they all been enthusiastic at one time, when? through and through, about nothing in particular, without a particular destination or adventure, simply enthusiastic, about nothing, nothing at all? When? As infants? Yes, as infants, long ago, in their time. Yes, in their time—but when was that?—hadn't all of us new arrivals in the world presented ourselves as enthusiastic? Wasn't there a time or a story in which everyone was born enthusiastic, with an enthusiasm meant for the long haul? But why did it seem now as though these people, coming into the world enthusiastic, the enthusiastic newborns, were the rarest of the rare? And what has become of all those who were enthusiastic in their day, those destined to remain youthful even as they aged, and all the more so, people to whom the adjective "young" applied as to no others?

But even if a hint or spirit of continuity was nowhere to be found anymore, at least there was the sporadic or episodic enthusiasm of parting. Every person thanked every other one, just like that, for nothing in particular. And each asked every other one to say hello for him to the place for which he was setting out, even if the place was unfamiliar to the person sending greetings.

She, however, knew the Yuste Monastery, several days' journey away, on the southern side, at the foot of the Sierra, below the lowest and easiest of the passes through the mountains, the Puerto de Tornavacas, and she gave the *emperador* this charge: "Say hello for me to the holm oaks, to the pool in the garden, to the giant palms, and especially to the sparrows, who are so absent from the northern Sierra, on the northern side of the *djebel.*" — He: "Also to the mausoleum and the sarcophagus?" — She: "No." And laying her hand on his shoulder, she stole, without his noticing, the soft tiger-striped falcon's feather from his ermine. And each person wished the other—a seemingly efficacious wishing—what he had secretly already wished for himself. Even if the stories they had launched together would not continue—so what? at least they had been launched.

This morning hardly anything suggested that the cones of mud and wood had served as an inn overnight; no sign, either "El Milano Real" or any other. By daylight the tent resembled all the others in Pedrada, except that it was somewhat larger. And by day it was only their (approximate) tent form that set apart all the new buildings that had appeared here since her last visit from the square houses that had been here before: all through the settlement the building materials, the mud, the blocks of wood, the granite ashlar, were the same, all the roofs here consisting of broom twigs and cork-tree bark, densely layered to make them rainproof and, with their stone weights, as storm-resistant as any roofing tiles— which were completely absent, both the flat ones of the north and the curved tiles of the south, as if Pedrada, and indeed the whole Sierra, no longer belonged to a specific geographical area.

The innkeeper of the previous night had been transformed into the bus driver again, who now drove over from the orchard and waited with his Cyclopean dog in front of the main tent for the passengers. And already these were coming from all parts of the seemingly fast-asleep village, long since ready for the trip, some of them also from beyond the tents and houses, from above, from the higher and apparently empty, treeless, and uninhabited elevations, loaded down with heavy bags, hanging every which way, dragging suitcases or, a bizarre sight on the trackless slopes with the ridges in the background, pulling them along on wheels.

And hardly any of those setting out on a long journey to town were unaccompanied. Although each was leaving the Sierra by himself, he was surrounded until he boarded the bus by a swarm of near and dear (who were perhaps not relatives at all, merely "near and dear" for the purpose of keeping him company).

It was still very early. Not a soul outside, except for the dense crowd of people saying their goodbyes around the windows of the bus, which because of the throng on all sides now seemed to be standing on a square disproportionately large for this mountain village. Despite the crowd, the scene was fairly quiet. Only now and then could a louder word be heard, and for the most part people's lips merely moved, delivering silent messages, whether inside behind the glass or outside on the square.

The driver had meanwhile left the bus and disappeared somewhere; his seat the only one not occupied. Behind the bus, the crest of the mountain, with a cloud bank to the south, the bank stalled, a so-called barrier cloud—as one of the companions explained to the person he was accompanying, as if to distract him from their parting, as the latter stood hesitantly on the bus step.

These were special farewells, bearing no resemblance to the cheerful goodbyes among the members of the fortuitous group. The necessity of parting forever, or for an undetermined length of time, now hung over them, after they had been so close, which here in their Sierra had always been precarious. These people inside and outside of the bus, taking final leave of each other only with their eyes, wide open, without winking or blinking, had survived something together in this place, something so terrifying and incomprehensible that it surpassed any local epidemics, famines, or natural disasters, something every moment of which would remain indelibly imprinted on their collective memory; memory? the present, memory as a present that would continue to rage. And after a shared survival like this, the necessity of parting was all the more painful: from now on, this person here and that person there would have to survive alone, bitterly alone with his remembering, with this experience constantly before his eyes.

The bus driver's return. The door closing. Pulling out. The accompanying friends rapidly disappearing. The square cleared. Along with the haze of bitterness, the square remaining filled with a powerful, lingering sense of intimacy or—equally heartrending—affection, which she, the fruit and feather thief, the last person left on the square, thought she could taste with her tongue and palate. "Really? Tasting a feeling?" — "Yes, feelings as sustenance! And what sustenance! It just depends on the feeling." Above the square, on the mountain crest far in the background, still the thick wall of the barrier cloud. And an apple had been lying on the roof of the bus.

Later, during her visit to the author in his village in La Mancha, she proposed another title for their book: *The Liturgy of Preservation*. Even very early in her life, it had pained her to leave a place that meant something to her. Not so much her village or one of the other places where she had spent time, but some way station or other, where, for a brief moment, "life had appeared" (didn't that phrase occur in one of the Gospels?), or where for a moment one had felt a breath of something, if only from a wind-tossed tree outside the window.

She had experienced pain, not for herself, the one who now had to leave the place, but for the place itself, "in person." She sensed, she thought, the place needed her and her attention, her scrutiny, her involvement in and appreciation for as many particulars as possible—something that went beyond recording, posting, and adding. That was how it should be, for the place deserved recognition, as well as gratitude; that was fitting ("Do people still say that?"—the author).

And thus every time she set out from such a "coach stage," she felt she must—observe again her smile at this "I must"—record the place visually, one look at a time and at every step. Wherever she went, or, as now, stood still, she impressed upon herself one spot and one thing (such as a person) after another; she noted the number of steps leading up to a front door here, the creaking of a wooden staircase there; took in the color of a rock, the shape of a door handle, the smell from a sewer grating, and so on: a consistent process despite the marked differences among the objects "entrusted" to her, which lent a coherence and a rhythm to the way station she was about to leave, a process she referred to as the "liturgy of preservation," and which she wanted the author to translate into images and sentences, into the coherence and rhythms of prose, so that it might endure as long as possible. "Yes, I am seeking whatever eternity is possible for human beings," she told the author, who replied, "And I want to be transitory," whereupon she could be heard to say, "That is not a difference or a contradiction."

Accordingly, that morning she surveyed Pedrada, the stone-casting settlement. She must not make a sound; must not wake anyone. Down-river on the Tormes, mill wheels were turning, new ones, which had nothing to do with the mills from previous centuries, in ruins now, overgrown with brush. Electrical pylons marched in from the opening of the valley, far off to the west, where the town of El Barco de Ávila lay, making their way up here, likewise new, as if installed overnight.

On the other side of the village stood a telephone booth, already partway out into the snow-dotted rocky wilderness, empty, with the rising sun shining through it, showing the impressions of the users' hair, forehead, and fingers on the glass. The feeder brooks still had no fish, as did the first stretch of the river, where they converged—but past a certain spot, right after the first bridge, suddenly the lengthwise flashing of hundreds of trout through the water, tiny little finned bodies, but masses of them, water-colored, almost transparent, and not a trout in these dense swarms would have passed an invisible line on its way upstream, even if it was swimming ahead of the others, as if this line straight across the río Tormes barricaded its source area, reserved for frogs and dragonflies and off-limits to any kind of fish: their sudden hesitation there, hovering for a while motionless on the riverbed and then slowly turning and whipping back downstream.

At last she had bestirred herself and was zigzagging through the late-sleepers' village, treading as lightly as possible. The notion that the items included in such a liturgy of preservation would also constitute a sort of letter, addressed to someone or other who was already waiting for it far away, and at the very moment when she was still engaged here in looking and listening, the letter was in the hands of its recipient; actually writing a letter was thus superfluous.

But could one really use the term "liturgy" for this kind of organizing, connecting, coordinating, rhythmicizing, setting in motion, loading the givens with the energy to reach a distant vanishing point? Wasn't it more a sort of strategy? A strategy that was the very essence of the professional activity she had allegedly given up? Wasn't it rather the case that even here, in the high Sierra, after she had, by her own admission, voluntarily withdrawn from the contemporary banking world, she could not resist looking for the "value" in objects, the element of value that could not be left to gather dust but had to be put into circulation, in combination with as many other such elements as possible, into constant, fruitful circulation?

Liturgy of preservation? Liturgy of accrual, with objects as capital? "That is true," she replied, "insofar as on that morning in Pedrada it disturbed me to see that the only bank branch there, a very small one established at one time by my bank, had been converted into a sheep shed, and also chiefly because that bank building was perhaps one of the most remarkable in the entire world: the last cottage in the village and at the highest point, directly behind it ravines and the jungle of broom, hardly even a building, simply a hollow boulder used for money transactions, the one and only banking facility in a natural cavern: a block of granite equipped with a counter and a vault, the stone head or stone brain, so to speak, above stony Pedrada, the most remote branch of the twenty-story plate-glass headquarters situated by the mouth of the two northwestern rivers.

"And it is also true that I am looking for the capital in the givens. And I should like never to give up this search. And on that morning in Pedrada, too, I was looking for the one bronze dewdrop among the other water-clear ones. But there was no dew. Instead I found, here and there, baked into the granite outcroppings, a little chip of mica, which for moments in the sun became dark bronze among all the others that merely glittered. And from a number of tent-houses hung black mourning bunting, faded and torn, many years old. And several of those leaving the village and those accompanying them had worn similarly quite faded mourning bands on their arms."

The morning's seeing and listening, her liturgy of preservation, was then interrupted by a sound such as she had never heard in the Sierra or in any village, not even in the village of her childhood: a siren. It sounded less like an alarm than like a factory whistle. And a few blinks later the mountainous horizon was filled with a dull roar, and a heavy, dark airplane approached, very slowly for an aircraft, so close to the ground that it almost grazed the rounded cliff tops with its fat fuselage, despite the even whirring of its four propellers—she had always had an eye for numbers, seeing the number of objects along with the objects themselves—the wings teetering constantly in the air, hardly a rope ladder's length above the roofs of the settlement, which almost seemed to sway sympathetically.

The airplane, blackish, and appearing from the ground, and probably from the same altitude as well, to consist of a thick, opaque metal envelope, more massive and powerful than even the largest of the centuries-old granite buildings below, did not remain alone. It was followed by a twelve-plane squadron—she involuntarily counted again. One warplane (they did not have to be bombers) after the other crossed the horizon, a ridge of the Sierra facing the sunrise, which thus took on some of the character of a rampart, and each plane then wobbled over the village, almost within hand's reach, and seeming to set Pedrada in motion.

But none of the twelve followed the one ahead. Each flew breathtakingly close to the ground—as was intended—but then chose its own course over the houses and tents, having appeared from the same point on the horizon. And this course was painstakingly plotted: no spot, no bark-covered roof, no chimney, no satellite dish, no fruit stand—no corner in Pedrada without one—no root cellar, no structure occupied in any way, was to remain untouched and undarkened by "the rest of us" and the shadows of our air-supreme force (which, according to the external observer in his report, first and foremost gave the old and the new settlers a sense of being protected).

Before people even had a chance to get a good look, the morning flyover ended. The twelfth plane had flown its course over the village, then had gone shooting off to the common point on the next horizon, of which there was one after the other in the Sierra, and had promptly been swallowed up by it, along with the hearing-loss-like sudden cessation of the dull roar; only an echo, as if from a dozen distant waterfalls; or were those actual cascades?

With the siren and the flyover, the village of Pedrada in the remotest and innermost Sierra had finally emerged from its slumber, which, as time passed, had come to resemble hibernation (as if the residents had turned overnight into dormice). Village? Quite a few large iron shutters, not very village-like, were raised. A garbage truck—and not only one—thundered along, and here and there on the paved roads urban street sweepers turned up. One man stepping out of a tent-house was wearing a necktie, and he did not remain the only one. Convoys of delivery vans were forging their way across the farflung mountain region, almost the only vehicles in the area, except for the very similar ones belonging to hunters. Other than in size, their vans differed from the delivery vans only in that their contents—if there were any—remained out of sight (barely even a trace of blood in back on a loading door). The goods being brought in and shipped out remained in equilibrium, and among the goods that were, so to speak, exported, local crops and products—venison, fish, honey, fruit—did not particularly predominate, and among the goods imported, those unique to cities or industrial areas similarly tended to be in the minority.

Now, although around Pedrada there were droves and droves of rather small white mountain pigs running around loose, whole truckloads of different pigs were arriving, those enormous black-bristled ones with black hooves, fattened up with acorns from the plains of Extremadura to produce that famous flavorful meat, now destined to be processed—winter, pig-slaughtering time—in the Sierra factory up here.

And, likewise, the square in front of the local oil press, to whose existence nothing had previously called attention, was unexpectedly darkened for a while, in a way that differed from the shadow of the air squadron, by the trucks uninterruptedly rolling up, filled to the top with blue-black olives from the "sunny sides" of the Sierra: winter, olive-harvest time. And among the goods—the usual herbs, cheese wheels, juniper berries, rowanberry schnapps, etc.—which moved in the opposite direction, out to the rest of the country—were equal numbers of refrigerators, washing machines, flashlights, knives.

In this respect, too, the place had become quite different since her last visit. And there was a local school again (all the previous times it had been closed, as if for good). The odd thing was that the teachers seemed to be in the majority—until she realized that these adults, although without book bags on their backs, were going to school just like the children, pupils among pupils. Such things occurred otherwise only in nightmares. But this was nothing of the sort.

Had all of Pedrada in fact lain in a deep slumber until now? The not infrequent columns of smoke from the stone chimneys had spoken against such an assumption, and in particular the silence, less dozing than breathing. And then when the grilles, the curtains, the doors to the stores—every third tent-house was a store, a stand, a business—and the cafés opened—every ninth tent an eatery—an image presented itself to her such as she had never seen or experienced before, either in the Sierra de Gredos or anywhere else in the world: in all the interior spaces of the village, the day had long since been under way or going full blast.

The activities inside the stores were not just beginning or being prepared for. Nowhere were the goings-on in these places taking place in expectation of the first morning customers: the hairdresser, for instance, was not straightening a pile of magazines (he was long since busy cutting hair); the jeweler was not taking items out of the safe and arranging them in his window (they were already there); the restaurant managers and waiters were not removing chairs from the tables (which were already set); the butchers were not spreading sawdust on the floor (it was already there, in many cases showing fresh footprints).

Wherever one looked, the daily routine was not just starting but rather was going on as before; not a new beginning but a continuation. Before this, after the opening of curtains and doors, turning out of lights, raising of shutters, opening of barriers, there had indeed been a moment when the stores and businesses of Pedrada had been not empty but at a standstill, which, if the paused images had not revealed an almost imperceptible swaying and quivering, one might have taken for paralysis or doll-like rigidity. The hairdresser and the woman under the dryer formed an almost motionless ensemble, the comb and scissors in the hairdresser's hands suspended in midair, halfway to their destination. The already numerous diners in the small eating places, as if having a first coffee break, might here and there have their fingers wrapped around glasses and cups, but one did not see a single one of them drinking. The bicycle dealer, kneeling by a child's bicycle, seemed to pause in the middle of pumping up the tire, next to him his customer, the child, with its hand motionless on the saddle.

The impression that this barely perceptible moment, when events were at a standstill, had been preceded by moons and entire years of the same. And that now, let us say, "ten years later," all at once, let us say, at the boom of a gong or a blast on a whistle, the interrupted game resumed, as if nothing had happened, no multi-year interruption, not even a momentary one.

Wherever one looked in the village, suddenly a steady bustle of activity, as if it had never been interrupted, only much more audible now, a veritable racket—a great variety of sounds (reminiscent, in turn, of the coppersmiths' street in Cairo, or elsewhere). The rushing, hissing, bubbling of coffee machines. The bone-hacking of butchers. Now even the snipping of the hairdresser's scissors could be heard, the magazine-page-turning of the waiting customers, the thread-biting in the tailor's shop.

And although these continued activities and busynesses on that morning high in the Sierra did not yield any story for the tabloids, one saw all the people in the village engaged in them telling their own stories through their activities. That something could tell its story in this fashion, without anything added, was a sign that in this place things were all right again, or still, something by no means to be taken for granted, but rather, today, or from time immemorial, well-nigh miraculous.

2 4

As the story goes, in that early-morning hour she even forgot her wrath at the conversion of the bank branch into a sheep shed. Did she forget it? That she could be wrathful sometimes, in a way unusual for a woman, or indeed for anyone, also belonged in her book, as she insisted.

Far below, on the río Tormes, to the west, King Charles V and Emperor Charles I was walking along on his own two feet, without an entourage, alone, without hobbling. How he had yawned that morning after his night of dying—so plentifully and heartily, as only one risen from the dead can yawn.

And many people here in Pedrada yawned the same way. And almost all of them had, like the *emperador*—and like her, the fruit thief, former short-term film star, and current adventurer—their survivors' wounds, which they displayed openly and as if proudly. She fell in with the throng of her people. Yet unlike elsewhere, here no one recognized her, although this time she would actually have wished to be recognized. ("Wished": did such a word even apply to her: yes.) Yet not even the stonemason and his beloved seemed to recognize her. Overnight they had opened a store together, with *ultramarinos* and *ultramontañeros*, goods from overseas and beyond the mountains, where she purchased cheese and sausage, salt, ham, and above all olive oil for the coming crossing of the Sierra—and slipped one apple into her pocket.

She, on the other hand, saw in every inhabitant, most of whom had moved here from other parts of the world, the doubles of people who had been familiar and close to her at various times in her life. It was striking, by the bye, that as a result of the warlike turmoil in this region a couple of years back, never recognized by the rest of the world as a war (?), even the few remaining inhabitants from long ago had acquired the new arrivals' timidity and fear of strangers, if anything more noticeable than in the recent settlers.

When one of them, in whom she encountered the image of "my faraway life partner," had the gall not to acknowledge her, she stuck out her tongue at him (see "wrath"). And almost all the young people, including some males, appeared to her in the guise of her vanished child, yet these resemblances and this repeated phenomenon of a person's being cut from the same cloth afforded her no comfort. And then one time she caught herself turning in her thoughts—this had never happened before—to her dead parents: "Father, Mother—tell me: Who am I?"

The people of Pedrada, on the other hand, not only did not recognize her; they treated her initially as an enemy. Or was it only her imagination that she was not wanted here? That from inside the store and restaurant tents looks like daggers were hurled at her? That the legs people extended were meant to trip her up?

It was not her imagination. A woman came hurtling out of one of the alleys between the tents—she, too, looked familiar; wasn't she that neighbor from the Sorbian village who had once reported her to the police for a stolen apple?—and, her teeth bared, bashed her over the head with a heavy handbag, seemingly filled with rocks, and darted off down another alley. And children sprayed her with ice-cold water from one of the feeder brooks that ran in a canal between the houses, not in play but in earnest, with glaring, unchildlike expressions.

And finally, at one end of Pedrada, where only tumbledown field huts and abandoned beehives stood, just before the mountain wilderness took over, she was pelted from all sides with stones, the invisible throwers far away. The hail of stones around her refused to stop, as if she were supposed to be kept spellbound in this circle of missiles. Pedrada, the stone-casting village: So the ancient tradition of stoning intruders was still in force here? And none of the throwers showed his face or let out a peep. If they had revealed themselves, she would have known what to do. As it was, the only solution was for her to break out of the magic circle and get back to the center of the village, where she arrived with blood on her forehead.

Again that image from the Orient came to her aid. One time there she had found herself in a part of town with no other women (or they were hidden away in their houses). Nothing but men on the street, not a step without encountering a cluster of men. The street was actually an alley, so narrow that it offered hardly any room for walking and getting past those who were sitting and standing around. Wherever she appeared, each of these otherwise peaceable gatherings and groupings turned into a mob. They hissed, groped, jostled, grabbed, spat, and this was not playful but rather menacing, hostile, on the verge of violence, and the threat persisted at every step of the way, without any prospect of her getting through. The alley, narrow as it was, seemed endless, and the side alleys were, if possible, even more crowded with bodies, and were also, without exception, cul-de-sacs.

So she did what had worked for her since childhood. In her youth she had often gone about alone and repeatedly found herself the target of hordes of boys from neighboring villages. Whenever these hordes descended on her, the child, and later the adolescent, did not run away but instead stood her ground; turned and advanced toward her persecutors; plunged into their midst as though nothing were happening, and indeed nothing did happen; the rabble dissolved into individuals, and sometimes the individuals even became well disposed toward her—or at least she, the girl, became invisible as far as the boys were concerned.

A decade later she had similarly made herself invisible to the male fiends in the Arab casbah; from one minute to the next she turned aside from the gauntlet and headed into the midst of the men who formed it, sat down among them on a stool at a table belonging to the terrace of an eatery that narrowed the passage to almost nothing; like them she drank tea, mint, or whatever (to go so far as to suck on a waterpipe would have been excessive); like them, she did no more than sit there and gaze into the alley with eyes as wide open as possible: and thus it was out of the question for even one of the men to turn and stare at her, or reach for her, or pull her hair; she had hardly ever been left as much in peace as she was by these Arab men; and then, among them, precisely among these men who moments earlier had made her situation a living hell, she experienced a peace such as she had seldom felt—a profound peace, peace as the most all-encompassing sensation.

In the same fashion she decided that morning in Pedrada not to duck the hostility anymore. Instead she plunged straight into it. And the knife-throwers made her a present of the knives? Yes. One did, at least—it was a very tiny knife, by the way, with a blade hardly longer than a thumbnail. And the stone-throwers ceased to throw stones? Yes, when she threw stones herself, one of which collided in midair with a stone tossed by one of her presumptive enemies. What a sound, and what a peaceful silence after that.

In the center of the stone-casting village, where she went into a shop-tent that also housed a bar, she promptly elbowed her way to the spot most crowded with potential attackers, and, after a critical moment (for which there was a special word in that region, *trance*), during which the faces grew more savage by several degrees—the eyes blazing like nests of dragons—hands reached for her from all sides, tugging, plucking, pulling, stroking her hair, her cheeks, her shoulders.

Yes, the people of Pedrada reached for her this way out of joy. What had appeared to be hatred and rage in their faces had in actuality been distrust, and not born merely of the current situation—a seemingly chronic disappointment vis-à-vis the rest of the world. She was the one walking around this village with evil in mind, she who had come from elsewhere, the stranger. The settlers in Pedrada expected nothing but the worst from those who came from elsewhere. And no sooner was she standing among them, no sooner did she look around her, than instead of beating her, they plucked, scratched, and jostled her, shouted and spit-sprayed her, out of sheer excitement, eagerness to talk, cordiality and hospitality. Disarming people simply by looking around? Yes. And yet she did not look at anyone in particular. No one felt personally targeted by her gaze. Her gaze merely brushed each one.

It was quite rare, by the way, for her to look someone in the eye. And it happened most rarely with a man. But when it did! Once in a lifetime! Woe unto me. What a lucky man I am! There was that one time when he was pierced by her wrathful gaze, from the depths of a wound that cut into him like his own. No, not a wrathful gaze—rather a pure and simple opening of the eyes, not so much aimed at the man as dedicated to him and intended for him; that blackest of full gazes with which she surrenders entirely and at the same time calls on the man, me, me? for help, silently, and at the same time, with the same widening of her eyes, places trust in me as in no one else, or am I deceiving myself? a trust to which to the end of my days I shall do more than merely be equal, for which I will be the rock. But did I manage to be that?

And now no help for it but to return to the episode in the bar-shop with her and the Sierra folk. By looking around, the stranger had mollified these people, who generally felt passed over and despised, and made them whole; with her in their midst, they no longer felt marginalized.

Although she, this beautiful and well-intentioned guest—at long last such a guest—merely glanced or looked sideways at us natives or settlers, reputed to be obstinate and backward, and who therefore actually were this way at times—her idiosyncrasy, to turn her profile toward each of us as she looked—or even looked us up and down, which, since the days when Homer's single combatants faced each other before wielding their weapons, has signified disrespect and arrogance, or merely glanced fleetingly around, her eyes invisible behind a veil (afterward each of us will have imagined a different eye color for her), we knew our value had been raised by her scrutiny. No, we were not the way the observers portrayed us, and beneath the gaze of our dear guest we were no longer forced to play that role. For once we could be high-spirited. And in this high-spiritedness, which to our regret lasted far too short a time, we recognized that this was no exception but rather one of the most valid and exemplary things we deserved, part of our worth, part of our tradition. Under the gaze of this particular person, we were no longer shriveled nonentities, but each of us lived in his own space and breathed his innate and indigenous time.

The story tells us that the people of Pedrada did not want to let their guest depart. And we are told that at the parting one person hung around her neck a medallion with the white angel (but wasn't that her own?). And the story tells of a couple of others who bickered high-spiritedly over which of them would escort the stranger up to the crest of the Sierra (yet of those who wanted to climb up there with her, none had yet ventured to the peaks, in this respect more strangers to the mountains than the guest, and when they finally set out, she, the new one here, was repeatedly asked for directions, even before they left the center of the village, even just to get around the corner). And the story tells of local children, who, unlike big-city street children nowadays, did not budge from the woman's side as she eventually set out alone, but gazed at her expectantly, hand in hand with her (children from the very horde that had previously pelted her with stones?). And she, according to the story, continued to recognize in each of her hosts someone she had met in another part of the world, primarily those from the northwestern riverport city, here the outskirts idiot, there her would-be lover (and she remarked to herself that moving to the air and light of these remote inner regions of the Sierra de Gredos had not done them any harm).

And here is the place to insert the reporter's account of his visit to the Pedrada region. Enough glorification, which, as he wrote in the introduction, amounted to the same thing as obfuscation. It had been his assignment, he wrote, simply to observe, rather than to glorify and prematurely pave the way for a conciliatory attitude toward these people, which might actually make things worse.

In his reporting, he said, he had been guided exclusively by the recognized and accepted rules of rational thought. To be sure, now and then feelings had slipped in among the sober observations—indeed, it had sometimes been almost impossible to "ward off" feelings—but there was no place for them in a purely rational account, not even as a "makeshift device." No feelings. Or at least not allowing oneself to be [mis]led by them. They merely distorted the given facts, disfiguring them and destroying their structure.

Similarly he had avoided in his report all evocations of atmosphere. To place particular emphasis on the atmosphere of a region under analysis would falsify the actual circumstances and veil the causes of local problems. Atmospherics were fine for the soccer field and the circus, "or, as far as I am concerned, for a Western or an adventure story, but not a research project intended to elicit facts or establish the truth." Feelings, like atmosphere, were incompatible with the urgently needed information on the Pedrada region, from which almost nothing but rumors reached the outside world. And likewise any fleeting images or scraps of words picked up in the course of a day did not constitute hard facts.

Incidentals and details unrelated to the main point: dozens of these had come to his attention during his stay in Pedrada. He had repeatedly been at risk of being distracted by them from his assignment, which called for capturing the essentials, had been at risk of ascribing to insignificant factors and small incidental images a meaning that they by no means possessed and above all were "not allowed to have," as far as the problem of Pedrada and the Sierra de Gredos was concerned.

Even now, as he was compiling his report, the reporter admitted, images were constantly breaking or barging their way in among the rational statements, "in veritable toadlike fashion," "and likewise in dark swarms," not only inappropriate, deviant, and confused, but also illogical or at least intent on keeping him from staying on track, images "like will-o'-the-wisps or demons!" And such images, intermittently flashing and flickering, were not information, and certainly not the information that was called for. The facts and "the disjointed interior worlds of images" were "mortal enemies."

The same was true, he wrote, of knowledge and intuition. In his report, his assignment was to transmit what he knew to be proven, documented, witnessed, and certified as far as the Pedrada population was concerned. Anything intuited had to be omitted, "alas." Yes, he wrote "alas": for quite a few of the intuitions that had come to him while he shared his life with the Sierra folk had impressed him at least as powerfully as all his accumulated factual knowledge; these "intuitions that unexpectedly came flying to me" had from time to time been even more convincing than the known facts, in defiance of the laws of rational thought. Intuitions "like eagles' shadows, or at least the shadows of raptors, which threatened to darken my reason." Above all, no making things up out of thin air. Both feet on the ground.

And it went without saying—thus he ended the introduction to his report—that in the following compilation of data and statistics, geared toward ease of understanding and general applicability or usefulness, dreams had no place—"although it must be admitted here that during my assignment in the innermost Sierra, probably as a result of the altitude, I dreamed as nowhere else (although my life as a reporter has taken me to the most remote and dream-stricken corners of our planet): dreams that pursued and persecuted me all day during my fieldwork, and often thoroughly muddled this work, along with the data and facts. But it is also out of the question that these dreams—what an unfamiliar pounding of my heart they caused, and still cause—should be considered straightforward information that leads to the heart of the matter."

According to the reporter's account, the life of the Pedrada settlers was primarily characterized by regression to forms of civilization thought to have been long since left behind. "Among the population, one can observe a degree of atavism unequaled anywhere else, not merely in Europe, but in the entire modern world, now well advanced into the twenty-first century."

This atavism, he wrote, was evident already in the fact that none of the inhabitants cared what was happening outside the borders of his region. The local station, whether radio or television, carried almost exclusively local news. The satellite dishes, as numerous here as elsewhere, served only to receive broadcasts of old movies. People were uninformed, either about the shipwrecks in the Indian Ocean, or the floods in Alaska, or the bombing of the Eiffel Tower. There was no newspaper, and if one happened to find its way to the village from elsewhere, brought, for instance, by a bus passenger, it went unread. The few announcements were disseminated orally, as in much earlier times, on Sundays after mass, after the Shabbat service, after Friday prayers in the mosque.

Further evidence of regression was the rejection of cashless financial transactions and indeed any kind of banking. All that prevented the reintroduction of piggy banks and money chests was the fact that no one saved, let alone hoarded valuables: the money in the region was in constant circulation, with uninterrupted buying and selling, in the course of which objects and money passed from hand to hand without anyone's thinking to amass capital with which to undertake some long-term project or gain a substantial advantage over others.

The atavism was such that even the old-fangled barter system was sending forth its sickly tendrils on the entire northern side of the Sierra de Gredos, which in any case suffered from sun deprivation. More childishly than children, the Pedrada population would spend hours haggling over barters, which exchanges, once they were concluded, were so crazy and pointless that merchants from the outside world—though none came—would have had an easier time of it with these ninnies than Columbus with the West Indians, Pizarro with the Incas, or Cortés with the Mayas or the Aztecs. One person bartered a gold pocket watch for a chess piece made not even of ivory or crystal but of wood. The one who had received the gold watch promptly exchanged it for a glass marble, for which he was offered by the next person a bench, a first edition of *Don Quixote*, or a crate of apples allegedly blessed by one of the hermits up on the crest of the Sierra, and so it went in the local bartering frenzy.

What was more worrisome was that the inhabitants of Pedrada and its surroundings still lived as people had before the discovery of play. True, in their daily dealings and in their evening leisure activities they displayed something oddly playful—every head movement was playful, likewise every placement of their feet, every blink, every exchange of objects, even the words that they literally sent flying back and forth among themselves—but beyond that they never played an actual game, and apparently knew of and were acquainted with none (the chess piece, like a ball, a deck of poker cards, a Ping-Pong paddle, was merely an object of exchange).

And "since they never played particular games—or if they did perhaps play, without any rules—the people of Pedrada seemed imprisoned in their own countries, not deflected for a moment from their separate and isolated existences, in which, without any social games, they had no opportunity to escape from themselves even for a while, or, by way of the much-needed detour provided by regulated play, to interact with their fellow human beings freely and uninhibitedly, and the result was that they—a serious regression—had all mutated into those 'idiots,' which might be translated literally as 'go-it-aloners' or 'odd ducks,' for whom the first progressive society, the Greek polis, had had no room within its system"—by which the reporter meant to suggest that membership in contemporary societies, whose model "of course had to be the polis," was out of the question for the entire population of P., a straggling horde of obsolete idiots, too stupid to play.

Even more worrisome, the outside reporter continued, was that the legal and judicial system in the Comarca of Pedrada was no longer based on the world or universal convention that had finally been adopted everywhere else, but that these people—certainly at the behest of precisely those who had moved here from the most advanced civilizations!—had reverted to a concept of neighborhood justice, for the regulation and enforcement of "local coexistence," that had allegedly held sway in the mountains in olden times and had been preserved there: a system not even captured in writing and codified, but merely passed down from one generation to the next in some obscure fashion.

In the Sierra de Gredos, according to the report, respect for one's neighborhood, for the other person's, the neighbor's, space, had become the starting point for all decisions as to what was allowed and what was prohibited—and that among these idiots, who skittishly kept to themselves!—a principle now almost "sacred" to these people, like the law of hospitality and the law of "niceness" (!) (as if they wanted to turn their backs in willful defiance on the present and take refuge in a dark, gloomy past).

Yes, in this remote world an unwritten law was in effect, in all seriousness: when it came to one's neighbor, good repute—or none at all—or complete silence about the person; but in particular: not a word about a foreigner, no matter how unwelcome. Wherever Pedradeños (they had another name for themselves, but they guarded it jealously) came together, as usual looking past one another, over each other's shoulders, into space, their topic was generally those who were absent, their neighbors from the upper, middle, or lower feeder brooks of the río Tormes, and the murmuring, whispering, and growling, accentuated by the hissing, guttural, fricative, and spitting sounds characteristic of the Sierra, had as its subject, if not various legendary heroes or other whimsies, the positive and lovable features of various fellow residents, as well as their lovable defects and mistakes—apparently only the lovable kind could be mentioned.

How well these others all came off in such conversations, how seemingly human and as if without negative qualities—anyone listening without preconceptions, and without the blinders of an obsolete, narrow, artificially revived law based on custom and tradition, had to be filled with doubt from the outset—when the reporter was privy to such obstinately favorable comments on others, he almost felt like bursting out laughing, almost. How beautifully white XY's hair had turned over the past year. How he and his wife still loved each other after a quarter of a century, still held hands and opened doors for each other. How so-and-so's children were even more beautiful than their mother, who was a beauty herself, what a beauty. How forever young this woman looked, like women in medieval epics. How what's-his-name was always so punctual about pruning his fruit trees. How kindly he had left a bottle of sparkling cider outside the speaker's window yesterday. How attractive the new color of his window shutters was. How reassuring it was to hear the man next door banging the garage door shut every evening, or to pass every day the large family's laundry just hung out to dry, with the rips and holes in the clothing and socks—this morning only single stockings, all missing their mates! What a pleasure to hear the voice of a newborn behind the fence, to see the freshly polished shoes in the attic window across the way, to smell the eldest daughter's perfume through the wild broom, to find, upon coming home, yet another ball in one's own tent garden or courtyard and to be able to toss it back into the garden next door.

What a happy feeling to know that one's neighbors were home again when they had been away—a rare occurrence in these parts—or on vacation—an even greater rarity, to see their vehicles in their parking spaces, their colors all matching the gray of the granite and the silver of the mica and the yellow and white of the broom, and then, in the evening, the glow of lights from the tent-houses across the way, shining through the cracks, and the familiar voices, after all these days and weeks of darkness and silence. How only an hour ago a neighbor thought to have vanished had turned up, and he and the speaker had fallen into each other's arms and even hoisted each other into the air, and how the absent one had not only been in the best of moods but had also brought his neighbor a gift, along with gifts for his own wife and children, and not some bauble, either, no, a most valuable and beautiful gift, for him, the neighbor, the speaker.

No wonder, the reporter wrote, that in a social order like Pedrada's, restricted in this way to glorification of neighborliness and good repute—and this was the most worrisome feature of all—a kind of smugness had taken hold among the settlers there that did not pertain to neighbors and those telling stories about each other but increasingly became a menace, a danger to areas outside the narrow confines of the region, a true public menace.

And in his report he made it very clear that precisely the ominous hospitality rules of the Sierra, allegedly the third pillar of the prevailing system of justice, the buttress, so to speak, that made for apparent equilibrium, apparently also intended for those on the outside, was merely the presentable face, only feigning friendliness, of the lurking public menace.

It was true that he, who had come flying and rolling in from afar, experienced within his field of observation the kind of reception that a guest could only wish for, and such as "one finds out in the world only as a ghostly presence in legends of ancient tribes or primitive peoples, stricken in bygone times from the book of human progress."

But this hospitality was also all there was. Beyond that, nothing. Not a word. Not a look. Wherever he went, he was served, assigned the best seat, tucked into the warmest bed. And at the same time, from his first day to his last, the people of Pedrada were completely indifferent to him. No one took any interest in this man who came from the hubs of the planet, or in anything he could have conveyed to them from there or from anywhere else on the outside. No one cared about him—where he came from, what he planned to accomplish here, or where he wanted to go.

Such indifference toward him, a man belonging to the great outside world, struck him as barbarous. It impressed him as a particularly brutal form of aggression, and turned the region under observation into a blot on the world map, which was finally meeting contemporary standards everywhere else.

And in his report he compared this indifference to the emphasis on mandatory niceness in this place, whose all the more ugly underside was that when one spoke of a neighbor one could not say a word about his illnesses, his lying on his deathbed, the death of his wife, of his children. Not a word about the other person's misery, misfortune, sorrows.

Yes, not a soul, not a man, child, and certainly not a woman in Pedrada cared about him. Not even an animal cared about him, the foreigner, no dog and no cat. The bulls ignored him. The kites and mountain jackdaws fell silent in his presence. The dragonflies zigged and zagged away from him. The trout, when he waded into the río Tormes in his researcher's hip boots, acted as though he did not exist, but the moment he reached for them they slipped through his fingers.

The lovely yellow lichens on the granite boulders also manifested the malevolent indifference characteristic of the area, causing him to slip and fall repeatedly. Even the coarse grass stalks were standoffish and hostile like all the Sierra folk, cutting into his skin. Damned thistles. Damned brambles, *malditas zarzamoras* (wasn't he in the process, just for his studies here, of learning the local language—which then no one admitted to understanding?!). Damned cow flops, foxholes, and wild-boar trails. And curses, too, on the infants here, who—where else in the world did this happen? didn't little ones everywhere intently seek the eyes of others, of adults?—looked right through him.

Yes, did these most backward inhabitants of the world think they were something special? Did they imagine that their shit was better than his? What were they so proud of? What gave them the right to be so standoffish? Why, whenever he urged them to tell him about themselves and this place, about the suffering, atrocities, murders, storms, catastrophic winters and summers, did each of them simply turn his back on him and not want his story told, absolutely not? At the very most, one of them would spit, as if to say, "All right, I'll tell my story—but not to you. Have my story told, but, by God and all the saints, not by you."

Yes, didn't the inhabitants of this mountain enclave, the old-timers as well as the new settlers, know that continued resistance was pointless—their current resistance to observing and being observed (objectively) just as much as their earlier resistance to the unfortunately necessary use of arms against them by outsiders? Why couldn't they grasp that they had lost, and, furthermore, were lost, defending here a cause long since lost in what merely seemed to be their own country but in actuality was not a bright mountain summit but a dark crevasse? Why did each of them, confined to the tiny corner that had been graciously left him here, without the slightest elbow room—instead of looking this fact in the eye—behave as though he were free to roam his kingdom, or a kingdom altogether?

Didn't it move the reporter almost, almost to tears one evening when he was in the main tent, The Red Kite, and observed the people of the Pedrada and Hondareda Region (that was its full official name) engaged in what was, at least at that time, their nightly dancing? How they hopped and stamped, hoofed it and whirled, dressed festively, even splendidly, until the first glint of morning entered the barnlike hall. How they clung, if not to each other, then at least to their dance, which incidentally was a fairly chaotic wheeling, combining elements of American square dance from the Wild West, rock and roll, flamenco, and an old-fashioned round dance that seemed a bit rancid, in which often one dancer or a couple would abruptly move from one figure into the next, with constant backward movements being most characteristic! How clueless these dancers were, in reality despised and shunned by all of modern enlightened civilization—it was not merely as if they still belonged to civilization and had a right to enjoy themselves like the rest of us today; some of them even let out more or less primitive shouts of joy, *tahallul!* in the new settlers' idiom, a variant on "hallelujah"?—but also as if, instead of being the damned and accursed of the earth, they were something like an avantgarde, an elite, the elect, the new and only salt of the earth!

These dancing idiots had not the slightest suspicion (no, not "suspicion," but "realization") of how far off the mark they were, how played out and danced out they were, how the scenario had been continuing without them for a long time—how it was all over for them, for good, till the end of time—how their dancing and, accordingly, all their actions, their entire life and their obstinate survival, even their death, had become meaningless, devoid of content, and, along with their rejoicing, foot-stamping, and round-dancing, was headed for the void.

And it was then that tears almost came into the eyes of the traveling observer. As a man trained as a social scientist, whose research specialty was anxiety and fear, he was familiar with the phenomenon whereby an individual who was profoundly frightened by something would later make involuntarily "empty chewing movements," with nothing in his mouth, so to speak, but the breath that had been dammed up by fear: and, as he now recognized, the dances, like the other manifestations of life among the people of the region, were similar empty chewing movements. Empty chewing movements caused by nothing but terrible fear, which also explained their recourse, or, more precisely, regression and reversion, to long since faded regional legends, myths, and sagas.

Empty chewing movements: that atavistic fiddling, often merely on an instrument with a single string, and the plucking of a Jew's harp, which he observed with particular frequency. Empty chewing movements: the constant looking away from each other, the abrupt, rude, almost dismissive behavior of the sexes here, the men and women toward each other— in his report he wrote of the "absence of any culture of eroticism," of the "disheveled art of wooing," of the "complete lack," at least in public, "of mutual displays of affection"—and at this he almost, almost jumped up, either to shout at one of the dancers or another, or to take one by the hand, or to throw his arms around one, and only the fact that as a child, when he had run toward others to touch them, to embrace them, he had always been pushed away or ignored, as an intruder, a superfluous and ridiculous extra wheel, restrained him, at the last moment, fortunately for him and his report.

Accursed Pedrada. Confounded Sierra de Gredos y de Caponica.

2 5

She had crossed the Sierra de Gredos quite often, in every season, taking all the various passes, including passes that still bore that name but had been out of use for generations, either for the driving of cattle from north to south, the *transhumancia*, or for transports of any kind, and had meanwhile become almost impassable, even on foot.

And now the plan called for her to set out on another crossing, which she wished or wanted to be her last—did she really wish that?—by way of the so-called Puerto de Candeleda, a route from before the war, on today's map merely a name—but wasn't a name something, at least?—and recognizable by the complete absence of any indication of a road or even a footpath down the steep southern flank of the Sierra directly after the "pass," more like a random spot up on the ridge.

And at the same time she was confident that by evening she would be down in Candeleda, at the foot of the southern flank, over fifteen hundred meters below the out-of-service pass named after the small town that did not belong to any *meseta* or plateau but, rather, lay on the edge of a lowland, surrounded by groves of palms, oranges, olives, and who knew what else. (She instructed the author to insert words like "confidence" and "confident" into her story, from way station to way station, from section to section, but to avoid expressions for "hope," including the Spanish *esperanza* and even the Arabic *hamal*—"I do not want this word, and I will not learn it—any more than the word for 'guilt,' *hithm!*"—so she had learned these words after all?)

So in spite of the short winter day she was confident? Yes. Time and again, especially in the morning, as now, in the mountains, one (one?) was seized by the scruff of one's neck, so to speak (so to speak?), by a confidence that was all the more powerful the more baseless and senseless it was, and hoisted into the air. And although she did not have much time, it seemed to her as if she had plenty of time. It seemed to her? She made up her mind again to have time, and it was so. "Plenty of time!" that was also the farewell used by the people of Pedrada—the farewell used by all those moving out of the region. And she heard another farewell, one introduced since the last time she had passed through, astonishing in light of what had happened in the region since then: "Have no fear!"

Everywhere in the spaces between the granite houses and the clay-and-wood tents, the ridgeline could be seen, and somewhere was the pass or crossing. No, every point was a possible crossing. And it seemed close by. It was a clear day. Or was it? (More than once, just such clear and promising days in the Sierra de Gredos had ended with a life-threatening storm or, if the clear weather persisted, with a no less dangerous loss of all sense of direction or a close call, perhaps simply the result of a slight misstep.)

In spite of the many snowy and icy patches, it was a day outside of any season, windless, and warm from the mountain sun. And it seemed to one as if it would be that way forever. When one placed one's hand on a granite outcropping, on the yellow lichen there, or reached into a tuft of grass by a spring or one of the broom thickets, a quiet warmth, a heating warmth, penetrated one's body to the bone, such as one had never felt so comfortingly in an actual calendrical summer—in the middle of the purported Sierra winter, a fullness of summery warmth experienced previously at most in a dream. "It is summer!"—and as one said that, it became summer, even if it was perhaps still late winter.

And at the same time the adventuress was of course thoroughly aware not of some specific danger or other but of the unidentifiable and yet by no means less serious danger. This danger simply had to be there, as already described, not that she particularly wanted to look for it. One could not manage without it, at least from time to time. This danger, whether connected with the Sierra or with something else, was the be-all and end-all. Without it, no story. Danger and the story were necessities—and again she saw herself in this respect as anything but alone.

Did anyone else intend to cross the Sierra de Gredos from north to south on foot that day? She posed the question not to the people of Pedrada, who were visibly relieved to be staying down below in the settlement, and understandably had no intention of undertaking long journeys into the unknown, but to one of the Internet screens in the village—it goes without saying that there were locations in the village for them, as for almost everything. No answer, or rather yes, there was one, from someone who wanted to make his way up into the Caucasus that same day, to the Sierra de Armenia there. So no one else was heading for the Puerto de Candeleda? Terrific. Gusto: for walking, climbing, tracking, cutting a trail.

And it occurred to her then that she still lacked something important for the expedition: bread. In the whole of Pedrada she had not come upon a single bakery. How could that be, with the new mills downriver on the Tormes? But there had to be a *panadería*, and hastening up and down the yurt alleys and around corners, she said this word to herself, first under her breath, then out loud, as an exclamation, or merely "Bread!" "¡Pan!" and finally, involuntarily, in Arabic, "Chubs": and almost in the same breath she smelled from around the corner the aroma of freshly baked bread, which she then followed—to be sure, it was still quite a distance to the bakery, halfway across the village. The precincts and geography of the bread aroma. Cozy oven fragrance in the midst of the far-flung, deserted rocky mountains.

The bakery was the smallest of the hundred shops in Pedrada, installed in a hut of worked stone that had perhaps once been a rabbit shed. And now it was one of the few buildings there (the tents were also "buildings," of course) with a glass door and strings of metal beads in front of the opening. And as she entered, the glass door reflected for a moment her vanished child. A glance over her shoulder: no one there.

After the girl's first disappearance, when they had found each other on the island in the Atlantic, after months of searching, near Los Llanos de Aridane, she, the mother, was then received with everything "from soup to nuts" by her daughter in the hut where she had taken refuge, no, her home, and she had been served, among other things, "homemade bread." And now, buying bread in the Sierra bakery, she asked after the girl she had lost track of for the second time. Except that she did not manage to describe a single feature of the young woman, her own flesh and blood, not a single one. Yet she had an image of her, and such a distinct one. Name? What is the child's name?

And at that she realized that she no longer even knew her name; in the course of their long separation, it had escaped her! So what was the vanished girl's name? Only a moment ago she had felt strong enough to bring a mill wheel to a stop with one finger, and the next moment—

The liturgy of preservation continued as she left the settlement behind and climbed toward the summit plain of the Sierra. For as she departed, she was convinced she was seeing the Pedrada region for the last time. Because she, the visitor, would not be around much longer? Because she would never pass this way again, would never set out again for anywhere? No. It seemed to her rather that in the fairly near future the entire tent- or yurt-town, together with the village's old stone houses, would vanish from the face of the earth, perhaps already after the snowmelt, perhaps with the emergence of the summery swarms of flies.

Back home in the riverport city she would stock up on images from all the possible channels, images of the clean-swept mountain and feeder-brook landscape, aerial photographs of leveled ground, where even the granite outcroppings had been flattened; the former tent sites, like the footprints of the houses, recognizable only from fragmentary dark patches here and there in the churned-up ground, portions of circles and rectangles, as from a plane one can see in a plowed field below the darker lines among the otherwise evenly light-colored furrows that indicate where buildings once stood, decades, centuries, millennia earlier, and were cleared away or sank into the ground, and the meandering courses of brooks and rivers that may have disappeared, dried up, or flowed in entirely different directions as much as a million years ago: thus—and certainly worried about herself, "Do not worry!"—she took leave of Pedrada.

A pregnant little dog with piglike bristles ("dog," *kalb* in Arabic) and a belly whose teats dragged on the sand and stones accompanied her well beyond the upper limits of the town and then even much farther, deep into the mountain steppe; at times remained standing some distance behind her, as if to turn back, but was then beside her again, gazing up expectantly.

And then who had claimed that in the Pedrada region even the children had forgotten how to play? Not that she saw any of them playing—school was still in session—or any proper toys, but at every step of the way, far up into the wilderness, she saw signs of play. While still in the village, where the bedrock had been eroded, forming sandy patches, she saw rows of little craters, like sand and dust baths for small birds, sparrows? (So there were sparrows after all at this elevation? Yes. And as previously mentioned: it is not necessary to avoid a contradiction here and there in her story.) And these bathing hollows, as was clearly recognizable from the markings, were alternately used by the children, or by whom else? for shooting marbles. Likewise she came upon signs of ninepin games, with wooden sticks set up as the pins, now fallen every which way, and among them, serving as the bowling balls, more or less round fieldstones.

"Or did I merely imagine these Sierra children's games? Did my Sorbian-Arab village interpose its image again? Or, even more likely, my long-ago film set in the Middle Ages, in which the children had to play typical medieval games, with marbles and ninepins?"

The only person she really saw playing, on an athletic field carved out of a wasteland of stones, actually the mere suggestion of one, was the observer from abroad (she passed him unobserved): he was playing basketball by himself, at his knees a cluster of quite small children, not yet old enough for school. The basket, with mere shreds of a net, was bolted to a cliff, high up, and the reporter repeatedly jumped up to it with the ball for a "slam dunk." He was playing in the sweat of his brow, cheering himself and the children on. They were supposed to join in and get the ball away from him. They were supposed to participate. They were supposed to play, please, please. He almost pleaded with them to play with him. But it was true after all, they did not play. They did not want to play—they were incapable of playing. All these children of Pedrada knew how to do was look on.

And it was even unclear whether they were watching him or something else altogether, for instance a trail of ants crossing the rocks or an invisible joust taking place behind him, fought with lances and swords by two men on horseback, their faces hidden in their visors; who said that the remote playing field there could not just as well have been the lists? Wasn't this the place and the time to approach the solitary player, so that he could accompany her, at least for part of the way? "Not here yet, not now."

In the telephone booth, up there way beyond the outskirts of Pedrada, surrounded by brambles and honeysuckle vines that formed a sort of lane, she dialed her own number, that of her property on the edge of the riverport city. She had entered the booth without any particular intention, desire, or decision, and had picked up the receiver. In this region there was still, or permanently, no service for her hand telephone.

The booth was far from everything, she later told the author, but besides, it was the one from which she had always called her daughter when crossing the Sierra de Gredos on foot; usually her daughter had stayed home alone (the girl was independent at an early age, or at least wanted

to be). "Everything all right?" — "Yes." — "Not too lonely?" — "No, no."
And so on. And now? On the first ring, the telephone was picked up, and
she had her child's voice in her ear.

And now she also knew her name; it popped out, her only word. But
then the voice said, "I am not your daughter. I am the boy from next door,
the son of your neighbor in the porter's lodge. I am taking care of your
house until you get back."

And it remained the voice of her vanished child nonetheless, and it
continued: "It is my wish that you not be too lonely on your journey. Here
everything is all right. I have set the alarm and turned up the heat. The
house is warm. The morning sun is shining in. Ah, behind the quinces
there I can see the idiot of the outskirts going by. He is rowing with his
arms and whistling. And now a train is blowing its whistle. And a few
ship's horns are blaring from down on the two rivers, several, many! When
are you coming back? You have been gone so long already, such a long
time. At night your admirer still circles the property. And each time he
leaves a letter in the box for you. I have burned them all, but read them
first and committed them to memory—in case you want to hear them. I
am not reading a newspaper anymore—no longer need to. Ah, and now it
is starting to snow, even though the sun is shining. One letter had no return address; I did not read it. The stamp had mountain peaks, the Sierra
de Gredos. No one has asked for you. A hedgehog is going through the orchard right now, slaloming past the trees; shouldn't he be hibernating? A
ladder has tipped over. An outdoor table has collapsed. A statue, the one
in back by the beech, is missing its head. Your bed looks used. The toys in
Salma's or Lubna's room are lying all over the place. Otherwise everything
is fine. Ah, now the fireplace screen is rattling. I have made a fire. And the
oak roots in the forest that were ripped out of the ground by the storm are
more and more matted, and hard as rock."

She had hung up without a word and had continued on up the mountainside, with her daughter's voice in her ear, even if it had broken now
and then like that of a teenage boy whose voice was changing—with
nothing but the voice, not a moment's thought for the news it had imparted. It was still the voice of a child, which, although it articulated
every word carefully, spoke as if only in vowels. The vowels shaped every
one of the words, and the sentences, too.

In this sense, that voice had had nothing Arabic about it, a language
in which even children's speech consisted almost entirely of hissing,

fricative, throaty, coughing, and choking sounds? Or maybe not? The vowels carried the words, transported them, breathed soul into them, lent them wings. They had come from afar and at the same time from an abundant source and had set more than just her hearing to vibrating. These gently wafting vowels, forming an acoustic garland, created in the listener a sound chamber that made him able to reply in the same trusting, candid tone, and so on, back and forth, forth and back.

In the mountain telephone booth she had not answered, yet the voice continued to resonate in her long afterward, so she now made up for that. As she climbed, she spun around, and now gave her replies: "Here it is warm, too. Or does it only seem that way to me? Ah, a lizard, look. Show yourself. Do not hide. You do not know how to hide, my child. You never knew how to hide. When you played hide-and-seek with the others, you were always the one who could be seen right away, even more clearly than before the game began. You can play anything else and turn anything into a game, but not hiding. Ah, look, the first eagle. And oh my, here the wild boars have rooted up the grass. Ahoy!"

In the immortal old books that had preceded her own story, this stretch would probably have been one of those that were described thus: "He [the hero, for it could only have been a 'he'?] walked, rode, sailed [so and so many] miles and hours without encountering anything worth telling [or even 'worthy of telling']."

But of course her story was supposed to take place in a time when it was less the purely external surprising, astonishing, and unusual happenings that provided material—a time when mere actions as a source for the plot seemed to have been exhausted long since—than the astonishing and unusual juxtapositions of external and internal, the interactions and indeed the resonances, thus also appropriate to the time or era of her story, or even "lighting the way" (like the rose in the old poem)? Or lighting her way home, or around the corner?

And accordingly she then emphasized in a conversation with her designated author that the aforementioned stretch was an episode worthy of telling, even if nothing happened other than her climbing up the mountain, the wafting of the air, and the blueing of the sky.

And again her wrath, almost an outburst of rage, and this from her, the financial manager, the expert on money and numbers, when the author had the audacity to ask how and with what she, traveling without cash, had paid for the hotel and her provisions that morning in Pedrada, etc.: No: that was of no relevance or reality when it came to their book, at least in this part. "That is not it. That is not how it is." The question was "completely idiotic" and gave reason to fear that he, the author, had not yet understood what she had in mind for the book. "Or are you merely trying to provoke me?" There were already hundreds of articles about her, crammed with banking and money matters. "Don't tell me, and us, every little thing."

She actually did ride part of the way, bareback on a Sierra horse, long-legged, gleaming brownish-black, which was waiting, as if just for her, under an overhanging cliff, as was the rounded rock on the ground from which she swung herself onto the horse's back; both ready for her as if for the repetition of a scene in her old film.

She could have ridden up to the ridges (the precipitous southern slopes were too much for even a native horse); the animal carried her as if she were nothing, or as if she were no one. But very soon she dismounted from its rather narrow back and continued her journey on foot. And again, when she turned and looked back from higher up, the horse was standing under an overhanging rock, but now with others, of the same color, in a row, as if at an abandoned hack stand; on each horse sat an even darker Sierra jackdaw, picking something out of the horse's coat and mane and teeth and nostrils.

And still, as had been the case ever since her departure from the settlement, pairs of cattle horns stared at her here and there from amid the broom or escoba bushes (otherwise there was hardly any taller vegetation, only scattered scrub pines, most of them long since dead and stripped of their bark); the horns were very wide and curved, almost always ending in a pointed, straight section, and occasionally one of the powerful, always anthracite-black bodies would loom up from amid the tangle of broom branches in the omnipresent chest-high thicket, the cow's or bull's eyes seemingly aimed and guided on both sides by the horns' dagger tips; this time more Ávila cattle than usual were spending the winter high in the Sierra.

She walked without stopping, without changing pace; without in any way deviating from her pace. She did not stop even when she passed the corpses of the stonemason and the woman from Friuli or Lefkadia, lying side by side at a spot in the tundra, with gunshot wounds in their scalps, in their crowns, their eyes still open, hardly broken, in which she saw herself recognized, unlike in the *ultramarinos* shop earlier, and again this dead couple stood in for her parents, killed in an accident.

During earlier crossings of the Sierra de Gredos, whenever she came upon an animal, especially in open patches, she had headed straight for it, not in a hurry but speeding up a little, until she stood body to body with it, for a moment, *"el trance,"* as if grown together with it—in the same way in which she rendered potential human attackers defenseless by leaving them no surface to attack—and then briskly continued in her chosen direction, even if it might be the wrong direction at first.

With her walking, with her manner of walking, she protected herself, made herself invulnerable to attack. True, it was a kind of loafing. But because it had a rhythm, it had value. And furthermore, so she imagined, or was almost certain, she also protected others by walking, and by walking as she was walking now. With her walk and her walking now she was protecting her distant, absent brother. And in particular she was protecting him in this fashion from himself.

By walking this way through the Sierra, his sister was doing her part to make sure that he, who had previously committed violent acts only against objects, was restrained from his first outbreak of violence against a human being. Once he crossed this threshold, which had been calling to him or even drawing him magnetically for a long time—"ever since I became aware [his words] of my mother- and fatherlessness"—there would be no turning back. Her brother would then take aim at more and more people, at the whole human race, at life. As he had long fantasized to himself and also to her, he would run amok in a way precisely calculated and planned, and intended for the duration, with that treacherous glow in the corners of his eyes and mouth that women in particular saw as a kind of magical smile. And precisely on this day, at this hour, after another of his nocturnal wanderings, this time in an uninterrupted circle around an encampment of occupation troops in his chosen country, his ultimate (she to the author: "Occasionally it is all right to use a term of non-Germanic origin") crossing of the line was imminent—his first murderous blow.

The air around her as she headed up the mountain was jolted, ah, how much more sharply and harshly than by the bulls' horns, by her brother's "Now I'm going to do it! Now! Now! Now!" And then all that helped was her walking. She walked. She walked with everything she had, with her soles, her kneecaps, her thighs, her vagina (yes), her stomach, her shoulders, with her mouth, nose, and eyes, and with all of them at once; all these things together had to walk, and had to walk together.

She walked with everything at her disposal, her thoughts, her memory, her desire, her will, her intentions. She walked exactly as she worked in her "business," or had worked. Her way of walking, as a form of averting, bringing to safety, calming, clarifying, gaining perspective, preparing the ground and plowing, went beyond mere walking. Of course it was the movement of someone who had time, much free time, but simultaneously it was a form of action, which, because it includes, according to Adam Smith, John Maynard Keynes, Schumpeter, or also Marx, Lenin, and Kardelj, that special kind of political, moral, and aesthetic action, can render unnecessary all those other overspecialized and thus destructive forms of action (no examples here): walking as comprehensive action—as (topic) stewardship ("of course only in Utopia"): as another invisible hand.

She walked with everything she encountered and came upon, with everything she saw, tasted, heard, and smelled.

And in particular she walked with the images, the images that flew to her from distant times and places in the course of her steady progress up the mountainside, which provided zones of protection and safety and prospects for the future entirely different from memories, thoughts, feelings, and sensory impressions.

These kinds of images assured continuity, and something above and beyond that. They made magic. With this walking, she imagined, and was almost certain, she was saving not only her brother, not only her own blood relative. Wasn't that one of the reasons for her walking? Ah, keep everything in proportion, otherwise we are lost. She had not been lost for a long time, and the next time it happened, it would be for good. One false step and it would become evident how cut off one was, from everything and everyone.

Walking, healing, organizing, managing: magical walking? So had the foreign woman already been infected by the natives' atavism? And her repeated deep sighs in the course of her seemingly so light-footed walking? *Tahallul*, rejoicing; *tanassul*, sighing.

Dear observer, first of all that need not be a contradiction, and second, this sighing is perhaps merely a family and tribal trait, "typically Sorbian-Oriental," passed down to the present day from long, long ago.

And when she asked the author later whether it wasn't the same with him during long, steady walks, especially when he was crossing the mountains—all her experiences could only be universal ones—he replied, no, he was familiar with the concept of assuring continuity, keeping alive, lending a hand, in short, of "managing"—instead of setting out to write he actually used the term "setting out to manage" in his mind—solely from his own "doings" now and then, writing down, writing up, writing on, but that was no form of certainty, not even "approximately"—"or was it?"

One was walking up the mountain. ("One?" —One.) Walking was taking place. Walking will have taken place. Like the falcon: when one looked for it, it was no longer, yet still, in the spot where it had been when it had screeched. "Falcon, kite, drop a feather for me." And it dropped one.

She had distributed the weight she was carrying in such a way that instead of slowing or hindering her walking it gave her a rhythm, like set sails. Thus, carrying in front her knapsack, *mochila*, *michlatuz-zahr*, which, as long ago with women travelers, was reminiscent of a bolster, *almohada*, *michada*, with the bare necessities and a bit more stuffed into it, and with other bulky items hooked onto her belt, and this thing or that swinging around her hips, she sailed up the Sierra, a solitary seafarer.

On earlier crossings she had sometimes set out without any baggage, with nothing in her hands, nothing to carry, thinking she would be freer and less encumbered that way. But she had soon noticed that the walking, climbing, scrambling, was not any easier as a result but rather the opposite. One needed, one had to have on one's body, properly balanced loads, but especially the kind that balanced the bearer. They kept one alert, not as snakes did, but similarly, as one groped one's way through the pathless, trackless waste, alert from top to toe, and thus prevented the sort of precipitous actions that could be fatal, especially to one walking alone; they constituted a sort of armor of mindfulness, guided one and blazed a trail on the middle path, the only viable one, at least in the Sierra, between gravity and free flight.

"Never again," she had then sworn to herself, "will I hike over the Sierra de Gredos without something suitable on my back and on my tummy"—how could she call her flat, muscular stomach a "tummy"?!

She, the solitary seafarer, all alone far and wide. Astonishing, almost incomprehensible, that there were no others scaling these sky-high heights at the same time, perhaps nicely dispersed across the northern flanks that sloped gently skyward. What in the world was everyone doing? How could they stand moping around at home, down in the lowlands, in those gloomy cities that made them narrow-minded (to say nothing of the contemporary "villages")? How did it happen that she never ran into a single one of her thousand and three enemies in these remote, lonely, sheltered, quiet, and expansive spaces that generated harmony, but only in places where, with the best will in the world, one could not help remaining enemies?

Why didn't her mortal enemy (for she had one, or imagined one, as almost everyone did at the time of her story) suddenly appear around a granite cliff, three thousand six hundred miles from Wall Street and the Ginza, and the two of them look at each other wide-eyed, laugh, for the moment completely forgetting or losing track of the fact that they were mortal enemies, and realize they had to hang on to the moment or do something constructive with it?

But it was not actually true that on this day she was walking through the Sierra alone. Soon she saw ahead of her human footprints in the stretches of granite sand that often simulated a path through the broom and juniper thicket, and in the increasingly frequent patches of snow: fresh tracks, as if from that very morning, and not single ones but many, then innumerable ones, close together and behind each other and finally overlapping. Except that she did not get to see the people they belonged to, although she could feel, smell, and taste their presence—did not see them for such a long time that she forgot them again.

One was walking. Walking was taking place. The inimitable sound of the granite sand underfoot, less a crunching than a grinding and rustling of the coarse particles, which at the same time massaged one's feet: the most prominent walking sound on the Iberian peninsula—even if one might encounter a similar sound during a crossing of the Alps, or in the Andes, or, for all she cared, in the Himalayas ("The highest peaks are not for me," akin to: "We have no business going into outer space").

More and more stretches bare of all vegetation, without a bush, without a blade of grass, even without those lichens, an ornamental smear of the most varied yellows, greens, and reds that resembled geographical maps and were also named after them: "geography lichens"; yet also no wastelands of scree and stones, but often glass-smooth, slightly rounded rocky plateaus, polished long ago by the Sierra glaciers, slippery smooth not only where they were snow-covered but just as much in the dry patches.

The glowing sky reflected in what looked like subterranean boats not yet completely surfaced and shot through with alabaster-white veins of quartz. Crossing these gentle, stadium-size rocky mounds as if one were all dressed up, even if one had not put on anything special for the journey (or had one?).

And nevertheless closest to the blue of the sky above the ridge, either lightning blue or in the next moment almost outer-space black, whenever one took in the sky not nakedly and directly but glimpsed through a shrub or a tree—so now and then there still was a tree, if only a dwarf one—a blue, merely as background. Merely?

Every long story, she later told the author, has a certain color, a predominant color. And the color she wanted for their book—just as its sound should be the steps of a solitary person walking through the granite sand of the otherwise silent, still Sierra—was that sky-blue shining intermittently through the mountain brush. It was the blue found in the background of medieval stained-glass windows, with the twigs, branches, evergreen leaves, needles, berries (juniper berries or rowanberries, for instance), fruit capsules (rose hips, for instance), and pods (of broom) as the figures against this background. Smoke-colored sky-blue. For the smoke color lent objects their sharpest contours.

No, when the blue glowed and shimmered through the slits, gaps, and holes in the Sierra vegetation, filling the smallest openings and being simply blue and still, it resembled the blue of work clothes hung out to dry as far as the eye could see. She knew that blue from her ancestral village, and not only from there: the blue of her neighbors' work pants and jackets, seen through the foliage of bushes and fruit trees. And upon seeing that blue one thought simultaneously of "work" and "festivity." The blue behind the leaves presented the image of work clothes that could also serve as party clothes, just as they were, without having to be altered in any fashion. It was the blue of patches, but also the blue of brides' trains and scarves and flags—flags with this background-blue as their only color. It looked like cloth, as no other blue and no other color did; it had nothing heavenly or ethereal about it, but rather hung, stood, rested, waited for one in back there as a material, as something material.

Despite its being winter, some thickets of broom emitted a summery vanilla scent as one slipped through them. When one had painfully forced one's way between two boulders, one's hands had a singed smell, as after rubbing flints together. When we bit into the withered and blackened rowanberries, which hung in bunches from bare trees that were hardly taller than we were, seemingly frozen and long since dried out, our mouths, parched from the climb, were filled with the taste of the fresh berries and even their juice, both bitter as can be, but how refreshing! and promptly lengthening our stride—the rowanberries' taste so evocative of midsummer that we saw before us the unique light red, the rowanberry red, of newly ripened bunches, in a way that we had never encountered during an actual summer, different from a mere daydream red.

Involuntarily we stuffed our pockets with the surprisingly weighty—but not "heavy"—clumps of berries. We would need them later, especially on the descent into the southern lowland, where, winter or not, we would feel hotter and hotter; as if for a weeklong expedition—one never knew—at the little island of trees amid the sea of cliffs and snow, we supplemented our provisions (the author suggested using the word "provender" occasionally, even if this term was no longer in use in his far-off linguistic homeland).

And now as we plucked more and more bunches of fruit, with the practiced motions of those who had been fruit thieves from childhood on, and finally stood on tiptoe to reach the clusters (yes, more "clusters" than "berries"), we finally understood why the common name for these berries was "bird berries": for concealed behind them, completely hidden from view, perched the small birds so rare in the Sierra—mountain titmice, wrens, robins—behind the clusters but also in them, inconspicuously and silently pecking at them—and when you stood on tiptoe and reached for the berries, they whooshed out of the little rowan tree, not all at once, but each one just as its berries were about to be picked, each of them scolding and shrieking as the rightful owner of the bird-berry bunch, robbed by you of its due.

As the story went, there was once a time when the hunters of the Sierra, not those hunters whose story remains to be told here, even planted rowan trees hither and yon in the mountain wilderness, in order to lure the small birds that were prized as delicacies, and at any rate the rowan trees that often stand alone, as if artificially planted, in the Sierra de Gredos have a second name, along with "bird berry" also "hunter ash." Bitter-as-can-be berries or clusters? Yes, bitter as can be. Not bitter as gall.

But as other fruits first tasted sweet and only later manifested their bitterness, deep within, a bitterness that caused the person eating them to spit them out suddenly, a bitterness that not only turned his stomach but "shook him up" (a village expression?), the rowanberries by contrast revealed to the palate, after the initial off-putting bitterness, a taste that was more than mere "sweetness": an inwardness (did that exist, an "inward taste"?) all the more inward because the initial bitterness remained present in it. Ah, ow, oh—only no "ugh!"—the rowanberries in the rocky clefts of the Sierra de Gredos. (Was it appropriate for her, the heroine, to stand on tiptoe? Yes.)

26

During one period—which one, again, hardly matters for the current story—she had viewed possessions and property as a kind of "accomplishment" (though different from the accomplishment of "having a child," in which she continued to believe, now even unwaveringly). And at the end of that period? She was no longer so sure.

And now, while crossing the Sierra? Was she happy to be as far as possible from her so-called possessions; to get through the day without ever thinking about or looking at things the way a property-owner would—in other words, to be rid of something that over time, rather than cushioning or liberating a person, tended to make one petty and rigid, which plagued and preoccupied one (and there was nothing positive in being thus "occupied")?

What: Was she, a banker and economist, which she continued to be, in her apparently traditional fashion, an enemy of property?

Yes: at least as far as her personal existence was concerned. And besides, she saw here, too, a problem that was beautiful = worth describing, but not a contradiction. Even a few top people at the World and Universal Bank—before her journey, one could easily have pictured her as one of them—had recently come out in opposition to the position on property espoused by this super-powerful institution, which merely pretended to want to help the have-nots of the world and in reality was out to enhance its own power and prestige, and had left their posts with that institution to do something altogether different—something in opposition. And perhaps these people, one at a time, were also making their way through a similar moonlike region, devoid of human beings, relieved to be released for the time being from their eternal preoccupation with power and possessions, perhaps even contemplating an entirely new paradigm?

No, owning property could be an accomplishment for a while, but it was not one's mission in life—which it seemed to have become in the current era. Money and possessions had become the be-all and end-all. The money-changers in the temple? No, the temple of money-changers—and it was the one temple that still counted. In the face of the silence, brightness, and sanctified aura of the money temple, everything else could not help degenerating into dark, agitatedly flailing, recidivist raging. But to her, and precisely to her, the formerly fruitful and liberating notion of property seemed exhausted once and for all, yes, a complete failure. Property no longer represented an ideal.

And because, as she made her way through the Sierra, no "property" crossed her path and disrupted her rhythm, she became, and was, so free that she could do the smallest thing, or, with reference to others, the majority, could "undertake" them. At least this conception accompanied her, and for a stretch her "I" or "one" became a "we" and a "you." We laced our boots. We would bring this rock crystal back for you, and this sheet of mica for you, and this snakeskin for you.

Yes, just as she was making the journey for herself, she was undertaking it for others, and in the rhythm of her stride she felt constantly accompanied by others. It was crucial to stay away from property, as far as possible. We have been property owners long enough. And there was very little that got in the way of observing and perceiving—of seeing the big picture—as much as property ownership. And if we lost the ability to observe, we ceased to be worthy of observation, of being kept in the picture.

And at the same time she remained aware that one false step, one stumble, not even a broken foot, merely a sprain, would be enough to put an end to this cocky "we." One momentary slip, and the veil of universality, the epic sweep, would be ripped off our big picture of the world, and all such words as "we" and "you" and "one" would be blown away, and only the teeny-tiny "I," more solipsistic still than the property owners' "I," would be left, more wretched, ridiculous, and, in her eyes, now "not worth describing."

And even more powerful than her constant awareness of the external danger of falling, which was mechanical and merely threatened her body and could also be anticipated and to some extent forestalled, another awareness was at work inside her, one that had pursued her since her first time in the Sierra de Gredos, when she was halfway to the top and suddenly found herself without her companion, the father of her child, which she could feel, ready to be born, in her protruding belly; under her heart.

Just as then, when she had stood alone with the fetus in the blazing granite-cliff sun, there would again erupt from deep within her something that would turn everything upside down, uncontrollably: labor pains, which would have nothing to do with giving birth, bringing something into the world, and which, also, instead of just hurting, produced sheer, revolting horror—turning not only herself but the entire exterior world upside down, so that again she would be unable to distinguish her head from her feet, but also north from south, earth from sky, horizontal from vertical, mountain from plain, up from down, large from small, body from surfaces, eagles from lizards, ants from ibexes, cliffs from houses, rock-slides from metropolises—all hopelessly mixed up before her eyes. Hopelessly? Hopelessly.

Yes, infinitely more to be feared than a false step was the repetition of that tumbling and stumbling of her insides, casting her, and with her the world and everything in it, into a chaotic state in which the cosmos (which meant "ornament" and "order," did it not?) seemed utterly insane and the entire creation fell out of joint—and far outstripped the so-called primal chaos in its frantic confusion.

"To get a grip on things," she went on, "I sank my teeth into my arm, and as I did so felt my arm growing teeth and biting me back in the face . . . The tops of the cliffs, although they were standing still, began to tip in all directions. The kite circling in the distance grazed me with its beak. The shoe I had kicked off became a person in his death throes, his mouth gaping wide. A circle of dead tree trunks bent over to become a herd of elephants, about to stampede over me and the child in my belly. I jumped backward at the sight of a cloud. I leaned over to pick some blackberries that were hanging high above my head. When a butterfly approached, I jerked my head to the side as if it were a mountain vulture. Like someone cutting her own hair in front of a mirror—no, not like that—I reached to the left for something on the right, in front of me for something at my back, and vice versa, and vice versa again. And finally, in a panic, I even looked for the doorbell in a rock wall . . ." For once she did not interrupt her story in midstream, but was all afire (the author: "an expression still in use?") to go on and on, describing the episode.

So was the narrow, rigid gaze of the property owner therefore preferable to the threat of such dire confusion? The halfway-safe "What's mine is mine"?

"It is true," she then told the author in his village in La Mancha: "Even far from my earthly possessions, on my way to you, I allowed myself to be influenced, incidentally and not even all that reluctantly, by one of my belongings, as if that could keep me from being thrown off course. Yes, among other things, while crossing the Sierra this time I was guided by the thought that in a bush or somewhere I would come upon a certain object I had lost on another crossing, nothing special, nothing valuable, some small thing, insignificant in itself, but linked with a memory. I am repeating myself? As I should. You should repeat it as well, author of mine." — The author: "A scarf? A glove? A pocketknife?" — She: "A scarf. I was constantly on the lookout for the black scarf I lost maybe ten years ago, one summer, in the Sierra."

The author: "So that means a yes, within limits, to owning such personal items? But not real estate, not house and land? When it comes to the latter, your story should say the exact opposite of your immortal predecessor's, in which house and patience are named in one breath: 'He abandoned his house and his patience.' So instead: 'She abandoned the house and impatience'; 'She abandoned the house and intolerance'; 'She set out for distant parts and patience'; 'She set out for foreign parts and tolerance'?" — She: "Yes, something along those lines."

Despite all the measures and precautions taken, the moment nonetheless came when up again turned into down, houses became cliffs, cliffs became lodgings, and chaos took hold.

Except that this soon lost its power to terrify. For the first time now it was right and proper. It started—so the story goes—with her pausing on one of the outer shelves of the main Sierra ridge that were staggered in an even rhythm all the way to the horizon and looking back into the high valley of the río Tormes and its headwaters, where she had begun her ascent that morning.

She saw Pedrada lying below, the stone-thrower village. But was this still her Pedrada? Weren't the tents she recalled actually a cluster of those conical and pyramid-shaped haystacks typical of the Sierra de Gredos, far from any settlement, fenced off from the mountain wilderness by stone walls, which surrounded the stacks, always in a circle? And these hay cones, precisely in the middle of the otherwise empty stone enclosures—no cattle or sheep in sight—looked as if they had long since been abandoned there, blackened with age, stacked perhaps years, if not decades, earlier, the hay unusable, the tarpaulins covering them tattered to shreds.

Her, and our, Pedrada no longer existed; the stone buildings were blocks of granite heaved out of the ground; "Pedrada" a mere name, with no village to go with it, similar to the way in which, on the route ahead of her, the Puerto de Candeleda had long since ceased to be a pass or a crossing and merely bore the name, with not even the suggestion of a notch there at the top of the ridge.

And she did not see that phantasmagorical Pedrada at her feet, far below; rather the tent-shaped haystacks and the boulders, strewn about as if by an explosion, appeared as if high above her; although she had been climbing for all those hours, they now seemed to be above eye level—just as in the game German children call "Heaven and Hell" the players see themselves rolling along the ground through an undulating landscape bisected by furrows, down into one furrow and ditch, then up, then down again, and up again, until in the end below becomes above, heaven above becomes hell below, and vice versa again.

But unlike what had happened during her first time in the Sierra, this time one experienced such reversals as part of a game involving the terrain or region, the result of the particular sequence and rhythm in which one experienced this mountainous area as one walked, climbed, descended, and ascended again, and this time the constant transformation of earth-low into sky-high did not produce dread (yes, dread, horror) but contentment, not unlike that of children tumbling and rolling over hummocks—a sense of lightheartedness and levity at finding that for once "heaven" was "hell" and "hell" was now "heaven."

And likewise, when we turned toward our destination, the crest, we saw it, along with the still merely imaginary Candeleda Pass, not at the level of our brow or crown, but sunken, hardly reaching our beltline, as if the shelf where we had paused were already the main ridge up above.

And here between our feet and the crest of the Sierra (hardly a stone's throw and birds' or electric pylons' swoop away?), over there where the mountain range actually should have presented a landscape of peaks, reaching for outer space: a gigantic hollow, hemmed in to the west and the east, toward sunrise and sunset, by the steep cliffs of the "summit plain," which formed a fragmentary half-circle around the hollow; hollow? more like an area of collapse or a depression, and all this up sky-high, with the bottom of this depression having the appearance of a mammoth arena.

And although it was not her first time here, she did not recognize this arena. The dark spot at the bottom was a forest, if only a small one, and it had not been there earlier. But the pool at the bottom of the depression—or was it a lake, if only a very small one?—was not new to her; it was the Laguna Grande de Gredos, a lake! Except that its water was not even frozen, and had clouds drifting over it, of frost? smoke? haze?

Familiar to her from before were, likewise, the tumbled boulders, both on the floor of the arena and—even more helter-skelter, fractured, and varied—on the slopes or "tiers" of the natural amphitheater, in which ten times ten theaters the size of the already enormous one at Epidauros would have fit easily. She knew that the entire hell-deep depression there had once been filled to the rim with glacial ice, and that it was the glacier that had left the boulders, towers, and fragments all higgledy-piggledy, leaning against each other, crashed on top of each other, some seemingly standing on their heads (or on their hands, or on only one hand)? Yes, in bygone times, chaos had reigned clear across the Sierra arena, hour after hour, day after day, and for thousands of years, an incessant crashing, smashing, splitting, pounding, with sparks flying. But then, once the ice had melted and was no longer eternal, the chaos had died down. Now it was recalled only on maps, in mountaineering books, in the guide to the "Dangers of the Sierra de Gredos": "El caos de Hondoneda" (or "Hondareda"), the Chaos of Hondoneda (*hondo*, deep); "chaos" was the name used the world over for all the areas formerly chewed up by the glacier—nothing quieter than a "chaos" like this, and even the rock formations that seemed to be resting on only one hand were stable for the duration (the duration?).

But no: the smoke or haze in the depths of Hondoneda or Hondareda, high up in the Sierra, did not emanate, or not exclusively, from the "laguna"—where the glacier had sliced most deeply—but rose from one of the chaos-boulders, no, from several, from all of them.

These were lived in, were human habitations. It was the smoke from fires—wood smoke, root smoke—that we smelled all the way up here. Of course we knew from earlier crossings that down there in Hondareda, the most remote part of the Sierra, lived a hermit. But these people were no hermits anymore: so close together, and also so many crowded into one place. We had already noticed earlier, as we crossed the trackless wastes, in addition to the innumerable footprints, the mussel shells amid the granite, in the sand and in the crevices.

We had even come upon oyster shells, gleaming with mother-of-pearl. And these could not be fossils, could they? There had been no ocean here, had there? And what hermits ate mussels and oysters? Had them delivered up here in the mountains? And the legions of shell-casings on the way up—in every tenth thicket a blue capsule (which one soon stopped mistaking for a glimpse of the sky on the other side)? Hermits who in the meantime were also hunters? Had mutated into hunters? And now also shots, from shotguns, again and again; in the forest down there?

The longer she stood and gazed down into this broad depression, so close to the summit plain (or the "cirque," *circo*, as it is called in the area), the more contradictory the image became, less in the sense of off-putting than of attractive: contradictory? erratic, jumpy. Here in the trackless wilderness, to reach the colony below she had to strike out at random, clambering, jumping, also slithering down sandy slopes, then fight her way through, and on the opposite slope, up to the former pass, a real vehicular road in serpentines, this, too, not there on her previous visit to the Sierra, or overlooked. So was the Puerto de Candeleda in use again? even widened as never before, and likewise on the steep southern descent more or less passable, at least with an all-terrain vehicle? But this road leading so straight up to the bare horizon that one involuntarily thought: "Not suitable as an escape route."

And in the midst of the chaos a helicopter landing pad, not built as such, but already there, a square of quartz and granite polished by the glacier, and a helicopter there just about to take off? no, that was merely the full-sized outline of one, with broad, blazing red stripes, in the middle of the square, intended to mark the destination for pilots heading for the depression. And there was a constant crack of shotguns, and at the same time, as she descended, from far below as well as from the slopes to the right and left of her, people were waving. From all sides dogs came racing toward her for a moment, each of them guarding a herd of sheep, goats, or calves, and they all jumped up on her at the same time and licked her from top to toe.

The shepherds, or whatever they were, who went with the dogs, without exception young and speaking into walkie-talkies, belonged to different and in every case quite mixed races, one with Asian eyes in an

American Indian face, another dark-skinned and red-haired, a third with the lips and forehead of an Australian aborigine, but tall and narrow-hipped, the next, a kerchief under her mannish hat, a girl with such a white skin and such black eyes that the two women, when they encountered each other, jumped backward for a moment, and all the young shepherds, not dressed in shepherd style, but positively elegant—which actually seemed even more practical and also appropriate to the *circo* of glassy, green, gray, blue-tinged rock walls—were intently focused on their work, the result of their not having been at it long—having started only yesterday or this morning. And as they carried out their "shepherdly" duties, they were also engaged in other activities, not only playing musical instruments, above all lutes, *oud* in Arabic, and steel harmonicas, whose brittle sound went well with the granite, but also juggling, walking on their hands, turning cartwheels on the edge of precipices, as if indeed practicing to perform in a circus, but also following the lines of a book with their fingers, rubbing flints together, tasting the mountain fruits, and many more such things.

How transformed these faces seemed, too, faces one might have encountered on a grand boulevard in Madrid or Rome, in the light of the high Sierra, in the broad-spectrum reflection that deepened and clarified the colors and lines of individual details, which the granite gallery encircling all of Hondareda, as well as the flat ledge underfoot, emitted; a light and refraction that showed the features of the faces not as isolated details, as mouth, nose, ears, but all in one.

"As a visage?" the author interrupted: "insofar as that word can still be used . . ." — She in reply: "At least for this book of ours you should describe less the mountains or the natural phenomena of the Sierra than the way the faces of people appear in the glow of the high Sierra!"

27

Not that the great depression, or basin, or bowl, below the uppermost rocky crest was thickly settled. And yet, on what was for now Ablaha's final crossing, it appeared to be full of people. And that impression did not stem merely from the fact that during her previous times up/down there in Hondareda not a soul had crossed her path, or at most one to three hermits.

Altogether, this place presented fundamentally different numerical conditions, or, to put it another way, perceptions of quantity. A scant dozen figures, moving about or merely expelling visible—at long last visible—puffs of breath in the otherwise motionless stony expanse at her feet, made the impression of being "numerous."

Earlier she had received a similar impression from seeing the mountain goats in this high-altitude depression: even when it was only a single pair, grazing at a distance from one another, the peculiar nature of the location made it appear to her like a sizable flock. Or: whenever a pair of moths fluttered around each other, it looked like a whole swarm. Even the perception of space as one gazed down toward the floor of this supersized stadium, as well as around at the slopes or tiers, was unusual. The body of water at the bottom was at one moment a mere puddle, at the next a good-size lake. The dimensions of the lone building one encountered before the Puerto de Candeleda shifted between those of a vast mountain hotel, a half-collapsed little shelter, or a toolshed on the edge of the southerly access road (or was it nothing but a former glacial trough, full of light-colored scree?). And were those swaths of snow or trails of spilled flour?

She climbed down, down, down, for an hour? for two? for half a day? and yet had hardly come any closer to the first of the rock dwellings, which had at first seemed no farther away than a hop, skip, and a jump, or an ibex's leap. Along with the confusing—confusing? no—numerical conditions in this Hondareda went measures of distance that at first seemed unconventional, then somewhat amusing, and finally familiar from long ago, becoming, the longer one was exposed to them, just as clear and self-explanatory as the commonly used meters, kilometers, miles, or, if you will, "leguas" or "versts." As in earlier tales, she literally and figuratively—the path was heading downhill again, steeply—saw before her, after the treeless stretch, a dwarf conifer at a distance of "a stone's throw," then only a "chamois's leap," and then one member of the observation team, strangers to the area, at "crossbow-shot distance."

A while later, she again had in her field of vision down below King Charles V / Emperor Charles I, or the man playing or replaying him, making his way without his litter and bearers, alone, hopping "over sticks and stones" with no sign of his gout, despite his almost sixty years, also with no signs of his king- or emperorship, his mouth open "as wide as a barn door," as when he was a child and stood there "as if to catch Spanish flies," at what distance from her? perhaps in "paper-airplane range." And the abandoned litter tipped over among the broom branches, how far away? Approximately a "spear's toss," no, "a bowshot" away. So does this make it a tale from an earlier time, too? No, from now (and now, and now).

The observer dispatched from the outside world to the new settlers' region of Hondareda—who had just jumped out of the barely landed helicopter down below, along with several others of his ilk—noted, however, in his later report that in fact it appeared that up here people had completely taken leave of the present, by even a few gloomy degrees more decisively than in Pedrada, halfway up; a regression was at work here that set them back not merely by decades but into the far-distant past, by centuries, perhaps millennia, actually an "atavism of an atavism."

And his report bore the heading "The Has-Beens, or" (like contemporary headline-writers for newspapers and advertisements, he had a proclivity for verbal paradoxes and wordplay): "The Mountain Castaways."

What was accurate in his report, or whatever his testimonial (pun!) was—which is not to say that it was "true"—was that the closer to the bottom of the depression, with its lake, the people there lived or "resided," the more "down and out" they appeared. Observers, and not only the observation teams flown in, could not escape the impression that of the mixtures and crosses of all the human races (if that word was still appropriate), the ugliest and most profoundly neglected, as well as most savagely, unsalvageably, and hopelessly battered representatives, individually or in pairs, had dragged themselves to this spot in the high Sierra and had tumbled headfirst into this enormous, rocky, prehistoric glacial pit.

Yes, that was correct: the figures in the settlement down there at the bottom corresponded to the image one had, although one should know better, of humans from prehistoric times. Were they even human beings like us, today, in the present? Did they even possess consciousness, a mental awareness as sharp and alert as ours, and our richly developed modern emotional life? Or wasn't the sight that met our eyes at the bottom of the depression actually something we had shaken off once and for all, a deposit, the "dregs"?—even the observer would probably have been appalled at such an expression?

Yet it was only from the threshold of the dwellings down there in the valley that the people of Hondareda appeared this way to her. (Yes, it was a valley, with meadows along the outflow of the lake, and a stretch of forest, although the trees were hardly as tall as a man, along one section of the lakeshore.)

Once she had arrived and entered the settlement down there, the people became recognizable as close relatives of the unmistakably contemporary young people she had seen all over the steep slopes: their parents? More likely their grandparents, and not old at all, as well as uncles and aunts, all of whom had something foster-parent-like about them.

And if the goings-on, the doings among those dwellings, did seem odd for this day and age—again the observer had observed accurately—and were not entirely up-to-date, this hardly indicated that they had "turned their back on the present."

It must be conceded that along with, or in addition to, the unusual surface and spatial conditions in Hondareda, something like a different kind of time was in effect. Yet it did not prevail or hold sway, but rather accompanied and undergirded normal time, as a melody and a rhythm— like everywhere else, when a person did not know what time it was by the clock, the next person would know.

The presence of a secondary type of time simply came from the fact that with every few steps down into the granite basin one encountered a different microclimate, a wind that was wintry, then warmer and vernally mild, then hot and summery, suddenly bitter cold again for a bit, until down at the bottom all these climate zones and winds were jumbled together.

And she acknowledged later that the reporter was right to some extent—when the two of them, since he, too, was out there all alone, crossed each other's paths at some unspecified time in the wilderness beyond his observation post, close to the Candeleda Pass, and fell into conversation: it was not completely inaccurate to call the Hondareda population the "has-beens."

The very ambiguity of the term has something to recommend it. Didn't each of the new settlers remind one of an athlete whom an opposing player had sidelined once and for all, while this opponent had long since gone away, vanished, was no longer there to be challenged, continuing to play somewhere else? As if the has-been were not even benched but merely left shaking his fist impotently in the air?

But the inhabitants of Hondareda, as she urged the outside observer to consider at the end of her stay there, appeared to be has-beens even more, and infinitely more lastingly, in a different respect: as if of their own accord and free will they had decided, in rank and file (they who never lined up anywhere), not to play anymore, or at least not to play games in which one played, either openly or surreptitiously, primarily against another person or persons—not to play even a single one of those games known as "grown-up games."

"So that means voluntarily renouncing all games with winners and losers, and certainly all games of annihilation? Forever? Such games are played out for good down in the pit?" (A playful question on the part of her partner in conversation.)

Her response: "Played out for the time being, in this period of transition, until perhaps, no, necessarily, a new and entirely different kind of play crops up. In this transitional period at least, your has-beens have decided to cultivate the greatest possible seriousness, each in his dealings with himself and likewise with his fellow settlers—which by no means manifests itself—why did you not see it that way as well?—in gravity but rather in a special gracefulness ('Latinate words'). Where you may have observed, or rather *wanted* to observe, wild shaking of fists in the air, someone else might have noticed lunging and hopping steps, of a sort seen nowhere else, or maybe that peculiar clumsiness of someone dedicated to total seriousness, but what a lovely clumsiness, not all that different from floating."

A question from her opponent: "The clumsy seriousness of the has-beens and castaways, in which the rudiments and elements of a new form of play can be discerned?"

She: "That is right. Yes. To be discerned and ferreted out. And there is another way, a third way, to read your 'has-beens': apparently they have lost all the images, ideas, ideals, rituals, dreams, laws, and, finally, also the first and last images that made it possible for them to picture a world, communal life on the planet, and prefigured it for them, prescribed it, lent it a rhythm, or perhaps merely feigned or conjured it up. And being stranded in this fashion is by no means voluntary. The loss of images is something that befell the people of Hondareda. The images, laws, rhythms, and so on that give the world meaning were violently destroyed for them, for each of them in his seemingly inherited place, by all sorts of external events—war, the death of loved ones, betrayal, crime, including crimes they committed themselves, and so on—generally at one blow.

"From one moment to the next, something ceased to mean anything at all to them: the image or the idea, for instance, that the Olympic flame is carried every four or however many years across the continents to the site of the next games, or the previously always valid rhythmic and pre-dictable image of belonging to a country, a culture, even a people; or the images of Mars transmitted to Earth—and these are only the most harm-less and tolerable losses of images. All the others—and the loss of images is total for those who found their way to Hondareda, or rather washed up there—are far more grave, infinitely more grave! A person stricken with such a loss can think only one thought: endgame! It is all up with me and with the world. Except that those who are affected, instead of drowning or hanging themselves or running amok against the rest of the world, have made their way here.

"To find a new image? Among this horde of castaways high in the mountains? To which you also belong? When you speak of the loss of im-ages, are you speaking of yourself?"

While she, the adventurer, and he, the transcontinental observer, were thus engaged in conversation, they were standing, by now on the other side of the meanwhile legendary "Great Depression of Hondareda," on an almost glass-smooth granite outcropping in the midst of the mountain wilderness, far from the colony down below, but also far from the newly graded Candeleda Pass road.

It was not unusual for her to deviate from the path on her crossing of the Sierra. For him, on the other hand, such a deviation was almost unheard of. This was the first time during his stay here that he had been thrust into an area devoid of human beings. At first he ventured only a few steps from the path, then a few more, and finally, without having made a conscious decision, he was already so far from his fellow observers that they, together with their top-volume communication and other devices, ended up out of his earshot, and even sooner out of his sight.

He was drawn more and more forcefully off the beaten track, and eventually he no longer hesitated to give in to the pull or undertow. He even hastened away from the others, no longer pulled but going of his own accord. And what did "off the beaten track" mean? How could a place to which he was going of his own accord, on his own recognizance, be off the beaten track?

And then, in what resembled the "eagle's solitude," as the area through which he was walking felt to him, alone beneath the blue, nearly black sky—he had unexpectedly come upon this other human being. Even before he so much as registered that it was a woman, the woman, he realized that he and this other person were acquainted with each other, and not in a good way. In the place where they had met previously, the two of them, if not declared enemies, had crossed swords.

But how? And where? And when? The reporter—no, at this hour and in this part of the world he was no longer that, nor was he an "observer" anymore—could not for the life of him remember, and from the moment he first caught sight of the other person there in this remote area beyond Hondareda-Comarca, it no longer mattered. To his immense astonishment, the moment he became aware of a second person, obviously out there roaming around as freely as he was, something inside him took a great leap, a joyful one, toward this fellow walker: it did not matter now how she had once crossed swords with him!

That he then contained his joy, and in their exchange continued to play the observer's role, at least for a while, was another story—but it, too, no longer mattered to him, now that he was with this other person, who made him whole here in this half-lost condition.

So what did matter to him? For instance, that she had fulfilled a wish of his, of which he had not even been aware earlier: the wish to meet,

in a remote place, as far as possible from the usual everyday and current happenings, someone he had once known all too well, or known in a
bad sense, even in mortal enmity, appearing now as nothing more than
a face, and thus to speak face-to-face as he had never spoken with anyone before; for instance, to experience in the flesh that the hostilities
and dislikes of daily life were perhaps merely evil illusions, but all the
more potent, despite being "neither conclusive nor inclusive" (his playful
wording).

Mere wishful thinking? Yes. But how can one really object to wishful
thinking? the observer asked himself, while he continued for the moment
to play the role of the field researcher and reporter in his conversation
with this former enemy, the lovely vagabond, or whatever she was, there
on the glassy rock, surrounded by brush, scree, and ice: Hasn't precisely
my unconscious wishful thinking become awareness and possibility,
which means I can, I should, I may make it a reality, as is perhaps the case
with no other way of thinking? I may? I should? It is up to me.

To be sure, and this was not to be denied, that first moment of catching sight of his adversary up here in this remote spot had also created an
acute conflict: on the one hand, there was that leap of joy inside him
toward the other person, kept secret until now but irrepressible—but on
the rebound, no, simultaneously with that leap or reconciliatory urge,
another impulse shot through the observer there in this alien Sierra
territory—to clear that repellent figure out of the way—to kill her—
destroy her—this was his chance!

And the other person, too, that was certain, had the same impulse in
the first moment, was conflicted as he was: Jumping for joy or (a play on
words) about to jump into a life-or-death duel?

And nonetheless, during that conversation on the stone outcropping,
with both of them just playing at arguing, his amazement when in the part
quoted above ("When you speak of the loss of images, are you speaking
of yourself?") the mountain vagabond seized him, the official outside observer, by his ponytail—some of his colleagues on the team also wore
their hair tied back this way—and hacked it off, lickety-split, with her
pocketknife and tossed it into the stony waste.

And it is this action by which he recognizes the woman: she was the
one who gave him a kick the previous evening, or a few weeks ago, or when
had that been? Except that now this cutting of his hair is no hostile act.
What is it? "A new ritual? A new image?" And in this spirit the two of

them will continue for a while to discuss the nature of images and the loss of images.

But we have not yet reached that point. One thing at a time—the episode or way station described just now was a case of our getting ahead of ourselves: first the story must deal more thoroughly with the wanderer and her encounter with the people in the pit of Hondareda up by the summit plain.

2 8

She stayed in Hondareda, as it turned out, longer than more or less planned, consistent with a favorite greeting in the colony: "Let it be a surprise!"

How long? For hours? days? Time played no part in these events, or at least not the usual part. Just as the customary categories of place and space continued to exist but hardly applied to what took place, the hours, minutes, seconds, and such were, if not inoperative, at least units of measurement best left out of consideration during this particular period, and whenever they nonetheless popped up in the story, they proved disruptive and unnecessarily sobering.

Time did continue to have an influence in this highest inhabited spot in the Sierra, but its units were less calibrated to, and measurable by, any clock rhythms from the outside world.

Entirely different units of time were in effect during the Hondareda episode, units lacking a beat, as it were, powerfully concentrated, condensed, and yet prolonged, oscillating and, for that reason, even without the usual tick-tock, by no means less regular, continuing on and on.

When normal clock times sneaked in among these temporal spaces so different from the ones we customarily traverse ("sneaked"? yes)—"for just a second," "two minutes later," etc.—they weakened the temporal magic, which, according to the reporter, was "in any case questionable," but, in the view of the woman who had commissioned this story, reinforced the realness and the nowness and gave the story fresh impetus. In contrast to the measures of distance that had spontaneously come into use in the hollow, units of measure from long ago as well as newly minted ones—"a stone's throw away," "at the distance of an ibex's leap," "at telescopic distance," etc.,—for the temporal units now in force no particular terms offered themselves; for instance, not "in a dozing-off moment," or "after a second dream-night," for it was not a question of a dream.

At most they might refer to "a wind-gust later" or "after another hammer blow" or "before the next page-turning," or use a now clichéd expression, which, however, had acquired meaning again in Hondareda time, "in a jiffy" or "after a while."

The time in effect during her crossing of the valley perhaps revealed itself to be most clearly distinct from chronometricized standard time— yet no less normal or natural?—in that she, lingering along the way, also walking in a circle, as if getting lost on purpose, later described it to the author not with the usual "then . . . and then . . . and then . . . ," but rather "and so on . . . and on . . . and on . . ."

In her eyes, a connection existed between those local time measurements, which eschewed any kind of precision, and the fact, "yes, the fact," that the inhabitants of the Hondareda colony, in another regression? preferred to have their money, to the extent that any was in circulation among them, in the most archaic forms or incarnations possible, or in seemingly impossible shapes, such as lumps of rock crystal, or, preferably, sheets of mica, or, better still, clumps of droppings from the Sierra chamois, or, absolutely the best, hazelnuts—anyone who paid with empty shells was a counterfeiter!—and dried chestnuts, and the further fact that in the colony the units of weights and measures recognized the world over, the gram, hundredweight, ounce, pud, and ton, had not merely been eliminated but were also frowned upon, and this although the new settlers had arrived only recently and amid the confusion were busy setting up temporary housekeeping arrangements.

Anyone who slipped up and said that "in two hours" he had collected "ten liters of cranberries" or "twenty pounds of bovists in half an hour" or shot a "wild boar weighing half a ton" or had already harvested from his greenhouse "two hundredweight of potatoes, four bushels of barley, an ounce of tobacco, and eight grams of saffron" was punished with scorn.

In the depression, the only measures of quantity that counted— according to a law, unwritten, like all the others there (see "atavism")— were ones such as "a handful," "two palmsful," "a bent armful," "all pockets full," "a back full," and the like; although founded only a short time ago, the colony was already well stocked with customs and a sort of common law.

And the observer called this "simple and childish"; see currency transactions, see units of measure. He also asserted that Hondareda was less a "colony" than a "camp," self-imposed and voluntary, an arrogant one. She understood the man (without particularly acknowledging that he was right—which he also did not expect, for he assumed in any case that he was).

How strange at least the inmates of that high-altitude depression could appear when looked at in a certain way and from a certain angle. Weren't they in fact prisoners, of themselves or whomever, or refugees who had not adjusted to their refugee existence in the slightest; still acutely in flight with every step they took up here, where they were seemingly safe, or maybe not? So in contrast to their descendants, those young people up on the bright, rocky slopes, who had perhaps not been old enough to remember much of the flight, and crossed paths with the strange woman without suspicion, enjoying complete peace of mind, as she made her way to the settlement at the bottom, passing through the chaos boulders, the members of the older generations, who seemed to be in detention there, almost all shied away in alarm.

What had looked from a distance, from the valley's upper rim, like people waving to her: wasn't it rather a communal shooing-away, in unison, so to speak, of the intruder? The people of Hondareda recoiled, each in his own place, at the appearance of this unknown person among the inhabited blocks of stone, as from an enemy, who, having pursued them here from the place they had fled, was threatening their lives; the people of Hondareda existed in a permanent state of war, if not in their conscious minds or their unconscious, at least on the surface of their bodies, in their nerves, their skin, and their hair; and the enemy, even in the singular, like this woman now, had a crushing power advantage over them, just like the enemy from an earlier time and a great distance away; even when armed, all they could do when face-to-face with this enemy was cringe defenselessly and squeeze their eyes shut—pretend to be blind, as they had done from time immemorial, as if that made them invisible.

This is how the new arrival encountered the population of the hollow, though only at first, and briefly. A while later, a few eagles' circles, mountain jackdaw flocks' caws, under-ice chords from the half-frozen lake later, it became clear to her that a general and persistent recoiling, cringing, and shying away was typical of this place; not merely at the sight of her, or of outsiders (in the twinkling of an eye she was no longer viewed as such) but also at mere nothings—if the sudden shadow of a bird or a cloud overhead and an equally unexpected sound were nothings.

The noises in particular, also the most distant and tiny ones, which took on a ghostly, oversized presence down there in the huge stone amphitheater, leaping from cliff to cliff, exploding now on the left, now on the right, now in front, now in back of me, made me and the person next to me, my fellow hermit right around the corner, my neighbor in the next chaos-alley over, duck involuntarily or even throw myself flat on the ground or to one side.

The reporter commented that these behaviors stemmed from typical hearing damage, which affected not only the people in the Hondareda enclave but by now almost the entire earth's population: this phenomenon could be observed nowadays wherever civilization's noise no longer physically assailed people at its source but instead took on other forms, like phantom sounds, beyond the ordinary sounds, tones, and signals characteristic of civilization, and in these phantom forms jumped us from behind in precisely those places assumed to be isolated: in nature, in places without machines and devices and crowds, assaulting our organism more ruthlessly than the original racket in the inhabited hubs of our civilized planet.

"Take, for example, the solitary hiker, who thinks he has put behind him all the so-called curses of civilization, tramping, say, through a semi-desert in Arizona or a full-fledged desert in Mongolia: a hissing of wind behind him, and he, his ears deceiving him, jumps to one side in confusion to avoid what he thinks is a horde of bicyclists descending on him—while at home on the city outskirts he would have calmly let real ones pedal past him. Then a chirping of crickets is heard all across the silent steppe, and he perceives it as the ticking of thousands of office clocks, more piercingly tormenting there than they ever were in his actual office. The softest bird's peeping in a briar bush—and he hears it as a telephone ringing, so harsh, so deadly to daydreams, and so hostile that he has hardly ever heard its like in reality.

"So we can observe precisely in the—admittedly peaceable—sectarians of Hondareda that there is no escaping our civilization—and why would there be? That it catches up with anyone who flees it—and only then, in catching up with him, as a phantom, becomes the actual evil that he earlier merely imagined!"

She, on the other hand, saw in the Hondarederos neither refugees from the world nor victims of civilization. Both as far as they were concerned personally, and in the name of the story to be told here: they were survivors. They—with the exception of the young ones—had all, each alone and in his own way, crossed the valley of the shadow of death. They were all equally timid and tremulous, also those for whom the crossing had taken place quite long ago.

It was true that in their confrontations with strangers or even those with whom they had no connection, these people seemed reduced almost entirely to reactions or even naked reflexes. Yet in such reactions and reflexes, only the first and entirely superficial layer of the body or being of these survivors found expression. Below—behind?—beside? in the middle of? everywhere else, in body and soul, she, the interloper, sensed, as only in certain survivors, an enthusiasm, a joy in existence, and gratitude, if still concealed and not (yet) capable of being expressed freely.

How she sensed that? She herself was a survivor. And when their turn came, it took only a brief exchange of glances, after the initial head-tossing, for the "handful" of people down at the bottom of the valley, the core of the new settlers there, to recognize that she was one, too. And then they opened up to her, without further ado, though not collectively— Hondareda also lacked anything resembling a village square or any other sort of communal gathering place—but each one individually; each in his hideaway, which appeared to turn its back on his neighbor's, and was also seemingly as different from it as possible, on purpose.

And did they expect her to open up to them as well? Until the departure of the strange woman, "a considerable time," "a moon," several moons, later, no one among the inhabitants of the Sierra summit-plain valley knew who she was. For the first time on her journey she went unrecognized. But there was nothing left to recognize, not the queen of finance, or the film star, or anyone else, given how she had been making her way across the land and the continent for so long now, without a profession, without status, without a role.

They did not want to know anything about her, either; no name, no family, no previous life, no loved ones, no mother or father tongue, no land of origin, no destination—each person's dealings with her took place as if in the absence of all feeling—and rightly so—rightly so? "The only thing the various individuals of this strange tribe lacking all tribal organization" (the reporter's expression), of this "tribe of hermits" (ibid.), and all of them, wanted to ask of the beautiful stranger, "whose beauty meant nothing to this neoprimeval horde" (ibid.), and the very first thing they said after coming to trust her, their fellow in experience, each in his own idiom, different from that of the person next door, was: Which route had she taken through the Sierra de Gredos, to bring her up here / down here to Hondareda—which, among them, was absolutely not to be called "Hondareda," but rather, exclusively, and each time with a different pronunciation, "the Pleasant Plantation."

She had then omitted not a single detail in her recounting of the journey; in particular the deviations and detours aroused enthusiasm in listener after listener, or, to use another term, their solidarity, and so from way station to way station she invented more and more details for them. How gullible these "planters in stony acres" (the observer) were when it came to anything that involved storytelling—all that was needed was the appropriate wind-up, the sentence structure, the tone of voice, and the rhythm, and each of them was all ears, and their lips parted in astonishment—even when the contents offered nothing at all to be astonished at. ("What do you consider human?" she asked the author, and his reply: "To ask you the right questions and in that way get you to tell stories." In that way? Yes. And here his use of the intimate form of "you" was just right.)

This was how she also discovered that her listeners, like her, the storyteller, were survivors in a particular sense. Was she, who had once, quite emotionlessly, made major decisions affecting banks and the money market, also gullible? Yes, and always had been, since her village childhood. "You could tell her anything!" ("Me, too!"—the author's exclamation.)

Beyond storytelling, however, when it came to other utterances and events: just as among the people in this place—if not a villager's caginess, certainly a fundamental skepticism ("basic," the author's suggestion); a probing and testing, or an insuperable incredulity, impervious to the most logical argument.

And common, furthermore, to them and to her, who had wafted in, was clumsiness; a clumsiness that in her case, as well as that of the individuals here, broke out only after a series of noticeably skillful, no, noticeably graceful, actions and movements (dexterities, kinesthetic harmonies, gravity-defying shifts in equilibrium, dancing hither and yon through the air almost acrobatically), and interrupted these round-dance-like movements that were seemingly executed with the greatest of ease.

And all the more noticeable, when they had been in control of themselves and of objects so long, this outbreak of clumsiness. All the more alarming. All the more "embarrassing" (the observer). All the more "disappointing and disillusioning" (ibid.). "The unexpected stumbles and trips, slips, blunders, misspeakings, confusions of up and down, steps into thin air, falls, heads bumping against rocks and trees, all went to show that the equanimity and superiority of which each individual in the Hondareda troop made such a show was nothing but dissembling. Their general clumsiness, as well as the way it manifested itself just before the completion of a sequence of actions, carried out, up to then, with remarkable delicacy, and destroyed the entire action, the work, the product, in the last or next-to-last second or even microsecond, reveals to us the swindle that the Hondarederos want to put over on us, and even more on themselves, with their plan for a New Life—which, by the way, has not been written down or finalized, yes, has barely been suggested, with not even the plan of a plan drawn up."

And once more she agreed with the reporter. She even felt a kind of admiration for his observation regarding this most peculiar clumsiness. Except that she, the fellow survivor and sister in clumsiness, again also saw something that transcended this phenomenon. Where the reporter, with the perspective of a complete outsider, saw nothing funny in the sudden tumbles, collisions, and heaps of broken glass, nothing but further proof of the local life-lie, she, the eyewitness and kin to these people, first felt moved to laugh, and "after that" to cry.

Her own manifestations of clumsiness could never have brought tears to her eyes, unlike those of her people here, often heartrending reversals of the "last-minute saves" familiar from old-time films: falls just before a perfect ending or before a brilliant freestyle dismount. Was it because she saw in the others' vicissitudes the course her own life was taking? "No." Because she saw the world this way? "No. Actually, the truth is," she told the author later in his village in La Mancha, "that I realized, upon seeing these repeated, apparently axiomatic, misfortunes that mirrored my own (often just minor ones, which, however, because they thwarted people on the verge of success, took on the dimensions of major accidents), that they for their part and I for mine, we survivors, had probably not survived that successfully after all.

"A part of us, of me and of these people, still lay knocked to the ground, close to death, in a hapless heap. And the other part of us, dancing its dance of survival on the lightest of feet, was always in danger, magnetically drawn by the overwhelming gravity of this heap, of stumbling off course and tumbling toward it.

"On the one hand, my people and I were the quintessential survivors: live wires, full of spark and spunk—and, on the other hand, since the moment of that great fall, survivors merely in appearance, dashed to the ground dying, dying."

Yet in her view there was something positive after all in this precarious survival: of all the senses, the sense of taste had become the most acutely developed. True, the other senses seemed to have been refined as well. But there the result tended to be more in the nature of intensifications, excesses, even deviations and aberrations.

The mistaken, if not panic-filled, sense of hearing has already been mentioned. Seeing, especially seeing that involved things beyond the safe thresholds of the new settlement, took place too much out of the corners of the eyes, and thus inanimate objects seemed to come alive, motionless things seemed to move, and so on. And their apparent motion always signified misfortune or calamity to the new settlers. Someone, a person in one's care, a child, was hurtling off a steep cliff. Or a mortal enemy seemed to come tearing at one at full speed (yet it was merely one of the frequent sudden wind gusts whipping a solitary broom bush).

Similarly subject to mistaken perception was the survivors' sense of smell. There was not a single lovely scent—and what scents one could sniff in the high Sierra, where even the pure air had a delicious smell to it—that could not suddenly acquire the reek of decay.

The sense of touch, or skin sense, however, turned out to be atrophied among the Hondareda population, hardly present anymore, at least among the "squad" (her term) or the "band" (his) of original settlers down there; and that was hardly a function (here the two outsiders were again in agreement) of the more advanced age of all of them.

Nonetheless, the reporter then promptly called into question the comment made by his interlocutor, the strange yet familiar adventurer, to the effect that these people's fingertips had grown numb and dulled this way in the hour of their near death. "How do you know that?" — She: "I know it from experience." — "Knowledge from experience does not count in our case." — She: "'He (or she) knew from experience': you find that in the most ancient books, in all the early written languages, and from the beginning this formula has always been valid."

For him, however, such knowledge had not a whisper of probative value. A fact, demonstrated with reproducible data, researched by a representative number of "contemporary survivors," was their "positively superb" sense of taste. No normal person could taste food and drink as such survivors could, foretasting and aftertasting, salivating, letting them melt on the tongue, rolling them between the lips and the palate, and, as if without swallowing, without any detour by way of digestion and circulation, solely by virtue of a consummate tasting that went on and on, letting them flash from the eye, transformed into living atoms, letting them spark from the ears, puff from the nostrils, glow from every pore of the skin, but primarily from the cheeks, foreheads, and, most especially, the temples.

On the other hand, what was supposed to be positive about this? It was no secret, after all, that the Hondarederos, no matter how shabby and stranded they appeared, were certainly not poverty-stricken. Even if they had not exactly accumulated fortunes in their previous lives, they had by no means been without means (pun), something they perhaps had even more in common than survival.

And although here in the Sierra depression they were not seen with money, that did not mean that they had renounced property and possessions: in the valleys beyond the mountain crests, and beyond those all the way to the Atlantic and the Mediterranean, and likewise across the oceans, these self-appointed repeaters of a *vita nuova* enjoyed unlimited credit, each and every one of them. World champions in tasting, true— thanks to the trinity of survival, the mountain air, and, above all, a life of luxury. After all, hadn't these folks, after they had become has-beens everywhere else, made their way here more to indulge themselves in peace in good eating and drinking—see the oyster shells scattered about?

As the two of them conversed in this fashion, standing on the porcelain-smooth granite outcropping in the remote area just below the Puerto de Candeleda, she, in her time among the new settlers of the Sierra, had already been invited several times to dinner—in each case, only the host and she at the table, each meal accompanied by a monologue spoken by the host and chef—and now she offered more or less the following reply to the observer:

First of all—she demanded of the author that he reproduce her part of the conversation with the observer in indirect discourse—the oyster shells were not left over from the inhabitants' cooking but had been left there by transcontinental drifters, or, as they called themselves, "novo-nomads" (a temporary phenomenon long since passé) when they had visited the glacial basin that had become a greening, grain-yellow, and water-blue valley and thus an attraction: an oyster picnic in the mountains had been as much in vogue among them as a chamois-sausage afternoon snack in their desert bivouac and penguin-in-pastry-shell on a trans-Antarctic excursion train.

And furthermore, her people did allow themselves the occasional luxury, but none that consisted of anything extra, or of imported ingredients. Every luxury came from substances extracted from the most hidden and, at the same time, magically fruitful—a natural magic, following the laws of nature—crevices and deposits in the area. These were the usual products and plants from such altitudes, as scarce and scanty as anywhere, items like juniper berries, bilberries, rowanberries, rose hips, acorns, Sierra olives, and so forth. Except that, because of the warming climate, the sun heated the rocks in such a way that, in all these fruits, in their classic miniature mountain forms, their pure essence was concentrated.

So there were no apples or grapes of the size found in the Garden of Eden or the Land of Canaan; but the few one could detect with the naked eye—for that reason alone they constituted a luxury, no, a treasure—were, whether added as garnish to ordinary meals or eaten separately, a whole meal in themselves, a delicacy, something for which the word *delicatesse* would be appropriate for once.

Altogether, the Hondareda depression was in reality less disadvantaged and inimical to life than one would have concluded from the name, and not only from first appearances. All the rounded granite boulders that had emerged from the thawing ice, hundreds and thousands of them, scattered hither and yon across the valley and up to the summit plain, polished to a high sheen, veined with sparkling white bands of quartz, reflecting each other many times over, especially now in the cold season, with the sun at an oblique angle all day, represented a system of natural solar collectors, by no means weak, and radiating heat even at night, which were used by the settlers—in the village and throughout the village, even the clumsiest and most awkward of them having become in the twinkling of an eye technical experts and engineers—to heat their dwelling niches, carved out of the cliffs, as well as their patchlike plantations, easily mistaken for rockslides, and the occasional greenhouses (mistaken by the observer for piles of debris, with half-broken panes of glass, sheets of corrugated tin, cardboard, and splintered window frames, beneath which, in his eyes, poisonous green, sulphur-yellow, and moldy gray weeds flourished).

To that extent her people, the handful there in the Pleasant Plantation, were indeed creatures of luxury, hiding, whether intentionally or not, under the cloak of being cast adrift in this region and wretchedly eking out an existence; that side of their being, too, which the reporter accurately characterized as a "reversion to hunting and gathering," was part of the luxury, if only because of the rarity and—not only for that reason—deliciousness of the wild animals they bagged.

Which brought her back to the Hondarederos' sense of taste, far surpassing all the other senses. Not once had a meal to which she had been bidden borne the slightest resemblance to gluttony or carousing. Rather, these few meals, rare in every sense, had consisted of tasting, sampling, nibbling; yet they had been as filling and thirst-quenching as any food and drink could be. In the same way that the new settlers had of their own accord become technicians, repairmen, and inventors, without training or study, simply in response to local conditions, so, too, taking the fruits of the area and ennobling them, they had, without lessons or planning, transformed themselves into culinary artists.

And these chefs consumed what they themselves had prepared with an enthusiasm experienced hardly anywhere else. They—and the guest in their company—inhaled their dishes. If there had been no devouring, even in the presence of intense hunger, it had nothing to do with "good manners": devouring the items, yes, "items," had been absolutely out of the question.

In their sense of taste, all feeling for being alive and surviving had been concentrated. And the other senses, those affected by their near deaths, had become concentrated ("No, gathered," she to the author) in such tasting. Seeing, hearing, smelling, and tasting, or, to put it differently, all sensitivities, had been drawn into these meals and had either regained their rhythm or, in the sense of touch, their function.

This manner of eating had helped heal and unify the senses, and furthermore had never become routine. — "Unified senses, sensuousness?" — That, too; but the unified senses had had an even stronger effect on the thinking of the immigrants of Hondareda—whose nickname among them had been *La Mojada Honda* (The Deep Mountain Pasture, The Deep Enclosure); not so much on their abstract thinking as on the way they considered and contemplated a specific thing or problem.

Every mealtime in the village had also been a time of contemplation—not an intensified but rather a heightened and elevated contemplation—where external and internal reflection had gone hand in hand, accompanied by a cheerfulness otherwise rare in those parts; the result being a likewise uncommon loquacity, a speaking in tongues very different from ordinary table conversation, more like the conversations of the mute with themselves, going in circles; thus also close to exuberance and pure, hearty nonsense—as was generally the case when, after spending time in a death zone, people regained the air of life, and with it, language.

The eating and drinking had had an effect on those confused folk and their jumbled senses, thoughts, and words, an effect similar to that which a certain kind of reading had on other survivors, a reading that was neither skimming nor poking around nor devouring, but a reflective tracing, in places also spelling out and deciphering, and if ultimately it was a form of consuming after all, it was a kind of inhaling, a breathing in (and out). Such meals represented time saved in two ways, much as reading did, and also rhythmic (recreational) walking.

Like those survivor-readers glancing into a book, the survivor-eaters there had been impelled by tasting to look up and raise their heads for contemplation, some for release from themselves, some for relaxation, some for excitement, and finally some for the pleasure of communicating and sharing—as among the previously mentioned readers out of the desire to read aloud or even to act on something they had long ago resolved to do, an action postponed almost past the time for it—which only now, with reading, with tasting, became possible and accessible—even if such an action, in the presence of food, just as in the presence of books, should express itself merely in a seemingly meaningless hug given to a random stranger.

29

The reporter presumably replied to her as follows: "The Deep Enclosure? The Pleasant Plantation? We outside observers have another name for the basin of Hondareda: The Dark Clearing. And this is no paradox or play on words now; I do not want you to have sawn off my ponytail in vain. The term 'Dark Clearing' actually stems from an observation shared by all who were dispatched here: as a result of the belt of trees planted around the bottom of the basin or arena, the area it encircles has taken on the character of a classic clearing, a *clarière*, a *tschistina*, a *claro*—the expressions in all languages have to do with brightness. But in Hondareda, darkness mixes in with the brightness that remains trapped in the light, smooth rocks and rock dwellings, evident each time one looks, a gloom specific to the place. Contrary to the assertion that they live in a clearing, darkness prevails there. The interior of the surrounding dense conifer forests is an opaque black. And this black does not remain confined to the forest. It is constantly reaching for the open area. True: the mountain sun, together with its reflection in the glacial lake and its more colorful, varied, warm reflection in the indeed wondrously smooth granite hilltops—you see, I am not merely an observer!—provides a heightened light to the circle of the settlement, light such as I have never encountered in any other clearing in the world.

"This much is also true: when one sets foot in this space for the first time, one involuntarily says to oneself: How beautiful this is. What beauty. Where am I? One does not want to leave. One? I. Something has begun to happen. Something is beginning to happen. Something will begin to happen. I will begin to do something. My thinking will change— will become larger, wider—and correspondingly brighter. Warmhearted. Moved by love and intent on love.

"And on all subsequent occasions as well, when, after the long climb from the Tormes valley below and the descent to the bottom of the basin, I had the clearing before me, in the first tenth of a second something surged up in me—something like a moment of being airborne (which, now that we come here by helicopter rather than on foot, no longer happens—peace at last, thanks to objectivity).

"But even that first time, upon my stepping into the clearing, after five to eight paces toward its center, it became obvious that the special light there is an illusion. It is only a feeling. It does not count. What does count, and what in fact prevails, is the pitch blackness that confronts one in the middle of this allegedly new land, as it glows in the sun and all the colors of midday, the blackness emanating from the surrounding stand of trees, which has the character of a jungle-like primeval forest, although it was planted only a short while ago. The blackness, instead of perhaps softening the brightness, relativizing it, or, if you will, grounding it, cancels out the promise or the prophecy that seems initially to radiate from the local light, and makes my feeling null and void, and properly so. Dark Clearing.

"And as befits this kind of a dark clearing, those who have immigrated there, the objects of my observation, exist and conduct themselves according to its standards, under the spell of its darkness. In settling there they have certainly not struck out to find the light and the air of a different era, but are lying in wait, which is what the hunters and gatherers did in dark prehistoric times, and gloomily—more gloomy and numb than prehistoric people can possibly have been—otherwise they would hardly have evolved.

"I am speaking in paradoxes? This tribe of bumblers *lives* them. These folks produce nothing, not even contradictions, which would be a kind of productivity: they cling to the unproductive dream of an upside-down world. Even in their shadowy hunter-gatherer ways the signs have been reversed: gathering—listen to this!—is considered, and not only officially, by my dear Hondareda idiots, to be an activity that brutalizes the individual as well as the group and carries with it the danger of spiritual decadence, while hunting, on the other hand, is seen as an opportunity for achieving greater humanity.

"It, yes, hunting, first of all, hones one's attention, and in a fundamentally different way from gathering: in contrast to the latter, hunting does not narrow one's field of vision but rather widens it, literally to infinity.

According to them, hunting, tracking, and the like involves the entire body, increases circumspection, makes one aware of the terrain—in distinction to the gatherer's mere knowledge of the best places to find things—and in particular develops in those who practice it endless patience.

"But gathering threatens to cripple the body and the soul. It even interferes with and distorts the erect posture. And altogether, collecting is the province of impure ulterior motives and top-heaviness, the province of envy, greed, avarice, and other cardinal sins. More than hunting, gathering can degenerate into hostility, not so much the activity itself as the motives and sidelong looks associated with it. Gathering makes people small, in particular by shrinking all the others with and around the gatherer, not only because of his gaze, which is constantly focused on the ground, on crevices, on the underbrush, instead of scanning the sky or staying at normal eye level, and eventually makes them disappear and/or magnifies them into seeking-and-gathering rivals.

"And thus those who populate the dark clearing live in other respects, too, as prisoners of their paradoxes and of their upside-down and constantly backpedaling worlds. Listen to me. Not only do they live in shacks, caves, and dugouts like the first and last human beings. They speak more to their cattle than to each other, even to the most puny animals, and to objects. And they treat the objects and the livestock more attentively and tenderly than I ever observed them treating their next-door neighbor.

"Time and again during the year I have spent up here I have witnessed some person or other waving to an eagle swooping around the peak of the Almanzor, also to a mountain raven, a vulture, a marmot—whose whistling elicited a response,—an Alpine hare. Like certain mentally retarded people, they have the ability to find something that pleases them in literally everything, the most nondescript plant, the most shapeless and useless stone. And they show their true colors perhaps most distinctly in one custom they all share—although each goes his own way, they have developed what an outsider can recognize as shared customs—of tracing in the air with their hands or fingers the living beings and also the inanimate objects to which they address themselves all day long—that almost seems to be their chief occupation—while they are talking to them.

"As they pass by a rocky hummock, a silver thistle, an ant heap, they one and all sketch the essential outlines of these things in the air and even run their fingertips over them, probably to regain their almost lost sense of touch. They draw a fish that has leaped out of the laguna or a bird that has whirred over them, following its lines in the air until they have registered them accurately; only then, according to the custom that in the meantime has acquired the force of law, are they allowed to turn their attention to something else.

"The astonishing part, however, is that the following happens with some of the animals they have thus portrayed in the air: the animals turn up again; the salmon or the trout leaps out of the water a second time, the kite that had whizzed behind a towering rock comes back and circles again, and so on. It is as if the creatures of the earth, water, and air now wanted to salute in turn the person who has just reproduced their structure, along with their specific leaping or flying motion, with his tender, yes, loving air-sketching.

"This salutation-like copying or modeling in the wind can, admittedly, even prove useful from time to time and have its good side. More than once I have observed an otherwise dangerous animal being calmed in this fashion, or at least stopped in its tracks for a few seconds, which, however, were life-saving seconds. A raging mountain bull, a wild sow hurtling toward a Hondaredero who has unintentionally cut her off from her young: the form of the bull or the sow drawn in large strokes—yes, always in large, swirling, harmonious strokes!—and at once the sow and bull stopped for an interval, shorter or longer, as if spellbound, and let the human being pass. Instead of cliff drawings, air drawings. The Dark Clearing.

"And besides, what hunters these people up here claim to be! To be sure, they lie in wait in the strip of forest from dawn till dusk with their thoroughly modern shotguns, and occasionally take aim and fire, too. But to this day I have not been able to discover what animals they are hunting. I think, no, I do not think, I am sure, that they have no intention of hunting down and killing anything. They are merely practicing. They are practicing hunting and being hunters for its own sake, not for some future emergency or for putting their skill to work. Practicing is enough for them.

"But what are they practicing? When I tried to research this question, I received the same answer, verbatim, from every single practice hunter, although they never compare notes with each other: I am practicing so as to become composed.—Composed for what? And here again all the answers were identical, though in all the different languages: Composed, without any why or wherefore. To gain composure. To acquire composure, not for any particular purpose, for everything and nothing. Composure is all.

"And not merely because this last dictum, spoken, what is more, in unison, has a sinister after-tone: talk like this again points to the regression syndrome of my new settlers, in the sense that in positing a vague, undefined, undefinable composure that defies rational documentation, it aims to smuggle back myth into this world of ours, which for centuries has had nothing more to say, interpret, and convey in this genre—the myth of one who went forth to gain composure, thereby propagating a new knighthood, one that in reality had long since become obsolete.

"The knights of the Dark Clearing! The world has never seen more unsightly knights, and that, now, is my last play on words (speaking to you, I realize that in my previous life I spent too much time as a headline-writer). They are a cross between would-be knights, clay-pit dwellers, and vagabonds, the ugliest cross possible.

"By birth they are all crossbreeds. Did you know that your ancestors all came from here in the Sierra de Gredos, from the mountain valleys and gullies along the río Tormes in the north, from the villages and towns down there at the southern base of the range, between the steep drop and the lowland of the río Tiétar, from San Martín de la Vega del Alberque, from Aliseda, from San Esteban del Valle, from Santa Cruz del Valle, from Mombeltrán, from Arenas de San Pedro, from Jarandilla de la Vera, from Jaraiz de la Vera, and, yes, from Candeleda? That your ancestors departed from the Sierra region centuries ago and emigrated, leaving Europe for all continents, often venturing to the borders of the known world of the time, which their travels then expanded?

"One such ancestor, for instance, comes from the town of El Barco de Ávila, the bark of Ávila, in the west, where the río Tormes flows out of the central massif, and he was the helmsman, *el tripulante*, of the ship on which Christopher Columbus discovered America, no, plural, the Americas, just as in those days it was not yet called 'Spain,' in the singular, *La España*, but *Las Españas*, and similarly not *La Italia* but *Las Italias*.

"A century later, another ancestor traveled as a missionary to China, there dropped out of his order, married a native, and established his crossbreed family. A third, long before that, at the time of the Crusades, fathered a child with an Arab woman, with whom he stayed. A forebear of yours settled at the far end of each of the gold, silver, platinum, silk, and spice routes and intermarried with Mongols, Indians, Jews, Slavs, blacks.

"And today, as if by prior arrangement, their descendants have come here from the most distant continents and islands to be together in this place, which they regard as their ancestral land, and not without justification—but for what purpose? to regain composure? and have they really come together when each keeps strictly to himself?

"That, too, presumably forms part of their would-be myth: a return to their ancestral land; even though, when asked, each one of them, all of them again in complete agreement, will insist that the Hondareda basin is neither the land of his fathers nor a homeland; the Pleasant Plantation—in truth, an almost felicitous expression, at least at times—remains foreign territory to them, so foreign that it could not appear more so to any human being, foreign root, branch, and sky—but not the kind of foreign territory described in a saying common in these parts, passed down from those ancestors who emigrated—not the foreign territory, not at all the kind of foreign territory 'where the doors slam shut on your heels.'

"This place where they are living, as each of them asserts, uninfluenced by neighbors and houses next door, is the foreign place visualized and reserved by them for the duration and for good—though precisely not the kind of foreign place of which a poet's description was passed down from their forefathers: a foreign place where, when music from afar reached a person's ears, the sound rent his heart, because it made him realize: Never shall I return to my home. But if music from afar was heard here in the Pleasant Plantation, it 'heartened' one and strengthened one in one's resolve to stick it out in these foreign parts and never to reinterpret them or transform them into something other than what they essentially were and—another of those unwritten laws—should remain: foreign, foreign, foreign.

"Foreign land: another topos of these seekers after a new myth. They see themselves, and again that means each by himself, as people without a country, as stateless people, yet they are also proud of their country- and statelessness.

"We could let this pass, were it not associated with the aforementioned ugliness. To us, in contrast to those down below, beauty is the overarching law in the following sense: What is ugly cannot be good; the ugly is evil and bad, and it must not be allowed to stand.

"And my knightly vagabonds of the Dark Clearing are of an interminable ugliness, even when one considers only their weapons and their bivouacs, an ugliness that is an insult to human dignity and makes a mockery of existence. Does not the aesthetic world order, the law of the beautiful, include the ethical as well, the distinction between good and not good, right and wrong, or am I mistaken? How the appalling ugliness of these crossbreeds—their clothing, their hovels, their rocky gardens, fields, and stables, their greenhouses, their tools, their materials—has pierced me to the quick from the outset, preventing me from living and breathing freely.

"Not that they constantly go barefoot. But why do they always wear unmatched socks, as if on principle and out of malicious, ugly defiance, and possibly unmatched shoes as well, on the left foot a black oxford and on the right foot a yellow pigskin boot? There is nothing they are, have, or do that is not breathtakingly ugly. Even the way these denizens of the Dark Clearing move: where elsewhere people thrust themselves into the foreground, these people, each separately and yet all of them together forming a mass, huddle in the background, as if by prior arrangement.

"The ugly and the bad aspects of those who thrust themselves into the foreground are almost tolerable by comparison, allowing one at least to sense the presence of gaps and the horizon; while the masses huddling in the background block the view, the light, and the sun, and thereby any possibility of seeing the big picture, and once this is thwarted, the ugly crowd, there, and there, and back there, appears doubly ugly, ugly to the second power, ugly to the nth power.

"Whenever I go looking for them and approach them—for that is my mission here, after all—they skulk, hide, huddle in the background. Whether I want to track them down in their hovels or sheep pens or solar collectors or radio shacks, they are always way in the back. And I can never get at them there. They have installed threshold after threshold between us as obstacles, often what may not even be intentional thresholds, consisting of infinite uglinesses in the form of sights, sounds, and smells— and that seems to me the most criminal aspect of their criminal ugliness: that it makes these ugly people of mine even more inaccessible to me. Their ugliness means inaccessibility. Ugliness and inaccessibility, or un-approachableness, grievously sad, and are they not ultimately one and the same after all?

"To this day I have not succeeded in crossing these insurmountable thresholds of ugliness to get to my dear Hondarederos. How ugly even their voices are from a distance. Ravens' cawing, blue jays' screeching, and wildcats' hissing are the most mellifluous harmonies by comparison. It must pierce the heart of every natural enemy of ugliness and make his blood boil when these voices assault him, amplified by the cliffs around here and this vast natural mountain amphitheater.

"And every word spoken, as if spat out, coughed out, vomited from the deepest and most distant background, strikes one's ear like a giant fist. I am forced to hear distinctly even their most faraway speech in all its ugliness, word for word. Although each of them by now talks almost exclusively to himself, he always expresses himself in a hideous jargon, which, adding to the ugliness, they all use, unwittingly, albeit in the most varied languages—and are not jargon, ugliness, exclusivity, and inaccessibility in the final analysis one and the same?

"And listen: this jargon echoing from the fissures in the rock consists for the most part of obsolete expressions, drawn chiefly from the language of seafarers, as if these re-immigrants wanted to recapitulate and claim for themselves the linguistic formulations of those ancestors who left the Comarca centuries ago to sail the oceans.

"How presumptuous of them to refer to their huddling here in this out-of-the-way mountainous area as 'lying at anchor' and their various movements as 'sailing'; to shout, upon seeing a trout, hardly as long as an arm, leaping out of a glacial pond, 'Dolphin ahoy!' or, upon chewing a juniper berry or dipping their toes into the icy water or moistening their eyes with the admittedly special dew of the Pleasant Plantation, to screech, bark, scold, shriek into the granite wasteland: 'Je suis embarqué! I have embarked! I am on the high seas! I will remain on the high seas! No land in sight! No, no land in sight! Oh joy: no, no, no land in sight!'"

Here the reporter on the rocky island amid the wilderness of broom paused for an eighth to a half a second and then continued in a voice even more shrill, if possible: "After all, our assignment here goes beyond mere observing. We are supposed to investigate the causes of and the reasons for things. For what reason do the people shipwrecked here no longer have a language? Why have they tossed the laws and rules of beauty overboard? Why are they bobbing here in their Dead Sea of inaccessibility?

"So hear me out: the source of this Robinson crew's terminal ugliness can be traced to the loss of images. And the additional assignment with which my team was sent up here is as follows: to cure, or at least contain, this new image-loss disease, dangerous because it is epidemic or even pandemic. Quarantine hand in hand with therapy. Curing these ominously ugly folk, but how, and by what means? By delivering images, importing images, injecting images, without let-up. Produce, transport, and deliver an image to a person, and his soul will regain its health, his language will be revitalized, his voice will become hearty and his eye clear, accessible, and beautiful.

"For a year or more we have been struggling to steer these denizens of darkness back into the bright world of images. To stop the leakage of images. But how, you ask. Why do you not ask?—First of all we wired the enclave of Hondareda, ran underground cables, set up reflectors all around, and installed image-producing machines every few feet, at a density ten to fourteen times greater than that of the traffic lights in Frankfurt, Paris, New York, or Hong Kong: machines that reproduce images not only from external and outside sources, from civilization, but, above all, images of those Hondarederos who wander into their reception and broadcast area, images of the inside of their bodies, projecting onto this bit of cliff the heart cavity of a passerby, onto the next the inside of the head, onto a third the genital and abdominal region.

"These image-producing devices function as mirrors, reflecting not the person's face but what lies behind it. Except that none of the immigrants so much as glances at the images, whether external or internal. From the outset, the people up here did not even look away from the images we supplied; they simply ignored them. And yet we had introduced a process by which even the shadows, instead of showing mere outlines, took on shape and color: shadows with the mouth, nose, and eyes clearly inscribed in the shadow of a face, along with the eye color, even richer than in the actual face that cast the shadow, also more glowing and beautiful—the very image of beauty.

"And our equipment provided the image-loss folk with similar shadows of trees, rocks, clouds, airplanes: leaves, needles, limbs, lichens, sheets of mica, veins of quartz, strands of alabaster, strips of sunlight, blue holes, aluminum, etc., shimmered in the shadow images of these objects of the air or ground, in colors more brilliant or pure white than the objects themselves ever displayed. And did the people we were treating so much as mention these miraculous works? Why will you not hazard a guess?

"That even the moving images of films failed to make a dent on these people robbed of their image sense is superfluous to report. Neither the classic series of twenty-four images per second nor accelerated image-bombardment more in tune with the contemporary way of seeing could straighten things out. No penetration occurs when the image receptors have been removed, you understand. Why do you not understand?

"Yet we set up an open-air cinema for them, probably more lovely than ever existed anywhere and at any time—films projected without a screen onto the smooth rock faces of the Sierra. But even the young people who moved there with the core population are already completely image-resistant, or have become so in this place.

"Even the young people, who can otherwise be distracted by any little liver spot on someone else's face and any speck of color in a dewdrop, however small, simply let the images be images—or, rather, categorically refuse to let the images be images, that is to say, they categorically refuse to let images, no matter which, pry open access to the world of today and, instead of leaving them as hostages to their parents and grandparents, connect them with their own kind, wherever they may be, beyond the mountains, no matter where—everywhere.

"Granted, my people here in the Dark Clearing do not represent a new generation of iconoclasts. Not once have our image-projecting de-vices, which hardly allow them to choose to look in directions we have not populated with images, been attacked or vandalized by them. It is as if their eyes simply veered past the walls of images erected on all sides, seeking the narrow, imageless strip along the horizon, as once the Is-raelites during their exodus from bondage in Egypt moved through the passage that opened up for them through the Dead, no, the Red, Sea.

"Each of them avers that he has not suffered a loss of images, but rather that he has sworn off images. Each claims that no image, not a single one, exists or is valid, at least during this transitional period, and not merely for him, but in general. But what matters to him, precisely in this transitional period, is perception. Along with his life in the place from which he emigrated, he has lost not the images, whether natural or cre-ated, dreamed or lived, external or internal; what he has lost, or what at least is threatened, is the ability to perceive.

"And, he says, what he misses more and more painfully in the world, and in this world, is seeing. And regaining the ability to see is what motivates him up here, on the 'Isthmus of the Transitional Period'—such an appropriate term—in the Pleasant Plantation or the Deep Enclosure, the *Mojada Honda*, and not for the sake of one image or another, no, simply for the sake of seeing, conflict-resolving, existence-justifying, 'world-anchoring,' dignify-ing, renewing, connecting, seeing. As Goethe says, 'Born to look, appointed to see . . . thus the world is pleasing to me,' thus the world is created for me, thus the world coalesces for me, or something like that.

"And accordingly the primary activity of each individual and solitary person here, independent of his neighbor and next-door property owner, is seeing, on the strips or isthmuses, wherever in their view there is something to see, no matter what. Daybreak and seeing. Deep night and more seeing, for instance of the trees' shadows on the rock faces (in the image-free strips or passages). 'To see and let appear'—the settlement's motto, similar to 'Dream and work.' Or is it a form of working? Or of leisure? Impossible to tell the difference.

"What do you think? Why do you say nothing? This is what the returnees believe at any rate, as always in complete unanimity, without prior consultation with one another: images are certainly essential; without them no transmission of the world and no sense of life. But in the previous century in particular, images were overexploited as never before. As a result, the world of images has dried up—has, without exception, become blind, mute, and stale—incapable of being refreshed by any science. And thus, in this transitional period, all that is possible is seeing—in which, by the way, all science is included, and out of which science must develop, one step at a time. The Hondareda idiots consider themselves scientists!

"And the childish things on which they spend their time in their Dark Clearing are, for them—even if they use entirely different terms, as for almost everything, old-fashioned and obsolete ones—'sight-enhancing measures.' That includes not only their posing as hunters, their acting as though they were stalking, taking aim, and so on: time and again one sees them walking backward, more often than forward; that kind of thing, they assert, enhances seeing as much as their constant squatting, close to the ground (whereas standing on tiptoes is prohibited—their standard dictum: 'Standing on tiptoes is no standing').

"When they unexpectedly whirl like dervishes, one person in the background turning to the east, then, without any connection to him, another in back to the west, it is of course no dance, either; the people of the Pedrada-Hondareda region have neither games nor dances, and that includes the young ones—but rather, well, you already know this, or do you?—an exercise in seeing!

"Instead of putting things where they belong or filing them away like adults, these people of the depression are also constantly tossing things into place, and from as far away as possible, and, furthermore, not straightaway and forthwith—now I am using such obsolete expressions myself—but always in an arc, and one that is as high as possible, and to what end? You know this. To facilitate seeing, seeing, nothing but seeing.

"If only such exercises, measures, and exertions led to something: to moldability (ah, another word from horse-and-buggy days); to mobility; to awareness of another person—I don't necessarily mean of me—to neighborliness, or at least a hint of everyday togetherness. But as I have observed for one year, three days, and five to nine hours, each of these Hondareda desperados is holed up, stiff as a board, deep inside his hovel, shack, and barbed-wire enclosure, immobile and immovable, having taken leave for good of the present.

"While in the meantime we have lit up even the North and South Pole, as well as the peak of Everest and the Aconcagua, only the Hondareda region persists in its self-imposed darkness. The only semblance of a joint activity I have been able to observe in my subjects here is that whenever one of them thinks he has spotted something for which he has long been searching, or something precious, or simply something beautiful—precisely in their ugliness they are obsessed with beauty, or, as they express it, with the 'uncommonly beautiful'—but then realizes that he was mistaken—as he was every other time, by the way—that he was thoroughly mistaken and rashly pounced on what he mistook for a treasure or something uncommonly beautiful, but which turned out to be worthless, ordinary, or nothing at all, the person experiencing such a disappointment, and that is what can be astonishing, at the moment when he realizes he was deluded, turns out to be not bitter in the slightest, but rather, without any premeditation, cheerfully disappointed. Disappointment fills the person in question, no matter who in this glacial basin, with cheerfulness.

"And in this state of cheerful disappointment, and only in this state, the individual at the same time always gains the ability to turn to the others in the settlement. At the moment when he is fixated on the deceptive object there, in a rock crevice, the crook of a tree, a fissure in the ground, he calls, whistles, and drums together the entire core population of the Dark Clearing. And the others promptly cluster around him. And he tells them what value, or rarity, or uncommon beauty he allowed himself to project onto this thing or stuff or trifle or garbage or piece of junk.

"And as they stand there with him and inspect the spot or the mess or the nothing-at-all from every side, they share his disillusionment, but likewise, by virtue of the enduring effect of imagination, his cheerfulness. How they all perk up. And these are the only occasions up to now on which I have heard them laugh. Otherwise they cannot laugh, you see, either at others or at themselves—at anything at all. To be sure, disappointments like this and the resulting shared amusement are everyday occurrences down there.

"And the contemplation of mistakes and disappointments, and of absent treasures or treasures they missed again, or other objects of longing, represents for them the acme of seeing, constitutes their way of celebrating, their kind of celebration. These poor, aloof Hondarederitos—have you noticed that I even have a term of endearment for this tribe of new savages! Their dangerous solipsism: What unspeakable war, unlike any that ever took place, are they hatching?—for there is no doubt that they are on a war footing with people like us. Why will not a single one of them look at me? And why will not a single one of them speak a word to me?

"Just as you, foreign lady, have not looked me in the eye once in all this time. Why not? Not for a single micromillisecond during the year or decade of my observing and recording up here in the high Sierra have human eyes looked at me. And what about your fellow observers, you ask. (Why do you not ask?) Not a word about them. Except this: that they are not intentionally mean nor behave as if they were—their mere presence and hanging around is mischief enough. I say that? Yes, I do. In the course of time, I have even tried to meet the eyes of the animals here, the ibex, the *Capra hispanica*, the snakes, the bulls, the vultures, the dragonflies on the laguna, the wagtails—by the way, the only time I was eyed affectionately, it was by the latter, from a broom bush, from a boulder in a glacial brook.

"In the Pleasant Plantation not one pair of human eyes has ever met mine. Here in the Deep Enclosure not a brown or blue or green or gray or any other color of eye has ever taken me in. Not a single person sees me. On the other hand, I am not kindly ignored by anyone, except perhaps by my co-observers.

"I cannot take a single step unobserved. But what a manner of being observed. Yes, it is different from being observed reproachfully. Yet there is no doubt that these gazes are meant to punish me, if any ever were. No, these gazes are not meant to kill. Instead they declare me dead. In their eyes, I, their observer and reporter, have already been dead for a long time. The way their gaze scans me, they doubtless see a cadaver in their field of vision, or a living corpse—which does not count in this field, however—what does count there? you ask; what counts in their field of vision: light, wind, gaps, sand, also flies, spiders, and Sierra beetles. In contrast to the apathy and fatigue they exhibit toward me, what their eyes manifest at the mere glimpse of a wild boar's droppings or a snowflake can be described as a glow.

"Everywhere in today's world, the borders have long since been eliminated. This regressive crew, however, has reintroduced all the old barriers in this crisis-ridden region. Not only against those of us coming from the outside, but also among themselves—another result of the loss of images: they have created the most dense network imaginable of not only old and ancient boundary lines but also previously unthought-of, inconceivable ones: actual ones in the form of thresholds, barriers, and beams, and likewise imaginary ones, which are often even more effective.

"Women, and men as well, go around shrouded and veiled, or do you think I merely have that impression? That it looks that way to me—but doesn't that say something, too? Not only their houses are barred, off limits to people like us, as well as to their nearest neighbor, and besides completely out of sight; also around his garden—for there is no cramped cave and hut that lacks a large garden—every one of the resettlers has erected a wall made of clay, tarpaper, tin, manure, and the like, unless the beds and fruit trees are already shielded from prying eyes by the enormous boulders broken off from the cliffs or moved there. This wall is higher than any I have seen around a garden anywhere, as high as a prison wall.

"Even the graves are strictly separated from one another—during my time here, nine to thirteen of them have already been dug or hewn out of the granite: there is no such thing as community cemeteries; rather each planter unit or monad has its own grave, each clearly isolated from the other, miles away, somewhere way out in the mountain wastes.

"The living observe an equally strict distance: when two or three of them happened to come together, I hardly ever saw one of them as close as arm's length or closer to his fellow resident, and it is even more frowned upon here to follow close behind someone, on his heels; and whereas, in a crowd, we contemporaries romp along freely next to each other, having often just eliminated the last barriers, in this desolate spot all it takes is for a second person to appear in a deserted area for me to feel I have no room to breathe!

"Borders upon borders here, one more grotesque than the next. And most grotesque of all is perhaps the fact that they communicate with each other primarily in writing, that is to say, in letters—orally or over the telephone only in the most extreme emergencies—otherwise that is frowned upon: if a person so much as addresses another person coming toward him, out of the blue, the others go out of their way to avoid him, and he is left standing there alone. Nothing happens here that does not involve drawing boundaries, putting things in bounds and out of bounds.

"Man is a stranger to man, and a stranger he must remain: that is one of the fundamental decrees in this loners' corral. And so it goes in their crazy, upside-down world, wherever one turns: as a stateless person, each acts only on his own behalf, as if that were part and parcel of his loner's consciousness, and at the same time, between one and three thousand consistent rules, norms, and unwritten authoritarian edicts have found their way into this loners' outpost.

"Of late I even see a communal flag waving above the rocky crest in the middle of the glacial lake, which is just about the precise center of the Hondareda colony, although otherwise not a soul goes there, a flag with the peak of the Almanzor woven into it, and to the right and left of it, as the heraldic animals, the almost black, hardly spotted Almanzor salamander and, no, neither the red kite nor the Hispanic chamois, but the extraordinarily small Sierra hedgehog, which one might mistake for a silver thistle. Thistle or hedgehog? What can you make out at this distance? You have better eyes than I, who am myopic, farsighted, and astigmatic to boot.

"And although they are all intent on preserving a veritably mythic namelessness and nobodyness, bit by bit names have been adopted for the most nondescript places and wretched spots in their hardship post, official and mandatory names. And although they have beyond any doubt said goodbye forever, good night, and fare thee well to history, the present, and the light of logic, these names for the most part refer to time, light, reason, and presentness.

"A patch of meadow, for instance, with nothing but a few granite outcroppings and arching wild rose canes, is called, God only knows why, 'The Meadow of Reason,' 'El Prado de la Razón'; a beaten track that zigzags among the randomly situated living cubes—not even a real path or walkway, a mere system of gaps, where time and again one must flatten oneself to slip through, almost labyrinthine—is called 'Passage of Things to Come,' 'Passage de l'Avenir'; and the rocky island in the laguna?—'Corso of the Third Era,' 'Corso di Terzo Tempo,' *corso* because it is approximately circular and level—but a *corso* on which the likes of us have never yet seen a single Hondaredero strolling? either in the evening or at any other time? let alone the entire population of the town, as would be the case on a normal *corso*?

"Altogether, although these people have obviously left the great cities behind them, all their placeless and faceless urban features carry names like 'Plaza . . . ,' 'Avenida . . . ,' 'Boulevard . . . ,' 'Rambla . . . ,' 'New Square,' also 'Esplanade . . . ,' 'Promenade . . . ,' 'Quai . . . ,' and the like.

"And I see the world most grotesquely turned upside down in a cult of dew in which my Hondarederos indulge—yes, you heard me right: dew, *nadan*, *rosée*, *rocío*—which, besides the wetness from the clear sky, is, here on the Iberian peninsula, also a lovely woman's name, without doubt the most lovely.

"Just think: in their crazed eyes it is not a cult but a science: the science of dew, and they view themselves as the dew scientists of the Pleasant Plantation, located in the central massif of the Sierra de Gredos, like the nuclear or microchip or macro-hard scientists of Silicon or Micomicon or Peppermint Valley.

"What feeds their folly, to be sure, is the fact that in this mountain basin the dew falls more heavily than perhaps anywhere else, and that in the daytime sun, which does not dry it up but rather allows the dewdrops to flow into each other, the dew forms veritable torrents, brooks, and cataracts, falling with a strange softness and almost soundlessly over the smooth cliff walls—massive quantities of water from the merging of dewdrops, collecting in the natural basins created by the glacier on the granite floor of the valley, and also captured in specially installed ponds, from which the settlers draw the dew water directly or channel it through gutters and pipes, pipeline-like! to their houses.

"That they use it for drinking, washing, and cooking is actually almost a fine thing—after all, precisely in the mountains the rest of the water is contaminated by grazing animals, by airplanes, and in general, and thus unwholesome, even toxic; I, too, have grown used, over time, to drinking the special dewdrop liquid—I like the taste—and to washing with it every morning, even my hair, without shampoo, and how soft it comes out! but everything else they do with their dew up here already crosses the line of foolishness into the kingdom of fools—their dew-fools' kingdom, which is also dangerous.

"Now listen to this: by now the entire region is dotted with dew wells, roofed over, fenced in, also strictly guarded, as are elsewhere drilling towers in the most productive oil fields. With the exception of a few pathetic little rock crystals, the entire Sierra de Gredos has almost no mineral resources, and accordingly the people here speak of their "air resources," among which the dew is the primary one. They treat dew as their chief capital, and also intend, as I have observed, to exploit it commercially and market it.

"I know: my Hondaredians will bottle the dew water in flasks, spray cans, tubes, canisters, barrels, in order to sell it and to become powerful through the dew business. I can prove that you fellows are poised to sell your dew not only as drinking water but also as medicines to treat all imaginable deficiencies and disorders, for external and internal use: dew products for acne, insect bites, snakebites, eye problems, cellulite, as well as for heart palpitations, colic, chronic fatigue, nightmares, loss of appetite, obesity, and, finally, even for melancholy, loneliness, fear of death, murderous impulses, schizophrenia, hopelessness, malaise, inability to love in all its manifestations, or, more precisely, forms of atrophy and wasting. Dew water boosts your libido!—that is the slogan they plan to launch. And another: Dew from the Sierra de Gredos: the secret of a radiant skin!

"With a view to such a market, which you intend, not without justified optimism, to expand step by step into a worldwide market, you plan to manufacture your dew products in solid form as well, as powder, pastilles, pills, buffered with atomized mountain fruits, such as juniper berry, rowanberry, moss berry, and so on. If one of you actually happens to be a dew scientist, I must tell you that to me this science is by no means pure anymore—dew, schmew: as the scientist conducts his dew research in apparent innocence, examining the dew under a microscope, mixing it, assaying reactions, he has his eye fixed firmly on profits and a monopoly.

"I have obtained copies of all of your scientific papers, most of them lengthy and seemingly tedious, on topics such as 'The Form of Dewdrops on Grasses in Contrast to Dew Formations on Stones, Sand, Gravel, and Glass,' 'Multiplicated Accumulation of Dew on Smooth Granite Surfaces as a Result of Increased Nocturnal Solar Radiation in the Mountains,' 'The Dew Sphere as Collecting Lens for the Color Spectrum,' 'Erroneous Flights of Sierra Moths to the Dew Meadows, or Simulation of Mating

Invitations by Dew Glitter,' 'Varying Dew Phenomena on Oak Leaves, Larch Needles, Bird Feathers—in Particular on Jackdaws, Mountain Cocks, and Peregrine Falcons—and Further on Wild-Boar Bristles, Human Hair, and Animal Pelts, with Particular Attention to So-Called Dew-Licks and Dew-Spirals on Cows, Goats, and Sheepdogs,' 'The Riddle of Black Dew: An Attempt at an Explanation': but not one of these dew deliriums did not have thrumming in the background your insane notion of achieving fame and fortune by means of this natural resource.

"Without a doubt it will be proved that you are seriously considering establishing a dew mafia and then using typical mafia methods to found a human-rights-flouting despotic state among the universal-rights states that have finally cleaned up their act since the last century. From economic to political power, and from political power to the new religion that you will impose on the rest of the world, as I need not demonstrate because it is the logical outcome.

"By now you already worship dew as your idol. I was not mistaken when I heard each of you singly, but all of you in exactly the same words, intoning veritable dew litanies: 'O dew of the new moon! O dew of the solstice! O dew on the mountain apple! O dew in my shoes! O dew on my mother's headstone! O dew that I drank from the lips of my beloved! O dew in the night as I lay dying! O dew on the cellophane from the crushed cigarette pack! O dew, my eyebrow pencil and my moisturizer! O dew that in the expressions of lands all over the earth maketh the meat, the vegetables, the wheat kernels, and the fruit soft and tender as only thou canst! O dew, by definition the fruit of the reflected rays of our earth! O dew, atom of truth and beauty! O dew of the night of pain and suffering! O dew of the hour of awakening! O dew on the eyelids of the white angel! O dew in the child's cowlick! O dew on the pencil point! O dew on the blood spot! O puddle of dew, in which the sky with its jet contrails is mirrored! O dew that sprayeth in the colors of the rainbow and turneth a somersault when the ball rolls through the dewy grass! O dark crisscrossing trails in the dew of the savannah where the wild beasts have trod! O drop of dew, measure of measures! O dewdrop, fullness of being and of our brief sojourn in these parts, and not only in the hours of morning!'

"And I will testify that you have developed an entire creation story or cosmogony that has its origin in dew: no big bang or whatever at some point or wherever—rather, the silent multiplication into infinitude of one dewdrop! Already, before you read a book, you first leave it out in the dew, open to the page you will be reading. And already I can observe how for you people dew literally functions as the measure of measures, as the basic standard. Instead of the basic metric: the basic dew.

"Every second word you utter is 'dew'! Instead of 'money,' 'dollar,' 'mark,' 'peseta,' 'real,' 'maravedi': dew. Instead of 'a kilometer from here,' I hear 'three dew fields from here,' and you also calculate time according to the dew: instead of 'after a night,' 'after a dewfall.' Where others write or calculate in the air, you write in the dew—on an outdoor table, on a tree trunk, on a car's fender. Where others sniff gasoline or drugs or other substances, you dew-fools sniff dew. Where elsewhere storms measure eight to eleven and earthquakes measure seven to ten, you measure Dew Strength One Hundred, using the dew gauge. And when I bring up all these things to you dangerous dew-fools, you look at me as though I were the fool.

"And you thereby embody beyond any doubt that divine utterance that hits the fool nail on the fool head, my dear Hondarederos and Hondarederitos and Hondaredians: you see the mote in your neighbor's eye, but the beam in your own eye, as thick as a tree, you do not see, no, no, no!"

Thus the reporter standing on the ledge in the middle of the wilderness continued to speak for a long time. It was as if the dew, or the word, or speaking of the dew in the Hondareda region, had loosened his tongue—or several different tongues at once. His speaking sparkled with enthusiasm, independent of what he was saying. Had he not earlier, in time out of mind, been one of those classic enthusiasts who are supposed to figure prominently in our story?

And now, in this remote locale, far from his observer's routine, in the presence of the woman, the stranger whose identity he had no desire to know, nor where she came from, nor where she was going—it was enough to be standing there with her—his former enthusiasm had caught up with him again, at last. He had flushed cheeks like an adolescent, and now and then he began to stammer, like one who for the first time in his life begins to say what he has long dreamed of saying.

Except that he also jumbled things up quite a bit. Did not enthusiasm have to be accompanied by clarity, the ability to make distinctions, and, if grounded in criticism, in self-criticism above all? On the other hand: didn't such speaking, although this and that might be far-fetched, pulled out of the air, tossed out to test the waters, as people used to say, create a reality, which, unlike a merely observed and registered reality, simply through the rhythm of the speaking, suggested—narrated—proposed, a possible alternative world?

And the reporter, speaking so heatedly that despite the cold up here in the Sierra his astigmatic's glasses fogged up, was astonished by, amazed at, all the things that enthusiasm made possible in the way of words and sentences, if one just let it have its way, parallel to the facts and the tangibles. And she, the stranger, the adventurer, or whatever she was? She remained silent.

The story tells us that she remained silent long after he had finished speaking and was waiting expectantly for her reply. A troop of chamois, no, a veritable herd, gazelle-like, filed past between the two of them, the younger animals leaping, and trotted down the steepest part of the ledge as if on a level surface tipped up vertically.

Later another member of the observation team passed them, running as always, storming along and stamping straight through the underbrush and around the piles of dead branches that increased in number toward the ridge but did not slow him down: before he came into sight, a squeaking and squawking that was his panting. He must have noticed the two of them, the temporary pair, on the crest, but seemed not to recognize his colleague. And the vagabond of the mountains that this woman was, to judge by the rips in her clothes and her hair blowing in all directions, received the most cursory of glances from the cross-country runner, not merely a greetingless and malevolent glance but a death-dealing one, reinforced further by being tossed over his shoulder. And at the same time he stuck out his tongue—what a thick tongue—and fired through the air at her with both index fingers.

Yes, there were also people like him, whose mind could not be changed by a fairy-tale-like encounter, who, even when they ran into another person up here, far from the usual world with its hostilities, did not promptly forget the unpleasantness that had arisen between them simply by virtue of their being opposite types or genders, but rather, in this third location, face-to-face with the image of an enemy—of which he had at least one to three thousand lurking inside him—found these images confirmed; and if the two of them had spotted each other on Jupiter or Venus, in the remotest corner of the universe, as the only surviving human beings: as far as he was concerned, such a thing would have merely sealed his hatred and his irreconcilability.

And the story goes on to say that the mountain-crossing woman persisted in her silence, although with a constant, ever more lively display of facial expressions, which the observer followed as intently as if he were reading the longed-for words from her lips. She, too, was astonished. She, too, was amazed at what the other person had said.

Yet she was not astonished at the same things as he was. She was astonished, rather, to realize that if she were to speak now, she would have something to say about the mountain basin and its inhabitants that would not merely contradict his observations and explanations but would negate them entirely. This although the man had already been in the high Sierra for a whole year or even far longer, while she had been here only—

And again she was astonished: for it suddenly seemed to her, who had come to the region so recently, as if she had lived in Hondareda a good deal longer than the reporter. "Yes, the time there," she remarked to the author much later, as if long, long afterward, "seems to me in retrospect like a piece, a thing, an object, a mass of material; something spread out, spatial; spacious."

3 0

Not merely one phenomenon or another: from the outset, to her, the very rhythm in the Hondareda basin that carried, connected, and indeed first generated the phenomena and allowed them to appear was fundamentally contrary to that of the red-cheeked, red-haired man. And this rhythm had established itself, after the climb from Pedrada, when she first caught sight of the amazingly deep mountain basin, and of this settlement at the bottom and on the slopes that was entirely new to her, and it had provided the beat for the next phase in her one-woman expedition.

Precisely because of the depth of the cavity at her feet and the massive dimensions and extent of the granite depression, which quietly exploded all usual expectations, the individual features, both near and far, appeared as if through a lens that sharpened them and lent particular emphasis to their contours; and furthermore the contours thus emphasized revealed themselves to be in harmony with one another: in fact part and parcel of the special prevailing rhythm that manifested itself in a flash.

The scattered boulders, the dwellings, the hayricks, the lake (laguna), its outflow, the herds, the people, the entire high-altitude lowland instantaneously took on the appearance of a script, complete with links connecting the individual features or letters, and likewise spaces, paragraphs, or punctuation marks, but in a clearly organized and, at least to her, lovely regularity (see rhythm, above).

And also worth mentioning: that to her the writing looked Arabic, with the identical squiggles of the dwarf bushes everywhere, the repeated and often parallel loose ends, splits, similar curved fissures in cliff after cliff, the dots, points, waves, accents, breathing marks of lichens and mosses on the rock, an Arabic script that she also, involuntarily, "read" from right to left.

And the rhythm of the phenomena in the sprawl of Hondareda went approximately as follows: A swarm of wild doves rattled. A family of grouse ran, hustled, flitted. A snowflake fell. The sky was blue. A rock was a dinosaur egg. A gust of wind hissed. A cloud of dust was yellow. An old man had freckles. The pattern in the dried mud was pentagonal or hexagonal. My grandfather sang in the distance. A flint gave off a singed smell. In the conifer forest the light-colored cones glowed and were cone-shaped, and the raven that flew by was raven-black.

And continuing in the Hondareda rhythm: In the sheltered spots behind the hawthorns the sun shone summery-warm as in summer, and in the leafless rowan trees no birds were sitting, and the bunches of berries were shriveled, and in the middle of winter or fall or May the crickets began to chirp, and I let them wind up my heart anew, and the grass quivered, and a stick was snakeskin gray.

And in the glacial lagoon the water smoked where it was free of ice, and reflected, and the dark part in this reflection was the steep peak of the Almanzor, so steep that precisely this highest peak among the peaks of the Sierra was the only one without snow, and *al-mansûr*, yes, clear as day now, means "the place" in Arabic, and *kathib* means "dune," and behind a stone fortification actually appeared, as if conjured up by the word, a dune, sand from weathered rock that had been blown there, yellow like the feet of bees, and another man was red-haired, and on a mountain acacia the thorns were pointed like sharks' fins, and all joys and sorrows of the world were gathered in one place, and there was a grove of chestnut trees the size of a small orchard, distributed over two terraces, and a single leaf there was whistling, and a few burst fruit husks hung there, empty and showing off their spines, and I leaped over the stone wall and snatched the forgotten chestnuts from the ground, and from an overhanging ledge hung icicles.

And the smoke in the settlement smelled like the smoke in Tiflis, in Stavanger, and in Montana, and next to the Almanzor the mountain water now mirrored the façade of my office building at the confluence of the two rivers in my riverport city, and farther to the left there was a clattering in an oak gall, and in the black broom pods the seeds rattled, yes, rattled, and way over to the left, down at the end of the lines, stood *bint*, Arabic for "girl," and another word for daughter was *ibna*, and someone actually was standing there, and everything was all right again, and nothing was all right again, and everything and nothing was again as it had been, and in a dormer window a candle was burning, and my brother tossed a hand grenade, and one was filled with bliss, with a desire to help, with helplessness, and with a general lostness and neediness, as never before and as always, and the flock of wild doves rustled, and the phoenix rose flaming from its ashes, and one was swept across the first threshold one happened upon, in the first house one happened upon on the floor of the basin.

Long ago, during her first time in the Sierra de Gredos, with the child in her womb, when the child's father, her one and only, had disappeared on the way into the mountains (a disappearing that was characteristic of his tribe?), and when the world before her, at her feet, had suddenly turned upside down, had been stood on its head and acted insane, she herself, in the face of that spectacle, had gone insane, not just almost, but from top to toe.

For years she had denied it, she finally admitted, almost inaudibly, to the author, had denied it energetically and determinedly, and this energy had then been partly responsible for her "worldwide success"—a criminal energy, so to speak (no, not so to speak).

"Everyone has his own madness inside him," she dictated later, when she had recovered her voice, to the author, "and this madness has already come to the surface once, or several times. Except that we all behave, or most of us do, as if nothing had been wrong."

Now, however, at the sight of the depression of Hondareda, with its unexpected new settlement, which upon one's approach looked positively urban, indeed metropolitan, head-down in the glacier-clear valley, a city as if under a glass bell, or altogether as if in a different, as yet unexplored and even undiscovered element, a scene replayed itself in her mind, one of the last before the somewhat happy ending of that film whose heroine she had portrayed long ago: fleeing from her mortal enemies, she found herself in an utterly dead landscape with nothing but volcanic ash, some of it still smoldering, at the edge of the world—as everywhere, such ends, edges, and precipices of the world could occur practically cheek by jowl with the apparent middles and centers—and she wandered, abandoned, half-blind, empty-handed, pleading to the invisible heavens, calling for her parents, her brothers and sisters, her homeland, cursing her fate and human existence altogether, through the scree and fallen rock, stumbled, fell, struggled to her feet, fell again, and finally remained lying facedown on the ground. The camera showed her in close-up, prostrate. Sparks of what looked like lava shot nightward past the figure lying stretched out there, in a coma or dead. A temporal leap. A change of lighting, with the close-up unaltered. The searchlights of the pursuers? No, daylight. The end of night. During the temporal leap, day had broken. Her head still in the smoking volcanic ash and basalt. Over? The end?

Yet gradually some movement, or is it merely the wind in the hair of the corpse? Slowly her head rises and is bathed in light, morning light. Her skin, also her brow, and especially her temples seem made for this light. (Of course the lighting man has done his part, with additional spots and reflectors on the sides and especially on the ground.)

The eyes opening: black, which at the beginning of the shot looks just as dull and veiled as the cratered landscape all around, but then begins to glow, and now, as the camera slowly pulls back, almost imperceptibly, from a close-up to a full shot, here and there the glassy humps of basalt also begin to glow, the fiery cataracts of all the long-ago volcanic eruptions now chilled, hardened like crystal, and heaped up in the wasteland of petrified ash.

It is a rather dark glow, almost scornful, or even, with all the hopelessness concentrated in her gaze, full of quiet rage, unlike her futile fleeing of the previous night, with hands and feet groping and tapping pointlessly in every direction. Then—although the camera remains focused for a full shot, I seem to recall seeing as a moviegoer a shot of only her mouth, just for a moment: the lips parting. Astonishment. Yes, astonishment. Not to be forgotten: her film was set in the Middle Ages, and the occasional astonishment expressed by the characters was not merely believable but was a basic trait. This astonishment of hers, however, exceeded the customary medieval astonishment, was an astonishment at nothing, nothing at all, and it was decisive.

For it saved her life. More than that: it gave her the strength to start a new life. That decisive astonishment in the moment of awakening after a night of despair enabled her to shake off her old story once and for all, and made room for a new scenario, one that was not merely a thousand times but infinitely more beautiful and true, and this story was now about to begin. (Except that the film did not show what happened next.)

At the time, several interpretations were put forward to explain that "decisive astonishment" on the part of the heroine: a dream, a predawn dream, of the sort that sometimes plays out in heavenly colors and tones? the light of morning shortly before sunrise, and the sky, again very medieval, as the domed firmament, and the lava earth, on which the woman lay outstretched, as the surface over which it arched? Or a prematitudinal dream of Paradise and the light and the air currents of the real or waking world intermingling with it?

For my part, I believe that the fresh astonishment of that persecuted and despairing woman there was actually unfounded, or stemmed from almost nothing—just as I, too, from early on and to this day, though less often, and less and less frequently, in my often damnably askew and sometimes accursedly worthless life, occasionally see, newly astonished and astonished anew, an immense, powerful, unshakably peaceful world flash by, which I cannot be dissuaded from considering the actual one—more will be said here later about the rather despised word "actual"—and such a world never appears to me in the form of the sun or of pure light, but only in rather dim, flickering, twilight-gray flashes resembling distant heat lightning, as the most inconspicuous of the inconspicuous: for instance as a rusted nail seen years earlier on a dusty road in the place of my birth; as a curb seen one time on the Peloponnesus; as the shadow of a child in Oklahoma; as the boat gangplanks in Cappadocia. And I, too—and with me my "actual world"—are threatened with the loss of images, or has it already taken place, irreversibly? And since it is a question of my life, and not of a film plot, my astonishment was also never able to play a decisive role.

Her first experience of the surprisingly populated mountain depression matched to a T the way her eyes had been opened to the world in the scene she had played at the end of her film. The world one experienced in Hondareda was virginal and bridal, yet equally, as one sensed the first time one gazed down into that camp in the hollow, a lost cause, or perhaps not? (For this sentence she again insisted on "one," and when the author, who had long since left his father- and motherland for his village in La Mancha, hesitantly asked whether "bridal" and "virginal" were terms still used in German and suitable, she told him that what mattered was the adjectives' relationship to the nouns, and in this case: yes!)

By the way, she said, her story would have to return later to that upside-down hour, with the outbreak of insanity, that had occurred during her first journey through the Sierra de Gredos; for that had also become the hour of her guilt, and the fact that now, on this last, or perhaps not last? crossing, she had made up her mind, and, in the worst moments, intensely imagined, that she would speak of it at long last, had kept her from giving up and just letting herself fall, or perhaps not?

On her previous adventurous journeys, she had encountered that virginal world not so infrequently—and again she interrupted the author and ordered him occasionally to replace "adventure" and "journey" with "roaming." Almost every time it manifested itself, it had been when the roamer, or, in Spanish, *la andariega* or *andarina*, from *andar*, "to walk," had stretched out somewhere in the open and fallen asleep, just as had happened in the film with the heroine she had played.

Unlike in the film, she slept there, on the bank of a brook, in the steppe grass, under an overhanging cliff, only very briefly, usually for just a few breaths. And the falling asleep occurred in broad daylight. And it was never preceded by sorrow or despair, at most by a certain weariness from walking, a listlessness.

Awakening from such a slumber, always accompanied by the rushing of water, the whistling of wind, and several times the more or less distant roar of a highway: not an easy awakening: as if poked by the forehead of an animal watching over her or some friendly creature. And also each time a scenery that, although unchanged, now seemed thoroughly unfamiliar and above all incomprehensible, without north and south, noon and afternoon—if any time, then morning, if any land, a land in the Orient.

What freshness wafted toward one from this indecipherable setting. Except that it soon gave way to the tried-and-true familiar, and already the rejuvenation and the brideliness were wilted and dissipated. But in her Hondareda period this was not the case. She had never experienced anything similar.

But then something comparable did come to mind. As a young woman she had often taken the train from her university town home to see her grandparents and her brother, still quite little, in the Sorbian-Arab village. Although the village lay in an almost flat landscape, before arriving at the railroad station, located a short distance from the village, the train went through a real tunnel. That got one's attention, and not only the first time but every time, and even more remarkable was the length of the tunnel. Each time it seemed as though it would never end. What a long journey, with darkness to right and left, and in a tunnel on almost level terrain, too!

When she traveled home this way, it was always evening already, if not night. And often she was tired, from being in the city or just in general. And as time went by, she would fall asleep in the tunnel, more and more often, and eventually every single time. And she fell asleep there even when she was not tired. The train had hardly entered the tunnel, at which it always more than doubled its speed, and its rattling and banging turned into a high-pitched whirring and whining, when her eyes would close and she, her body and her consciousness, and everything and everyone in the car with her, would drift along, while the iron wheels and rails took on a stronger and seemingly hardened rhythm between the very narrow tunnel walls, deep in the wide, hollowed-out belly of the dugout of the grander time. And: in the tunnel one man raped her. One? One for all.

At the end of the tunnel, with the train's sound now more distant again and softer, while the train slowed before reaching the station, she awoke. And every time, and with every repetition of the trip just as powerfully as in a fairy tale, she had the transformed-world experience. And unlike the times when she awoke as a vagabond with the sky above her, the awakening in and after the tunnel was lasting and reliable and above all valid. As a result of the tunnel, momentary, everyday experience, the mere present, was transformed and elevated into something of epic proportions. When one's eyes closed in the tunnel, one saw afterward with much bigger eyes.

And just as later, when she was in upside-down, downside-up Hondareda, surrounded by the summit plain of the Sierra walls, she had thought back then, at the sight of the entirely unadorned village, which, however, seemed after her tunnel sleep to be decked out as for a festival: "What has-beens, how superfluous we are. How played-out we are. What dream merchants and castle-in-the-air-builders we are. How lonely and lost we are."

And just as after the tunnel sleep her former home had seemed incomprehensible, so the Hondareda world seemed incomprehensible to her now, and from beginning to end: which did not mean that she was looking to comprehend it. For, just as when she awoke under the open sky after the tunnel, this not-comprehending-anymore was basically invigorating, and despite all one's awareness of being a lost soul among lost souls, it gave one confidence, of a very strange sort. What? Was she, the boss, a lost soul? That, too, the story will touch upon later. And besides, she had long ago ceased to be a boss. Or perhaps not? Or all the more?

There was almost nothing ordinary about the "mead of Hondareda," one of the names as numerous as flower petals that had been coined for the glacial basin. So she stood there, and stands there, and will have stood there, one day looking at a sundial painted on a granite slab. It was not merely that it had no hands, and behind the shadow-dial nothing but a landscape in circular form, a miniature of the region: the sundial was located at a spot in the settlement that the sun seldom reached, and then only for moments, and besides, a granite cliff stood in the way of the sun's rays: so that the sundial's indicator cast its time-revealing shadow at most for a couple of moments.

Similarly, right after her arrival there, beneath the mountain-blue sky, the zenith of whose great dome already hinted stormily at outer-space black, she had again been pelted, as earlier in Pedrada, from a broom thicket: except that this time, instead of stones it was almost weightless juniper berries, and, after another stretch, shiny red rose hips, not even as big as quail eggs, and, after a few more boulders, Sierra nuts, elderberries, and pine nuts. And it was not so much that she was pelted with these things but rather that they were thrown to her by persons who kept out of sight, in a high arc, as if she were supposed to catch them (which she then did).

Likewise a brand-new, shiny bulldozer was suddenly parked there, surrounded by quartz and alabaster cliffs so smooth that one's hand could not gain a purchase. And on another day, somewhere else entirely, far from the settlement, from the grainlike tall steppe grass, among which actual blades of wheat could be found, emerged freshly sieved sand cones as high as houses, in each one a weather-beaten rusty shovel, as if left there long ago. And the first, or third, or last of the original inhabitants of Hondareda—the observer had observed correctly—a man visibly stricken with years, was busy day in, day out, transporting boards on a small ladder wagon, back and forth, forth and back, sometimes also in a circle, without unloading them anywhere.

Another Hondareda person clambered into the one crane in the place, which towered above all the rock spires on the floor of the basin, and stayed up there, motionless, in his cabin, sitting below the still arm of the crane, reading? watching? finally fumbling around, doing things with his hands that had no connection with the lifting apparatus, something like shaking a skillet, something like threading a needle, something like writing, with his nose close to the paper like a first-grader—writing with his entire hand, his fist, meanwhile rolling his shoulders, throwing his head back, swaying his torso, and thus involving his entire body, or was this actually lovemaking, with his "partner" shielded by the cabin's screen, and look, now he is gazing quietly out his crane window again, not moving a muscle, look how far away he is, and how, at fingertip distance, his iris iridesces and his pupils pulsate.

And one day or night, or again and again, the roamer in the temporary Sierra capital must have pushed open one of the seemingly unoccupied wooden shacks, pushed aside the partition, and seen two lovers there, more real or in the flesh than anything one could imagine: there lay two people, very young, and the girl, the woman, was the most visible.

She did not react in the slightest to the intruder, who in fact immediately took one step backward, but then became a spectator, wordlessly asked and invited to do so by the woman. As glistening as the girl lying there naked was (where in the world was the source of light in the dim shack?), the epitome of pride and surrender in flesh and blood, but especially in flesh, she seemed even prouder when she knew herself observed, and her surrender, becoming hard to define, transcending the person to which it pertained, the boy or man, appeared to be not merely somewhat but infinitely greater and more self-aware—will have appeared thus, appears thus.

Enough of myths, this gaze said, this skin and this hair: enough of myths in which male gods descend on the woman in the shape of a cloud, a swan, a bull, a dragon, a billy goat, and the like; look at me: entirely different myths are in effect, and not only here and now, myths in which longing during absence and fulfillment during presence finally coalesce, and these myths are not made up out of whole cloth! A knothole in the shack opened into a spiral, and through the wide-open door the summit plain of the Sierra, peak after peak, the Mira, the Little Brothers, Los Hermanitos, the Little Knives, Los Cuchilleros, the Three Galayos, the Almanzor, the Galana, came riding in, one after the other. What were the two doing there? Was this even lovemaking? And the observer again understood nothing, nothing at all: and that was as it should be. Whatever the case: those two in the shack, copulating in such a creaturely way, majestically, displayed it to the world; displayed it to the universe.

3 1

On her property—the former stagecoach relay station and orchard—at the edge of the riverport city, she had once had an experience that presaged her interlude in Hondareda, an experience with a quince tree, known to her in one of the few remaining Sorbian words in her vocabulary as *dunja*, along with *kwita*.

That year the quince, aka *dunja*, had bloomed, with its inimitable white blossoms, shaped like small, shallow bowls and gleaming from amid the dense, dull-green foliage, but then not one single fruit had developed. And nevertheless she went out to the tree every morning that summer, and then also in the fall, and looked to see whether there was not at least one quince, no, *dunja*. As time passed, here and there in the yard next door, so much smaller and more shaded, that ineffable *dunja* green, later yellow, appeared again, together with those rounded forms that surpassed any apple or other tree-borne fruit, and the shimmering fuzz on the surface. Only, in her orchard, no matter how often she climbed the ladder and poked through the leaves: nothing, and today again nothing.

And nevertheless she had not ceased to be on the lookout and to search. Was it not possible that in the fork of a bough or elsewhere, concealed from sight, a *dunja* might be hiding? Yes, one day it would present itself to her eyes, a body, a curve, a fruit—with weight, volume, and fragrance among all the flat, odorless, and weightless leaves, which here and there were rounded, mimicking a fruit. And her looking would contribute to the fruit's taking shape and its eventual appearance; would help bring forth the quince, the one quince on the tree. And if not, she, the experienced fruit thief, would simply take one from next door and attach it by a string or something to her tree—exclamation point!

And then, one morning in late fall, when the foliage had become sparse, crinkled, and often blackened, with yellow spots like the special Almanzor salamander up here, from a distance her gaze, without being intent on anything for a change, unexpectedly—"out of the blue," the author's suggestion—behind, between, no, in front of, next to, and especially above the salamandrine spots, encountered a form, a ball no larger than a wild apple—which in that spot, on the previously so empty and barren tree, created a sphere in which the entire tree, without any wind, and with the *dunja* lancets at a standstill, strangely rigid in their wilting, at the moment when she caught sight of the quince ("So there!") seemed to be turning. In this fashion a second and a third fruit then appeared, one more meager and nondescript than the next, and she left them all hanging on the tree, to shrivel and turn wintry black.

And looking as a form of intervening, contributing, and inducing manifested itself again during her time in Hondareda, going far beyond such influencing of a plant. The observer had observed correctly when he spoke of the shapelessness or homeliness or chaotic ugliness of both the entire settlement in its layout and the individual hovels, "sleeping crates," "pre-Promethean holes in the ground," "termite mounds without termite architecture." And yet he had not looked long enough, or often enough?

Had he ever stepped over a threshold and eaten, lived, and so forth with the inhabitants in a sense fundamentally different from that in which some other, particularly assiduous, travel writers "participate in the natives' lives"? Not once—although his reports do attest that everywhere entry had been silently refused to him, despite the absence of any visible, physical barrier-threshold in front of the living-holes; and as a result, he, together with the other members of his team, instead of crossing a threshold in Hondareda considerately and like a polite guest, had blindly forced his way in and remained blind to the spaces and conditions inside, or had he, or perhaps not?

She, on the other hand, the unmistakably foreign woman—which did not mean outsider—discovered in this new settlement high in the mountains—which was a place of transition, and not only because of its proximity to the Candeleda Pass—a painstakingly worked-out, precisely defined, and, in the last analysis, positively artistic system of thresholds, or, in the inhabitants' water-dominated vocabulary, locks? And once one's eyes and all one's senses caught on to this system, the apparently chaotic image of the settlement, seemingly mimicking the postglacial chaos of boulders scattered around without plan or rhythm, as well as the human habitations, acquired form (and forms) and relevance.

True, it was a correct observation that each route into the colony took an inconvenient and seemingly illogical course, involving twists and turns, and going around bends that without apparent reason led one far from one's destination; even a path or rocky trail to the neighbor's place directly across the way followed a seemingly needlessly roundabout detour. But these detours had been there from the beginning, before the inhabitants settled in and constructed their dwellings, had been laid out after his arrival by one camper to the next: a sign and indication of the mutual commitment to preserving distance between oneself and others, a polite measure precisely in these cramped quarters, perhaps an even more distinct signal of giving one's fellow immigrant a wide berth, intended as a salutation: "I mean well by you!"

And it was from these original detours, established without much ado (or actually with much ado) between the new arrivals—perhaps prefigured for all of them in the human circulatory system—from this kind of both external and internal pre-tracery, then, that without much further effort the entire seemingly pointless network of diverging and deviating streets, alleys, and passageways had developed in the village of Hondareda.

And with some variations the same was true of the individual buildings, or the natural features that had simply been adapted for living, storage, parking, cellaring: the caves, the holes and niches, the clay pits; and equally true of the now abandoned huts of the hermits, a succession of whom had followed each other to the basin over the centuries, huts that on closer inspection turned out to have been altered in all sorts of ways and only from above appeared to have caved in; and likewise true of the one-time "king's refuge," which only an outsider would perceive as a threatful (was that word still in use?) mountain fortress in ruins, and which, to be sure, continued to be marked on all maps of the Sierra by a small black triangle (= ruin), but in reality had meanwhile been rebuilt by the Hondarederos step by step as something else entirely, starting deep inside this obsolete castle, where, invisible to observers, a new cornerstone had been laid: as the seat of government of the—self-declared? nothing up there is declared, and precisely that is part of the international Hondareda problem—enclave, the seat of government hidden away in what still looks like a pile of stones and beams from the former royal refuge, and can be reached only with difficulty from the inhabited basin below: far, far removed from this government seat or center in the sky-high wilderness, at least sixty times sixty hammer throws or ten to thirteen sonic seconds away.

No matter over which thresholds in the Hondareda region you step or let yourself be sluiced or carried into the center of the habitations, and not only the geometric center: everywhere you will find yourself enclosed by that sphere that categorically refused to be recognizable from the outside. Even in a mere shack, even in a culvert-like structure resembling a segment of a pipeline (which upon your entry turns out nonetheless to be heated and equipped with bull's-eye windows like a cruise ship), you immediately encounter the quince, as it were, the *dunja,* both in the singular and the plural, the fruit; the flavor and color radiate from the living area into the other spaces, and out into the open.

One could also believe the observer, and it was not a question of ill will on his part, when, in his reports, he described the people of Hondareda as regressing to a much earlier time, something already perceptible in their living conditions. For even she had felt during her first period there as if she had been transported back to the storm-wracked forest beyond the outskirts of her home riverport city. For, to greet her, one Hondaredero or another clambered out of a trough not unlike those left behind when the huge trees were uprooted. (In fact, not a few of those root hollows, as her neighbor's son from the porter's lodge had told her over the telephone, were now being used as sleeping places by the increasing numbers of homeless in the region, made habitable with cardboard boxes, blankets, and animal skins, also valuable carpets, with people climbing in and out through the gaps between the earth and the up-ended rootwork, now situated vertically; later he, too, would spend the night in such a hole, and perhaps more than once.)

The holes in both places resembled each other in that they had come about as a result of a sort of upheaval of the earth's surface: there the centuries-old oaks, chestnuts, and cedars had left behind hollows deeper than graves and wider than bomb craters, while here it was the granite boulders, left standing upright in the scree and debris of the former glacier, as tall as trees and with a diameter of at least ten tree trunks, that had lost their footing, without any help from a storm, simply as a result of the gradual sinking of the subsoil and eventually their own top-heaviness.

But, no again, my dear observer, these pits, the hollows left by what had previously anchored all the stone trees of the glacial-chaos forest, now tipped in all directions, were by no means evidence of an attempt to slip away from any sort of present day.

It was not even a question of pits, at least not inhabited pits. These numerous additional hollows, almost completely sheltered from wind and weather, within the larger Hondareda depression, served rather as trenches, among other things for the storage of firewood and for heating-oil tanks, and above all for marking—though not, as the observer thought, for blocking and complicating—access to the actual living quarters, which in this fashion were initially shielded from view: as passageways, or outworks, or, if you prefer the term, "connectors."

And only after these passageways or outworks—why had this remained a mystery to the nearsighted, farsighted, and also astigmatic observer up to now?—the actual dwelling, both fortuitous and constructed (with ancient as well as contemporary materials), as modest and prepossessing, as run-down and at the same time elegant, as its inhabitant, hailing from Hong Kong, Mexico City, Haifa, Freetown, Adelaide, or Santa Fe, let us say. — Did this mean that she was enthusiastic about Hondareda and those who had moved there? — "Yes." — And therefore predisposed toward them? — "Enthusiastic does not mean predisposed." — But didn't enthusiasm threaten to run away with one? — "If it is enthusiasm, never." — But didn't it add something to the object that was not naturally part of it? — "If it is enthusiasm, always." — And what did it add? What did it do? — "Yes, it does something. It makes something. It creates something." — But how could one regain one's lost enthusiasm? How did it make a new beginning possible? — "It seems to me, it begins as a great pain often begins, but then works in the opposite way. Are you familiar with that? After a long period of being free of pain, you suddenly think of the absent pain, in your head, in your soul, in your heart, in your stomach, in your intestines. Completely free of pain, you think of pain, here and now, or merely think of the word and the possible site of pain—and the next night, or an hour later, or immediately after your thinking of the word, pain breaks out in you, in the very spot you were thinking of, and with great intensity, and you think you will die of it this very instant.

"And this is the way enthusiasm sets in, right?, or returns, usually with thinking or becoming aware—not of pain, of course, but rather of an object that should actually be present, but, strange to say, is not. Long ago in the village, and not only then—let us say, in my fruit-stealing days, which are not over yet—often, very often the mere name of a fruit would come to me—'apple,' 'wild plum,' 'cherry,' or 'quince'—with nothing of the sort far and wide, and why should there have been, and then a few steps or roads or farm paths farther on: there was the thing, the object, the tree of early apples, or the good Louise of Avranches, conjured up by the name, as it were; no, not as it were, and at any rate, simply thinking constantly of the names, the names, and again the names had put me on the trail of the apples, pears, quinces, plums.

"And so one day in Hondareda, for example, I thought about the word 'children': yes, where are the children here? Are there no children here?— and with the conscious thought, my asking, listening, and raising my head at the same time, they promptly revealed themselves, if at first only in a brief clattering of feet on the smooth, natural glacial rock surface, which echoed louder than any man-made paving—a clattering that had long since been in her ear but had been mistaken for hands clapping. And then the cries of infants from more and more rock huts. And then immediately, upon the repetition of the word, a screeching of many voices, seemingly unending, such as could come only from a school playground . . .

"And enthusiasm, at least enthusiasm for the objects, places, and living beings in the depression of Hondareda, meant that in each word or name that added something to those that were already there, pain was all the more certain to be present, a pain that exceeded my own and was inescapably bound up with the things there, the things here; see the expression for being dead that had soon established itself in the region, without prior discussion: 'No longer being on earth.' And this enthusiasm, which makes things appear, brings them to light, with or without the concomitant pain, is something you should insert into my story again and again! It should provide the accent, the accent of plenitude and at the same time of dearth—that certain accent that all the inhabitants of the Pedrada-Hondareda region actually have when they speak." Thereupon the author: "As you do as well here."

3 2

When the author in his spot in La Mancha (and *mancha* already meant "spot"), far from the world but not world-forsaken, set to work later on her, and his, book, several versions of her crossing the Sierra de Gredos had already reached his ears, and they all had to do with the sojourn of that roaming woman, *andariega*, in the Hondareda-Camarca region.

Although by nature, or for whatever reason, he was a gullible person, it seemed to him that what was "attested to" and "recounted"—such things were always particularly emphasized in the preambles—was not merely false but also falsified. For these falsifying narrators, who further-more never identified themselves and claimed to "require anonymity as a shield against predictable acts of revenge," were plainly intent, and this was revealed by their very first sentence, in the choice of words and even more in the grammar and sentence rhythm, on first selling their story and second maligning their subject, with the latter motive, at least in their opinion, the absolute prerequisite for the former.

But actually they were attempting, in content as well as in form, to accomplish something far worse than mere character assassination, which could have produced exactly the opposite effect on various people in the market they were targeting: the little folks of Hondareda had to be por-trayed from A to Z, and from the first adjective to the last verb, as the new Gothamites, dragging sunlight in bushel baskets from outside into their windowless houses or cellar holes, and so on. By treating the life of these settlers, who had made their way to the mountain basin from all over the world, as the stuff of fables and legends, they meant to render it harmless and, yes, unreal.

And these anonymous and apocryphal narrators thought that a partic-ularly clever way to undermine the Hondarederos and those enthusiastic about their existential experiment, to render them ridiculous and insignificant, was to ascribe to them a belief in utopia, which everywhere else on the planet had become the butt of ridicule, and thus had great commercial potential as a humor-product.

The basic feature of all the apocryphal stories: that a first commandment of the H-people was "to be good and nothing but good." Which suggested never doing good intentionally; it was enough to be good, with whatever flowed from that. And a variation on such a first commandment in that remote world was allegedly "not to do good but to behave well."

What followed in the individual false fables, narrated in an exaggerated pseudo-legend style, was, for instance, that one of the new settlers, intent only on being good and behaving well, out of the clear blue sky fell upon a fellow citizen he happened to encounter and almost killed him, with the explanation that those responsible for the misery and wretchedness of the current era, his own as well as everyone else's—and they existed in the flesh, if also hardly in blood—were so inaccessible and so beyond his reach, and anyone's, that he, "good as he was" (apocryphal irony), could not help taking out his impotent rage against all those absentees on the next person who crossed his path . . . (Typical also of the apocryphal narrators: that they suggested to the imagined reader simply by means of those three dots what he was supposed to think about a subject.)

The local residents were also shunted off into the nonserious realm of the fable by these narrators, under the guise of seriousness, when they asserted that "the citizens of Hondareda" had, by their own testimony, revived a long-dormant tradition of the region, according to which, if one of them had to be the decision-maker—"for heaven's sake, not a leader or master"—he had to exercise this authority not like an Old Testament or even cannibalistic father but "as a brother" (this was the resurrected traditional phrase)—which gave rise to tall tales describing a series of "brother presidents," whose despotic regimes were not so much intentionally brutal as clumsy, but, because they appeared in "brotherly" guise, turned out to be especially brutal.

And then the author found at least partially believable what he learned from the apocryphal legends: that many of those who had moved to Hondareda from the most distant parts of the globe had gone well beyond borrowing for their new houses here just a few features from the indigenous architecture of their lands of origin: the multiracial person from

Colorado who had returned here to the land of his distant ancestors had added onto the existing cavern in a granite cliff a perfect replica of one of the sandstone dwellings familiar to him from the Navajos back in Colorado (he himself also their descendant . . .); another had built on a ledge extending far into the mountain lagoon the spitting image of one of the limestone saltworks houses from the distant land of his birth, such as he had inhabited in Dubrovnik, in the former Yugoslavia, with mounds of raw salt stored in the windowless ground floor; a third had used boards and sticks and broom branches to hammer together a lean-to that represented a copy, if a poor one, of a field hut in his "motherland, Styria, New Austria" . . .

What made these versions credible in the author's eyes: one detail or another was indubitably true, a date here, a place description there, even an occasional rhythm—which he dubbed "oscillating truth"—: many individual elements were true and effective—had the effect of making the whole thing, the whole story, ring true. But what was ultimately false and falsified, the essence of falsification, was the way in which the apocryphal narrators strung together the accurate details—the swindle resided in the linkages; denying the Hondareda folk any right to exist in the present by transporting their lives into the realm of legend, and thereby reducing them—who was being despotic here?—to manifestations of infantile, self-pitying homesickness. "Does no one notice?" the author shouted (and in his writing shed alternately pounded the table and struck himself on the head).

And at the same time it was precisely the circumstance that he had already heard the story told numerous times, one way or the other—was familiar with it from hearsay and still more hearsay, and discovered that it was constantly being offered to him again—that tempted him to commit it finally to paper in his own way.

Precisely the fact that many versions of a story already existed had always motivated him to become its author far more than anything else, whether tragedy, comedy, unique occurrence, or whatever, and to him it was no contradiction that "author" means "originator"; when so much and so many different things were told about a topic, there must be something to it, something to mine from its "original" form.

And now every day there was a sort of Hondareda story in installments again—to the author the clearest indication that what was taking place, or had taken place, there represented a problem, in the sense that it gave him a push or rather got him moving, a subject, one that lit a fire under him. What troubled him this time was only that the story had been commissioned. But was the initial assignment still in force? When the once powerful woman from the northwestern riverport city arrived in his house on the edge of the steppe in La Mancha, after crossing the Sierra de Gredos, was she merely pretending to be his client, and then? not even pretending anymore?

Yes, it was true—thus her reply, which for a long time consisted only of a silent play of expressions, to the reporter from abroad up there on the granite outcropping—each of the new settlers of Hondareda lived primarily in isolation, at most sharing his time in the morning and evening with his young housemate, usually a grandson, often still a child.

And, yes, except for particular occasions, people there seemed to go out of their way to avoid each other. How skinny, how exaggeratedly skinny, they made themselves when they passed each other in the rocky alleys. What glassy eyes, almost rigid with fear, they had when they looked at each other, only at each other? no, also when they were walking by themselves, and the fear in that case was decidedly more noticeable, though at the same time related less to something in the present than to the lingering effect of an earlier experience, actually mitigated a bit by the encounter with a neighbor.

Yes, the way they had of giving each other the widest berth possible—even out on the open mountain tundra, even while swimming in the lake, with its patches of bog-warm water—a way of backing off and wheeling to go in the opposite direction, and if a person turned to look at another after all, he would then walk backward, backward as if rigid with fear.

And there was some truth to the observation, made in Hondareda by her opposite number up there on the rock outcropping, that the neighbors spied on one another. True: the extraordinary technical skills the new settlers all possessed were used primarily for finding out what the neighbors were up to. Yes, they had things like peri-periscopes, more sophisticated than those in submarines, in every one of their dwellings, which from the outside seemed to be shielded, or, you could say, armored, and with these devices one person could see around a thousand and one corners into another's cooking pots and books, under lamps and cap visors, even under eyelids, could see the top of another's head, his hands, his mouth.

But, no, it is not that they want to spy on their neighbors so as to catch them doing something or corner them. Rather, they hope this spying will allow them to be in the company of others—to feel at one with them—to be with them. Ah, now my neighbor over there is running a bath for his grandchild. And now the other neighbor is sweeping out his workshop. And now my third neighbor is finally coming home, turning on the light in his glassed-in veranda—in the Hondareda enclave they have generally reintroduced rotary switches, likewise rotary dials on the telephones—and is pacing up and down, up and down—is he not feeling well?—is turning the light off again, sitting down, bowing his head, holding his head in his hands, rocking it, moving his lips, singing, yes, the grandfather over there is singing, and even though I cannot hear the song, I recognize it, I know it, and I am singing along over here.

And it is also correct that the Hondarederos, whenever they have time—and they almost always have time—post themselves on their property lines, each on the edge of his fairly narrow lot, and lie in wait for one another. But what we are lying in wait for, with ears cocked, hands poised, and knees and feet ready to break into a dash, perhaps for instance toward a shirt blown by the wind over the wall marking the property line, a dress, a handkerchief: so that we can promptly hand it back to our neighbor, ladder to ladder against the wall, or it is a ball: if only it would fly by accident again onto my land, and I, in an elegant, utterly natural gesture, could kick it back, without a word, with sleight of foot, as if the child next door had sent it my way on purpose.

Or we intentionally lob our own ball over the property line and wait to see what will happen next. Or we lie in wait, with our whole body pressed against the wall, the impenetrable fence, the barrier of broom berries and intertwined roots, for a call for help from across the way, for sobs, for whimpers, not out of ordinary curiosity or malice, but in the sense in which we also lie in wait for a singing or humming—not random singing or humming—and also for simply a kind and gentle voice from next door.

We watch our neighbors from all sides in this fashion because we wish them only well, and because, for our part, we feel protected and reassured by whatever we see and hear them doing, just as we, for our part, allow something to blow, or throw something, over to their side, in the hope that it will be brought or thrown back.

Or we engage in small, tolerated violations of each other's bound-
aries, and also of each other's property, and thereby show that our neighbor's land, what grows on it, and thus also our neighbor himself, attracts
us and is dear to our hearts. There is no greater proof of our respect for
him than for us to let him catch us—to make a point of letting him see
us—as we enter his greenhouse (neither dwellings nor other buildings are
locked here) and, as calmly as you please, go over to his apple, pear, or orange tree and let one, never more than one, fruit, just for our own consumption, drop into our hand, and promptly bite into it. (In Hondareda
the word "let" is one of the most frequently used verbs.) And I am flat-
tered and appeased in turn when my neighbor clambers into my yard.

And thus a saying has come into use among us: even though we give
each other a wide berth when we happen to meet, etc.—which does not
mean the same thing it means elsewhere—sometimes the other person
calls out to me, "I saw you!" which implies, however, neither a warning
nor a threat, but the opposite, and along with "Not to worry!" and "Who's
counting!" is one of the greeting formulas regularly heard in the Hondareda region.

And besides, it is only superficially accurate to say that the immigrants hardly communicate with each other and at most utter a few empty
phrases: precisely by means of these empty or coded formulas, which
sound strange to an outsider, they convey a number of things to the other
person, even beyond ordinary communication; in which case it is always
the voice, yes, the voice of the fellow resident, that provides this additional element.

Nowhere else in the world had she, the adventurer, the roamer, heard
voices like these here. They were not trained voices, not those of announcers or actors, such as various members of the observation team had.
These immigrants' voices took one by surprise. She understood the observer
when he was put off by the inhabitants' appearance, more vagabondish
than hers by x rips in their clothing and y tangles in their hair and z scaly
patches on their faces. Yes, they resembled a peculiar cross between
knights and beggars.

But: once, long ago, on a street in Paris, or in Palermo, she had passed
a similar figure that looked terminally scruffy, and had heard issuing from
this seemingly abandoned heap of misery, which had long since lost any resemblance to a human being, a tremulous voice, God! what a voice! And
in her mind, she/one had fallen on her/one's knees at the sound of that

tentative and pitiful but oh so vital voice—the voice of a living being if ever there was one—and in reality? one had stopped and listened to that voice, on and on, with one's back to it, and was sure that the other person was conscious of establishing contact with his voice, at least getting through. How could she be so sure of that? She/one could taste it.

And this same surprising voice rang out, yes, rang out—despite the complete absence of tonality and resonance—from each of her people here in Hondareda.

Without exception they were broken voices, rough and hoarse even in the young people and children. The dying sometimes had such voices, when they were fully conscious—as no healthy person is or any person freed for the moment somehow of all limitations—when they saw their lives, and life in general, pass before them, and were at once filled with zest for life and acceptance of death; or survivors also; or people gratefully exhausted after some mighty task or effort.

These voices resonated for her like—as—no, neither "like" nor "as": the voices resonated, that was all. (The author likes to slip in the word "resonate," whether obsolete or not.)

No one else had such a voice nowadays. And besides, the people of Hondareda were not really shabby or ragged in the least—she almost shouted at the observer and scolded him—even the older ones went about in the finest fabrics, with the most elegant cuts, and there, under the mountain sky and close to the trails of wild animals, this seemed infinitely, to the nth power, more appropriate than on models on the catwalk and their imitators sashaying through the megalopolises with rolling shoulders and high-stepping legs—except it happened that the Hondarederos' garments, which they wore everywhere, even on the spiny savannah and in the coniferous forests, had gradually acquired rips and tears, and in that region people even took pride in this, just look at me! and as far as mending, etc., went, they followed the example of that literary hero of many centuries ago, who left the rips in his garment unmended as a token of the adventures he had survived.

And how could this be: Were my people down there in the glacial trough unemployed, without regular occupations?

This much had again been observed accurately: none of them ever let himself be seen by outsiders engaged in any organized form of work. And, in particular, whatever the Hondarederos did, and especially what they left undone, never looked like work. Except that it was not enough to watch them during their days and nights. And besides, it was wrong to interrogate them about it, or about anything. The trick was to get them to talk by some other means. To get them to talk of their own accord!

In this manner, for example, you would have learned that they do things every day, make things, move things along—without any sign of working or toiling. Yes, they not only have no conventional occupations; they also reject separate professions, along with their labels. And yet, although this is not obvious with any one of them, each is many things in one: producer, manufacturer, tradesman, engineer, entrepreneur, dealer, processor, distributor, and also a knowledgeable customer (of the others). Every time they allowed me to watch them while they were doing something or intentionally leaving something undone, I thought to myself: These are my people, or: These are my kin—and every time—this shows how much I continue to live according to the rhythm of the profession I gave up—I misspoke in my thoughts and said: These are my clients!

And every time I entered their dwellings, even the sight of their shoes in the entryway, of a dog-eared book, of a few hazelnuts, slivers of mica, chunks of alabaster, juniper branches, a black boar ham hanging from the doorpost to cure, made the property seem well managed to me.

Did I just say "property," rather than shack, grotto, bunker, hut, and so forth? Yes. Where from the outside you see nothing but windowless hovels, I, escorted with the proverbial "inconspicuous hospitality" into the interior, see, if not "crystal palaces," at least spaces offering rich vistas of the outdoors, all the way to a variety of horizons, and that is no mere glorification, or my reaction against the palatial dwellings that I often perceive as worthless rubble, but also the eye of the trained manager: of a person who sniffs out value and makes sure it bears fruit.

As was already stated: I have always felt driven to bring something to the others, "my kin," not so much to help them as to help some undertaking along, to suggest ideas to them in conjunction with it—to speed them on their way. What all did I not bring back for my brother and then for my child, and in what direction did I not speed the one and the other? I? Yes, I.

But I came here to Hondareda empty-handed, with nothing but my gaze. And with it I saw, and let the people here see, just as they first let themselves be seen—a seeing, one move at a time, as in business negotiations, yet fundamentally different—that their actions as well as their inaction—apart from any impression of work, effort, strain, muscular exertion, brow-furrowing—prefigured, or sketched, a kind of management that had never before been practiced in just this way, of entrepreneurship, value creation, treasure extraction.

What was new about them was that they never approached their diverse forms of action and inaction (which included reading, looking, etc., as action? as inaction?) with a plan for the day, let alone the year: another unspoken principle shared without prior consultation by the Hondarederos, adopted from a loafer of the previous century, a Swiss loafer! according to whom it was incompatible with human dignity "to make preparations."

Very often, when she was the guest of one of them, deep inside his house or in his hidden garden—how cordially she was welcomed every time—and observed him going about his day, it happened that the other person, male or female, just sat there for a while or squatted on his or her heels, alternately gazing into space and reading, reading and gazing into space, or likewise gazed into space and alternately tasted something, sipped something, or, in general, from the beginning and also in between, stared absentmindedly at the book, into the air, at the flowerbeds, into the trees, or into the cooking pots, as she had once observed among many inhabitants of her vanished Slavic-Arab village (for which the expression "He [she] is gazing into the idiot box again" was used, or also, borrowed from the game of chess, "the Slavic defense").

But then suddenly, with a light-footedness very different from the sluggishness and groaning of her fellow villagers back home, who were worn out at an early age, her host would get up from his place, silently and swiftly, and perform some operation on a piece of work in a distant corner of a room or the orchard, write something at the desk in an even more distant room, push a tub containing a fruit-bearing plant into the light in a third room fathoms away, hang out a piece of wash to dry in the wind on the line above the boundary wall, and was already back in his place, reading, tasting, doing nothing, as if he had not moved at all and had accomplished everything only with his fingertips.

And she was even tempted, in the presence of such effortless managing—entailing nothing but looking at things, combined with finger dexterity—to come up with one of those wordplays of which the observer next to her was so fond: a new form of brilliance was coming to light.

In any case, this was no longer the contemporary economy, in which the forecasting and bringing to fruition she saw as appropriate to her profession had been displaced by sleazy, greedy speculation. In the new economy here—her silent speech almost became audible at this point—instead of such dangerous, fantastical notions, something else was at work, in operation, and in effect: that incomparably more productive and constructive form of imagination that represented a value in and of itself and deserved that designation, which, again according to the Swiss loafer, is "warming-up," illumination, revelation "of that which exists."

Yes, in the Pedrada-Hondareda area economic activity consisted of imagining, and lighting a fire under, and putting in the right light, that which already existed. And a corollary was that letting things go and leaving things alone for now was more fruitful than action; and that in the case of such an innovative economy, the word "inspiration" applied first and foremost to things that it was both good and necessary to leave alone. What a boost leaving things alone gave in the direction of even better things. How I would have contributed to their economy if I had not arrived too late; or if only theirs had not been a lost cause from the outset here in the former glacial hollow—and not because of the glacial hollow.

Yes, indeed, if she had not arrived too late and if they had not been a bunch of losers from the moment they immigrated here, and a lost people (and here the observer threw her a glance, as if he understood what she was saying, although her speech to him continued to be silent), she would have established, together with them down there, a type of economy never before attempted. For such an economy was sorely needed, and all over the world.

Together with the founding fathers of Hondareda she would have taken the elements that were available there so plentifully and so full of promise and developed a new system of use and consumption, of saving and spending, of storage and distribution.

Nothing usable would have been thrown away anymore, even the smallest fragments: use, expend, buy, employ, yes, time and again, in a constant and stimulating cycle and in invigorating variation—but for heaven's and the earth's sake, not an iota, a flake, a drop, a knife-tip, a tea- or tablespoon, a smidgen (detergent, fruit-tree fertilizer, pepper, salt), not a grain (pill, sugar, flour), not a crumb, screw, nail, scrap of firewood, match, soap bubble, fingertip, not a dozen, three, two, or even just one of any item of use and consumption over and above what was strictly necessary—although in this new economic system the very strictness would have had a liberating effect, and how!

In such an economy, instead of the brutal distinction between sinister winners and wretched losers, equilibrium would have finally prevailed and, as could be observed at times between vendors and customers in public markets, a general cheerfulness; to paraphrase the saying that God loves the cheerful giver, spending, saving, storing, paying, taking money, producing, trading, consuming, would have gone hand in hand, all intensely cheerful.

Simply in the way the individuals in Hondareda allowed themselves to be seen in their daily life, this possible economy was prefigured, she thought: in the way each living space in their dwellings was simultaneously a studio and workshop and storeroom and shed and laboratory and library, and so forth.

For if I had not arrived too late and if the people of Hondareda had been a little more open to outsiders, their pattern of action and inaction could also have helped shape a new way of life, as is fitting for an economy. I could use such a new way of life. And so could you, my observer. And now enough of this talk of a different world order. Let us leave the question open. This is a story, and it should remain open.

Just one last comment on the money economy: there is no other realm in which God's will and the work of the devil seem to lie so close together. And: when it came to money matters, one could not help making a hash of things. And: in the meantime, money was causing more pain than gain. And yet: engaging in economic activity as a sort of salvation, "I have kept the faith—I have engaged in economic activity." And then again: "So much money!" just as one might say in disgust, "So many people!" And then again: Perhaps the power of money was the least cutthroat, in that it did not hide behind religious dogma? Managing economic activity was bringing things together?

Why, during your entire time here, did you remain the reporter on the outside? Your guiding principle, "No, I will not go inside, for no one is there!" may be accurate in most situations, but not in the case of this high-altitude hollow, which may be stripped of its future as early as tomorrow.

It remains true: no video- and no audiotape could capture what I experienced in Hondareda. And no film could tell the story of the Hondarederos. They are not a subject for a newspaper feature, nor does their story fit into a film, not even one set in the Middle Ages or whenever. For all that exists of their story is internal images: it takes place primarily inside: inside the garden and house walls, and in general indoors. For if you, my freckled observer, had entered even one time and had let yourself enter in, once inside you would have recognized from the interior images that the people here, in contrast to the externals you observed, are by no means incapable of playing, or played-out. There is sometimes a playing and dancing inside them that is a joy to behold.

The same thing applies when, as often happens, their head is in danger of dropping from exhaustion: whereas elsewhere people nowadays deny tiredness as something shameful, the people here try to resist it by transforming it into a game, recognizable as such only to themselves.

One of the most common games here: in a crowd and in narrow passageways, to avoid each other, squeezing into the most confined space and making oneself thin, thinner, thinnest. Altogether, these games or dances take place in the most confining space and often for no more than the twinkling of an eye—and are therefore also utterly inconspicuous and altogether invisible from the outside. But how much composure they gain from a dance like this, lasting only a second.

All their internal games and dances consist of these avoiding and skirting and countering motions, a balancing of contradictions: and in addition to recaptured composure, they give them fresh strength and a new outlook, contribute to conversions: of tiredness into alertness, of timid recoiling into calm gazing around, of getting out of the way into discovery of new ways, of getting lost into finding one's way to some other destination entirely. These are transformative games and dances that produce a reversal, growing precisely out of failures and false starts. One could thus, with more justification, characterize the dancers of Hondareda as "transformers" than as scientists, engineers, planters, animal husbandmen, bakers, shoemakers, shepherds, hunters, gatherers (yes, really), readers, writers, technicians, carpenters, breadwinners, gardeners, merchants.

They transform the bustle in the streets and town squares—after all, up here in the mountains they are not out of this world—into a dance of haste: by slowing down inwardly, not outwardly, they transform slavish haste into briskness. And they accomplish all those actions and operations that are otherwise inevitably accompanied by annoying sounds and noise either by merging the sounds into a sequence, like relaxing dance music, or, when the person nearby, a grandson, a neighbor, a person entrusted to them, is sleeping or ill, by becoming quieter and quieter in their actions, a special art, which, entirely unlike a disturbing complete absence of noise, fans the person sleeping or sick in bed in the next room or next building with relief and rocks him to sleep. A dance and a ballet like this quieting dance is something you, my observer, have never seen, and you will never see it anywhere else, and you will not see it here anymore, because with my departure it will no longer be here to be seen.

And you, my Herr Cox or Jakob Lebel, you reporters sent here from elsewhere, suspect these players and dancers of the internal world of being the evil enemies, the mortal enemies, of those who sent you on this mission, and therefore also your enemies. And the chief reason for your suspicion: the contrariness among the new settlers here, culminating in their relationship to numbers and, a critical element in the remote-controlled furor against the new settlers, above all their relationship to time.

And it is true: you outsiders have a way of experiencing and measuring time that strikes the Hondarederos as harmful to reality. Not that they would have the temerity to throw myths at you and charge that in your attitude toward time you are repeating the murder of the first of the gods, the god of time, progenitor of all the other gods. But they do accuse you— and see you in turn as their enemies—of stripping time of its reality, humiliating and desecrating it, with your way of measuring, dividing, manhandling it; instead of letting time play an active role in life, actually enlivening life, time as the life of life, even if one does not see anything supernatural or divine in it.

They are aware, of course, that they do not stand a chance against you and your kind of time, and therefore they will never foment a war against you, contrary to what one hears. Instead they sometimes—though very seldom—feud with one another, to the point of hurling insults and even beating each other up, which occurs when one of them uses your sense of time in conversation with a neighbor: "It was a year and three days ago that I moved here and began a new life." —Don't say that! "Those lovely minutes four and a half months ago on the peak of Almanzor." —Be still, you blasphemer, you are committing a sin against time!

Not that the people of Hondareda have no calendars and clocks. They have the most modern clocks here—and use these time-counters and measuring devices wherever they are useful, in the workshop, the laboratory, the studio, in the wine, cider, or olive cellar. Such things are abhorred, in the sense of being proscribed and banned from the entire settlement area, only outside of normal, or mechanical, arithmetic, practical time. The many curses directed at the prevailing time here: in the form of deep sighs.

The time that is supposed to come into play now is by no means each person's subjective, emotive, internal time. Yet time as experienced by me, you, my neighbors, by all of us neighbors, is supposed to contribute to the project of a different time system, one that would have nothing to do with calculation—a system in which time, instead of merely ticking to count things off and count them out, would commence to dance, as the friend of life—a dance like all the dances in the Hondareda region: internal, momentary yet also more lasting in its effects.

A project? Yes, a new form of time like this would have been the Grand Project, invisibly inscribed here on the horizons, in which all the new settlers' fragmentary basic impulses—a new form of time must be found for you, for me, for him, for us, for them—could have come together. New verb tenses, time-grammars, a new way of thinking and speaking of time: accompanying existence, yes, escorting our being, illuminating it, lighting the way for it.

To date, however, tentative efforts at best have been made, and today every Hondaredero is left to his own devices in his attempt to achieve the grander time in concert with his neighbors, and all of these efforts are again negative dances, in sentence form: "Not like this! Not like this! and also not like this way of thinking and speaking of your time here on earth!"

Hasn't every individual in the depression of Hondareda cursed himself over and over, also scratched his own face and bitten his hands, whenever he has contemplated his life, past, present, and future, and found that the numbers and norms of clock and calendrical time have converted what had been lived, was being lived, and would be lived into a mere calculation of before, now, and later; rendered even the most piquant of life's images flat and tasteless; stripped memory's richness and potency of its reality and value; covered the precious Now! with rust; and metronomically deprived the longing for day or night of its body and soul.

"Not to destroy my experience yet again by adding the thought that I met my first and last love nineteen years ago; that today, at my departure, it is eleven o'clock on the second of February."

But did not my, your, and our story demand and require for its completion that we add the notion of a time element? Yes, with the mental addition of a time element, the "three minutes" last night and the "microseconds" this morning would be transformed into the continuity that historians otherwise attribute only to centuries or millennia. What kind of time should we thus think of in conjunction with our life, our story—for here, in Hondareda at least, every person can think: "My life! My story! I exist!" Who else can say that?

So, what tenses? what images of time? what time-styles and time-rhythms, time-signs, time-words, or also merely temporal arabesques, should be added to our existence to make it shine forth beyond the boundaries of our existence and life?—And that, in a rough outline, would have been the time-reconceptualization project up here, for which, however, from the beginning it was no longer, or not yet, the time.

I know, too, observer, that for once you would agree with me, if here, on this granite outcropping under the mottled black high Sierra sky, I were to say to you that the Hondareda region is particularly suited for outlining and integrating forms and sequences of time that are less wedded to numbers.

Even just the stratospheric sky here—and not only on those nights when there seems to be not a single patch of sky without stars, and when the most distant and closest planets' orbits are crossing, with the sparkling of their innumerable reflections in the mica, quartz, and alabaster at your feet: a different universal time from the one posted elsewhere in airports, banks, and also here and there in the remaining no-man's-lands.

And this region is also favorable for the construction, yes, construction, of a new sense of time free of the compulsion to count, favorable precisely because of the "chaos" created and left behind by the giant glacier, the granite boulders, towers, arches, and outcroppings scattered over the broad bottom of the basin where the settlers live. It is true: all over the earth there are no longer distinct seasons for blossoming, ripening, and lying fallow. But down there in the summit-plain depression, this constant shifting of the seasons is particularly noticeable. And what is also true: those who have migrated here have helped the effect along through technical measures. But summer and winter, fall and spring, are also all mixed up naturally, with abrupt switches from windy to windless in the rocky chaos, from sunny to cloudy; it can be freezing cold in the cavernous alleys, yet hardly a step farther on, without the actual presence of the sun, merely from the heat radiating from the granite boulders standing, leaning, and lying there in a favorable spot, shone on previously by the sun: a warmth tangible like the warmth that sometimes wafts over one from a field of grain, or the warmth that streams from ears of corn being shucked, even in late fall—a silo warmth, no, an oven warmth, a broody warmth. And similar conditions in the lake in the chaos, where the ankle-freezing still water suddenly gives way to smoothing, caressing warm currents, followed by almost scalding whirlpools.

And this is true as well: at present one can observe everywhere in the world that fruit-bearing plants in particular often bloom several times a year and produce fruit all year round, even in wintertime. Whether it be elderberries, rose hips, or strawberries: next to the dark-black, heavy, sweetly ripe bunches of elderberries, in fall or summer you have surely noticed, against a barn wall, at a crossroads, by an electric pylon, April-like cream-colored clusters of bloom or still unopened buds.

And the mountainous regions are even more favorable to this magical transformation of one season into another. And the village of Hondareda, with this chaos that does not merely create blockages or obstructions but also has a dynamic or propelling effect, enhances this phenomenon, acting like a glass bell in some places and spaces, independent of the seasons. The budding, blooming, fruit-setting, greening, darkening, and ripening, the shriveling and wilting of an elderberry cluster can be seen all at the same time on the bushes.

Thus Hondareda-Comarca is both the natural glacial chaos as well as a protected enclosure, used as such by the settlers and unobtrusively enlarged by them, sheltered from the surrounding mountain wastes, and if exposed, then primarily to the stratosphere above: perhaps more related to it than exposed.

All of this could have provided fertile ground for the time-economy project. At least there were some points of departure in the speaking style and sayings of Hondareda, which seemed extremely odd when one first heard them.

Thus a verb tense in current usage again was one that had disappeared almost everywhere else, the pre- or postfuture or future perfect tense: "We will have met each other. We will have exchanged clothing." Or we often used the equally archaic prepositional phrase "at the time of": "at the time of our evening meal," "at the time of his life," "at the time of your absence," and we used this phrase more frequently than "with," "before," "after," and "during," and also in bizarre expressions such as "at blackberry time," "at book time," "at brother time," "at grain-of-rice time," "at the time of your lips," "at night-wind time," "at our deal-making time," "at apple time," "at grass-blowing time."

Yet for the most part the project remained limited to this: in our thinking and speaking, our action and inaction, we rejected, often filled with anger at ourselves, the bad forms of time that had a destructive effect on being.

It was even more beautiful then, and an even more powerful reality, when, as happened all too rarely, one became aware of a time more in tune with existence, and one could finally give "time" full play as a noun: "sand-between-the-streetcar-tracks-time," "sky-in-the-treetops-time," "night-blindness-time," "Orion-and-Pleiades-time," "eye-color-time," "steppe-roaming-time," "baby-carriage-pushing-time," "Death-and-the-Maiden-time," "crumple-letters-in-the-fire-time."

Time beyond counting and measuring? Yes, and also, in an expression found in the book that accompanied me on my journey, my vanished child's Arabic anthology: time "beyond weighing." Away with those ugly standard times that anger us, and distort reality—and bring on the uplifting, inspiring time beyond weighing.

Does this mean that the immigrants to the mountains despise numbers and figures? On the contrary: they worshipped numbers for their imperviousness to all dodges and tricks.

And naturally—in the sense of a law of nature—the group of new settlers in Hondareda must have aroused worldwide indignation with this new time-management plan?, no, time-management initiative, like a dangerous sect?, no, even more passionate indignation than the most notorious sect, engaged in abducting children, emptying bank accounts, and practicing human sacrifice. And yet those who sent you and the others here, my dear observer, will not even step forward to oppose the impending attack, intervention, or whatever up here in the Sierra de Gredos. They see nothing wrong with it. They also have nothing against the people here, and when they assert that, they are almost pure of heart.

They think nothing at all when the intervention, as they say without lying, "forces itself" on them. What will happen up here is completely independent of their thinking, their decisions, their will, their person. As far as they are concerned, and this is believable, the Hondarederos are not their enemies. That the Hondareda enclave must be wiped off the face of the earth has nothing to do with two different worldviews, economic systems, concepts of morality and aesthetics, but rather with the laws of nature. Hondareda must be eliminated simply on the basis of the laws of physics. Motion produces countermotion. Every action produces an equal and opposite reaction.

A vacuum—and in the Hondareda region one of these voids that, as we know, are abhorred by nature, has developed, simply as a result of the negative thinking here, a widespread "not that!" "not that way," "not him," etc.—a vacuum provokes, attracts, and creates fullness, in this particular case a violent fullness, in the form of a natural pushing, penetrating, over-turning, rushing from all sides into the vacuum created here, which brought on this purely physical violence by keeping this space open.

And if there is any physical mass here in the basin, it is almost negli-gible, and furthermore hardly moving and heterogeneous, while the mass all around, to the borders of the ecumene, as far as the Arctic and Antarc-tica, in the meantime seems completely homogeneous, thanks to its ex-clusively positive signs, "that way!" "precisely so!" "you, you, and you!" etc., a constantly moving and expanding mass, and above all one infinitely larger and more powerful than the one here.

As the laws of nature dictate, energy and matter—as you will soon be able to observe here—produce motion and force. To speak of aggression, therefore, of hostile actions, forays, violations, war, or even planned liqui-dation, in connection with what is in the offing for the people up here is inaccurate and inexcusable anthropomorphism in view of such purely physical processes. Sweeping Hondareda from the face of the earth will be neither an act of revenge nor a punitive operation. It is imposed by the laws of nature and inevitable.

In your reports, however, although you, the observer, may not have likened the immigrants of Hondareda to a sect, you have described them, particularly in the context of their attempt to achieve a different relation-ship to time, as "on their way to something like a new world religion." According to you, the Hondarederos are in unspoken agreement that everything to be revealed, from A to Z, has already been revealed, once and for all, and captured in the writings of the most diverse peoples in the most diverse ways, yet always with the same meaning, where it can be read and used as a guide to life. In the settlers' opinion, as your report will have it, no new revelations of any sort can be expected, and none are needed—for which reason this is no sect, according to your observations.

As far as any essential or thought-provoking contrary notion of time goes, they think that anything that needed to be revealed has been revealed, from Isaiah to Buddha, from Jesus to Muhammad. Except that what you call these "unintentional founders of a religion" distinguish between uncontested religious revelations, which they accept without reservation, and prophecies. Of all that is prophesied in the revealed religions, they believe that only the prophecy of a different kind of time is a promise that has gone unfulfilled—that indeed, in the current era it has perhaps even more prophetic force for each individual and solitary person than ever before, precisely because it does not aim to be extracted from one's thinking, one's innermost feelings, one's self-awareness, and imposed on the external world, to conquer or achieve power over others. As your report puts it, "What for the Jews remains the promise of the Messiah, is for them, though quite different and above all different in focus, the promised time."

And you continue: "To be once more, as before story became history, *children of time*, of the god Kronos, and also to behave like children of time, unlike the original time-god-murdering children: that is the prophecy, a sort of unplanned universal religion, according to which each individual in Hondareda wants to live, with such obscure watchwords as 'to restore time's veil,' 'back to veiled time,' and the like." Yes, I have studied your reports closely, by means of my own peri-periscope.

And in them, in the course of your assignment here, you have hinted more and more that you are drawn to the region and the immigrants here, even filled with enthusiasm, although of a sort that differs from mine. You, too, dear Jakob Lebel—the name of this old variety of apple, named for a farmer, suits you to a T—you, too, are, or at least once were, an enthusiast: except that your original enthusiasm emerges in reshaped and often peculiar forms as a result of your profession as observer.

Thus, in your reports, the way in which each of the Hondarederos, for himself in his cave and hideout, speaks of and rethinks time, day and night, in toneless monologues, you compare with people talking in their sleep, and furthermore not adults but children.

That impression on someone passing by outside stems primarily, you say, from the voices (which you could not hear as I could when I was inside as a guest) of those people talking to themselves in the dwellings: these sounds and syllables, seemingly uttered with great effort, which to your ears seldom resolved themselves into comprehensible words and even more seldom into an audible sentence, in fact have the ability, you write, "to transport an unprepared listener out of ordinary time and to suggest to him a subliminal time, a downright violently contrary time—an underground time" (later in the report you once use the verb "to murmur" pejoratively, as proof that you are immune to what is imputed to you, but on the other hand you note, in referring to yourself personally, that "in the meantime, however, I am more likely to prick up my ears whenever something is murmured to me, than in response to all the usual speaking in no uncertain terms, explaining, clarifying, intoning, and articulating").

And, according to you, something uncanny emanates from the people talking to themselves in Hondareda, as elsewhere from people talking in their sleep. But in your report, where those who gave you your assignment would perhaps, for obvious reasons, like to see the word "threat," you unexpectedly used the word "threatened." Which brings us back to your comparison with children talking in their sleep: like them, you wrote, especially when they were lying alone somewhere, far away or separated forever from any kin, "utterly forsaken," and stammered and stuttered into the nocturnal stillness, and finally could not produce one coherent sentence, the people up here "exuded with their entire existence, not only at night, but also on the brightest, sunniest day, an unparalleled sense of being threatened and exposed."

And so, you conclude, they do not represent any danger to the world—simply because they would never, ever want to proclaim themselves an enclave in the valley they cultivate, and would never lay claim to property, either personal property or real estate—but on the contrary are themselves the ones who are threatened, yes, "lost and abandoned."

3 3

And at this moment, so the story goes, she, the mistress of her story, standing opposite the observer up there on the granite slab in the midst of the wilderness near the Candeleda Pass, suddenly switched from thinking to speaking out loud, and directly, and continued, clearly audible to the other person: "And your enthusiasm, my dear, and mine for the people up here come together in our recognition of their loss, of everything that gives an impression of abandonment and lostness."

And the red-haired, freckled observer promptly replied: "Yes, that is how it is. I have already been dispatched to hundreds of places and battlefields. But to Hondareda, and back and forth through the Sierra de Gredos—this has been my first real journey, and if I am ever sent anywhere else, it will be only to places like this, just as painful and just as alive."

And she repeated out loud, though in somewhat different words, what she had previously said in her thoughts: "This is a one-day people here, most definitely. Their time reckoning does not include a year, let alone a century, and even months and weeks: canceled. Not to mention halves and quarters: how they laughed at me when, after my arrival, I slipped up once: 'I have been here for half a month now.' Nothing more ludicrous in Hondareda than 'a quarter of a year' or, heaven forbid, 'a trimester,' 'a semester.' If there is any unit of time, it is nothing but a day, a whole day. This is a one-day people, and a twilight people, and the glacial floor down there is the arena or the dance floor for their twilight dance, which will not save this people and its day and its time, and will at most postpone the extinguishing of the lights for another rowanberry or rice-grain moment."

And he: "And the old man who has been searching day and night since he came here for his son, who went missing somewhere else entirely, and if only he could find his bones, if only he could bury one small bone of his son at least!"

And she: "And the way the person who just died kept trying for a while afterward to form one word with his lips."

And he: "And the unusual or perhaps not so unusual crying of the children here, sounding so unusual in this rocky basin because it carries everywhere, a crying without an *a* or an *i* or a *u*, without vowels, only in consonants, *b, d, g; k, l, m; r, s, t*. Or the crying in general here."

And she: "And the way all their books are dog-eared, and the way they manhandle the books further before they read them, tossing them in the air, bending them almost to the point of breaking the spine, leaving them out in the open, exposed to rain, wind, dew, and snow, letting them be pounded by hail."

And he: "And the way they have made a daily ritual of sniffing deadly poisons, together with their children and grandchildren, whether in mushrooms or flowers, many of which contain the same poisons as they do elsewhere, but in a more concentrated form up here."

And she: "And the way they use one of their favorite words, a word that is rightfully or wrongfully shunned elsewhere, the word 'actually,' in a sense that expresses happy amazement at a characteristic, a condition, or a phenomenon thought to have disappeared long ago, to have been abolished, to have become no longer possible—their constant 'That's actually beautiful!' instead of a mere 'That's beautiful,' finding beautiful something of which one would no longer have thought that, of which one would not even have dreamt that—hence the astonishment."

And he: "And the way, when, in exceptional cases, they involuntarily, spontaneously, turn to us, even to us observers flown in from elsewhere, because the matter itself calls for it, as it were, and exclaim simply, 'Isn't it beautiful up here in our Hondareda?!' without any 'actually'!"

And she: "And the public library there, with the books even more beat-up than those in the houses: transparent glass structures right on the edge of a cliff, with a view from the reading room and from the reading ladders into the still-open crevice at the end of the melted glacier."

And he: "And in their disdain for gatherers they are not serious in the slightest; they themselves gather whatever they can, crouching down, crawling on their stomachs, on all fours. But they do not look like gatherers, or even grabbers, snatchers, on the one hand because while gathering, instead of becoming utterly immersed and absorbed in it, they broaden their outlook—precisely through their searching and gathering and 'collecting,' which somewhat resembles harvesting—and acquire a three-hundred-sixty-degree sense, a sense that has no specific focus but lets them become open to all sides, especially when, in contrast to contemporary gatherers, instead of doing their gathering in secret, shamefacedly, with a guilty conscience, they do it openly and proudly and thus relieve us of our gatherers' guilt—and among them the young people also gather cheerfully and with an infectious matter-of-factness, dressed in the latest styles from the cities and at ease with the latest technology!"

And she: "And have you heard how the children up here can launch into storytelling from one word to the next, and then do not want to stop, while elsewhere—or at least this is what is claimed—storytelling is dying out more and more, and hardly any children surprise the people around them with stories—yet how wonderful and redeeming it used to be to hear, and also see, one's own child, or any child, unexpectedly turning up as a storyteller!"

And he, with an expression he had never used in his reports: "It is true: with my own eyes I have seen the way two butterflies up here, when they flutter around each other, amount, as the Hondarederos say, to more than a pair, and as they gyrate in the air defy being counted, in harmony with the principle here, that time 'defies measurement.'" The expression he had never used before? "With my own eyes."

And she: "And look: the water in the lake down below is flowing in a circle."

And he, turning his head to look down into the basin: "And look, the untouched piles of freshly split firewood everywhere in the settlement, as if in Hondareda it were simultaneously winter and early spring and already summer again, or fall. And look, the branches bending under the weight of fruit there in the garden of the man who is dying. And I have experienced personally"—another new expression for the observer—"that walking the town squares and the streets of Hondareda, naturally paved with smooth-polished granite, is infinitely easier on the feet and more unimpeded than anywhere in the great cities, where even the most central squares and avenues have become so uneven, dangerously uneven, despite their general appearance, from the constant digging-up and repaving of small patches, that with one step I stub my toe on a bump, with the next stumble or go flying into the air, with the third slip and fall, and so on. And look over there, the frog in the crown of the tree. And there, a lost pizza-delivery man!"

And she, shouting at him: "Isn't it beautiful in Hondareda? Couldn't it have been beautiful?"

3 4

While the mistress of the story, *la Señora de la historia*, and the reporter conversed thus and gazed down from their rocky platform above the brush at the settlement in the hollow, twilight fell and the moment of departure drew near: for her last crossing of the Sierra de Gredos she had chosen this night, a clear one, to be sure, but one without moonlight, a new-moon night.

The granite outcroppings stretching as far as the eye could see—the normal unit of space in the Sierra—shimmered yellow-red-blue, almost sparkling, as if it were early morning, shortly before sunrise.

In Hondareda not a light was burning. From the giant hollow in which the town lay, its houses indistinguishable at the moment from the glacial chaos of boulders, a shot or explosion rang out—in fact, it was merely a heavy piece of firewood crashing from its pile onto the rocky ground, the bang amplified as it echoed through the mountain basin.

From innumerable chimneys the smoke from stoves and workshops had been rising, steadily and everywhere straight up in a column, and now, in the interval it took to close one's eyes and open them again, the smoke seemed here and there to have suddenly ceased.

How shrunken the capital of the Sierra appeared. And what an indecipherable and bizarre pattern it continued to present. High up in the sky the sun was still shining, its rays visible in the jet contrails of a plane that was already out of sight, the trail ending abruptly, as if the plane had crashed or been shot down. In the shadow of the summit plain, the wheeling of a kite, above that the wheeling of a mountain eagle, still in the sun. The settlers appeared, seemingly in their best clothes, to bid her farewell, dressed as if for their last days on earth.

Now above the entire region, from this clear sky, came a rain of pamphlets, with the sound of falling leaves, and one of them also landed at their feet. They did not have to bend down to read it. Written in all the languages of the world was one sentence in bold type: "People of Hondareda! We have not forgotten you!" And that was not meant to be reassuring; that was a threat.

From the corner of her eye she saw what she had not noticed before—that the observer, Jakob Lebel, had swollen and reddened eyelids, and that he was wringing his hands, like a woman or a very old man.

The rattle of tank treads that reached them from the depression came from suitcase wheels: a few people were leaving the settlement with bag and baggage, dragging themselves along the newly rebuilt road up to the Puerto de Candeleda. And the rattling also came from the Venetian blinds being lowered in some windows, something that had previously not been customary anywhere in Hondareda in the evening (they were used otherwise only to keep out the sun).

On the other hand, she saw the shutters open, providing a framed image, as if brought close by a telescope, on the only residential building that during her entire time here had been locked up, as if permanently abandoned, and the iron pegs, which otherwise hung down on chains, were stuck into the sockets along the entire façade to fasten the wide-open shutters; and this one stone building, now that it was apparently inhabited at last, allowed them—simply because it was lived in?—to hear the beat of music (a kind that had never, and would never have, been heard in Hondareda otherwise, a music seemingly vanished and unknown).

And in this "blockhouse" the first light appeared, and there was singing, no, not there, somewhere. And no, it was not singing, merely humming. "If you're going to sing, then sing so we can hear you!" Who said that? She and the man next to her shouted it in unison. And at this command someone, who? promptly sang, at top volume, the single line of a song that was immediately swallowed up by the increasing late-afternoon racket and the rumbling of the garbage trucks (a song which later, as the apocryphal storyteller, who chimed in again, reducing the story to a legend, would have it, was "supposed to become the anthem of the vanished region"). And this single line, audible through the din, went, "I know who you are!" and, unlike the sentence in the leaflet, this was an expression of trust and respect.

And the rumbling also came from the other members of the observation team, which included as many women as men, who were just running their final laps of the day around the settlement, eight to thirteen of them, shouting and at the same time exchanging incomprehensible small talk, while the rotors of the helicopter that was to bring them back to their lodgings on the other side of the Sierra ridge were already whirring (and another line of the song, not added until later, referred, according to the apocryphal narrator, to these runners in circles: "I do not know who you are!").

Yet these runners from elsewhere were the only ones whose faces—primarily the nose and chin—became visible. A kind of artificial light lit them up, as if they were running for a movie. Their running kicked up dust, even when there was nothing on the bare rock to form dust. And compared to the incessant, loud slobber of words emanating from their mouths as they ran, the slobber of any animal would seem like a string of pearls. The population of Hondareda, or what remained of it, appeared on its pre-twilight *corso,* which resembled more a back-and-forth of individual residents, as mere outlines.

Although each of them had just stepped out of the nearby cave where he lived, the silhouettes there seemed to come from afar. And at the sight of the troop of runners they walked even more casually ("with provocative slowness," as another observer's report put it). As is customary everywhere, dogs accompanied them, of whom the false author then wrote that in H. they barked "as dogs nowhere else do, with sounds as strained, feeble, and soft as the voices of the people there." And along with the Hondarederos strolled the local mountain goats, pack mules, a couple of pigs, and, "as legend has it," even the silhouettes of some Sierra hedgehogs.

It was no invention, however, that, as she then told the rightful author, those strolling through the town were joined time and again by children who had already been put to bed and now came out of the houses and asked their foster or grandparents: "Did you call me?" And not a few of these children had gray hair, as she now saw upon taking leave of Hondareda. And the pairs of grandparents or foster parents all looked like twins who had grown old. And the young couples who stood in silence with their arms around each other, from the beginning to the end of the alleys and squares, were again the same from chaos boulder to chaos boulder, the first couple. Yes, there she had been among people she could understand.

And one of the settlers—wasn't it the town elder—had departed not on foot but by way of the freight cable car, without luggage, alone in the open gondola, from which only his head protruded. And one of the neighbors had secretly fertilized the plants in the greenhouse for another in his absence. And the signal earlier, marking the end of the workday in the glacial basin, had been like a temple gong, church bells, a minaret call, a shofar, a siren, a ship's horn, a train's whistle, and a school bell all at once. Finally a silence that rose from down there, a mighty and, to both their ears, precious and exquisite silence. What did the Hondarederos call themselves in private? *Indios?*—The name for people who had once emigrated and in some fashion or other become rich.

Now he, the observer, was the one who gazed sidelong at the woman next to him on the rocky outcropping. And she let him see her. No woman had ever let herself be seen by him this way. (The author, in his village in La Mancha, later suggested that at this point in the story the Spanish expression *se dejó ver,* "let oneself be seen," be inserted.)

He had never encountered a female adventurer like this. There was also one woman or another on his observer team who called herself, officially, and listed as her profession on her passport, or for her regular appearances on television, "adventurer," *"aventurière," "aventurera,"* and had in fact crossed the Gobi Desert alone, swum the Channel, sailed across the Pacific, climbed the north face of Mount Eiger and a year later the south face of the Karakorum range, thinking, all the while, according to her published diaries, of her one to three children back home, whom her husband was taking care of, proud of his wife the adventurer.

But this adventurer here, even if she had an absent child like the others, belonged to another species, never before observed, let alone back home in the media. Jakob Lebel, or whatever his name was (certainly not Cox—that did not suit him), felt his heart pounding. While the woman let herself be seen by him, she looked at him.

He had never confronted such eyes before. Her gaze pierced him through and through. It was an open and disarmingly friendly gaze. (This rocky mound in the wilderness of broom had something special about it.) But there was another element at work in the gaze of the adventurer: and that was an almost boundless neediness and a delicacy of feeling of the same sort, and what seemed strangest to him was that it immediately became clear that her gaze did not apply to him, not to him, and it was quite sufficient for him that she let herself be seen by him.

Adventurer: that meant here that in her presence, in the presence of this stranger, he, the observer, was seized with the spirit of adventure, yes, spirit, and yes, seized. It would never have occurred to him that this creature, as straightforward as she was proud, as loving as she was in need of love, was a former film star or a current or former queen of the financial world—although such information would have neither added anything to nor subtracted anything from the moment: after all, nowadays it had become almost routine for people to shed their so-called professional roles from one moment to the next and, not perform other roles or leisure activities, but rather not perform at all anymore and simply become unrecognizable, unrecognizable and transparent in a lovely way, just letting themselves be seen without one's having to think "doctor," "architect," "entrepreneur," "artist," only not as she was doing now, in which connection another factor was that the person offering and revealing herself so freely was a woman, and what a woman—one who, among other things, never felt cold, even her hair exuding warmth.

Jakob Lebel returned her gaze. Ah, to embrace her on the spot. But hadn't that already happened, when she let herself be seen this way and he saw her this way? And her hand, which she held in front of her, bent upward, not cramped but loose, like a bowl, showing there, too, neediness. Ah, to take this hand. But hadn't that already happened? That her hand let itself be seen this way was sufficient for him.

The light, too, the last of the day, added to the effect, a glow, the "alpenglow"? no, the Sierra glow, the glowing of the Sierra de Gredos, of the granite peaks far to the south—what kind of glow? go there and see for yourself.

"I must go," the adventurer said with that smile she had smiled every time she used the word "must." He debated for a moment whether he should give her his copy of the "Guide to the Dangers of the Sierra de Gredos" as a parting gift, but it was obvious that she did not want any advice for the journey.

He, too, had to go (without a smile, even inwardly). On this night he would not, this once at least, board the helicopter, but would stay in Hondareda, would stride decisively over someone's threshold, going from one connector to another into the house proper. A wind arose, a wind from the south, a mild one, and the German word for gust, *Windsbraut*, bride of the wind, occurred spontaneously to Jakob Lebel as the two of them parted and he turned once more to watch her as she began to climb. How glad he would have been to go with her, as her page, her *escudero*.

The dew had already fallen and collected in a rocky basin, forming a little pool, and he moistened his temples with it. He had always been at the head of his class, in elementary school, then in high school and at the university, and now also on his team, yet he had never found his place, and would never find it?

And what was she doing and thinking in the meantime, the woman? Now, very close, a stone's throw, from the Sierra ridge, she jingled something in her pockets, but it was not coins but hazelnuts, chestnuts, juniper berries, and who knows what else. And if she was thinking anything, perhaps it was something along the lines of the words to be found in the orchardist's text that her brother had used during his training at vocational school, on the variety of apple called "Jakob Lebel": "On its sun-facing side, Jakob Lebel is checkered and spotted . . . in the cellar its skin becomes waxy . . . slightly sour taste, without aroma . . . bears even at high, cold elevations . . . naturally lacks a straight habit of growth and must therefore be pruned frequently. . . . Back in the day when I was a fruit thief, the apples known as Jakob Lebel were my favorites. Jakob Lebel, you are not yet sufficiently lost . . ."

The last mountain crickets chirped, up above and down below. And upon hearing them, Jakob Lebel recalled that, after all, there was a kind of plan for the day in Hondareda, repeated time and again, and it went: "Go out and listen to the crickets!" And he wished that the crickets, with their incredibly tender voices, might perform for his burial here. Did he want to die, then, here in Hondareda? Yes. But first he wanted to live here.

"Jakob Lebel"? That simply could *not* be the name of an enemy.

3 5

No doubt she, too, looked back at the hummock on which she had been standing only a short while ago, and at Hondareda, or Hondoneda, down below. Sometimes, when one stepped out of a house or a pub onto the street and looked in through a window at the place one had just left, didn't one feel surprised at no longer seeing oneself inside, sitting at the table or wherever one had been a few seconds earlier, reading, writing, talking to someone, and might that not give rise to a hallucination—of oneself?

This is what the woman experienced as she set out and glanced over her shoulder at the now vacant rocky mound, and this is how she later described it to the author. The hallucination, the residual image, of herself was so compelling that her astonishment was accompanied by shock. She recoiled at the flickering silhouette there, as if that "Me!" were something sinister, or rather something that made one shudder, not the way one would shudder at a ghost or some other alarming phantom, a menacing one: Didn't this recoiling, followed by pausing and doing a double take, also make one stronger? (Like her brother, she was both brave and easily startled, and there was the family legend that this propensity for being startled went back to that night when they were still children and someone came dashing into the house with the news that their parents and their other brother had died in an accident.)

And Hondareda in the glacial trough? As she looked down, it seemed at first not even to exist anymore, and for this verb "to seem," according to the author in La Mancha, the Spanish term *traslucir,* or "shine through," would probably have been wrong: for all that showed of the Dark Clearing was the darkness, a black hole in the middle of the otherwise brightly dusky high Sierra.

But then the labyrinthine settlement appeared all the more distinct in the darkness, with a more intense glittering of the mica, a glowing of the veins of quartz, a shimmering of the lichen: the latter, coating the cliffs as well as the rocky roofs throughout the basin with a yellowish-greenish-grayish film, made the town look like a city of millions, like Shanghai or São Paulo, photographed from a satellite halfway between the earth and the moon.

But to the same backward glance how small our Hondareda looked, and then, as she walked backward, how it gradually shrank still more. And at the same time a roar rose from the former ice basin, a roar such as might have come from a normally quiet area that was flooded in all directions as far as the horizon, the roar coming from the bottom of a river, still coursing along its channel even as it spilled over its banks, "the roar of the Mississippi." And in the roar one could also make out a kind of buzzing, which brought to mind the many newly installed apiaries on those slopes that were bathed in sunshine at almost all times of day—nowhere was the sun warmer and more constant than up here in the mountains—the apiaries also serving some of the settlers as dwellings, which one of her hosts took as a pretext for renaming Hondareda "El Nuevo Colmenar," which translated approximately as "New Beehive" (a reversal of a name very common on the Iberian highland, "El Viejo Colmenar," "Old Beehive"). And from this evening-warm incessant buzzing a single voice emerged, that of a child, not crying but shouting, rising unmistakably above all the underlying sounds: "Warte auf mich! Wait for me! Attends-moi! Espérame!" Now at nightfall the mighty rushing sound of the bees, and many bright, piercing tones.

Finally, when she was already an arrow-shot away from the ridge of the Sierra and the crossing point—off to one side of the Candeleda Pass—to the steep drop of the massif to the south, and the settlement behind her already out of cannon- and mortar-fire range, if not of rocket range, she could make out down below distant silhouettes, which, as they strolled alone along the only remaining bright feature of the landscape, the lake, the sky-mirroring laguna, were constantly ducking for no apparent reason, and in the trackless mountain steppe, before they crossed from one granite mound to another, whipped their dim profiles around, as if they were about to cross a dangerous boulevard with vehicles whizzing by.

And in the end she could no longer see any clear image of Hondareda or Hondoneda (the most recent maps mention the place only in parentheses, if at all), and instead, to the accompaniment of her steps crunching in the stones and scree, with stretches of quartz sand and snow in between, a litany consisting only of place names came to her: Nuevo Colmenar, Deep Enclosure, Dark Clearing, El Barco de la Sierra, Fondamente Nuove, New Briar Hole, Wandering Dune, High Lowland—just as the mountains of the summit plain, now at eye level, became transformed into pure names, and more and more were added to Galana (The Elegant One), Hermanitos (Little Brothers), Mira (= Look!), Morezón (from Moro: Moor, Arab?), Almanzor. Liturgy of preservation! It had been a long time since she had attended mass. "Attended"? Yes, attended. Yet there was hardly anything that completed one more than being present for the holy liturgy. Liturgy: oh, my goodness.

So had she left no farewell present for the transitory people of Hondareda, whom she had once spoken of as "mine"? Nothing—nothing at all. She had even taken something away from them—pilfered something (see "fruit thief"). While she was making the rounds in the plantation there as a guest, and told one of her hosts about her early days as a fruit thief back in the village, he replied that for him, too, now soon to be an old man, climbing into a tree still meant a good beginning to a day or a happy day. She, "friend of thieves and lost souls"? A thief and lost soul herself?

In the course of time each of the immigrants in Hondareda had shared his story with her. The main point, for each, was his reasons for being here, but then came a whole slew of events that had nothing to do with that. The more the individual got into the swing of his narrative, the more the elements of the story became jumbled, which did not mean that his story was confused. It seemed rather to have taken place so long ago that now it was true again. What became clear, even without reasons: the way he or she had left a familiar region, homeland, state, confederation, etc., and that he or she would remain here now—where else?—though not necessarily forever.

Some of them invented their reasons, for the most part obviously flimsy ones—"I was running away from today's women!"—"I wanted to escape the male world!"—"I did not want to die a rich man!"—so as to hint that in reality they had had entirely different reasons, or none at all, or that the reasons were not all that important to their story.

What gave an impetus to the speaking as well as the listening each time was first the sharing of a meal between the two of them (even days and months afterward, when she was already somewhere else entirely, she had an aftertaste, all the more fresh, of those Hondareda meals in her mouth), and then also the fact that the new settlers' individual dwellings, despite their markedly private nature, all had the feel of a public or generally accessible space—not in the sense of gathering places, public offices, community halls, or churches, but of alehouses or dives, albeit without the ill repute; divelike simply because the dining table was always set up in the innermost recesses of the inhabited cave, and could have accommodated, in addition to the two of them and perhaps a child doing homework at the other end, various total strangers, who also seemed to be expected. To sit deep inside these caves with the aura of dives sharpened one's attention and helped one collect oneself (was this expression still current?).

Thus one day, or one evening, she heard from a settler to whose table—at other times a workbench and various other things—she was invited, that he had left the land of his origin "out of sheer boredom. It was not my country in particular that bored me. Nor was it the climate. Or my work. It was sheer boredom, total and all-encompassing.

"True, even as a child and then, in a different way, as a youth, I was sometimes bored. But only sometimes, in certain places, in conjunction with certain activities, and primarily when I had no one or nothing to play with, and in my adolescence when I was terribly alone. Except that this kind of boredom became increasingly tolerable as I got older, for I imagined that later on, in my profession, I would no longer be alone, and that in love, or what I imagined love would be like, everything would be different.

"And what I imagined did not deceive me. From a time that cannot be pinpointed, once love arrived? once hate arose? once I found pleasure in action and inaction, also in taking care of things, in acting and thinking in concert with others, also in mere watching, I was no longer bored. At last I felt alive, one way or the other, even in sorrow and rage, and always, and in the thick of things—never lacking for excitement.

"And I imagined that from this moment on I would continue to be like those I had once envied, those who seemed to be basking in a realm inaccessible to me, who said of themselves: Bored? I have no idea what that means!

"My imagination turned out to have tricked me after all. In another period—known as the transition, right?—which cannot be pinpointed or dated, boredom returned, neither from one moment to the next nor from one day or year to the next. It did not come over me all of a sudden, but sneaked up on me—certain clichés, only a few, can hit the nail on the head, if not used too often—interposing itself between me and events, persons, things, places.

"First, I do not know when, one thing bored me, then several things, then everything. And even then I did not know that it was boredom— initially I felt only slight discomfort, which in the end became huge. For, truth be told, this was not a recurrence of the boredom familiar to me from my childhood and youth, an appropriate, healthy, or at least not un- healthy boredom, but rather a sickness, something without a name, and calling it 'boredom' or 'nameless' was merely an expression of my confu- sion and helplessness. Sickness and madness. It became a boredom as hopeless as it was deadly: on the one hand, I was hopelessly sick with it, and on the other hand, I was driven in my insane boredom to extermi- nate and destroy. 'You bore me' meant the same thing as: '*My child* bores me,' as: '*My house* bores me,' as: '*The forest* bores me,' and also, yes, '*I bore myself*'—and it meant a compulsion to do away with you, my child, the forest, and myself.

"And so I had to get out, to come here. And at least here I am rid of that kind of boredom. And by now I even imagine that I am on my way to a third kind of boredom here, one in which, just as before, time will seem to stretch, but in an entirely different way. This morning I walked across a snowfield and kept sinking in with my left leg, never with my right. In front of me in the snow, I swear to God, a snake was crawling along, and then a giant dragonfly with a yellow head was swooping over the ice floes in the lake."

Another person whose hospitality she enjoyed for a while said that he had originally come to the region to do glacier research—his specialty: the hollows left by the melted glacial masses, together with their micro- climate, vegetation, and so forth—and then he had decided on the spur of the moment to stay here, to continue his research and simply to stay.

The next person who took her in presented himself to her as someone who, in his place of origin, had been obsessed with searching—searching for treasures, as well as for this little thing or that—with searching in gen- eral, and in Hondareda, where there was nothing to search for, and all the treasures, if there had been any to discover there, had already been ex- tracted, he finally felt free of his compulsion, especially of his narrow, and narrowing, searcher's gaze, and free, for what? For now, simply free.

Others among the founders told her their stories: of being descended from a tribe of missionaries, involved for centuries in converting everything they came across, anywhere in the world, and of having put this tribe and its missionary zeal behind them once they set out for or returned here; or: having become, in their distant country of origin, in the course of life as petty-minded as their neighbors, in fact several degrees more crotchety, more narrow-minded, more malicious—more mean and nasty, lying in wait for some misfortune to strike next door, an accident, a separation, a death—one simply had to escape from an environment that turned one into a person like that!; or they told of inheriting from their ancestors, handed down from generation to generation, over there in Peru, Arizona, Ecuador, Honduras (!), the sense that the mere mention of the Sierra de Gredos and of Hondareda was the magic word at the right moment, "like a lit match"; or having been inspired to come here simply by the names, or by the sound of one name or another along the way, the sound of "El Almanzor," "El Puerto de Candeleda," "río Tormes," "río Barbellido," "La Galana," "La Angostura," "Ramacastañas."

One of them explained to her, and he was perfectly serious, that he had come to Hondareda from Tokyo, or was it Honolulu? or Cairo? and then settled there because he wanted to feel that he was "finally in a hub" again, in a place and a region "where something mattered," "where something could be seen happening"—what could be seen?—no answer—but then she had not asked, either.

And then another in his dinner-table monologue (she always had the impression that the entire colony of settlers was sitting at the table with the two of them): here in the trough in the high Sierra he had begun to dream again; the closed-off or remote nature of the region produced (yes) particularly cosmopolitan dreams, also—expansive dreams, in which he himself participated only as part of an audience—"but how I participate! More involved than I ever was in my time as a protagonist!"—epic dreams, whose vividness stayed with him when he woke up, and represented "capital" for the day, for being and acting awake, value (it took no special talent to guess that the speaker here was her former co-director at the world or central bank, or whatever it was called or may have been called—who seemed, by the way, to have forgotten his partner, or at least acted as though he had).

And for a while she had been the guest of a former judge—as for her other hosts, she unobtrusively took over the household chores, or served as a sort of barmaid—who among other things at one point wound up to offer more or less the following account: "In the thousands of years of recorded human history, we have already had one age of judges. It is supposed to have been a heroic era, a pioneering time, a time of preparation, the time before the age of kings and then of emperors. The people's judges were also the rulers or leaders, the generals, the administrators, and the high priests. But their chief title was that of judge." As fate or chance would have it, at this moment the ex-judge's grandnephew or foster son stuck his head into the cave, which, as everywhere in H., grew increasingly grand the deeper one advanced into it, and asked, "Did you call me?" Her host said no, and continued: "And in my time out there and down below, it was an age of judges again, a different one, and with different judges. I myself come from a family of judges. All the men and then all the women in this family practiced the judge's profession, without much effort, simply following a tradition that had the force of law. But I wanted to have been the last in our family line! With me and through me we were to become extinct as judges. And so I have broken out of the family tradition, at least for the time being, and am no longer in office. Never again to judge, to hand down verdicts, to convict. Never again to base my entire existence on being a judge, and at the same time to destroy another's existence, or at least put it in jeopardy. For this second age of judges, as it was still in force down/out there until just a while ago, yes, or is still in force, was, as I know, for I was part of it, no return to that pioneering era but rather an age of terror, a new one and a new kind.

"The second age of judges was, or is, one of unlimited, arbitrary, and uncontrolled despotism, masquerading as an obligation to intervene in anything and everything—and a despotism no longer confined to individuals but all-inclusive. For anyone can claim to belong to the family of judges, and every man and every woman can cast, and casts, him- or herself with unequaled self-aggrandizement as the judge of everything and everyone, as the judge of the whole world. And these judges of the world want to be something that fortunately no one else wants to be anymore, or perhaps not? They want to be world rulers in their own way. And a result of that was, and is, that now none of the innumerable judges will himself tolerate being judged by the world."

Again the boy poked his head in the door, but this time he said, "I knocked over the milk can"—whereupon his foster father replied, as if in jest, "An hour of detention in the cellar, without light, and for a month a hard cot and lights on, you useless good-for-nothing!" and continued, "Anything but to be a judge again! *In my time*, that means the time now, after my time as a judge!" (And was not he the one who had proclaimed that stealing an apple from a stranger's tree should be viewed as daybreak in the middle of the day?)

For a while the abdicated queen of finance was also hosted by the likewise abdicated "king" and *"emperador."* He was one of those in Hondareda who lived entirely alone, without grandchildren or other descendants. And it was not only because during her time as his guest she did the household chores for him in his "royal palace" or Palacio Real that the old man viewed her as if she had been the one who took him in when he was abandoned in the high steppe.

His palace was located in a cul-de-sac, part of the rocky chaos like the majority of the other buildings, though even more huddled, more crooked, and more like a hideout, and like the others who had found their way there, this Charles the Fifth or the First exuded the quiet sadness of a widower, and occasionally the delicate loneliness of an orphan.

Another factor in his case was that he was gravely ill and knew that he would die today or tomorrow, and up here in the high Sierra, not in the monastery of Yuste in the southern Piedmont, like the historical Charles. He had dragged himself, alone in the end, without his litter and bearers, up here and down into the pit of Hondareda, to end his days in this place, and that would occur in a manner entirely different from down near the plain—just the way he imagined his death, if it had to be now; wished it; wanted it.

Besides, he had had enough of kingship and emperorship, his own and in general. Over and done with, once and for all. What was it they said about kings? During their entire lives they had to be there for others and do nothing but listen from morn till night. And what had poor Louis the Sixteenth, on the evening before his beheading, impressed upon his son? A stern, bitter dictum: "Beware of being king!"

And yet this Carlos remained of two minds up to the hour of his death, or he was, as another of those apocryphal authors chimed in, "downright schizophrenic": his abdication and also the general disappearance or disempowerment of kings struck him as perfectly fine—and a second age of kings, like the "second age of judges," heaven forbid!—and, conversely, as he looked back on the life in society that he, split personality or not, imaginary king or not, had left behind when he set out for the

Sierra de Gredos, his own renunciation seemed a bit hasty, to say the least, as he saw before him, like a waking nightmare, the individual members of that society, in which meanwhile almost everyone had become his own king and self-appointed emperor, with ears for no one and nothing else, day in, day out, and if at one moment he was the soul of serenity and even wanted to lay his hands on his contemporaries, who had become so foreign to him, to perform the miracle of healing, in the next moment he wanted to curse them royally, as in bygone times. Wasn't he striving, after all, to regain his kingship? Yes, but more in the sense of a counter-king. He wanted to serve as a counter-king and a counter-emperor for his contemporaries.

Not until the day of his death was he in fact completely reconciled to what he had renounced. His being or playing at being king no longer mattered. The dream was over, and with it the split personality. He was simply the person he had been during his time there in Hondareda: the archivist, not in Simancas or some such place in the historical world, but for the new settlement—his cooking/living/sleeping hovel, with stacks, drawers, cupboards full of documentation, documentary stones, documentary plants, a concentrated memorial to everything that Hondareda would have been.

And at the end the abdicated king and emperor was also no longer an archivist but simply the dying man, with the Spanish flies around his mouth more numerous than ever, who muttered that he hoped he "hadn't spoiled the party for you"—what party?—and whose lips, after his death, still moved, in total silence, as if to continue speaking, and finally, for a long, long time, only the lower lip, that protruding lip characteristic of his royal line. And not until after his death did the sounds of pain he had suppressed all his life escape. Before that, he—with his soul already between his teeth—to her: "I regret only that I cannot read your, and my, story to the end." Although he was letting himself die, he broke off several attempts. And when he finally succeeded, a child standing by his bedside clapped. Then a few adults standing around clapped as well. And toward the end they all applauded him, and how.

And she? had looked that day away from the man who had just died and gazed through the opening in the rock to the outside, which was not at all deathly still, or rather into the window slit in the back of the building next door, slightly off center, which let one see through a third house, and beyond that through the next of the little windows in the rock, and thus through the house with the corpse to the next and the next and the next, all the way to the end of the row and on through the last of the windows and finally at a tiny yellow-gray-blue segment, all the more clearly in focus, of the granite surface that formed the summit plain of the Sierra, and against that backdrop the inhabitants bustling hither and yon, from dwelling to dwelling, or lounging, or reading, just as on a moving train one can look from a car up front, near the locomotive, back through all the other cars, and see the passengers from compartment to compartment to compartment, and behind the train the vanishing landscape.

Another of the transitional travelers, after he had beckoned her into his cottage, no doubt told her that the reason for his being here, if indeed there was a reason, was the light. Another: here at long last he did not understand a word, no longer had to hear his own language, its sounds and accent. And one person explained that he had left his country not because, as was often said, it was too limiting or insignificant or trivial, but actually the opposite, for at least to outward appearances, with its natural resources and especially its economic power, which gave rise to other forms of power, it had suddenly no longer been so limiting and insignificant, and then had become so powerful and finally even more powerful than in its glory days. And one person said he had set out for this region as a reader, as the reader of a long, long story that was set here in the Sierra, about a woman and her vanished lover.

And one day in Hondareda she also came upon her own would-be lover from the riverport city: as she now wanted it to be for her story, he had forgotten her, or had he? and he was thriving. And in the course of time she saw yet another person from home: the idiot of the outskirts—and the change of locale to the high Sierra seemed to have done him good likewise. His idiocy, which when expressed day in, day out, on the outskirts, with their identical curbs and the front lawns all mowed to exactly the same height, wore thin, flourished up here near the stratosphere, among the lichen-covered cliffs, got a second wind—was that expression still in use?—and adapted to the doings of the others.

And finally the story wanted the *andariega* to see in one of the new settlers her brother, recently released from prison, who she thought was in an entirely different country, committing his first act of violence directed not at things but at human beings, from which there would be no turning back.

And the person who appeared to her as her surviving brother—although outwardly there was little similarity to discover—or out of whom the supposedly lost brother spoke, said, as they shared an evening meal, at an hour unusually early for the Iberian Peninsula, in his living shed/storeroom/warehouse, approximately the following:

"I could already feel killing in my upper arms and my fingertips. Now! I said to myself one morning when I woke up lying next to yet another stranger, a woman who had called to me on the street the previous night as I was heading for yet another railroad station: 'Wait for me!' The woman claimed to have known me for a long time. And my absence, to quote her verbatim, had lasted 'for centuries.' How rough and at the same time tender her sex was. I had never encountered anything so rough yet so soft before. And as with all the other women, I never saw this stranger again. And with the passage of time I became her admirer. If you meet her, give her my best. I adore her. And I am sure she knows it, even if she will never hear me say it. And perhaps she will read in your story that we met not here and not there but in a third country that was at war.

"And I was in that country because of the war. I wanted to be in the war to take part in the killing. So there would be at least one less of these mindless and soulless two-legged creatures who are everywhere and nowhere nowadays, taking up space and even being paid handsomely for it! And that morning the moment had finally arrived! Off to clear the decks! And even though I was armed, I would do it with my bare hands, or with a stick—the whole combat zone was strewn with sticks and stones. And I would not kill an adversary or an enemy—I considered those of us on the two warring sides to be not enemies but woeful comrades in arms or whatever—but rather someone who was not directly involved, one of those bystanders who, as has become customary or fitting in wars in third countries, instead of trying to prevent war actually incite and whip it up, at the same time turning it into a business opportunity, or rather the sidewalk superintendents and kibitzers with whom the place was swarming.

"My grandfather was in the first world conflict and my father in the second, and both of them told me that it never crossed their minds to want to shoot at a so-called enemy, and to the very end they made a special effort to aim so as to miss. In contrast, however: death and destruction to those on both sides who had sent them off to fight one another and turned the killing and dying into a spectacle—except that neither my grandfather nor my father ever had a chance to look these 'devils' or 'charlatans,' as both of them called those responsible, in the eye or lay hands on them.

"On that day in my war I was assigned to a unit that was actually deployed to keep a fire-free zone open, secure a transit route, provide safe conduct. With a few others I was posted along a river in the mountains, at a ford where the road crossed the river at a shallow spot. At some point during the day, I saw, way off down the road on the other side of the river, a man walking alone, making his way through the bushes that had grown far into the travel lane since the war began. He was obviously not native to the area—although the civilian natives in the war zone had long since lost any native characteristics, by which I mean any sense of time and place, and were constantly mistaking yesterday for today, or for a day in the previous year, and constantly losing their way in their own village and even in their own house and grounds. No, that is not the one I am going to do away with, I thought, not yet. But the next one, from the Third Column, that of the sightless ones, in the armored personnel carriers with nineteen times nineteen banners waving!

"The lone pedestrian came to the ford. And at the same moment a vehicle actually appeared behind him, not armored, true, but instead seemingly disguised, and the car stopped, and a few actually masked men jumped out, some of the ones who were waging their own special, uncontrollable, and also, thanks to the masks, absolutely ruthless war-within-a-war. And one of the masked men, all of whom were wearing long, dust-colored greatcoats as if to be ready for being filmed, promptly took aim at the man who was wading through the ford with his pant legs rolled up. With the rushing of the water it was almost inaudible at first. But then I heard nothing but gunfire.

"And the gunfire—in the parents' cries here in Hondareda I hear the pow-pow-pow again—continued even after the corpse was already floating downstream. The masked man at the ford went on shooting at the dead man while his masked comrades kept us pinned down. I opened my eyes wide. Can one even say that of oneself? Yes, I, I opened my eyes wide. And my eyes were opened. And above the murdered man I saw the open sky. And I, I was innocent. I am innocent, I thought. And never, never will I kill anyone. And altogether: an end to revenge!

"And I was almost, almost grateful to that killer, grateful that he had saved me, saved me from my chief obsession, my obsession with murdering people. How tender was the sex of that woman who had called to me from behind that night on the street leading to the railroad station. Clasping me tenderly. And how noble. Noble and dark and wide, and above all special. And it was not only we who were together there in the night. Outside her apartment window stood a birch tree. A kind of millrace flowed past the house. And in the next room her child was sleeping."

The evening on which she saw the person out of whom she heard her brother speaking was bright, with spring just around the corner, and outside on the mountain steppe a few of the reporters were running to their helicopter. And at the sight of them her host involuntarily made a gesture like aiming a machine gun at the string of runners, pressing the trigger and spraying them with bullets.

He had even leaped to his feet and pushed open the window. The last deep-yellow rays of the sun shone on the walls of smooth-polished granite, and one equally yellow Sierra hornet, smaller than those in the valleys but with wings that droned all the more loudly, came shooting at the shooter, swerving just in time to miss him, and he jumped back, as only her brother could jump back, easily startled, especially by small things, and it was almost, almost all right with her that even Hondareda did not lie outside the labyrinthine world.

3 6

She scaled the gentle northern slopes and reached the crest of the Sierra with the last light of day. In the old books the word used for ridge or crest was "eyelash."

At one time there had been a crossing here, a path used mainly for driving the livestock over the ridge, worn by the cattle themselves, the only human addition being the road markers on the rocks consisting of very small, narrow columns of stones. These still existed here and there. But they had either toppled over or been overgrown by the little forests of broom. It was better not to try to locate them and risk being misled by these unreliable signs, which might just as well be chance heaps of weathered rock. Instead one should feel one's own way, one step at a time.

And that had to be possible on the almost bare, steep, rock-strewn descent to the south. Standing on the ridge, she saw the lights far, far below in Candeleda, where it was already night in the small town that now appeared much larger from her sky-high vantage point, the lights forming an island of light in the sea of blackish gray and black black that stretched to the horizon in almost every direction. Only in the west could one still see blue strips, one above the other, and the top one almost bright blue. It was the same blue as in the uppermost and outer wing portion of that white angel on the lost or stolen medallion. "If the angel had not gone missing," she said to herself, "I would not see its wing color in that blue over there."

Although no path leading down the mountain was evident anywhere, along this section of the ridge one could safely cross and head downhill. The air was clear way down into the lowlands. Far in the distance the outlines of the Montes de Toledo, the mountains of Toledo. The wind wafting up from below was mild. The remaining snow patches and snowfields apparently behind her. The jagged peaks and escarpments of the summit plain of the Almanzor, the little knives, the Galayos, and the Galana disappeared behind the nearer, more rounded peaks. Gone, too, the depression of Hondareda. As she looked around, only the faint glow from a few seemingly inaccessible villages on the slopes, above the high valley of the río Tormes; Pedrada, too, the stone-pelting place in the headwaters region, gone.

Now came the moment when she wished she were home on her own property on the outskirts of the riverport city, or under her fruit trees there. Never had she experienced such indecisiveness in herself, just at the point in her journey and her hike where her destination lay at her feet, and not only figuratively. This amused her even more than it took her by surprise. One step forward, one step back, one to the left, one to the right. And her initially jerky, puppet-like indecisiveness—her gaze, likewise, jerking forward, then back over her shoulder, then up to the summit, then down to the ground—produced a kind of harmony, as if the indecisiveness and the hesitating gradually became dance steps (and, accordingly, she later told the author about her "dance of indecision" up there on the crest of the Sierra de Gredos).

And then emerging, thanks to this dancing, from her back-and-forth hesitation, she really, without any as-if, gained the momentum for a decision, the indecisiveness now transformed into decisiveness: time to be on her way! onward, down into the nocturnal blackness, which, once one plunged into it, had a clarity of its own. That wood-road with protruding tree roots at home on the outskirts of the city came to mind, but not because she still wished to be back there, where in the layered and intertwined roots the mountains and foothills and base of the mountains here had appeared to her in miniature, in peaceable and harmless form: no, this purely playful format of the Sierra de Gredos now revealed itself on location: it was a matter of crossing and leaping over the mighty Sierra in her mind's eye just as light-footedly and quickly as over the layered roots at home in front of her own house.

And already she was running and leaping downhill, in imaginary serpentines, an *asendereada*, which usually meant "a woman who has strayed from the path," but not here, where for the first stretch of the path (yes, path), as she drifted off as if in a drift originating inside her and safeguarding her, nothing could go wrong, and for the moment she was the mistress of her story again.

Leaping from ridge to ridge, as back there at home from one root branch to another. What contributed to her current sense of security was the phenomenon that one of the settlers in Hondareda, a rock expert, had once described in her presence as the "rhythm of the Sierra de Gredos." According to him, the Sierra was a rhythmic formation in the sense that, whether on the gentle northern face or the steep southern face, the many chimneys, clefts, gorges, rivulets, and torrents fanned out evenly, the result of reciprocal action of water and the granite bedrock, which had created a relief characterized by rhythmic regularity, without the distortions, gaps, dislocations, and "unpleasant surprises" one often encountered in sandstone or limestone mountains, which consisted of masses that had been blown in or been deposited from elsewhere, rather than of original bedrock.

And that rhythmic quality, according to her geologist, also communicated itself to anyone hiking through the Sierra—the rhythm of the ground under his feet assured evenness, order, and controllability in his movement, "at least for the time being" ("for the time being" was also a much-used expression among the new settlers).

And as the *asendereada* cast her thoughts back to Hondareda once more, she said, again to herself, in the very penetrable darkness surrounding her descent from the mountain: "Lost country. Authentic country. Leaving behind the authentic country for one's own lostness! What a rhythm that creates. What energy. I know who you all are. Of mixed blood, like me. How fortunate to be alive in the time when the last homogeneous people ceases to exist. A rich time. Fullness of time." She almost sang this, like an old hit. But the moment had not yet come for her song. It was only the time for a greeting, sent in the direction of the glacial basin settlement, a greeting *after* the farewell, as if imagined in an Arabic poem.

She was dressed for the nocturnal crossing of the Sierra as at the beginning of her journey. Only a few small things had been added, a chin strap for her hat, knee pads, a juniper walking stick, which, when one waved it in the air, produced a hissing sound. Stuck into her belt—not her hat—were the feathers of various birds, each one a singleton, dropped as the birds took flight, a gray-blue-white one from a wild dove, a tiger-striped one from a falcon, a shiny black one from a jackdaw, a dull brown one from a vulture, a feather bordered in ultramarine but otherwise transparent from a blue jay, a kite feather partly dusted with gold. Sewn onto her garment everywhere were little pieces of mica, which—according to the intermittently superstitious people of Hondareda—were supposed to ward off lightning and protect one from fire: from her clothing, as otherwise from the mica-strewn ground, there now came a reflection of the night sky, and not all that dim; and from the fringes of her jacket sleeves dangled smooth little granite pebbles, which constantly bumped against each other in an even rhythm as she walked.

If "Gredos" came from the word *greda*, meaning clay, or potter's earth, or scree, or grit, the steep southern slopes of the Sierra deserved the name more than the northern ones, which consisted almost entirely of solid rock: for her descent repeatedly took her across stretches of soft, almost muddy earth, also slate scree and gravel, where she sometimes slid more than walked; a sliding which, because she was always prepared for it, instead of carrying the risk of slipping and falling, was used by her for making more rapid progress, a sort of riding down the mountain.

The rucksack also helped her maintain her balance. The expression she used later in conversation with the author was that it was "nice and heavy," for one thing from the fruit she had pilfered before setting out—her own form of superstition?—and then somewhat less from the almost feather-light bread than from the olive oil that had proved its worth on all her previous crossings, and the large container of salt: the salty air that had unexpectedly reached her nostrils up on the crest along with the suddenly mild southerly wind—did it emanate from the salt that her body, heated from the climb, caused to steam? Or did the salty cloud come from her body itself? The only other provender she had—yes, she assured the author, he could be so bold as to use this word—were the mountain walnuts, the hazelnuts, the chestnuts, and dried rowan and juniper berries, which she constantly jiggled in her various pant and jacket pockets, making them click and jingle.

"Time is money?" she said out loud in the darkness, which grew denser as she descended: "Yes, but not the way most people think. No one has established yet what wealth one can acquire by means of time. I have time now, and nothing else has ever made me feel freer or wealthier. Yes, and having time is definitely a feeling and has nothing to do with leisure or a sense of leisure. It comes from inside and is added onto whatever I am engaged in at the moment, and it alone provides a sense of completeness and meaning or specialness. Listen: having time is the overarching? no, the basic feeling that first makes possible the other feelings, the specific and also the grander feelings, that is to say, the more warmhearted feelings and life on a grand scale."

Talking to herself in the dark: Was she afraid on this solitary descent? Forget that question—anything resembling fear was out of the question for the *asendereada* and her story; and besides, where she was at the moment, far above the tree line, it was not pitch-dark, for the spatially pliable chiaroscuro still held sway, in which she even descended backward at times, with her eyes fixed on the Sierra mountaintop, which was noticeably receding from her—while, strangely enough, the lowlands and the plain below were also receding, even though she was nearing them, step by step, probably also receding because the only lights, those of Candeleda, had soon been swallowed up by the foothills and low ridges, leaving not even a pale shimmer in the sky.

But if no fear, what about the skittishness typical of her tribe or village or ethnic group? "That was out of the question during this nocturnal crossing," she told the author. "Besides, it had never reared its head on all my previous solitary crossings of the Sierra. Was it the evenness, the rhythm, or the constant state of alertness? At any rate, when an entire forest of bushes, which a moment ago had been completely motionless, began to sway, advancing toward me like a huge black wave, I stepped out of its path as if nothing were wrong, and in fact it was only a herd of cattle, of the deep-black Ávila breed, which had been sleeping in the patch of bushes and had all stood up at once.

"And time and again, when I slid past snakes at a thumb's and a throat's distance, after slipping, which happened to me more often in broad daylight than in the dusk, I merely observed them wide-eyed, like the sharp horns of the bulls poking out of the foliage, and my only thought was: Well, well, aha.

"The startle response that comes when one trips and almost falls, or falls off something, is entirely different. I experienced that constantly during all my crossings of the Gredos massif, except during the last one, when I actually would have welcomed it after a while: for the shock that goes through one when one thinks one is losing the ground under one's feet merely affects the body, and puts it on a particular kind of alert: afterward one sees more clearly, hears more distinctly, and, most important, a person who has been 'pulled up short' this way, as our village expression has it, at once shakes off any brooding or self-absorption."

In the previously mentioned "Guide to the Dangers of the Sierra de Gredos"—which she knew almost by heart, as if she had literally written it herself, the descent from the ridges at the summit to Candeleda, at the edge of the valley of the río Tiétar, was described as "extremely challenging." One was advised not to try it alone, or at night. On the other hand, the descent was said not to take more than "approximately six hours," and "as the crow flies" it was a "mere fifteen kilometers."

Yet she found the descent to be not challenging at all, or at least that was not the proper word for this journey on foot. Nevertheless, the *asendereada* needed not six hours for the descent to Candeleda but the entire night, and the entire following day, and another night? and when she finally reached the fig and olive trees on the edge of the small town, in the darkness before dawn, or after dusk? she had lost more than just a day and a night. Lost? Really?

In his youth the author had occasionally read one of his attempts at epic literature—he had always been intent on achieving epic breadth, without being familiar with the term itself—aloud to a friend, male or female: and the first thing he always asked was whether it had been "exciting" (although even in those days, if the answer was yes, he was oddly disappointed, as if he had hoped to hear some adjective other than "exciting" applied to his creation).

A similar mechanism was still at work now, when it came to the episode of the crossing of the mountain range, and he felt tempted to resort to the sort of dramatic style that he had eschewed all his life as a feature that would distract one from what was really happening. (That author who was apocryphal in this or some other respect, that twister of words and facts, who made things either better or worse than they were: that could also have been him at any number of junctures.)

In a dramatic account, during that first night, shortly after reaching the tree line below and plunging into the pitch-dark, yes, pitch-dark first belt of woodland, the heroine of the story would have encountered a hermit and been raped by him. On the following day, as she lay, more dead than alive, in a thicket of ferns, giant toads would have crawled over her, spewing venom in her face. And the next night, as she stumbled around, half-blinded, she would have been attacked by a wild bull, which, had she not seized him by the horns, and in that position—with her hands gripping the horns!—hurled the story of her life at the bull's head and into the bull's eyes, would have fallen upon her in an entirely different way from the hermit monk of the night before.

And like the heroine of a nineteenth-century English novel, for example, she would have taken refuge that second night in a hole in the ground, surrounded by so-called fairy circles of mushrooms, to her mind always the most uncanny of plants, enormous, black-gilled mushrooms that glowed in the dark and beamed their disgusting odor of decay at her in the middle of the circle, their giant umbrellas having the form of black suns. And there was lightning and thunder. And an avalanche—in the southern gullies of the Sierra it was early spring, with a constant danger of avalanches, especially when the mild winds blew from the south— roared by so close to her that she felt its draft for a long time, like an ice-cold spray on her flushed face.

And that one zone in the stretch of forest that had had a fire, where she had constantly stumbled over nothing but dead birds, all the cadavers close together, as if they had been blown there, the hawk with the mountain titmouse, the sparrow with the eagle, the wren with the sparrow hawk or hawk, and in all cases only their bare bodies—what had happened to their feathers? And that scene in a storm, as she cowered in a sheltering niche under a rock shelf, and little by little a fox, a viper, a scorpion, a salamander, a family of wild boars, a snow-white weasel, and even more animals that were otherwise mortal enemies by nature, had gradually joined her, and how they had all waited quietly and peaceably for the storm to pass. And one time, as she slept in a sitting position, the blow on the back of her neck.

None of this happened during her descent from the Sierra de Gredos, or perhaps some of it did, after all, but under different circumstances, in a different light, and especially in a very different rhythm. She encountered drama at every step, whether walking, standing, or lying, but not of the cheap variety sketched out here.

Accordingly, on that first night, in the first stretch of forest, a jungle-like tangle, she saw a fire flaring up in the pitch-darkness, though well contained in a circle of upended stones, and in fact she did come upon a solitary person, the only one during this phase of her journey, a nocturnal Jew's harp player. And she asked him whether he wasn't afraid, of what? of other people in this unsafe time and area, whereupon he—was this the rape?—looked at her with burning eyes and replied that he was never afraid, for "I love human beings" (yet the author, when she repeated this, word for word, so that he could write it down, looked at her as if in dismay; as if such a thing, both as a fact and as a statement, had long since become impossible and unthinkable; dismayed? disarmed?). The hermit had exuded a strong smell; he smelled of having gone astray.

And during the second night, as the *asendereada* was crouching somewhere, she in fact, almost literally, had her head knocked off. Yet the blow came from her own head, which, as she nodded off from exhaustion, struck her chest with practically lethal force: "One could have died of it, as if executed by the weight of one's own head." And it was also true that she lay in a ferny hollow for almost a day, "more dead than alive," but without the "poisonous toads" that "crawled over her"—but what did this mean? wasn't this a way of being truly alive for a change?

How it came about that she then lay dying, as it were—no, leave out the "as it were"—and without anyone else's doing, that was, or so it seemed, exciting enough to the author and reader caught up in the story—and exciting in a way that annoyed him less than those many stories that were written, and even more often filmed, as if "excitement" were the be-all and end-all—as if it were required nowadays that all books and films be exciting.

Even the steep southern face of the Sierra was punctuated by granite ribs, rock spouts, and ledges, poking up amid the fallen rock and scree. As the woman passed them on her way down, for a while she was still so preoccupied with the settlement of Hondareda that she was repeatedly tempted to knock on one of the rock piles and step through a doorway as into one of the dwellings carved out of the former glacial trough. Except that these were no delicate chaos-rocks resembling houses or inhabited towers. For here on the southern flank there had never been a glacier. The topography was too steep for a gradual flow of ice. And where the author's client had initially, just past the crest, wanted to push open the door to what she thought was a stone dwelling, the rocky ruins—not as rounded and polished as those of Hondareda—came from a peak that had gradually crumbled in some prehistoric era: parts had sheared off one after the other and hurtled into the depths, over the course of ten thousand or a hundred thousand solar years—until finally all that was left of the former mountain, at one time perhaps just as pointed and almost as high as the Almanzor, was the flat, slightly jagged rump, today's ridge, the crossing point. The largest and heaviest pieces of that former mountain had fallen almost halfway to the valley, and stuck out in the middle of the steep slopes, in the form of spurs, onto which one stepped on the way down from the Sierra as onto an almost horizontal platform, easy to walk on and seemingly intended as resting places—whereupon one suddenly found oneself on the edge of a vertical rock wall, falling off into a veritable abyss, not a good idea to scramble down, at least not during the night.

Time and again she knew she must turn back there—still that smile upon turning back? her smile glowing in the dark? and go slightly uphill again, until she finally ignored the spurs and the smoother stretches they seemed to offer, and in fact all apparent shortcuts. Better to stick to the reliable step-by-step serpentines through the trackless scree. She had everything she needed. She even felt increasingly enriched, "in the sense of being showered with presents," as she described it. In contrast to all her previous crossings of the Sierra, where the moments of fulfillment—the sense of experiencing the entire possible range of existence, body and soul—had been pierced almost immediately with the pain of guilt at being farther than ever, infinitely far, from love and her loved ones, this time she did not see herself as alone, and at one point said out loud into the night: "I can do nothing better for you than to keep on doing what I am doing. In doing that, in doing it in rhythm, in a conscientious rhythm, without sloppiness, finding my own rhythm and getting it to vibrate, oscillate, and show the way, I am doing for myself and for you the best I can do, for myself and you." — "What do you mean by rhythm?" (the author chiming in here). — She: "Intensification of what is already there."

And as she walked, climbed, and scrambled, there appeared to her for a moment, as briefly as a single snowflake flitting by before the real snow came, the old nursery in her house on the outskirts of the northwestern two-river city, lying there silent in dim light, where the toys lined up on the floor for a game were suddenly illuminated, then gone just as suddenly.

That must have occurred at approximately the spot where the *asendereada* left the treeless, and also almost vegetationless, high-altitude precinct of the Gredos massif and began threading her way past the first Sierra pines, all of which along the edge of the woods were denuded, stripped of their bark and their tops by lightning. A lone star above one of the split crowns: an accessory, an essential one. But contrary to her supposition, it was not one of the stars forming the forehead of Orion, the central winter constellation. Indeed, there was no more Orion to be seen anywhere in the entire vast sky. Also no more Pleiades. No more Castor and Pollux. Not a single winter constellation left. No more winter? So that is how long we have been traveling together. A good long time. A swath of time. A wave of time. A hedgehog's snout of time. A plane tree's notched leaf of time. A bomb crater of time. And now, too, an expression from the Arabic book, this also flaring up like a snowflake or a falling star: "And the breath of the Merciful One wafted in from Yemen."

And now something squishy beneath the hiker's sole, a sinking into something soft: a piece of a garment? an entire garment? a garment shrouding a decomposing corpse, stretched out there on the forest floor, already half transformed into a cadaver, gelatinized?

No, the softness came only from the fabric and the thick moss growing all over it. And the fabric? Was, and is, that shawl or stole we had lost during the previous crossing of the Sierra de Gredos, a year or five years ago, and had been determined to find this time. Is such a thing possible? Yes, it is possible. "And we will not lose you a second time, my shawl!" she said, as she involuntarily traced the word "shawl" in Arabic letters in the night air (it was the same word).

3 7

She walked. We played. And our playscapes extended far beyond the four walls of your nursery, farther and farther beyond. At every step a playground, a playing field, a play space, and one followed the other; followed on its heels; went hand in hand with it.

And this succession of spaces also presented itself as a succession of settings—for what? what was set there? what happened there?: where the spaces themselves were the happening, the game, the spectacle. And the places through which she was walking alone now formed trails and fords and passageways and walkways and tunnels to the locales, the same ones or others, of once-upon-a-time: where we two—did Arabic, like the Slavic languages, have a dual form, between singular and plural?— had been at one time, or had passed through: every few steps, these places in the Sierra turned out to be augmented by settings from her childhood village, from her school and university towns, from megalo- and metropolises, but more often by settings off the beaten track, remote places where she had once been with another person, or with several people who had become close friends, and at the same time will have been—this is how clearly the places, sites, and spots of the past that were played into her hand presented themselves.

And each of these once and future settings, here and there (she demanded that the author avoid the term "place images" or even "image" for this stage of their joint story and use it only at the end, if at all), revealed a pivot and a hinge, a connecting element that allowed it to pass into the following setting, to continue turning the stage and the page to the next.

Wasn't this whirl of settings, from her own life and others', contemporary ones and ones from hundreds of years ago, predestined for this section of her route and as if planned in advance for her book? Perhaps;

but if so, not such a rapid whirl: with time less whirling than swirling like a meteorite and crossing its own path. And remarkable, too, that it happened as she was walking downhill, instead of uphill, as had been her previous experience, and at night instead of in the morning.

A setting that came flying to her was the kitchen where her half-grown daughter, after they had located each other again (before she lost the child for the second time), was playing hostess, serving her (that had never happened before between mother and daughter and would never happen again in this way?) in that house by the Atlantic cliff near the small island town with the name "Los Llanos de Aridane": yes, each setting and everything in the series passed before her, together with the terms for it, as the-signified-and-its-signifier.

And almost with the same step there came flying to her the edge of a square in another small town ("Where, when, in the ring-around-the-rosy of places, names from now on are unimportant for our story," she told the author), where the two of them again, the woman and child, had eaten at the end of a market day, and all that had happened was that they had sat there together in the otherwise emptied-out marketplace and that a strong wind will have been blowing, making the empty fruit and vegetable crates left behind from the market skitter all over the square, and that scraps of paper and plastic will have swirled around their heads, and that the sky above the square was, and is, and will have been pale gray.

And with the next step, the two of them—in the dual, *mi dva* or some such—are driving home in the car on a rainy night, and all that happened was that during the entire trip tools, hammers, axes, pliers, together with apples or whatever, rolled back and forth on the floor of the car, and knocked against each other, and that the shadows of the raindrops on the windshield, whenever they were struck by the headlights of an oncoming car, dart across their clothes and faces in the form of dark, round spots, and that it is warm inside the vehicle.

And a building that had once been a schoolhouse had a triangular gable with a relief in the middle representing an empty circle. And from a harvested cornfield far from the Sorbian-Arab village, a waterspout (an archaic term?) swept the chaff up above eye level and across the abandoned field in a column. And a caisson pulled far ahead of us along a cemetery's main avenue, and the autumn leaves drift down around it. And on the railroad embankment the tall grass appeared and then was gone and out of sight, as it blew in the direction we and the train were traveling. And the hedgehog appears, the one that got stuck in the fence and that we will have freed. And now that swing appears on a certain playground in the dusk, still swinging without the swinger, who has disappeared, and then it will have continued to be pushed by nothing but the wind.

And with yet another step she saw in a flash the mouth of one of the rivers where it meets the other in the riverport city, with its sandbanks and the northern sky mirrored white in the water, one of the rivers black like the río Negro, the other blue and yellow like the Amazon, and the waterfowl from all the world's rivers swarming there at the mouth. And with the following step she saw in a flash the shriveled onions sending out green shoots in the cellar of the bombed-out house. And with the following step there flew to her the neatly set table at the foot of the cliff. And with the following step, the fire seen through the little mica window in the door of the stove. And with the following, the sobbing from the telephone (which thus also became a setting).

At last she reached a patch of woods where it was no longer merely dark but in fact pitch-dark. No, "pitch-dark" was not the word either, or "pitch-black," for even with the juniper branch, which she held out in front of her like a blind person and tapped on the ground, she could not make any headway. Yet the moonless starry sky remained just as clear as before. The trees simply formed such a dense canopy between her and the sky that although a faint sparkle penetrated, it did not light her way even a thumb's length ahead. What was that expression from the Sorbian-Arab village?—"a darkness you can hang an ax on."

One could not see one's hand before one's face? That was how it was. True, it would not have prevented her from pressing on. So why did she finally stop in her tracks? Because she no longer knew whether she would still have solid ground beneath her feet; because not another step was possible. To feel her way forward with her hands was still possible; but impossible to do that at the same time with her toes and soles. Another village expression came to mind: "no farther than a hen's step."

For a while she tried shuffling along, without raising a foot. And could one make headway like this? Each step covered hardly half a span, and in the end perhaps just barely a toenail's length. On this night there would be no finding her way out of this forest. And where she now stopped, total darkness reigned, without a glimmer, without any outlines, a darkness such as she had encountered only underground and in a tunnel. Since this was the case, and nothing to be done, she sat down to wait for morning.

She did not have a flashlight on her, but she did have matches. Where she was crouching, she could feel brush under her fingertips and could have made a fire like the Jew's harp player and lover of humanity much higher up in the Sierra. (Higher? She had been going downhill and uphill so constantly that the two of them were probably at the same elevation, but separated by ridges and yet more ridges?) But she preferred to remain in this unparalleled darkness, at the same time under an open, cloudless sky. She also did not want anyone down in the lowlands or elsewhere to see her fire and think she needed help.

Did she need help? No. She stretched out, on her back. Even once her eyes had grown accustomed to the darkness, the earth and the world around her remained invisible; not a thing could be made out in the light of a star here or there, no leaf, no cluster of needles; what could be made out was only the darkness—but it could be made out after all—which took on shape, became a form, provided companionship. A bit earlier she had been walking along a brook at the bottom of a gorge that turned out to have no outlet, and thus for a while she had had to go uphill again, winding back and forth: from the water far below now barely a distant rushing. Otherwise, all around her not a sound to be heard.

Not the slightest wind was blowing now, either. All night long, no breeze. Neither cold nor warm, no breath of coolness or mildness. In the total darkness the air stood still, could not even be felt as an element. Occasionally, astonishment that one had no trouble breathing. Involuntary sitting up and leaning back—was this a tree? Yes, it was, and to judge by the pattern of its bark, an oak. That meant one had already covered half the distance, from the heights above the tree line and through the belt of conifers. I have hardly ever seen this woman lean on anything, certainly not on a person. And now she sat on the bare ground and leaned back, and how.

Then there were noises after all, sporadic ones, at intervals, and always the same: something hitting the forest floor, small yet very hard and heavy, after falling from a considerable height. And these were acorns, and they fell all night long, now farther away, now very close to her, now on the right, now on the left, now up on the mountain, now toward the valley. Was fall already around the corner, then? No, she had experienced just such a falling of acorns before, during a very different night spent out of doors, in a different part of the world. And during that Sierra night she heard it again inside her, and thus it deserved its moment in her story.

The falling acorns, for all their distinct clinking, clanging, and eventually veritable "cymbaling," produced mysterious sounds like those otherwise made by a single leaf or twig in a barely perceptible wind. At first they were joined by the last airplanes, at great altitudes, on the threshold of audibility, the planes on long-distance flights to overseas destinations, having taken off around midnight. Then came the night after midnight, and nothing but the tinkling of the acorns and the acorn xylophone, more and more also an acorn vibraphone; yes, the darkness vibrated with the sound of falling acorns.

For a time she dug into her provisions: "How groping for something to eat enhanced its taste—the greatly intensified quintessential bitterness of the rowanberries!" For a while also mere lying and resting. For a while sitting and taking notes, for me. What? writing in tunnel-like darkness, forming letters and words? Yes, and precisely under these circumstances with a particular presence of mind.

And all the while, even though she now lacked the even rhythm of walking, there continued—except that by this time it was at an almost dizzying speed—the carousel of places and settings, darting, hot on each other's heels, into the middle of whatever she was doing, and shooting through her; eventually also more like a cable or valley railroad.

And in the meantime the series included places and things that did not belong to her in particular and did not originate in her own experience. Yes, that spot along the brook now, under the ash by the cow pasture, in the autumn rain that sounded so entirely different in the wilted, fallen, brittle foliage than in summer, that spot had also been hers at one time.

But the hand that she saw next, a hand writing in the glow of an oil lamp, writing and writing and writing—in a rhythm she had never seen before—with a steel pen and black India ink, that was not her hand, or any hand from her own century, and the shoulders and profile of the writer that swept in along with the hand had transported her for a millisecond into the company of a man who, did he not belong to an era long past, would have been the author she dreamt of for her story? And I, the contemporary author in the village in La Mancha? What was I in comparison but a sort of stopgap?

And how had he come to appear to her on that mountain-crossing night, her ideal writer for this commission, her Miguel de Cervantes? "As Miguel wrote and writes and will have written in a certain way, one felt in one's own body, in one's own shoulders, one's own profile, one's arms, one's hips, one's legs, how oneself and one's story was, and could have been, and was being, traced by the moving writing instrument, and underlined, underlined and emphasized, emphasized and clad in beauty, clad in beauty and rendered truthful."

And yes, now, brushing past her like a falling star, the abandoned railroad spur, breaking off at a road through the fields, complete with rusty warning signs in the grass, that was part of her life again, her era, and she could have told me the name of the place, and where to locate it. But then: a woman as foreign to her as she was familiar, driven off course onto a new continent, in an odyssey never before told: How had the lightning flashing through her shown her this stranger?—Odysseus in the shape of a woman, and not alone on her odyssey, but with her child, and this odyssey, according to the information accompanying the flash, would have been the contemporary equivalent of Homer's, the odyssey of a mother with her child! What a double-edged sword these flashes of places and constellations were: on the one hand confirming one's existence, on the other hand—well, double-edged.

3 8

With the first light of morning, pale as distant daylight inside a cave, she set out, heading for the valley. She was almost in a hurry to get out of the Sierra de Gredos. Although outwardly she still had time, she no longer felt as though she did: Was it necessary for the *fact* of having time to be joined by the *feeling*, if one was to be able to benefit from having time?

Did she lack for anything? Nothing, except that she was thirsty, and with a vengeance. For the first time on her journey she was almost driven. She rushed; walked as if being rushed. Yet she had long since left behind the overgrown stretch of forest and was passing through an unexpectedly day-bright section. This revealed itself as a transitional area, no longer in the midst of the Sierra yet still without signs of the foothills region, the plain as well as the peaks hidden from view by the belt of trees; also no sounds of civilization, neither honking nor cars passing each other, sounds that otherwise penetrated from the lowlands into the most remote reaches of the mountains. The area was devoid of trees, scruffy, with hardly any rocks, but the ferns were impressive, constituting the main vegetation here, their fronds overlapping, way over her head, a kind of fern forest.

There was, however, one sign of human habitation: a road, or actually more of a footpath, leading diagonally down through the fern forest, with snapped fronds on either side. So she was no longer a pathless one, an *asendereada*. And what name did she give herself now? "*La aventurera*," she said, "the adventurer." Hadn't she already been called that earlier in the story? That was her name again now, on the final stretch, with even more justification. She, such an orderly person, an adventurer? Yes, for she was at once orderly and bold, an orderly adventurer.

Instead of in S-curves, the path now led straight down, but quite gradually, which suited her at the moment; the steep stretches of the Sierra lay behind her. And among the ferns she then also found something to quench her thirst: ground blackberries, whose runners crisscrossed the floor of the fern forest. Many of the berries were shriveled, or still green, or not yet formed, in bloom—all this again in a delightful confusion—and a few already ripe, altogether very few, "to be counted on the fingers of one hand." Yet what a gift even one of these *zarzamoras* was. Gift? "Yes, at the sight of them I literally said: 'a gift!'" she explained. What an ability this little ball of fruit, no bigger than a rabbit dropping, had to magically banish her parching thirst.

The thirst had grown so fierce that one had, so to speak, to shut down one's mouth, together with one's tongue and throat, avoiding any movement, such as the tongue's bumping against the palate, swallowing, taking a deep breath, for fear that with the slightest contact between parts of the mouth—if the tongue even brushed the gums—the need for water, water, water would turn one inside out. Now one tiny little blackberry was enough, and the burning in one's gullet was a thing of the past.

Unimaginable thirst? Yes, impossible to imagine that one had been thirsty just now. Besides: with the instantaneous relief, practically salvation, a sense of pleasure. The pure deliciousness, all-pervasive—and from such a tiny thing—made one open not only one's mouth but also one's eyes and ears.

When she then ordered her author to come up with a hymn in praise of the Sierra blackberries, the man with the assignment replied that in his life as a writer he had already praised enough things, occasionally even one person or another—actually more "another," and then he gave in, as usual: "If you insist—but only a short paragraph."

That she ran through the fern forest—she, who otherwise never ran; in her village no one ran—and finally even raced, was not, however, the doing of the couple of blackberries or the energy they gave her. The quick succession of world settings was still darting through her, passing faster than a heartbeat, and also no longer, as earlier, in a rhythm that coincided with the beating of the heart and reinforced it. (Anyone running or racing in her Sorbian-Arab village had to be a refugee or someone being pursued.)

There was no longer any rhythm at all. A setting from her own experience, or increasingly from a universal human past in which she had not participated personally, would come suddenly, while the next would flash by so rapidly, overlapping it and getting tangled in it so that it made one dizzy. One could no longer speak of sequence and regularity; instead of a lovely jumble, an increasingly hopeless one.

For the first time, no, not for the first time, in her life, the *aventurera* felt close to madness. Madness? "Going crazy—and I would have preferred hellish thirst to that." It seemed appropriate that in one of the places or settings that came flying to her she saw herself as the former queen, shut up in the tower of Tordesillas in the sixteenth century, that queen whom history had dubbed Juana la Loca, Crazy Joan (she, too, had not gone mad, but, worse or maybe better, simply crazy). The crazy woman's eyes were mirrored in the río Duero, the bright river, at which she stared down, unseeing—as if all that remained of her eyes were the whites. And the monk painted by Zurbarán fleeing past her into the darkness, after his vision had shown him, where he had thought to find a light glowing, a whitish, desiccated, scabby tongue dotted with congealed blood, like the tongue of an animal run over on the road.

That was the last of the settings, places, objects, fragments, in the overlapping, swirling series. The adventurer stumbled head over heels down the not very steep path, trying now to steer toward something like a port between the menacing shoals—like the people of Hondareda, she was now thinking in nautical terms. After the disappearance and obliteration of the río Duero, of the queen's eyes, of the monk's robe in the darkness, nothing more—no square, no place, no figure, no tongue.

And then came the loss of images. (Not until this point was the author allowed to use this expression.) Loss of images? For the time being? No, once and for all. Personal loss of images? Her own? No, general. Universal. A general, universal loss of images. Who said that? How could one say such a thing? The story said it. Hers and mine, our story said it. It, the story, wanted it this way. This was how the story had visualized it.

And it was in her, this adventurer as orderly as she was bold, that there, in the fern forest far below the summit plain of the Sierra de Gredos, the story wanted the general loss of images to be consummated.

This was, to be sure, a problem of this period in history, and the loss of images, and of the image, took place in each person only gradually, not as suddenly as in her case now (which is perhaps partly an invention, yet not an untruth). But according to the story, the problem had to be described in conjunction with her, the solitary and isolated individual.

According to the story, the adventurer was the last one who, while the loss of images had already taken hold of and infected people in general, was still in the picture, living among and from images. And maybe now I, the current author, am more the right one to tell the story of the loss of images than her Miguel (de Cervantes Saavedra, or whatever his name was), for whom this problem or topic would have been inconceivable? Or perhaps not?

The stumbling became a tripping. The tripping became a fall. The fall became a general capsizing. The adventurer tumbled head over heels into the fern forest, which was full of holes and hollows not mentioned in the "Guide to the Dangers of the Sierra de Gredos": no reason to fault it, for these depressions were all rather shallow and quite well padded with the fallen and rotting fern fronds from the past, and thus, in the terms of the "Guía de peligros," no real danger, and certainly not in comparison to the actually dangerous *neveros*, or snow holes, where, on a seemingly smooth surface, one could sink from one step to the next up to one's neck, and deeper, into an apparently harmless patch of snow.

The danger here in the fern forest was of an essentially different kind. Her fall, caused by the abrupt loss of images, was a small fall on the outside and a large fall on the inside. Yes, first came the loss of images, and only then did she get tangled in her own feet, which caused her to tip sideways, fall, and roll over and over, although she had not fallen from much of a height. What the images, the image, and the loss of images mean and bring about: that will be the subject of the epilogue—her conversation with the author in the village in La Mancha.

For the moment she lay on the ground surrounded by ferns, invisible from the outside as well as from above, on her stomach, motionless. In a close-up her torso would have been heaving violently yet almost inaudibly as she breathed, like that of a sheep sleeping. Just so, people with severe injuries, even if they were fully conscious and felt no pain, instead of trying to get up, would instinctively remain lying on the spot without moving, as if simply to raise their head or bend a toe would mean the end of them. So was she injured? No, it was worse: felled by the extinguishing flash marking the loss of images, coming on the heels of the hopelessly jumbled series of image flashes, and now visited on her and the world, she was going through death, as it were (without "as it were"). That was how the story wanted it to be. That was the story (which is neither a fable nor a legend, and also no fairy tale).

And she accepted the idea of perishing. Hadn't she, hadn't one, foundered long since, in existence, in life, in relationships, and didn't that now finally become obvious in the loss of images, brought on almost intentionally? The sweetness of acceptance. To disappear from the face of the earth: as it should be.

On the other hand, acceptance did not mean wanting to die. She had never felt anything like a longing for death, and certainly did not now. How incomprehensible she found the sentence "I look forward to dying." True, even before the crossing of the Sierra, she had counted on perishing. But if she were close to it, one thing was clear: she would fight for her life to the last. For her life? For life.

And so now she girded herself to resist, at first only inwardly, yet where else would one begin? And as had always been the case with her, this taking action, like all her doings, was a form of management—and didn't one say, instead of "I must find a way out," "I must manage to get out of this situation"? While she lay there, not moving a finger, her thoughts were already focused on managing again: budgeting, measuring, calculating, ordering, surveying, projecting, taking precautions, planning. Except that no plan for forging ahead presented itself, or, in her words: no managerial opportunity. For in her terms, rather than "It's all over," the conclusion was "There is nothing more to manage!"

It was of her own free will that she then decided to remain lying this way in the ferns, in the death zone, for the day and one night, el día y una noche.

At least she had one thing in common with the hero of her Miguel's story: she looked for adventures where there were none to undergo, at least no external, visible ones. And accordingly he, that good-for-nothing, that inept soldier and galley slave, that one-armed son of a quack, would have been the right one to tell her story after all, the only one? But this man Cervantes never did narrate primarily internal adventures such as hers? Or did he? Was it not true that his adventure stories, too, no less than that of the loss-of-images-and-how-one-can-manage-one's-way-out-of-it, belonged primarily to an interior world, and were for that very reason universal?

39

First of all, so the story goes, the woman who had fallen into the image-loss pit turned onto her back.

Through the gaps in the fern-frond canopy, the daytime sky, high and blue. A period of just lying there in the heart of the Sierra. Springtime or late-fall sunlight penetrating all the way to the ground. On a sunlit stone there, the feathery shadow of a fern, like a fossil from prehistoric times. Or was that not a shadow at all but an actual petrified fern? Intentionally reaching out to touch one of the stinging nettles, which, according to the danger guide, like to "cohabit" with ferns and in the Sierra de Gredos sting "both piercingly and persistently." (The author, though not particularly familiar with the Sierra, shared her experience one time.)

But even this pain did not help in the absence of a management plan. The only thoughts: meaningless wordplays and spoonerisms—crime waits for yeoman, or: a penny paved is a penny spurned; and so forth.

And then, on the other hand: what a relief no longer to have to be master or mistress of the story, *la Señora de la historia,* and once and for all. Just as in the chaotic or panicky helter-skelter of the external world one could find a kind of peace or even shelter for a while, so one could in the frantic inner world, at least for as long as it took to inhale and exhale. The tranquil blue sky above the ferns, and another nonsensical thought: all souls' sky. Nonsensical? The roar of a squadron up there, heading for the high Sierra. The bombers snored, the entire sky filled with their snoring and their terrible heavy load. Hondareda! Did no one but you see and hear this? No one whose heart broke like yours at the sound?

The camera panning from your face to a grasshopper next to it, its eyes—are those eyes?—black like yours, the antennae flailing in midair. Grasshopper, *dzarad* in Arabic—but even thinking of this word did not help you out. Another pan to—a toad?—no, a frog, not toadlike at all, and too skinny for a toad, so small, hardly as big as a pencil point, as if he has just been transformed from a tadpole, in water, into an amphibious being, and is trying out his first hops on the earth, like a flea (that is how small he was), and now his attempt to get out of the hollow, observed from extremely close up: the tiny fellow scrambling, all his limbs operating alternately as he climbs, the spitting image of the first and last human.

Image? Yes, image, but not of the sort under discussion here. And how had the man-frog come to be here beneath the ferns, so far from his primal element, water? The camera panning back to you, not merely to your face this time, but to your whole body. In her film long ago there had been many such pans.

How glorious—find a different word—a body could look—and not only because of the particular camera angle and the special cinematic lighting—awakening the oldest dreams ever dreamt about a woman, about you. How glorious? How majestic. How childlike—find a different word—how pure—find a different word—like man, woman, and child all in one, but also how simple and touching, for instance a glance at your hands, those fruit-thief hands, which did not even have slippery fingers. But how pulse-quickening, too—find a different word—how heart-pounding (in medieval stories, and thus also in your film, such expressions were never used, yet those love stories were infinitely more physical, corporeal, and steamy than those of today!), how igniting, how kindling, how flame-fanning, how . . . —God alone knows how, and above all: how delightful such a body can be, how heartening, how amusing.

In the story about you and your man, you were as much admired as desired. There admiring and desiring went together again, and anew. The more you were admired by him, the more intensely—find a different word—the more unconditionally you were desired by him. "My body!" is what he called you in those days, and both his secret exclamations of astonishment, of joy, of wonder, and his equally secret oaths, even when they had nothing to do with you, began with "O body of my woman!" or "On my woman's body, I swear . . . (pledge . . .)" What body-travels the two of you undertook, then and there: even when you were both as naked as only a woman and man can be when they are together, you continued to strip each other, of a thousand and one garments, one at a time: another one gone, and another, until you came together truly naked.

Except that even then, from the outset, he, the only one you loved and wanted, saw himself as not your equal and equal to your body, or to put it differently, he was not synchronized with you, or, to put it differently, the fullness of love, or, to put it differently, the fulfillment of love, did not come about for him until you were absent. "Yes, I was never equal to this woman of mine."

And his vacillating feelings reached the tipping point as the two of you were going through the Sierra de Gredos, you with the child in your womb, shortly before the birth. After you had lost sight of each other for an hour or so, instead of zooming to you from a bow-and-arrow distance, he took to his heels, or he simply stayed where he was and let you climb on alone, in the knowledge that once under way you would not turn back. He fled from you, he hid from you, he left you in the lurch, believing he had led you astray, and not merely outwardly, there in the Sierra, but above all led you astray as a man, with his wanting to be your man.

And as the years passed, he left you without word of himself. And in doing so, he had no sense of privation. For he knew he was incorporated into you from a distance, perhaps even more intensely than you into him. Night after night he disappeared, experiencing himself and being extinguished in you. That sufficed for him.

And one day it no longer sufficed for him. For at last he knew that he was synchronized with you. The discrepancy between his, the man's, time and your, the woman's, time was at an end. Or at least that was what he pictured: now, at least, instead of "in his own time," both your time! Or that is what the story called for. The story decided that the man and woman who have lost each other, seemingly forever, shall come together again, and that is also no myth. "That we may no longer come together on earth, but only in some heaven or paradise—that must not be. And that will not be!"

She lay among the ferns the following night as well. She felt almost at peace. Had it not been for the thirst, which returned, this time a thirst that no blackberries could quench (besides, the last ones had been consumed long since). Again the starry sky, now showing its Sierra multiplicity above the translucent fern fingers, and with it the pencil-thin sickle of the new moon and the Milky Way, which brought to mind her vanished daughter's Arabic book: the figure of the "teacher" in the book had "the form of milk." Ah, her vanished child: one could draw strength and resolution from the dying, but from the vanished . . .

The air that night was no longer still, but wafted, barely perceptible, past her temples. Nocturnal birds, far, far off, called—not owls, but bird calls such as she had never heard before, like those of crickets at a great height, and she could not get enough of them. What hurtled across the sky intermittently were showers, not of bright stars but of dark foliage, blown through her field of vision. This foliage created at least a transient horizon, and horizon meant: relief. (Loss of images meant: lacking a horizon. And at the same time this gave her a remarkable sense of filiation.)

Now and then, as if for a short journey in a sleeping car, she also fell asleep and dreamed, the same dream every time, in which she was walking through a ford, with shoes on, and the water was getting deeper and deeper, and then there was no more ford, and she lost her shoes, would have to appear in public barefoot.

Wasn't that something like an image? So there was not a complete image blackout? Nonsense: the loss of the image and images had nothing to do with dream images. For it was not, or had long since ceased to be, dream images that refreshed existence and constituted the world, but rather almost exclusively those that came when one was wide awake, the matitudinal ones—or those had been the ones.

She woke up. The blackness of night still around her. But a morning breeze was already blowing. And then the notion came to her that she and her story could continue only if she spoke of her "guilt." It was time to confess it, in detail, out loud, distinctly. But to whom? For she could not address her confession to the air or to a rock or to the human frog. Or could she? Why not tell the story to the underside of a fern frond, for instance? With impatience—which was rare in this woman to whom that expression from the Sierra, *tener correa*, hold your shoelace, meaning "Be patient!" applied nicely—she awaited the light that would herald the dawn.

There: the first fans, jagged like a lizard's tail, and after a moment of grayness already greening, and on the underside of the delicate dwarf fern leaves the pattern of dot-shaped spore sacs, like the dots on dice, here two eyes, here five, here only one, many sixes! and, as was proper for dice eyes, nowhere more than that, never seven, eight, or more of the dots, though in some cases little fingers that lacked them altogether. All right: speak, tell your story.

And as she opened her mouth, she saw that all around her in the ferns other people were lying. They were in uniform. They were soldiers.

And they were all asleep, as exhausted as one could possibly be. The one closest to her was even sleeping with his eyes half open.

And she promptly turned to him and told him, who, like his comrades, would have heard not a word, even if she had begun to shout, that during her first time in the Sierra de Gredos, when her man went missing, she had wished that the child in her womb would die, or at least she had entertained the idea.

So? Hadn't many parents, and perhaps mothers in particular, wanted for a moment to be rid of their children, or, at least—what was the expression—"entertained with approval" the thought of their going away? And did one not hear every day of mothers who had actually killed their children, not in the tradition of that sorceress in antiquity—to take revenge on their vanished father, who had abandoned her—but out of despair?

"Yes, but at the time of my death wish for my unborn child, I made up my mind to be successful and to become powerful," she told the sound-asleep soldier, whom neither a Katyusha launching multiple rockets nor a Lincoln's drum or whatever right by his ear would have awakened—maybe only a cry of pleasure, she thought involuntarily.

So? What was objectionable about success and power? "It was the kind of power and success," she said. "I wanted to be a player on the world stage. And for a while I believed in that, and especially in the ability of an individual to make a difference in this day and age. And how easy it was to achieve the sort of success and power I acquired. But what was my success? A pattern without value. And my power? There was and is no more power, only the abuse thereof. In addition, my guilt was that I wanted to win. That I made a profession of my business of foreseeing, seeing what's what, seeing clearly. That I wanted to show the world. That I wanted to conquer the world."

Well? Why not? "Yes, why not? But not that way."

Several versions have been narrated of the reasons or stimuli that got the victim of the loss of images back on her feet early that morning in the heart of the Sierra de Gredos and sent her on her way. Let the reader decide which of the reasons seem credible—perhaps less important—or sensible—perhaps more important—or so crazy that they, without being one or the other, are perhaps most important.

One of the versions went as follows: the heroine, and thus also her story, was able to move on as a result of admitting her guilt and betraying her secret (so according to plan).

The second: it was the voice. She could have spoken about any-thing—the main point was that she opened her mouth and spoke, even if only to herself—"for with the sound of her own voice she pulled herself out of the pit."

A third version: it was the declaration of love, or whatever it was sup-posed to be, by that narrator who had intervened before, the narrator "from above," which lit a fire under her and gave her new legs and arms, and so on.

A fourth or seventh version (the one appealing most to a certain reader, which would mean, however, that it is because of him, the reader, and his particular ways?): the strength to get up resulted from a mistaken impression, when she first mistook an object in the fern hollow, or an an-imal, for instance a bird, for something else, then realized her mistake, and in observing the object in question, a robin, let us say, teetering on a fern frond above her and eyeing her and clearly not a wren and certainly not a hawk or a fern rat, saw the difference between the two objects, the one before her eyes and the one for which she had at first mistaken it: the adventurer of the loss of images derived the strength to get up and continue on her way, as this version has it, from the breeze of observa-tion, which wafted toward her from the thing she was observing, as in the Arabic saying "The breath of mercy wafted hither from Yemen."

And the last of the versions: neither the breeze of observation, nor the confession of guilt, nor her own voice after a long period of silence, nor . . . no, she owed her newfound ability to contract all the sinews of her body and leap to her feet to the morning wind: "It was the morning wind."

What confusion again until she finally reached the path. First she crept on all fours, wriggled, crawled on her stomach like a seal, as if lack-ing arms and legs, slid sideways, clumsily, not in the least bit soldierly (the warriors whom she passed on her way out did not react in their sleep to being shoved aside; that was how deathly exhausted they were, sleeping so soundly that no snoring was to be heard).

While she was still pulling herself together, she had uttered a cry, no, a rattle, a stammer, consisting only of consonants. And now a barking, hoarse and grating, issued from the beautiful woman's throat, followed by a grunting, as if from a creature wallowing in mud, a wolf's howling, as if not belonging to her, from beyond the horizon, an old man's cough, a sound that combined mooing, baaing, and bleating, to which actual ani-mal noises seemed to respond from the distance, here a jay's squawking, there the fluting of a nightingale, there the whistling of a red kite, shriller than any referee's whistle.

For the first steps on the path she hopped along in a squat, her mouth awry, her tongue hanging out like an idiot's. She stank, and was smeared with her own excrement. But at the same time, her eyes: what pride, what clarity and calm, such as one sees only in the heroine of a film, in the most disturbing scenes as well.

She of all people, whose ideal was the Taylor system, originally devised for the assembly line in factories, to assure that every motion would represent the ultimate in coordination and efficiency, focused on the product, although she applied it to life apart from the assembly line and production—she, in a mess that could not be uglier, more unworthy of a human being? No. For this was not a hopeless confusion but an almost holy one. *Negra aventura,* black adventure? Black and white?

She stood up. Her lips twitched, particularly the lower one; yet not for speaking. She jingled the last few chestnuts and other nuts in her pocket: in the old tales these had been the basic sustenance of the most solitary adventurers. A rumble of thunder directly in front of her: her own breath. She moved backward, and not only for the first few steps. For a while she swayed as she walked, even staggering now and then. Later she noticed that she really was barefoot.

Farther down the mountain she found herself in a strip of forest, and encountered the most harmless and at the same time most terrible plague of the Sierra (actually there were no other plagues, only dangers): the flies.

Even before the sun, with the warmth rising from the lowlands, they buzzed around one, small, almost delicate, also soundless, hardly corporeal, except that there were myriads of them, as in the old stories, and as soon as one paused for a moment, myriads upon myriads, not biting flies, but rather the kind that merely brushed against one, though constantly, and not only brushing but also flying into one's mouth (see above), or, when one shut one's mouth, into one's nostrils, far in, likewise into one's ears, and in particular into one's eye sockets; no sunglasses and no scarf could be so tight that they would not slip inside, and scads of them.

And this tongue of forest—the flies kept to the forest—went on forever. The flies clustered on one's face, in one's eyes, in one's nose—buzzed and circled around all the small orifices in one's head, without letting up for a breath, without letting one breathe at all. And now you could not even stop, despite your thirst, at a trickle of water that finally turned up: already the myriads have whirled through your eyes into your sinuses, and thence under your scalp—a diabolical breed, even if they do no more than tickle, brush, and bump lightly against you.

But, strange to say: that morning this did not upset her. Any other hiker would have slapped at his head every few steps, just missing his face, hit his nose, knocked his glasses off (see "author's own experience," as with the Sierra nettles)—a grotesque sight from a distance, where the dot-sized flies are not visible: she went on unaffected, even in the (close-up) blackest swarms of flies.

Was she already, or still, lying there dying? But wait: would a dead person walk in hops, as she did intermittently, or slide along on the balls of her feet? And one time, at a sharp bend in the road, she waded through a pile of leaves, a sort of leafy dune that reached way above her hips, and she heard her footsteps becoming heavy and slow, like those of an old man with whom she had walked through leaves long ago, those of her grandfather, the singer. And wasn't that an image, an "auditory image"? "Auditory images are not the images that were lost," she said. "And was she now, at last, ready to sing?" "No, not yet."

It was also in the forest with the flies that when she spread her arms one time and "stretched," her child came to mind, who had once re-sponded to just such a posture, such a stretch, with a look of dismay and shame, for her, her mother. Her raised arms, victorious, in the pose of a victor, had been slapped down then by her child.

And in the same instant, in that deserted forest, a cork-oak forest dense with foliage, she felt herself seen by the vanished girl, through the leaves, which were reminiscent of the oak leaves on playing cards. Time and again, when the two of them had agreed to rendezvous somewhere, she had hunted in vain for the child. And every time she had been spot-ted by the girl first, at a distance, even in a large crowd, and every time the child would then be standing in front of, next to, behind her, no matter how the mother had scoured the scene; or she, the mother, crammed in among thousands of heads, heard her calling, as if she were miles away and at the same time right by her eardrum. A mother-daughter odyssey? In spite of everything, that was not enough for her. Her face-seeking eyes, her eye-seeking eyes, no longer sought only her own child.

Out of the fly forest, and with that, out of the Sierra de Gredos. Be-fore her on the plain the big little town of Candeleda, olive trees, figs, palms. A crisscrossing of the warm, almost sultry air currents from the south and the breezes from high up at the summit plain, and above there a cloud in which one now saw another "barrier cloud," then the fluffy little formation known in the region as a "butterfly cloud"; in her mouth the taste of tar steaming in the heat, blending with that of new-fallen snow.

Advancing toward the town at the foot of the mountains by a side path that snaked along a narrow, vertical depression, not unlike a foxhole, quite typical of the southern spurs of the Sierra. She asked a child for the date and time, and received precise information. At sunrise, on the sunken path, in the midst of the fields, among orange trees, she turns back once more toward the massif, already shrouded in the blue of distance. And so, walking backward again on the last stretch to Candeleda: the Sierra veiled, an enormous box taking up the whole horizon, yet light in weight.

One of the torrents from above, broadening beside the path into a stream, which widens as it leaves the mountains into deep, clear pools, called *"piscina natural."* Letting herself down on the bank and plunging her entire body into the water, diving under, at first not to swim but simply to drink. And drinking and swimming along with her, the little animal brought from the Sierra, the tiny little man-frog.

And if this were a fairy tale, she would have drunk the brook dry in a few gulps. She lay on her stomach, her head underwater, and—yes, gulped. Our orderly adventurer gulped and gulped and gulped. And her thirst was of the sort that not even the waters of the torrent called Garganta Santa María, formed from the confluence of the Garganta Blanca, the White Torrent, and the Garganta Lobrega (from "wolf" or "she-wolf"), could quench.

With her thirst still unquenched, next came swimming. Swimming while drinking more. Then washing her clothes. Strange, the flakes of ashes in the fabric, as if from lava. Quick drying on a block of granite in the sun. Mending, darning, ironing (with a smooth, heavy, hot stone). Polishing her shoes (with a cream manufactured up there in Hondareda: wasn't there a time when quite a few companies produced, along with their main products, almost all the little necessities for their employees?). Makeup (from Hondareda). Perfume (from Hondareda, where else?). Upon slipping off her shoes: what a liberation that had been; one could suffer from shoe rage, as from prison rage.

Only much later the appearance of other people by the water. This turned out to be a region of late sleepers, like the entire Iberian Peninsula, by the way (except for Hondareda, of course). A man spoke to her as she strolled in a wide arc through the town to the railroad station—now a train route ran through the valley of the río Tiétar; on her previous crossings of the Sierra there had been no mention of it. And what did the stranger say? He asked: "¿Sois amorada? Are you in love?"

Remarkable how many men spoke to her, without a moment's hesitation, and not merely in this particular hour, simply addressed her, in a casual way, as good neighbors, or, to use a local word, "compadres." Might that have to do with the fact that this aventurera was not like many other women, who with strangers put on an absent or even forbidding expression, lighting up only when they caught sight of the one man who was theirs? That this vagabond looked at any stranger with open, laughing eyes that promptly instilled trust—precisely their deep-black color had that effect—almost like an idiot, if it were not for her sovereign, yes, sovereign, and at the same time cheerful and, yes, compassionate beauty?

Yet remarkable, on the other hand, that this woman, once she catches sight of the one man who is hers, will have assumed a veritable scowl, the kind of look that, given the dark black of her eyes, almost, and not merely "almost," inspires fear?

4 0

When, precisely, she traveled from Candeleda to the village in La Mancha, she told the author there, was of no significance for their tale. It was enough that it was long after Candlemas (= Candelaria) and the month of Ramadan and the festival of unleavened bread, and sometime between Sukkoth, the Buddhist Dugout Festival, and All Souls' Day. "The angels of the night and the day follow upon one another and watch over you," she read during the train trip in the Arabic book belonging to her vanished child.

The Sierra de Gredos had still been visible from Liubovia, then still from Navamoral (= Mulberry Hollow) de la Mata, and, finally, on the bus trip from Talavera de la Reina in the direction of Toledo and Ciudad Real: until long after Talavera and after the crossing of the río Tajo, whenever she turned around in her seat in the back of the bus, the blooming of the blue mountain to the north, far, far off, with white crags at the top: so, up on the summit plain the first snow had fallen again.

She had taken her time once more: spent the night in Talavera (= Cutting Edge)-of-the-Queen in the hotel by the bus station; in Toledo she had herself poled across the río Tajo in the one-man ferry, from the city to the rocky steppe, and, far out in the meadow on the other side of the river, tracked down the remote church dedicated to the patron saint of Toledo, who was unfamiliar to most residents, and from whom she had taken one of her daughter's several names, along with Lubna, Salma, Ibna, etc.

The following night she spent in Orgaz, already deep in La Mancha, quite barren and also well above the altitude of the Tajo valley. And the next day she strolled through the capital of La Mancha, Ciudad Real, spent hours gazing at the prehistoric archeological finds there, and toward evening took the only bus to the spot where she was scheduled to meet the author.

The return to conventional time was not as distasteful to her as one might have assumed. She could still feel inside her the alternate time dispensation of her crossing of the Sierra, providing an additional impetus that would not leave her that soon. Also no brooding as to what the future held.

Since the loss of images, there was, to be sure, no more "and," that sweet, duration-forging link between her steps. Yet on the other hand she had her story inside her, there to pass on to others. She took in current events as current events, and these brushed against her story without disrupting it—indeed, some news, world happenings, or historic events that had occurred in the meantime actually reinforced what she had experienced, precisely by way of contrast, lent her experiences colorful outlines and backgrounds.

While she had been crossing the Sierra de Gredos, the first manned spacecraft had landed on Mars. The highway signs throughout Europe and the rest of the world now indicated the hours, minutes, and seconds in neon lights. The final communiqué from a global presidents' summit conference announced: "At last we all speak a single language." The president of a poor country asked the Universal Bank for money, pledging that his country would "show itself worthy of the community of deal-makers." A new pope again asked in the name of his Church for forgiveness for something for which there could be no forgiveness, at most dissolution of the Church. Africa was declared the "continent of peace" for the coming decade (and the black faces pictured in that connection made that seem almost credible, and, above all, possible). Belgrade, the other riverport city and sister city of hers in the northwest, had been recently, for the second or third time in its history, conquered by the Turks, and the victorious second-in-command, the author of a book called *Jogging Through Turkey*, stood in his jogging suit at the spot where the Save flows into the Danube, waving a bundle of money, and at the same time pissing into the confluence of the rivers. Aquileia had become the capital of Italy. Ancient Greek had again become a required subject in schools from Alaska to Tierra del Fuego. Dog owners proclaimed that anyone who was not a friend of animals was an enemy of mankind. And—no "and"—her favorite team—no, not the one from Valladolid—Football Club Numancia, had in the meantime beaten FC Barcelona and Real Madrid and become the

Iberian champions: the Europe Cup game against Manchester United was about to take place. (To judge by that, wasn't everything about which she cared passionately threatened with extinction after all?) And: Spain had abolished the upside-down question mark at the beginning of questions. ¿True?

Upon the bus's arrival in the La Mancha village it was already night. The bus station was almost as big as a city terminal. The village itself, though only a hamlet, spread far out into the *meseta*. Centuries earlier it, not Ciudad Real, had been the capital of La Mancha. Nonetheless it had had in those days, as it did today, the air (yes, air) of a village, a *pueblo*. The author took her home with him for the night and the telling of her story; his house, as he told her at once, should help her feel at home, for it had been in the village's days as the capital a sort of storehouse for goods and money, owned by her colleague and predecessor Jakob Fugger, a branch of his business in the middle of sixteenth-century Spain, turned over to the banking emperor by Emperor Charles as compensation for the imperial debt to the House of Fugger.

The bus station was a barracks in the middle of the otherwise empty square ("not to be confused with the Plaza Mayor, the main square"), housing both the ticket counter and a bar. At first she did not recognize the author; took him for a *labrador*, a land or field worker, a rather haggard and ragged one.

Yet he, too, looked right past her as she got off the bus with the last passengers. Had she changed that much? It was true: it had not been possible to cover the scrapes and scabs with makeup. Yet her face always remained the same!: so it was probably the fault of the author, who was often uncertain about precisely those people of whom he had a clear mental image when they, whom he was expecting, suddenly stood before him.

So for the moment she let him go on hunting for her and behind his back ordered something to drink at the bar (her thirst from the Sierra was still with her). Only then did she come up behind the man and grab him under the arms, and at last he recognized her. And he seemed familiar to her now, as if not from their first encounter but from somewhere else entirely.

As the two of them made their way to his storehouse in the village, the night was chilly. Altogether, on this last leg of her journey, even though she had been heading south all the while, it had become noticeably colder. The huge village square was strewn with sand, which crunched under their feet as only frozen sand could crunch. Not another soul was out on the village streets then, despite the rather early hour; no *corso*, no evening strolling by the population; yet the *aldea* so deep in the Iberian south.

The author's *almacén*, or warehouse, lay on the edge of the village. It had no windows on the sides overlooking the street and alley. The windows it did have faced on the grass- and scree-covered steppe that surrounded all the rather sparse settlements in La Mancha, which were often half a day's journey apart. The other village houses, as well as the astonishingly many churches, also seemed to be built on the edge of the savannah; one of the churches was even located far out in the grassland, and was dedicated to Santa María de las Nieves, Mary of the Snows; from the window of the guest room she could see this snow church—without snow—standing in the moonlight.

They had passed through a spacious, empty vestibule and entered the inner courtyard of the former warehouse, where a gallery running all around the one upper story—marble columns and shallow Moorish arches in a delicate, light-colored clay brick—gave the impression of a miniature palace, not a royal one but a rustic, peasant one. In the inner courtyard the giant seedpods of a baobab tree rustled in the night wind.

She had been shown up to her room and left there while her host put the finishing touches on the evening meal, for which he refused to accept her help. "My housekeeper has the day off"—these were his words.

In her room, again something between a chamber and a storeroom, she changed her clothes. The supposed chef's tunic that she had had with her the entire time in her pack was in actuality a dress, and it was also not white but revealed, when she had put it on, at least here and there, completely different colors, which flowed into each other as she moved, and for which there were no names—at least none recognized by the master of the house, who could distinguish about a thousand colors but hardly knew a name for one of them.

As she descended the broad brick steps—so broad because they had been used for moving goods to the storage areas—he also noticed that she was barefoot. Yes, since the loss of her shoes on that morning of leave-taking from the Sierra, she had gone barefoot, and he was the first to notice this, or rather, the first she allowed to notice; for she continued to have it in her power, if not to be invisible, then to be overlooked by the world around her.

They ate their evening meal in the hall or main storeroom, adjacent to the patio—crammed with junk, or at least stuff that looked like junk—with a glass door (no window in the room) looking out on the Mancha steppe. As befitted her, and their, story, and especially its last chapter, there was a fireplace by the table, quite a tiny one, and not only in proportion to the hall, and the fire in it smoldered more than it burned or blazed, and the author then allowed it to go out, intentionally, as he said: "For gazing into a fire has always tended to distract me; unlike running water, it puts me to sleep, hypnotizes me, pulls me away, in an unproductive sense, from the matter at hand, or what should be the matter at hand." — "Me, too," she replied. But they did not feel cold, and that was the result, among other things, of her telling and his listening.

While she told him the story of crossing the Sierra de Gredos and the loss of images, she noticed that the listener was increasingly usurping her story, the story. Usurping? Absorbing it? More the latter, if also in the sense that it, in turn, the story, was passed to him, and at times also literally entered him, like a demon? yes, but not an evil demon, rather one that one might almost wish would circulate inside one as long as possible, working its magic. The stooped author pulled himself together and sat up straight. To be sure, at moments this also caused him to sway.

And she, the storyteller? Time and again as she recounted her adventures, she was filled, in retrospect, with a horror of which there had been not so much as a hint at the moment of the experience. At one point, in the middle of a paragraph, she even found herself on the verge of breaking off the story—a child's crib on the edge of a precipice, tipping (another image after all?)—and for good: the story would end there, would thus not even come into being. For she saw herself still lying in the fern hollow, helpless and unable to move, completely and utterly alone.

And wasn't she in fact still lying there in the dark? Was in reality not here, safe and sound in human company? The retroactive trembling familiar from so many adventure stories came over her. But wasn't this, on the other hand, the unmistakable sign of a proper adventure? Trembling and faltering, she and the author went on to the next sentence. In between they both shuddered. But without this shuddering the journey would not have deserved the name. That alone was what validated a journey.

Before the two of them, now calm and wide awake, discussed the loss of images, the author remarked, at the end of her tale—which, nota bene, was only the provisional end—perhaps not in complete seriousness, that he, as a man who had of necessity turned his back on the world, at least the social world, would have wished to hear more about money and banking. Her response: first of all, there was enough written about her as the powerful banker, a modern-day Jakob Fugger ("That was once upon a time"); and, second, there had been plenty said on the subject in the current story, directly and even more indirectly; and, third—this she now dictated to the author: "Yes, money is a mystery. But here more mysteries are at stake than the mystery of money or secret bank accounts."

It goes without saying that the author, like all the earth's inhabitants at the time of this story, had experienced the loss of images long before her, the heroine. Yet, nota bene again! the loss of images did not mean that images no longer flashed and flared through the world or that no one noticed and/or registered these flashing and flaring images at least now and then. And here began the nocturnal discussion between the adventurer and her author of the loss of images—which at the same time was a conversation of both parties with themselves—each one of their soliloquies was evoked by the other's, and so forth.

"The image sparks, the will-o'-the-wisp images within us—no, these are no will-o'-the-wisps—continue to occur, flashing and flaring into our midst." — "Except that they no longer have any effect. Or no: they could perhaps continue to have an effect. But I am no longer capable of taking them in and letting them affect me." — "What affects me instead is the ready-made and prefabricated ones, images controlled from the outside and directed at will, and their effect is the opposite of the old ones." — "These new images have destroyed those other images, the image per se, the source. Particularly in the century just past, the original sources and deposits of images were ruthlessly raided, in the end disastrously. The natural vein has been stripped, and people now cling to the synthetic, mass-produced, artificial images that have replaced the reality that was lost along with the original images, that pretend to be them, and even heighten the false impression, like drugs, as a drug."

"But anyone who has recognized the loss of images in himself can at least say what the image and the images once meant to him." — "Yes. The images, the instant they appeared, meant being alive, even if I was dying, and peace, even if war was raging all around; which makes it clear that an image of terror or horror is incompatible with the kind of images of which our story should speak." — "Those images seemed, in the face of the transitoriness and destructibility of the body, indestructible. Even if only one came to me in a day, just a brief flash, I saw it as a sequel and continuation, as part of a whole: the images as the comet's tail of the world's survival, sweeping over the entire earth and revitalizing the smallest nooks and crannies."

"A single image spark from any place whatsoever—strange that its name always accompanied the flash as well—allowed one to see the entire globe—what used to be called the ecumene, the inhabited world, and reinforced the conviction that we all belong together; made sure that one was face-to-face with the world, including the world of the future, which accordingly seemed eternal, and could exclaim, in all seriousness: Oh happy day!" — "The images were epiphanies. They were epiphanies in the sense in which people used to say: I have had an epiphany. True, they were always the briefest of the brief. But who is to say that the other ones, the reported epiphanies, lasted any longer? And before the loss of images: who said that there were no more epiphanies? Perhaps there has never been anything more than our suddenly appearing and promptly vanishing lightning images?" — "The images were the last inspirations."

"In the image, internal and external seemed to be fused into a third element, greater and more lasting. The images represented the value to end all values. They were our seemingly safest form of capital. Mankind's last treasure." (Three guesses as to which of the two said that.) — "With the images I plunged into the maternal world." (Three guesses as to who . . .) — "It was perhaps not my man, but rather merely—merely?—the image inside me that binds me to him forever, and it was my man after all, the one I wanted, body and soul!" (But that, too, came from her!)

"Whenever an image allowed me to see it, it was the answer to an unconscious prayer, a prayer I was not aware was on its way. In the image I was redeemed every day, and opened up, but not for any religion. In the daily image I became a different person, but not for an ideology, not for a mass movement." — "In the images appeared what was beautiful and what was right, but not the way they appear in any philosophy, sociology, theology, economics—simply appearing, instead of being asserted, thought, or proclaimed. And they were also different from memories, including the so-called collective ones." — "The image manifested itself outside of legend and myth. The image—how marvelously myth-free it was—just the image, both the switchboard and switch." — "Physicists: instead of smashing atoms, etc.: map a physics of the images!"

"The loss of images is the most painful of losses." — "It means the loss of the world. It means: there is no more seeing. It means: one's perception slides off every possible constellation. It means: there is no longer any constellation." — "We will have to live without the image for the time being." — "For the time being. But isn't precisely such a loss accompanied by energy, even if this energy is undirected for the time being?" — "*Cuerpo del mundo*. Body of the world. We, the banished, full of passion."

The author then said, among other things: "How appalled I am at myself that the images that once meant everything to me have been shattered. A leaf had only to move, and I would become a player in the widest world. A scrap of blue morning sky in the blue night sky. A train passing in the dark with all its windows lit up. The eyes of people in a crowd, the eyes especially! The stubbly beard of the man condemned to death. The mountains of shoes from those who were gassed. The thistle silk blown in little balls by the wind across the savannah. In the image I embraced the world, you, us. Images, refuges, dark sheltering niches. Nothing meant more to me than the image. And now—and you?"

The images he had evoked there: Were those, after all, not the sort she meant? Had she been mistaken in the author? Was he the wrong one? But then he launched into the following litany, which reassured her: "Images, you world-arrows. Images, you world-encompassers. Images, do not let me be orphaned. Image, you grounded perception. *Imagen, mi norte* (= guide) *y mi luz*. Images, let life appear to us. Image, word in the universal language. Image, as light as a shed snakeskin. Image, most lasting of all afterimages. Images, you capital realities. Image, give me the world, and let me forget the world. Image, acknowledgment of what has been lived, impetus for what is yet to be lived. In the image the hospitable and enduringly hospitable globe. Image, you who indicate to me that I am still on the right path. Images, you pure opposite number. O image, my life spirit: show me the space where you are hiding."

And she: "Perhaps I will found an image bank, a new, different world bank, on the basis of the science of images, which, as I picture it, will create a sweetness and prove fruitful like hardly any science before it. A science that will encompass all the others. Or I will act in a film again."

For a while they then laughed together, silently and from ear to ear. And finally the author made a speech about today's pencils, which were utterly worthless; above all, the leads, often enclosed in two halves made of different kinds of wood, kept breaking off during sharpening; wood and graphite—if they still were wood and graphite—no longer had any "smell and taste," in the sense of musk, in which, according to the old Arabs, "smell and taste combine"; also the sound of pencil on paper was no longer the same as before, and the cracking, grinding, and squeaking when one sharpened them and held one's ear to the sharpener, or vice versa, was outrageous; just putting the finally sharpened lead to paper was a game of chance; even the good old Cumberlands now had low-quality wood and were badly glued; only his "school pencil" had not left him completely in the lurch when it came to managing; down with modern pencils! (His activity, too, was "managing.") Or not so after all! His favorite pencil bore the inscription EAN, which means "let" in Greek. And she saw that the cuffs of his pants were full of pencil shavings.

That night they alternated among languages. In every language, the two of them had a similar accent: that of villagers, of *aldeanos*. Like her, the author came from a village, and she and he had met here in a third village.

Finally they were no longer speaking. The light in the hall or storeroom, consisting in any case merely of a few bare bulbs, was switched off. Through the glass door, the moonlit steppe; darkness inside the *almacén*. The author poured her another glass of steppe wine and left the room. The quince, *safurdzul, dunja*, from the other tree in the inner courtyard, lightly steamed, that he brought her as dessert, was doubled by the one she had earlier secretly plucked herself. Perhaps thinking that in him, the author, all the threads had to come together, he also brought her the telephone, for a nocturnal call to her property on the outskirts of the distant riverport city.

As she placed the call, out of the corner of her eye she saw on the glass door a single leaf of ivy, or whatever, moving, and taking on the form of someone long awaited. On the telephone: the half-grown neighbor boy from the porter's lodge. A Spanish proverb occurred to her: "Wipe the neighbor boy's nose and put him in your house." And she spoke to him as the guardian of her house. That morning, he told her, the idiot of the outskirts had come toward him, carrying heavy loads in both hands, and while still far off had shifted the load to his left hand, so as to offer the boy his right. And now the idiot was making his rounds, singing and yelling through the empty streets, as reliable as the local night watchman.

But then she heard him say: "I would like to go to my room now." — "Where is your room?" she asked. — His reply: "Where all the toys are."

And only then did she recognize that she was speaking not with the neighbor boy but with her vanished daughter. In her absence, her child had come home. Lubna. Salma. Ibna. Alexia. After all the news, this was the greatest news. "A favorable wind for the homeward journey"—who said that?

The two women remained silent. One as well as the other—yes, in Arabic there was a dual!—they pursued their thoughts in silence, each in her distant place: enough of being apart. Stay together, whatever it takes. That was what the story called for. So it was only a story? Only?

Then all this time her vanished child had been near her house, her home? Was that possible? And did the expression "my home" still exist? Vanished within eyeshot. And in a flash of thought it seemed possible to her that the half-grown boy from the porter's lodge really was her own child, with a slightly altered appearance. Was that possible? Well, well, well! And at the end of their wordless conversation the *aventurera* felt herself to be absolved by her child: on the one hand because the girl was alive and well; and then by the simple fact of the child's existence, that she had a child. Never again to feel she had to do something special for her. Just to be with her. The doing would happen by itself.

Was guilt rearing its head again? I would have expected a woman, and a woman's story, to spare us and me, the author, who sees himself first and last as a reader, a reminder of our eternal guilt, or original sin. Adam and Eve were innocent. Oedipus or whoever was innocent. Enough guilt stories. Mystery, not guilt.

And in the end the *aventurera* and *asendereada*, "the pathless yet undeterred one," had opened her mouth after all and recounted to her child, named after the patron saint of Toledo or somewhere, how a man had introduced himself to her as she made her way through the Sierra: "I live with my wife, my children, and my friends."

And in the following *parágrafo* of the last chapter of the tale of the loss of images, the woman in the warehouse palace opened the large glass back door to the Mancha steppe: "door" and "chapter" were the same word in Arabic, *bab*. She raised her arm to throw the book, her child's property, which had accompanied her on the entire journey, far out into the night, in Arabic *laila*.

One second before she let it go, it occurred to her, however, how every time she had thrown something—she had a passion for throwing, and almost always hit her target—her daughter had been horrified and hurt by the sight of the thrower, just as by the sight of her mother as a victor. "Don't throw, Mother!" And so she laid the book on the ground instead, in the steppe grass, which glistened in the moonlight with dewdrops, some of them already hard, frozen. At that moment, on the horizon, *ufuq* in Arabic, perhaps precisely because she had broken off her throw, a feathered spear flew past the doorstep at eye level and would never fall to the ground.

The Mancha village, although many of its inhabitants had moved to the cities, turned out to be not so terribly deserted after all. From the solitary church out there on the steppe a small nocturnal procession emerged, with a baldachin borne on ahead, under which was the statue of Our Lady of the Snows: after spending the summer in the hermitage there, she was being moved, as every year, for the approaching winter, to another church in the heart of the village. That was how long the hike through the Sierra de Gredos had taken. It was October, and it was starting to get cold for our Señora de las Nieves out there on the savannah.

But the person who by contrast was not cold in the slightest was the ablaha there, the beautiful idiot. Barefoot, she went out into the scree of the old old Mancha. The many dark, symmetrical parts of her dress, rippling rhythmically as she walked, corresponded to the dark cavities and craters up there on the moon. And then she even ran, sprinted; hurled herself into the moonlit darkness.

In a film, that would have seemed like a flight. In the reality of the story I saw her run toward a group of gypsy musicians—was it still permissible to write "gypsy," *gitano*?—that was accompanying the Madonna with flamenco tambourines, trumpets, and drums, and the *cante hondo*, the song from the depths, to the cathedral. Andalusia was not far from here in La Mancha.

In the following paragraph, one of the last in this last chapter, I saw the woman—the procession with the musicians now silent and gone with the wind—out on the Mancha steppe, going in circles, setting one foot deliberately in front of the other.

In a film that would have signalized danger. (Now and then, since I have been living abroad, away from my country and my people, I occasionally use such a foreign word.) But perhaps she simply liked walking here on that special Mancha earth, the best earth one could wish for, with firm, granular sand, scree, ash, slag, countless burned patches in the short grass, where the rain and dew puddles were just freezing, in the shape of arrows or giant feet, mirroring the night sky.

And suddenly I then saw her going backward, toward the Fugger warehouse with the glass door. In a film, that would have signalized "fear," as if she had suddenly stumbled upon her place of execution. But now, already on the threshold, she hurtled forward again. So wasn't she running toward something or someone instead? A film shot would have shown only her nocturnal eyes. All through the years she had run that way, and crossing the Sierra de Gredos had been her last running start. She flew forward, as only a female idiot in her idiot's tale can fly toward a male idiot, who for his part flew toward her, could fly toward her. And that was as it was supposed to be. She released her hair net, black, longer than her long hair, as she flew forward.

Actually the song that she struck up as she ran in circles, after the disappearance of the procession and the gypsy band, should have been inserted into the previous paragraph. She sang it, not boomingly, like her singer-grandfather in his day, but almost inaudibly and, to my oversensitive ears, at times slightly off-key, but perhaps as it was supposed to be sung. And at first her singing appeared to imitate a child's crying. And that song went more or less as follows:

> I did not know what you were like
> I did not know who your parents were
> I did not know whether you had a child
> I did not know where your country was
> I did not know how many reals, maravedis, and dubloons you had
> I did not know when you came into the world
> I did not know what your intentions were
> But I knew and knew and knew who you were
>
> I knew the lines of your hand
> I knew the length of your stride
> I knew your scars
> I knew your childhood diseases
> I knew your passport number
> I knew your voice
> I knew your habits

I knew your tastes
I knew your circle of friends
I knew your rhythm
But I did not know, did not know you

I no longer knew the color of your skin
I no longer knew your shoe size
I no longer knew your neck size
I no longer knew your blood group
I no longer knew your favorite trees
I no longer knew your favorite animals
I no longer knew your preferences
I no longer knew your Zodiac sign
I no longer knew your name
I no longer knew your day- and night dreams
I no longer knew your direction
I no longer knew the day of your death
I no longer had an image of you
But I knew and knew and knew of you

What a young voice to go with her face, so ageless. And at last, in the middle of the song, she had found the pitch, and one time even uttered the shrill Sorbian-Oriental whistle. And the song was called: Guilt Was Healed. Healed and avenged. The song was called: Vengeance Is Mine. And that alone was the best revenge.

This tenth- or twelfth-from-last paragraph of our tale of the loss of images, as it is supposed to be told, on and on, for the centuries to come—for what else? and for whom else?—for him and her, and for all souls—was transsected by the gravel highway, in Arabic *tariq hamm*, where the *aventurera*, the *asendereada* and ablaha, paused in her running. Her footprints were erased by the hem of her dress. A single dwarf tree stood there, a little oak, let us say, from whose leaves the dew no longer merely dripped but showered, in a pelting downpour, while round about silence reigned. In the sky a false Milky Way from a plane's jet contrail. The wind was blowing, but it had no strength to stir the tree's leaves. Next to its dark form, the bright spot glowing in the exact shape of the tree: its nocturnal afterimage. (This sentence I stole from Miguel de Cervantes Saavedra. And the word "highway" reminds me that in an earlier time the inhabitants of the village in La Mancha, when one of their loved ones fell ill, had the habit of running out on the highway and begging one of the foreigners, who passed that way more often in those days, to come into the house of the sick man and heal him—but it had to be a total stranger!)

Then her hand on her hip, which reminds me of two lovers who had agreed to meet after years of separation, and then unexpectedly passed each other on the road before the appointed time, and acted, or had to act, as though they did not see each other, and both thereupon betrayed the meeting and their love. But now they went into the house, and the story was over? Not yet.

Sitting inside in the dark. To be seen there, on a table in the back, the author's pencils lying higgledy-piggledy, smeared with mud, clay, mica, as if he had dug in the ground with them. Next to them his collection of Jew's harps, most of them rusty, each one propped up like a praying mantis; to strike one after the other supposedly added depth to the epic.

Was this really his own house, his warehouse or *almacén*? Or had he merely rented it for the night and filled it with props?

Sitting there created a connection and a link at the same time with what was happening out in the empty and now Madonna-less Mancha: one sat there, in the company of a yellowish, almost red, camel that was swaying along the *tariq hamm*; in the company of a child making its way home, pushing a twig ahead of it through the dust as a divining rod; in the company of the cloud dunes covering the moon, to which down on the residual earth a white, barely noticeable sand dune corresponded.

But were the windmills missing? No. They were turning on all the horizons; their old wooden vanes creaking. And still that thirst, a burning one. And still the obstacles, as there should be, and still the mutual storytelling, about what? "The pages tell their life, the knights their love" (again your Miguel). And in spite of the coolness of an October night in La Mancha, a warmth in the hands, there especially, as if they were sticking in sun-heated hay. *Saghir-aisinn* was the strangely long Arabic word for "young." She, the mature youthful woman. Covet the body when it trembles.

Were their two bodies, then, not in such a hurry? No—because all that time they had been literally inscribed in one another. And *compás* was a Spanish expression for "rhythm." Yes, he had been expecting it only from her, the woman, the *aventurera*, the *asendereada*, the ablaha, the *aldeana*. What? It.

Two falling stars, one with a long tail, one with a short one: Who was who? The castanet-like clicking in the deep pockets of her dress, what did it come from? From the last couple of chestnuts and hazelnuts, the last remains of her provisions, her survival rations. And still the last gulp of wine in her mouth, unswallowed.

This night was supposed to go on and on; no day and no additional sun were needed now.

Once she had dreamed a dream with nothing but taste in her mouth; in which the entire dream was nothing but tasting and taste. Hondareda! She would rename the settlement "La Nueva Numancia," after Numancia, the original settlement in the *meseta* to which the Romans had laid siege far more than two thousand years ago and which they had eventually leveled completely. No one had ever lived, done things, worked, left things undone, like the people of Hondareda or Nueva Numancia, and never again would anyone live, do things, work, and leave things undone like the people of Hondareda or Nueva Numancia far off in the Sierra de Gredos—fortunately? unfortunately? Only a story? Imagination: the crown of reason. There was a form of searching in which the thing sought seemed to have been found already, far more real and potent than if it had really been found. And such searching was the searching on behalf of someone else and for others.

And finally, the bed made up with old linens, shimmering as white as snow, somewhere in a remote spot in the Fugger warehouse-palace, as if in another country (the author had situated it in the cellar, in the underground vault)—at last! And the great rush of blood toward the other person set in, at last. And the river of return flowed, unlike any other. And the in-between spaces glowed: one was ready for the other person. Twitching of lips. Stumbling along in the dark, as over the hummocks in a stalactite cave. All as it should be. Standing on tiptoe in the dark was not easy. And who held whom? And: that was still not it, not yet completely. But it came close, as close as it could.

And for the last series of sentences in the tale of the loss of images, the author for a change allowed something that he otherwise abhorred: that a story, instead of dealing with problems, asking questions, and taking detours, narrated itself, without problems, without questions, and without detours, so to speak—no, without "so to speak." And he sensed that the story was true. And what made him sense that? (No questions!) He sensed it from its beginning or commencement—no, already before that (no detours!)—in his heart; and toward the end he felt it in his hair—no, in the roots of his hair, in his scalp (do not turn this into a problem!)—and especially in his legs.

And with that the story was done, and we went home. In the story-telling site the lights were turned off. On our way home, it started to snow. It was as if a garment were being draped over us. A bird flew through the flakes and played with them.

A vehicle halted at its destination, at the end of a long, long journey, and continued to sway after coming to a standstill. And this swaying did not end all that soon; will not have ended all that soon.